"A FAST-PACED, EXCITING NOVEL THAT'S HARD
TO PUT DOWN. . . . I think it's one of the best histori-
cal romances I've read, and that Nicole and Christopher
are real, strongly portrayed characters who won't easily be
forgotten by any reader."

Rosemary Rogers

"A BIG, BOLD, TEMPESTUOUS TALE full of action
and passionate romance by a stunning new writer headed
straight to the top."

Jennifer Wilde

Other Avon Books by
Shirlee Busbee

DECEIVE NOT MY HEART
GYPSY LADY
WHILE PASSION SLEEPS

Lady Vixen

Shirlee Busbee

AVON
PUBLISHERS OF BARD, CAMELOT, DISCUS AND FLARE BOOKS

LADY VIXEN is an original publication of Avon Books.
This work has never before appeared in book form.

AVON BOOKS
A division of
The Hearst Corporation
1790 Broadway
New York, New York 10019

Copyright © 1980 by Shirlee Busbee
Published by arrangement with the author
Library of Congress Catalog Card Number: 79-56781
ISBN: 0-380-75382-0

First Avon Printing, March, 1980

AVON TRADEMARK REG. U.S. PAT. OFF. AND IN
OTHER COUNTRIES, MARCA REGISTRADA,
HECHO EN U.S.A.

Printed in the U.S.A.

WFH   10   9   8   7   6

This one is for three *very* special people,

TOM E. HUFF, who over the months has given me so much encouragement and who told me repeatedly that the second book is the hardest . . . Tom, you're absolutely right!

HOWARD BUSBEE, my husband, my favorite critic, my favorite proofreader, my favorite fan, and my mainstay.

And finally, ROSIE, who keeps me on the right track, and drops those little gems of wisdom at precisely the right time.

PROLOGUE

THE RUNAWAY

England, 1808

1

It was one of those warm, lazy days in August that occasionally caressed the gentle hills and valleys of Surrey, near the small village of Beddington's Corner. The sunlight was streaming into Nicole Ashford's room, golden strands of gossamer that beckoned irresistibly and yet, for just a few minutes longer, Nicole refused to leave the soft comfort of the feather mattress. She determinedly ignored the urge to arise and meet the day, snuggling deeper into the welcoming pillow and pulling the fine linen sheet further up across her slim body. But sleep eluded her, and with a relaxed sigh, she slowly turned over, lying on her back in the large eyelet-cotton-draped bed. Dreamily, her topaz gaze drifted around the delightful room, unconsciously noting the polished rosewood highboy and the cherry-wood armoire and the jeweled tones of the gaily flowered carpet that covered the floor. Crisp white curtains, trimmed with the same fabric that formed the hangings of her bed, hung at the tall windows; a mahogany chest, filled just now with discarded toys, was underneath one of the windows, and to its left sat an oak rocking chair, the crumpled gown she had worn yesterday thrown carelessly across one arm.

Seeing the gown reminded her that soon she would have to be up, because today was a special day—today her parents were having a garden party, and she and Giles, her twin brother, were going to be allowed to attend. A garden party might not sound especially exciting to some, but as Nicole was not quite twelve and it was her first grown-up party, her pleasure in the coming day was understandable. Besides, it wasn't often that Annabelle and Adrian Ashford were in residence at Ashland, their country estate, and Nicole treasured the few moments she had with her parents.

With a sense of happy anticipation, the long hair tumbling about the already-striking features, she flung back the sheets, only to stop abruptly as the door to her room flew open and Giles catapulted into the room.

3

"Nicky! Are you still abed, you lazy slug? Hurry and dress, Shadow had her foal last night!" Giles cried, his young voice full of pride and excitement. The topaz eyes so like his sister's were gleaming with tawny sparks, and a lock of dark brown hair fell across his forehead as he entered her room.

Nicole's own small face suddenly alight with the same blaze of elation, she slipped from the big bed, filling the air with questions. "Oh, why didn't you wake me sooner? Were you there when the foal was born? What color is it? Is it a filly or a colt?"

Giles laughed. "Give me a chance, chatterbox! No, I wasn't there when it was born, so take that look off your face—I didn't steal the march on you. It is a filly, a beautiful black little girl, just like Shadow and she was born just after midnight. Oh, wait until you see her, Nicky! She is so beautifully formed and so soft, with great brown eyes." His boyish chest swelling with pride, he finished loftily, "Father says she is to be mine!"

"Oh, Giles! How lucky for you! I am so glad!" Nicole returned with genuine pleasure. She had received her own horse, Maxwell, last year and was truly delighted that now Giles would have his.

Hurriedly she scrambled into the gown she had worn yesterday. Mentally preparing herself for the strictures she would receive from her maid later, she quickly washed her face and dragged a brush through her tangled mass of curls. A second later the twins raced down the graceful, curving staircase, across the wide, elegant hallway, and then out the massive double doors at the front of the house. It took only a moment for them to leap down the wide steps of the entrance and to disappear around the side of the magnificent country mansion.

Hand in hand, nearly out of breath, they reached the stables at the rear of the house a few minutes later. On tiptoe, breathing in the pungent smell of warm horse flesh and sweet straw, they approached the large box stall at one end of the sprawling stables. Adrian Ashford, tall and handsome in buff breeches and a slim-fitting coat of blue with silver buttons, was already standing there, as well as the head groom, Mr. Brown. Glancing over his shoulder, Adrian smiled at the children, beckoning them nearer.

"I see you woke her. Couldn't you wait?" he inquired, a warm smile curling his fine mouth, a teasing glint coming and going in the wide dark eyes.

"No! Besides, Nicky would have been a spitting fury if

4

I hadn't told her immediately. You know what a pepper pot she is!" Giles answered, his eyes dancing.

Nicole stuck out her tongue at him and flashed her father a sunny smile, saying demurely, "I am growing up now. Young ladies are *not* pepper pots!"

Giles hooted with laughter and both Adrian and Mr. Brown joined in, much to Nicole's discomfort. Taking pity on his daughter, Adrian swung her up in his arms, murmuring in an affectionate tone, "You're getting almost too big for this, my pet. In a year or two, I'll have to remember that you are not my *little* girl any longer."

"Oh, Father! I shall always be your little girl!" Nicole promised fiercely as she threw her arms around his neck, hugging him tightly, almost convulsively. Her father kissed her on the forehead and set her on the ground. Gently pushing a strand of the shining sable-fire hair behind one of her ears, he said softly, "I'm sure you will sweetheart. But come, let us admire Shadow's lovely little daughter."

The filly was just as Giles had described her—black, black as ebony, and with great soft curious brown eyes. With a sigh of pure pleasure, not caring about possible damage to her gown, Nicole sank down onto the straw-littered floor, crooning gently, "Oh, you pretty thing! How beautiful you are!"

Shadow, a long-limbed thoroughbred as black as her foal, nuzzled the spindle-legged small replica of herself, blowing softly through her nostrils, and Nicole laughed. "I think Shadow is very proud of her daughter." Turning the enchantingly lively features up toward her brother, she asked excitedly, "What are you going to call her?"

Looking a little self-conscious, Giles muttered, "I thought you would like to name her—you let me name Maxwell."

"May I? Really, Giles? You'll let me name her for you?"

"Of course, silly! Who else would I let do it?"

The topaz eyes shining like precious jewels, Nicole turned back to stare at the foal. Her forehead wrinkled in thought, she said after a few minutes, "I know it isn't very clever, but I like the name Midnight. You said she was born just after midnight and she is certainly black as midnight!"

"That would be perfect, Nicky!"

"An excellent choice," commented Adrian. Then pulling Nicole to her feet, he said, "Now I think we have all lingered here in the stables long enough. Your mother is probably wondering where we have all disappeared to. Don't forget that we have guests arriving in a few hours."

"As if I would!" Nicole protested.

Giles shot her a teasing look, murmuring, "Well if that's what you are going to wear and if you're going to leave that mane of yours straggling down your back, it certainly does look as if you have!"

"Oh, pooh! You know very well I have not! Just you wait until you see me in a little while." And with that she scampered off, the long sable-fire hair waving like a banner behind her.

And two hours later, as Nicole stood on the broad marble steps leading to the entrance of Ashland, greeting the arriving guests, no one would have connected her with the hoyden who had knelt in the straw of the stable. Standing confidently between her father and Giles, dressed in a most becoming soft muslin gown of buttercup yellow, the lace of her exquisite pantaloons just peeping from beneath the ankle-length skirt, the long hair pulled back into a wealth of gleaming ringlets that cascaded nearly to her waist, Nicole was everything an aristocrat's daughter should be. From the bright yellow ribbon that held her hair back to the little white kid slippers on her feet she was a daughter any man would be proud of. That Adrian Ashford was pleased with both his son and daughter was very apparent in the smiling and encouraging looks that he sent them as they continued to welcome the guests.

Nicole loved every movement of it. Her only disappointment was that her mother, Annabelle, had decided to greet their friends and neighbors in the gardens rather than on the steps with her husband and children. But it was such a minor flaw in this wonderful day that Nicole shrugged it aside.

The party was a huge success; the rose-scented gardens were dotted with gaily attired members of England's wealthier class and white-and-gold liveried servants bobbed about offering gigantic trays of temptingly arranged refreshments. Under the stately oaks and spreading chestnuts were dainty white tables and chairs for those who wished to sit in the shade and observe the antics of the others.

Nicole and Giles, full of icy lemonade and melting cream-cakes, darted from one group to another, enjoying the attention they were receiving. Yet both were very conscious that it was their first grown-up party and consequently they were behaving surprisingly well. Surprisingly, for in the neighborhood everyone knew what mischievous little devils the Ashford twins could be.

"Not an ounce of evil in either of them," remarked Colonel Eggleston pompously. "But the trouble those two can cause! Did I tell you of the time they caught a fox and put it in Lord Saxon's hen house? And that little Nicole is a harum-scarum scamp, if I ever saw one. Why just last week she climbed to the top of that old walnut tree near our entrance gate! Hardly a young ladylike pursuit!"

Nicole, approaching the Colonel and Mrs. Eggleston as they were standing and talking with the vicar and his wife, heard that comment, and for one moment she was shaken by a gust of quick anger. The Colonel would have to tell everyone! she thought furiously. Old windbag! But the burst of temper disappeared as quickly as it had come, and with a smiling face, she said, "Good afternoon, Colonel Eggleston, Mrs. Eggleston, Vicar and Mrs. Summerton."

"How pretty you look today, my dear," Mrs. Eggleston said quickly, having noticed the scowl that had momentarily darkened Nicole's lively face.

And because Mrs. Eggleston, with her white sugar-spun hair and gentle blue eyes, was the nearest thing to a grandmother that the twins knew, and because she really was on her best behavior, Nicole promptly forgot the Colonel's comments. She didn't remain with them long though, for seeing her father standing alone at the corner of the house, she wandered over to him. Almost absently he placed an arm around her slender shoulders and pulled her against him. "Happy, poppet?"

"Oh, yes . . . but I am getting a little tired of smiling at everyone and being so very good. Won't they all go home soon?"

Adrian laughed out loud. "So tactful! But that echoes my sentiments exactly!" Glancing around, he asked casually, "Where is your mother? I haven't seen her for some minutes now."

"She's walking in the rose garden with Mr. Saxon, I think. At least that's where I saw her last."

With surprise, Nicole felt her father's body stiffen and she looked up at his face curiously. It suddenly seemed tighter, the laughter lines grim. But then he laughed, a peculiar laugh, and said, "Well, why don't we go find them?"

And as she liked nothing better than to have both her charming father and her very beautiful mother with her, she tagged happily along as her father took off with long strides in the direction of the formal rose gardens that lay to the left of the lawn area.

They found Annabelle and Robert Saxon a few moments later at the far end of the garden. Annabelle, in a high-waisted gown of leaf-green jaconet that bared more of her full bosom than was precisely proper, was leaning languidly back against the bright yellow cushions of a lawn lounge placed under a shading willow tree. Robert Saxon was seated beside her, his black head bent attentively in Annabelle's direction. With a burst of innocent pride, Nicole couldn't help admiring her mother's startling beauty, the flaming red hair, the flawless features and the cat-shaped emerald eyes. Annabelle Ashford was undoubtedly one of the loveliest women in England.

"Ah, here you are, my dear," Adrian said coolly. "Don't you think it a bit rude to desert your guests?"

Annabelle shrugged indifferently, then holding out her arms to Nicole, she smiled her dazzling smile and eagerly Nicole went to her. It wasn't often that Mama was affectionate and Nicole hoarded these moments. Her head against Annabelle's lovely breasts, Nicole smiled shyly at Robert Saxon, who rather mockingly returned the smile.

Casting her husband a calculating glance, Annabelle murmured, "It is so warm, Adrian, and you know these country parties are really not to my liking. I shall return in a moment, but I simply had to have a few minutes of peace and quiet, and Robert so very nicely offered to escort me away from all those babbling country yokels."

Her eyes round with astonishment, Nicole looked up at her mother. "Don't you like the party, Mama? I think it is lovely!"

"Of course I do, darling! It is just that this kind of affair is not as exciting as the ones your father and I attend in London. That is all I meant. Don't bother your head about it."

Satisfied, Nicole rested comfortably against her mother, unaware of the charming picture they presented. It was Robert Saxon who commented on it: "You are to be congratulated, Ashford, on possessing such a lovely wife and, it appears, an extremely lovely child. With that hair and mouth and those great topaz eyes in a few years' time you'll have the suitors clamoring on your doorstep."

Nicole blushed and turned her head away, although she was very pleased. Adrian sent Saxon a long unsmiling look and made some noncommittal remark. Sensing that the three adults were only making conversation in front of her, after one last hug Nicole stood and said, "If you will excuse me, I shall go and find Giles."

"Run along, sweetheart," Adrian replied, and without another thought Nicole wandered down the neatly manicured flagstone path on her way to the house.

There was a faint smell of lavender in the air that mingled with the heavy perfume of the rosebushes that lined the path. Taking a deep breath, Nicole savored the heady, rich fragrance that surrounded her. Today had been so special. So perfect she would remember it forever. Her first grown-up party, and Mama so lovely and Father so handsome and kind. It was wonderful. Wonderful to live here at Ashland, wonderful to have Giles for a brother and to be the daughter of her parents. With a sense of growing pride she approached the stately house that she called home, thinking of the generations of Ashfords that had lived in this very house; of the Ashfords that had sailed with Drake, of the Ashfords that had fought against Cromwell and had gone into exile with their prince, of the Ashfords that had been advisors and friends of the various monarchs, and she felt her heart swell with pride. Someday she would do great things too! She really would! And Giles and Mama and Father would be so very proud of her.

Then laughing at her own sudden intensity, she began to run in search of Giles, finding him, as she expected, in the hayloft of the stables. The hayloft provided a perfect place to overlook Shadow and Midnight, and together the twins spent several moments watching the still-clumsy movements of the young foal. Rising to her feet and brushing away the bits of clinging straw, Nicole said, "We had better go back, Giles. Father thinks it is rude to leave our guests."

Reluctantly Giles agreed and slowly he began to climb down the ladder that led to the floor of the stable. Nicole was following him when her foot slipped and she started to fall. She tried to save herself only she couldn't regain her balance and her body came hurtling down, down, down . . .

With a smothered gasp, Nicole sat up in the bed, her eyes feverishly searching the room. It was her bedroom, just as it should be, only it was different. The furnishings, were the same, but toys no longer filled the chest under the window and no dress lay on the arm of the chair. It was different within herself, different because she realized with a sickening lurch in the region of her heart that she had been dreaming again. Dreaming of that won-

9

derful day, just over a year ago. Dreaming of the way it had been then, dreaming that Giles and Mama and Father were still alive.

Choking back a sob, she threw back the covers, staring hard at the door to her room, knowing that never again would Giles come bursting through, never again would Father call her his little girl, never again would Mama clasp her near. A low moan of pain escaped from her and with awkward movements, as if she were in agony, she stumbled to the window that overlooked the back lawn, that lawn where only last year the wonderful party had been held. Staring blindly out the window, she wondered bleakly at how swiftly it had all changed. Six weeks after the garden party they had traveled to Brighton, Adrian having decided that the sea air would be a delightful change for them all. And it was . . . at first.

Giles and she loved the sea and frequently the entire family had sailed on the bay at Brighton, reveling in the crisp air, the swell of the ocean beneath their feet. Adrian had even purchased their very own small yacht, christening it *The Nicole*, much to Nicole's nearly bursting pride. Oh, yes, it had been a wonderful time . . . until *that* day.

The day had been slightly overcast, a stiff wind had been blowing across the bay, making the waters choppy, the weather uncertain. It had been somewhat hastily planned for Adrian and Annabelle to take out *The Nicole* by themselves, Annabelle claiming she wished to have her husband to herself for once. But Giles, full of high spirits and mischief, had decided to surprise his parents by sneaking aboard and hiding in the cabin, determined not to reveal himself until the yacht was far enough away to make it impractical to return him to the dock.

Perhaps if Nicole hadn't sprained her ankle and been forbidden to walk on it, Giles would have remained with her. Except for that sprained ankle there had been the very distinct possibility that Nicole might have joined Giles, the pair of them giggling over this latest prank. But fate decreed otherwise, and so it was that Nicole had been confined at their summer residence, watching from the balcony that overlooked the bay when the accident occurred. Her foot propped up on a pile of fluffy pillows, she saw *The Nicole* slip away from the dock and skim lightly across the choppy bay. A smile on her face, she imagined Giles's appearance on the deck. And then, her smile vanished, for *The Nicole*, running before the wind, suddenly veered crazily and floundered onto her side. Before Nicole's shocked and horrified gaze, the gleaming white yacht had sunk, disappearing almost instantly beneath the white-capped blue waters.

The hours following the mishap had been filled with suffocating fear as she watched and waited with increasing panic for word of her family. They couldn't drown, they *couldn't*, she kept repeating over and over like a prayer. Friends of the Ashfords had arrived instantly, including Mrs. Eggleston. It was to Mrs. Eggleston, her arms wrapped tightly around the white-faced child, that the task had fallen to tell her that her parents had drowned; their bodies had been washed ashore by the tide just before dawn. Of Giles nothing was ever found, and it was believed that he had been trapped in the cabin of the yacht, unable to fight his way to the surface.

Thinking of that, of Giles forever in the ocean depths, brought it all back so vividly that Nicole couldn't bear it, and with an anguished cry she closed her eyes, willing it to have been a nightmare. But it wasn't.

In a way Nicole missed Giles more than she did either Annabelle or Adrian, for in the manner of many of the wellborn, her parents had oftentimes been too busy for their offspring, and Nicole and Giles were more familiar with nursemaids and nannies than the company of their parents.

For Nicole the death of her family had been a tragedy in more ways than the obvious. Not only had she lost a beloved brother, a twin, her father and mother, but their deaths left her without any family at all. And that might not have been so very desperate if Colonel and Mrs. Eggleston had been appointed her guardians. At least with them she would have been loved and cherished. But Annabelle did have a stepsister and Agatha, along with her husband William Markham, had claimed to be a very definite connection of the family.

The Markhams were only remotely related, but since their claim was greater than that of a concerned neighbor, as in the Egglestons' case, Agatha and her husband had been appointed guardians. Guardians to Nicole Ashford's young person *and* her very, very large fortune.

It had been, and still was, a grim adjustment for Nicole. Strangers now occupied the rooms where her mother and father had slept. Even Giles's rooms had not been left untouched—Edward, her seventeen-year-old cousin, had arrogantly commanded them for his use.

The Ashfords had never been particularly intimate with the Markhams, for the two stepsisters had regarded each

11

other with acute aversion. More importantly, Annabelle had come from a wealthy noble family, while Agatha, despite her widowed mother's opportune marriage to a widower of wealth and position, had been barely genteel. And now Nicole was completely under the control of an aunt she had little in common with, a person she barely knew, and an uncle whose vulgarity was disdained by the local gentry.

Leaning her head forlornly against the window jamb, Nicole viewed the day through eyes filled with tears. If only Giles had lived, then things might not seem quite so bad. If Giles had been with her then the Markhams might not seem as beastly. At least then she and Giles could comfort one another. But now . . .

Her heart like a stone in her breast, with lethargic movements she wandered over to the marble washstand and almost numbly began pouring water into a bowl from the pitcher that stood nearby.

It was only as she pulled on her gown for the day, that she remembered Mrs. Eggleston was coming to see her this morning and she felt a flicker of interest stir. Thinking of Mrs. Eggleston's own very recent tragedy, she forgot some of her own troubles. The Colonel had died not two weeks ago, and now, Nicole told herself, it is time for you to comfort Mrs. Eggleston. We can comfort each other, she thought unhappily, and together we can face anything.

2

"You can't leave me!" Nicole blurted out. "You can't possibly! Oh, Mrs. Eggleston, say it isn't true. Why must you leave?" Nicole cried, her face going white with shock at what Mrs. Eggleston had just divulged. The two of them were in the blue room at the front of the house, and Mrs. Eggleston had just very gently told Nicole the extremely unpleasant and unwelcome news that she was leaving for Canada tomorrow morning.

There was such forlorn dismay in Nicole's voice that for a moment Mrs. Eggleston's resolution wavered. She had known the child would be upset and had deliberately, cowardly, put off this last meeting. Nicole's reaction had shaken her more than she cared to admit, but smiling determinedly Mrs. Eggleston said, "My dear, as much as I would like to remain and as much as I shall miss you, I simply cannot stay here in Beddington's Corner any longer." Her faded blue eyes almost pleading for understanding, Mrs. Eggleston continued softly, "We all have to do things occasionally that we would rather not, and this, I'm afraid, is one of those times for me. Believe me, child, I would give anything not to have to leave you at this time, but it is impossible for me to continue to live at Rosehaven."

"But why?" asked Nicole, the huge topaz-brown eyes wide with appeal, the unmistakable sheen of tears not far away.

Feeling even more wretched, if that were possible, Mrs. Eggleston stared at Nicole, wishing she could give some crumb of comfort. Poor child, she thought compassionately, remembering the way the light had died out of the little face when the news of her parents' death had been given to her. A light that had, as yet, never come back. Deliberately, Mrs. Eggleston refused to think about the Markhams and what they were doing to the child, and it was only by sternly reminding herself that she could do nothing to help Nicole that she was able to continue the conversation.

"My dear, I know things are very difficult for you just now, but in time perhaps it won't seem so terrible. Why in a few years you'll be a grown-up young lady attending balls in London and this will all seem like a bad dream."

It was an unfortunate choice of words, for with the dream of how it had been still fresh in Nicole's mind, the tears she had held back this morning in her bedroom suddenly spilled over, running down the thin little cheeks. Mrs. Eggleston felt her own eyes fill, and with an inarticulate murmur she clasped Nicole's shaking body next to her own. "Oh, my dear, do not cry so! *Please* do not! In a moment I too shall be wailing and it will accomplish nothing."

Fighting to control herself, eventually Nicole brought the tears to a stop, her breath coming in rapid little hiccups. Forcing herself to step away from Mrs. Eggleston, she said almost inaudibly, "I am sorry for acting like a baby. It is just that I never thought you would leave me."

Her heart twisting, Mrs. Eggleston murmured softly, "Nicole, my dear, it is not the end of the world, you'll see. I shall write and you must promise to write me back. We shall continue to know how the other is doing, and while I know it is not the same as seeing one another whenever we wish, it will suffice. You'll see that I'm right."

"Oh, how can you say so! You know that my aunt begrudges every penny I ask for—I can just see her paying the shocking cost of mailing a letter to Canada," Nicole said vehemently, a little spurt of spirit returning.

Mrs. Eggleston bit her lip. What Nicole said was true. The house, the lands, and the fortune were all Nicole's, yet the Markhams, moving in with their son with indecent haste, did act as if Nicole were some unnecessary encumbrance with which they had to live. More than once Mrs. Eggleston had seen Agatha order the girl about as if she were some thieving waif who had inadvertently strayed into her hallowed presence. And Edward, Edward made no bones about disliking his younger cousin, treating her with a callous spitefulness that dismayed Mrs. Eggleston. As for William, Agatha's husband, Mrs. Eggleston's little bosom swelled with indignation—he was forever making disgustingly vulgar remarks and it seemed always pinching Nicole's cheeks or nipping her arms, laughing about their little benefactress.

Looking at the slender figure in the white muslin gown, it seemed incredible to Mrs. Eggleston that the thin little girl with the wan features and dull eyes standing so dejectedly across the room from her could possibly be the same Nicole that had romped so happily the day of the garden party. Would the child ever regain that air of gaiety, ever sparkle with happiness again?

Reminding herself that she could do nothing to change the unhappy situation, Mrs. Eggleston firmly closed her mind to more distressing thoughts. Realizing that to prolong this sad little interview would be painful to them both, she said with forced cheerfulness, "Well, write to me when you can, my pet. And now I fear I must be off."

It took a great deal of resolution to leave that lonely little figure, yet knowing she could offer no alternative, that she was, in fact, in a worse position than Nicole, for at least Nicole had a roof over her head, Mrs. Eggleston walked briskly from the room, but her heart was heavy in her breast.

The heaviness in Mrs. Eggleston's breast was not all for Nicole. Mrs. Eggleston herself had troubles, a great deal of trouble, but not for the world would she have let anyone know—certainly not poor little Nicole, the child had burden enough as it was.

Colonel Eggleston's unexpected death of an inflammation of the lung had been a shock, but an even greater one had awaited his widow—it was discovered that not only had he left no fortune of any kind, but that he had been deeply in debt. The gracious home, Rosehaven, where Mrs. Eggleston had lived for over twenty years, was to be sold as well as every item of value that had been gathered throughout the forty years of her marriage. She was to be thrust penniless into the world at a time when she should have been looking forward to a safe, sedate future.

No one, least of all Nicole, knew of the disaster that had befallen her, and with a gentle, stubborn pride, she intended that no one ever would. To her friends, and there were many, she told with a bright smile that there were too many memories at Rosehaven—it was such a big house for one old woman and anyway she wished for a change, saying to those who asked that she was going to live with some distant relatives in Canada. In reality she had been most fortunate to gain employment as a companion to an elderly French émigré lady who was leaving England for Canada. And as Mrs. Bovair planned to sail on Wednesday, this was Mrs. Eggleston's last day in Beddington's Corner.

She returned to Rosehaven and spent the remainder of the morning packing. She would be staying the night at the Bell and Candle, Beddington's Corner's only inn, leaving the following morning for London. And so, depressed and sad, she folded what clothes she felt would be most suitable for her new role in the stoutest valise that she possessed. Afterward there were still a few hours before the carriage would take her into Beddington's Corner for this, the last trip, and she wandered through the empty rooms of her home for the final time.

So many memories, she thought wistfully, some sad, some happy. She stopped before a bay window that overlooked a curved fishpond, and as if it were yesterday, she could see Christopher Saxon, laughing, his young face dark and the thick blue-black hair giving him the appearance of some wild brigand, as he fished a screaming four-year-old Nicole from the shallow depths of the pond.

What had happened to that shining youth, she mused with regret. She hadn't thought of Christopher in years, for it was a painful memory, and she wondered if the boy were even alive. He had been so handsome that spring nine years ago—tall, his smooth skin a dark tawny of bronze, with eyes such an incredible gleaming amber-gold —it seemed impossible to think that such a vibrant young spirit could be dead, or that he had been capable of doing the terrible things they whispered about him.

Christoper, like Nicole, Mrs. Eggleston had known from childhood, and he too, like the twins, had once been a frequent visitor to her home. With a wry smile, she acknowledged that it appeared to be her fate, always to be drawn to children, yet to have none of her own. But Christopher had been almost like the grandchild she would never have, and she still could not bring herself to believe the stories about him. Shrugging aside the unhappy thoughts, she scolded herself—there was no use crying over spilt milk. Decisively, she turned away from the fishpond, but yet, remembering what had happened the last time she had left Beddington's Corner, she hesitated. If she hadn't gone with her husband to Spain that summer, perhaps Christopher would still be here, a young man of twenty-four and not, if he were alive, heaven knew where and in disgrace! She dreaded leaving Nicole, knowing the child was in an unfortunate situation. But knowing there was nothing else she could do, Mrs. Eggleston told herself that just because she had left Christopher and he had come to grief was no indication the same fate would overtake Nicole. Surely not!

And yet, unbeknownst to Mrs. Eggleston, her departure from Beddington's Corner would indeed be the start of a new life for Nicole—a life fraught with deception and peril. Her leaving had in some way awakened Nicole from the almost apathetic state that she had fallen into since her parents' death, and it was in an extremely thoughtful and introspective mood that she joined the Markhams and their son, Edward, for lunch.

After lunch Edward, his blue eyes gleaming with unkind mockery and his blond handsomeness spoiled somewhat by the slightly malicious cast of his lips, said nastily to Nicole, "Poor baby, now you're all alone. Oh me, whatever shall you do?" His eyes narrowing at Nicole's lack of response, he went on, "Well, now that old 'Eggie' is gone, maybe we'll have some peace in this house and not be constantly tripping over her. And maybe now you'll be a little more friendly to me—won't you, dear cuz?"

Nicole flashed him a glance of disdain. Most times he could taunt her into losing her temper, smiling smugly when his parents scolded her for her apparent lack of control. But today Nicole was too distressed by Mrs. Eggleston's departure to rise to his bait.

Edward, seeing that she would not provide him with any sport, shrugged his shoulders and left the dining room, presumably in search of more lively company than his cousin.

With a beaming fondness, Agatha watched her only child saunter from the room, her plump features still retaining a modicum of prettiness. The faded blond hair was skillfully arranged in a cluster of curls that would only have been suitable on a girl half her age, and the gown she wore, while stylish, must have been made for a woman several pounds lighter than Agatha. Watching her aunt's ample bosom swell with maternal pride as Edward walked out the door, Nicole stared, fascinated at the way the seams strained almost to the breaking point yet managed not to burst.

When Edward had gone from the room, Agatha picked up the letter she had been reading to William. It was from a particularly close crony of hers in London.

"Oh, listen to this, William! Beth writes that she has met Anne Saxon!" And with that Agatha began to read aloud.

" 'I was most fortunate last week to meet some neighbors of yours. Didn't you say that Ashland was near Baron Saxon's estate? I'm sure you did. Well, my dear, there I was in Hookham's Lending Library and who should I meet but young Anne Saxon! She is truly a beautiful girl with all those blond curls and blue, *blue* eyes. She is here for the season, I understand, and the gentlemen are already calling her the "incomparable." They say that they are even betting that she will be engaged before the season really begins.' "

Laying down the letter, her aunt shot Nicole a pettish look. "Did you know Anne was to be in London?"

Nicole sighed. Her aunt was most ambitious to join the ranks of the *ton* and she had been mortified and angry when it had been rather forcibly thrust on her that while every door was open to orphaned Nicole Ashford, the same doors did not necessarily swing wide to her less wellborn aunt and uncle.

Consequently, not wishing to be subjected to one of her aunt's frustrated tirades about the unfairness of "certain" people, Nicole replied quietly, "No. Anne is eighteen, she is almost grown. Why should she tell me that she was leaving for London?" And deciding it was wise to shift the attack into her aunt's large lap, Nicole asked curiously, "Why are you so interested in what Anne does?"

Throwing her a look of displeasure, Agatha snapped, "You keep a civil tongue in your head, miss!"

William, his full face flushed from the effects of several glasses of wine served with lunch, said heartily, "Now, now, pet, mustn't ring a peal over our little Nicole, remember how much we owe to her. I expect when she is a little older she will be more interested in all the scandal broth that is so dear to your heart."

For once Nicole was grateful for her uncle's intervention, but that didn't make her any fonder of him. She kept her eyes lowered to the table and wished for the hundredth time that she, too, had been on the sloop that terrible day. She hated these constant scrabbles that erupted over nothing and her uncle's patronizing defense was sometimes worse than her aunt's scolds.

Agatha, still not entirely satisfied, muttered, "I doubt it! She is the dullest child!"

Placidly, William soothed, "Don't fly up in the boughs, my love. When Nicole has her season, she will change. I have no doubt."

"But Nicole won't have a season," Agatha blurted.

Nicole's head jerked up at that, and she intercepted the angry warning look her uncle flashed to her aunt. "Why won't I have a season?" she asked in a puzzled tone.

Her aunt appeared flustered and ignored the question. "That's enough out of you! You may leave the table."

Knowing something was vitally wrong, Nicole stiffened, her little chin hard with resolution. "Why won't I have a season?"

Glaring at her with open dislike, Agatha snapped, "Because you are to marry Edward! There is no need to waste all that money on a London season to find you a husband. It is all arranged."

Speechless for a moment, Nicole could only stare at her aunt. *Marry Edward!* Marry that lazy, malicious son of the two people she most detested in the world? *"Edward!"* she burst out at last with loathing. "I will not marry him! You must be mad to think that I would!"

Suddenly her uncle, his face even redder with temper, commanded, "Now, my girl, you don't get so uppity and you listen here! You have a great fortune and we are your only relatives. We don't want to see you taken advantage of." In a calmer tone he continued, "Marriage with Edward will make certain everything is kept in the family. We won't have any fortune hunters marrying you for your money."

"No, *you* are fortune hunters enough!" Nicole spat, her topaz-dark eyes nearly black with fury, a becoming flush staining her cheeks. She jumped up from her chair, and in a voice trembling with rage she said, "You forget that you are not really any relation of mine at all! That the fortune you worry about does not belong to your family, but to *mine.*" Then turning on her heels and ignoring her uncle's shout for her to stay, she ran from the room, out of the house, and toward the stables.

In the quiet of the stables, breathing heavily, she leaned her hot face on the silken neck of her horse. No longer only hers, she thought bitterly, for rather than waste the money to buy Edward a horse of his own, William had ordered that her horse would be used by Edward whenever he wanted.

Maxwell had been a gift to her from her father on her eleventh birthday, and it galled her to have to share the thoroughbred bay gelding with anyone who mistreated an animal as Edward did. With tender fingers she traced the half-healed wound made by Edward's spurs on the gleaming hide. Oh, why couldn't Edward ride some other horse, she thought with unhappiness.

True, there were others in the stable, but none so fine as Maxwell, for her uncle, in what he said was an economy move, had sold all of her father's handsome hunters and thoroughbreds, leaving the stable shrunk to only a few hacks and a pair of carriage horses. Maxwell, too, would have joined the others under the hammer, only Nicole had roused herself from the grief of her family's deaths to defy him, demanding to know by what right he sold things that were actually hers. Her uncle had backed down, not wishing too many questions asked about where the money went.

The sound of footsteps brought Nicole back to the present and caused her to shrink into a corner of the stall. Just now she didn't want to talk to anyone. She was hoping desperately whoever it was would leave, but instead of leaving, a moment later someone else joined the first person in the stable. Nicole heard a soft mutter, a gasp of laughter, and then silence. Curious, she peered round the edge of the stall and stood transfixed at the sight of Edward, his breeches undone, sprawled in a pile of soft hay with Ellen, the kitchen maid. Edward's hands disappeared under Ellen's skirts and Nicole blinked, unable to believe what she was seeing.

"Oh, Master Edward, whatever would Miss Nicole think if she could see you now?" teased Ellen, her thighs spreading before Nicole's horrified gaze as Edward lay on top of her. Nicole was not so young that she didn't know what they were doing, and sick with disgust she turned away from the sight.

Edward gave an audible grunt, muttering thickly, "Little Nicole will do as she's damn well told."

Nicole tasted bile rising in her throat, and for a second she was terrified that she would be sick. But she fought back the wave of sickness, and with her eyes closed, her mind blank, she waited for them to finish their sordid little act. After what seemed an eternity, she thought she heard them rising to their feet and then Edward said, "Tonight, you'll come to my room?"

Ellen's murmur was lost to Nicole and for that she was thankful. She had heard enough, she didn't want to hear any more. She stayed there, frozen for several minutes after they had departed, and then driven like some vixen before the hounds, she stumbled and ran in the direction of the woods that grew beyond the stables. Blindly she found her way to the deserted summer pavilion that had become her favorite retreat.

The pavilion wasn't on Ashford land, but belonged to their nearest neighbor, Baron Saxon. It had always held a beckoning attraction for Nicole, and lately she found solace in creeping like an intruder into the attic of the building to daydream her woes away. The pavilion was associated with happier times, times when she had been very young and there had been a great deal of visiting between the Ashfords and the Saxons that brought her to it.

The pavilion had fallen into disrepair over the years, the once soft green couches and lounges with their faded scarlet cushions were dull, the finish cracked and peeling. The building itself was no longer a bright cheerful yellow, but a sad, depressing muddy color that gave little clue to its past charm.

Years before, she and Giles had discovered the small attic, which in the past had been used for winter storage. The twins had instantly made it their secret place—a place where no one bothered them, a place where together they would lie on the floor, arms folded under their heads, and stare through the hole in the roof at the blue sky, sharing small secrets and dreaming out loud. But that was in the past, Nicole thought sadly, as she slowly climbed up into the attic.

The events of today had only clarified the misery she felt when she viewed the future. No longer could she tell herself that things would right themselves. Obviously they would not. The Markhams firmly believed that her fortune and her life were theirs to dispose of as they wished. But she was not going to let it happen, she vowed grimly, the spirit and determination that had always been hers wakening and stirring from its long sleep.

What was she to do? she wondered dismally. She would not fall in with the Markham's plans! Edward, she decided dispassionately, was revolting. Fastidiously her straight little nose wrinkled with distaste as she remembered the faint sounds that had drifted from the shifting bodies under the hay—Edward was not going to do that to her!

Resolved upon that point, she felt somewhat better. But knowing that unless the fates were kind or she took fate into her own slender hands she was doomed to wed Edward, she seriously considered escape. Somehow she would remove herself from their greedy clutches.

With half-hearted enthusiasm she began to dwell upon the methods she could use to accomplish this, and because thirteen is very young she was either unaware of or ignored all the obvious obstacles in her path. First, her fancy alighted upon becoming a barmaid at an unknown posting house far away, where the kindly owner and his wife would take her to their bosom. Next, she decided that instead she would run away to London and offer her services as a parlormaid . . . or perhaps a companion to some old charming woman . . . or was she too young? Or best, she would disguise herself as a boy and have an adventurous life in the Army—or, better yet, the Royal Navy—hadn't Giles planned to be a naval officer, hadn't Admiral Nelson been her hero as well as Giles's? And when she was informed laughingly by her father that she couldn't follow her brother to sea, hadn't the twins planned to smuggle her aboard her brother's ship, where they would have a jolly time fighting the French! The more she thought of it, the more the almost-forgotten plan appealed to her. She gave a great sigh, wishing suddenly and forlornly for Giles's comforting presence.

The sound of someone's noisy approach to the pavilion scattered her thoughts and warily she peeked down from her attic hiding place, breathing a sigh of relief when she recognized Sally's slightly plump figure.

Sally's father had been the head groom at Ashland before William, in another economy mood, had fired him, and Nicole and Sally had known each other all their lives. Sally Brown was older than Nicole, soon to reach her sixteenth birthday, and of late the friendship had begun to suffer because of Sally's increasing interest in the opposite sex—something that at the moment bored Nicole intolerably.

"Nicky are you up there?" Sally called once she had walked to the middle of the pavilion.

And with a groan Nicole answered grudgingly, "Yes, I am. What do you want?"

"Well, come down here you silly goose and I'll tell you!"

Nicole made a face, certain that Sally was about to regale her with some silly tale about the Squire's son's supposed amorous interest in Sally's ripening body. But still Nicole was almost pleased to see Sally today, for Sally was a pleasant jolly sort and her foolish chatter would take Nicole's mind off the Markham family and the impending departure of Mrs. Eggleston.

Her eyes dreamy, Sally breathed, "Oh, Nicky, you should see the gorgeous creature that is putting up at the inn. He just arrived but Peg says he'll only be staying tonight. Oh, how I wish I worked at the inn! Peg gets to meet the most handsome coves and gets paid for it too!"

Nicole grimaced and returned in a bored tone, "So what! I thought you had something interesting to tell me."

"But it is! You ought to see him—tall, with hair so dark it really is blue-black, and his eyes remined me of a

22

lion's, gold and"—Sally gave a delicious shiver—"just as dangerous."

"How do you know that? Have you seen him?" Nicole demanded, interested in spite of herself.

"Oh, yes! Peg let me serve him lunch, and I can tell you I could hardly keep myself from touching him—he is so unlike everyone here. His name is Captain Saber, he's an American, and Peg says that he had stopped here to visit one night with friends and then tomorrow is leaving for London. Just think, he has a ship all his own! According to Peg he's been in England buying cargo for sale in America, but she heard him say he wouldn't mind if one or two of our Surrey lads wanted to sign up with him." Sally giggled. "Can you imagine, Jem or even Tim going away to sea? If Captain Saber only knew—Beddington's Corner is no place to find seamen!"

An arrested expression in the topaz eyes, Nicole stared at her friend. "Seamen? You say this man is after seamen?"

"Well, I guess so, at least that's what he told Peg when she asked, ever so politely, you know, what brought him here." As if to excuse her sister's curiosity, Sally added, "It isn't often that we get strangers here and Peg just wondered what a gentrycove like him was doing in Beddington's Corner."

Nicole, her mind already busy with an incredible plan, asked impatiently, "Where is he now?"

Sally shrugged. "I don't know, he left right after lunch. He probably won't be back until late." Sally gave a sigh. "I'll probably never see him again."

"Shush!" Nicole bit out sharply. Her head turning in the direction that Sally had come, she listened for a second and then said, "Quick! Up in the attic, someone is coming!"

"What difference does that make?" Sally asked, but Nicole paid her no heed, already hastily scrambling up into the attic. Sally hesitated a half second and then with a resigned air followed the younger girl. She had barely joined Nicole and positioned herself so that she could look down into the pavilion, when a tall man entered the building.

Sally gave a smothered gasp. "It's him! It's Captain Saber."

The tall man below them apparently didn't hear those barely audible words for he never glanced up. Instead, he stood in the middle of the building and seemed to survey it slowly, as Nicole watched, fascinated in spite of herself by the view she had of his dark, bearded features.

For several moments the man stayed in the pavilion looking around, and Nicole had the odd sensation that this place held memories for him and that they were not happy ones. He picked up one of the faded scarlet cushions and then with an angry exclamation threw it violently away from himself.

Nicole heard the second man's approach at the same time the man below her did, because she saw the way he stiffened and turned to stare at the door. And astonished, she and Sally watched as Lord Saxon's only living son, Robert Saxon, entered the building.

"I wondered if you would meet me after all," Robert said by way of greeting.

Captain Saber smiled, his teeth very white in the black beard. "I'm not a youth anymore to be manipulated at will. And I'm prepared for you this time—last time I trusted you."

Robert regarded him for a moment, taking in the tall, lithe frame, the broad shoulders, and the long, lean legs. Giving no sign that the other's words disturbed him, he said calmly, "It was fortunate I met you on the way to the house. It would never do for Simon to see you and be distressed."

"So you said—but you'll excuse me if I doubt your word!"

Robert smiled thinly. "But you don't exactly doubt my word, do you? If you did, you wouldn't have agreed to meet me here first. Now do you want to hear what I have to say?"

The gold eyes narrowed to dangerous slits, the man called Captain Saber replied in an ugly tone, "Not particularly, but since I was foolish enough to meet you instead of continuing on my way, I shall have to, won't I?"

"So it would appear," Robert agreed and then went on. "My father suffered a nearly fatal seizure just last month and for a while it was feared that he would die. He is quite ill and I rather doubt that your presence will be of any help to him. He has surprised all of us and is very definitely on the mend, to allay any fears you may have that he is on his deathbed. But any shock, any, shall we say, unpleasant surprise could very well bring on a fatal attack. If you are so set upon seeing him—seeing a man who does not want, I might add, to see you—I would suggest that you wait a few weeks."

"I cannot! It was only a whim that brought me here today as it was." Captain Saber hesitated. "I would like to see him, Robert," he said at last. "My ship sails at the end of this week, and I rather doubt that I shall ever return to England. My life is in America and there is nothing here for me—you have no worry that I shall force myself on him, to start tongues wagging once more. I only wanted to see him, to make things easier between us."

"How very admirable," Robert said dryly, apparently unmoved by the passionate thread in the other's voice. "But unfortunately not possible. I would suggest you leave for your ship tonight and forget about ever seeing Lord Saxon again." But then recognizing the stubborn set to the other's fine mouth, he said carefully, "I know that you do not trust me and perhaps with good reason, but what I did I did only for your own good." At Captain Saber's furious step forward, Robert held up a hand and commanded, "Hear me out! I do not want to haggle with you! As I began to say just a second ago, you do not trust me, but in this case I think you should. I will try to prepare the way for you if you insist. Let me talk to Simon first. I shall try to broach the subject gradually and make it less of a shock. But I ask that you be prepared for me to fail."

"Why should I trust you. How do I know that you are not lying to me?" Captain Saber growled in a thick voice.

"You don't," Robert replied carelessly. "But the state of Lord Saxon's health can be verified very easily. And believe me when I say any sudden unsettling event could precipitate a fatal attack. If you want to take that chance then go ahead and force yourself on him."

"Goddamn you!" Captain Saber burst out hotly. "You know that I dare not after what you have told me. Very well then, in this case I shall do what you say. But so help me, Robert, if you—"

"My dear young man! You forget he is my father and that I would do nothing to upset him. As for you— you interest me not at all but I shall try to arrange an interview for you. Now where are you staying?"

His jaw tight, Captain Saber muttered, "At the Bell and Candle. Robert, I meant it when I said I have no desire to create a scandal. And I must return to London tomorrow. You will have to act this evening. I cannot delay my departure beyond tomorrow afternoon." Almost apologetically he added, "I know I should have notified someone of my return as soon as I arrived in England, but I had no thought then of even trying to see him. It was only

25

yesterday that I wondered if perhaps I couldn't try to lessen the constraint between us."

"Mmmm. It is too bad the idea ever crossed your mind. But since it has, I shall do what I can. And, young man, if you do not hear from me by ten o'clock tomorrow, then I shall have failed and you can be assured that any attempt on your part to intrude upon a sick old man will have dangerous consequences."

Captain Saber swallowed with difficulty. "Very well, I understand. If I do not hear from you then I shall know that nothing has changed."

The two men exchanged no further conversation, leaving together, going in opposite directions as soon as they quitted the pavilion.

The pavilion now deserted, Nicole and Sally regarded each other.

"Well!" Sally burst out at last. "I wonder what that was all about? Why does this Captain Saber want to see Lord Saxon so badly?"

Nicole said nothing; the conversation she had just overheard was not of much interest to her. What did interest her, though, was that Captain Saber was here in Surrey and that he wanted seamen. That thought was uppermost in her mind and she was almost oblivious to anything else. Who cared why he wanted to see old Lord Saxon? Or why Robert Saxon was willing to intervene for him? She didn't! Out loud she said, "Who knows. He probably was an underbutler and pinched some silver and now wants to ease his guilty conscience."

"Maybe. But I don't think it was that. More than likely though," Sally said with disappointment. "Wouldn't it have been exciting if it were something more than that, though? Like if—"

"Oh, Sally, will you shut up about it," Nicole muttered with exasperation, suddenly wishing that Sally would leave her alone with her thoughts.

Not unnaturally Sally took offense at Nicole's manner and remarked huffily, "Well, if that's the way you feel! I'll just let you sulk up here by yourself. You are so *young*, Nicole. I honestly don't know why I bother with you."

Nicole, instantly contrite and not really wanting to hurt Sally's feelings, said quickly, "I'm sorry and I'm not sulking. But, Sally, I would like to be by myself, if you don't mind."

Resignedly Sally replied, "All right. I'll go. Shall I see you next week at the horse fair or has your aunt forbidden you to go?"

Her mind elsewhere, Nicole answered absently, "Probably. At least I think so."

Left alone, Nicole sat thinking for several moments. The sea, perhaps that was the answer. America, far away from the Markhams. Here was an unhoped-for opportunity of the greatest magnitude. Surely a kind fate had led Sally to her today. Her young mind filled with schemes and plans, a flame of elation flickering through her body, she scrambled down from her place of concealment and scampered off to Ashland.

It wasn't until well after dinner, a strained and uncomfortable meal, that she was able to put her hastily concocted plan into motion. But once she had been dismissed for the evening, amazing her aunt by not arguing, she climbed the stairs to her room and locked the door behind her. Flying across the room, with hands that trembled with feverish excitement, she rooted through the few precious effects she had managed to keep of her brother's. Amongst them were the objects she sought—a pair of faded pants, one of his shirts, and his favorite jacket, a soft much-worn brown tweed. Quickly she ripped off her dress and pulled on the unfamiliar clothes, using the sash from one of her own gowns to hold up the pants. Not to be daunted by such minor things as baggy pants and a jacket whose sleeves nearly covered her hands, she surveyed herself hopefully in the mirror.

What a laugh she looked, she thought with a giggle, staring at the clownish figure she presented. But then serious, she considered the long sable locks with the glinting auburn lights. *That* would have to go! Ruthlessly she hacked off the long silky hair, carefully gathering the shorn locks and stuffing them into a pillow covering to be dropped in the nearest well. Her hair, what was left of it, stuck out in odd patches, but it definitely gave her a more boyish look—a pretty boy but boyish nonetheless! Feeling more satisfied, she once again examined her appearance. Thank goodness she was still bosomless, but frowning she peered closely at her face. Large, wide-spaced topaz-brown eyes, fringed with exorbitantly long black lashes, stared back, causing her some dissatisfaction. Her nose was pert and straight, if still childish in its appearance, and her wide, generous mouth with a full bottom lip and decidedly firm, little chin completed the picture. After some closer scrutiny she agreed with herself that she made a handsome boy, except for those very feminine curling eyelashes. Well, desperate actions called for stern measures, and carefully, her face pressed close to the mirror, the scissors in one hand, she painstakingly trimmed the offending lashes until they were practically nonexistent. Then taking another long look, she was positive no one would guess her sex, and darkly she vowed that whatever the outcome, she was not returning. She would see the man at the Bell and Candle tonight and she would *make* him take her to sea with him! Without another glance or a second thought she climbed lithely out the window and down the old oak tree that grew near the house.

3

If Nicole's spirits were considerably lighter as she fled through the window, Captain Saber's were not. Seated in the private parlor of the inn, a foaming tankard of ale in his hand, he found his present situation intolerable. Yet at the moment he was unable to do anything about it. Discreet and careful questioning of a number of village inhabitants had elicited the information that Robert's assessment of the situation was correct. Simon Saxon *had* suffered a seizure in January, and the old man's rages and sudden flights of temper were legendary to the townfolk. But in spite of this news it galled him to allow Robert Saxon to have any say in his affairs. Unfortunately, it appeared he would have to trust Robert's diplomacy. He knew he was a fool to have returned, a fool to think perhaps Lord Saxon had forgiven him or learned the truth. And to have returned alone and unarmed was dangerous. It was dangerous to have left London by himself and dangerous to have said so much to Robert. With greater hindsight he realized he should have brought Higgins with him. But he had let it be known that he had no intention of remaining, Saber thought doggedly. He had stated that he was leaving shortly, not to return. That knowledge should keep Robert from planning any unpleasant surprises—surprises such as the last one the man had arranged. He wondered viciously if Robert had told that bitch Annabelle that he had returned.

Bitterly Saber's mouth thinned, and an unattractive light glinted in the amber-gold eyes. Four long years it had cost him. Four years of unspeakable brutality and cruelty in the British Royal Navy—all neatly arranged by kind Robert Saxon! Four years in which he grew from an idealistic boy into a hard, calculating man who had fought bloody sea battles and felt the lash of the cat-o'-nine-tails on his back, leaving scars that would be with him until the day he died.

Remembering those years, his hand tightened about

29

the tankard until the knuckles shone white. Angry with himself for allowing the fury to rise so quickly, he drank the cool ale in one long swallow and slammed the empty tankard down. Grimly he forced himself to push the memories away and to remind himself that in a way Robert had done him a favor. That Robert had not had him impressed into the British Navy for his own good was a moot point! A sharp unhappy laugh broke from him and he rose impatiently from his chair, wishing that he had not bespoken the private parlor. He needed the companionship of fellowmen tonight—not the solitude of this small room.

Beddington's Corner was a small community, and the Bell and Candle, typical of the inns to be found in such places, catered primarily to farmers and village folk. The private parlor was seldom used—few ladies and gentlemen of quality stopped in Beddington's Corner. Seeking more congenial company than his own black thoughts, he left the private parlor, missing Mrs. Eggleston by a few minutes, and joined the noisy group in the dark oak-beamed common room. When he caught the roving eye of that buxom barmaid, he abandoned his plan to drink himself senseless. A few minutes later she was warming his lap, giggling at his bold advances. Between squeals of laughter and false protestations, she let him know her name was Peggy, she was finished at midnight, and was perfectly agreeable to sharing his lonely bed. Smiling, he found himself a small table in a quiet corner and watched with interest the behavior of the boisterous farmhands at the bar. Peggy good-naturedly slapped aside their amorous advances, turning frequently to the tall, dark-haired gentleman who lounged with careless elegance in the corner.

Coo, he was an handsome cove, she thought delightedly, and a *real* gentleman too, with his neatly trimmed beard, white starched cravat, and clean long-fingered hands. A shiver of expectation slid down her spine as it neared midnight. Soon she would creep up the backstairs with that gentleman, and as she caught the lazy, amused glance he sent her through his thick black lashes, a sharp, pleasurable ache hit her stomach.

Saber, knowing he would be pleasantly occupied for the remainder of the night, drank little of the dark, heady ale that flowed so copiously throughout the evening. His head was clear and his step steady, as a few minutes after midnight he and Peggy made their way up the stairs. They reached his room at the top of the stairs a few moments later, and Saber pushed the door open and ushered the eager Peggy inside. She stepped into the dark room and gave a small cry of pain as a crushing weight smashed into her head and she crumpled to the floor. As Saber realized what had happened, he leaped against the wall of the hallway, pressing himself tightly against it. Alert to the sudden danger, his fingers sought the heavy seaman's knife concealed under his clothing. With his body hard against the wall, he turned his face toward the open doorway, straining to see inside the room.

Two shadowy figures seemed to detach themselves from the gloom of the darkened room. A foul expletive broke from one of them as he bent over Peg's still form. "It's the bloody barmaid! Where's the man?"

They both whirled quickly and ran out into the hall just as Saber, knife in hand, stepped out from his place of concealment. Startled, the two hesitated, then rushed him, but he jumped agilely from their path, and with a well-placed kick sent one man sprawling into the other, causing both men to tumble down the narrow staircase. Then leaping down the steps he was on top of them before they had time to recover. He restrained himself from killing them both only when he realized that for him to be found near the courtyard of the inn with two still-warm corpses would benefit Robert as greatly as his death or disappearance. He bellowed for the innkeeper, and kept the two ruffians busy avoiding the murderous aim of his highly polished boots.

It was an hour before all was settled, and then not to Saber's satisfaction. Peg was conscious—but with a throbbing head that would make her think twice about entering a strange gentleman's room in the future. The two men cried loudly of their innocence, claiming that they had mistaken the room and hadn't touched the woman—she must have fallen and hit her head on the floor. Peg quite honestly couldn't remember and Saber guessed there was little to be gained by pressing it, so he coldly accepted their false apologies and allowed the innkeeper to hustle them away. Apparently they were well-known local bullies and the innkeeper wanted no trouble from them.

Glumly Saber surveyed his evening. Dalliance with Peg was out. But more importantly he knew he wouldn't sleep now, remaining in Beddington's Corner would only give Robert Saxon another chance at him. He paid his shot and ordered his horse brought round. Those men had *not* mistaken the room and if, as he had planned originally, he'd drunk himself into a pleasant state of euphoria, they would have easily accomplished their task—whether it was murder, as he strongly suspected, or merely seeing him back in the British Navy. He doubted Robert would try that trick again and felt confident that the plan had been to slit his throat then and there. Tonight's disruption let him know there was little to be gained by staying, and that there existed no likelihood he would have access to Simon Saxon—Robert would see to that!

The landlord was understandably unhappy at the outcome, and while Saber waited impatiently for his horse to be saddled, he attempted to smooth the incident away. Saber found no comfort from his words and strode away toward the stables, intent upon finding out what was taking the hostler so confoundedly long. By the light from one dim lantern he watched the clumsy movements of the sleepy boy until exasperated, he snapped, "Let it be! Go back to bed, I'll do it myself."

The boy, perfectly agreeable, stumbled away back to his bed in the hay and with quick, sure motions Saber finished the job. He was on the point of leading the horse, a deep-chested bay gelding, from the stables when a gruff little voice halted him.

"Please, sir, are you the gentleman from London who is looking for seamen?"

Startled, Saber turned on his heel and gazed with astonished amusement at the small figure before him. In an ill-fitting set of clothes, the boy stared back, his wide eyes fringed by a set of stubby lashes. From underneath a black, floppy brimmed hat, short ragged ends of dark hair stuck out, adding to the boy's odd appearance. He was young, not more than ten, Saber guessed, and smiling kindly he said, "News travels fast—I did need seamen, but I'm afraid circumstances are such that I find myself compelled to leave earlier than I had planned. Were you interested in a life at sea?"

Her heart pounding so hard she felt certain he could hear it, Nicole gasped, "Yes, sir. Will you have me? I'm much stronger than I look and I would work *very* hard!"

Shaking his head slowly, Saber tried to soften the blow as he confronted the urchin's pleading topaz eyes. "I'm positive you would, but you are a little . . . too young. Perhaps next time?"

He gave the boy a polite nod and turned to mount his

horse. One foot was already in the stirrup when a desperate hand clutched his arm and an impassioned voice cried softly, "Oh, please, sir! Take me with you! I promise you'll never be sorry. Please!"

Gazing down into those wide, begging eyes, he hesitated, strangely touched by this boy. Sensing he was weakening, Nicole pleaded, "Please give me a chance, sir!"

Saber might have ridden away, regretful at having turned the child down, if the stableboy hadn't been aroused by their voices and chosen that moment to interfere.

Though only a country inn, the Bell and Candle was a very proper inn, one that didn't put up with its guests being plagued by beggars and nasty riffraff. Bristling, the stableboy approached and ordered Nicole away. Grasping her collar, he attempted to throw her out of the stable and shouted, "Be gone with you, you little tramp! Go beg somewhere else. Don't bother this gentleman."

All her hopes disappearing, Nicole gave into a wave of undiluted anger and nearly spitting with rage, she fought back, clawing and kicking like a wild little animal, even going so far as to bite the unprepared stableboy on the arm. "Let me go! I shall go to sea. I shall! I *shall!*"

The stableboy was nearly twice Nicole's size and once his first surprise vanished he flew at her, intending to give this little beggar the thrashing of his life. But Nicole was fighting mad and she gave as good as she got, receiving a bloody nose in the process. It was an unfair fight and had but one ending until Saber took a hand. Plucking her bodily off the stableboy, as she pummeled him wildly, he said laughing, "Very well, my little fox cub. You shall go with me!"

Astonishment held her motionless, and then ignoring the pain of her bloody nose and a rapidly puffing eye, she grinned. And Saber, unable to understand his motives, found himself grinning back.

Mounting his horse, he reached down and swung her light weight up behind him, and then riding out into the black night, they left Beddington's Corner behind them. Her head pressed tightly to Saber's back, her skinny arms wrapped around him in a death hold, Nicole could hardly keep from shouting out loud for joy. It had worked! She was off to sea!

PART ONE

1813
YOUNG NICK

"Let tomorrow take care of tomorrow,—
leave things of the future to fate."

—Charles Swain, "Imaginary Evils"

4

The lagoon was like glass and dreamily Nicole stared into the smooth turquoise depths, her thoughts drifting in lazy rhythm with the waves. She was lying with a companion on the warm white sands of one of the many small islands that comprise the Bermuda Islands, having left the ship a short while ago for a few hours of quiet and privacy. The islands had long been one of Captain Saber's favorite stopping places, and the fact that a large portion of the British Navy was stationed at the main island added a bit of spice and danger to his continued use of it.

The more than three hundred tiny islands, strung out like a hilly green necklace across the Atlantic Ocean, were ideal hiding places for many of the American privateers that preyed on the British, French, and Spanish shipping fleets. The Bermudas were the last bit of land until the Azores, and the warm Gulf Stream that carried the ships, loaded with spices, tobacco, and sugar from the West Indies, toward the colder, greener waters of the north Atlantic flowed just beyond their coral reefs.

There were too many of the islands, most uninhabited, for the British Navy to patrol effectively and American privateers were quick to take advantage of that fact—besides *they* were not frightened of the greatest sea power on the ocean. Impudently they outsailed and outmaneuvered the heavier, more cumbersome warships of the British. The brash Americans were not beyond attacking and, worse, occasionally capturing a British naval ship. The war declared in 1812 by President Madison gave the privateers the added glory of performing a patriotic duty with every ship they took. Their depredations upon the English fighting fleet were not great, but it wasn't the British Navy that the Americans menaced. It was loaded merchantmen on their way to Europe from the West Indies that drew the privateers and outright pirates, like sharks after a bloodied corpse.

Captain Saber, like many others sailing with letters of marque from more than one country, had grown rich off those fat carriers of the wealth of the islands.

Of late though, Nicole decided thoughtfully, the Captain seemed almost to play at privateering. He acted much in the manner of a well-fed tiger, replete but unable to resist the lure of the plump pigeons that paraded beneath his nose in the guise of the trading ships of the British. *La Belle Garce,* his sleek heavily armed schooner, had taken merely two prizes this past six months, and Nicole suspected that Saber had captured the two—an English barkentine late of Jamaica, and a Spanish merchantman, sailing for Cadiz—to quiet the rumblings of the crew and simply because he was bored!

Frowning, she stared blankly at the inviting waters of the small cove where she lay wondering about a man who could name his ship *La Belle Garce,* The Beautiful Bitch. Saber had been acting strange for months now, and she wondered uneasily if he did indeed suspect her disguise. She moved restlessly on the warm sand, not liking the path her thoughts were following.

Why couldn't things stay as they were, she wondered pensively. She had thrived during the past five years, for they had been filled with excitement and danger. Sometimes she even forgot that she was a female and not the tall, slim cabin boy from *La Belle Garce.* Her charade had been relatively simple during the first year or so, for nature, as if abetting her masquerade, had endowed her with a height that was somewhat above average in a girl and a deep husky voice that would be unusual in a woman but would pass unnoticed in a youth.

The Captain, who didn't understand the queer whim that had possessed him, had carelessly dumped her on the deck of his ship and promptly forgot her. Nicole spent several weeks living in unspeakable misery and fear in the cramped hold of the ship before he noticed her again. In the meantime she slaved such long hard hours that at night she tumbled into her hammock, slung between the decks along with the other crew members', almost completely exhausted. Every filthy job came her way, from the emptying of the slop jars in the officers' quarters to the hard sweaty work of scraping the hull of the ship. Being the lowliest member of the crew, as well as the youngest and newest, she was at the beck and call of every member of the ship, and it seemed to her in those first frightening weeks that she spent more time running errands between decks than anything else. Astonishingly she managed to endure it all. The thought of having escaped from the Markhams lifted her flagging spirits and the cool, clean salt-sweet breezes that blew over the ocean soothed her inner qualms about the rash step she had taken. And there were other compensations too, for she loved being ordered into the riggings, and like an agile monkey, she would swiftly clamber up into the sails, unafraid of the danger and nearly intoxicated by the dizzying height. And there was the power of the sea to drug one, the many moods, from placid gentleness to the exhilaration of the thunder and crash of a storm. And excitement—oh, yes, excitement . . .

Never, she thought dreamily, would she ever forget her first sea battle . . . That day when a Spanish merchantman had been sighted and *La Belle Garce* had swooped down on its prey like a hawk. When the first warning shots were fired, she had felt a quiver of youthful terror, but then the blood of other sea fighters flowed in her veins and eagerly, her topaz-brown eyes sparkling with adventure, she joined the fray, willing and almost impatient to do her share. When the Captain had noticed her slight figure dashing about the smoke-filled decks, he had harshly ordered her to one of the cabins and out of danger. Fiercely she had demanded that she be returned to the deck, but he would not allow it.

Moved perhaps by the obvious youth of the boy, Saber then designated Nicole as his personal servant. There were sneers and sly remarks about Captain Saber's "pretty boy," but Nicole, too aware of the danger, for once wisely held her tongue and pretended not to hear . . . or understand their meaning.

Once she became the Captain's servant, much of the danger of discovery was alleviated for he, with the same amount of indifferent concern he would bestow upon a forward puppy, had ordered her to sleep in a corner of his cabin. And so indignantly she had strung her hammock in the corner farthest away from the now-not-so-worshipped Captain Saber and with little enthusiasm saw to the task of keeping his cabin, as well as his gear, in excellent condition.

Her disappointment in her new status was obvious, and the darkling looks she cast his way, as she busied herself doing his commands, seemed to afford him a certain amount of wicked amusement. And often he chided his erstwhile cabin boy for lack of gratitude:

"You know, young Nick, I could name a half dozen boys below decks at this very moment who would be delighted to be in your shoes—and do a better job to boot!"

Nicole's unruly tongue moved her to speak unwisely, as well as disrespectfully, and she received a sharp box on the ears that left her head ringing for an hour. But the Captain's point was well taken and she resigned herself to the monotonous task of caring for his personal effects. Muttering under her breath that she would have been better off as a parlormaid, Nicole gritted her teeth and set to work. But relief from this trying set of affairs was in sight, although, again, it wasn't precisely what she would have wished for. When he discovered by accident that his ungrateful cabin boy could also read and write, a circumstance that made him take a more appraising look at the boy, he promptly put him to use in compiling legible lists of the plunder they captured. Eventually the disgruntled Nicole found herself not only his personal servant but his secretary as well.

In her calmer moments she realized that had she been left with the rough crew of *La Belle Garce*, it was doubtful her sex would have remained a secret for long, certainly not for five years! But as the Captain's property and secretary she was removed from close association with the men. As for the Captain, himself, as long as she obeyed promptly, he never wasted a second glance on her. But she sometimes wondered if he suspected her secret, and turning over on her side she faced her companion and asked abruptly, "Allen, do you think Captain Saber knows that I'm a girl?"

"God in heaven, I should hope not! Your life wouldn't be worth last year's scuttlebutt, if he did," Allen answered with unnecessary promptness.

Looking at his dark, open face, the brown, curly hair moving slightly in the soft breeze, Nicole questioned again his reasons for joining Captain Saber's crew.

Allen Ballard was an enigma to Nicole. He had joined *La Belle Garce* after deserting the British Navy less than a year ago, and she often puzzled over his reasons for doing so. She knew little about him, but from the neatness of his clothes and his beautiful manners, it was obvious he came from a much better background than the majority of the crew. His air of assurance as well as his manners and dress, indicated that he must have been an officer, so it wasn't surprising that Saber had chosen him as second-in-command for this last journey. Nicole had been drawn to Allen instantly. He reminded her of

Giles, with his quiet, thoughtful manner, and one of those odd shipboard bonds had sprung up between them.

Because they spent most of their free time in port together, it hadn't taken Allen very long to discover that Nicole was not the slender boy she appeared.

It had been on an occasion much like today, when he had stumbled across her lying naked on the warm sands of a secluded little cove. At first he couldn't believe his eyes. Nicole had instantly pleaded with him not to betray her. He hadn't liked it, and liked it even less when she confessed, reluctantly, the whole story. Vainly he had argued with her to let him arrange for her return to England, to the bosom of her family, and stonily Nicole had stared back at him. She resisted every plea he put forth, but she had noticed it was queer that he never put forth the one argument against which she had no defense —that the Captain would have to be told! She had often wondered why but chose not to dwell on it.

Sometimes, though, she suspected Allen was more than he appeared. He was inordinately interested in all that went on in the Captain's quarters, especially his official papers and lists of ships and cargoes taken. Nicole had thought Allen was merely unduly involved in the profit that would be made until recently when she had caught him searching through Saber's private papers. She had read murder in his eyes in that instant before he recognized her, and then an odd expression had flitted across his face—Regret? Embarrassment? Resignation?

It was an awkward confrontation and Allen had quickly bound her to secrecy by the simple promise that if she did not betray him, he would continue to hold his tongue about her!

Surprisingly it had brought them closer together, for Nicole had come a long way from the almost worshipful manner in which she had first viewed Captain Saber. But she didn't want to think about anything today. She wanted to enjoy these moments of freedom and impatiently she wriggled under the scratchy feel of her rough cotton shirt.

Normally Nicole would have shed her clothes the moment she reached the beach. But Allen was rather peculiar about things like that, so she was wearing an abbreviated version of her usual clothes, the shirt tied under her high bosom and the cotton pants cut off near the tops of her slender thighs. She had another pair of long black pants to wear back to the ship, for no one seeing the delicately curved long legs would have any doubt about her sex.

Rising gracefully to her feet, she regarded the prone Allen. He was wearing much the same costume, except his strong muscled back was bare to the heat of the sun and there was a long seaman's knife strapped about his hard waist. No shirt for Allen, she thought resentfully. Then her mood shifted quickly, as always, and she asked, "Shall we dive from the rock?"

Though Allen liked it, this particular cove was not really one of Nicole's favorites for it possessed a brooding air that made her uneasy. Perhaps it was because of the black volcanic rock that rose so steeply on either side, reaching out like sinister arms, and because the lagoon was deeper than most, the water was a dark, rather menacing blue instead of the clear azure of the coves Nicole preferred. But it did possess a high outcropping of rock at the end of one of the arms that made an excellent point from which to dive into the cool blue depths.

His blue eyes lazy, Allen murmured sleepily, "You go ahead, Nick. I'll be there eventually."

And so Nicole slowly climbed the rocks alone. Reaching the top, for a long minute she stared out at the open sea, then down into the crystal blueness of the lagoon. Here the waters were almost fifty feet deep, and the fact that there were no hidden rocks made it ideal for diving. She glanced over her shoulder, and seeing that Allen was at last beginning to climb to the top, she gave him a cheerful wave and then, a graceful figure of hair flamed by the sun and long golden legs, she dived into the water. Down she plunged and then her legs moving in a scissorlike fashion, she propelled herself to the surface. The water was a silken delight after the warmth of the sun, and for several minutes she swam in lazy circles, waiting for Allen to appear at the top of the rock.

She had no feeling of impending danger, just sheer enjoyment at the caress of the satin seawater. Allen appeared, and floating on her back, she kicked a high spume of water in his direction, laughing. "Join me—it's like heaven."

Allen, some fifteen to twenty feet above her, grinned down at her, appreciating the enticing picture she made. Then he stiffened and in a voice harsh with urgency and fear he shouted, "Nick! Below you!"

Instantly stopping her antics, she let her feet sink down and stared into the water. And there it was, circling, not fifteen feet below her—the long deadly shape that every seaman dreads—shark!

A chill slithered down her spine and terror made her clumsy as she began with awkward strokes to swim the one hundred yards that separated her from safety. The beach was her only hope, for the steep sides of the lagoon offered no chance of escape from the water. Fervently she sent up a little prayer that the shark was only curious, and as her first spurt of terror abated she swam with her usual strong and swift motions. But the shark was more than just curious. There was something so frightening and threatening in the creature's increasingly narrow circles that Nicole sensed it was only a matter of minutes before the monster struck at her long, flashing legs.

As if undecided, the shark glided to a position some yards in front of her, effectively, whether by accident or design, cutting off her retreat to the beach. Nicole stopped her race for safety, treading water and swallowing a lump of fear as she watched the shark swim back and forth some twelve feet in front of her.

She cast an uncertain glance back at Allen. He still stood on the rocky outcropping, his own face as white as hers, his eyes intent on the sleek, menacing creature now swimming not ten feet in front of her.

His voice encouraging, Allen shouted, "Keep swimming, Nick. For God's sake don't start to panic and flounder around—that will only disturb it. Keep swimming!"

Swallowing a mouthful of pure fear and grimly telling herself that her life was not going to end in a shark's belly, she followed Allen's advice. But she saw that the shark was once again directly under her, and she watched with glazed eyes as it drifted slowly upward toward her defenseless body, the jaws opening, the rows of teeth like gleaming saw blades. She knew she was indeed going to die—now!

Dimly she heard the splash of Allen's body as he entered the water, the noise and vibration abruptly startling the shark, for it stopped its deadly attack and darted away as if frightened. Seeing Allen's head breaking the surface of the water, she cried, "What the devil are you doing? Now we're both in danger."

"I suppose," he yelled grimly, "I was just to stand there and watch you be torn apart. Shut up, Nick, and start swimming."

The shark, never having gone very far, returned, this time nearer to Allen. He kept a wary eye on the beast before him and firmly gripped the handle of the razor-sharp seaman's blade. "Get going, Nick, goddamnit!" he shouted over his shoulder.

"But you!" she argued, knowing he was right, but unable to leave him.

"And what the devil can you do! If you would kindly get the hell out of here, I could do the same! Now is not the time for you to get heroic!"

She stifled a hysterical giggle and wondered what he would call his actions. Then with a speed that was prompted as much from the fear that any second she would feel those saw-toothed jaws tearing into her body, as the knowledge that Allen would not attempt the shore until she was safe, she hurtled to the beach. Splashing into ankle-deep water, she turned, thankful to see that Allen was still alive and not more than fifty yards from the shore. But from the slow, steady strokes he was taking and from the way he stared into the ocean depths, she knew the shark still followed him. Desperately her eyes scanned the small deserted beach, searching frantically for something, anything that could be used to help Allen, but nothing met her eyes.

Gingerly, Allen kept swimming, his eyes never leaving for more than a second the gray streamlined shape that followed so silently and unnervingly on his heels. It was not a huge shark, barely ten feet in length, but even a shark half that size was a deadly enemy to a man in the sea. The knife held tightly in his hand gave him some comfort, as did the nearing shoreline, but Allen was familiar with sharks and this one's actions did not deceive him.

It was, just now, swimming parallel to him, not five feet to his left, and once or twice it had suddenly changed directions, swimming directly under his body, the dorsal fin a scant few inches from his powerful kicking legs.

They were closer to the beach now, and Nicole could see for herself the long destructive shape that seemed to be growing more and more daring in its approach to Allen's brown muscled body. Oh, God, she thought with anguish, save him! He saved me—don't let him die! *Please!* She took a step forward, intent upon flinging herself into the water, but knowing Allen's bravery could very well be for nothing if she did, she stood frozen, her body chilled to the bone as she saw the shark swim once more under Allen. Then turning in one sinuous motion, the creature began the same deadly rush that only moments before had menaced her.

Allen sensed the shark's imminent attack, and the razor-honed blade he clenched in his hand seemed a flimsy protection against the saw-sharp teeth and sandpaper-rough hide of his adversary. But he knew a man *could* win against such a monster, for he had seen it done once, and with a prayer he hoped he could duplicate that feat.

In a tremendous surge that brought the head and shoulders from the water, the shark came at Allen with a speed that took his breath away, but he held onto his courage as he faced that deadly charge and the distance between them became a matter of inches. Then only a heartbeat away from the ravaging jaws, Allen jerked to one side, the knife held in both hands, the blade aimed toward the tail, and drove it deeply into the underbelly, the force of the shark's momentum causing the blade to gut the beast from gill to tail. Barely risking a glance, Allen saw the shark, mortally wounded, guts and blood spilling from the opened cavity, crazily swimming toward the open sea. Then swimming with an unbearable urgency he reached the shore and stumbled into Nicole's welcoming arms.

They held each other for a long moment, both shaken to the very deepest recesses of their beings.

"Oh, my God, Allen! I was so frightened!" Nicole muttered, her face still pale.

His breath coming in deep, agonizing gulps, Allen grinned. "I, too, was just a little uneasy!"

Nicole giggled then, a giggle verging on the hysterical, and a moment later they were both laughing on the sand, glad just to be alive. But Nicole was first to recover and soberly she said, "I owe you my life, Allen. How can I ever repay you?"

For a second the blue eyes roved over her face and the slender body, the alluring curves obvious in the wet clothes, but he merely smiled and said, "Nonsense, young Nick! But I don't think we'll go swimming in this place anymore, I wouldn't want to go through that again!"

With a shudder Nicole glanced out at the still waters of the lagoon. "No! Certainly not!"

Not wishing her to dwell on how close to death they had come, he affectionately ruffled the sea-wet head. "Come now! Forget it and just remember next time don't swim out so far."

Giving a subdued smile, she nodded in quick agreement. "The shallows it is for me, for a long time."

They dressed quickly without further conversation, but Nicole knew that she was forever in Allen's debt and that she owed him her very life. It had been an inordinately brave thing that he had done and she would never forget it. *Never!*

5

La Belle Garce was almost deserted when they boarded her some time later. Now Nicole's hair was combed back tightly in a queue that stretched her features, hardening them and hiding the feminine softness. She wore the cheap cotton loose-fitting pants and shirt, and did indeed look to be a tall, slender youth of fifteen.

There were a few men dicing near the foredeck, and with ease she recognized Jake's sandy head amongst them. She glanced at him, wondering anew at all the questions he asked. And as if feeling her gaze, he looked up, his ever-present plug of tobacco bulging in one cheek. He was not a prepossessing person and Nicole decided that he deliberately cultivated that unremarkable appearance. No one would remember him five minutes after meeting him. But Jake asked a lot of questions, Nicole thought, as she nodded at him and quickly walked to the Captain's quarters. Jake was new this trip, and she couldn't quite shake the conviction that Jake, like Allen, had something to hide. But then she shrugged her uncertain thoughts away and entered Captain Saber's quarters.

"Oh, hello, Mr. Higgins," she said cheerfully, seeing the first mate bent over a map on one of the room's long tables.

"Morning, Nick. Looking for the Captain?"

Nicole liked Mr. Higgins. His brown button eyes were always merry and he appeared to have a soft spot for her, because more than one time he had covered up some minor transgression of hers from the captain's gimlet eyes.

"No. Not really. But I thought I should report back to the ship. I've been gone all morning," she admitted with a guilty smile.

"Well, the Captain's gone visiting." A sly grin wrinkling his already creased face, Higgins murmured, "And we know who he's visiting, don't we?"

47

"Louise Huntleigh," Nicole said flatly, wondering why the news depressed her.

Higgins nodded, his brown eyes twinkling. "Ah, yes. If the Captain isn't careful, his sea-roving days will be over."

"I hardly think so," drawled a deep lazy voice unexpectedly from the doorway.

And turning around, Nicole felt her heart lurch in her breast as she met the amber-gold gaze of the Captain. Lately it seemed the sudden sight of him always did that to her, and she resented it—resented, too, his unashamed masculinity as he stood in the door of the cabin, a brief towel tied around his lean hips. His skin was burned a deep dark bronze, his chest wide and well-muscled with a mat of fine black hair, his legs long and lean like the rest of him, and he reminded Nicole vividly of a sleek, untamed tawny-pelted panther, his gold eyes gleaming mockingly between thick black lashes. He had obviously just returned from a swim in the sea, for drops of salt water were staining the wood floor of the deck. Disregarding the two occupants, he casually undid the towel, and Nicole swiftly averted her eyes from the sight of that tall, broad-shouldered, naked figure as he walked with a lithe nonchalance to his private quarters.

Higgins saw her instinctive movement and there was a question in his eyes. Nicole sent him a feeble smile, and after a minute, still wondering at her shyness, Higgins shrugged and went back to studying his map. But before she could escape from the Captain's disturbing presence, his voice halted her. "Nick, where the hell did you put those black breeches I bought in Boston last trip?"

With a resigned sigh, knowing the hours of freedom were over, Nicole reluctantly walked into Saber's private quarters.

Saber, still naked, was standing with his back to her, before an oak chest with one drawer open, as he rummaged through the clothes that filled it. And for a moment Nick was caught by the sheer beauty of that sun-coppered, undoubtedly hard, masculine body. He was tall, an inch or two over six feet, a perfectly proportioned Apollo from the crown of his well-shaped black head to the soles of his aristocratically narrow feet, and she wished desperately that she could view his nakedness, his almost pagan beauty, with the same indifference that she gave any other member of the crew. But she couldn't. Saber unsettled her, making her unconsciously aware of her hidden femininity, and lately those unwelcome feelings had increased to a point that rendered her normally confident movements clumsy.

This time was no different, and as Saber turned and glanced impatiently over his shoulder at her, she crossed the room and stumbled over a small wooden stool. Saber's quick action, as he leaped and caught her by both shoulders, saved her from falling flat on the floor in front of him.

"Hold it, youngster. Just because I'm in a hurry doesn't mean I expect you to fall at my feet," he grinned at her, his teeth very even and white in the blackness of his neat beard.

Again that unwanted breathlessness assailed Nicole and she was so very conscious of his naked body, of the warm, sea-scented nearness of him, that for one horrifying moment she thought she would melt into his arms and turn her mouth up to the hard experienced fierceness of his recklessly curved lips. But with a suppressed gasp she quickly recovered herself, as her brain clamored—remember he thinks you're a boy!

Jerkily she moved away from his arms and muttered, "Those breeches are here in the sea chest, right where you told me to pack them."

"Oh, so I did," he returned carelessly enough, but there was a puzzled frown between the sardonically carved black eyebrows as he accepted the garment in question from her. "Something wrong, Nick?" he asked unexpectedly.

Finding her tongue swiftly, she mumbled, "No. I'm just having trouble finding my sea legs this trip." She breathed a sigh of relief when he dismissed her after a hard look from narrowed eyes.

She would not have been so relieved if she had known his gaze followed her, the puzzled frown deepening as she slipped from the cabin. What the devil was the matter with the boy, Saber thought. Nick had been as jumpy as a gigged fish lately, and he damn sure wanted to know why. Thinking of it, he finally decided that he had better ask Higgins—Higgins seemed to know everything that went on with the crew. And recalling all the years he and Higgins had spent together, he smiled.

They had been companions from the moment the older man had shielded a bewildered and confused young man, thrown suddenly into the less-than-tender embrace of the British Royal Navy. Those first months had been hell, even with Higgins running interference for him. His back bore the results of those times when Higgins, himself a felon convicted of forgery, had not been able to prevent his hot-headed young friend from coming to grief. Looking back, Saber often thought he would have gone mad if it hadn't been for Higgins's quiet and cool counsel. But even Higgins had run afoul of the brutal system, and when Saber had vowed to jump ship, Higgins had come with him—their roles suddenly reversing, for it was now Saber who led and Higgins who followed. There were few men and, at the moment, no women whom Saber would ever trust, but Higgins was one—the other, people would have been surprised to know, was a black ex-slave named Sanderson.

Sanderson, too, had known adversity, when Saber and Higgins had come across him shortly after their own desertion. He had been on the slave block in New Orleans, and was being sold, it was said, for insolence to his master. It was by accident that the two were there in the square that hot, sunny morning, but the sight of that powerful body, wearing his chains with pride, affected Saber deeply, as he remembered his own recent chains. Pooling their resources, they had bid on the man and shortly found themselves close to being penniless, their only asset a slave noted for his undesirable traits.

It had been a strange trio that had walked away from the slave sale—a little gnome of a man, a tall, broad-shouldered youth, and a sullen, slender negro. Their steps took them to the Lafitte Brothers' smithy, and there, his mouth twisting in a grimace of distaste at the sight of the heavy iron shackles around the man's ankles, Saber had demanded that they be struck off—all of them. The task done, he had roughly pressed the purchase papers along with his last gold coin into the startled man's hand and told him that he was free. In that instant he gained a slave for life.

His lips curved in a relaxed smile, Saber shrugged off thoughts of the past and sauntered into the office of the ship. Higgins was still there, and the recent scene with Nick on his mind, Saber asked, "Higgins, have you noticed anything odd about Nick lately? The boy regards me as a monster and I can't figure out why."

For a moment Higgins hesitated answering him, instantly recalling the peculiar shyness that seemed to overtake the boy whenever the Captain, clothed or not, was around. Finally he said, "Can't say that I have, I think the boy is just growing up and maybe feeling a bit resentful of being no more than your skivvy. Mayhap Nick has ambitions."

Saber snorted. "I doubt it. He's either being downright cheeky to me or trying to blend in with the bulkhead. But you may be right. I'll have to give some thought to his future."

Nicole would have been horrified at the thought of the Captain planning her future, but fortunately she didn't know of this conversation or the expressed opinions of the two men. Consequently she went about her daily tasks as if nothing had altered, although she was conscious that Saber seemed to watch her more closely, and once again she worried that he had discovered her deception. At night while lying in her hammock, thoughts of the Captain invaded her mind and angrily she cursed him. Damn Saber! Even when he wasn't around he possessed the power to distress her.

Some days later the thought occurred to her again, as once more she lay on the warm sands of yet another private little cove. She was alone this time, and she had partially recovered from the fear that struck her heart the first time she had entered the sea after the shark attack. The abject terror was gone, for she believed that it had been a fluke and was not likely to happen again. But she avoided the lagoon where it had happened and she never swam too far from the shore—something she felt certain that the Captain would mock as lily-livered, if he knew. Sighing, she shifted her naked body on the warm sand, wishing that her thoughts didn't always drift to the exasperating and commanding Captain Saber.

Until recently she had not given her relationship with Saber much thought. He was just there, in the background. Reflectively she admitted silently that she had admired him intensely during her first few years on board *La Belle Garce*—he had been that godlike creature who had made her wildest dreams come true, who had lifted her from the Markhams, and who had filled her life with excitement. It hadn't been until the war with England that she had begun to question her emotions.

It was odd, she thought suddenly, that in the five years they had been together, he had never shown any curiosity about his young secretary–cabin boy. He had never evinced any interest in why she had wanted so badly to go to sea or even if she had any family to worry over her.

51

She supposed it was partially due to the fact that one didn't question the motives or backgrounds of the hard-eyed, grim-faced individuals who sailed on the privateers and pirate ships, and he had merely extended that same lack of interest to her. It was an unspoken rule that no one, not even the Captain, pried into a man's reasons for wishing the anonymity of life at sea. Saber had never paid any attention to her beyond seeing that she did as he wanted. He had never been unnecessarily cruel, although he had been a demanding taskmaster. She never questioned their relationship on the ship, nor the way he ran *La Belle Garce,* and somewhat to her confusion she discovered that there was a great deal to admire in him. But that was before, she thought grimly, before he had displayed his complete cold-bloodedness.

It had happened just three months ago—one of the crew, a youth not above eighteen, had smuggled a woman aboard as they left port from France for New Orleans. The woman was a whore, one of the many who walked the waterfront areas, and Nicole had often wondered how Tom, the youth, could have been so enamored by the hard-faced, sly-eyed creature. But he was and, worse, had allowed himself to be convinced by the woman that without him her life was nothing. He was so blind with love and cleverly manipulated by the older woman that he broke one of the cardinal rules of the ship—no women on board when on the high seas. They were two days from France before the whore was discovered, and Nicole shivered remembering the cold rage that had emanated from Saber when Tom and the woman had been brought before him. Tom, he dealt with swiftly—thirty lashes before the crew and the remainder of this trip in the brig.

Nicole had watched the flogging without flinching, the boy's back a mass of torn and bleeding flesh by the time it was over. The punishment was harsh, but Tom had known the risks, and Nicole was uncomfortably aware that an iron hand was necessary to enforce the rules the privateers lived by. She might have disagreed with Saber's punishment, but she didn't hold it against him. No, it was his disposal of the woman that sickened her.

The flogging done, Saber's cold gaze had fallen on the woman. He stared at her a long time, as if undecided what to do with her, and then his eyes had narrowed when she misinterpreted his interest and threw him a coy look of invitation. Watching her, his face expressionless, he said softly, "Take her below and for this trip let the crew enjoy the services of a resident whore!"

The woman's eyes had widened with shock, and pleading and screaming, she was forced below by a group of leering and grinning crewmen. Then, knowing what was in store for the woman, Nicole was well and truly sick. Saber, she decided angrily, was a cold, brutal, unfeeling beast!

Nicole's heart had bled for the plight of the whore. No woman, she thought fiercely, not even a woman of the streets, should be forced to service unceasingly the demands of the entire crew of *La Belle Garce*.

Recalling the incident in vivid detail, she fidgeted unhappily on the beach. It distressed her still and gave her a hollow feeling in the pit of her stomach. Men were such savages, she thought contemptuously. Then a slow slight smile curved the wide, generous mouth—no, not all of them, not Allen.

Thinking of Allen, Nicole's face broke into a pleased smile. Dear, *dear* Allen. It had been Allen who had apologetically suggested to Saber that it wasn't precisely quite the thing to have Nick exposed to *all* that went on in the Captain's quarters. Saber had thrown Allen an icy golden stare, and then those thickly lashed eyes had fallen on Nicole's interested young face. And no doubt remembering the many times he had entertained ladies of less-than-moral character in his room while Nick supposedly slept dreamlessly in the corner, Saber's mouth had quirked in a lazily amused grin and he had ordered Allen to find something nearby for the boy. Consequently, shortly thereafter Nicole found herself the proud possessor of a small cupboard next door to the Captain's quarters.

It really had been a cupboard, but Allen had ordered the ship's carpenter to make some minor revisions. And so Nicole had a tiny room just large enough for her hammock and a small leather-bound chest in which she kept her few belongings. As the months passed she was frequently thankful that Saber had taken Allen's suggestion.

The sun was becoming too hot to remain lying motionless any longer, and Nicole stood up and walked slowly to the edge of the beach. The last vestige of fear of shark attack left her, and she waded out till the silky water was nearly waist high and then swam a short way out into the beckoning blueness. She swam until she felt pleasantly tired and then lazily propelled herself toward the shallows. Thinking herself to be unobserved, she was as natural and unself-conscious as only the young can be, and laughing, she stood up, turning her face up for the kiss of the sun, the green-blue waters swirling about her slender hips like some glorious gown of shimmering satin. But Nicole was not alone.

The man who stood transfixed by the sight before him was hidden by the lush green undergrowth of the tropical forest, and frozen into immobility he made no sound. At first astonished and stunned, he could only stare at the tall laughing girl in the water, her dark auburn hair like a damp mantle of sable fire about her shoulders.

Nicole had grown up into a tall, slender girl, a very tall girl, but not ungainly. She was small boned and finely formed, with beautiful sloping shoulders and a high, proud upthrusting bosom—not voluptuous, but still *very* womanly. Observing the slender waist and delicately rounded hips, the watcher wondered sardonically how anyone could have been in ignorance of her sex! And as she waded to the white sandy beach, the long, supple legs flashing wetly golden in the sunlight, his breath caught in his throat at the sheer, long-limbed beauty of her. The smooth apricot-tinted skin was unblemished, and her full-lipped, almost sultry mouth unleashed a desire to capture her in his arms and taste the sweetness of those tempting lips. He started forward when a sound to his left halted his step, and he recognized instantly the man who stepped out onto the beach.

"Goddamnit, Nick! How many times do I have to warn you? Anyone could come along and discover you!"

Startled, Nicole glanced up apprehensively, but seeing who it was she grinned. "Oh, Allen, you fuss far too much. The ship is on the other side of the island and the men never leave the town—they're too busy getting their fill of rum and whores. Why on earth would they come this far?"

"That's not the point! Someone could and then we'd really be in the soup. I've told you time and time again that if you want to go bathing let me know, so I can at least be on the lookout."

Grimacing and completely unconcerned about her nakedness, Nicole grumbled, "I think you worry overmuch."

Allen shook his head disgustedly. "I don't think you realize the risk we're running. Get some clothes on!"

Good-naturedly, Nicole scrambled into the long cotton

pants, and not taking time to bind her breasts as she usually did, she slipped on her coarse white linen shirt. "There, satisfied?" she challenged.

A smile crossed his darkly tanned face and, a twinkle in his blue eyes, he laughed, "Yes, I'm satisfied. But I think I'm man enough to much prefer you the way you were! Now come over here and let me do something with that tangled mane of yours!"

Obediently Nicole walked over to him, stopping directly in front of him. He seated himself gingerly on one of the boulders of the rocky outcrop that formed the encircling arms of Nicole's cove and, forcing her to kneel in the sand in front of him, proceeded to untangle the heavy auburn hair. Then ruthlessly he scraped it back from her face and bound it tightly in a long braided queue that hung down her back. Finished, he stood up and reached down a hand and helped her to her feet. Gazing into the wide-spaced topaz eyes, their darkness intensified by the heavy black lashes and golden sheen of her skin, he wondered uneasily how much longer this masquerade could last. Her mouth was too sensitive and full to be manly; her nose, with its straight purity of line, only broken by a slight, ever so slight, tip at its end, was much too feminine.

The fact that she had left off three years of her age originally helped enormously, and he supposed a delicate youth of fifteen could look like Nicole. He smiled at her, but couldn't help asking seriously, "How much longer do you think you can continue to carry out this disguise, Nicole? Sooner or later, you'll have to end it. You don't plan on turning into an old salt, do you?"

Nicole hunched a shoulder and turned away from Allen's probing gaze. Staring off into the ocean, her eyes squinting against the glare off the water, she said slowly, "If I were to do as you say and return to England, I would have accomplished nothing but to have given myself a five-year respite. I'm still underage, female, and the Markhams would still have control of my person *and* my money! I have only two courses—to wait until I reach my majority or to marry." Spinning around she asked with a teasing note, "Will you marry me, Allen?"

Dumbfounded, Allen stared at her helplessly and Nicole's laughter bubbled out at his expression. "You see —I have no choice but to wait until I'm of age."

Realizing his lack of speech was less than complimentary, Allen attempted an explanation and found himself stammering to a halt before Nicole's amused stare. Her self-possession occasionally alarmed him. She had no maidenly attributes, and thought as clearly and hard-headedly as a man, so much so that sometimes Allen wondered despairingly if she was even aware that she was a woman! He wasn't in love with her, but he did have a great deal of affection for her and was as fond of her as he would be of a younger brother—and sporadically even *he* was hard pressed to remember she was a woman! But sometimes, as now, he was extremely conscious that she was a female and a young woman of good birth, with a family in England who must often wonder at her fate.

Nicole had no coyness, no airs about her. She was straightforward and there was nothing missish about her! No vapors and maidenly blushes, and he smiled in unwilling amusement as he pictured the stunning effect that she would have on proper London the first time she opened her beautiful mouth and uttered one of the more colorful curses which she had learned from close association with a crew of rough seamen. Throwing a companionable arm about her slender shoulders, he guided her toward the path that ran through the forest. "You know, young lady, if I thought it would work, I *would* marry you! But I'm very much afraid you would lead me such a merry dance, I'd go to my grave long before I plan to!"

"I wish you would marry me, Allen," Nicole said slowly. "Are you certain you couldn't bring yourself to do it? After all, we deal together admirably, and I know you could oust the Markhams."

Allen only shook his head at the coaxing note in her voice. "Nicole, Nicole, what an unnatural girl you are! Don't you dream of falling in love?"

Astonishment halted her steps and perplexedly she stared at him. "But I *do* love you! I love you better than anyone in the whole world!" she protested.

Gently, Allen said, "That's the wrong kind of love, Nicole. Someday you'll know what I mean, and then you'll understand when I say what you feel for me isn't enough."

Frowning, she looked at him doubtfully and Allen flicked her lightly on the nose. "Don't worry about it," he said softly. "Forget it. You'll learn soon enough what I'm talking about, once I get you into some proper clothes."

Inclined to argue, Nicole opened her mouth to pursue the subject. But Allen gave her a determined shove and reluctantly she moved down the path.

And to lighten her mood Allen laughed, "Come along,

young Nick, I've got a surprise for you—one I hope you'll like."

They wandered slowly out of sight and hearing of the hidden watcher, and after a few minutes the man stepped from the concealing greenery onto the path. Though he had not been able to hear their conversation on the beach, he had observed closely their air of intimacy. There was an unpleasant smile about his chiseled lips as he thought grimly that young Nick wasn't the only one due for a surprise!

6

Nicole and Allen, completely unaware that they had been observed, continued on the little dirt path through the lush tropical undergrowth until they reached an area where the forest stopped and signs of encroaching human occupancy could be clearly seen. The forest had been hacked back to make way for the fields of tall green sugarcane, and here and there in the distance a house or building gleamed white against the vivid backdrop of bright blue sky and a multitude of shades of green. Skirting the field where they had come out of the forest, they eventually reached their destination—a small single-storied lime-washed house.

The house belonged to the overseer, a Scotsman, one Ian MacAlister, whom Allen had met about the same time Saber had discovered the not-inconsiderable charms of Louise Huntleigh, the only child of MacAlister's employer. And while Saber paid lazy court to Louise, a deep friendship developed between Allen and MacAlister. Consequently, whenever *La Belle Garce* put into the Bermudas and Allen was free of his duties aboard ship, he spent his time with MacAlister, most times with Nicole in tow.

It hadn't taken too many visits for the canny Scot to stumble across the secret that Nicole and Allen attempted to hide. But beyond muttering that they were both daft to continue such a masquerade, McAlister turned a deaf ear and a blind eye. If the bonnie lass wanted to be a lad, it was none of his concern.

If Ian was prepared to turn a blind eye, Marthe, his woman, a small and comely quadroon, who was also Louise's maid, was not. The whole situation affronted her sense of propriety, but a harsh look and a stern command from her beloved Ian stilled the words of censure on her lips. But for all Marthe's obvious disapproval, she had a soft heart and secretly admired Nicole's cool effrontery. When Allen approached her to help him, she was more than willing to fall in with his plan.

Entering the coolness of the interior of the house, Nicole glanced curiously around the room, searching for anything that could possibly be Allen's surprise. But the house, with its highly polished dark wooden floors and the soft white walls, appeared as it always did.

Rising from the cane-backed chair in which she had been seated, Marthe, wearing a crisp white gown, smiled encouragingly at Nicole. Ian, his ever-present pipe clenched tightly between his teeth, a twinkle in the light blue eyes, laughed. "My, my, lassie, between the two of them they'll maze ye brain with all those fripperies Marthe had been gathering."

Suspiciously, Nicole eyed Marthe and Allen, and Marthe was moved to protest in her soft musical voice, "Hush, you! Miss Nicole, you come with me and don't you pay no attention to him."

Very much in the manner of an animal scenting danger, Nicole cast a wary look around the room. Allen smiled at her obvious uneasiness and gave her a gentle push. "Go with Marthe, Nick. She won't hurt you."

Marthe, impatient and eager to begin the transformation, grasped Nicole's nerveless hand and led her into a small bedroom. Shutting the door on the amused faces of the two men, she turned and surveyed her charge.

Nicole stood stiffly in the center of the room, eyeing the brass tub filled with delicately scented water much as she would a scorpion. A gown of bright butter-yellow muslin was laid out on the bed, and with a growing sense of dismay her eyes fell upon the brushes and combs as well as odd pots of God knows what that littered the low dresser. Swallowing, she took a step backward, but Marthe, the light of determination burning in her black eyes, coaxed, "Come now, Miss Nicole, wouldn't you like to see what Marthe can do? It's only for our own amusement. Besides wouldn't you like to take a nice warm bath in soft rainwater instead of that nasty seawater?"

Gingerly Nicole approached the tub and dipped a hand into the water. It did feel soft, she discovered, delightfully so, and because she knew it would be churlish and ungrateful to spurn what Allen and Marthe felt was a pleasant surprise, she gave in resignedly. Unenthusiastically she allowed Marthe to settle her in the tub and suffered the woman's ministrations. To her astonishment she found the bath enjoyable and she was feminine enough to decide that she liked the lavender scent of the soap that Marthe used with such efficiency. She did not enjoy having her hair washed and protested vehemently until

Marthe calmly poured a bucket of cold water over her head. After that she sat in wet dripping rage, while Marthe ignored Nicole's muttered threats and continued just as if her charge were a young lady used to the services of a lady's maid and not a glowering young savage. But once the bath and subsequent hair washing were behind them, Nicole, wrapped in a huge white towel and sitting in a comfortable chair, found herself so relaxed she nearly fell asleep as Marthe brushed the long dark auburn locks dry. Deftly Marthe piled the glowing hair high on Nicole's head in neat curls. After dusting her lavishly with powder, Marthe coaxed Nicole into a gossamer-thin chemise before slipping the butter-yellow gown over her head. It was a very fashionable gown, but of course Nicole didn't know that, or that it had been included accidentally in an order of Louise's some months ago. Marthe, even then with Allen's half-formed plan in mind, had begged it from her mistress when the gown was discovered to be much too large for the tiny Louise. Marthe had altered it slightly from her memory of Nicole's tall, slender shape, and now the gown flowed about Nicole as if made for her.

Slightly dazed, Nicole stared at herself in the mirror, unable to believe that the regal creature who stared back could possibly be herself. The gown was cut low across the bosom, leaving her shoulders exposed, barely covering the young upthrusting breasts. A moss-green satin ribbon passed under her bosom and was tied in a small bow underneath her breasts, while the remainder of the gown fell in soft folds to her feet—her bare feet. Unfortunately Marthe had been unable to procure slippers of a size for Nicole's long, slender feet. But Nicole never gave her lack of footwear a second thought. Excitedly, like the child she was, she burst into the room where Allen and Ian sat comfortably discussing the latest events of Mr. Madison's war.

Both men looked up and the expressions on their faces were a tribute to Marthe's skill. Not even in his wildest dreams had Allen expected Nicole to look so beautiful, and he stared as if seeing her for the first time. She was truly a lovely girl, he thought, astonished, his gaze lingering on the shining dark fire curls before traveling down the wide forehead and the surprisingly black eyebrows and thickly lashed eyes. Unnecessarily Marthe had lightly darkened her eyebrows and lashes and had applied a light coating of rice powder before gently rouging the soft, full mouth and silently Allen applauded her skill. But there was nothing artificial about the sparkle in the topaz eyes, and as Nicole danced into the room, the yellow gown swirling out behind her, she cried, "Look at me! Am I not grand? Do you think I'm pretty?" Then lowering her eyes, she asked mischievously, "Tell me, Allen, am I as pretty as the women at Madame Maria's that you and Saber visit?"

As Madam Maria's was a very well-known bordello in New Orleans, Allen looked everywhere but at Marthe's outraged face. Clearing his throat uneasily, he said scoldingly, "Nick, Nick, you are not to compare yourself with them—and young ladies do not talk of such things!"

"But I am not a young lady, and I don't know any other women," she confessed with paralyzing candor, then added impishly, "except Marthe."

Allen was torn between the desire to laugh at her artless statement and a strong desire to box her ears. Deciding amusement was the safest course, he said, "Well, hopefully, we're going to do something about your *not* being a young lady!"

At Nicole's sudden mutinous expression he held up a warning hand and commanded, "Now hear me out, Nick, and listen to what I say fairly."

A very unladylike snort was his answer, but surprisingly, without further argument, Nicole sank down onto a nearby sofa and muttered, "Leave well enough alone. I'm perfectly happy the way I am and it's really none of your concern what I do!"

Ignoring her angry words, Allen seated himself across from her, and grasping one of her hands, he said coaxingly, "Now listen to me. What I propose to do won't hurt you—in fact it will help you. You have got to learn to be a girl *and* a lady sooner or later. Marthe and I intend to help you to remember how a young lady should act. If you ever take your place in society again, you can't do it wearing men's clothing and cursing like a sailor. Think about what I'm saying," he finished sternly.

Nicole's lips thinned at his words and she snatched her hand from his loose hold. She would have liked to storm from the room and tear off the gown she was wearing, but common sense made her sit still. The truth of his words were obvious and Nicole hadn't really thought about her eventual return to her ancestral estates. It was something that would occur in the nebulous far-off future. She just expected that someday she would return, sweep the Markhams from her home, and then live happily ever after. And biting her lip uncertainly, she acknowledged within herself that what Allen proposed made sense. At this point she wasn't even sure that she wanted to return to England. Grudgingly she asked, "What exactly do you want to do?"

Allen smiled to himself at her apparent reluctance. She was such a child—no, she wasn't a child anymore, not even the sight of her bare feet peeping out from underneath the fashionable gown could hide the fact that she was a very beautiful young girl. But she was a stubborn little minx too, and he knew his task was not going to be simple. He hoped that by clever maneuvering he could instill in her the desire to *want* to take her place as a wellborn young woman. Carefully, feeling his way, he answered her question.

"Marthe and I have decided between the two of us that you might enjoy being treated as a young woman. We thought that if you would agree, whenever the *La Belle Garce* is in port here, Marthe would act as your maid and Ian and I, with Marthe's help, would coach you in the manners of a lady. It will be a different experience for you, one I'm sure you'll enjoy, if you let yourself. You certainly have nothing to lose."

Frowning, Nicole regarded him. She couldn't see any flaws in Allen's reasoning yet she was suspicious of it. What was the point of learning to be a lady if she had no immediate plans to put that knowledge to use? She glanced at Ian and Marthe, then at Allen. All three faces showed only affectionate interest. Reluctantly she decided that if it meant so much to them, why not?

And in the evening that followed she discovered she enjoyed herself very much indeed. Allen was charming, paying her teasing compliments that brought a flush to her cheeks and increased the glitter of the topaz eyes. Ian and Marthe joined in treating her as if she were a visiting guest. The only thing she didn't like were those times when the three of them corrected her unruly tongue or pointed out that young ladies do not flounce down in a chair in such a manner, nor do they gulp and splutter when drinking champagne, and laughingly Allen commented on her fascination with her image in the mirror.

She couldn't help it. She was mesmerized by her own reflection, yet it was not conceit that drew her eyes to it again and again—it was astonishment! She had to keep looking to reassure herself that the girl in the mirror was really her.

Allen was rather elated with the results of the evening,

but he kept his thoughts to himself as the two of them made their way to the ship. She had a long way to go yet before he would wish to see her in Almack's, but tonight had been the first step forward in making her aware that there was another way of living. He wished not for the first time she would have agreed to stay with Ian and Marthe. They would have been delighted, and while with an overseer and his quadroon mistress was not precisely where he would have preferred Nick to be placed, it was a damned sight better than having her on *La Belle Garce* under Saber's discerning eye—lecherous eye, he amended silently.

He would have been even more elated with tonight's success if he'd known that Nicole had shed her gown and watched Marthe remove all traces of powder and rouge with a definite feeling of regret. She wasn't ready to admit she wanted to keep her first grown-up gown, but she had been struck by a queer, confusing desire for the infuriating Captain Saber to see her arrayed in the butter-yellow muslin, her hair piled high on her head. The thought alarmed her as well as confused her, and she was decidedly uneasy as she climbed into her hammock in her little cupboard on *La Belle Garce*.

This afternoon and evening had stirred old memories and half-forgotten precepts. She never thought of her "other" life, the pampered life of Miss Nicole Ashford, but tonight had awakened reminiscences—memories of her laughing beautiful mother, the candlelight gleaming on her flame-red hair and her satin gown swirling about her feet as she leaned on her husband's proffered arm. Her handsome father would be wearing silks, the white lace of his shirt foaming near his throat. Together they would descend the curving oak staircase to greet their guests while she and Giles peeped down between the railings of the banister; the carved doors to the dining room would be thrown open and the children afforded a glimpse of the long mahogany table hidden beneath a snowy white tablecloth, the crystal twinkling in the candlelight and the silver glowing brightly in the room. What a long time ago it all was, yet the memories were clear as yesterday.

Conscious that she was spending an inordinate amount of time thinking about Saber and things that were best forgotten, Nicole determinedly attempted to fall asleep. It was useless. Her brain was too busy and for the first time the smallness of her sleeping quarters seemed to

63

press in on her. Damnation and hellfire! Why did Allen have to meddle? Her restlessness was all his fault! If he would just leave well enough alone she would work it out herself.

What was she going to do? She owned little beyond the clothes on her back. Her share of the plundered cargoes they'd taken within the past years had been minimal, and she had not saved any of it. She had merely drifted, letting each day take care of itself.

Returning to England, she suddenly realized, was going to present a multitude of difficulties that she had never imagined. It occurred to her, dampening her spirits, that she wouldn't just be able to deposit herself as she was on the family doorstep. Certainly she would more than likely have to prove her identity—and somehow live until her claim was justified. Appallingly the idea presented itself that no one would believe her and her mouth tightened. She *was* Nicole Ashford and she *would* regain her fortune . . . but how?

She turned restlessly in her narrow hammock. Damn Allen! Why couldn't he leave well enough alone? She was happy, she told herself fiercely. Who cared for silly old gowns and scented soap? She didn't! She *liked* seawater baths and her well-worn coarse linen shirt and cotton pants. But then contradictorily she gave a sigh as the memory of that silky chemise came to mind. How soft it had felt lying against her skin!

Allen's worry that Nicole sometimes forgot she was a woman was unfounded. Of late, the last year or two to be exact, she was becoming increasingly aware of a restlessness that had everything to do with her masquerade. She wouldn't acknowledge it to herself, but she had unknowingly begun to take a great interest in the dress and mannerisms of the few women she came in contact with—not the whores the seamen tumbled carelessly below decks on their first night in port after weeks at sea, but the somewhat higher-class ladies whom Saber entertained in his quarters.

The hour was late and crossly Nicole tossed off the light covering that lay across her body. She didn't want to think about it anymore. She was tired and slightly fuzzy from the unaccustomed amount of wine she had drunk tonight. Thinking about the evening, a pleased smile curved her lips and she sighed deeply. Sleepily she wondered if Saber would have been impressed by the change in her, and then angrily chastised herself for even thinking of him in such a connection. What did she care what Saber thought—about anything? She already knew what type of woman appealed to him—dainty little blonds like the lovely Louise—not a tall auburn-haired minx who was more comfortable in boy's clothing than in silks and laces.

7

Nicole was glowering at Saber. It was something she did frequently, but since they had left Bermuda it seemed to her that he had gone out of his way to annoy her. He kept her on her feet continually, racing first after one object and then another that he needed *immediately!* When not running useless errands, he had her painstakingly copying in her neat copperplate hand a complete duplicate list of every cargo they had taken for the past year. Nicole could see no need for this task and suspected angrily that he wanted it merely because it kept her chained to the table where she worked. But what really grated on her nerves was his sudden slipshod manner. He took delight in deliberately creating havoc. Then instead of leaving her alone to get on with it, he lounged in the doorway and watched critically as she straightened his quarters, daring her to complain. Nicole bit her lip and ignored the challenge in his eyes as she finished the rumpled bed. "Will that be all, sir?" she asked woodenly.

"Hmmmm, I suppose for now that will do."

Nicole, glad to escape his increasingly disturbing presence, took a few steps forward, but he remained in the doorway. She halted a short distance from him, uncertain of his mood and slightly uneasy. There was a strange glitter in the yellow-gold eyes, and she didn't like the way those same eyes were regarding her. The assessing quality of his gaze fed her growing uneasiness and nervously, hating herself for the nervousness, she inquired, "May I pass, sir? Or is there something else you require?"

Saber straightened slowly, his tall form filling the doorway, his gleaming black head almost brushing the wooden beam. "How old are you, Nick?" he asked abruptly.

Startled, the topaz eyes grew wide and she stuttered, "Eigh—fifteen!"

An unpleasant smile flitted across his face. "Fifteen, mmm. A bit old for a cabin boy, wouldn't you say?"

Momentarily caught by surprise, Nicole watched him

warily as he walked past her to an array of sturdy decanters that sat on his desk. After splashing a goodly amount of dark Jamaican rum into a glass, he turned and half sitting on the desk, one long leg swinging aimlessly above the floor, stared back at her. For a moment she was filled with a curious trembling in her mid-region as she looked at him. He was, she decided erratically, one of the most vital, virile creatures she had ever seen. And just now, with the white shirt opened nearly to his waist, revealing a muscled chest covered with dark curling hair, the slim hips and long legs clad in black form-hugging breeches, he made Nicole uncomfortably aware of him as a man—a man of extraordinary appeal to the opposite sex! Certain intimate memories of him with other women in this very room crowded her thoughts and an uncontrollable blush suffused her features. Furious with herself, she glared at him and asked aggressively, "Are you telling me, you no longer require my services . . . sir?"

"Did I say that?" he drawled, that unpleasant smile curving his lips once again. Tautly he added, "If you would listen to what *I* say Nick, as readily as you do everything *Allen* says, things would be much easier between us. But that aside, I merely stated that fifteen was a little old for the duties you perform. I probably should assign you to the ship's carpenter, or perhaps you might be interested in training for a gunner's mate. Would you like that?"

It was what at one time she had longed for passionately, but now she was appalled. She could not continue her masquerade in close proximity to the crew. The first time she was unable to carry out a task that required only simple masculine muscle the fat would truly be in the fire! Trusting that her face had not betrayed her, she lifted her chin pugnaciously and said brazenly, "I would like it above all things! Particularly being apprenticed to the gunner's mate."

His mouth tightened disagreeably at her brave words and the challenging tone. Setting the glass down sharply, he replied acidly, "Well, you can forget it! After five years I've grown rather used to your insolent efficiency!"

Unreasonably angry at the fright he had given her, forgetting again as well the danger of letting her ready tongue rule her, she placed her hands on her slender hips and snapped, "You were the one that brought the subject up. I was merely proceeding with my usual insolent efficiency!"

"Careful, Nick," he said softly. "Don't push me too far or I'm likely to treat you as you deserve."

Recalled to her senses by the underlying menace in his voice, she dropped her eyes from his and said expressionlessly, "I apologize, sir. If you'll excuse me, I'll continue working on the cargo lists?"

The lists she had been working on were still scattered over the desk, and after pulling out a heavy oak chair, she sat down stiffly and began to write. She found it an enormous effort to concentrate with Saber just a short distance away. She was too distracted by his lean maleness and loose-limbed strength. From the corner of her eye she could see one sun-browned hand playing idly with a bit of twine that lay on the desk and she wished vehemently that he would leave. She knew he was watching her, knew he was staring at her down-bent head; she could feel it and the muscles in her neck tightened. Worse, she could have sworn aloud when she noticed a slight tremble in her hand as she reached for another slip of paper.

"Relax, Nick. I won't bite, you know." His amusement was obvious and Nicole gritted her teeth. Then once again forgetful of the role she played and ruled by the fire in her hair, she shot him a venomous look.

He grinned back at her, a mocking gleam in the amber-gold eyes. "Young Nick, it occurs to me that in spite of five years' close association, we know very little of each other. Now why is that do you suppose?"

Forcing herself to reply calmly, she said stiffly, "I doubt that most captains are greatly concerned with their cabin boys." Unable to control the impulse, she added sarcastically, "All we have in common are dirty linens, slop jars, and unmade beds—hardly exciting topics of conversation. There is little to know about me as long as I perform my duties satisfactorily."

"But you don't," he said darkly. "You're insolent and you dislike me—a fact you make little effort to hide, I might add. Considering I took you to sea at your very urgent request, I should think you would have a certain liking for me." His voice hardening, he inquired, "But you don't, do you, Nick?"

"I didn't think my likes and dislikes were that important to you," she said cautiously. "You have never commented on my attitude before and if my . . ." She hesitated a moment before saying, "Dislike was as apparent as you seem to feel it is, surely you would have said something previously." Boldly she finished, "I think, sir, you imagine things."

"Do I, Nick? Did I just imagine the look you flashed my way not too many seconds ago? And have I been imagining those baleful glances that frequently follow me from this room?" he asked dryly.

Oh, God, where was Allen? she thought uneasily. Where was anyone who could interrupt this strained conversation? Steeling herself, her eyes met his and she said quietly, "I can only apologize if you have found my manner less than pleasing. I'm sorry to have annoyed you, and I shall try in the future not to give you cause to complain."

It was pompous and she knew it, but she wanted this meeting over with and she wanted Saber gone from this room.

Saber's lip had thinned at her words and slamming down his glass on the desk, he snapped harshly, "I don't want your apologies, damnit! You're very adept at avoiding questions, my friend!" Leaning forward, his face inches from hers, he growled, "Now tell me, young Nick, why you find service with me so distasteful? I want an answer this time—not an excuse or an apology!"

Staring at the hard bearded face so close to hers, Nicole was assailed by a variety of emotions. Uppermost was an acute awareness of him as a man, with the faint scent of tobacco and salt sea air clinging to him. Unbearably conscious of the fact that his mouth was barely a breath away from hers, she wondered foolishly what his reaction would be if she were to lean forward and press her own tremulous lips to that firm mouth.

"I'm waiting, Nick."

His words shattered her erratic thoughts and brought her back to the matter at hand. All wide eyes and innocence she said slowly, "I think that all boys have times when they are rebellious and resentful of those who have authority over them. If I appear to dislike you at times, it must be because of that."

An exasperated snort from Saber preceded his words. "Clever, Nick. An answer that is not an answer." He moved back into his original position and picked up his glass. "Some day soon, you and I must have another little talk. You are after a fashion my . . . er . . . ward, and it has occurred to me that I have not been doing my duty by you. I think perhaps that I shall take more of an interest in you in the future . . . more interest in you than I have in the past."

He stood up, having downed the remainder of his rum. Staring down at Nicole's astonished and faintly dismayed features, he smiled sweetly and said, "You'll enjoy *that*, I'm sure!" He sauntered from the room.

For several seconds Nicole stared after him. Now what the devil did he mean by that? she wondered. With a sigh she turned back to the cargo lists but found she was unable to concentrate. It wasn't like Saber to probe, and she could have sworn, before this morning, that he was hardly aware of his cabin boy's existence. What was behind his odd mood?

She hadn't liked the way his eyes had wandered over her body either. He had seldom glanced her way in the past, but today there had been, at least to her mind, a searching quality in his gaze. Had he guessed? Was her face now too obviously feminine? Had that discerning golden-eyed stare discovered a flaw in her disguise? She glanced down nervously at her flat bosom; her breasts as usual were bound tightly beneath her shirt. No, if anything he would only wonder at her lack of manly muscle. So her disguise hadn't failed her, she was certain . . . almost.

Perhaps, she concluded, he was just bored and enjoyed baiting her. If he had known or even suspected, she wouldn't now be seated before her table. A shiver snaked down her spine as she recalled the red-headed whore's fate and grimly she set about her work.

She worked steadily for some time. The room was quiet and there was only the soft splash of the sea against the hull of the ship and the pleasant whisper of the wind in the sails to disturb her.

La Belle Garce had been built four years ago to Saber's specifications. She was a four-masted schooner, long, low, and rather narrow. The ship was three hundred and nineteen tons of menace, carrying twenty twelve-pound carronades with two long eighteens as chase guns.

The room where Nicole was working was clearly his office; despite the fine rug on the floor and the damask curtains that hung on the portholes across the stern, the heavy oak desk in the corner as well as the charts and maps that lined the wall gave evidence of this. Nicole's table was on the starboard side of the ship, and in the center of the room was another highly polished table with several squat leather chairs pushed beneath it.

The sound of a door opening caused Nicole to look up sharply. "Thank God, it's you, Allen," she muttered.

Settling himself on the edge of the table where she

worked, he laughed. "What's the matter, Nick? Has the Captain been annoying you again?"

Nicole threw down her pen and asked seriously, "Allen, do you think Saber knows that I'm a girl?"

The twinkle in the blue eyes vanished instantly. Concerned, he inquired, "What makes you ask? Has he said something?"

She hunched an impatient shoulder and muttered, "He's acting damned strange, I can tell you that! This morning he talked a lot of nonsense about our not knowing one another and taking an interest in me."

A soundless whistle came from Allen. Frowning, he rubbed his chin thoughtfully. "Mmmm, I don't like the sound of that! Saber is no fool and anyone that took a careful look at you would tumble to your disguise. Nick, this settles it. When we reach New Orleans you have to let me take care of you."

"Oh, Allen, not *that* again! He can't know. If he knew, you can be assured I wouldn't be sitting here now."

"Don't be too sure. He resembles a cat in more ways than one, and he's not above playing with a auburn-headed little mouse. I'm serious, Nick, when we reach port this time you're disembarking with me and I'll make the arrangements for you. My mind is hard on this thought, Nick—you are *not* continuing as you are! If you balk me you'll leave me no alternative but to tell Saber."

Dismayed, Nicole stared pleadingly at him. But his face was set and there was an iron cast to the firm chin. "I mean it, Nick. It's over as soon as we reach New Orleans."

Silently she regarded him. It was curious that he was at last using the ultimate threat. And she wondered why he chose now to use it. Of course, she could retaliate . . . "Aren't you forgetting what I can tell Saber . . . about you?"

Allen's face froze and an ugly look gleamed briefly in the blue eyes. "Are you threatening me, Nick? I should warn you not to. You can run to Saber if you like, but you can't prove anything, and you can be assured that your masquerade will be revealed no matter what you do. On the other hand," he continued smoothly, "you could keep your mouth shut about whatever you suspect and let me keep you until you're in a position or frame of mind to return to England." Gently he added, "I like you, Nicole, and I'll see you safely to your family the instant you say the word."

"I see," she said coldly. "Very well, I'm afraid I have

no real choice but to accept your kind offer." Her voice grated on the word *kind* and Allen winced.

He reached for Nicole's hand and held it between his own. "Don't take it like this, Nick. If you think about it, you know that I'm right. It's the only solution now and I should have demanded it long ago. You mustn't mind too much that I shall be paying your bills—I'm happy to do so. If you dislike it excessively you can keep an account and repay me once your own affairs are settled." Coaxingly he begged, "Let us remain friends, Nicole. We have been close companions too long to part in anger—especially when I'm only thinking of your welfare."

An unwilling smile curved Nicole's mouth. "Oh, damn you, Allen! Have your way. I'm tired of fighting you and perhaps your plan is wiser." Ruefully she admitted, "I've certainly got nothing to lose by it. But I shall repay you—every penny."

There was a discreet cough behind them, and jerking around, Nicole stared aghast at Saber leaning against the door; his arms folded across his chest, he was watching them. Caustically he drawled, "Something wrong with Nick's hand?"

Allen dropped the member in question as if it had suddenly become a red-hot coal, and standing up abruptly he muttered, "Er . . . Nick thought he had a boil coming and I was merely checking."

Sarcastically Saber murmured, "A physician too, no less. I must tell the ship's surgeon when next he requires an assistant that you will be happy to oblige." Then pushing away from the door with one lithe movement and opening it, he said icily, "You're needed on deck, Ballard. In case you haven't noticed, there's a great deal of activity going on. We've sighted another ship and I think it's a damn sight more important than a possible boil on Nick's hand. Besides," he added silkily, "Nick, is my concern—*not* yours!"

Allen's face was carefully blank, but his mouth compressed at Saber's parting shot, and there was a rigid cast to his shoulders as he walked past him. When Allen was gone, Saber slammed the door shut with a violent motion and spun around to face Nicole. "And how often does that go on?" he asked harshly.

Fencing, she fought to keep her expression unworried. "What? I don't understand what you mean." Innocently she asked, "Is Mr. Ballard not supposed to be in here?"

Saber strangled an oath and glared at her. "Don't play me for a fool! I think, young Nick, we'll have that talk very soon, a nice, quiet, private, personal talk—just you and I!"

A rapid pounding on the door forestalled any further conversation. Throwing the door open, Saber barked at Jake, who was standing there before him, "Yes, what is it?"

"Sir, we're closing fast. The ship is an English packet heavily armed, but trying to avoid a fight. Do we go after her?"

Saber grinned and clapped Jake on the arm. "Now what do you think?" he teased.

Then throwing Nicole a look over his shoulder, he commanded, "You stay here! I don't want to see your face topside. Understand?"

Nicole nodded, a knot already tightening in her stomach. Overhead she could hear the sound of the barefooted men as they prepared for action and the rumble of the carronades as the guns were positioned and primed. The sharpshooters, their rifles loaded and ready, would already be climbing up into the riggings, and Nicole knew the main deck would be a hive of industry as every item not needed for the coming battle was cleared and stowed below decks. Saber, from his vantage point on the bridge, would be bellowing out last-minute instructions as the two ships came closer to one another.

She didn't mind when they fought a Spanish ship or even a French one. But when the ship was English, she was at war within herself. Afterward when the prisoners were brought on board and the prize crew transferred to the beaten ship, she felt troubled and shaken that she should join in preying upon her own countrymen.

Trying to ignore what was happening around her, she forced herself to work on the cargo lists. But unable to ignore the thunder of the carronades and the raging noises of battle, she watched the fight from a porthole.

The battle that followed was fierce. The roar and boom of the guns reverberated across the sunlit sea, and the air was filled with smoke and the cries of the wounded. As Nicole looked on, the packet, in a desperate attempt to cripple *La Belle Garce*, unloaded a tremendous broadside. But it did little good for she hadn't the range of the carronades of *La Belle Garce*, and Saber, having guessed her captain would try such a maneuver, had already ordered *La Belle Garce* to jibe sharply and the shots never reached their target.

When at last quiet fell, Nicole went into Saber's private quarters and peered out of a porthole. The packet had put up a gallant fight, but she had been no match for *La Belle Garce*. Her main mast was gone, her sails in shreds, and she was floundering badly. Her deck was littered with wounded men and even as Nicole stared, the ship struck her colors. A cold lump in her throat, Nicole turned away from the scene of carnage. Why did he have to attack English ships? she wondered dully.

It was easy to forget that the United States was at war with Britain; it took an event like today's to remind her of Mr. Madison's war. The campaign in Canada was far removed from Nicole. It was almost as if different countries were involved. The violent battles on the Great Lakes and the blockade on the Chesapeake meant little to her. She could see little reason to become excited about a battle that was weeks or even months old and the outcome already established. New Orleans and the Caribbean were a great distance from the British attack on Fort Stephenson on the Sandusky River in northern Ohio. But now with the victorious crew of *La Belle Garce* boarding the disabled packet and her officers and men being taken prisoner, Mr. Madison's war—the "Printmaker's War"—was very real and very close.

The door opened and she looked up quickly, her heart lurching a little at the sight of Saber. There was a streak of blood across his forehead and under one arm he carried a small hide-and-brass chest. His eyes were blazing yellow-gold with victory, and his black hair was wind ruffled, adding unnecessarily, Nicole thought waspishly, to his already unfair attractiveness. Flashing her a jubilant white grin, he tossed the small chest down on the table and said, "We've found a treasure, Nick! One which the British Navy would pay highly to recover from us."

Her natural curiosity prompted her to come closer. The lock that had previously sealed the chest had been blown apart from the shot of a pistol, and what was left of it clattered to the floor. Peeking inside, Nicole was disappointed to see only a few small black books and some papers.

A perplexed look in her eyes, she asked, "What are they?"

It was Allen coming up quietly behind her who answered, "British code books."

An ominous silence followed Allen's words. Staring blankly at the opened chest Nicole was aware that Saber was watching her closely. She kept her features as unrevealing as possible, hiding the dismay that filled her. Unhappily she wondered how Allen felt about the capture

74

of those little books—those little books that unlocked the British dispatches that had been unfortunate enough to fall into the hands of the Americans; those little books, Nicole thought with confused emotions, that would give the Americans an unfair advantage over the English.

Saber sat down on the table near the chest, lit a thin black cheroot and lifted a book from the chest. Allen couldn't help himself and made an involuntary movement forward, almost as if he meant to snatch the book from Saber's hand. Saber glanced over at him, an unpleasant smile on his mouth, and drawled. "Interested in them, Ballard?"

Allen controlled himself and answered calmly, "Not particularly. But they explain why the packet fought so desperately. I only wonder why the captain didn't destroy them before allowing them to fall into enemy hands?"

Saber shrugged. "He was foolish enough to wait until the last minute before trying to dispose of them. He was caught as he was about to shove them over the side." His eyes on Allen's face he added, "A pity, isn't it, that he wasn't quicker."

Allen remained silent and Saber, apparently losing interest in him, idly flipped through the pages. "Hmmm, I can't make much sense of it, but I'm certain the military at New Orleans will be delighted with them." Then as Allen made no move to leave, he looked at him pointedly and said, "Haven't you something to do on deck?"

A dark red stained Allen's neck, and without another word he spun on his heel and walked stiffly from the room. Saber watched him until the door closed on the retreating back and then his gaze swung to Nicole's face. He seemed to be waiting for her to speak, and for the life of her she could think of nothing to say.

At odds within herself, torn between loyalty to America and Saber, too, and the knowledge that those little books could cost hundreds of British lives, it was all she could do not to snatch the books held so carelessly in that lean hand, scoop up the chest and throw it out the nearest porthole. Her thoughts must have betrayed her, for Saber gave a harsh snort of laughter and murmured, "I wouldn't try it, Nick. And if I were you, I'd learn damned quickly not to wear what I felt so openly on my face."

Boldly, her eyes fighting his, although her heart thudded like a drum in her chest, she said, "I'm afraid I don't understand you, sir. What do you mean?"

Taking the cheroot from between his teeth and tossing the book back into the chest, he stood up. The action put

75

him alarmingly close to Nicole, and she couldn't help taking a nervous step backward. His laugh was more like a pleased growl, she thought warily, as he moved close to her. It was all she could do not to keep retreating from him, and she had the feeling that was exactly what he was trying to make her do. Compelling herself to remain where she was, she stared up at him, his mouth with its wicked slant only inches from hers. For a moment their eyes locked and she had the insane notion he meant to kiss her. She had seen the flicker of desire that danced in his eyes when he wanted a woman too often to mistake it, and she could have sworn that for just an instant, a tiny second, it had flashed in his eyes. But if it had it was quickly shuttered. Growing more confused every moment, Nicole swallowed painfully and repeated stupidly, "What did you mean?"

"I think you know very well what I mean, Nick." Then he quite literally paralyzed her by running one long finger down the side of her face and muttering, "Such soft skin for a youth, Nick. I wonder, are you really a boy?"

Galvanized by pure fear, she jerked her head away and speedily put the width of the room between them. Gruffly, the huskiness of her voice deepened by fright, she said, "Don't be ridiculous! Of course I'm a boy! What else could I be? I think you're in a strange mood lately, sir, and I wish you would not take out your odd humors on me!"

"An odd humor, is it? I wonder?" he mused slowly. Then he gave her a level glance, his eyes enigmatic as they rested on her, and she wished most fervently that he would leave. For a minute she thought he would continue his unnerving questions, but his eyes shifted from her to the code books. Shrugging his shoulders as if he had grown tired of this particular game, he walked over and picked up the small books.

"These, I think, are best locked in the safe." So saying he sauntered from the room into his own quarters. With warring emotions she watched him deposit them in the safe near his bed. He possessed the only key that unlocked it, and its size, larger than a man and several times heavier, prevented it from being stolen.

There was nothing she could do to stop him, she realized bleakly, uncertain if she even really wanted to. At least with the books locked in his safe, they did *no one* any harm!

Not so strangely Nicole found herself very much in a quandary—she had a great fondness for the United

States, yet she still thought of herself as English. And those little black books put her in a very uncomfortable position indeed. One part of her wanted them destroyed and yet, deep inside, she sympathized with the Americans. Sighing unhappily, she discovered that she no longer knew what she thought of the war between England and the United States.

Seeking a breath of air that night, she saw Allen as she walked alone near the bow of the ship, and she told him that she wished the books would vanish. Allen threw her a peculiar look and asked, "Doesn't it bother you that the Americans will use the information against your own countrymen—that a lot of British sailors are going to die as a result?"

Feeling inexplicably guilty, as if it were her fault that the wretched books had been found at all, Nicole said in a small voice, "Yes, it does. But, Allen, we are at war and I'm certain that the British ships manage to steal American secrets too!"

Allen's face tightened. "Listen, you little fool," he snarled in a harsh undertone, "Britain is fighting for her life—do you think this war is being fought for amusement?"

The struggle within herself increasing, Nicole whispered unhappily, "No. But, Allen, please understand—it is very hard for me to take sides—I have been away from England for five years and all I have known during that time are Americans."

Allen's features froze and the blue eyes went nearly black with some strong emotion. His fist clenched as it rested near Nicole's own, and she had the troubling feeling that if they were somewhere safe from prying eyes, he would have shook her with anger.

Then slowly she asked out loud the question that had lain between them for so long. "You're not truly a British deserter, are you, Allen?"

She couldn't read his expression in the darkness but she felt his tenseness. There was silence for several long seconds; both of them stared out over the rail at the sea that flowed endless and black before them.

Finally Allen said, "Let's just say I would like to see this damn war over! And that I'll do everything within my power to see that it ends as quickly as possible."

Nicole swallowed, uncertain whether she was glad or not that Allen had refused to answer her. Did it really matter? The important thing was that the war end, and was it truly imperative that one take sides? Nicole thought not.

Pensively she murmured, "I, too, would do anything to help bring about the end. It's not right that two countries with such close ties should be at war with one another."

Quickly Allen said, "Then help me, Nick! Those code books will lead to more bloodshed, more men and ships lost to both sides. But if we were to steal them from Saber—steal them and destroy them—then neither side would have them."

"Steal them from Saber?" she asked uncertainly, not liking the idea of pitting herself against him.

"Yes! We have to, Nick. If those books and papers are destroyed, then not only will the Americans not have them, but neither will the British! Don't you see—it will save the lives of many men—Americans and British. Help me!"

Still Nicole hesitated, knowing Saber would be furious and that she was being disloyal. But then, convinced that she would be helping to end the war, and in some hidden recess realizing that by throwing in her lot with Allen, she would be severing forever her strange relationship with Saber, she agreed. It was not a wholehearted capitulation, but determinedly she pushed her doubts aside. She would help Allen and do her part to end the hostilities between America and England.

Her eyes reflecting her inner turmoil, she said reluctantly, "Yes, I will help you. What do you want me to do?"

Allen stared at her very hard, aware that her heart was not fully committed, but then he shrugged—he needed Nick's help and knew she would prove a willing tool when the final moments came. Quietly he said, "It will do us no good to act now—even if we could. We have no way of escape, and once the books were missed, Saber would know damn well that they had been stolen by someone on board this ship. We'll just wait until we reach Barataria. All you can do in the meantime is keep an eye on Saber and let me know the instant he removes them from that safe."

They parted shortly after that, Nicole going silently to her little cupboard and Allen remaining leaning on the railing, staring out blankly over the shifting sea. He wanted those code books so badly it was all he could do to control the impulse to steal them right now, tonight, whatever the risks. His only consolation was the fact that the books did Saber little good. Unfortunately in no time they would be in the hands of the American authorities. If only he had been the one to discover the frantic young officer, a Lieutenant Jennings-Smythe, attempting to destroy that damning information. Now instead of reposing safely on the bottom of the sea, where they belonged, he thought viciously, they rested snugly in Saber's safe. Those books must not fall into the hands of the Americans, Allen decided fiercely. They must not!

8

Though Saber created no more disturbing scenes, Nicole was in constant conflict with her conscience in connection with him. She dreamed of those wretched code books disappearing into thin air, thereby relieving her of the necessity of aligning herself against Saber. Alone in Saber's quarters she spent hours staring at the massive safe, trying to will it to vanish. But it did not and she knew she was committed to stealing those little black books.

The return to Barataria Bay was accomplished easily. It was with a sense of homecoming that Nicole saw the outlines of the islands, Grand Terre and Grand Isle, heave into sight.

For five years Grand Terre, the main headquarters of Jean Lafitte, the notorious and aristocratic smuggler, had been like a second home to her, the first being *La Belle Garce*. It was here on Grand Terre, lying to the east of Grand Isle, that Lafitte had erected enormous warehouses to hold the plunder taken by the many ships that filled the bay. Here he had built a large and frequently well-stocked slave barracoon, bordellos, gambling houses, and cafés for the entertainment of the pirates. Lafitte was king of the smugglers, and he wandered brazenly through New Orleans, a tall, handsome man, rubbing shoulders with the wealthy and highborn, as if daring anyone to question his right to be there.

Few did, for smuggling was *almost* a respectable pastime in lower Louisiana, and there was more than one aristocratic family that owed its good fortune to smuggling—much to the consternation and confusion of the Americans. The Creoles saw little wrong with it, and when the American businessmen and officials attempted to point out that it was unlawful, they were met with blank stares and shocked tones. "Surely, Monsieur is wrong, my grandfather was a great smuggler! It is just a way of life, n'est-ce pas?"

It was a way of life, and the many bayous below New Orleans made an ideal setting for the smugglers. The swampy area was like a catacomb, with hidden places for storing goods before transporting them secretly over the watery bayou roadways to the warehouses in the city.

There were many small smuggling operations carried on, but Lafitte's group, situated on Grand Terre, was by far the largest, numbering over a thousand men. Barataria Bay was filled with ships of all sizes; feluccas, red-sailed luggers, and schooners; some captured vessels being refitted; some pirate ships and a few privateers; and there, arrogantly, with her three prizes following her, *La Belle Garce.*

As always with the return of a ship, there was a great deal of activity both aboard ship as well as onshore. Ordinarily Nicole loved this period of intense excitement, but this trip had been different in many unpleasant ways, and she was tense and edgy, knowing that soon she and Allen would be out in the open. Once those code books were in their hands, there was no going back. No more would she sail on *La Belle Garce,* the Captain's secretary—cabin boy, and never again would she sleep in her little cubbyhole, hiding her identity beneath a boyish exterior. It was the finish of an adventure that had started the moment she'd been pulled behind Saber all those years before, and truthfully she couldn't tell whether she was happy or sad.

She and Allen had settled upon a simple plan. Knowing the majority of the crew would be ashore and that the Captain would remain on board until after the first exodus, they planned to overpower him in his quarters on the nearly deserted ship. After gagging and binding him, it would be easy to remove the key that hung around his neck, open the safe, remove the books, and row themselves to shore. They would leave him tied in his bunk, to be discovered at some later hour. No one would think anything about their arriving together; young Nick usually tagged after Ballard. Nor would anyone think it strange that they carried a small trunk with them or that they set off immediately in the direction of New Orleans. Many of the crew were already making plans for the orgy of drink and women they would find in that wide-open city. Only Nicole and Allen would know that their ultimate destination was not to be New Orleans.

The tiny flaw in the plan was that Saber might leave

with the code books earlier than anticipated. It was essential that the ship be nearly deserted; it would be disastrous if a crewman should blunder into the Captain's quarters with some last-minute request! Allen would remain outside but nearby, and it would be up to Nicole to see that Saber stayed inside the cabin until after the crew had dispersed. For this purpose Allen had slipped Nicole a small ivory-handled pistol, cautioning her to use it only if Saber attempted to leave. They hoped he would not make that attempt until Allen was ready for him.

Nicole was as jittery as a high-strung filly before her first race. The small pistol, concealed about her waist, felt as if it were a cannon, and everytime Saber spoke, she knew he had discovered the plot. She forced herself to remain cool and aloof and pretended to be straightening her table, as she resolutely ignored Saber's upsetting nearness.

Higgins came in for a brief conversation, during which Saber ordered Nicole to run an errand to the storeroom. She almost balked, but with Higgins standing right next to him, she could only obey. She hurried as fast as she could, fearful that Saber would leave before she returned; she raced back with the information he wanted and entered the room slightly breathless. Saber was alone and gave a disinterested grunt at her information, paying her no further attention.

He seemed in no hurry to leave. For that she was thankful. Not that she doubted her ability to hold him. She knew that few men will argue with a pistol, but she would have felt more confident if Allen had been at her side! She was, if the truth be known, just a bit torn. Deep down she knew she owed Saber a certain amount of loyalty, yet she simply could *not* allow him to turn those wretched code books over to the Americans. Unconsciously she frowned at the unhappy thoughts.

"Worried about something, Nick?" Saber asked softly, and Nicole started at his words.

She left off her shuffling of papers and turned slowly to face him, willing the frown to vanish. "Why no, sir. I was just concentrating. You know how it is when one's mind is busy."

A disbelieving snort greeted her prim words. Saber was relaxing in one of the large leather chairs near his desk. He was in a state of semi-undress, with his white linen shirt gaping open, and Nicole was suddenly prey to an unnerving desire to run her hands over his muscular chest. One hand rested lightly on his desk and clasped a tumbler of dark rum, despite the morning hour. He was smoking a thin black cigar, and its heady scent drifted lightly in the air. Glancing at him beneath her lashes, she was again uneasily conscious of the feeling of leashed power that emanated from him. For a tiny second she questioned the wisdom of earning his enmity; she knew all too well what a merciless foe he would make. There was silence except for the slap of the bay on the hull. Feeling something more was expected of her, Nicole asked tartly, "Didn't you like my answer, sir?"

Crushing his cigar in a small china dish, apparently absorbed in the task, he said thoughtfully, "No, I didn't like your answer, but then, I *never* do . . . do I?"

Not wishing another argument to spring up between them, Nicole held her tongue, and at her lack of retort he swung his golden gaze to her face. "Nothing to say, young Nick?"

Nicole shook her head, deliberately turning her back on him. She heard the movements as he rose from his chair, and her heart leaped within her breast when he remarked, "A quiet Nick is unusual. Are you planning something, I wonder?"

Studiously, Nicole kept her head bent, willing him to leave well enough alone. She couldn't bear it if he started another of those queer, unsettling conversations that seemed to lead nowhere.

It was fortunate that she couldn't see Saber at the moment, for he was staring at the back of her head with a narrowed, speculative gaze. He did so for several seconds but, as Nicole refused to rise to the bait, he shrugged his shoulders indifferently and walked into his personal quarters.

Nicole guessed he was getting dressed, preparing to leave the ship. Her mouth felt dry; she knew that unless Allen appeared soon she would have to stop Saber from leaving. Surreptitiously her hand slid to the small pistol, and she turned her head, glancing through the doorway just at the second that Saber, fully clothed, with the black leather-bound trunk under one arm, wandered back into the room. Well, she told herself stoutly, the moment has come!

Saber quirked an eyebrow at her as she rose from her table and walked toward the outer door. "Leaving, Nick? If you'll wait a minute you can come with me."

Obviously unaware of the treachery that was about

to be committed, he paid no further attention to her. He placed the trunk on his desk and with his back to her, opened it. After checking the contents, he slammed the lid and locked it. Putting it once more under his arm, he turned, stopping abruptly as his gaze fell upon Nicole standing very straight before the door, the pistol held determinedly in her hand.

"Dear me," he drawled, almost amused, "does this mean what I think it does?"

Nicole swallowed, ignoring his facetious question, and gritted, "Put that trunk on the desk."

"Certainly. Whatever you say, m'dear. I *do* hope you're not a nervous person, Nick. I'd hate for you to accidentally put a hole in me," Saber murmured as he followed her instructions. The trunk safely deposited on the desk, he leaned against the edge of it, folded his arms across his chest, and asked, as if fascinated, "Do we wait for Allen to appear now, or are you doing this on your own?"

His words gave her a start, especially that reference to Allen. Had he guessed their plot? Certainly his tone was undisturbed and Nicole was completely baffled by his attitude. Fury she had expected, but not this amused indifference. Her gaze flitted uneasily over his face, noting that while he appeared at ease, there was a taut line about his mouth and his eyes were deliberately blank.

"Not going to answer? Well, that's wise. I see Allen has taught you admirably." His eyes suddenly left her face and lifted to a point somewhere behind her. "Ah, here's the good Allen now."

With relief Nicole swung around toward the door, and in that instant Saber struck. Nicole had only a second to realize that she had fallen for one of the oldest tricks in the world. Like iron bands, Saber's arms closed around her, his grip crushing her hands as he wrestled the pistol from her. Struggling, her hands flailing against the arms that held her, she fought to escape, but he mastered her thrashing body effortlessly and pressed her tightly against his chest in a painful, captive embrace.

"Little fool!" he breathed in her ear. "Did you really think you could get away with it?"

Too infuriated to be frightened, Nicole's eyes went black with rage. "Loose me!" she spat. "Let me go!"

She fought silently until she became aware that those strange amber-gold eyes were staring at her, that his mouth had a satisfied grin on it, and that the hands that held her securely were almost caressing in their touch.

Her head snapped back in quick suspicion and her eyes widened at what she saw on his face.

"You know," she said flatly.

If it were possible, he pulled her even closer, and dizzily she heard his muttered, "But, of course, little witch," a second before his mouth closed over hers.

His breath was smoky, his lips hard as they moved half savagely and half tenderly on hers. Her senses went spinning at their touch; she was unable to think clearly as she stood stiffly in his embrace, willing him to release her. After what seemed like hours, his lips left her bruised mouth and his hold slackened. A quizzical expression on his face, he inquired, "Is it just me, or is Allen the only one you share your charms with?"

Tightly, speaking through her teeth, she snapped, "Why don't you ask him?"

A heavy black brow tilted. "I intend to, baggage. I intend to ask the good Allen so many questions!"

As if on cue the door behind them flew open and two burly seaman, a bloodied and disheveled Allen held between them, entered the room.

Nicole, seeing Allen, started toward him, but Saber's hand jerked her back to his side. "Behave," he threatened softly. "Would you like to join him? I'm certain the men would enjoy it."

Frozen by the implication of his words, she remained still, unable to take in exactly how their plan had failed, or how Saber had known that she was a female. How long had he known? she wondered sickly. From the beginning? No, surely not—even he wouldn't have knowingly exposed a child to this crude, often cruel way of life. Then when? She was dimly aware of the murmur of conversation around her, but it was Saber's, "Take him below and chain him. I'll tend to him later," that roused her from her stupor.

"No!" she screamed, and catching Saber by surprise, she almost twisted from his bruising hold. His hand tightened hurtfully around her soft arm, and knowing it was useless to tear at the steel-muscled hand that held her, she viciously raked one side of his bearded face with her fingernails.

Swearing, Saber released her, only to catch her other arm and, swinging her around, struck a blow across her face. Astonished and shaken, she blurted, "You hit me, you bastard!"

His eyes gleaming and narrowed, Saber snarled gently, "And I'll hit you again if you repeat that trick!"

Ignoring her, he snapped to the gaping seamen, "You heard me, get him out of my sight! And," he added menacingly, "keep your tongues between your teeth."

If Nicole had thought it silent earlier, that silence had been almost thunderous compared to the one that fell on the room after the men had hurriedly departed, dragging Allen between them. Nicole refused to look at Saber but remained with her back to him and stared stonily out the porthole. Her mind was so filled with confusion at what had happened, and shock and fury at Saber's knowledge of her sex, that for a moment she felt dull and drained, not quite certain of her next move. It dawned on her rather painfully, as she stared out the porthole at the green, white-maned waves that gently rocked the ship, that she wasn't likely to have any say in what would happen next.

Though young and personally untouched by passion, Nicole knew more about the animal urgings that drove men than she should have. She knew Saber wanted her . . . his body, as they had struggled earlier, had betrayed that fact *most* definitely! Even now she remembered the warmth of him as he had held her prisoner, and most vividly she could recall the pressure of the hardened shaft of male power that had leaped to life as their bodies twisted together.

She swallowed with difficulty, her throat suddenly parched. It seemed unfair, she thought sadly, that she would become a woman before she'd had the chance to be a girl. Her thoughts coming to the inescapable, she wondered if Saber would treat her virginity gently . . . or take her with brute passion. At least she knew what to expect from him, which was more than did most of the sheltered girls of her age and breeding. But then, in spite of her bravado, dismayingly clear and in detail, certain better-forgotten memories of Saber bedding other women—some in this very room—returned and she swallowed again. She knew he could be kind because she had seen him so; she also knew he could be an animal, and she could only hope that he would be tender.

Resigning herself to her fate, she squared her slim shoulders and slowly turned to face Saber. He was leaning near the doorway, his eyes narrowed against the thin curl of smoke that drifted from the cigar. His hair had become disarrayed during their struggle and a few errant locks fell across his forehead, increasing his piratical appearance. Meeting his hard eyes across the width of the room, she was uncomfortably aware of her increased heartbeat. To combat her own nervousness, she thrust up her chin angrily and kept her voice cool as she asked, "What do you intend to do with us?"

Smiling unpleasantly, he said conversationally, "You've handled it all wrong, you know. Instead of stony silence, you should show all the signs of outraged innocence and demand to know what the good Allen has done to be in his present situation. You accepted defeat much too easily. I'm disappointed in you, Nick. I was certain you would try to brazen it out."

Nicole stiffened at his provoking manner and, unable to help herself, spat, "What good would it have done? You obviously knew the whole."

"Hmmm, true—but never, little vixen, *never* betray so blatantly that you have lost. You might have convinced me that you were uninvolved with Allen's attempt. And if we had retained our present relationship, you could have helped your confederate. Pity you weren't more clever."

Nicole restrained herself with utmost difficulty and stared resolutely at a point somewhere above his head, ignoring his goading words.

Saber smiled to himself. What a stubborn little vixen she was. And how completely unaware of her own beauty. A feeling of intense satisfaction swept over him as he continued to stare at her. No longer would he be tantalized half out of his bed by thoughts of the lovely long-limbed body sleeping a short distance away—and no more would the memory of her as she rose from the water of Bermuda return to haunt him!

Who she was, he didn't care. Why she was here on his ship in disguise interested him even less. She was a woman, a desirable woman, who had conspired against him. His eyes narrowed and grew hard at that thought, and for a long moment his gaze rested on her dark hair, the auburn glints flaming in a shaft of sunlight. What else could he expect from her, he thought unfairly. Women with red hair, whatever the shade, were not to be trusted. How well he had learned that lesson, he thought bitterly. Suddenly Annabelle's face rose up before him . . . Annabelle of the flaming hair and green eyes . . . Annabelle who had lied and cheated and schemed his very downfall even as he had laid his young heart at her feet . . . bitch! Lying, conniving bitch!

Nicole, still staring beyond him, was growing tired of this wretched uncertainty. She was *not* going to let him provoke her or frighten her. Unfortunately, she wasn't adept at hiding her emotions, and her belligerent attitude showed very clearly on her face.

Seeing it banished Saber's black memories, and with something approaching laughter, he drawled, "Do you intend to stay like that forever? I assure you, you'll become quite bored with it after some hours."

Frostily she regarded him. "Pray, what else should I do?" Her voice dripped with ice, and at his quick grin she could have cheerfully thrown a knife at his head.

He pushed himself away from the wall and walked slowly over to her. Tipping her face up to his with one finger, he lowered his head and teasingly caressed her lips with his. "You sound impatient. Are you so eager for your new duties to begin?" he murmured against her mouth. Then his lips traveled across her cheek, and he lightly kissed her ear and said, "Of course, if you wish it, we can start immediately. It's been a long while since Bermuda, and I can't think of anyone I would rather have break my enforced celibacy."

Nicole jerked away from him and flashed, "Not even Louise Huntleigh?"

His eyes gleamed angry gold between the thick black lashes, and Nicole was aware of his sudden spurt of hot temper. "We'll leave her out of this!" he snapped.

Driven by some inner compulsion, she argued, "Why? Isn't she your mistress? Do you think she'll be pleased when she discovers you've been toying with another?"

"You're very young, aren't you, Nick?" he sneered. Then struck by a new thought, he asked, "How old *are* you? Certainly not the fifteen you've led me to believe. While you're at it, you might as well give me your real name too. I can't continue to call you 'Nick,' can I? Although, I confess that in spite of everything I probably shall always think of you as Nick."

She was of two minds about answering him, but they were such unimportant questions to balk at that resentfully she gave him the answers he wanted.

"Well now, *Nicole,* another answer if you please. How long have you been Allen's mistress?"

That sharply barked question gave Nicole pause. She didn't think he would believe her if she asserted that she had never been Allen's mistress—or anyone's for that matter. On the other hand, when he took her, as surely he would, the fact of her virgin state would be evident. Resignedly she muttered, "I've never been his mistress."

"My dear child, do you expect me to swallow that?" he asked scathingly.

Her eyes meeting his, she challenged, "There's one way we can find out, isn't there?" At the leap of speculation in his eyes she added, "I promise you I'll fight you, and you can be assured you won't enjoy it!"

"What? Not enjoy being the first!" he mocked. "You *are* awfully young if you think that. Virginity in his woman is highly prized by a man."

"But I'm not *your* woman, am I?" she shot back, angry and yet strangely exhilarated.

"No," he replied with a small smile lurking about his mouth. "Not at the moment! And we haven't proved the truth of your claim either. I must admit I find it hard to believe that Allen hasn't taken advantage of your accessibility. Of course," he finished lightly, "I'm willing to be shown otherwise."

Ignoring the taunt in his voice and feeling it was prudent to change the subject, she demanded, "What do you plan to do with Allen?"

The smile left his lips instantly, and his features fell into their familiar hard, implacable lines. Coldly he stated, "It would be best for you to forget Allen. He is no good to you now."

"Forget him? You must be mad! I love him! I cannot push him away as if nothing happened!" she cried, impassioned.

"You love him?" he inquired dryly. "A moment ago you claimed you were not lovers. Make up your mind, Nick. Which is it?"

"Damn you! You twist everything I say. I shall not tell you anything more. Make whatever conclusions you wish." Resentfully she ended, "You will anyway."

Nicole's eyes were nearly black with distress as she hurled the words at him, but he appeared unmoved by her outburst, watching her as though she were an amusing child. Goaded by his actions, Nicole stamped a foot with rage, and her hands on her hips, she shouted, "God damn you, Saber! Don't just sit there! Answer my question. What do you intend to do with Allen?"

A laugh burst from him and he mocked, "Aren't you forgetting that I'm the one in the position to do the asking. Calm down, little hothead."

Gritting her teeth, Nicole fumed with impotent rage. How dare he remain so cool, so unemotional, when he had turned her world upside down and imprisoned Allen, Allen who had saved her life at the risk of his own! She spun on her heels, intent upon slamming from the room, but Saber's voice, no longer amused, halted her.

"Sit down, Nick. You're not going anywhere, at least not at the moment.

"Your loyalty to your . . . er . . . confederate, while admirable, is unnecessary. He is perfectly capable of fending for himself. YOU are not! If I didn't desire you myself—God knows why—you would be chained in the hold with him. You would," he added deliberately, "also hang with him."

Shocked, Nicole cried, "You can't hang him! You have no right!"

Imperturbably he replied, "*I* will not hang him. That task will be left to the authorities at New Orleans." His voice hardening, he went on, "Your precious Allen is an agent for the British."

"How do you know? You have no proof!"

"I don't need any proof. I happen to know he is a member of the British Royal Navy—a captain, in fact. In case you've forgotten it, America is at war with England. Even if he had not tried to steal the code book, his being found on board my ship could hang him."

"What can you tell? Allen has done nothing while on your ship. You cannot even prove he was doing any wrong today," Nicole said scornfully, hiding the fear that clutched at her heart.

Saber took a deep breath and quelled the desire to turn her over his knee and beat some sense into her. She didn't seem to realize the seriousness of her position, and her blind faith in Allen annoyed him considerably. "Allen was a member of the crew on two other American ships before he joined *La Belle Garce*. Would you say it was a bit of a coincidence that both his previous ships were taken by the British within days after he came aboard and that both times Mr. Ballard miraculously escaped, only to reappear on another United States ship?"

A shaken Nicole squirmed in her chair, but hung on to her aggressive attitude. "You're making it up to discredit him. Besides," she persisted, "why would a captain in the British Navy remain on *La Belle Garce?* We're a civilian ship—we don't carry military secrets."

Saber almost smiled at her possessive reference to the ship, but his voice gave no hint of his thoughts as he replied, "Allen is not a fool! He had only to remain safely undetected on *La Belle Garce* and supply his superiors with sailing dates and routes of other privateers."

At Nicole's look of disbelief, he added, "I too have my own methods of finding out things. It was a simple task to have a certain . . . er . . . friend in Jamaica

90

inquire briefly after a supposed crony in the Navy. Naturally no hint was given as to Allen's orders or his whereabouts, but the information received revealed clearly that the Admiralty Office in London thinks very highly of young Captain Allen Ballard."

Appalled and not a little distressed to think that Allen actually was the spy she had suspected, Nicole paled. She had no doubt that Saber would present his information to the proper authorities and Allen would hang! For the moment her own peril took second place to Allen's greater danger, and she studied Saber with consideration.

He was, from all appearances, unmoved by the day's events, almost disinterested. If it had suited him for Allen to remain on his ship, he would have allowed him to do so, just as he would have ignored her own disguise indefinitely. She wasn't positive of her own role, but suspected that he had grown bored with the situation and had decided to end it. She had the inner conviction that his desire for her had been a final factor, and she sought a way in which to turn his possible passion for her into an advantage. She asked carefully, "If it were beneficial to you, would you forget about Allen's identity and allow him to escape?"

"My dear Nick," he asked quizzically, "are you attempting to bribe me?"

She nodded slowly, a sense of excitement coursing through her veins. But Saber shattered her mood by laughing cruelly, "What have you to offer? You're penniless, and I don't believe Allen is in position to bargain with me."

It was a delicate situation and Nicole was playing on the very risky assumption that Saber desired her willing, instead of kicking and clawing. It was all too true, but taking a deep breath she said boldly, "I have nothing to offer except myself. I propose a trade—*I* come to your bed willingly and remain as long as you will, and *you* release Allen—you have my word on it!"

9

Nicole's wild proposal left Saber nonplussed. After several unnerving moments, he asked curiously, "Are you saying you'll become my mistress, if I release Ballard?"

"Exactly!" she said with more confidence than she really felt.

For a long minute Saber's gaze traveled slowly over her body. Unconsciously she stiffened with anger at his blatant appraisal of her body, and forgetting herself, she lifted her chin angrily and snapped, "Well, is it a bargain?"

A slight mocking smile curving his mouth, Saber moved away from the desk and walked unhurriedly up to her, his body warm and hard as he pulled her slowly into his arms. Nicole was conscious of a trembling in her legs that had nothing to do with fear.

"Why not?" he murmured and then his mouth, seeking and exploring, covered hers.

Telling herself she was doing this for Allen, Nicole stood unresisting and uncertain in Saber's arms. Her lips were soft and untaught under Saber's, and after a second he raised his head and teased, "You'll have to do better than that, Nick."

Incurably honest and slightly nettled, Nicole shot back, "How can I, when I don't know what I'm supposed to do?"

One eyebrow flew up again, this time in derisive disbelief. "Are you going to continue this virginal pretense? I wouldn't if I were you. I saw you that afternoon when you met Allen at the lagoon, and I was witness to your eager embrace. Don't ever, my dear Nick, play me for a fool."

Grimly she said, "I'm telling the truth, and I would be silly indeed to attempt to deceive you about something that can be so easily proved."

She watched the dark bearded features closely and

wished he were not so adept at hiding his emotions. What was going on behind those inscrutable amber-gold eyes? His face did not betray him, and Nicole stirred uneasily in his arms as the seconds passed and he remained silent. Finally he said quietly, "There's only one way to find out, isn't there?"

Nicole nodded slowly, her heart thumping madly. Watching her face intently, Saber released her and said abruptly, "We'll leave here." A sudden grin creased his face, and with a wicked glance at her he added, "I foresee a very pleasurable respite for us."

Nicole said nothing. He had accepted her rash offer and she was committed to seeing it through. At least she had the comfort of knowing Allen was saved. She remembered uneasily that Saber hadn't agreed exactly, but had only implied in so many words that he did.

Her troubled gaze fell upon the trunk as he placed it on his shoulder; seeing her interest, Saber smiled coldly and said unkindly, "It wouldn't have done any good at all, Nick. Those code books left the ship this morning while you were in the storeroom for me. Higgins should be a good way down the road to New Orleans with them by now."

Nicole went white, and nearly stuttering with rage, she demanded, "H-h-how could they be? You never went near the safe this morning."

"You're not as clever as you think, Nick. It was a simple task to remove them last night and entrust them to the first mate this morning. A very *loyal* individual is Higgins," he finished in that irritating drawling manner of his.

Nicole felt a sweep of guilt at the emphasis on loyal, but she hated the sarcastic inflection in his voice, and keeping her body as stiff and unyielding as possible, she let him propel her out of the room. The deck was deserted except for a few necessary crewmen who were standing idly about.

No one spoke as the dinghy was lowered and they clambered aboard. It was a silent journey to the shore; the creaking of the oarlocks, the swish of the waves, and the occasional cry of a gull were the only sounds in the salt-scented sea air.

Saber paid little attention to Nicole, and for a second as they walked away from the dinghy, she contemplated making a sprint away from the beach and into the safety of the palm-thatched buildings that lay just beyond the fringe of trees.

"I wouldn't try it if I was you, Nick." Saber's cold warning caused her to nearly stumble in the sand, and quelling the unnerving thought that he must have read her mind, she inquired innocently, "Whatever do you mean?"

He gave a grating laugh. "You know very well what I mean! Stop trying to gull me." Deliberately he added, "Remember poor Allen."

Dispiritedly she acknowledged she *had* almost forgotten Allen, and with a twinge of regret she put aside the thought of escape.

Some hours later, as they drifted up to a small pier, Nicole realized that she had been lost in her own thoughts as they slowly traveled up the black murky waters of the bayou. She sat staring blindly at the huge cypress trees with their trailing, ghostlike veils of gray moss. With a start of surprise she noticed that they had reached their probable destination, and like one awakening from an unpleasant dream, she shook herself mentally and assumed a mask of calmness to hide her inner turmoil.

Thibodaux House was an old plantation. It had been wrested from the antediluvian wilderness when New Orleans was just a cluster of wooden shacks huddled together along a swampy, fever-infested bend of the muddy Mississippi River. Where there once had been swamp and forests of cypress and water oaks, now fields of cotton and sugarcane stretched to the very banks of the levees that held back the river and the constantly shifting bayous, which would have eagerly engulfed and covered the land again.

The original house had long since been destroyed, and another more elegant dwelling had replaced it. The present house was less than twenty years old, and yet the massive oaks that lined the broad avenue leading to it were nearly a century old. Their huge knotted limbs almost met overhead, and from them Spanish moss hung like a soft gray-green mist, creating a long, shady arch through which Nicole and Saber traveled. The avenue ended abruptly and there before them stood Thibodaux House, majestic in the winter sunlight. Magnolias, pecans, and the ever-present oaks were scattered in studied carelessness near the house, like a frame for a beautiful painting. And the house, as if aware of its great beauty, rose in proud splendor from the parklike expanse of emerald lawn that surrounded it. Galleries, wide and cool, encompassed all sides of the house; a railing of airy latticework across the upper story was tinted a soft green, while below the graceful brick-plastered columns that surrounded the lower floor were an incredibly glistening white. Shutters that adorned the many long, narrow windows repeated the same soft green of the upper railings, as did the two staircases at either side of the house.

For just a minute Nicole allowed a feeling of pleasure to run through her as she admired the quiet, almost arrogant beauty of the house. But she wondered at Saber's presence here. Did he have such easygoing wealthy friends that he could call on them at will? Or had he, somehow by iniquitous means, acquired the house himself? And because she was suspicious and wary, she was able to conceal any admiration she might have felt.

Even the black-and-white marbled floors of the huge main hall, the slabs laid out in a lovely diamond pattern, aroused no comment from her. Stiffly she stood at Saber's side as he talked in an undertone to a tall, slender negro dressed in a severe suit of dark cloth, the blackness of his skin intensified by the startling white of his shirt. She paid no attention to their soft conversation, but stared blankly down the hall, hearing nothing, seeing nothing. So lost was she in her efforts to appear indifferent that Saber's light touch on her arm, as he piloted her in the direction of the imposing front door, came as a shock, and she gave a start of surprise.

Smiling down into her upturned face, he said coolly, "Nervous, m'dear? Don't be. I assure you I have no intention of falling upon you like a starving wolf."

Nicole took no comfort from his mocking words, but then she suspected she wasn't meant to either. Pulling herself together, she cast him a look of undiluted hatred. Saber laughed, and his hand tightening around her arm, he propelled her out onto the downstairs gallery. Ignoring her obvious reluctance, he continued to force her in the direction of one of the staircases. At the bottom step they were met by a smiling young negress, her head wrapped in a gay red-and-white bandana. Saber greeted the girl with pleasure, and Nicole, sourly watching the black face light up with enjoyment at his easy words, wondered how he was able so effortlessly to charm whenever and whomever he wished. Well, he certainly wasn't charming *her*, she thought nastily!

He glanced down at her and, as if guessing her thoughts, said lightly, "I'm sure you'll overlook my servants' pleasure at my return, but they for some, I'm sure you'll agree, odd reason happen to enjoy working for me. They haven't your clear-sighted view of my character."

With bored nonchalance she said, "My dear sir, your relationship with your servants is none of my business. All I care about at the present is my bed and bath!"

"Then you will no doubt enjoy the services of Galena. She will be your maid as long as you remain here. Be sure," he added in a hard voice, "to let her know if there is anything you require."

"I intend to!" Nicole purred sweetly.

Saber grinned; then he strode away in the direction of the overseer's office, a small brick building that was situated just beyond the plantation's kitchen.

As was typical of the houses in Louisiana, the kitchen was a separate building behind the main house; then came the overseer's office, and behind it the dovecotes, and beyond that the two rows of small brick cabins that comprised the slave quarters. In the distance behind the slave cabins, Saber could see the green fields of sugarcane and just barely the tip of the sugar mill. For a moment he spared a thought for the family that had lost all this wealth merely on a throw of the dice, but he promptly forgot them as he pushed open the door to his overseer's office.

Nicole wandered around the large pleasant bedroom in which she found herself, wondering how Saber came to find himself in such luxury. It was a marvelous room —soft woolen carpets covered most of the gleaming wooden floor; an enormous carved mahogany bed with cheerful yellow silk hangings was against one wall; small inlaid tables were placed here and there; a few chairs covered with excellent damask were arranged near the fireplace; and above the mantel a majestic gilt mirror reflected the entire room.

Turning her back on the fireplace, she walked over to one of the long, narrow windows hung with drapes of satin in the same shade of yellow as the bed hangings and stared out gloomily. Life was the very devil, she decided unhappily. This time yesterday she and Allen had everything in the palm of their hands and now . . . Saber had blasted it all to hell! She stood looking out at the green expanse of lawn in the fading light and tried to imagine how she would feel this time tomorrow . . . after tonight!

Silently she watched the sun sinking and wished as it disappeared slowly behind the towering oaks and cypress swamp that it was already tomorrow and that this evening were behind her. But in spite of an inward shrinking Nicole was not a coward and she had made a bargain. That she would like to change her mind was true, and as Galena bustled around in the background and laid out a robe of some silky material in a shade of deep green and a gown of a lighter shade, but not any less transparent, she had a wild urge to flee from the room and plead with Saber to forget her earlier foolish words. Yet the thought of Allen's fate stilled the motion. She knew that whatever plans Saber may have had for Allen, her intervention had changed them, and Saber would hold her to her word.

Grimly, like a gladiator preparing for the arena, she let Galena unbind and wash her hair, and submitted with the same resigned air to a bath perfumed with the scent of jasmine. Closing her eyes, she willed her tense body to relax in the warm water and was surpised when she did so. She left the bath with regret and was enfolded in a large fluffy towel and coaxed over to the bed. Galena's soft hands massaged her body, and Nicole felt all stiffness leave. A lightly perfumed oil evocative of jasmine and honeysuckle was poured over her and smoothed into her skin. Numbly, she slipped into the flowing gown and robe, wondering where her will to fight had flown, and then reminded herself that there was to be no fight—she was to be *willing*, it was her own bargain.

That same numbness was so strong that not even the appearance of Saber in a heavy gold silk robe that rioted with black Chinese dragons could shatter it.

Acting as if it were a common occurrence to receive gentlemen in her bedroom, she watched impassively as Sanderson, the slender negro to whom Saber had spoken upon their arrival, set up a small table and proceeded to serve them dinner. It was a meal worthy of royalty, but for the pleasure she derived from the succulent shrimp, the *filet de boeuf aux champignons,* and the wild rice and oysters, she might as well have been eating black dried bread crusts. A deep red Burgundy was served with the main course and Nicole emptied her glass as quickly as it was filled.

Saber, lounging leisurely in his chair and savoring an after-dinner cigar with his brandy, smiled as she defiantly tossed down another glass of wine. She looked to Sanderson, but he, intercepting the decisive shake of Saber's head, pretended not to see and, correctly interpreting the glance his master sent him, quickly cleared

97

all signs of their meal. Leaving only a decanter of brandy for Saber, Sanderson departed.

With dismay she watched him leave, and then rashly deciding attack was the best defense, she took a deep breath and demanded, "And now?"

Saber flashed her a lazy grin, but then after he stubbed out his half-finished cigar, his smile vanished and he said thoughtfully, "And *now*, little vixen . . . we find out just how much of the truth you have been telling me!"

10

The words hit her like a blast of icy wind. Frozen, she watched him, her eyes dark with emotion, as he rose from his chair and approached her. For a moment he stood beside her and looked down into her face, his eyes gliding lightly over her faintly agitated features—eyes nearly black with turmoil and a full, inviting mouth. The gleaming, dark fire hair tumbling about her shoulders and framing her face gave her the look of some wood creature—a wild creature untouched by man. His eyes lingered for a moment on that half-parted mouth, and then they slid down to the gentle swell of her breasts, staring as if bewitched at the increased rise and fall of her bosom beneath the misty green veil of her gown.

Nicole had never been so conscious of her body, but then she had never worn such a transparent excuse for a garment before nor, and more importantly, had she ever been the object of Saber's sensual interest.

She felt a queer sense of detachment—almost as if this were happening to someone else. Even when he pulled her up into his arms, the feeling persisted. It wasn't her he was kissing, his lips warm and passionate against hers, his arms holding her pressed next to his tall, lean body, it was some other girl, and she, Nicole, was merely an onlooker.

Saber, feeling her lack of response, and aware of her air of insularity, raised his mouth from hers. He could feel it in the slim body, so close to his, and in the indifferent softness of her lips under his. Speculatively he looked at her, his gold eyes narrowed and hidden by the thick black lashes. Perhaps she was as she asserted—a virgin—but he doubted it. And because he thought she was stooping to trickery, he wasted little time in preliminaries. Grasping the low neck of her gown in one quick downward swipe, he tore it from her body.

Nicole stood naked and unmoving before him, her

slender body bathed in candlelight. Gazing at her slim beauty—the high pointed breasts with the soft coral nipples, the narrow ribcage resting above a slender waist, the flat tautness of her stomach, and the dark lovely triangle between her long legs—Saber's breath caught in his throat, his desire erupted like a blazing volcano. Sweeping her up into his arms, he carried her to the bed.

He slid onto the bed beside Nicole as she lay motionless on the scented sheets, her hair spilling out like a cloak of fire around her shoulders. Lying on his side next to her, barely touching her, he leaned over and leisurely, in spite of the driving urgency of his body, he kissed her, again evoking no response. With a frown of displeasure, he propped himself up on one arm and stared down at her face.

Gravely, the feeling of detachment fading only slightly, she stared back at his harsh bearded face. An animal desire emanated from him, further disturbing her calmness.

"Look at me, Nick," he commanded quietly. Capturing her chin, he forced her to meet his eyes. His voice betraying his rising anger, he snarled, "When I kiss you, damnit, I want to know I'm kissing a *woman* not a stiff-lipped spinster!"

He crushed her mouth with his, forcing her lips to open. Plundering and searching her mouth, holding her chin firmly in his grasp, allowing her no respite from his hungry assault. Shaken by the naked urgency of his mouth, Nicole was helpless against a sudden surge of frightening desire that struggled into life throughout her body. Unable to help herself, her lips became soft and responsive under his. Feeling her surrender, Saber released his hold on her chin, his fingers gently caressing her jawline and neck before his hand slipped down her shoulders and spine, leaving a tingle of awakening awareness in its wake.

Nicole felt as one possessed, as if another creature, a hot-blooded, sensual animal, had entered her body. Her arms reached out with a tranced will of their own to embrace Saber. Her hands, commanded by her own need, caressed the dark head and then daringly slid down to explore his long, lean body, the broad back with its scarred ridges and the arms with their iron-smooth muscles. His own hands were like tongues of fire as they skimmed delicately over her, his mouth no long plundering, yet still hungry and demanding as it wooed her into desire. She was sinking in a sea of new sensations, no longer thinking sanely, only filled with a fiery longing that was burning brighter and more vibrant with his every touch. His hard body seemed to drive her deeper into this yearning for possession—the fine rasp of his chest hair against her breasts, the strength of his legs as they pressed to hers, and the symbol of his very manhood between them, warm and throbbing.

As his growing desire blotted out coherent thought, Saber was no longer in control of his emotions. No longer could he only lightly touch and explore the silky flesh so near his. Forgetful of her possible virginity, his hand blindly sought the satin softness between her legs; his fingers thrust without warning within her.

At that first ungentle touch between her thighs, Nicole's whole body stiffened with shock. Memories of Saber with other women suddenly flooded her mind, and she knew she couldn't go through with it. Her thoughts banished the passion that had so recently engulfed her, and tearing her mouth from Saber's, she squirmed away, managing to evade his hands. Half lying on the bed, half kneeling on the floor, she stared back at him as he frowned at her, his eyes still glazed with desire. Earnestly trying to explain to him the motives behind her sudden reversal, she stammered, "I—I—can't! Please understand!"

Her words seemed to stun Saber, and for a long minute he stared at her, obviously unable to take in what she was saying. But then he remembered her possible virginity and his whole manner changed; his eyes were suddenly warm and compelling as they rested on her apprehensive face. "Hush, sweetheart. Come to me and let me teach you. I won't hurt . . . I promise. Ah, God, Nicole, let me love you," he said huskily, and disarming her with gentleness, he gathered her unresisting body next to his. For several seconds they lay together, Nicole conscious of the hard length of him next to her naked body, and when he kissed her, his lips moving in soft sensual rythmn across hers, she felt herself again slipping into the intoxicating headiness of desire. His hands explored the slender curves and hollows, this time slowly, maddeningly, caressing her, touching her gently. Giddily she tried halfway to fight free of the web he was spinning around her, but her body was already trapped in the awakening desire he so skillfully wrought. A small feverish moan escaped her when his lips left her love-bruised mouth and slid slowly to her hardened nipples. She was not prepared for the delicious pleasure his teeth created as he gently bit the tender flesh, sending a shiver of pure animal desire down her spine. His hands moved with sensual power over her skin, gently fondling the nape of her neck, down her spine and over her hips, luring her beyond the point of rational thought. He pulled her to him so that they lay side by side, her breasts brushing the coarse silk of his chest, and deliberately he made her aware that he was full and ready for her. Swiftly he took her hand and, ignoring her startled protest, guided it to him.

Instinctively Nicole knew what he wanted, and she experienced a warm wave of tenderness when she felt him catch his breath and stiffen as her untaught hands explored the essence of him. A half groan came from him as she continued, and he felt his need for her growing, until he knew that soon he must have her—or shame himself!

Slowly he laid her back on the bed, his mouth exploring hers with growing urgency. Nicole was too caught up in too many new sensations of the physical to have even one coherent thought in her head. When his hand gently probed between her legs, she gave a leap of half-fear, half anticipation, but Saber stilled it and said against her mouth, "Don't move, love . . . don't fight me, sweetheart. It'll be good . . . I promise."

With a shudder Nicole melted against him, and he shifted slightly, his fingers gently and expertly easing the way for his possession. He moved between her thighs, holding her legs apart with his knees and, releasing her mouth for a second, muttered thickly, "Let me in, love, let me fill you and lose myself in you."

Dazed and in the grip of such frenzy of longing, Nicole barely heard him—she felt her hips raised and the first swelling pressure of his entrance. He took her gently, so gently there was just one small moment of pain, and then he slid full-length into the softness between her thighs. In a welter of shock and arousal she could feel her body expanding to take him, to accommodate this intrusion of her body. Kissing her, he whispered almost tenderly, "So, my little one, you were a virgin after all." But then that slightly caressing note vanished and he said in a half-guttural, half-groaning voice, "Ah, God, I don't know if I can hold back—I want you too badly." His mouth captured hers and his body, despite his words, mindful of her inexperience, began to rock against hers until he could stand it no longer—and he thrust hungrily and almost painfully into her. Though he tried not to hurt her, Nicole wasn't quite ready for the sudden, almost brutal movements of his body and she cried out in pain. Hearing it, Saber compelled himself to lessen the force of his movements, but the soft body beneath him was driving him to fill her, to take her as he had never taken a woman in his life. Driven by something he didn't understand, he wanted to brand her with his possession, to take her with such intensity that she would be forever his. And Nicole, unaware of anything except the hard body joined with hers, was suddenly, feverishly caught up with him, her body rising to meet the thrust of him, her hands holding him closer as if she could not have enough of him. And when at last the incredible emotion had spent itself in a wild flurry of exquisite pleasure, Saber cradled Nicole's shaking body in his arms. She was exhausted from the storm he had aroused and was confused at how easily she had succumbed to his lovemaking. She hadn't thought once of Allen, and now she guiltily remembered that it was supposedly for Allen that she had given herself to Saber.

She lay there in his arms, aware of a certain discomfort between her legs, and suddenly her heart was filled with sadness. Saber had been gentle, she couldn't deny it, but it still couldn't erase the feeling that what had passed was something she would never be proud of. She told herself that she had done it for Allen, and she didn't begrudge it to him—she owed him her life and this seemed a small price to pay. And yet there was the nagging thought—had it just been for Allen that she had given herself to Saber? She couldn't answer it and she didn't want to face what might be the truth. Uneasily, she moved away from Saber's relaxed body and after a few minutes fell into a fitful doze, but she couldn't sleep. And so perhaps twenty minutes or so later, the ache of unshed tears in the back of her throat, she sat up stiffly, ignoring Saber who lay on the bed beside her, one hand flung out on her pillow, where he had been teasingly playing with her hair.

"Where are you going?" he asked idly.

"I—I—don't know. You've had what you wanted. There's nothing more you could take from me."

Saber only smiled, his eyes gold and warm as they played over her face. "Oh, no. You, I shall want again and again for some time. I'm hungry for you again already, did you know that?"

She looked at him, then quickly averted her eyes from the growing proof of what he said. Lying there beside him, her mind in confusion, she came to a decision. Allen would hate the bargain she had made and she knew that she couldn't continue it. She had already given this man her innocence. She could give no more and wanted no more, afraid of what it would reveal about herself.

Unaware of her turmoil, Saber was running a caressing finger down her spine, his mouth sliding on her shoulder. "Come to me again, Nick," he said huskily.

"No, never!" Nicole spat, suddenly sickened by the sordidness of it all, and she leaped away, her eyes dark with shame. "It was a stupid bargain I made. I cannot stay as your mistress. I thought I could, but I find that even to save Allen, I cannot turn myself into a common slut . . . especially not one of *your* common sluts!"

Saber's mouth tightened and he felt fury take him by the throat at her notion that it might end as easily as that. "Rest easy about your bargain!" he snarled. "I have no intention of releasing Allen Ballard and nothing you can do will change my mind." At her look of disbelief, he laughed softly, "I never *said* I would let him go, did I?"

"B-b-but you—you . . ." The words trailed off as she desperately sought to recall precisely what he had said.

"I said, 'Why not?' I'll admit there is an implication there. But, brat, you should have made certain before you assumed I had agreed."

Some of his fury died at the stunned expression on her face, and almost gently he added, "He's not in American hands in New Orleans at the moment, so you could say I kept the bargain. But hear me, Nicole, I will not free Allen—at least not immediately. When I decide he can cause no more trouble, I'll consider it."

"But, you promised!" Nicole protested heatedly, not really quite comprehending what Saber was saying.

"So did you!" he shot back. "You promised to be my mistress as long as I wanted you—but you were going to back out, weren't you?"

"That's different!" she retorted defensively.

Saber snorted. "The difference escapes me, I'm afraid. And despite the fact that events are not turning out quite as you planned, I have kept my end of it. Allen is still alive and as yet he is not in the calaboose in New Orleans."

"You double-crossing, monstrous beast! You deliberately misled me!" Nicole cried angrily, the topaz eyes gleaming with sparks of fury. "You know that I thought you would free him after tonight!"

"And you would be gone in the morning, wouldn't

you?" he growled dangerously. "Gone to join your confederate, after so cleverly gulling the Captain."

Nicole was genuinely appalled that he thought her capable of such double-dealing. In a small voice she asked, "Could we please forget about Allen and the bargain? Could we just pretend that I changed my mind? I don't want to be your mistress, Saber . . . and Allen has nothing to do with it."

"But you're going back on your word, aren't you? You gave your word, remember?" he snapped coldly.

"So did you—and you haven't kept it either. You knew I assumed you would let Allen go free tomorrow. So you're breaking your word too!"

"Not quite!" he said with an icy smile. "I never gave my word. You did and now you're breaking it! Well, let me tell you, brat, I don't like people not paying their debts to me! We'll forget about your bargain all right! We'll forget about it, and I'll treat you like I should have when I first discovered your little treachery." Viciously his arms snaked out to capture her. And in that moment before he erupted out of the bed, the thought crossed his mind that women were all alike—liars, cheats, and betrayers—and this one was no different from the first woman who had caused him to be banished and sold into the British Navy. *Sluts*—every last one of them!

Nicole had seen his eyes narrow with intent a second before he moved, and she scrambled behind the table where they had eaten. A chill of apprehension slid down her spine as he advanced. She sensed that some strange emotion drove him, an emotion that she was only part of, and with growing dismay she watched his approach.

The black hair was tousled from her caressing fingers and the wavering candlelight created sinister shadows over his bearded face and tall body. His eyes were cold and icy and the tight line of his mouth told her that nothing short of murder could save her.

Slowly they circled the table, hunted and hunter, and searching frantically for escape or some way of halting him, Nicole's eyes fell upon the goblet he had used during dinner. With a quick movement she grabbed it and smashed the top off in one downward crack against the table; she was left with the stem with which to hold it and the jagged edges to fight with.

A grim smile flickered through the gold eyes and he laughed softly. "Do you think *that* will stop me?"

Nicole nodded vigorously, her eyes huge with grim determination.

"It won't, you know," he said coldly. "I intend to have you, and *nothing* will stop me!"

He lunged across the table, and Nicole had to leave its protection. Now there was nothing between their naked bodies but the goblet's glittering edge. She held it as she would a knife and cautiously backed away from him. Her heart was thumping madly in her breast and she felt almost dizzy. She must have been insane to have even suggested such a monstrous bargain and even crazier to have let things go so far. And as Nicole continued to back away his mouth went hard, and the gold eyes glittering icily, he charged. Nicole, startled by his sudden movement, stumbled into a chair and was unable to regain her balance or protect herself. Saber caught the hand that held the goblet and twisted her arm behind her back. Propelling her across the room, he shoved her face down into the softness of the bed.

The pain in her arm was excruciating, and for a moment, with her face buried in the feather mattress, she thought she would be smothered. But then the cruel grip was released, and before she could do more than draw in a great gulp, his hands captured her hips, and he partially lifted the lower half of her body from the bed. She struggled to escape, but he had one arm wrapped around her waist, holding her securely, and with a shock of disbelief and an odd tingle of anticipation, she felt his other hand slide between her thighs. Knowing instinctively what he meant to do, she fought even more wildly, unwilling to give in to the giddy ache that was stirring in her loins, but her actions aroused him further. His arm left her waist, and with both hands gripping her hips, he entered her suddenly from behind.

Helpless to free herself, not even certain that she wanted to be free, Nicole was only aware of his big body driving into hers, and with horror she experienced a shocking burst of pleasure as he continued to thrust himself deep within her. And then this half-savage, half-exciting possession was finished as Saber gave a guttural growl of carnal satisfaction and withdrew from her. Her ravished body sank down onto the bed. Between her legs there was a throbbing ache, and in her brain a raging fire clouded rational thought. Dimly she heard Saber say flatly, "I'm sorry, you didn't deserve that and I should not have lost my temper . . . but, Nick, I'm afraid you brought it on yourself." His cool uncaring ignited her turbulent feelings, and with a feral snarl, she reared up and swung blindly in his direction with the broken goblet.

Saber, though he moved with the speed of a striking snake, could not escape unscathed. Her wild slash caught him diagonally on the ribs, down across his stomach and groin, ending on his thigh. It wasn't deep, but blood was seeping from the jagged wound. He backed away from her, but Nicole stalked him like a maddened animal, intent upon destroying that portion of him that had so recently taken her virginity.

Saber eyed her warily. That she had every intention of castrating him was obvious—that she would enjoy it was even more apparent. Cautiously he stepped back, keeping away from the razor-sharp piece of crystal. His eyes never left hers as they moved around the room, their roles being reversed—*she* the hunter and he the hunted!

But Saber was not without an agile brain. He would let her draw near; then at the last moment he would twist away from her weapon. Over and over again he danced out of her reach, cleverly leading her exactly where he wanted.

Infuriated further by his actions, she swung more frantically. Suddenly careless in her fury, her eyes left his—and in that moment he snatched up his silken robe. Whirling the robe like a matador's cape, he swung it around her arm, entangled her hand and rendered the goblet useless. Immediately he closed in on her and imprisoned her in his arms, one hand clenched tightly around the wrist of the hand that still clasped the weapon. "Drop it, Nick!" he commanded, but Nicole only increased her exertions. Saber held her fast, his grip growning stronger and more painful as they fought.

"I won't," she panted, twisting her slender wrist in its iron embrace. "I won't!"

Saber's hold became even more intense, and Nicole knew he'd break her wrist if she didn't let go. The pressure was nearly unbearable and then suddenly it was over. They both heard the sickening sound of the bone cracking, and she sagged against him, the goblet sliding from her numb fingers.

A great sigh of relief escaped Saber as he felt her go limp, and almost gently he lifted the defeated Nicole in his arms and laid her on the bed. Her wrist was aching in a dull, pounding fashion, and as she lay there, she felt foolish feminine tears gathering. I *won't* cry, she thought furiously. Her humiliation was great enough without dissolving into a flood of tears. She lay on her side, ignoring him, curled in a tight woeful curve of misery.

Saber, his face expressionless, stood gazing down at

her, prey to a multitude of emotions. Confusingly he discovered he wanted her—again, now! Mixed with desire was a flicker of tenderness and a feeling of sharp regret at his treatment of her. And incredibly, he admitted to himself, he felt an odd satisfaction that she had told the truth about her virginity. Deeply annoyed by his conflicting thoughts, he turned impatiently away from her.

The room was in turmoil from their battle, and striding to the bell rope, he rang for a servant. Then he walked back to the bed, threw on his robe, and pulled the covers lightly over Nicole. When Sanderson answered the summons, Saber curtly requested several items and demanded that the room be put into some sort of order. Sanderson's features did not betray what he thought of such a request at this late hour or the state of the room. Quietly and efficiently he straightened overturned chairs, meticulously stationed the satinwood tables in their normal positions, and swept up the shattered glass. He returned and brought with him, on a large silver tray, the brandy and other things Saber had wanted. After putting them on a table he inquired formally, "Will that be all, sir?"

Saber dismissed him with a curt nod and poured himself a glass of brandy and lit a cigar. For some seconds he stood staring thoughtfully at Nicole's motionless form.

Nicole, herself, was emotionally spent. At the moment she wished she were dead! No, she thought suddenly, she wished *Saber* were dead. She rolled painfully onto her other side—it was best, she reminded herself, always to keep one's enemy in sight.

Imperviously Saber returned her stare, although one brow rose quizzically, as though questioning her wisdom in showing so openly what she felt. He unhurriedly gathered up the ewer of warm water and a bowl, as well as the cloths he had requested, and walked over to her. As he looked down on her he was reminded of a vixen he'd seen once, her foot nearly gnawed in two from her frantic efforts to free herself from the teeth of the trap that held her. The creature had looked at the nearing poacher in that same way—half-fearful, yet ready to fight for its very life. Touched by her look, he hesitated. At last he said, "I don't intend to hurt you again." Then destroying any kindness the words may have imparted, he said bluntly, "Unless you force me to."

Nicole shrugged, her soft mouth tightening with rebellion, the topaz eyes damning him.

Unmoved by her hostility, he stripped back the covers, laying her body bare to his gaze. Nicole forced herself to remain motionless as his hand traveled lightly over the line of her thigh and hip. But with a regretful sigh Saber curtailed the urge and gently grasped Nicole's injured wrist. She winced at his touch, slight though it was, and Saber smiled in commiseration.

"Sorry, brat. I wouldn't have hurt you on purpose, but I had no wish to spend the rest of my life squeaking in a high girlish tone of voice."

In any other circumstances Nicole would have giggled at his words, but she was in no mood to be amused. Yet try as she did to resist it, she was undeniably drawn to him. Her eyes flat and resentful, she stared at him and wondered bleakly why she could look at him and still find him attractive. But he was so disgustingly striking, she thought angrily, with his harsh, sardonic features, the yellow-gold eyes bright in the bearded face, and the hair so black it held blue shadows.

Saber's touch was gentle. He was sure her wrist wasn't broken, as he knew exactly how much pressure he had exerted, but it was quite swollen and obviously extremely painful. With almost professional skill he bound it, using the splints and linen strips he had also requested earlier. It wouldn't hurt for her to rest it a day or two, and he had some laudanum for the pain. Pouring the laudanum into a glass, he added some brandy to it and offered it to her.

"Drugging me now?" she jeered.

He smiled faintly. "Precisely, my little vixen. For your own good. Be a good child and drink it down."

With a resigned grimace she took the glass from him and swallowed the contents in one gulp. Lying back against the pillows, she glanced up at him, curious about his next move. Her earlier faintheartedness was vanishing. Her paining wrist strapped, the warm glow of brandy in her veins and the worst behind her, she suddenly found she could look forward with more spirit than she had thought possible a minute before.

Saber set down the empty glass on the table beside the bed. And then to Nicole's astonishment, he proceeded to bathe her entire body with the remaining water. There was no trace of desire in the dark bearded face as he bent over her and gently sponged away the signs of her lost virginity and his own brutal passion. How strange that after such violent events he could now be as tender as a lover. It made her wary, this unexpected kindness. The laudanum was making her drowsy and she wished he would leave her in peace. He had taken what he wanted, hadn't he? She stirred resentfully under his hands, glad when he at last threw the cloth into the bowl.

But it seemed that Saber was not done with her. She stared wide-eyed as he discarded his robe and lay down on the bed beside her. The laudanum made her reflexes clumsy, but she raised her fists to beat against his chest. He laughed and captured both hands, taking care not to cause more pain to the injured wrist. Her arms were pinioned on either side of her head, and as Saber towered dark and determined above her, she spat, "Not again! Not even *you* would dare to be such an animal!"

His mouth curved in a mocking smile. Then lowering his body's warm weight against hers, his knees pressing her legs apart to let him enter, he whispered against her lips, "You will find that there are many things that *I* would dare."

11

As was his habit, Saber woke as the first pale fingers of dawn were creeping into the room. Nicole's body was warm and soft as she lay sleeping next to him, and he lay there half-awake, savoring the sensation.

Saber smiled slightly, suffering at this moment a trace of remorse. Nick was such a little firebrand, he thought tenderly. If he were to awaken her, no longer would she rest so confidingly next to him, but with her eyes spitting black defiance, she would leap instantly into the fray, damning him and hating him with every word she uttered.

Pity . . . that, he thought drowsily. If only she could accept what had occurred as the natural course of events. It was bound to have happened sooner or later, if not with him with someone else.

It was such a simple thing. He had always treated his mistresses well, as Nicole damn well knew. Grinning, he recalled the astonished look on her face when he bestowed, as a parting gift to one particular ladybird, a carriage and four matched bays. Surely she was aware that he would do no less for her, more in fact, taking into account her untouched state. Why couldn't she be logical? She offered a commodity he was willing to pay for—simple!

Nicole's nearness disturbed his wandering thoughts, and with unsatiated hunger he could feel his own body hardening with desire. Lightly he touched her outflung arm and lazily nuzzled her ear. But even in sleep she rejected him, turning her head away.

Regretfully he let her be. Perhaps it was the sight of her bandaged, curiously defenseless wrist, or it might have been the sweet softness of her face in repose that stopped him. Whatever the reason, it didn't cool his awakened passion, but he restrained his natural inclinations and left her to sleep.

An hour later, after having dressed and breakfasted, he was on his way back to Grand Terre. There were things he had to attend to—not the least of these was Allen's fate! He would discuss it, he decided thoughtfully, with Lafitte. Together they would explore the most profitable method of disposing of his one-time lieutenant. Ransom, perhaps . . . or an outright sale to the American officials? Wouldn't Nick just love that! But he shrugged his shoulders. It made little damn difference to him.

Several hours later Grand Terre came into sight, and shortly after dismissing his coxswain, he walked up the beach. Behind the thin, straggling line of trees that fringed the island had been built the thatched cottages that housed many of the pirates and smugglers, with their women. Bordellos, gambling houses, cafés, and other establishments that catered to the wild drinking and excitement-seeking pirates were clustered near the middle of the island. The slave barracoon was at the south end, the massive warehouses not too far distant, and in the center of the colony, rising like a lily from a refuse heap, stood Lafitte's brick and stone mansion.

The mansion was sumptuously furnished: fine carpets lay upon the floor, paintings by the foremost masters of the day and heavy gilt mirrors adorned the walls, and crystal chandeliers winked and blazed above. Businessmen, shopkeepers, plantation owners, and slave dealers all came to Lafitte for the best of any merchandise. There was hardly a segment of commerce in lower Louisiana for which Jean Lafitte did not supply at least a portion of the goods. From his warehouses only the highest quality of silks, laces, brandy, wines, tobacco, spices, and numerous other costly and sought-after items were sold.

Since the importation of slaves had been banned several years before, it was only here on Grand Terre that the thrifty planter was able to buy, at reasonable cost, additional stock. In his slave dealings alone, he had a thriving concern. And his was no secret backstreet operation—respectable and prominent individuals came openly to trade with him. In New Orleans Governor Claiborne and the American officials gnashed their teeth in impotent rage, unable to put a halt to this extremely lucrative and highly illegal commerce.

Claiborne had forgotten himself so far as to have circulated a poster offering five hundred dollars reward for anyone who would bring him the notorious pirate, Jean Lafitte. Lafitte had laughed and promptly made a counter offer—*he* would pay fifteen hundred dollars to anyone who would bring the governor to Grand Terre!

Remembering that not-too-distant incident, Saber was smiling as the servant ushered him into Lafitte's office.

"Mon ami, it is good to see you! I have been expecting you hourly since word of *La Belle Garce*'s arrival reached me. What has taken you so long?"

Grinning, Saber helped himself to one of the excellent cigars that reposed in a crystal case on Lafitte's desk and said as he did so, "I had a little matter that required my attention."

Lafitte looked arch, murmuring, "Ah yes, the affair of the young boy who is *not* a boy whom the Captain was discovered embracing in his quarters."

"I'll be damned!" Saber growled, looking annoyed, but shrugging his shoulders, he selected one of several crimson velvet chairs arranged comfortably about the large room and sat down, crossing one booted foot over the other.

Lafitte, still smiling, reseated himself behind his desk. Evidently, from the litter on top of it, Saber had interrupted him at work, but this was not an uncommon occurrence, and Lafitte was always pleased to see one of his best captains.

Both were tall men, Saber perhaps by a little the taller of the two. Lafitte, a few years older than Saber, was an extremely handsome man with attractive regular features. His complexion was dark and the lively black eyes betrayed his French ancestry. His hair was black, as blue-black as Saber's, and there was an air of culture and elegance about him. Certainly no one would ever take him for a smuggler.

Lafitte's background was shrouded in mystery, and beyond the fact that he and his brother Pierre had opened a blacksmith shop in New Orleans some years ago, little was known of his earlier days. Even then the brothers had dabbled in smuggled goods, and from the smithy they expanded to a pleasant cottage near St. Philip and Bourbon streets and to a warehouse on the docks. Not content with the slipshod method of the pirate suppliers, Lafitte, along with his brother, had boldy traveled to Grand Terre and commandeered the whole disorganized structure of the many pirate gangs; welding them together with the privateers, he had produced one of the greatest networks in the history of smuggling. Men like Dominique You, rumored actually to be a member of the Lafitte family; the notorious pirates Gambi and Chighizola, called Nez Coupé; and the experienced seaman, smuggler, and cannoneer, Renato Beluche, whom Lafitte called *oncle,* all acknowledged him as their leader, their *Bos*. And Captain Saber was one of his most trusted lieutenants.

For a few minutes Lafitte and Saber conversed desultorily. Then Saber brought up the issue that concerned him most—Allen Ballard.

A frown creased Lafitte's forehead. "How do you wish to dispose of him? He is, after all, your prisoner, and as long as he is in no position to pass on more information, I do not greatly care what his fate is. We can turn him over to the Americans, thereby gaining their guarded goodwill . . . or we can sell him back to the British. It makes little difference; we benefit whichever way we chose." His frown lightened, and flashing a singularly charming smile, he murmured, "A pleasant state of affairs, no?"

"I think I should like to keep him prisoner for the present," Saber said slowly. "I should like a bit more information from him. We can always dispose of the man . . . but I may have a use for him in the meantime. Do you mind if I have him transferred from the ship to your calaboose, here on the island?"

Lafitte gave his consent readily and at Saber's request summoned a servant to carry a message to *La Belle Garce* for Allen's removal. The servant gone, Saber asked idly, "Do you wish to come with me when I question him?"

A sardonic gleam in the black eyes, Lafitte retorted, "Hardly, and you would be dismayed if I did. I am not deceived by your casual attitude, *mon ami*. You wish this man for your own purposes, and for your own reasons you want him in my so-very-secure calaboose. If it were not for that, you would never have mentioned his existence to me!"

Saber grinned, not a bit abashed by Lafitte's correct reading of the situation. "Well, it did occur to me that there might be a member or two of my ship that might not agree with my actions," he admitted. "Ballard was very popular with the crew."

"But naturally! A spy would be," returned Lafitte dryly. "But, speaking of spies," Lafitte continued, "word reached me just after you sailed this last time that there were some very pointed questions being asked about you on Grand Terre."

Surprised and showing it, Saber asked, "What kind of questions?"

"Mmmm, some questions like: What is Captain Saber's true name? Where did he come from? When?"

Puzzled, Saber stared at Lafitte. "Why would anyone be that interested in me? Do you know who it was?"

"That I do not. Words travel like wildfire on Grand Terre, conveniently losing their sources in the process. It may be nothing, but I thought it wise to warn you. Perhaps someone wishes you evil. A jealous husband, no? Or someone who would benefit if you were to come to grief? Who knows?"

For a second Saber thought of Robert Saxon in England, but pushed the idea away as absurd. Even Robert's arm was not that long.

Not greatly alarmed by Lafitte's news, Saber dismissed the subject with a shrug and adroitly changed the topic of conversation. Staring out the window at the glimpse of the bay over the straggling treetops, he asked, "What sort of price would you give me for *La Belle Garce?*"

"Pardon?" Bewilderment was apparent in Lafitte's voice. "I must have misunderstood you . . . I thought you just asked if I would buy your ship."

"Hmm, I did. I've decided to sell her. I've a mind to become respectable."

If Saber had stated he wished to become a nun in the Order of Ursuline in New Orleans, Lafitte could not have been more horrified. In a faint voice he repeated, "Sell *La Belle Garce* and become respectable!" He spat out the last word with a great deal of distaste. Staring at Saber's bearded face with consternation, he cried, "You must be mad! Why?"

At the moment Lafitte could find no words to express his feelings. It was simply incomprehensible, and Saber, taking pity on him, said gently, "I've enjoyed our association, profited by it, but I'm not the wild hotheaded youth that I was ten years ago. I grow weary of playing the pirate, even if it is cloaked by the polite term of privateer. Bluntly, I have no more need of *La Belle Garce.* I've acquired fortune enough to make it unnecessary for me to continue in the role of privateer, or if you prefer plain speaking—*pirate!*"

Recovering himself somewhat, Lafitte sighed. "So you would leave your friends and become like the so-proper gentlemen in New Orleans."

Saber laughed. "I would never turn my back on a friend and I doubt I shall be able to become a model of decorum."

Lafitte allowed a shadow of a smile to cross his handsome face. "I agree." Then seriously, he asked "You are certain this is what you plan to do? You will not, six months from now, change your mind?"

All laughter banished from the gold eyes, Saber regarded

his cigar rather somberly. "Yes, I'm certain and I would offer you a little advice . . . if you will not take it amiss."

Lafitte cocked an eyebrow and looked amused. "You will teach your granny to suck eggs?"

A quick grin was flashed to him, but then Saber said carefully, "If I were you, I would follow my example and disassociate yourself from Grand Terre and all that it implies."

Lafitte stiffened, and aware of it, Saber met his angry stare. Softly he said, "Jean, listen to me. The wild days are almost over. We're in our waning stages, if you will just read all the signs correctly. The Americans are not going to stomach you on their doorstep much longer, and what is worse, they're convincing the old die-hard Creoles that we really are a menace and should be stamped out. It's only a matter of time until they take definite action." Deliberately he added, "That small slave rebellion in the Parish of St. John the Baptist, a few years back, did you little good."

Lafitte grunted in agreement. That much of what Saber said was true. There had been a rebellion planned on the order of the bloodbath that had overtaken Haiti many years ago. And when it was discovered the ringleaders were slaves who had been smuggled in from Africa by Lafitte, the more respectable portion of the population had been outraged and frightened. But unlike Saber, Lafitte did not read into that little contretemps the beginning of the end. He had outraged others before; it was certainly nothing novel. Without heat he inquired, "Are you a rat leaving what you think is a sinking ship, *mon ami?*"

Saber's mouth thinned and his hand tightened around the wineglass. "No. If I were, I would wait six months or a year before leaving." Flatly he said, "Get out, Jean, before you lose everything."

"Ah, bah! You annoy me! Feeling as you do, I think it is best that you will no longer be part of the organization. I have no use for men that doubt me."

Saber stood up, put down his wineglass, and very, *very* properly bowed. He turned to leave but Lafitte muttered, "Wait!"

Only polite curiosity showing on his features, Saber looked at him. Rising from behind his desk, Lafitte said, "I apologize. We are friends, are we not? As friends we should be able to speak our thoughts without the other taking offense. I admit I am vexed, greatly, but I do not wish us to part in anger."

Saber's mouth lengthened into a slow, lazy smile, a twinkle glinting in his eyes. "You were angry, I was not. I merely felt it politic to let you get over your . . . ah . . . sulks before I saw you again."

"Sulks!" Lafitte was plainly affronted by such a word being applied to himself, but then realizing Saber was right, he smiled and extended his hand. As the two shook hands he said, "I will give you a good price for your ship *mon ami*. How soon do you want all the final details settled?"

Saber shrugged. "I'm not in a tearing hurry, although now that my mind is made up, I would prefer to have it finished at the earliest possible date. Shall we say within the week, the first of December? I should have also decided what to do with the good Allen by then."

"Very well. I'm most regretful to lose you as one of my captains, but I hope I shall retain you as a good and frequent customer in the future. You will, of course, be staying with me tonight and I shall see you at dinner?"

Saber nodded and laughed, "Always the businessman, are you not?"

"But of course, *mon ami*. What else would I be?"

Departing from Lafitte's a few minutes later, he was glad of the warmth of his greatcoat against the bite of the chill wind that blew in from the bay as he slowly walked over to the sturdy brick building that comprised the calaboose. Strange to think that this part of his life was now ending, but it had served its purpose and now he was resolved upon another path of life.

Entering the calaboose, he discovered much to his satisfaction that Allen had arrived only moments before and was presently chained in one of the cells toward the rear of the building. The calaboose was not large, consisting of a small main room and beyond that four tiny cells—there was not much use for one on Grand Terre. Most disputes were settled by a knife or fists, and the calaboose was merely Lafitte's token of law and order. But that was not to say that the calaboose was weak or just an excuse, for it was quite sturdy.

Allen was in the last cell, and Saber's nose wrinkled with distaste as he walked down the narrow dark passageway that led there. The stale smell of unwashed bodies and other even less pleasant odors came to his nostrils, and he wondered sardonically if his new quarters gave Allen any joy. Evidently not, judging from his haggard appearance, Saber thought, as he viewed dispassionately the man manacled to the wall before him. His clothing was torn and bloodstained; bruises discolored his face. Eyeing a new bruise, Saber asked interestedly, "Did you try to escape as they were bringing you ashore? I don't remember you being quite so untidy when last we met."

Allen's head jerked up at Saber's words and instinctively he pulled against his chains.

"You bastard!" he snarled, anger darkening his eyes. "What have you done with Nick?"

"Don't you mean Nicole?"

Allen caught his breath. "She told *you?*" he finally croaked incredulously.

"Let us say I was able to . . . ah . . . discover it for myself. She was, like you, not very forthcoming."

Allen eyed the man across from him. His own danger he took as a matter of fact, he had always known the risks. Nicole was another story. Grimly he inquired, "Where is she?"

Saber's eyebrows rose in disdainful reproof. "Her fate is my concern."

"Saber, listen to me!" he started earnestly, then throwing caution to the winds, he blurted out the entire story, telling far more than Nicole had. She had told Saber nothing beyond her age and first name. But Allen, his very real worry for Nicole driving all other considerations from his mind, told Saber everything: her full name, her background, everything! It was only when he faltered to a stop that he became aware of the curious stillness of the other man, and the cold, derisive smile on his lips. The smile was a mirthless one, and if Allen could have known Saber's thoughts he would have been stunned and dismayed.

The Ashford name was well-known to Saber—he had cursed it for years. It was forever seared in his mind, associated with disgrace, dishonor, lies, and betrayal. Saber wondered at the ironic implausibility of it all, that orphaned Nicole Ashford should fall into his hands.

"Don't you understand?" Allen demanded, breaking into his thoughts. "Nicole Ashford is from a good family. She must be returned to her home before she finds herself in worse trouble."

Recovering himself, his expression openly skeptical, Saber asked, "Why didn't you say something earlier? It's a little late to worry about her now!"

Allen bit his lip, unwilling to confess that he had had his own reasons or that his motives had been anything less than altruistic. Saber waited silently, unperturbed, but as Allen offered nothing further, he grew bored. When the silence became awkward, Allen demanded, "What do you intend to do?"

Carelessly studying the nails of one finely shaped hand, Saber said coolly, "Do? I intend to do nothing. I shall find it much more amusing that way. I shall probably find it diverting to view her antics as she strives to hide the real facts from me—the real facts that you, her good friend, were so eager to impart to me."

"Saber, hasn't a word I've said made sense to you? Are you so completely without scruple that you will ruin a young and innocent girl?"

His gold eyes gleaming with mockery, Saber surveyed him pityingly for a moment, then said blunty, "Yes, of course I am!"

Allen's lips drew back in a snarl of helpless rage, but Saber only laughed and walked away from him. Stopping in the doorway to the cell, he turned and looked back at his prisoner. "Don't concern yourself with the future of young Nick," he taunted. "I intend to take her under my protection." His eyes suddenly shuttered and unreadable he murmured, "And I'm sure you know what that means."

Furiously Allen fought against his chains. "Saber, goddamnit! Listen to me!" But the words fell on uncaring ears, for with a mocking inclination of his black head Saber had departed.

Left alone, Allen's thoughts reverted irresistibly to Nicole. He was genuinely horrified at the thought of Nicole becoming Saber's mistress. And what of his own fate? How long would Saber hold him captive, and what did he have planned for him? Objectively he tried to view the events that had taken place, but his thoughts were erratic. Somehow Saber must have learned of their plan. Why else had he set those two sailors on him? He had known from the minute they'd entered his cabin yesterday that things had gone wrong, and like a fool he had made a desperate attempt to escape. That action alone destroyed whatever hope he may have had of bluffing his way clear. Damn Saber! How the hell had the man known when to strike? Another half hour and he and Nick would have been safely on their way. And what of Nick? Had Saber already forced himself upon her? And most importantly—where the hell was she?

At that moment Nicole was on her way back to Grand Terre. She had awakened just about the time Saber was leaving for Grand Terre. She lay there quietly for a few

119

minutes, still groggy from the laudanum, gradually becoming aware of her surroundings. The bed was soft and her first inclination was to snuggle down deeper into its welcoming warmth. But an unwise movement of her injured wrist jerked her painfully awake and brought the past night's disagreeable events to mind.

Cautiously she glanced around the room and heaved a cowardly sigh of relief when she discovered Saber was gone and the room was empty. Clumsily, because of her still-aching wrist, she propped herself up with two fluffy pillows and coolly surveyed her situation.

The worst had happened. Her masquerade had been discovered, Allen was in chains, and she herself was Saber's prisoner. She had become a woman at Saber's experienced hands and in the process acquired a damaged wrist. Her body felt stiff and bruised and she was aware of a slight discomfort between her thighs. Thank God it was over. She was alive, granted a bit torn and battered, but nonetheless whole and alert.

The soft sound of a door opening distracted her thoughts, and unconsciously squaring her shoulders, she watched the door being pushed wider. At the sight of Galena's round face she giggled with relief.

Cheerfully Galena asked, "Would you like some coffee or perhaps some chocolate?"

Nicole smiled at her, determined to act as natural as possible. "Some coffee please." She hesitated, then asked carefully, "Where is Saber?"

Galena looked slightly puzzled. "Saber? Oh, you must mean the master! He has left on business and won't return until tomorrow or the next day. In the meantime, he left orders to make you as comfortable as possible and to see to it that you have whatever you wish."

Rather thoughtfully Nicole regarded Galena. How much had Saber told his servants? Did they know of the real situation? And how far would they go in obeying her? Unless Saber had given orders to the contrary, there was nothing to stop her from disappearing while he was away. Well, there was just one way to find out. Abruptly she said, "I'd like a bath, some clothing, and something to eat. Please see to it, will you?"

Galena departed and returned shortly with several garments lying across her arm. A doubtful expression on her face, she said, "The master wasn't certain if there was anything here that would fit you. These gowns, I'm afraid, might be too short."

Nicole stiffened at the obvious implications and choked

back the hot words on her lips. She smiled thinly, saying, "I'd go naked before I'd clothe myself in a gown discarded by one of his mistresses. I'll wear my own clothes."

Galena was truly disturbed. "But you can't! Ladies don't wear breeches."

"I doubt your master has ever had a *lady* here before!" Nicole spat. "Get my clothes or get me something else to wear. Surely there must be a clean shirt and pants belonging to one of the servants that I can borrow. I'm not particularly selective at this moment."

Galena's eyes grew wide with shock, but she backed from the room and scurried down the hall. A lady wearing servant's clothing—and men's at that! Shaking her head at the strange goings-on, Galena quickly acquainted Sanderson with Nicole's request. He gave a start, but then rapidly recovering himself, provided her with a clean white shirt and gray cotton pants.

Bathed and wearing her boy's clothing, she explored Saber's house. Unconsciously she was searching for certain items, and her eyes lit up with excitement when she discovered the gun room at the rear of the house on the first floor.

It was a very masculine room. A few stuffed animal heads—a fox, a cougar, and a deer—were hung on one wall, and on another were some wooden-framed hunting prints. The furniture was large, comfortable, and worn. A well-stocked liquor cabinet was against one wall, but it was the sight of the gun racks that interested Nicole.

Boldly opening the oak gun case, she rummaged through the various weapons until she found what she wanted: a razor-sharp hunting knife, a small, deadly double-barreled pistol, and some shot and powder. After much thought she concealed them in the drawer of a long, narrow satinwood table and left the room.

She ate a hearty breakfast, discovering she was, despite last night, hungry. Life went on, she brooded, no matter what happened. But her spirits were recovering with every moment, and after finishing her meal, she brazenly borrowed an old hunting jacket, presumably belonging to Saber, and sauntered outside.

The cold sun of late November offered little heat and there was a chilly wind in the air. Glad of the warmth of Saber's jacket, she wandered down the broad avenue of oaks that led to the river. Stopping at the edge of a long wooden-planked pier that jutted into the mud-colored waters of the Mississippi River, she contemplated her next move.

Saber had obviously not apprised anyone of the true situation between them. The servants acted as if she were a guest, a slightly mad guest, but a guest nonetheless. But would they obey her odd requests to the point of allowing her to demand a guide to take her to Grand Terre?

Nicole knew she would only end up lost or wandering in circles in the swamps if she tried to leave unaided. Absently she kicked a clod of dirt into the river, her mind busy with the problem at hand. She would not wait meekly for Saber's return; her escape must be immediate.

Turning her back on the river, Nicole strode purposefully toward the house. Meeting Sanderson in the main hall, she said carelessly, "I've decided not to wait for your master's return. I shall leave within the hour. Please have a basket of food packed for a journey and find someone to escort me to Grand Terre. I'm sorry at the abruptness, but if I am to make the island before dark, I shall have to leave now."

Ignoring the disapproving expression on his face, she walked to the gun room and quickly stuffed the little horde she had collected earlier into the capacious pockets of the jacket. She fled the room and soon found her way to the room she had shared with Saber. She pushed open the door and entered, relieved to find it empty. Sparing not so much as a glance at the bed where just last night Saber had made love to her so very thoroughly, she walked over to a door that led to an adjoining bedroom. The door was unlocked, and after checking to see that this room, too, was deserted, she stepped inside, shutting the door behind her.

This was obviously Saber's bedroom. The massive furniture was made of dark wood, the huge bed was hung with burgundy velvet. But Nicole, not concerned with Saber's taste in furnishings, crossed the room swiftly and without hesitation rooted through his jewel box, which rested open on a large many-drawered bureau. She removed one of Saber's linen handkerchiefs and wrapped up a diamond stickpin, a fine emerald and pearl ring, and another stickpin—this one a ruby—as well as a number of other valuable trinkets. A few gold coins lay near the plundered jewel case and without scruple she scooped them up. She and Allen would need every asset that they could lay their hands on.

Her confidence blazing, she waited impatiently for some minutes in her own room. When she decided enough time had elapsed, she walked negligently down the stairs and, assuming a bored expression, she inquired of Sanderson, "Is everything ready? I should like to leave as soon as possible."

Before he could reply a small Negro boy, carrying a covered wicker basket nearly as large as himself, stumbled into the hallway. Glancing down at the child, Sanderson answered with reluctance, "I believe so. This is the food you requested and Jonah, who will act as your guide, is waiting at the dock." He paused, his indecision clear, but Nicole met his gaze haughtily, tilting one of her slender eyebrows as if daring him to question her actions.

"Will that be all, madame?" he said at last. "Samuel here will escort you to the dock."

Nicole inclined her head politely and followed the little figure with the large basket. It was all she could do to not snatch the basket from the boy and run like a wild thing to the river. Her heart was thudding in her breast, yet a satisfied grin kept tugging at her lips. Settling herself into the pirogue and watching the distance between herself and the dock widen, she couldn't control the little crow of laughter that slipped out. The young Negro piloting the craft gave her a strange look but she didn't care. She had provisions, a pistol, money, and freedom!

12

Nicole had been right in calculating that it would be nearly dark when they arrived at the island. Consequently, she was not surprised that dusk was falling when she reached her destination. Tossing a gold coin to her guide, she grasped the wicker basket and strode nonchalantly up the beach. Once she was out of sight of the pirogue, she quickly plunged into the sparse undergrowth at the edge of the island and, hidden from view, sat down to think.

She had escaped. She was armed and had food. The next step was to free Allen. Was he still on the ship? She hoped not! It would be virtually impossible for her to engineer his escape from *La Belle Garce*. By now word of her masquerade must have spread through the entire crew, making it highly unlikely that she could ever set foot on shipboard again.

A deep sigh welled up within her. Damn! Surely life could not be this unfair. She needed Allen—needed him badly!

Abstractedly she opened the basket, and discovering a whole baked chicken, she chewed ruminatively on a drumstick while studying her problem. Allen might not be on the ship. He could already be on his way to New Orleans. No, perhaps not. Allen must still be on *La Belle Garce,* unless Saber had returned to Grand Terre. She shivered with uneasiness, hoping desperately that Saber was nowhere within twenty miles of her. She should have questioned the servants about his destination. He could be on his way to New Orleans or—she swallowed nervously—he *could* be right here on the island.

Angrily she threw down her chicken bone and stood up, wiping her hands, boylike, on the seat of her pants. She wasn't going to let him frighten her. If he was on the island, more than likely he would be with Lafitte, and as long as she stayed away from the vicinity of the mansion, she should be able to avoid him. But it still didn't solve the problem of Allen.

From her hiding place, a little shrub-covered knoll, she had an excellent overall view of the island and the bay. Almost accidentally her gaze fell upon the small brick calaboose. She eyed it speculatively in the increasing darkness. Allen could be there. It was a slim possibility, but one worth exploring. Even if she discovered he was not there, it narrowed down the places he could be.

Hiding the food under a shrubby bush, she left her place of concealment, cautiously creeping across the island. She made her way from tree to bush, from house to building, and finally to the calaboose. She was breathing fast and her legs were shaky when she leaned against the back wall. Twice she had seen crew members of *La Belle Garce* meandering drunkenly from one bawdy house to the next. She had been hidden in the shadows each time, but it pointed out the danger she ran. If she were recognized, God help her! It would be worse than anything Saber could devise.

Recovering her breath and some of her courage, she began trying to locate Allen, stopping beneath each barred window to call his name. At the third window he answered. Relief washed over her. "Are you alone?" she whispered. "Are you safe?"

"For God's sake, Nick, what are you doing here?" Glancing nervously at the blackened hallway down which Saber had disappeared only an hour before, Allen added, "Talk quickly. Saber might return. Are you all right?"

Nicole nodded; then realizing Allen couldn't see her, she said, "Yes, but don't let us waste time talking. I've come to free you."

In the inkiness of his cell Allen smiled. Bless the child! How calmly she said that—as if it were the simplest thing in the world.

"Nick, I don't mean to discourage you, but I'm chained and the cell door has a very stout lock on it."

"Bah! Who cares? I'm armed, I have a pistol in my pocket. I'll think of something," she said with more confidence than she felt. Yet at the same time Allen's being so near made her feel certain that their luck was changing. Leaning her back against the bricks of his prison and watching for signs of discovery, she called up to him, "Who has the keys? Do you have a guard?"

"No. The only guard is old Manuel, and he's in the room at the front. He has the keys to the cell, Nick, but I'm afraid it's Saber who possesses the key that will unlock my chains." Allen's voice was bleak.

Damn the man! Was he infallible? The full import of

Allen's words sunk in. *Saber was here!* Her whole body stiffened with apprehension. After the first shock subsided she willed herself not to be terrorized. Saber was only a man, not the devil he resembled. He *did* make mistakes —her being here was proof of that. Even so, it was with increased suspense that her eyes pierced the darkness. The thought of Saber standing hidden in the night and watching her was unnerving, but she discarded it with a stubborn shake of her head. She wasn't a namby-pamby creature to jump at shadows.

"Are you certain, Allen? Wouldn't the keys stay with the old man?"

Allen frowned. Slowly he said, "You could be right, Nick." It was true, a separate key had been used to lock his chains, but there was no reason to believe it had not been added to the ring of keys that were hung in the jail's main room. He had assumed Saber would keep it. Yet Nick's query made more sense and he knew Saber had not planned on Nick escaping. He smiled grimly. Saber had underestimated young Nick rather badly.

Still smiling faintly, he said, "There's one way to find out, Nick. You'll have to get the keys from old Manuel. Can you do it?"

Nicole's jaw jutted in a stubborn line. She'd get those damned keys if it killed her! Optimistically she whispered, "Don't worry, if worse comes to worse, I shall shoot off the chains. Give me a moment, I shall think of something." And she did. Boldness had served her purpose in fleeing Saber, and if it had worked once, it would work again.

Discipline was lax on the island, and old Manuel's position as jailer was merely for appearances and because it gave him something to do. The few times the jail was actually used, it was common for the prisoners to have their cronies come to commiserate with them. It was not uncommon for old Manuel to hand the visitor the keys and let them show themselves in and out. No one had ever taken advantage of that laxity, mainly because while the prisoners might grumble, they were in awe of Lafitte. Jean was fair, and they knew better than to cross him.

From her visits to Grand Terre as a member of Saber's crew, Nicole knew that discipline was almost nonexistent. She walked calmly to the front of the calaboose and entered. She was uneasily aware that the old Spaniard might have been warned to watch out for her, but she thrust those cowardly thoughts aside and spoke boldly. "I've come to see Allen Ballard from *La Belle Garce*," she said crisply. "Where is he?"

The old man, sleepy from his nightly rum, waved a hand vaguely in the direction of the keys. "Help yourself. He's in the last cell on the left."

Her blood pounding like thunder in her temples, Nicole took down the keys, her fingers trembling with the elation of success. As nonchalantly as possible she walked down the narrow hall to Allen's cell and fumbled through the keys, trying to find the one that would open the door. Her hands were shaking so badly that she wasted precious seconds before at last the door swung wide. With her heart leaping in her breast, she ran to Allen. For a long moment they stood staring at one another, and then with a cry of distress at his haggard and bruised appearance, Nicole threw herself on his chest, her arms hugging him tightly. "Oh, Allen, your poor face. What has he done to you? Was it very bad?"

Allen gave her a warm smile and whispered into the soft hair that brushed his lips, "It's nothing, Nick. And now that you are here, everything will be fine."

Nicole hugged him again, her eyes swimming with tears of emotion; as naturally as a sister bestowing a kiss on a beloved brother, she pressed her lips sweetly to his. Unfortunately, to the tall bearded man who suddenly materialized in the open doorway, it had all the appearances of lovers reunited. His lips drew back in a growl of outrage and bright yellow fire gleamed in the gold eyes.

"Touching!" Saber snarled.

Nicole and Allen both froze. Her hand clutching the pistol in her pocket, Nicole whirled to face Saber, who loomed just inside the doorway, his feet spread apart and his bearded face very black in the dim light.

Allen sensed her intent and entreated, "Don't, Nick! The sound of a shot will bring a crowd. You won't be able to escape."

Sarcastically Saber murmured, "Are you sure you don't mean she wouldn't have time to free you!"

Allen threw Saber an angry glance, but it was Nicole who snapped, "Shut up, Saber! Or I *will* shoot you."

Mockingly he bowed. "Your wish, madame, at the moment, shall be my most fervent desire."

Eyeing him wrathfully, Nicole kept the pistol aimed at his heart and commanded, "Step over there, against the wall."

His mouth twitching with what could have been anger or, disconcertingly, amusement, Saber complied. With a bored expression on his face, he asked casually, "Do you intend to chain me like the good Allen?"

A curt nod was his answer. Nicole approached him cautiously. Saber's docile air didn't deceive her at all. Keeping the pistol on him with one hand, while she attempted to chain him with the other, was going to be awkward. She scowled at Saber and then cast a hopeful look at Allen. It would be wiser to free Allen first, then the two of them would have him at their mercy. But to Nicole's dismay none of the keys fit the locks of Allen's chains.

"If you had only asked, my dear, I could have saved you the trouble," Saber said smoothly. "The key you want is reposing on the bureau in my room at Lafitte's." She glowered at Saber as he lounged carelessly against the wall, apparently completely at ease.

"Be quiet!" she muttered tightly as she walked toward him. There was only one solution. She must chain Saber herself and then shoot Allen free. They would have to move quickly after that to escape the curious mob that would surely gather. It was not what she would have wished, but it seemed to be their only chance.

Standing in front of Saber, she said softly, "If you make one move that is not to my liking, I shall shoot you dead. Do you understand me?"

Watching her closely, Saber nodded his head slowly, his eyes, hard and speculative, locked on her white, determined face.

"Put your left wrist in the shackle directly above it," Nicole commanded. "Do it carefully, Saber, and remember that I would enjoy killing you."

But Saber only crossed his arms over his chest and said coolly, "I have no intention of doing anything so damned silly. Go ahead and shoot—if you dare!"

Nearly stuttering with rage, she shouted, "G-g-goddamn y-you, Saber, do as I tell you!"

"No," he replied calmly, unmoved by her actions.

Observing Nicole's face, Allen warned anxiously, "Be careful, Nick. He's deliberately goading you."

With an effort Nicole attempted to swallow her rage. But it was useless, the flame in her hair spoke of a truly ungovernable temper, and seeing her enemy before her, mocking her dilemma, she suddenly lost all caution. Storming at him, she dragged furiously at the arms that were folded over his chest and cried, "You *will* do as I say—even if I have to force you myself!" Forgetting her injury, she raised the pistol and struck him a vicious blow across one cheek.

A moan of pain came from her as her injured wrist betrayed her, but it quickly became a scream of fury as Saber exploded into action. Snaking both arms around her, he trapped her in a less-than-gentle embrace. Allen surged helplessly against his chains as they struggled in front of him, while with horror Nicole felt the pistol slip from her agonized grasp. She was caught like a vixen in a snare and she knew it. Her chest was pressed tightly to Saber's and his arms crushed her. Pride forbade that she beg and common sense told her it was useless to waste her strength. Damnable, *damnable* temper, she thought with self-disgust. Why had she let it possess her to the point of near insanity? Closing her eyes in contempt of her own foolish actions, she cursed herself for being the hotheaded nitwit she was.

"Do we cry quits, Nick?" Saber asked quietly.

Her eyes flew open; hating him and trying for some of his own arrogant coolness, she drawled, "You're asking me? How odd! In the past you've always commanded."

Smiling down into her upturned face, he was surprised to feel something next to admiration for her. With wry amusement he said, "What a little cocklebur you are! Do you never stay where you are put?"

Not deigning to answer him, Nicole stared mutely at the hard mouth above her. She wasn't about to cross verbal swords with him.

"Saber, hear me," Allen demanded from across the room. "You wouldn't listen earlier, but you must see that it is only just that you return Nicole to her family. Take her to New Orleans and place her on the first ship that sails for Jamaica—from there she can easily find passage to England. I have the money to pay for it, as well as enough to hire a woman to act as companion to her. What differences lie between you and me are between you and me. She has nothing to do with it. I beg of you, man, let her go!"

Saber's face went icy, the gold eyes staring with dislike at the chained man. "Let her go! Have your wits gone gathering? Why should I? What would I gain by it?"

Allen's own face was tight, the flesh stretched thin over his handsome features as his mind worked frantically on some inducement that would appeal to the man. He had nothing to offer and appealing to Saber's better nature was useless—Saber had no better nature!

Nicole herself put an end to the waiting uncertainty.

"Don't plead for me, Allen," she said softly. "What is done is done. It was none of your doing." She tossed her head back defiantly and added, "I shall make my own future and it won't be one that was bargained for with the likes of Saber." She glared up at her captor, despising him with her eyes.

Saber grinned at her and murmured, "You think not?" Flicking a taunting glance at Allen, he drew Nicole closer to him, and bending his head, he trapped her unsuspecting lips with his own. As if aware of the sick rage that filled the other man, he kissed Nicole deeply, his mouth seeking the sweetness from between her lips.

Nicole made no resistance to his searching mouth, surmising that he was doing it to torment Allen and to remind her of how completely she was his. The kiss gave her no pleasure—she endured it, and when it was over a shudder of relief shook her.

Saber frowned at her reaction, but released her with a careless shrug. Picking up the dropped pistol, he tucked it securely in the wide leather belt at his waist. Turning to Nicole, he searched her thoroughly, his hands purposefully lingering on her breasts and thighs, caressing her openly. Humiliated to the core of her being at such obvious intimacy in front of Allen, diamond-bright tears sparkled in the depths of her eyes. Saber's movements were not without reason. He was driving it home to Allen in the cruelest way possible that Nicole was *his*. The picture of Nicole kissing Allen was etched in acid on Saber's brain, and its memory made him want to take her now on the filthy floor of the cell in front of the other man. As if by possessing her before him, he could prove his ownership, like a small boy taunting, "See, she's *mine!*" But when he glanced at Nicole's rigid face, the feeling left him, and for the first time in half his lifetime, he let consideration for another human being sway him from his own desires. The sight of her face, with her emotions so clearly defined, made the thought of further degradation insupportable.

Without a word he pocketed the knife he found, as well as the gold coins and the jewelry. One hand clasping her arm, he guided her in the direction of the cell door. Reluctantly she obeyed the commanding pressure on her arm. It was so reminiscent of the scene of yesterday morning on *La Belle Garce* that a ripple of mirthless laughter broke from her.

"No, I'm not about ready to dissolve into frenzied weeping," she said as he glanced at her sharply. "I merely found it amusing that this is the second time in as many days that you have managed to gain the upper hand."

A glimmer of sardonic amusement in his gaze, he murmured, "You *are* rather stubborn. You seem to have the ridiculous idea that you can outmaneuver me. For shame, young Nick, you should know better!"

Incensed, she opened her mouth to join battle, but then recollecting past arguments, she turned away.

Saber grinned, his eyes dwelling appreciatively on the fiery glints in the dark hair. Then as he looked back at Allen, his grin faded and he remarked, "Cease your worry for her. As you can see, I meant what I said earlier —I have Nick's future well in hand!"

Silently, for there was nothing he could say, Allen watched dismally as Saber locked the cell, and with him pushing Nicole in front of him, they vanished from his sight. Dejectedly he slumped against the wall. Poor Nick! He should never have listened to her in the first place. The instant he had discovered her sex he should have sent her packing. And now it was too late. She was as much a prisoner as he and he was powerless to help her. Gad, what a plucky thing she was though; he remembered with sudden affection her determination to free him. Belatedly he realized that it would have been wiser if he had sent her to his supervisors with the news of his capture. At least she would be free, and his confederates would instantly set in motion plans to secure his release. Twice Saber had managed to outfox them, and he wondered wearily if it would always be so.

He knew he had made no mistakes. He had been so careful, and he doubted that Nicole had given away much. But then she knew really nothing to confess. Allen was struck by a new thought and his eyes brightened— there was no proof of his activities, of that he was certain. Yet against Saber's high-handedness, he was defenseless. Saber had not even accused him of any crime! But the man was a law unto himself and few, if any, questioned his actions. Even Lafitte was known to overlook certain of Saber's transgressions. And so Allen's unhappy thoughts went—concern for Nicole, regret that he had not acted sooner, speculation about Saber.

Nicole, with Saber her jailer, once more was not precisely in the most pleasant frame of mind herself. Her wrist was paining her fretfully, and she wondered if this time she had truly broken it. About Allen she could do nothing, at the moment. She spared him a second's regret and then turned all her energies into maintaining as self-

131

reliant a front as she could in the circumstances. It gave her a great boost of satisfaction to appear blasé and insouciant as she entered Lafitte's home beside Saber. Not for the world would she have betrayed the uneasy flutter in her throat or the knot of trepidation in her stomach. Her back was ramrod straight; her head was held high; and her eyes were gleaming with challenge. She wasn't beaten, but had merely suffered a slight reversal—that was all!

Having been only a cabin boy, Nicole had never been inside Lafitte's mansion, so it was with a great deal of lively curiosity that she noted her surroundings. After having glanced with penetrating thoroughness at the profusion of impressive gilt-edged mirrors that lined the walls, the innumerable intricately inlaid tables, and the hanging crystal chandeliers, she decided that Lafitte had tastes bordering on the vulgar, and her lip curled with disdain.

Observing her reaction, Saber smiled slightly and said, "It is a bit overpowering, isn't it? Jean feels that it is what is expected of him. But it is also a not-so-subtle way of reassuring his prospective buyers that he is perfectly capable of supplying their demands. Proof of that is all around you."

Having come to the conclusion that it would be best if she treated Saber as something highly distasteful that had to be endured, Nicole schooled her features into an expression of utmost boredom and shrugged her shoulders to imply that such things were beneath her and that only good manners, of which Saber would know nothing, kept her in his company. Saber's amused laughter did little to soothe her already rasped emotions, and she turned her back on him.

It would do no good to hurl abuse at him, and it was foolish to think that another physical attack would be successful. She was too much of a gambler not to know when luck was against her. She sighed, thinking that luck had truly deserted her lately. She knew that her feelings were still too raw from this latest catastrophe for her to think calmly and clearly. And with Saber one needed to be very calm and collected! Her only defense at the moment was indifference. Where temper had failed her, perhaps icy aloofness would prevail. Unwisely she glanced over her shoulder and caught him in an outright grin. Her eyes snapping with displeasure, she asked nastily, "Something amuses you?"

His splendid white teeth gleaming against the blackness of his beard, Saber replied provocatively, "Yes, you do! I swear I can't remember when, outside of bed naturally, a wench has given me as much enjoyment as you have."

Nicole's strangled gasp of rage was lost on Saber as Lafitte, an expression of pleasure on his face, entered the room and said, "Ah, you have returned, *mon ami*. You departed so suddenly after the message arrived that someone was skulking around the calaboose that I wondered if you would return this evening."

Catching sight of Nicole's tall, slender form, he halted just inside the room, his black eyes taking in her set face and rigid stance with open speculation. For a moment she was subjected to a thorough and unnerving appraisal, and then Lafitte looked at Saber murmuring, "But yes! One sees how it was done. She *is* tall for a woman, and in those bulky clothes, her shape would have been hidden. How old did you say she was?"

Blandly ignoring Nicole's wrathful face, Saber replied, "Eighteen and a few months, I believe. And of course, the hair being scraped back was also in itself a bit of a disguise. Freed it's an entirely different story. See what I mean?"

For one so large, Saber moved with a quicksilver grace, and before Nicole could guess his purpose, he had taken one long stride to her side and with rough, deft motions he loosened her hair.

Freed from the confining queue, her hair tumbled in soft waves of mahogany fire around her shoulders, and Lafitte's black eyes narrowed with appreciation.

"Very pretty," he said softly. "Would you be interested in selling her? I would give you a good price."

Nicole's eyes widened and her shocked gaze swung to Saber. Unaware of the imploring look in her dark eyes, she stared at him, willing him to say no.

He gave her a sardonic glance. Turning to Lafitte he said smoothly, "Perhaps, later. I've not yet grown used to her. Ask me again in a week or two."

Ordinarily Nicole would have reacted to those indifferent words, but she didn't like the calculating glint of Lafitte's eyes and decided instantly that she would like even less to share with him the intimacies Saber had forced upon her. She would delight in carving out Saber's liver and feeding it to the sharks, and yet at the same time she was reluctant to let Lafitte see that all was not well between them. Nicole felt rather than saw the curiosity in Saber's look, as she remained mute in the face of his taunt.

After waiting for a minute, he shrugged his shoulders and remarked infuriatingly, "You see, Jean, the *almost*-perfect woman—she knows when to keep her mouth shut!"

Nicole's eyes, burning with outraged dark fire, flew to Saber's face but wisely, for once, she said nothing. Saber grinned at her and dared her to prove him wrong.

Watching the pair of them, the black-bearded giant and the slender defiant girl, Lafitte smiled to himself. Saber, he felt certain, was about to discover that all women were not alike—that there existed a few who could resist his blandishments. Not that Saber appeared to be exerting himself to charm the chit, but he seemed to take pleasure in baiting her, something Lafitte had never seen before. It was all very interesting, especially in light of their earlier conversation. Could it be, he speculated, that at last Saber had been snared by the oldest trap of all? That this slender boyish female had slipped under his guard? If it were so, it was obvious that neither of the two principals were aware of it.

Next to making money, Lafitte loved romance best, and the thought of his cold-hearted friend caught in the throes of unrequited love made him smile. With a twinkle in his eyes Lafitte asked, "Do you intend to retire early, *mon ami?* I had thought we might play a hand or two of piquet. Of course"—smiling widely—"I will understand if you no longer find that plan agreeable."

Saber shot him a lazy look and shook his head. "That sounds fine. Just as soon as I get Nick settled, I'll join you in the library."

"How remiss of me! But yes, we must see to her comfort. I shall make arrangements at once."

Saber waved aside Lafitte's offer to ring for a servant and marched Nicole out of the room and up the wide, sweeping staircase. Pushing her down a large carpeted hall, he escorted her to the suite of rooms Lafitte had set aside for his use.

Shutting the door firmly behind him, he surveyed Nicole's angry face with displeasure, and it occurred to her suddenly that in spite of his baiting tone and his easy manner, he was in a rage, an icy rage that was all the more frightening for its lack of fire. But Nicole was not easily frightened and glaring at him she snapped, "Don't let me detain you. I'm sure Lafitte is eager for your company." Disdainfully she turned her back on him, only to

134

feel his hand hard on her shoulder as he spun her around to face him. No longer was his face bland and amused— his jaw was taut, his mouth thinned into a hard line, and his eyes as cold as frozen gold. His words, when they came, were like knives. "Lafitte can wait! You and I have something to settle between us first. You were, if I remember correctly, to remain at the plantation. I think I should remind you that I don't give orders merely to hear the sound of my voice. Just because you've become my mistress does not alter the fact that when I tell you to do something, I expect it to be done. Do you understand me?" He shook her slightly as he said the last.

"I understand, you—you shark's belly!" she retorted angrily. Stabbing a finger at him, she snapped, "You're the one who doesn't understand! I'm not a piece of booty you've captured and I will *not* be your mistress—or anything else!" Furiously she attempted to shrug off his hold, but his hands tightened until she thought her bones would snap.

Holding her temper in check with more patience than she knew she possessed, she demanded coldly, "Release me! You've already cracked my wrist, do you intend to break my shoulder as well?"

His hands loosened a fraction but he did not release her entirely. "Don't tempt me, little vixen! In the mood I'm in right now I could easily break every bone in your body, and what's more I'd enjoy doing it!"

"If you feel that way, why keep me prisoner?" she shot back hotly.

An ugly smile tugged at the corners of his mouth and he jerked her next to his lean body. Crushed to him, Nicole could feel him rigid with desire and thought that he meant to take her again, this instant. Protesting, she arched herself away, but his hands slid down to cup her buttocks, pulling her to his hips. Thrusting himself against her, making her unavoidably conscious that he was hard with wanting, he snarled softly, *"That* is why I keep you."

Shaken, more so than she could remember, she couldn't help crying, "Have you no mercy? No feeling for another person? Have you forgotten whatever morals you possess?" It was foolish, she knew, but the words were torn from her and she waited, her eyes dark, and bright with unshed tears.

He regarded her for a moment between slitted lids, and then he said icily, "I *have* no morals! I want you, Nicole, and *nothing* on this green earth will stop me from taking you as often as I please. Do not waste my time with pleas of mercy or tears. Pleas annoy me and tears bore me. If you will remember this conversation in the future, it will save you a great deal of anguish and heartburning. Be comforted by the knowledge that when I tire of you, I shall do well by you."

Dully she asked, "And if you never tire of me?"

Suddenly real amusement leaped to his eyes. Laughing, he taunted, "You flatter yourself, Nick. There's not a woman alive who would satisfy me for long, and remember, Nick . . . you are not in my preferred style!"

13

The room was like a tomb after Saber's departure. For several seconds Nicole just stood and stared like one in a nightmare at the shut door. He couldn't have uttered those ugly words, she thought numbly. Then a shudder shook her body. Yes, *he* could. He could say them and, worse, *mean* them. Dispiritedly she walked over to a satin-hung bed and threw herself facedown on it. For a long, long time, she just lay there, not wanting to think, yet unable to escape her thoughts.

If only there were some way to turn back the time, she thought wistfully. But then she shrugged. Saber had known she was female, and even if she had never tried to steal those code books with Allen, Allen would have been captured and she suspected that last night still would have found her in Saber's bed . . . willing or not. Saber had cleverly seized upon her rash bargain for his own use, and she had been fool enough to think him willing to strike a trade. But he had gulled her so easily that her stomach churned with embarrassment every time she thought of it. For a few fleeting seconds her mind dwelt lovingly on the picture of Saber reduced to crawling adoration, while she scornfully trod on his innermost emotions.

The idea had been at first merely a pleasant daydream of revenge, but frowning in sudden concentration, she began to pursue it in earnest. If she were to make herself so necessary to his needs that he could not do without her, might not their roles be reversed? And if she were artful enough to snare whatever tender feelings he possessed, wouldn't the balance of power fall into her own hands? Wouldn't Saber be willing, even eager, to please her? To do anything she wished? Such as free Allen . . . or, and her eyes glittered with animation, oust the Markhams from her estates in England!

How did one set out to enslave a man? She had watched, though not closely, several women work their charms on Saber, but to no avail. He played with them, manipulated them to his purpose, and then forgot them. Frowning, she tried to remember if there had been any who had held his interest, which told her one thing—her task wasn't going to be easy!

Her advantage over the others lay in the fact that she was not enamored of him, regardless of the physical fire between them, and that she was bent on using him in the same fashion he had used others. She also realized that part of her own allure for him was indisputably her professed dislike and defiance.

The thought of pitting herself against Saber, of beating him at his own game, restored Nicole's volatile spirit. Half-formed plans spinning in her brain, she paced the room until that first flush of excitement died, leaving her suddenly aware that the hour was late and that she was very sleepy. She eyed the bed uncertainly, not particularly pleased at the thought of Saber returning and finding her asleep. Yet at the same time she was enchanted with the idea that he would find it extremely disconcerting if, expecting a raging virago, he found instead a woman so indifferent to him that she could without a qualm calmly go to sleep! Grinning to herself she stripped and crawled under the blanket. As she drifted off to sleep it occurred to her that her unexpected arrival was bound to cause some change in Saber's plans; she hoped disagreeable ones for him.

Actually her arrival caused Saber little inconvenience, although he would have preferred not to have presented her to Lafitte. But that aside, her presence hardly changed his plans at all. He had intended to return to Thibodaux House in the morning, and that still held true, except now he would have Nick's glowering company on the trip back.

Returning to the library and ignoring the obvious curiosity in Lafitte's eyes, Saber helped himself to a glass of fine French brandy. Settling his long length comfortably in a chair, Saber proceeded to act just as if nothing had happened, and the two men spent the remainder of the evening just as planned originally, playing piquet, smoking cigars, and drinking contraband brandy. If Jean had expected Saber to cut the evening short he was disappointed. Saber stayed until the hour was well past midnight, discussing everything but the woman upstairs.

When it became obvious that Saber was not going to mention Nicole, Lafitte yawned and got to his feet. *"Mon ami,* are you ready to retire, as I am? Or is your silence because your thoughts are with the girl upstairs?"

Annoyed that he had allowed his thoughts to wander, Saber answered sharply, "If you wish to seek out your bed, do so. Don't let me keep you."

Wearing a pained expression, Lafitte remarked, "Truly it must be time for us to go to bed. You are becoming positively vile or," his eyes glittering with bright laughter, he added slyly, "is it that you are having troubles with *amour?*"

Giving a sigh of exasperation, Saber rose from his chair. *"Amour!"* He pronounced it as though it were a curse. "You damned French are always prattling on about it. That chit upstairs is nothing out of the ordinary. She means not a bit more than a half dozen others I could name." With less than his usual mocking manner he bid Lafitte a cool *bonne nuit* and strode down the hall to his room.

The darkness in the room surprised him—as did the sight of Nick asleep. The longer he stared at her, the angrier he became. By God! he thought furiously. She had more brass than a gypsy peddler.

As if aware of his presence, Nicole stirred, and opening her eyes, she met his golden stare with a shock that was almost physical. Quelling the instinctive urge to recoil at the sight of his black-bearded face looming above her, she remained motionless, her features, she hoped, betraying nothing. For several seconds their gazes locked, neither being able to look away. Then, his eyes still on her, he reached out and with slow deliberation removed the blankets covering her body. She made no move to stop him, and even when his hand lightly fondled one breast, the thumb brushing her nipple with insistent pressure, she lay motionless, silently fighting the sudden hot longing within herself.

She had told herself that when next they met she would give in to this . . . this . . . compulsion to have him make love to her, and yet, now that the moment was upon her, she found herself resisting the dictates of her own body. Helplessly she felt her nipple hardening beneath his hand and was ashamed at its betrayal. But her body had a different will, a different thought than the one her mind commanded. A warm, melting sensation was struggling in her loins, and with feverish determination her eyes clung to his, despising the cool, unmoved expression in their yellow-gold depths. She sensed he was holding himself back, toying with her as though she were of no real interest to him.

She truly hated him in that instant, hated him for the power he seemed to wield over her defenseless body. She wanted him in spite of all that had gone before, yet she was furious that he could gaze at her nakedness, caress her, and remain unmoved while she was being devoured by her own desires.

With his eyes still on hers, he left off fondling her breast and with agonizing deliberation trailed his hand down the narrow ribcage to her waist. Almost playfully, his fingers walked to her navel, and then his hand, spread wide, suddenly swept down her stomach. A faint tight grin, almost tigerish, curved his mouth as Nicole gave a gasp of half terror and half anticipation.

She couldn't help the increased thump of her heart, and she was sick, knowing her eyes were giving her away while still, damn him, he seemed unmoved. She tried desperately to maintain her composure, but there were a dozen signs that gave her away; her eyes were dilated and dark with passion, and her nipples rigid with desire.

It was a duel between them—she fighting to remain cool and frigid, and he deliberately arousing her and willing her to respond as he remained aloof and uninvolved himself.

Huskily she spat, "I *hate* you, Saber!" But he gave no sign he even heard her words. Giddily she wondered if he was somehow punishing her for last night. Then coherent thought fled as his fingers, no longer teasing her stomach, opened her and found her. The shock of that gentle caress shot through her entire body and built in intensity as he continued his movements. She fought the feeling as long as she could; then with an anguished moan she twisted away from him.

She lay half on her side, half on her stomach, her arms clasped over her breasts. She tried to capture a dozen fleeing thoughts and emotions as a tight, almost painful ache between her legs clamored for relief.

His face was no longer blank, and a thin film of sweat on his forehead betrayed his own fight for control. Saber stripped with ferocious speed, and before Nicole had time to recover her shattered wits, his hard body was pressed against her back. His breath was soft and warm on her ear, and she felt his body mold itself to hers as they lay there together on their sides. It seemed they touched the entire length—his chest against her slender spine, her buttocks curving into his stomach, and his legs following the position of hers. She started to jerk away but one sinewy arm came down in front of her and he whispered, "Last night was unfortunate and I intend to change that —right now. Let me, Nick, help me—let me *love* you."

She barely heard him, for already his hand had momentarily cupped one breast before it slid down between her legs once more. She was aware, yet unaware, of things besides the fire that was raging in her loins—his other arm sliding beneath her hips, his own rapid breathing as he felt her melt against him, giving herself up to him, and the warm pulsating length of him riding gently between her thighs. He did not enter her at once but again with his hand explored and deliberately gave her her first taste of sexual completeness. She knew that she cried out, as with his hand between her legs, he took her to the peak, but her emotions were spinning beyond her control and nothing mattered at that instant but that the feeling go on. It did. She had barely drifted back to sanity when he, still lying on his side, thrust himself gently within her, his body driving deep into the welcoming softness, his hands holding her tight against him. Like a dying fire leaping to renewed life, she felt her entire body respond to his and hungrily, unaware that she did so, she curved her body to make his possession easier, arching herself back against him. When the end came, this time it was as if every nerve in her body exploded with pleasure.

Panting, still in a daze, her eyes wide with the shock of it, she lay there hardly conscious of him beside her and slowly, very slowly, awareness came creeping back. She knew now irrevocably why those other women so shamelessly pursued him, and she would have given everything not to.

Reluctantly she rolled over to face him. He was lying on his back, one arm behind his head, watching her. For a long minute she stared at him and wondered how she could hate him and yet have her entire body turn to a quivering mass of yearning at the thought of his kisses. In a small, defiant voice she said, "I still hate you!"

Unbelievably he smiled, not the reckless, half-mocking expression she knew so well, but a rueful, almost tender smile. Softly he replied, "Do you know that's exactly what I thought you would say? You might hate me, Nick, but your body doesn't."

He turned onto his side, so that their faces were only inches apart. Gently his hand traveled down the center of her body and stopped when it encountered the dark triangle between her legs. She stiffened desperately, ignoring the sudden, unexpected leap of longing within her stomach.

"See," he laughed low, uncannily aware of her response. "I could make you want me again, despite what you say you feel for me." Roughly his mouth covered hers, giving her no chance to reply. It was like no other kiss he had ever given her. It was soft, yet compelling, warm and deep. Lifting his head, he looked down at her and whispered, his voice already thickening with passion, "Shall I, Nick? Shall I show you?"

Dumbly she shook her head, her eyes fixed painfully on his. There was no need, she thought unhappily, to prove what they both knew so well.

At her negative shake Saber sighed, moving away from her with reluctance, but he made no effort to change her mind. Instead, startling her just a little, he gathered her unresisting body next to his, brushed a faint kiss across her forehead, and murmured, "Go to sleep, Nick. We have a long day tomorrow."

Surprisingly, her body curled confidingly against his, and she did just that. Not so Saber—for quite some time after Nicole's even breathing revealed that she slept, he lay there thinking about the future.

He and Lafitte had concluded the sale of *La Belle Garce* this evening, and when morning came he and Nick would be on their way home with a hefty amount of gold. The disposal of the troublesome Allen Ballard had also been taken care of tonight—he would spend the next few months as an unwilling guest in Lafitte's calaboose. Saber had not yet decided upon Ballard's ultimate fate, but in the meantime he was safely under lock and key.

With *La Belle Garce* and Ballard removed, there was just one unsolved dilemma, and that dilemma lay warm and trusting by his side—Nick! Soon she would be privy to his secret, and he wondered what she would make of the fact that the Captain and Christopher Saxon were one and the same person!

Christopher Saxon. He was oddly satisfied to think that in less than twenty-four hours he would resume his own name once again; the dual personality of the bearded privateer Saber and the clean-shaven plantation owner would no longer exist.

The deception had begun long ago when he and Higgins had jumped ship. To escape detection by the British authorities searching for deserters he had called himself Saber Lacey. But when he had joined up with Lafitte, it had been Lafitte who had suggested there might be a great advantage in a dual identity. Thinking of his grandfather in England, Christopher had agreed. It was thus that Captain Saber had sailed on *La Belle Garce* and Christopher Saxon had won a fortune and Thibodaux House in the gaming rooms of New Orleans.

Saber had never appeared in New Orleans, though Saxon did periodically. Saxon lived several months of every year at Thibodaux House. True, Saxon disappeared for months on end, but who cared? And who would notice that during Saxon's absence, Captain Saber appeared at Grand Terre and *La Belle Garce* wreaked havoc on the seas? No one except Nick!

Coldly he told himself, it made no difference. And yet . . . Nicole could easily destroy his prestige with the more respectable members of New Orleans society. Did it matter?

Privateering was not a dishonorable profession, but certain eyebrows would be raised, whispers would follow him, and he would no longer be welcome in some homes. But it was a risk he would have to take—besides what did he care for "society"? Of course, he could leave Nick with Lafitte . . . but he disliked that idea excessively.

Memory is an elusive thing; as he lay there other memories of Nick came back—the sight of the small figure, nimble-quick, climbing into the riggings; the blazing excitement in the topaz eyes at the sign of a fight; the way her lip curled with determination as she worked at the table in his quarters. There were a thousand pictures of her as Nick that flashed across his brain, and he wondered how he could have been so blind not to have fathomed her disguise long ago.

Perhaps unknowingly he had. He had treated her with a teasing quality that no one else saw, he had tolerated her insolence to an astonishing degree, and somehow, whether deliberately or not, he had seen that she was safe during battle. He admitted with reluctance that there had always existed a careless though inconsistent affection for Nick. Definitely he had given no thought to Nick during those times he disappeared and became Christopher Saxon. He wondered how she had managed those times while he was away. Distastefully he remembered Ballard. Of course. She had probably lived on *La Belle Garce* while the ship was at Grand Terre, and as most of the crew kept to themselves, they would have paid her little attention. But she had run an appalling risk.

Unable to sleep because of his thoughts, he slipped Nick out of his arms and left the bed. Crossing to a table, he found a tray of liquors. Pouring himself a snifter of cognac, he wandered impatiently around the dark room, his thoughts drifting inexplicably in a direction he didn't like. If he was plagued by the memory of Nick as his cabin boy, that memory awoke another, one that, like a sleeping beast, he always kept in the deepest recesses of his mind. When he thought of Nick, it was inevitable that he would recall her mother and events best forgotten. But tonight those memories would not be denied—and with despair he remembered Nick's lovely mother, Annabelle, and his uncle!

Thinking of how they had so cleverly used him made him almost ill with fury. For how long, he wondered, had Annabelle's husband been suspicious that there was another man? It couldn't have been for too long or they could never had made him the goat. Looking back he could see it all so clearly—the affair between his Uncle Robert and the neighbor's sultry wife, both enmeshed in marriages they could not or would not end. Was it fear of exposure that had prompted them to sacrifice him? Or had his uncle had a more evil design? So easily, he realized now, he could have died in the Navy, leaving his uncle heir to his grandfather's and the Saxon estates.

A controlled fury seemed to burn within him as he brooded over those long-ago days. God! How he had worshipped her, the scintillating Annabelle, her hair like flame and a body that consumed a man like fire. Oh, how slyly she had charmed him, and he, like a fool, had lavished all his young love on her. He had been unable to conceal his adoration and knew the adults were amused by his calf love. But little did they know that she met him secretly at the pavilion, introducing him to mysteries of physical desire. That Robert had known of the meetings he was sure. But had Robert been aware that those secret meetings had been torrid, had he known how Annabelle had taken his virginity and initiated him thoroughly in the arts of love? Somehow he doubted his uncle had known *that!* Annabelle had been like a narcotic in his blood, Christopher recalled sickly, as she teased and played with him, mocking his avowals of love and teaching him deception. But for his goddess he could endure anything, even the way she treated him with amusement in front of others, because he knew that when night fell he would lose himself within her welcoming flesh. He snorted with contempt at his own fatuousness. He must have been out of his mind to believe that a woman, ten

144

years older and at the height of her beauty, would have fallen in love with a gangling, uncertain boy of fifteen.

She hadn't. Of course he knew that now, had known it since that awful, black moment when his grandfather, his face tight with rage, had hurled those condemning words at him while she, deceitful bitch, sobbed piteously into her handkerchief and cried that he had raped her and then held that over her head to compel her to give into his lustful demands. Even now he could recall the dull rage that had ripped through his body, his despair at this brutal end to his dreams. Annabelle's husband had stood stiffly at her side, his dark eyes plainly showing his galling frustration that Christopher was only a youth and unable to meet him on the dueling ground. And pride had forbidden Christopher to answer any of the accusations. His face had frozen, and something deep within him had died that day. On the verge of violence, he had flung himself from the room, only to fall into the tender claws of Robert. Unpleasantly he thought of how easily he had been manipulated. Still unaware of the relationship between Annabelle and Robert, he had been like wax in his uncle's hands as Robert sympathized and suggested that they leave the house for a while and retire to an obscure country inn, where they could thrash out this terrible development. Duplicitous Robert had soothed his bruised, confused young spirit as they sat over their beer in the private backroom of the inn, and then that too had been torn from him. With a great rush of rage he visualized that last ugly scene—himself bound and gagged, beaten viciously by his uncle, and Annabelle in Robert's arms. He had stared with fascinated repulsion as they, unaware or uncaring, had coupled like animals on the rough floor, and with distaste he could still see the look in Annabelle's eyes as she straightened her rumpled skirt and asked, "What about him? Now that he's served his purpose, how are you going to get rid of him?"

Robert had laughed, pulling her to him. "Don't worry over him. This time tomorrow he'll be somewhere at sea, an unfortunate victim of one of the press-gangs—only my father and your husband won't know that. They'll assume he's run away rather than face the shame."

She had smiled and her green eyes sparkled with glee. "You're so clever, Robert. Who else would have devised such a skillful plan to answer Adrian's suspicions. He believes fully that Christopher is the man I've been meeting." She giggled, obviously pleased with the situation. But her worries were not completely stilled, and with a

145

shade of anxiety she had inquired, "But what if *he* comes back?"

Robert had shrugged. "That, my love, is extremely doubtful. The rigors of the Navy should take care of him. Besides, we are at war with France. And if he should survive, he'd be unable to harm us. Who would believe him?"

"I suppose you're right." She had left without a glance at him, and within the hour Christopher had been in the brawny hands of a press-gang, after having been ushered into the room by a broadly smiling Robert.

Christopher's body trembled with the force of the emotions that surged through him, and his fist was clenched so tightly that the bones showed white beneath the tanned skin. Goddamn them! he thought with fury. Goddamn them to hell! His hands shaking with the rage of the powerful hate that consumed him, he poured himself another cognac. He swallowed it blindly overcome by fury. With an effort he pulled himself from the past. It was over and done with, he told himself heavily, and brooding on it would only destroy *him*.

Ah, you fool, he thought disgustedly, you can't be hurt, you tore out the ability for anyone to do that to you long ago. Have done with the past. You can do nothing about what happened, and Annabelle is beyond your grasp, dead, drowned in the sea!

But vengeance is a strong emotion, not easily put aside, and deliberately he focused on Nicole. How ironic that Annabelle's daughter should fall into his hands. There was, he admitted, a certain amount of pleasure in tormenting her daughter, in bending Nick to his will and—honesty made him say it—in punishing Nick for her mother's sins!

PART TWO

CHRISTOPHER

"But love is blind, and lovers cannot see
The pretty follies that themselves commit."
—Shakespeare, *The Merchant of Venice*

14

Christopher Saxon, his lean, clean-shaven face wearing an expression of weary disdain, was listening to the idle conversation around him. Why the devil had he let his friend Eustace Croix talk him into attending the Lavilles' *soirée* he would never know. Jesus Christ, but he was bored! He should have expected it. The Lavilles were elderly and so were most of their guests. When Eustace had begged for his company that night, he must have been mad not to have cried off.

Christopher Saxon was not a particularly sociable young man. He was silent and withdrawn, and he held himself aloof from those who would have sought his friendship. *Cold, callous, unfeeling* were epithets frequently hurled at his dark head. He appeared to be all of those things and would merely shrug his elegant shoulders and turn his back on whatever displeased him. This is not to say he was shunned or unpopular. Quite the contrary! Every morning during his sporadic sojourns in the city, his servant presented a small silver tray upon which reposed several invitations to attend this party or that ball, or to bear this or that acquaintance to a cockfight, or to see the latest beauties at the Quadroon Ball. By virtue of his wealth and handsome face he was a definite favorite of ladies with marriageable daughters. Most men thought him pleasant enough, if a bit cool.

But he never lacked for either companionship or amusement, and he had deliberately kept himself from making any close friends. Friends had a way of inquiring after one, of calling upon one when perhaps it was not convenient, and of interesting themselves in one's affairs.

At first he had withheld himself from intimate associations because of necessity, and then because it had become a habit. It suited him that there was no one who knew Christopher Saxon well.

Polite society accepted him as he was. His manners were correct, his family in England well connected, and no one could say much against him. To be certain there were those members of the Creole aristocracy who still remembered the disgraceful circumstances in which he had acquired his fortune—his comfortable mansion in the Vieux Carré, and the plantation, Thibodaux House—but they were few, and even they could not doubt that young Eugene Thibodaux had been a fool to game away his entire fortune.

A sharp inquiry from the formidable matron at his side abruptly brought Saxon back to the present, and with practiced ease he covered up his lapse and joined the conversation. The remainder of the deadly evening crept by, and he could barely restrain his relief when he finally escaped. *Never* would he be gulled into attending another of the Lavilles' interminable dinner parties.

Returning to his own grand stucco and brick home a few blocks from the Lavilles' he discovered he was not yet sleepy. He considered for a moment going to one of the bordellos or coffee houses in search of amusement but found the idea not to his liking. After ordering a decanter of whiskey to be brought to his room, he dismissed the servant for the evening. Stripping off his finery, he shrugged on a heavy robe of black silk. He poured himself a tumbler of whiskey and stepped through French doors onto the balcony that overlooked the courtyard.

He stayed there a long time, staring at nothing, sipping his whiskey. He knew he should have been well-satisfied, yet he was not, and places and amusements that had once absorbed his attention were now less than exciting. He was startled to realize that he was at a standstill, uncertain as to the direction in which he should exert his energies.

Captain Saber was no more! The plantation was organized to the extent that it required only the lightest supervision to run it perfectly. He was not a man to whom stolid respectability appealed—and right now he wasn't so certain that he had been wise in selling *La Belle Garce.*

Perhaps he wasn't cut out for a life of indolence and ease, he thought cynically. These past few weeks had not been as pleasant as he had thought they would be. Some spark of challenge and excitement was lacking. Yet this visit had been no different than any other. True, there was the knowledge that he would not become Captain Saber again, but that could not account for his dissatisfaction. He was just, he admitted ruefully, plain bored. He should have brought Nick along, he decided wryly.

She would have made for a lively time, he thought with a grin. And against his will, he wondered what she was doing tonight. Probably visiting a voodoo queen to obtain a potion to bring about his early demise.

To his intense annoyance he found his thoughts returning to Nick at the most inopportune times. Dancing with one of the reigning belles and gazing into her truly beautiful brown eyes, he discovered that he preferred Nick's. *Hers* were deeper, more lustrous, and certainly more lively. Attending a *soirée* where he was introduced to the charming niece of his host, he decided that while her mouth was delightfully curved, Nick's was softer and infinitely more kissable. Noticing at the opera one night a striking auburn-haired beauty, he thought her shining locks insipid and faded next to the memory of the burnished flame in Nick's dark hair. It was vexing and disturbing to one of his nature to have these unsettling thoughts, and he cursed his foolish preoccupation with this rebellious, topaz-eyed vixen. With a derisive snort he walked back into his room.

And when he awoke the next morning, wondering with disgust at his maudlin mood of the night before, he deliberately shoved all thoughts of the future away from him and threw himself into an orgy of activity. During the week that preceded Christmas he was seen at every party or *soirée* held in the elegant homes of New Orleans. Finding every minute filled with pleasurable commitment, he convinced himself that this was precisely what he wanted. This restless racketing to and fro might have continued indefinitely except for two incidents that occurred the night of the Governor's Christmas Ball. Christopher, along with a few hundred prominent members of Louisiana society, attended the affair, and it was there, about halfway through the evening, that he encountered a surprising specter from his past.

She was a small birdlike woman of about sixty-five with bright blue eyes and fluffy white hair; she was neatly but plainly dressed, clearly a governess. He didn't notice her at first, for who paid any attention to those drab individuals?

He was never sure why he noticed her. It may have been the way she held her head, or the quick movements of her body that struck a cord of memory. From across the crowded ballroom he found himself watching her, a frown of puzzlement creasing his brow.

He was sure that he must know the woman, and finally he inveigled an introduction to Miss Leala Dumas, who appeared to be her charge. He then learned the governess's name—Mrs. Eggleston!

When he heard that name the years vanished, and he was twelve again and wheedling a sugar plum from the colonel's lady. She had changed little in the intervening years, although the soft blue eyes were not as brimful with ready laughter, and her face, though still smooth, had acquired a faintly harassed air.

He was stunned when, having heard his name, she looked into his face and said, "Why, Christopher, how very nice to see you after all this time!"

He gave her a rueful smile and murmured, "And you, madame. But tell me, how is it that you are here?"

She hesitated and he didn't miss the uneasy glance sent her charge, the haughty Miss Dumas, whose expression clearly revealed her displeasure that the elusive Monsieur Saxon was paying more attention to her lowly governess than her own beautiful self. And so he wasn't surprised when Mrs. Eggleston twittered nervously, "Oh, it is much too long a story to bore you with. Did you wish to ask Miss Dumas for the next country dance? I believe one is forming now."

Gracefully Christopher followed her unspoken plea and led the now-beaming Miss Dumas out onto the ballroom floor. But he was not to be sidetracked, and he deftly extracted the information he wanted from his smug dancing partner.

Mrs. Eggleston was reduced to earning a meager living at the beck and call of whomever needed her services. Not content with what he gleaned from his partner, at the end of the dance he returned her to Mrs. Eggleston and waited in the vicinity until Miss Dumas was claimed for a dance by a handsome young Creole gentleman. Under the cover of polite conversation he convinced Mrs. Eggleston to meet him privately in two days. She looked doubtful, but had not been able to resist his blandishments. His aim accomplished, he drifted off in the direction of the card room.

He was frowning as he entered the room. Mrs. Eggleston had always been a favorite of his, and he was revolted at the idea that she should be at the mercy of a creature as demanding and conceited as Miss Dumas appeared to be. Ordinarily he would not have given the matter another thought, but he had liked Mrs. Eggleston! She had been kind to him when he was a youngster, and he was astonished to find that he cherished certain almost-forgotten memories of enjoyable afternoons spent at her home. But then his habitual sardonic self took over and he deliberately dismissed her from his mind. If he wasn't careful he'd find himself actually being concerned about another person. That, he decided, smiling harshly, would *never* do!

Mrs. Eggleston receded from his thoughts, and a second later he had joined a group of friends at one of the many tables scattered about the room. Many of the older men, happy to have escaped their wives' watchful gazes, were now enjoying a quiet rubber or two of whist. Most of the younger men were on the ballroom floor, but Christopher had little trouble finding three acquaintances who needed a fourth for a game in a secluded corner. It was only after he had played a number of hands that he became aware of a conversation taking place practically at his elbow.

Mention of Lafitte's name caught his attention, and idly his gaze shifted from the indifferent cards in his hand to the group of men at his left. Three of them he recognized vaguely, but he was much more familiar with the other two—Daniel Patterson and Jason Savage.

Patterson was in charge of the naval forces stationed in New Orleans, and it had been to him that he had anonymously sent the code books. Naturally Christopher had little to do with him, but because he was the master commandant, Christopher had considered it prudent to make his acquaintance. It never hurt to cultivate those who could harm one—and Patterson was an outspoken opponent of Jean Lafitte.

His knowledge of Jason Savage was not based upon any personal relationship. What he knew had been gleaned from gossip and drawing-room conversations, and he was well aware that Savage was not one to cross or ignore. He appeared to be deep in Governor Claiborne's confidence and was highly thought of by both the American faction and the Creoles. Christopher had been introduced to Savage's beautiful wife, Catherine, at a ball some years ago and agreed with those who said she was one of the loveliest women to grace New Orleans in years. But his beautiful wife aside, Christopher's interest in Jason Savage had been prompted by the knowledge that Savage was a man around whom things revolved. Though he seemed aloof and detached from circumstances, he was rumored to have his hand firmly on the life-beat of the entire state of Louisiana. And so Christopher took more than just polite interest in Savage's dealings. But it was Patterson's words that were arousing his interest at the moment.

"I tell you, I just don't understand it! Neither how they got into my office, nor why one of Lafitte's cutthroats would do such a thing."

In his drawling manner Jason murmured, "Perhaps he thought to gain something by it—a reward, or maybe even a pardon. Who knows?" His voice implied, "Who cares?"

Patterson became ruffled at the cool words and burst out, "No, damnit, Jason, it wasn't that! The books were spirited into my office. There was nothing with them— no letter, no identification, nothing! Just the books them- selves. I've questioned my men closely and no one knows how they got there. If the person who left them were af- ter money, surely there would have been some message with the damned books."

"Are you certain that they're genuine? It would be clever of the British to plant useless ones on you. They would, I'm certain, see to it that you received only those dispatches they wished you to know about."

One of the other men offered a ribald suggestion that appeared to annoy Patterson, and Christopher, eaves- dropping shamelessly, smiled to himself. With a good de- gree of hauteur, Patterson snapped, "This is no funning matter—and yes, the books are genuine, we are not nov- ices at our jobs!" The conversation shifted, and just about the time Christopher had become bored and was about to depart, Patterson again said something that captured his wandering interest.

". . . attack on New Orleans."

"Oh, come now, Daniel! The British aren't about to deploy more troops and naval ships for an assault on us. They're much too busy along the Canadian border and in the Great Lakes region to bother New Orleans," re- torted one businessman.

Patterson said nothing, as if realizing he had been a little indiscreet, and shrugged his shoulders. It was Jason, though, who continued the subject. Lazily he drawled, "I wouldn't say that, John. Attacking and conquering New Orleans would be a very strategic move on England's part. She needs a victory to bolster her continuance of the war, and possession of the city would give her a de- cided advantage at the peace talks in St. Petersburg. While I realize the British have refused the Czar's offer to mediate, they have expressed a desire for direct nego- tiations. And the reason they may not have pushed rather

154

strongly on direct negotiations could be that they wanted a decisive victory to strengthen their power when they actually settle down to talking. Right now I think it is simply as I said—they want a firm hand to sit at the peace table with. Don't dismiss an attack on New Orleans so easily." Jason's green eyes left his discomfitted companion's and swung to Patterson. "Is an attack on the city definitely planned? Have you proof—or are you just speculating?"

Uneasily, Patterson muttered, "There isn't any positive knowledge, you should know that. There's just been hints, and one of the dispatches captured recently mentioned a southern campaign."

"Daniel, do you mean to tell me that the governor is aware of this, and is doing nothing to verify it?" cried one of the men.

Patterson squirmed uncomfortably, wishing that he had never introduced the subject. He said a few words that Christopher couldn't hear, but the words seemed to put the other three men to rest, although one of them turned eagerly to Jason and said, "Your uncle is high in English government circles. Do you think that you could learn anything from him?"

Jason smiled sardonically, and in that moment his eyes met Christopher's across the space between them. Their gazes held, and Christopher had the curious conviction that Jason knew very well that his was more than just an idle interest. For perhaps a full sixty seconds green eyes locked with gold, and then as if having taken his measure, Jason's glance moved slowly from Christopher. With a hint of boredom in his voice Jason answered. "Roxbury is old and all his loyalty lies with England. If I were to be mad enough to travel to Britain in search of more definite proof, my uncle, a very astute man, would know the instant that I set foot on English soil why I was there. Not only would I be unable to learn anything of value, but *mon oncle* would see to it that my visit was exceedingly short and very unpleasant! Find another fool to run after your fairy thoughts!" And suddenly Jason's eyes flashed almost in challenge to Christopher's. Again Christopher was subjected to that emerald gaze, the bright eyes narrowed in speculation. With great effort Christopher ignored the compelling stare and gave no hint that he was aware of Jason's look. But as he left the card room a short while later, he was sure that those green eyes followed him and that a few blunt and searching questions would be asked about him in the very near future.

Actually, there was very little Jason Savage didn't already know about Saxon. For several long seconds following Christopher's departure, Jason stared thoughtfully after him, until a question repeated for the second time by Patterson recalled his wandering thoughts. With the appearance of being completely absorbed, he rejoined the conversation.

Presently Jason excused himself and strolled outside. To anyone watching it would appear he had escaped the noisy card room for a quiet breath of fresh air. Once outside and out of sight of any curious onlookers, his aimless pace quickened as he went past the governor's spectacular garden, now gloomy and damp from the persistent rain that had fallen for some days, and came to a lacy iron-work gate. Opening it he stepped gingerly across the quagmire that constituted a New Orleans street in winter and slipped quietly into a small carriage house.

"Jake?" he called softly.

"Over here," came a voice gruffly from a pile of straw in one corner.

A grin replacing the faint look of tenseness on his dark face, Jason relaxed slightly as Jake, a small untidily dressed man with sandy ill-cut hair and a scraggly beard, rose from the straw. Jake could have been any age between thirty and fifty. A large plug of tobacco, and a stream of brown liquid, spat carelessly over his shoulder a moment later, confirmed the impression of a rough-mannered fellow.

Jason's tall figure, elegant in evening dress of black velvet jacket and snowy white waistcoat, couldn't have been more in contrast with the other man's appearance.

"You see him?" Jake asked bluntly.

Jason nodded. "Just now. He is rather hard to overlook. Jake, you're certain we can trust him? I'd hate like hell for the British to know how worried Claiborne is about an attack on the city—or how undermanned New Orleans is."

"For Chrissake, Jason! Ain't I practically lived with the ruddy rakehell for the past four months?" Pausing only to shoot another stream of tobacco juice off to one side, Jake continued, "Saxon might be a bloody pirate, calling hisself Captain Saber, but he don't hold no love for the British. I was there when he took those code books. If'n he wasn't American to the bottom of his black heart, he'd never have sent Higgins with the books to Patterson. Besides, if you're spying, you don't attack your own kind. He sure don't hold no love for the British!"

His green eyes narrowed in concentration, Jason finally commented, "Very well, I'll have to take your word for it. And as you've never failed me in the past five years, I suspect you know what you're talking about."

"Damn right! I ain't called Jake the cat for nothing!"

Jason smiled at the vehement words, and dipping into his waistcoat, he placed several gold coins in the slightly dirty hand eagerly extended. "I think this will keep you a while, and I would suggest that you leave tonight for Terre du Coeur . . . just in case anyone has tumbled to you. I want you out of harm's way."

"I ain't frightened!" Jake said belligerently.

His smile fading just a little, Jason acknowledged, "I realize that! But, my *petit* friend, I didn't rescue you from having your head bashed in by that enraged flatboatman at 'Natchez under the hill' only to have you lose it now. Go to Terre du Coeur!"

Gruffly, Jake mumbled, "If'n I'd a known you was such a bloody, bossy bastard, I would a let my head be bashed in!"

"I'm sure you're stubborn enough to have done so!" Jason retorted crisply as he started for the doorway. "Do as you wish," he threw back over his shoulder.

"I'm leaving. I'm leaving," came the resigned grumble.

Smiling to himself, Jason quickly made his way back to the Governor's Ball. He saw Christopher Saxon once more before the evening ended and observed the young man's ease and grace as he moved throughout the ballroom. Yes, he thought, Christopher Saxon would fit the role planned for him very nicely.

15

Following dinner the next evening Christopher had adjourned to his study and was relaxing before the fire when his butler came into the room.

"Sir, a Mister Jason Savage is here to see you."

A moment later, surprised and more than a little intrigued, Christopher rose as Jason Savage entered the room.

"How fortunate that you are in this evening!" Jason said as he shook Christopher's hand. "I meant to call earlier in the day but circumstances conspired against it."

Christopher smiled politely, extremely watchful. "That happens to one occasionally. May I offer you something to drink? Sherry, port, or perhaps some brandy?"

"Brandy will be fine."

The refreshments taken care of, the two men settled in chairs before the fire.

Savage glanced around the elegant room with its green damask curtains, closed just now against the winter chill, the fine Brussels carpet, the impressive mahogany bookcases, and he commented, "I see you've changed little in this room since it was owned by the Thibodaux family."

Wary now, Christopher raised an eyebrow and took a sip of brandy. "Is that why you've come to call," he said dryly. "To see what renovations I have made?"

Jason smiled. "No, and I'm certain you realize it."

"Then why are you here? I do not mean to sound inhospitable, but I do not believe that you are here for polite conversation. Is there something I can do for you?"

His directness left Jason in a quandary. How was he going to approach the subject of his visit? Certainly he had hoped for more time, and he hadn't been sure he would discuss it at his first meeting with Saxon. Unfortunately Saxon didn't appear to be in the mood for exchanging pleasantries, nor for being fobbed off with polite nonsense. And as Jason preferred a direct manner himself, he said bluntly, "I'd like you to go to England for me!"

Christopher looked at him with astonishment. "I beg your pardon! Have you gone insane? We're at war with England!"

"Very true, but it is possible for someone such as yourself to go there."

"And why the devil should I?"

Jason gave Christopher a considering stare. Then softly he said, "Because I want to know exactly how serious the British are about attacking New Orleans!"

Christopher, his gold eyes suddenly thoughtful, sank slowly back against his chair, his mind flying in a dozen directions. Whatever he had expected from Savage's visit, it certainly hadn't been this!

"Why me?" he asked after several seconds.

Jason appeared to study the liquor in his glass. "Why not you?"

Impatiently Christopher stood up, and with his back to the fire he faced Jason. "One doesn't go up to a complete stranger with the kind of proposition you've just laid before me! I'm not a fool! I would like to know what game you're playing, Savage."

The emerald eyes bright between the thick black lashes, Jason regarded the hostile man before him. Almost indifferently he admitted, "I'm playing no game. It has been in my mind for some months to send someone to England—the thought was there before any hint of a British attack on New Orleans."

Still puzzled, Christopher demanded again, "Why me for such a task? I'm no diplomat, nor, might I add, have I ever displayed any tendency toward politics—and we're strangers. Good God!" he exploded at last. "I could very well be a spy for the British!"

"Are you?" Jason asked mildly.

Throwing him a look of dislike, Christopher snapped, "Of course not! But you don't know it, you only have my word that I'm not."

Jason smiled thinly. "But I do know, my friend. As I said a moment ago, I'm playing no game. And since the idea of sending someone to England occurred to me several months ago, I have been searching for a man I thought could handle the task." Smoothly he went on, "I didn't consider you at first—I'll admit it. But you aroused my curiosity, and for some months now I have had you closely watched." Jason stopped, then said deliberately, *"Captain Saber!"*

Christopher stiffened but gave no other sign that Savage's words affected him. Exposure was a risk he had always run, but it was not a fatal risk. He would have preferred to keep his two lives separate, but there was no reason to panic because his secret had been discovered. It depended on what Savage intended to do with the knowledge. And somehow Christopher didn't think he meant to turn him over to the authorities. Shrugging his shoulders, he murmured, "So, I admit to you, I am Captain Saber—but I am no infamous pirate! Less honorable men than myself have taken to the high seas and called themselves privateers. What difference does it make?"

Jason smiled with deep appreciation for Saxon's blatant arrogance. "*Mon ami,* you misunderstand me—I like a man of action. Your being Captain Saber interests me hardly at all. If I had discovered you were preying on American ships and were in fact a spy, as I first suspected, then this visit would never have occurred. May I be blunt?"

A snort from Christopher preceded his exasperated, "Haven't you been?"

"Perhaps. You asked why I have approached you, and I will be honest. There is no one else. I have your measure, thanks to a very adept spy of my own. I know you have played at privateering, but that does not make me think less of you. I know also that you have no love of the British—despite the fact that you are British yourself."

"Savage, I think we had better get one thing straight— I am *not* British and haven't been since I was press-ganged into the British Navy almost fifteen years ago. I am American by choice." Christopher spat the last words, almost ashamed of his ferocious pride.

"Very well, then. We agree. If you are as American as you say, I believe you would want to do something for her." Jason paused, but seeing he had Saxon's undivided attention, he continued briskly, "This war of Mr. Madison's is not going as was fondly foreseen, as you well know. If we are not careful, we shall end up being humiliatingly and very soundly beaten. The great conquest of Canada that started this damned business is a disaster. The United States will be lucky if she can hold her own borders, much less gain an inch of Canadian land. How Madison could have been swayed by such war hawks as Henry Clay and John Calhoun, I cannot conceive! And anyone who thinks this damned war is being fought over

160

the impressment of our seamen into the British Navy needs his head examined! It makes for a nice emotional issue, but it isn't accomplishing a damned thing—it was an excuse to hide behind for the invasion of Canada. I wish to God—" Jason stopped in midsentence, aware that he had become unnecessarily impassioned. "Forgive me! I did not mean to treat you to my own personal views on this war. But what I have said is true and brings me to my point—this damnable action must be stopped as soon as possible! And I do not want to see New Orleans dragged into it."

Christopher, frowning in concentration and with one arm resting casually on the mantel, asked, "Do you really believe the British will attack us? Granted they have a fairly effective fleet harassing us in the Gulf, but the bulk of their troops, ships, and men are in the north."

"True. But please remember, Napoleon suffered a shattering defeat at Leipzig in Germany in October and is retreating now from Moscow and suffering even further losses. From what reports I have received, he is in a very unenviable position. The British field marshall, Wellington, crossed the Pyrenees into France months ago, and though the fighting is heavy, I have no doubt Wellington will carry the day. Once all of Napoleon's forces have had their teeth pulled, nothing will stop the British from turning on us! The capture of New Orleans would strengthen their hand, and possibly strike a fatal blow to our country."

Jason ran one hand through his heavy black hair. "All my reports indicate that the British are preparing for a large attack, what they hope will be a surprise attack, somewhere in the southern United States. New Orleans has not been positively identified as that site, but logic tells me that our Creole Queen is indeed the city that the English hope to take."

Somewhat thoughtfully, Christopher picked up his brandy glass, having already decided he would go to England. Jason's words and ideas about the present war coincided with his own, and he was convinced of the gravity of the situation. The Americans were being forced out of Fort George at the mouth of the Niagara; the British had burned the town of Newark and were continuing their advance on Fort Niagara, while their Indian allies were intent on plundering the town of Lewiston, New York. The news was all bad, despite Lieutenant—now Captain—Perry's victory in gaining control of Lake Erie. Granted Tecumseh had been killed in September, and that had ended the Indians' hopes of a strong confederacy, and General Andrew Jackson had taken command in the Creek War, but the picture was not a happy one. There were too many fronts in this war. It was scattered from Canada to Florida, with skirmishes fought in a dozen places and no clear-cut victories or losses. The War of 1812 was turning into a seemingly purposeless and unrewarding fiasco.

The news about a possible attack on New Orleans, though, jerked Christopher out of his almost-blind acceptance of the war. And he found that he very much wished to do everything in his power to prevent such a happening. "If you want me to go to England, I will," he said abruptly. "But I must admit I do not see how I can be of any great help to you. I was a boy when last there, and I have few if any sources that would be of use."

"I do not expect a miracle, my friend. I know you may discover nothing. I'm aware of the situation, and I will not be able to open many doors for you—for obvious reasons."

Grimly Christopher inquired, "Your uncle?"

Jason nodded and asked dryly, "You know my background? Or did you, as I suspected, overhear the conversation last night at the Governor's Ball?"

A grin passed over Christopher's face. "Certainly! You want a man with ears and wits about him, do you not?"

"You see," Jason said with some amusement, "you are the man I need! But remember, you will be entirely on your own. There are certain people I can recommend that you see—but only between ourselves. My letters of introduction would do you more harm than good. If it were known we are acquainted, your every move would be suspect. As it is, you will have a very difficult time of it!"

Christopher shrugged. "I'll do what I can. But you must be more precise. What good will it do for me to discover that an attack is imminent without proof? And how much proof do you need?"

His fingers making a steeple, Jason stared at him for some seconds. He replied very slowly, "Your word alone will suffice."

At Christopher's start of disbelief, Jason said, "All I need is something more tangible than rumors to lay before the military. I will vouch for you, and without conceit I can assure you that they will take my word." With a grimace Jason added, "And if a man of my choosing comes direct from England with word of an attack on the city, and they do not send us troops and supplies, I shall be at my wits' end." His voice hardening, he continued, "Governor Claiborne writes constantly requesting reinforcements but is ignored. That situation, in view of a probable attack, cannot be permitted to continue—hence, my proposition."

"Aren't you taking a risky chance? How can you be certain I won't betray you?" Christopher asked curiously.

"You could," Jason admitted freely. "I may be taking a foolish chance. But I know your feeling for the British. I know, too, that you own lands here in Louisiana, lands I doubt you would like to see devastated by war. You made a place for yourself here in New Orleans, even before the war started."

Christopher still looked skeptical. And then Jason smiled that very charming smile of his and said gently, "And there are times when I must trust my own instincts."

"How much time do I have before I must depart?"

"Naturally I would prefer you to be on the next ship we can get out of port. But you must have a legitimate reason for returning to your homeland, or have you overlooked that fact?"

Christopher pulled a face. "The thought had occurred to me, and I do have an idea that might work. The problem is time. I'll need at least a month or two."

Frowning, his black brows meeting over the wide forehead, Jason asked heavily, "You realize that time is an important factor?"

"I'm aware of that! But by the same token, nothing is going to be moving very fast this time of year, and for now we know where the enemy is. You yourself admit that we don't know for certain that New Orleans is their target. With that in mind, I would hazard a guess that, whatever is planned, nothing definite will be set in motion before next fall, and that assumes Napoleon *is* beaten on all fronts in Europe. Until he is contained or completely annihilated, the British and their allies have their hands more than full." Christopher paused, trying to gauge the effect his words were having on Jason.

Jason was watching him intently, and Christopher had the curious conviction that despite Jason's earlier words, he was on trial. Picking his way with care, he continued, "If you agree with my assessment of the situation, I think you'll concede that as long as I arrive in England by the middle of April, I should have enough time to discover what is planned and to return ahead of the enemy. I'll admit, I could be cutting it fine, but without a *very* legitimate reason for returning to England, I am useless."

"Just what is this plan that takes two months to perfect?" Jason asked dryly.

Christopher hesitated. It was a flimsy idea, but at the moment it was all he could think of, and it depended upon so many different things. Not the least, Mrs. Eggleston and Nick. And he didn't like explaining himself to someone else. He was too used to doing what he damned well pleased!

Jason could guess at some of Christopher's dilemma. After all, Christopher knew very little of him. And from what Jason knew of Saxon, Saxon was not a man used to answering to another.

Having come to a decision, Christopher said in a perfectly expressionless tone, "Last night I met an old friend of mine, a Mrs. Eggleston."

"The governess to the Dumas girl?"

Startled, Christopher stared at him—was there anything that Savage didn't know? And nodding his head he admitted, "The same. Only when I knew her, she was living not far from my grandfather's estate and was the wife of a retired colonel."

"So?"

Quickly, keeping the facts to a bare minimum, Christopher explained about Nicole Ashford—leaving out their personal relationship. But Jason caught the slight change of inflection in Christopher's deep voice when the girl's name was mentioned and drew his own conclusions—young Saxon wasn't entirely indifferent to the chit. But his words gave away little as he asked thoughtfully, "You think you can eradicate the last five years in a few months and have her presentable by March?"

Christopher shrugged. "It shouldn't be impossible. After all, her first thirteen years were like those of any other young lady, and I think Mrs. Eggleston will be up to smoothing off the rough edges."

"Well, we can only hope. I give you credit for quick thinking."

Christopher bowed; his features lightening and a smile hovering about his lips, he murmured, "Thank you. I trust you will find the remainder of my activities as satisfactory."

An eyebrow rose in mockery. "Oh, I'm certain you'll get the task done. I am not often wrong in my dealings with my fellowmen, and I definitely don't intend to be this time."

Christopher merely nodded his head. Jason rose from his chair and said with surprise, "We seem to have covered the most important items in a remarkably short time. For the present, you will set about with your own plans, but keep me informed of any problems or setbacks. I will keep you abreast of any new developments that may necessitate our moving faster."

"Agreed. I'll meet with Mrs. Eggleston as I planned on Wednesday, and depending on the outcome of that meeting, I shall be returning almost immediately to Thibodaux House."

After Jason had departed, Christopher roamed the library like a caged jungle beast. At one point he decided he must be the biggest fool alive even to consider becoming involved in such a scheme, but he knew it would put to rest the dissastisfaction that had been plaguing him, while allowing him to do something for this country that he had adopted—or that had adopted him, he thought wryly.

Though he did not consider himself a patriot, New Orleans was *his* city. And he would hate for his lands to be destroyed by war. The thought of the British boot on Louisiana soil was intolerable, and he would be damned if he would meekly stand by and let it happen. He silently congratulated himself on having been able to concoct the plan to return the heiress Nicole Ashford to her rightful place.

Jason Savage, also pacing his own elegant library, was plagued by uncertainty. Saxon's plan to return Nicole was admirable, but Jason, older and less impetuous than Christopher, saw several pitfalls. After staring at the fire for some time, he seated himself behind his desk and began to write to the secretary of state, James Monroe. It was a brief letter, and after rereading it, he sealed it. Christopher, he decided, need not be apprised of his action. If it came to nothing, it came to nothing; but if Monroe fell in with his suggestion, he would have something of value to offer the young man.

Christopher, meanwhile, continued to view the plan from all angles. He distrusted it as much, if not more, than did Jason, but for the moment it was all he had.

Nick would give him no trouble. Mrs. Eggleston should be willing to fall in with his idea, *if* she accepted the story he gave her. Naturally he could say nothing of his real reasons for wishing to return to England, nor could he tell her the truth about his relationship with Nicole.

Seeing Mrs. Eggleston last night had been a shock. He still wasn't certain whether it had been unpleasant or pleasurable.

As a youth, left often to his own devices by parents more concerned and involved with the antics of the *ton* than their own offspring, it had been to Mrs. Eggleston that he had turned, and she had provided the only deep human affection he had ever known, except for his irascible grandfather. He had been barely in his teens when his parents were killed in their coach as it hurtled over a cliff. That tragedy had made him cling even more to the warmth and sanity that she represented. Perhaps, he mused, if she hadn't been away with the colonel that disastrous summer, he never would have fallen under Annabelle's dark spell and his uncle would never have been able to trap him so neatly.

It was unfortunate that he was going to trick Mrs. Eggleston, but he consoled himself with the knowledge that she would be much better off under his care than in her present situation.

He was still turning over half-formed plans on Wednesday when he set out for his meeting with Mrs. Eggleston. They met in front of a well-known dressmaker's shop, and after a little conversation, Christopher persuaded her to enter his carriage.

He had come to the conclusion that he would wait to spring Nick's presence on her. Once Mrs. Eggleston was under his protection, he could, he hoped, present a plausible story of why Nick was currently at his plantation, unchaperoned, and why she had been with him for the past five years.

Although he would admit to Mrs. Eggleston that he had done his share of privateering with Nick in tow, there was no need for her to know of his connection with Lafitte, or that he had sailed under the name of Captain Saber. No, Christopher decided thoughtfully, there was no reason for him to divulge everything.

He didn't doubt his ability to carry it off; the real problem would be later, in convincing Mrs. Eggleston to agree to lie about her own activities these past five years and to say that she and Nicole had been together. His first step must be to prize Mrs. Eggleston out from under the thumb of Miss Leala Dumas. He had decided that he would offer her the protection of his home, her position being much that of a favorite aunt. In this he was sincere, and even if Jason Savage had not called, Christopher would not have allowed her present situation to continue.

Now he would be able to use her dependent state, although, to give him credit, this was not what he had originally planned for her. Mrs. Eggleston would not be harmed in any way by the deception, and when it was complete, he would still see to her welfare. But first he must convince her that she was welcome under his roof.

He presented the idea to her in the politest and most graceful way possible, and was so certain of success that he had planned to have her settled in his home on Dauphine Street that very evening. But he had not reckoned with Mrs. Eggleston's gentle determination to make her own way.

Her eyes filled with tears at his kind words, and a tremulous smile quivered on her lips. "So kind," she whispered, but gathering her failing emotions she said sadly, "I cannot, Christopher. It would not be convenable. Someday you may marry and come to regret this fine and noble gesture you make now. I have managed so far, and while some of my charges have been——" She hesitated before saying, "high-spirited, I contrive to make myself amenable to whatever fate sends me. I cannot allow you to make such a sacrifice and saddle yourself with the care of one old woman. I have a little aside, and when the time comes that I can no longer find employment, I shall be able to keep myself, if not with the elegancies of life, at least with the necessities."

"And in the meantime," he bit out explosively, "you are at the beck and call of a supercilious young wench who is not worthy of sweeping the floor in front of you. By God, madame, I had thought better of you! Why must you act the drudge when I am offering you most sincerely a way of escape?"

His plan aside, he was genuinely furious that she would not accept his help.

"Such temper, Christopher!" she reproved gently. "I had hoped that you would outgrow it."

Nearly strangling on the hot words he longed to hurl at her small white head, Christopher snapped his mouth shut. Controlling his temper with an effort, he said in carefully enunciated tones, "Madame, you are behaving in a most unreasonable manner! You are saying you would *rather* continue at the mercy of spoiled beauties and be tossed from pillar to post as they marry and you are again looking for employment. Is this your desire?"

With a tremor of unease, she said, "Well, not precisely. I would love to have the charge of some dear little children and be able to stay in one family for the rest of my life." She sighed. "But everyone wants *young* nannies—they say I am too old and perhaps they are right. You see, there is nothing left for me but to act as companion or governess. Miss Dumas is not dreadful, Christopher. I had been companion to an elderly French *émigré* lady in Canada, and she *was* a trifle wearing on my nerves." Encouragingly she added, "Miss Dumas is an angel beside Madame Bovair," innocently giving Christopher a very clear picture of what must have been a hellish existence. Unaccountably moved, he concentrated on his horses, not trusting himself to speak. Mrs. Eggleston timidly laid a blue-veined hand on his arm and asked in a small voice, "You are not angry with me?"

He was. *Very* angry with her. But he didn't allow himself to say so. Coldly he replied, "Of course not. I enjoy having my generosity thrown back in my face." He meant it. Inexplicably he wanted to care for her, he who cared for no one, or so he had convinced himself long ago, and she would not let him.

Stricken at his words, she glanced away. They continued thus for several seconds; then unable to stand the sight of her obvious distress, he asked in a milder tone of voice, "What is it you actually object to? Living in the same house with a bachelor? If that is so," he said impetuously, "I will give you your own house. But let me assure you that we would not be in the way of each other. I confess that it would be pleasant to share my meals with another and to know that there would be someone waiting for me when I returned."

She smiled slightly and remarked, "If that is what you want, why not marry? Surely a wife is the one you would wish to have waiting for you—not an old woman." Then she gave a little sigh and said, "It is too bad that you are not married and have not set up your nursery—*you* wouldn't consider me too old to be a nanny."

"Are you saying you would *work* for me?" he demanded incredulously.

"Well, of course I would!"

Raising his eyes heavenward, he cursed a pride that was as stubborn as it was gentle and said out loud, "God, give me strength! Very well, madame, you will not live in my home without earning your keep. Give me a week, two at the most, in which to make certain arrangements, and then I shall be back to present you with another proposal that I hope you will find more to your liking."

A short while later he deposited Mrs. Eggleston a scant block from where they had first met, and watching her birdlike little figure disappear down the wooden sidewalk, he was filled with amused frustration—women!

16

The library at Thibodaux House was a long and narrow room. It ran the full length of the house, with tall windows at opposite ends that nearly covered the width of the room. On one long wall was a magnificent moss-green marble fireplace and a carved door that led to the main hallway of the house. Above the mantel rested a massive gilt-edged mirror, and before the fire burning on the grate were two dainty, but extremely comfortable, scarlet-covered chairs with a large satinwood table between them. At one end of the room stood a graceful dark Spanish desk, a black leather chair behind it, and at the opposite end, beneath one of the windows, was a long, narrow spindle-legged table in a dark wood. The floor was brightened by the jewel tones of the fine Oriental rug. Opposite the fireplace were two sets of French doors that led outside to the veranda. All in all it was a beguiling and elegant room, and Nicole spent a great deal of time there, especially on drizzly, gray days like this afternoon. Despite Galena's protests she was still dressed in her boy's garb. She vowed she would go naked before wearing a gown cast off by a discarded mistress of Saber's. The only time she released the gray trousers and white linen shirt was at night, and when necessity demanded they be washed.

Nicole habitually could always be found in the library in the late afternoon. She was staring blankly out the window, her thoughts far away. Christmas had come and gone. Eighteen-fourteen was already a week old, and Saber had not yet returned. A fortnight of the drizzling rain like today's had kept her chained inside, and without the relief that came from exploring the estate on a horse, accompanied by a grave-faced black groom, she was like a bound pantheress. There was a book lying on the floor where just a few minutes ago she had thrown it in an unusually violent attack of temper. Normally she wouldn't have misused a volume so, but this helpless feeling and the inactivity were trying her nerves badly.

The strain of the last few weeks could be very clearly seen about her person. Her faint apricot tan had faded, leaving her skin a smooth, milky magnolia color, that was, if she knew or cared, extremely becoming. She had lost weight and the fine bones of her face were more prominent. And there was, in spite of her tallness, a fragile air about her.

Sounds from the hallway suddenly jerked her from her wandering, unhappy thoughts, and frowning, she listened intently to the muffled noises that seeped through the book-lined walls. Saber had arrived!

She knew in her bones it had to be him—why else had she been in such a foul temper today? Ignoring the leap in her pulse at the thought of his return, she willed herself to stay exactly where she was. She didn't fool herself that she wasn't excited that he had returned—she was, but only because a fight with Saber, and she was certain there would be one, would chase away this terrible ennui.

Listening now with all her might and straining to hear his voice, she stiffened when it became apparent that there was a female with Saber. The words were indiscernible through the walls, but the soft murmur of a woman's voice was very obvious. Her mouth tightened disagreeably—probably another of his fancy women! So much for her hope to enslave him.

Several minutes passed, during which time Nicole could tell from the scrapes and bumps that Saber must have brought quite a bit of baggage back with him. Thinking again of the woman's voice, she snorted—*baggage* indeed!

She was so intent on willing herself to remain where she was and hiding her emotions behind a facade of indifference, that the sound of the library door opening and shutting firmly came as a distinct surprise. Hoping it was merely Sanderson coming to announce Saber's arrival, she glanced over her shoulder and suffered a momentary shock when she saw the tall, elegant gentleman standing near one of the scarlet chairs.

At first she didn't recognize Saber, dressed as he was in the height of fashion. He was wearing breeches of light drab, a coat of blue with beautiful silver buttons, and a gay waistcoat of striped Marseilles; he was the picture of a man of impeccable taste.

Nicole blinked at his splendor; then her eyes flew to his face. For the first time she saw his features unadorned

171

by the disguising beard, and she was startled at the difference it made. His mouth, with its inherent sensuality, appeared more firmly cut and aristocratically drawn than before; the hard line of his jaw and the aggressive thrust of his chin were very apparent. It was not a classically handsome face; the nose was a trifle too large and the eyes perhaps a bit deep-seated to claim true male beauty. But it was an arresting face, a handsomely hard face, and the shock of those incredibly clear amber-gold eyes shadowed by the heavy black lashes was enough to blind most observers, male or female, to the faults of his features.

A faint smile was curving those firm lips just now, and drawing off his buff leather gloves, he asked softly, "No greeting, Nick? I had thought that after such a long separation you would be happy to see me."

Aware of the sudden increased beating of her heart, she forced herself to remain unmoved, and raising an eyebrow sardonically, she murmured, "Are the fish that swim in the sea happy to see the shark return? I doubt it. And you should have known better—you forget that there is only one reason why I am still enjoying your . . . ah . . . hospitality, or have you forgotten Allen?"

Christopher's smile vanished at her words. "You are a little viper, aren't you? No, I haven't forgotten the good Allen, but I think you cling to that excuse a little too tightly."

Nicole gave him an infuriatingly superior smile and turned to stare out the window. She felt his presence behind her, but stubbornly she kept her back to him.

His breath was soft on her hair, and she was almost unbearably conscious of his nearness. "Why," he snarled in a low tone, "do I want to strangle you and yet at the same time kiss you until you melt in my arms?"

Not waiting for an answer, nor expecting one, he spun her around. And before she could defend herself or even guess his intention, his hands, strong and hurtful, closed around her throat, and bending his head, his mouth, hard and hungry, came down passionately on her soft lips. Nicole felt an uncontrollable flare of desire and without thought leaned into his body, feeling his instant response to her nearness. For a long moment they clung together, his mouth searching hers with an almost desperate urgency, his painful hold loosening on her slim neck, his fingers unconsciously caressing where a second before they had meant to hurt.

Lifting his mouth away with an effort, he stared down

into her upturned face, and then losing himself in the deep, dark pools of her eyes, he muttered, "Oh, God! You're a witch, Nick!" and then swept her into his arms, crushing her against him, his mouth moving feverishly over her face before settling on her mouth once again.

Mindless, Nicole didn't fight against her own emotions or search for reasons for what was happening—she was too wrapped up in the fierce pleasure of being in his arms again. Later she could condemn herself; later she'd curse her foolishness—but, oh, God!—not *now!*

How long they would have stayed lost in an embrace or how far this sudden surge of passion would have taken them was never to be known. There was a discreet tap on the door, and with a will he didn't know he possessed, Christopher tore his mouth from Nicole's and, almost flinging her away, called impatiently, "Yes, what is it?"

Sanderson entered, looking faintly apologetic. "Sir, Miss Mauer would like to know if you have any instructions for her before she begins to unpack?"

Breathing heavily and running his hand through the thick blue-black hair, Christopher growled, "Oh, the devil take her!" Then realizing it wasn't what was expected of him and ignoring Nicole's stricken silence, he asked in a quieter tone, "Have you settled her in her rooms?"

"Yes, sir. She is on the third floor as you ordered. She has just partaken of a light refreshment and is now ready to begin her duties."

"Very well. Just tell her to see to her own settling in. Tomorrow is soon enough for her to start her duties."

Sanderson bowed and left the room.

The conversation, short as it had been, had given Nicole the time she needed to gain control of herself. Fighting back an emotion curiously akin to jealousy, she sneered, "My, my, aren't we the greedy one! *Two* of us now! Aren't you frightened that we might wear you down? Of course," she said brightly, "if you're replacing me, I can't tell you how delighted I am. Shall I go and welcome my replacement? Oh, and I will certainly be most happy to change rooms. There is no reason for Miss . . . er . . . Mauer, didn't Sanderson say, to stay on the third floor with the house servants. I'll switch with her in an instant."

"Shut up, Nick," Christopher said amicably. He, too, had recovered himself and was as unshakable as ever. Staring indifferently at her angry face, he completely confounded her by saying, "Miss Mauer *is* a servant. You have a very nasty mind, my girl. Miss Mauer is your maid. The clothes referred to are a few I ordered for you. Miss Mauer will alter them to fit—I tried to accurately gauge your measurements and she will see to any . . . ah . . . oversight on my part."

At Nicole's look of outrage, he continued in a harder tone, "You will keep your mouth shut until I've finished! Mauer is a very expensive lady's maid. Starting tomorrow, she will begin tricking you out as befits a young lady of your station. *You* will keep a civil tongue in your head and follow her dictates. You will also stop using those seamen's curses you are so fond of, and you will follow my orders and start preparing yourself to return to England."

Completely dumbfounded, Nicole gazed at him in fascinated astonishment. "Return to England?" she finally got out in a voice that sounded nothing like her own.

Christopher nodded, aware of a sudden sharp pain in the pit of his stomach when he realized exactly what he was committed to. Whether it was the thought of the difficulties ahead, or the knowledge that Nick would soon be out of his power that caused the unexpected spasm, he preferred not to examine at any great length.

"My Gawd! The gent's turned respectable! Well, ain't I betwattled!" Nicole drawled in a vulgar manner, her hands resting on her hips.

Christopher's lips twitched. "You'll catch cold at that, young woman! I'm certain you can give me a good display of billingsgate language with little effort, but restrain yourself. From now on, you are to do everything within your power to become quite the thing. Mauer is a start, and shortly I hope to have a governess installed. We haven't," he added thoughtfully, "a great deal of time, and so you are going to be hard pressed, my dear, to turn overnight into a young lady of fashion."

"Why?" Nicole demanded bewilderedly.

"Because I say so," Christopher returned quietly, a wealth of meaning in his words.

Nicole's face tightened. "Do you *always* get your way?"

"Of course."

For a moment she glared at him, and then with an exclamation of disgust she marched to the door. Her hand on the doorknob, she stopped when Christopher said, "Your room has been changed."

Whirling to face him and with curiosity uppermost in her voice, she asked in a cold little tone, "Why? Observing the niceties?"

Christopher nodded. "From now on you will forget any

relationship that has been between us. You are, for Mauer's information, my ward. Your governess, a Mrs. Eggleston by the way, is not at present with us due to an inflammation of the lung. And because I have not the years to have a beautiful young ward living in my home unchaperoned without causing speculation, I have stayed away while your governess has been ill. It was only after Mauer consented to enter my employment that I could return. Even so, it will be best when Mrs. Eggleston arrives." He said the words with no emotion, as if reciting a lesson that Nicole was to learn immediately.

But Nicole had other ideas, and outraged, she cried, "Do you expect me to swallow that rapper?"

Crossing the room in swift strides, Christopher grasped Nicole's hands tightly between his own. In a determined tone he snapped, "You had better believe it—and *remember* it! From now on, it is the truth. You are my ward, Mrs. Eggleston is your governess, and you are going to tell that story to anyone who asks. If you don't, if you cross me, Nick, you'll discover that I am the devil you've always thought." Driven by his own demons, he added, "Remember, Nick, Allen's life depends on you. Defy me and I'll kill him with my own two hands!"

Nicole stared at him, and shaken by the violence she could feel in the air, she whispered, "Why? Why are you doing this? What do you intend?"

Looking down at her, he didn't understand any of the emotions he was experiencing. Because he was confused and uncertain himself, his voice was unduly harsh. "Because it pleases me! I am returning you to England as soon as possible. I hope you will have progressed to a point that will pass muster with your family so that we can sail by late February—perhaps sooner if you are very diligent. Mauer will be taking your measurements, and I will be leaving within the week for New Orleans again. A new wardrobe will replace the one you supposedly lost when the ship, also mythical by the way, sunk—it was taking you and Mrs. Eggleston from the north, where you both had been living until I could arrange to escort you here." Smiling thinly he added, "That's when Mrs. Eggleston became ill. It was very harrowing experience and you were lucky to have escaped with your lives."

"Why," Nicole asked in a numb voice, "were we living in the north?"

"Oh, that," he said easily. "Did you know that when you ran away from Beddington's Corner five years ago you went with Mrs. Eggleston?"

175

Staring at him as if she thought he were insane, Nicole said faintly, "I ran away with Mrs. Eggleston?"

"Yes. It was extremely irresponsible of you, but Mrs. Eggleston sympathized with your plight—and she didn't realize you had hidden yourself away on her coach until she had reached London."

Her eyes searched his face with something approaching hysteria. "You must be mad! No one would believe that tale—besides who is Mrs. Eggleston?" Her expression changed in an instant and she said in a tone of incredulity, *"Mrs. Eggleston!* Colonel Eggleston's widow?"

Christopher nodded. "The same. I met her by accident in New Orleans."

For a second he eyed Nicole with consideration. Then pulling her behind him, he walked over to the two chairs. Sitting down in one of them, he indicated that Nicole should take the other. She did so like one moving in a trance. Finally she got out, "How do you know Mrs. Eggleston?" And frowning she added, "And what is she doing here?"

Christopher hesitated. How much to tell Nick and how much to keep from her? He decided that the only thing that was vital to keep from her was Jason Savage's visit and the real reason for their return to England. Let Nick think he'd suddenly had an attack of conscience and was willing to return her home. Somewhat cautiously he asked, "Haven't you ever wondered exactly who I am or what I was doing in England five years ago?"

"You came to hire seamen," she said in a puzzled tone. "At least that's what Sally said."

"Sally?"

"Sally Brown. Her sister Peggy worked at the inn. Peggy heard you asking around."

Christopher grinned. "So that's how you knew I wanted seamen! I often wondered, but never thought of it overmuch."

Impatiently Nicole asked, "So?"

And reluctantly Christopher admitted, "Nick, I'm Lord Saxon's grandson. And from now on, you had best forget that Captain Saber ever existed and remember that my name is Christopher . . . not Saber."

For several seconds, Nicole looked at him, literally struck dumb. Eventually she managed, "The Christopher that ran away?"

His face falling into tight, bitter lines, Saber nodded. "The same."

"Then of course you know Mrs. Eggleston," she said

176

with wonder. "You know *everyone* at Beddington's Corner!"

"Not quite," he commented in a dry tone. "It has never been my pleasure to meet your guardians, the Markhams."

"Oh," Nicole said blankly. There were dozens of questions that flew in a dozen different directions in her startled brain. Why was he a pirate? And why the devil did he now wish to return to England?

A smile on his lips, Christopher mocked, "Is that all you have to say?"

She sought for words. "Um, no, it's just that it's a shock to discover that you're really someone I've known about all my life—that our families were neighbors, good friends even." Recovering herself somewhat, she guessed shrewdly, "Besides, you won't tell me anything anyway." And suddenly realizing the full significance of what he had revealed, her temper exploded and she exclaimed, "You're a foul beast, Saber, you know that! How could you treat me as you have! I could understand it partially when you were just Captain Saber, but you were raised a gentleman! Your grandfather is a lord! I would have expected better of you."

Christopher's eyes were shuttered and his smile vanished, leaving his face cold and forbidding. "Watch it, Nick!" he warned softly. "I haven't set you up as my judge. I am, what I am—for whatever reasons, and they don't concern you! All that concerns you is the tale that we're going to present. And present it, we *will!*"

Nicole bit back more angry words, and jumping to her feet, she said jeeringly, "Intrigue seems to be one of your talents! I'm certain you'll come up with a plausible tale—so tell me, why were we in the north? How have Mrs. Eggleston and I lived these past five years? And how did we have the great misfortune to come under your protection?"

Angry now too, especially when it occurred to him that if her damned slut of a mother had kept her legs together he wouldn't be in this ignoble position, Christopher stood up and snarled, "Misfortune indeed! You're bloody lucky I don't strangle you and throw you in the river. Don't push me too far, Nick!"

Having enraged him, Nicole now irrationally wished that she hadn't, and in a calmer tone of voice she said quickly, "You can't expect me to accept meekly what you have done—and I think if our roles were reversed, you, too, would fight back!"

177

Silently Christopher grudgingly acknowledged the justice of her words, but he only shook his head.

Christopher remained silent and Nicole said crossly, "Tell me the tale I'm to learn and let's get this farce done with!"

"Very well then, you ran away with Mrs. Eggleston five years ago when she left England. You have been living these past years quietly in a small town in British Canada. Due to the fighting along the border, Mrs. Eggleston decided it would be safer to leave the area. Besides she also felt that it was time you returned and claimed your estates. Unfortunately, your ship was sunk by an American privateer and you were taken to Charleston. I happened to be in Charleston myself, thinking of buying my own merchantman, when we accidentally met. Naturally"—and Christopher bowed mockingly in her direction—"learning of your plight, I immediately undertook to look after you both. We traveled to New Orleans, where Mrs. Eggleston's illness necessitated her remaining there. I deposited you at Thibodaux House and left right away again for New Orleans. I have just now returned with a suitable lady's maid and a few gowns to replace those you lost at sea. I will be leaving again in a few days to see to the remainder of your new wardrobe and to escort the fully recovered Mrs. Eggleston back here." He gave Nicole a hard look to see how she was taking his story. But Nicole could, upon occasion, hide her emotions too, and she had kept her face stony and unrevealing throughout Christopher's discourse. He ignored her lack of animation and continued, "Soon I'll see about arranging passage for us to London. And," he added provocatively, "if you do as I say and give me no difficulty, I shall free Allen . . . within a reasonable time period."

Christopher was rather pleased with his story. It hung together nicely. More importantly, there was going to be an ocean between them and the true facts—an ocean and a war going on. It would be almost impossible for anyone to disprove his tale—and who would want to? Mrs. Eggleston was a pattern card of respectability, and she had admitted to him that she had been too ashamed of her circumstances to let any of her friends in England know the truth. They believed she had left England, unable to bear it after the Colonel's death, and had decided to live with distant relatives in Canada. A coincidence Christopher blessed fervently.

With Mrs. Eggleston to lend credibility and he himself returning as the wild, young rascal who had made a fortune in America, they should brush through the first uneasy meetings with few problems. The explanation of the past five years was solid; Mrs. Eggleston's and Nick's wish to return also could not be open to conjecture. His own providential appearance on the scene was stretching it a bit thin, but only to someone who was unduly suspicious of his reasons for coming back to England.

The Markhams would present a certain amount of difficulty if they were as determined to control Nick's life and fortune as it appeared they were. But this time Nick would not be fighting them alone—she would have both himself and Mrs. Eggleston to stand in her favor, and he had the feeling that if his grandfather were still alive, old Simon Saxon would carry the battle right into the enemy camp.

Once Nick's claim was proven and she was safely in control of her own fortune, her usefulness was over. By that time he hoped he would have gained whatever knowledge he could and would be leaving her behind. For a moment he realized he felt saddened by the prospect, but he thrust it aside. She meant nothing to him— he had only grown used to her. And because he was angry at something he didn't or wouldn't understand, he snapped harshly, "Do you think you can remember what I've said? You're quick enough, you shouldn't have any trouble."

Nicole nodded, a lump of cold misery in her chest. Controlling herself with an effort, she asked expressionlessly, "Is that all? May I go to my room now?"

Angry and not certain why, Christopher snarled, "Yes, by God! Get out of my sight!"

Without another word, Nicole tore out of the library, and running out onto the veranda, she raced up the stairs to her room on the second floor . . . her new room. She met Galena in the wide hallway, who, with a carefully bland face, showed her the room she was now to occupy. It would have been more than she could bear if she'd had to ask Saber . . . or Christopher, as he now wanted to be called.

Not understanding herself, or why instead of mad elation there was only an empty feeling in her stomach, she ignored the trunks and packages that were scattered about the room, and with something approaching a sob threw herself down on the green silk-draped bed.

Of course it wasn't a sob—Nicole never cried, but she was dangerously near to it. Biting her lip to stop its quiver, she told herself she should be the most delighted girl in the world. Allen would be free . . . eventually. No longer would she have to endure Saber's, no, Christopher's lovemaking, and soon he would be taking her home to England, returning her to her rightful place and ousting the Markhams as she had always planned. Dismally she wondered why it mattered not one jot to her—why all she really wanted to do was to go on crossing swords with Sa—Christopher, fighting with him and then losing herself in his arms!

Her thoughts were not to be borne. Telling herself that it was the shock, the suddenness of having all her dreams come true that was responsible for this terrible feeling of depression, she wrenched her mind away from the painful subject and forced herself to concentrate on all the lovely things Christopher had brought back with him.

She rang for Galena. And within a few minutes, they began to unpack the trunks and packages. Christopher had said he had brought just a few clothes, but seeing the half dozen or so gorgeous gowns—one in Pomona green of gossamer satin; the dainty silk slippers; a delightfully curled silk bonnet; three simply enchanting night rails of the finest percale with matching robes delicately embroidered with roses; a very fashionable riding habit of bright green cloth ornamented with black braid *à la militaire*; a small riding hat of black beaver with gold cordon and tassels and a long green ostrich feather; two pairs of black half boots, one pair laced and fringed with green; a lace tippet *à la Duchess d'Agoulême,* edged with a border of Vandyke lace; and an amber silk cape—Nicole couldn't possibly see how she would ever need more!

For a young woman whose entire wardrobe for years had consisted only of the boy's clothes on her back, it seemed like an incredible wardrobe, and the knowledge that there would be more almost took her breath away.

One small trunk contained all the little odds and ends that most women so love and Nicole, despite herself, found that she was no different. With delight she lifted out delicate silk chemises, some spangled scarves, a matched set of combs, brushes and an oval hand mirror inlaid with mother of pearl, deliciously scented soaps and bath oils, as well as several crystal bottles of perfume.

With childlike glee Nicole ran from one lovely object to the other, her hands almost caressing the beautiful gowns and scarves. In simple enjoyment she slipped into a hastily prepared bath, liberally scented from one of the jars of bath oil, and reveled in the soft, silken water. Afterward Galena helped her into one of the new night rails with its matching wrapper, and Nicole sat lost in thought before the small fire in her room as Galena soothingly brushed her wavy locks.

Staring into the leaping flames, Nicole came to several decisions. She wouldn't think about Saber—or Christopher, as she would have to remember to call him. Somehow, though, she felt he would always be Saber to her, no matter what the future would bring. But from now on she would work very hard to regain her manners and follow the dictates of polite society. Whatever he was up to, the fact remained that he was going to do just as she would have wished. The only fault she could find was that Allen would not be freed immediately. She frowned as she thought about Allen. Christopher, and firmly she called him that in her mind, *Christopher* had said he would release Allen—but dare she trust him? Yes, she decided slowly after a great deal of thought. Christopher was a clever devil, but if he had said he would do something he would see it done. And he had stated outright that Allen would be set free. Unharmed? Her blood suddenly chilled. Christopher was perfectly capable of freeing Allen all right—right into the hands of the American military!

Realizing suddenly that she should have questioned him more closely, she started to her feet, only to be brought up short by Galena's admonition that she sit still. And of course she could not confront him in such inappropriate dress. How quickly the rules of society overtook one, she thought cynically.

She slept badly that night, tossing and turning, waking a half dozen times only to fall back into a restless doze. Though she tried to convince herself that her uneasy sleep was because of the new room, deep down inside she knew it had nothing to do with that.

Somewhere at the back of her consciousness had always been the thought that someday she would return to England and her home. How, when, or why hadn't been important. Nicole wasn't given to deep thinking, living for the most part on the surface of her emotions, but the abruptness with which this had happened made her, for the first time in her life, look inside at her deepest feelings. And she didn't like at all what she saw!

Trying to ignore the pull of physical attraction between herself and Christopher was futile. It existed and she would have been a fool to pretend otherwise. Whether she liked it or not, part of her restlessness was due to the unpalatable knowledge that her body wanted his, and that she would have given a great deal still to be in that room that adjoined his, knowing that he would be coming to her bed whenever he chose. She was secretly appalled and ashamed, but she knew it was true.

She wasn't so sure of her emotions concerning the return to England. Did she really wish to go back? She thought not—not if it meant being parted from Christopher!

Uncomfortable and just a little frightened at where her thoughts were taking her, she twisted the bedclothes into such knots with her constant tossings that close to dawn she had to get out of bed to straighten them. Climbing back into the bed, she lay there giving up all pretense of sleep. She was caught in a trap of her own making—pride would not allow her to back down from her once fiercely desired wish to oust the Markhams. And there was the further, lowering knowledge that even if she threw earlier dreams to the winds, Christopher was not likely to change his plans. Instead he would be more than certain to question and wonder at her change of heart—wonder and perhaps guess at something she herself wasn't even willing to name. Consequently, in view of the night she had just spent, it was a moody and heavy-eyed young woman that greeted Miss Mauer in the morning.

Miss Mauer looked precisely like what she was—a very efficient lady's maid—from the top of her graying dark locks, neatly combed and arranged in a bun behind her head, to the sturdy black slippers on her feet. She was not a large woman, nor an especially pretty woman, but her snapping black eyes, a lively smile, and her quick, deft movements gave her a pleasing appearance. She had a soft voice and when she spoke her French accent was noticeable.

After having ascertained with a swift glance that the clothes had already been neatly hung in the large cherrywood armoire near the corner of the room, she folded her hands and asked in a diffident tone of voice, "Would Mademoiselle care to dress?"

Nicole, seated on her bed and viewing the day with an uneasy eye, looked at her with consideration. She would have liked to order the woman from the room, but knowing it would only precipitate a scene with Christopher and that this situation was not of Mauer's making, she said reluctantly, "I suppose I should." Then in a burst of honesty that endeared her instantly to Miss Mauer, she admitted, "I've never had my very own maid before, you know, so you shall have to show me how to go on."

Nothing could have been more calculated to make Miss Mauer her slave. Used to spoiled women of fashion and aging beauties fighting desperately against the ravages of time, Nicole was a refreshing change. And once Nicole made up her mind to bow to the inevitable, everything was swiftly and agreeably arranged.

It was, as it turned out, a pleasant morning. Nicole, at Mauer's request, tried on first one gown then another. And very speedily Mauer made the necessary notations. As soon as the fittings were over, Mauer set about altering one gown for Nicole to wear that day, promising, as she was a notable needlewoman, that the others would be ready in no time at all.

An amber-bronze gown of serge with the new fashionable long sleeves and tiny buttons at the wrist was the dress finally selected to be altered first. It had the high waist that was once again in demand, and what would have been a shockingly low-cut bodice was filled with ecru-colored lace.

While Miss Mauer busily plied her needle, the two exchanged pleasantries. On Nicole's part the exchange was naturally guarded. She had to be careful of what she said and wished she had thought to question Christopher more closely on exactly what Miss Mauer had been told.

She needn't have worried about Mauer's reaction to her careful replies. Mauer knew better than to inquire too deeply into her employer's affairs, and if by chance she discovered something of a scandalous nature, her mouth was very firmly sealed—no one would hire a chatterbox who divulged all she knew!

The gown completed to her satisfaction, Mauer rather hesitantly suggested that perhaps before dressing, they should see to Nicole's hair.

Surprised and a little wary, Nicole asked, "What exactly do you mean?"

"Mademoiselle, you have beautiful hair, and such a dark, deep auburn, o la la, but perhaps it is a little, little long and ill-cut, n'est-ce pas?"

Looking in the mirror at the burnished mass of dark fire that fell almost to the middle of her back, Nicole admitted somewhat cautiously, "Yeees, it probably is a trifle long, and I haven't taken very good care of it."

Encouraged, Miss Mauer suggested, "Perhaps, if I were to trim a little off it would be easier to manage and to dress more fashionably?"

A gleam of mischief in her eyes, Nicole readily agreed, feeling certain that Christopher would forbid it if he knew. And so in perfect accord, if not for the same reasons, they set about creating the "new" Nicole.

Some two hours later it was a *very* fashionably dressed young lady who viewed herself in the long mirror. Her hair fell a little below her shoulders with a soft fringe across the forehead. Mauer had then arranged it in ringlets on top of her head with one long curl coaxed to rest on her shoulder. The amber gown fit to perfection, and the color was a pleasing foil for her burnished dark hair. A spangled shawl draped across her shoulders and bronze silk slippers completed the picture. For a long time Nicole stared at the tall, decidedly elegant creature before her. It seemed incredible that the fashionable young woman with the dark eyes and slender full-bosomed figure could be herself.

With a funny little catch in the region of her heart, she wondered if Christopher would find this "new" Nick more appealing than the old. Or would he continue to make half-savage, half-tender love to her one minute, and then snarl and snap the next.

17

If Nicole had been thrown off balance by the events of yesterday, so had Christopher. He hadn't expected the fierce surge of pleasure that had whipped through him at the sight of that slim figure in her boy's clothing, nor had he expected to feel any regret about their eventual parting. That he experienced both of those emotions left him torn between fury that any woman could arouse such feeling, and disgust, mingled with uneasiness, about the reasons for these very unnatural emotions.

He was not about to fall into the same snare he had years before—and certainly not with that slut Annabelle's daughter! Venting some of his anger by slamming from the library and demanding that Sanderson see that a tray of liquors was prepared and sent to the gun room, he stalked down the hall. Some minutes later, sprawling on the worn leather couch and staring at the fire, he proceeded to swallow one glass of whiskey after another. It was something he seldom did, if ever, but just now he didn't want to think about anything.

He told himself that events were working out for the best, and any regret on his part was only because he hadn't yet grown tired of Nicole's body. She meant absolutely nothing to him. She was a pawn to be used—as was Mrs. Eggleston!

Christopher was badly rattled. He thought himself a hard man, and he was. Yet since he had decided to give up all connections with Lafitte and privateering, the emotionless cloak with which he had clothed himself for so many years was showing quite a number of tears and rents.

He could remind himself that his concern in New Orleans's safety was purely selfish—he didn't want his own interests harmed, did he? He could also excuse his behavior with Mrs. Eggleston. After all, he argued with himself, she had always been good to him. Besides, he would be using her for his own ends, wouldn't he? And if he was doing the proper thing by returning Nicole Ashford to her relatives in England, it was only because it served his purpose. Having blackened his character to his satisfaction and convinced himself that he was indeed the filthy beast that Nick called him, he proceeded to drink himself blind.

He woke the next morning in a foul temper, but certain things had clarified themselves in his mind. He was not going to search and rack his brains to find reasons for why he was acting as he was—he was doing it because it suited *him*.

Dressing hurriedly in a pair of comfortable buckskins and top boots, he made arrangements to spend the morning with his manager, Hans Bartel, going over the plantation account books and discussing the plans to be carried out in his absence.

After spending an agreeable morning with Hans and making plans to inspect several innovations that had been made in his absence the next day, he returned to the house in a fairly amicable frame of mind, denying vehemently to himself that he was looking forward to seeing Nick in some of the finery he had brought for her. As it was, he returned to the house and was preparing to go upstairs and change for lunch just as Nicole was coming down. Catching sight of each other, for a long second they froze—Nicole about halfway down the stairs and Christopher with one foot resting on the first step.

Nicole's face paled; she was aware of sudden breathlessness at the unexpected sight of him, and Christopher couldn't quite hide the quick flame that turned his eyes bright gold as he stared at the lovely picture she made in the amber-bronze gown.

They both recovered quickly, although a muscle still jumped in Christopher's cheek as he drawled, "Very nice. You'll do me credit, m'dear."

Forgetting her role, Nicole spat, "I wouldn't count on it! Fine feathers do not necessarily make fine birds!"

Christopher only grinned. "In your case they make a delectably fine . . . er . . . bird."

"Ladybird, don't you mean?" Nick shot back. "A soiled dove to be exact."

Christopher's eyes narrowed and his voice sharpened. "That will be enough! You know full well that you are not supposed to know about ladybirds or soiled doves. Remember it!"

Coming slowly down the stairs, Nicole approached him, and when their eyes were level she smiled sweetly and murmured, "I wonder whose fault it is that I know of such things? Who soiled the dove?"

Christopher caught her wrist and pulled her abruptly against him. They both were angry now, and Christopher was also fighting the sudden desire to take her to his bed. Controlling himself, barely, he snapped in a low tone, "Talk like that in front of anyone else and you'll be ruined!" And because he was moved by the sight of her and the memory of her kissing Allen in the gloom of the prison, he had an urge to hurt and added grimly, "And Allen will die!"

"Bastard!" Nicole hissed under her breath, her eyes full of fury as she struggled to free her wrist.

Disgusted as much with himself as the sudden ugly scene, he released Nicole's wrist. Harshly he inquired, "Have I made myself clear?"

Glaring at him and rubbing her wrist, Nicole muttered, "Very."

Christopher smiled so coldly that Nicole ached to slap his handsome face, and he murmured, "Then I trust you will watch your unruly tongue in the future?"

Ignoring him and too angry to care what he thought, she spun on her heel and stalked off, her back held very straight. For a moment Christopher stood and stared after her, admiring the slight sway to her skirts and still fighting the urge to tip up those skirts as she walked away from him. Shrugging his shoulders, he ran up the stairs and quickly changed from his buckskins to a pair of buff breeches and an expertly cut coat of Spanish blue. Higgins, in his newly resumed role as Christopher's valet, slipped a pair of black Hessian boots on Christopher's feet.

Glancing at him, Christopher asked, "Have you settled in? Everything satisfactory?"

A grin splitting his weather-seamed face, Higgins answered cheerfully, "Right and tight, sir! It's good to be back, and I'm downright pleased that we won't be going back to sea. I'm getting a little old to be traipsing all over the world."

Christopher smiled, a smile few people ever saw. "Well don't get too used to domesticity, my friend. Remember we leave for England in six weeks, perhaps less."

Higgins nodded, but his grin faded and his face clearly revealed his doubt. "Do you think it's wise, sir? We're still at war with England and you and I are still technically deserters. And I doubt your uncle is going to be pleased when you show up."

187

"I'm aware of the danger from my uncle Robert, Higgins. But it is our duty to return Miss Ashford to her home. As for the war, remember it is no more popular in England than it is here. We'll manage to brush through unscathed." Christopher said the words easily, glad that he had not told Higgins the real reason behind their trip to England. What Higgins didn't know wouldn't hurt him, might, in fact, save his life, if by some mischance Christopher's real mission were discovered and he were captured.

And unaware of the thoughts running through Christopher's brain, but knowing from previous experience that there was no turning him from his path once his mind was made up, Higgins only shrugged and began picking up the buckskins that had been thrown casually across a chair. "As you say, sir, but I don't like it!"

Christopher didn't like it either—for several reasons, and not all of them concerning the risks involved—but he refused to think about it.

In the intervening time Nicole had managed to cool her sudden temper, and she was as furious with herself as she was with Christopher. She had meant to be very calm and polite, and then what had she done but lose her composure at the first sight of him. Pacing the library with long decidedly unladylike strides, she proceeded to give herself a mental scold that would have done a fishmonger's wife proud. Her temper gradually cooled and it was in a mood of icy politeness that she joined him in the dining room for luncheon.

She ate in frozen silence, and Christopher's remarks elicited only monosyllables. By the time they had finished the last course, Christopher was in a fine rage. Pushing his chair back with unnecessary force, he rose to his feet and snapped, "I'd like a word with you—in the library. Now!"

"Oh, I'm very sorry," Nicole murmured, "but Miss Mauer and I will be engaged this afternoon. Perhaps this evening before dinner?"

Christopher crossed over to her in two lithe strides, jerked her out of her chair, and dragged her past the astonished Sanderson into the library.

Her bosom heaving with suppressed emotion, she glared up at him. Fighting to maintain her cold facade, she asked, "Was that necessary? You expect me to act like a lady, but your actions are hardly those of a gentleman."

"If you wish me to act the gentleman, don't treat me

as if I don't exist. I don't expect you to be pleased with the situation, but you had better learn to afford me the bare courtesy of a guardian. I do not expect your gratitude, but I do expect a civil reply and not conceited bitchery."

Biting her lip with mortification, Nicole turned her back on him. Ignoring his harsh words, she said tightly, "I'm sorry if you don't like my manners, but you must remember that it is a long time since I have been part of *polite* society."

"Your manners are acceptable, my dear. It's your attitude that needs changing," Christopher commented dryly, his anger fading as quickly as it rose.

At his words Nicole glared at him. Grimly she said, "My attitude is no more than you deserve. I do not forget that you hold Allen's life over my head—nor what has gone between us."

Christopher walked up to her and took her by the shoulders. Staring into her angry face, he asked slowly, "Do you think that I enjoy holding Allen as a weapon against you?"

Nicole was suddenly breathless and frightened at the surge of emotion that rushed through her at his touch.

"Do you?" he demanded again.

"I don't know!" she cried.

Her answer afforded him little pleasure. "You leave me little choice," he admitted bitterly. "You must obey me, without question—and Allen seems to be the only person who means anything to you." Accusingly he added, "You were even willing to whore for him!"

Nicole flinched but her eyes met his. "I haven't forgotten," she said quietly. "Nor that you tricked me. Do you think that I will ever forget what has happened?"

"No," he agreed in a flat voice. "You won't forget, but"—and he gave a mirthless laugh—"neither will I!"

He released her and Nicole instantly moved away. For a second he stared at her, a brooding expression in his eyes. Finally he said, "Are you going to meet me halfway, or do we continue this constant war?"

Cautiously, Nicole conceded, "I will try to treat you as my guardian, but don't expect me to like it!"

Christopher nodded. "That will do," he said lightly. "More would be stretching your limits of acting."

For the remainder of the day Nicole drifted in a confused haze. She could not understand him—one minute he was cruel and brutal, the next demanding, then he would ask for her opinion as if it mattered to him.

189

Christopher was due to leave for New Orleans on Wednesday, and they spent the few days before his departure treating each other with a meticulous politeness.

On the morning before his departure, after their breakfast, Nicole asked a question that had been at the back of her mind for some time. "What does Mrs. Eggleston know of me? How have you explained my presence to her?"

"I haven't."

Startled, Nicole's eyes flew to his. "You mean she doesn't know that I am here?"

"No, not yet. But she will before she arrives. I intend to tell her a bit of the truth—that you disguised yourself as a boy and acted as my cabin boy until just recently, when I discovered your secret. Naturally," he said in a mocking tone, "once I knew who you were, I immediately took steps to set things right—hence your present situation."

Bewildered, Nicole stared up at him. "But—but," she stammered, "what of the tale you told me—that I've lived with her in Canada?"

"Hmmm. Don't worry. Eventually Mrs. Eggleston will support that entire fabrication, but for the moment she need only know what I want her to know." He hesitated a moment and then asked, "Can you keep your stories straight—an expurgated version of the truth for Mrs. Eggleston and later the Canadian tale for England?"

Grimly, Nicole answered, "I had better, hadn't I?"

"Let's hope so," he drawled. Christopher spent the rest of the day busy with the affairs of Thibodaux House—deliberately pushing all thoughts of Nicole from his mind, willing himself to deny how desirable he found her.

When he went downstairs that night, Nicole was already in the dining room. She was wearing an enchanting gown of gossamer silk, the Pomona green color complimenting the warm ivory of her skin. The gown was cut fashionably low, and Christopher had difficulty in tearing his eyes away from the satin expanse of smooth flesh that it exposed. Her hair had been arranged in soft ringlets that fell about her face in artless disarray, and he knew an impulse to kiss that spot where her slim neck met the soft nakedness of her shoulder. While he appreciated the sight of her, he was swamped by the almost overpowering urge to rip the gown from her body and to have that cleverly arranged hair in wild disorder from his lovemaking.

He could feel his body betraying him, hardening with

desire even as he walked over to her. The scent of the perfume she was wearing was tantalizing, and he resisted all his awakened carnal instincts and saw to it that she was seated before he walked to the other end of the table. Furious with himself and with her for arousing him, he signaled coldly for Sanderson to serve. Through the entire meal he was aware of the swelling in his skin-hugging breeches. Nicole's polite attempts at conversation were met with a curtness that soon caused her to give up all pretense of sociability.

Rising with relief at the finish of the meal, she bid him a frosty good night and swept from the room unaccountably depressed. Christopher barely acknowledged her departure—he was too occupied fighting his baser instincts to worry how his actions appeared to others. It was only after Nicole had been gone for some minutes that he was able to rise from the table, his body once more under control.

Angry and unsettled, he took himself from the house, intending to walk off some of his temper. Unfortunately it had begun to rain again, and after walking several yards in the damp drizzle, he gave it up and returned to the house, his mood, if possible, blacker and more explosive than before. He stalked off to his bedroom, donned a robe, and poured himself a whiskey.

He was in such a surly mood that Higgins, who usually enjoyed a short chat with him in the evening, took one look at his face and swiftly saw to the evening tasks, departing from the room with a sigh of relief.

The light rain had turned to a full-blown thunderstorm. Standing at the opened pair of doors that led to the veranda, he watched the jagged flashes of lightning against the black sky. He was not sleepy and the storm's awesome power awakened some primitive excitement in him. Stepping out onto the rain-lashed veranda, he let the rain blow against his face. For a moment he could almost pretend he was pacing the bridge of *La Belle Garce* as he had done so often in the past. As in a dream he found himself walking slowly in the direction of Nicole's room.

The storm had awakened her, and for several minutes she lay in the bed, watching the streaks of lightning out a window under the eaves of the veranda, and listening with sleepy contentment to the rumble and fury of the thunder. She sat up in the bed, the air cool against her naked flesh. Despite her delight in the new night rails, she found that she much preferred the sensual feel of the bedclothes against her bare skin. Her blanket-covered legs drawn up to her chest and her arms wrapped around them, she rested her chin on her knees and stared with fascination at the ever-changing sky.

Though she was sitting in her cozy bedroom, it almost reminded her of storms at sea, yet it was not quite as spectacular for there was not the surging feel of *La Belle Garce* under her body. She remembered with longing the taste of rain on her lips and the wind in her hair as she stood on the wave-lashed decks of the ship. Rising quickly, she slipped on one of her new robes and ran barefooted to the French doors.

Just as she opened them there was a particularly sharp and explosive crack of thunder, followed by a gigantic flash of lightning that lit up the entire sky and clearly etched Christopher in silver as he stood near the railings, his back to her, engrossed in the storm.

When she saw him, her impetuous rush halted, and she froze, one foot on the veranda. The force of the storm flattened the robe against her, outlining her pointed breasts, her legs gleaming softly as it parted and flew in the air. Shock at his presence weakened her hold on the doors, and with a suddenness that shook her, the wind whipped them out of her hands and slammed them against the wall.

At the sound Christopher whirled, and for a long timeless moment they stared at one another. His face was damp from the rain, and in the continuing flashes of lightning, his hair appeared shot with silver, as the light glinted off the raindrops resting on its inky blackness. Neither spoke, and Nicole was only aware of a sudden breathlessness, a tightening in her stomach, as the time spun out. Frightened of the emotions he evoked, with a small inarticulate cry she stumbled back into her room, but Christopher moved as swiftly as the lightning in the sky, and with a muttered "Nick!" he dragged her into his arms.

Fighting as much against herself as Christopher, she struggled to escape, but there was no escape, not with his mouth, warm and demanding, moving with half-fierce, half-gentle urgency against hers. Her arms were locked at her sides and her body crushed next to the hard strength of his. She was conscious of so many things as she twisted in his arms—the sweet taste of him, the feel of his long, muscled legs against hers, and most of all their naked state, for as her robe parted in her struggles so did his, and she caught her breath as she brushed against his groin, feeling him full and heavy with desire.

And Christopher, lost in his own hell, had no intention of fighting against himself and what he wanted. Nick was in his arms where he needed her, and he wasn't thinking of anything but the exquisite sensations of part-pain, part-pleasure it gave him to feel her soft, supple body twisting against him. She filled his arms as no one had before, her tall, slender body fitting as if she had been fashioned precisely for him and him alone. Somewhere at the back of his mind he probably wished she wouldn't deny him so, but now it didn't matter—all that mattered was that he be relieved of this demanding pressure between his legs. He ached with it, and it seemed that Nick was the only woman who had the power to satisfy it. And as he continued to kiss her, his hands now cradling her head, holding her to his mouth, Nicole's struggles gradually ceased, and she let the hunger that she hadn't understood before sweep over her, knowing that, for whatever reasons, only Christopher had the ability to assuage it.

Feeling her melt into him, he raised his head and stared intently with a narrowed hard look down into her wide dark eyes. His own were bright with passion, and seeing his own desires reflected tremulously back at him, he murmured beneath his breath, "Oh, God! I want you . . . I hurt with it, Nick. Heal me!"

Unaware of what he had said, or even what his words would have unwittingly revealed if Nicole had heard them, he slowly and deliberately undid her wrapper. And Nicole shivering with the knowledge of what he was going to do with her body—wanting it as badly as he— made no move to run when he released her long enough for his robe to be flung on the floor beside hers. Then he swept her up in his arms and took her to the bed.

And what followed was like no other time that they had come together in the past. They moved in slow sensual motion like people in a trance; Nicole for the first time in her life discovered what was meant by making love. For they did make love—not just satisfying lust or animal passion, but expressing what neither would admit in the most natural and beautiful way possible.

Christopher's flesh was a warm crushed velvet beneath her wandering fingertips as her hands slowly explored him, moving gently, almost dazedly, down across his face, his nose, his mouth, which curved with passion, to his chest covered with black, curiously soft hair, sliding across his back and feeling with an unaware frown the ridges and scars that marked him, then up again until her fingers encountered the dark rough silk of his head. And it was she who brought his lips to hers, holding his face in both her hands as she tantalizingly moved her mouth across his in sweet provocation.

At her first tentative touch Christopher had stilled, caught in the sensual web she was deliberately weaving. And trembling with the force of his ardor, he let her discover the dangerous pleasure of tempting and yielding as her fingers left his face and wandered down his body, her hands curving over his buttocks, exploring as they moved the shape and texture of him.

He endured it as long as he could, this exquisite aching pleasure, but when her breast lightly brushed against his chest and her hands finally found him, he groaned and, swiftly rolling over, trapped her beneath him. Catching her bottom lip tightly between his teeth, he growled thickly, "Torment me, will you?"

Loosening her mouth, his lips began a slow, searing trail down her neck to her bosom, his hands gently caressing as they followed the curve of her body to the swell of her slender hips.

His lips teasing the sensitive nipples of her breast, Nicole felt her entire body quiver as the nipples hardened with increasing desire, and her breath caught in her throat as his hands, with gentle insistence, slid between her thighs, seeking the softness within. His touch, delicate, yet demanding, as his fingers caressed the most private part of her, evoked a piercingly sweet agony of longing, and her body of its own will began to writhe in rhythm with the movements of his hand. But this time she was not content with a passive role, and with an urgent tug of his hair she brought his mouth to hers, and her hand went unerringly to where Christopher most wanted it. As her fingers encompassed him, swollen and bursting with desire, he made a low sound at the base of his throat, a sighing growl, and swiftly covered her, their bodies meeting and melting into one another as he slid deep into the warm silken sheath of her.

He filled her and stretched the delicate softness, until a low moan of pleasure-pain escaped from Nicole, but when at the sound of her half-animal cry, he hesitated, she tightened her legs around him and whispered huskily, "No! Don't leave me . . . not yet, *please!*" His body gave a convulsive leap at her words, and his eyes narrowing into gold slits of bright intensity, he began to thrust in a slow, almost lazy rhythm with her eagerly rising hips, his mouth moving with increasing urgency across her face.

Nicole was full of him, as was every fiber of her being. It was as if she were absorbing him—the scent of him, the faint lingering hint of tobacco, the sharp scent of whiskey, and the musky masculine odor that was essentially Christopher. She was spinning in a sensual dream, drunk on the taste of him, her open mouth sliding down his neck, her tongue tasting the salt of his shoulder, only to return hungrily for the tender savagery of his kiss, as he explored her willing mouth with a sweet fierceness that was as intoxicating as wine.

The soft prickly crush of his chest against her tingling nipples, the touch of his hard legs on her thighs, drove her to the point of madness, and she twisted uncontrollably under him. Christopher's hands came down swiftly to her hips, urging and guiding her movements with a desperate need for release. Both were engulfed by the searing flame of desire devouring them, their bodies coming together with a feverish intensity.

The ache in her loins grew until she was rigid with a sweet, piercing agony that suddenly exploded into a wash of pleasure so intense that unconsciously she dug her nails into his back and sobbed aloud, crying his name, her body trembling and damp from the force of the exquisite, shattering ecstasy that he lavished upon her slim body.

Floating, drifting, almost dizzy from the pleasure he evoked, she lay there in the bed, savoring the feel of him, the jump his body gave when at last he, too, could bear the intensity no longer and spilled himself deep inside her.

And afterward there were no words between them, just silence and completeness and that half-drunk feeling that follows such acute pleasure. Replete and satiated, Nicole blindly turned her head into Christopher's shoulder, and with a promptness that was startling, like a child she fell asleep, her body still pressed against the long length of him.

Sleep was not so easy for Christopher. And having considerably more experience with the physical aspect of desire, he knew that tonight had been something beyond just a casual mating. Reflectively he stared down at Nicole's sleeping face. In sleep her features took on the sweet innocence of youth, the dark lashes lying like thick black fans against her skin, her mouth soft and tenderly curved, and the burnished hair waving gently across one cheek. Staring at her, he was conscious of the queerest sensations—puzzlement, because of the odd conflicting emotions she aroused, and possessiveness. She was his! And that was a strange notion coming as it did from a man for whom women were playthings—not even quite human. And buried deep there existed a certain amount of fondness—if not for Nicole Ashford, at least for Nick. Even now he could recall vividly the feel of that skinny little body pressed against him that night five years ago as they had left Beddington's Corner. He grinned in the darkness, remembering too her ferocious attack on the stableboy. What a small hellcat she had been. And if there was one thing he admired it was spirit. Without a doubt his Nick was one of the pluckiest little devils he'd ever known. And suddenly, inexplicably, thinking of the danger she had been in all those years on *La Belle Garce,* his arms tightened instinctively around her. He'd kill anyone who harmed her. Then he smiled to himself. Poor Nick, she was safe from everyone but himself.

Drowsily, his cheek dropped to rest on her hair. Well, he wasn't going to waste any more effort thinking about Nick, tonight. It never did any good letting your emotions get involved with women—they were amusing creatures and making love to them was a pleasant way of spending an evening or two. Just don't ever develop a tenderness for one, he thought sleepily; therein lay madness.

18

Nicole woke slowly the next morning. She lay in the bed not quite awake, her body and emotions satiated and at rest for the first time in many weeks. A soft smile on her lips, she stretched luxuriously and reached for the pillow that bore the imprint of Christopher's head.

At what time he had left, she had no idea, but she suspected it must have been near dawn. And judging from the faint light filtering into the room, it couldn't be too many minutes past that time right now. The area where he had lain still held a trace of warmth from his body. Her arms enfolded his pillow as if somehow it had become Christopher's big vital body. She was drowsy and relaxed, quite filled with contentment.

Her cheek resting on his pillow, she admitted to herself that she was in love with Christopher Saxon. And for some inexplicable reason this knowledge did not engender the horror and revulsion that it should have. Whatever the cost to herself, and no matter what heartache the future held, she could no longer deny it.

Almost shamefacedly she realized now that half her fury and dislike of Captain Saber had been a form of self-defense, an attempt to ignore the growing attraction she felt for him. Even taking sides against him with Allen had been only to hide from herself the uncertain yearnings of her heart.

A sad sort of smile flitting across her face, she shook her head as she remembered the other women that had loved him and the other nights of passion in his life. But last night was different, she thought fiercely. Frowning, she eyed his empty pillow. He had left her without any explanation. Resolutely she told herself that he wouldn't want his household buzzing with gossip that he had been found in her bed. The thought that he didn't want their liaison to be food for scandal comforted her somewhat.

She sat up and rang for Mauer, thrusting the covers aside. He wouldn't have departed yet if he was still holding to his original plan. She prayed most fervently that what had happened between them had changed his mind about the future.

After bathing hurriedly, with Mauer's help she slipped into a jonquil-yellow gown of soft muslin and dragged a brush quickly through her burnished-sable tresses. Impatiently she sat still only long enough for Mauer to thread a yellow silk ribbon through her shining curls.

Christopher *must* feel something for her—something beyond just the ordinary—she thought stubbornly. If after last night he treated her with cool contempt, she would absolutely *hate* him. Her feelings were too new, too fragile to bear rejection or even indifference. She needed reassurance, some little sign to let her know that last night had been special to him too.

Crossing the main hallway and seeing his baggage stacked neatly by the door, she quelled a sigh of relief. He hadn't gone yet, but the very sight of those packed bags was not propitious. He still meant to leave this morning, and she tried to convince herself that he would have an acceptable explanation—possibly he had not departed already because he was waiting to talk to her.

Nicole wanted passionately to believe that her sudden recognition of her love for him had engendered an equal recognition in him. She was ready to meet him more than halfway in *any* relationship that they might have. If he wanted her as his mistress she would accept it, knowing in time she could make him love her. But if he turned from her, she didn't think she would be able to bear such pain. She didn't want to hate him—she wanted most passionately to love him. And she was certain that he must feel *something* for her.

For a moment she stood in the hall, uncertain where to find him. Then as she took a hesitant step toward the library, Sanderson startled her by coming out of the dining room on the opposite side of the hallway.

Seeing her standing there, Sanderson said in greeting, "Good morning, Miss Nicole, you are up early indeed today!"

She flashed him an almost-happy smile and asked, "Have you seen Mr. Saxon? He hasn't left already, has he?"

"Oh, no! He won't be leaving for an hour or so yet. I've just served him breakfast. Will you join him?"

"Thank you, that's exactly what I'd like to do!"

As she came in a second later, Christopher looked up in surprise. She was looking exceptionally lovely this morning, he thought, a pretty flush in her cheeks, the bright sparkle in the topaz-dark eyes adding to her beauty. The jonquil-yellow gown brought out the gleaming hints of fire in the sable curls, and remembering that hair sprayed out across her pillow, he felt something tighten painfully deep inside.

An uncertain smile trembling on her lips, she walked slowly to her usual chair and shyly murmured, "Good morning," in Christopher's direction. Sanderson poured her a cup of the strong chicory-flavored coffee Christopher preferred, and then he departed, presumably to see after her breakfast.

Alone, they stared at each other from the opposite ends of the table, and Nicole was suddenly horribly aware that she couldn't think of a thing to say. What *did* one say to a man after having shared the night with him—especially after a night like last night, and particularly to a man like Christopher?

Christopher was dressed in buckskins and top boots in anticipation of the trip up the river to New Orleans, and taking a surreptitious look at him, she saw with dismay that his face wore a closed, shut-in expression that filled her with dread. Yet when she noticed at the same time the heavy-eyed look that denoted a sleepless night, a pleased little smile hovered at the corners of her mouth. She *knew* what caused that lack of sleep!

It was a secretive, satisfied sort of smile that curved her lips. Christopher recognized it and could only remember that it was exactly the same kind of smile her mother had worn when she was especially delighted with something— Annabelle had worn it quite frequently in those days prior to Christopher's betrayal.

Staring grimly at the soft curve of her lips, he was suddenly enraged at how easily he might have fallen in the same trap again. But that smile reminded him vividly and painfully of something he preferred not to think of and harshly he snapped, "Something amuses you? I could use a good laugh this morning."

She was startled at his ugly and sarcastic tone, and her smile vanished. "I wasn't smiling at anything in particular. It's just a lovely morning," she said. Wary of his mood and not knowing what had angered him, she sipped her coffee, wishing there were some way that she could disperse the dangerous currents she sensed in the room.

But Christopher was not to be denied the argument he was spoiling for, and he asked nastily, "Do you always smile just because its a lovely morning? Must you sit at the end of my table simpering like some half-demented idiot!"

Nicole's cup clattered against her saucer, her volatile temper flaring like a summer storm. Trying not to start an argument, yet not willing to ignore his provocative manner, she inquired levelly, "Are you always in such a foul temper first thing in the morning?"

"Can't you remember, Nick? It isn't that long since we were on *La Belle Garce.* Surely a few weeks hasn't made you forget what I am like after a night of whoring!" He snarled the last words, his anger at himself driving him. He was beyond reasonable thought; all he could assimilate was that Annabelle's daughter sat there before him— Annabelle's daughter, lovely, possessing a beauty and warmth that would have outshone Annabelle's shallow shell as effortlessly as a diamond would eclipse a glass bead.

He was terrified—and unable to trust his instincts, for they had betrayed him once already. He was floundering, and at the same time furious—furious that Nicole had awakened emotions he thought long dead, and furious that he could not judge accurately whether these emotions were real or false. He wanted most intensely to regain his usual indifference to women and to convince himself that last night had not happened.

At his ugly words something snapped inside Nicole. Seeing her dreams destroyed, stunned by his word *whoring,* she erupted into the worst tantrum of her entire life. "How dare you!" she choked. She was vibrating with the force of her anger, literally scintillating with it, and without thinking, she closed her hand around the fragile china cup that she had so recently set down. With a cry of outrage she hurled it willy-nilly at Christopher's head.

He ducked and the cup missed him, but some of the hot coffee splashed him as the cup sailed by. He, too, leaped to his feet, and they faced each other across the long expanse of the white linen-covered table.

"That will be enough of that!" he thundered, his temper barely leashed.

And Nicole's lips curled in a sneer as she spat, "You think so? I haven't even started!" With that, the saucer whipped by his head, and he barely dodged the heavy silver-plated pepper mill that swiftly followed it. He was so astounded and at a loss that he wasn't quite quick enough to miss the deadly aim of the matching saltceller, and it struck him in the stomach like a kick from a mule.

Nicole's rage added to her strength. Encompassed by

fury, she searched angrily for some other object to hurl at her tormentor. Her eyes alighted on the beautiful wrought-silver candelabrum that dominated the middle of the table, and with an oath that would have done one of the crew members proud, she hurled it in Christopher's direction. It missed its destination fortunately, but unfortunately it smashed into the wall just as Sanderson innocently walked into the room with Nicole's breakfast.

Nicole wasted no time and wrenched from the startled Sanderson the silver tray on which he carried her plate of eggs and bacon. With unerring aim she pitched it at Christopher. "Bastard!" she spat. The plate caught Christopher full in the chest, the eggs clinging to his shirt front until, rather gingerly, he flicked them off.

His eyes wide with disbelief, Sanderson watched Christopher casually dab with a napkin at the mess on his shirt and jacket. Calmly Christopher said, "You may leave now, Sanderson, Miss Nicole and I will finish with breakfast shortly."

Sanderson stared at Christopher, but he simply said, "As you wish, sir," and departed.

Silence reigned in the dining room. Christopher's calm words had pierced the red mist of Nicole's fury, and with slightly horrified eyes she surveyed the shambles.

Christopher eyed her warily. He had known spitfires before, but Nick undoubtedly took the prize. While one part of him was furious at her, another part of him was fighting with a desire to laugh. He didn't really blame Nick for her outburst. He had been on the prod for a fight from the moment he had awoken this morning and he had gotten it! And thinking of the ludicrous figure he cut, he asked, "Is the storm over or shall I run for cover?"

Nicole was ill. The fury had left her as quickly as it had come, and now she just wanted to crawl off someplace and die. Blindly she stumbled toward the door, but Christopher caught her arm. "Don't go, Nick," he said softly.

Her distress was so obvious that he was unaccountably moved. "Ah, Nick, I'm sorry. I shouldn't have said what I did." Smiling almost tenderly he continued, "I'm in the devil's own temper this morning, darling. Forget what I said just now and let's start again."

Nicole stared up at him consideringly, not trusting the coaxing note in his voice, or believing the warm light that flickered in his gold eyes. He had tricked her too many times in the past, and she couldn't forgive him for belittling something that had been a momentous occasion for her. Even though her first outburst of temper had abated, she was still very angry.

"No," she said quietly. "We won't start anew. You've made your attitude very clear. Things are exactly as they were yesterday afternoon. Last night was a mistake. You may be sure it won't happen again!"

Firmly she removed his arm and said politely as she walked to the door, "I hope you have a pleasant trip and I look forward to meeting Mrs. Eggleston—she was once a very good friend of mine." Then she was gone, leaving Christopher, his face pale and tight, gazing at the shut door with real dismay and not a little anger. He was left with the uncomfortable feeling that he had damaged something irretrievably. Uneasily he discovered that he wanted the chance to relive these past few minutes. But he quickly recovered himself and with an effort reminded himself of Annabelle's perfidies, and then with a spurt of temper he cursed all women—Nick most vehemently.

What was the matter with him? he mused later as the pirogue moved slowly upstream toward New Orleans. What the *hell* was happening to him? Nick was on his mind continually! And he discovered emotions he had thought slain by Annabelle's cruel actions awakening with a vengeance. He didn't want *anyone* to get behind the hard front that concealed the inner man. And he decided resolutely that he would set Nick at a distance. He was not going to be beguiled into falling in love with her, not at his age, and certainly not with *her!* During the remainder of the journey to New Orleans he proceeded to arm himself against Nick. Meticulously he erected in his mind a very high, very cold barrier between them, and he was firmly convinced that he now had the situation well in hand.

Believing that, he was very pleased with himself when he went to call on Mrs. Eggleston that same afternoon. The Dumas family was gone for the day and Mrs. Eggleston was enjoying a respite from her willful charge. Miss Dumas had been particularly trying the past week, and Mrs. Eggleston was almost ready to sink her pride and take whatever Christopher had to offer.

Christopher's tale of Nicole's plight touched Mrs. Eggleston and she was eager to accept his employment.

She sat mesmerized as Christopher spun out his story of Nicole's adventure. "That Nicole Ashford!" she finally said with a twinkle in the faded blue eyes. "She was always a little hoyden. And while I am very shocked that

202

any young lady of her impeccable background would do anything so unseemly, I must admit I am not surprised. She was made most unhappy by the deaths of her family, and her guardians, the Markhams, were not very kindhearted people. Certainly, I shall be most happy and more than willing to chaperon her."

Shaking her white head, with an approving eye on Christopher that made him decidedly uncomfortable, she continued, "You are so good! And Nicole is most fortunate that it was you who discovered her masquerade. How terrible it would have been if she had fallen into the hands of some unscrupulous monster who would have taken advantage of what was, I am positive, only childish rebellion."

Feeling even more uncomfortable and coming as close to squirming in his chair as was possible for one of his nature, Christopher brushed her compliments aside. "It was my privilege, and, I assure you, nothing of great magnitude."

"Oh, but Christopher!" she cried protestingly. "What if she had found herself in the clutches of someone who would have"—her voice dropping to a mere whisper of horror—"destroyed her innocence? It doesn't bear thinking of! She is most, *most* fortunate that you were the one. Anything could have happened to her!"

Christopher had never been in a more invidious position in his life, and hastily he turned the subject. "Yes, well that is all behind her now."

He drew a long breath and shifted in his chair as he began the delicate part of his deception. Briskly he said, "And naturally I want to see her restored to her family. I think it important that we see that she is returned to England, despite this unfortunate war, just as quickly as possible."

A little pucker of worry on her forehead, Mrs. Eggleston offered hesitantly, "Christopher, I don't believe it will be that simple."

Hating himself for leading her so blatantly exactly where he wanted, yet feeling strongly the necessity for it, Christopher put an expression of great surprise on his face. "Why, what do you mean, madame?" Then, deliberately misunderstanding her, he conceded, "Of course, we shall have to see that she is brought up to scratch socially, but you shall be able to do that!"

Her frown growing, Mrs. Eggleston said slowly, "I wasn't thinking so much of that as I was of the scandal that will result if it is learned that Nicole has been sailing disguised as a boy on a ship these past years." Earnestly, she continued, "My dear, it just will not do! She would be completely ruined. We simply cannot allow that to happen!"

"What do you suggest?" Christopher asked in an expressionless tone.

She glanced at him nervously. Feeling that if she hadn't left Nicole, this wouldn't have happened, she was willing to do anything to set things right—even tell a lie, which went strongly against her principles. Because she didn't want Christopher to think she was the kind of woman to whom deceit came easily, she toyed with the worn lace about her neck and finally said with a rush, "We could tell a lie—we could say that she has been with me!"

Disliking himself very much, Christopher expertly took the conversation away from her and said crisply, "Yes, of course. I should have thought of it. Let me think of an appropriate tale, and then if it doesn't offend you overmuch, we shall use it to cover Nick's misadventures."

Thankful to have the decision made for her, she smiled gently and inquired, "How soon shall I give notice to the Dumas?"

"Today," he stated bluntly. "I want you out of this house by evening."

When she showed signs of being obstinate, he quickly convinced her that time was imperative, that every day Nick did without her chaperonage the more improper it was. Her tender heart was moved by the thought of poor little Nicole's possible disgrace, and without further argument she began to pack.

She left a note apologizing for departing from their service so abruptly and begged that they forgive her. Leaving in this manner went against her nature, but with Christopher giving her no chance to change her mind, she was swiftly and effectively whisked out of the Dumas's house.

Christopher and Mrs. Eggleston remained in New Orleans only two more days, attending to various tasks. He left off the measurements taken by Mauer at the dressmaker's and by guile and coaxing convinced Mrs. Eggleston that if they were to do the thing properly, she, too, would need an entire wardrobe.

She protested at first, genuinely horrified at the idea of any gentleman buying her gowns, but Christopher, so very innocently agreeing, went on to say. "Of course, you are right. I hadn't thought of how you would feel. I just hope that no one comments on Nick's rather extensive wardrobe and believes that you have denied yourself for her. Remember, no one will know of your straitened circumstances, or that you have been earning your own living. But there is this, though, so that there is not a great deal of difference between you, we should cancel some of these gowns I've ordered for Nick and have some different ones made up. You know, something more serviceable and durable."

Thinking of how much poor little Nicole had done without all these years, Mrs. Eggleston felt absolutely wretched, as Christopher knew she would. Searching Christopher's carefully bland face, she said distressfully, "Oh, no! I don't think that will be necessary. Little Nicole deserves something gay and frivolous after her boy's garb."

Christopher said nothing, and after struggling with her conscience for a few minutes longer, she murmured weakly, "Rather than have little Nicole do without, perhaps I should have just a gown or two to fill out my wardrobe." Her eyes brightening, she added, "And certainly I shall reimburse you from the very fine salary you are paying me."

Hiding a grin, Christopher watched her walk briskly to the back of the dressmaker's fashionable little shop. While Mrs. Eggleston was busy being measured and being shown swatches of material for her new gowns, Christopher had a very satisfactory conversation with Madame Colette, the modiste. By the time Mrs. Eggleston discovered his underhanded methods it would be too late, for she would find several more items of clothing than she expected—and what can one do with garments that have been made exclusively for oneself except wear them?

Besides seeing to the ladies' wardrobes, Christopher spent several hours with his banker and his business agent, discussing the conduct of his affairs for the six months he would be out of the country. And he managed to see Jason Savage for a few hours in the evening before leaving for the plantation.

After a pleasant dinner Jason said with a certain amount of satisfaction, "It appears you are wasting little time and that your plan is well on its way to success."

Christopher grimaced. "Oh, yes. I'm becoming adept at gulling little unsuspecting old ladies."

His eyebrow raising humorously, Jason asked, "Finding it heavy going?"

"Very!" Christopher said with feeling. "I didn't think using her would disturb me, but I find that it does. The only comfort I can discover is that it is for a worthy cause and she will benefit from it."

Those few words pleased Jason a great deal. It was risky, what he was doing, and even though he had Jake's report on Saxon and his own instincts to guide him, it was a relief to find that Christopher was not quite as calloused and unscrupulous as he appeared. Jason wondered exactly what sort of man Christopher really was. A gentleman of good family, a privateer, a plantation owner, a gambler, an associate of Lafitte's and now . . . patriot or spy? Which was the truth of the man? His green eyes wandering thoughtfully over the hard, yet almost unhappy face, Jason finally decided that there were hidden depths, places sealed away from others in the man. Time would tell how wise he had been in enlisting Saxon's aid. Putting aside such thoughts, he asked Christopher, "How soon do you think you'll be able to depart? You must give me a certain amount of warning, for I have to find a ship that is willing to risk running the British blockade of the Gulf."

"I will still have to hold out for at least a month, but weather permitting, I think we can leave by the middle of February. Nick is not quite the urchin I feared. And Mrs. Eggleston and I shall have the six weeks at sea to finish her transformation. The weather is going to be more of an uncertainty than Nick's progress."

Jason nodded, remembering with a shudder his own winter crossing some years ago. "Yes, I agree. I shall, though, start casting around for a ship's captain willing to risk British capture to take you. There is, after all, no reason to wait till the last minute."

Christopher shrugged. "It may be that your task and mine shall be completed at the same time. Having to leave a week or two earlier than originally planned would not be amiss."

"Yes. I cannot tell you how uneasy I am at the delay, assuming I had the ship and captain at my fingertips this instant," Jason admitted honestly.

"I thought we had decided that there would be no determined effort before the fall at the earliest, and that is saying Napoleon is finally beaten in Europe," Christopher said.

"Oh, you are probably right, but I dislike uncertainty," Jason complained with a wry twist to his lips.

Christopher merely smiled in commiseration; he was not particularly overjoyed with the difficulties ahead of him. The venture was filled with *too* much uncertainty. "If we had more to go on and a particular person to seek the information from, I'd like it better myself. But as we don't, I'll just have to blunder on my own and hope all comes out right in the end."

"True," Jason murmured unenthusiastically.

"Come, now," Christopher said exasperatedly, "if I could outsail the British, which I could, I see no reason to doubt my ability to outfox them on land." Grinning he added, "They have no brains anyway!"

Dryly Jason remarked, "You forget, I am part English and you are totally of English blood."

"Yes, but you see, we had the good sense to realize how lacking in clear thinking they are, and we quickly allied ourselves with our new homeland," Christopher shot back, mocking amusement dancing in the depths of the gold eyes.

Jason only grunted, "I was born here."

The gleam of amusement increased as Christopher said quickly, "So was Benedict Arnold!"

Laughing out loud, Jason shook his head. "You have a ready tongue—and a telling point, I must admit." But then his laughter died and Jason asked, "Speaking of traitors—how did you manage to desert Lafitte without being branded one?"

For a second Christopher paused, not exactly pleased with the turn of the conversation, but then with a shrug he said, "I was never involved in the smuggling; I am not trying to dissociate myself from Jean to excuse myself. I was a privateer. Granted I knew the items from my prizes would be smuggled into New Orleans, and I suppose that made me technically a smuggler, but I know little of that portion of Jean's activities. Jean knows I would not betray him, even if Claiborne were to raise the reward for him one hundred times. Jean is a good friend to me and to Louisiana. He feels that he is offering something the people want, and perhaps he is. Certainly he does not lack for buyers."

"But yet he breaks the law with every load of contraband that flows into the city," Jason argued grimly. "And, Christopher, Claiborne is not going to put up with it."

"I know," Christopher agreed soberly. "I told Jean

when I left that he, too, should pull out, but he will not. And in a showdown between them, I'm not so sure that Jean wouldn't emerge the winner."

"Perhaps, but he grows more flagrant with every day, and Claiborne cannot be expected to overlook such outrageous behavior forever."

It was on this rather strained note that they parted.

19

In the week since the disastrous confrontation in the dining room, Nicole had managed to master her hurt fury. She had come to realize bitterly that Christopher would never allow any woman to mean anything to him; she resolved to put all thought of him out of her mind. She concentrated grimly on allowing Mauer to transform her into a lady.

"Do not stride about like a man, *ma chère! Non*—do not sit in the chair like a mushroom, *petite, s'il vous plaît!* You must move gracefully, like a flower in the breeze— *oui! Non, non!* Not *that* way—like this!" And so it went. At first hurt and angry, she rebelled, storming from the room, muttering a black curse under her breath, only to return shortly, contrite and somewhat ashamed at her outburst.

Higgins had remained behind this time, for Christopher had not quite trusted Nicole after the scene in the dining room. Not so strangely, Nicole was almost content in the company of the onetime first mate of *La Belle Garce*. Higgins was familiar to her, and she had always liked him when they had been shipmates together. With Higgins she could reminisce over events of the past five years, laugh at remembered pranks of the crew; mostly she could be herself. It was with Higgins that she could sit on the floor with her long legs crossed in a decidedly unladylike fashion, winning and losing huge sums of money, all imaginary, as they diced.

Unfortunately Christopher and Mrs. Eggleston arrived one afternoon when the two were particularly engrossed in the dice. They were sitting on the floor in front of the fire. The rug was rolled back slightly so that the dice could bounce and slide with ease on the hardwood floor. Nicole, leaning forward eagerly, her eyes intent on the latest throw by Higgins, was unaware of their arrival. At the sound of Christopher's icy, "Are we disturbing you?" Higgins, a guilty look on his face, leaped to his feet, muttering something about how he had better see to the unpacking, and disappeared with remarkable haste.

Making no attempt to rise to her feet, Nicole leaned back on her hands, and slanting a provocative look up at Christopher's thunderous face, she murmured, "Oh! You're back! I wish we could have finished the game. I'm losing right now and I owe him half a million pounds."

His lips tightening, yet fighting back a regrettable desire to laugh at her outrageous behavior, he hauled her to her feet and said to Mrs. Eggleston, "You see, your task will not be an easy one."

And Mrs. Eggleston, regarding with dismay the tall young goddess before her, put aside forever all ideas of "little" Nicole. But then seeing the very becoming and stylish gown Nicole was wearing, a soft green finely spun wool that clung gently to her slender body before falling into a graceful full skirt, and the burnished hair arranged so tastefully in soft curls around her shoulders, she was somewhat reassured that Nicole was not a complete hoyden. And Mrs. Eggleston was thankful that Nicole *looked* a lady.

Her head held slightly to one side, a gentle smile on her lips, Mrs. Eggleston said quietly, "Hello, dear Nicole. Who would have guessed when we said good-bye that day at Ashland that we would be meeting once again in this new country? And I must say, how very like both your mother and your father you have grown to look."

Shrugging out of Christopher's grasp, Nicole grinned at her, an impish grin that hid the sheer delight at seeing her old friend again. "You were, as I remember, always very tactful," she said.

But despite her smile Mrs. Eggleston was extremely tired from the journey, and her conscience was still uneasy about the lies they were going to tell!

Seeing the weary droop to her thin little shoulders, Nicole walked quickly over to her, and placing a warm arm around Mrs. Eggleston's frail body, suggested, "Will you let me show you to your room? I'm certain you must be longing to put your feet up before the fire, which I shall see is lit this instant."

"Oh, yes. I would indeed!" Mrs. Eggleston replied with heartfelt relief.

"Perhaps even a cup of tea, too, would not be remiss?" Nicole tempted her.

"Oh, my, that would be most delightful. Dear Nicole, so thoughtful and so kind of you."

Christopher watched this little scene with sardonic

amusement. But he was satisfied that the two women hadn't taken an instant aversion to each other, and he was devoutly grateful that they had discovered Nick in no greater transgression than dicing with his valet! Higgins had better have a good excuse for the little tableau discovered just a few minutes ago—it could have so easily given Mrs. Eggleston a distaste for Nick and ruined his plans completely!

But Mrs. Eggleston, escorted by Nicole, was pleased to see that dear Nicole had not lost the warm spontaneity that she had possessed as a child. It was always so much pleasanter to instruct a pupil one was fond of, and Mrs. Eggleston was very fond of Nicole Ashford. She was sure she could teach Nicole everything she would need to know.

Nicole, too, was almost happily resigned to the first step in her eventual return to England. She had secretly dreaded meeting Mrs. Eggleston again. She did not know what she would have done if Mrs. Eggleston had snubbed her.

She realized now how outrageous her behavior had been. Looking back on it, she wondered at her own temerity and was deep inside overwhelmingly grateful that Christopher was, for whatever reasons, smoothing her path back to England.

Suddenly and unaccountably depressed, she gave a tiny sigh as she showed Mrs. Eggleston to her room.

It was a room admirably suited for an elderly lady—a cozy room, with soft pink walls; a thick carpet of muted pinks, blues, and greens on the floor; several small comfortable chairs in rose damask; and a very inviting bed draped in the palest pink imaginable.

The fire had already been lit by the efficient Galena, and after helping Mrs. Eggleston with her outer garments, Galena inquired in her soft voice if Madame would care for something hot to drink.

Nicole left Mrs. Eggleston in her room after seeing that she was comfortable and tea was prepared. "I'll see you at dinner," Nicole said, tactfully withdrawing to allow the older woman some time to rest and to gather her thoughts after the long journey.

Some minutes later, sipping an excellently steeped cup of tea, her feet resting comfortably on a small velvet footstool, Mrs. Eggleston stared thoughtfully at the fire. She was not as entirely satisfied with Christopher's story as she pretended. She had known him from a child and knew, as clearly as if he had told her himself, that he was lying. Some of what he had related to her, she was certain, was true, but she knew that Christopher was shrewd enough to include a trace of truth in his tale.

But where did the lie begin? And why? With an ease that would have startled Christopher, almost absentmindedly she considered the possibility that Christopher had dishonored Nicole. Sighing, she set her cup down. She didn't want to think that he was capable of such a thing, and remembering with a smile his treatment of herself, she pushed the thought aside as unworthy.

Yet, there was definitely some tension, some attraction between her two young people. After all, she had known them both from the cradle, and she had watched both change from toddlers into a young man and a young woman on the threshold of adulthood. She shook her head slowly and wished for the millionth time that she and the Colonel had not been away when Annabelle had told her spiteful story.

Mrs. Eggleston had known from the first moment she had heard the rumors that they could not be completely true, and remembering the almost gentle, sensitive youth Christopher had been and comparing the wary, hard man he had become, she hardened her heart against the dead Annabelle. She had always been aware that Annabelle was an unprincipled little harlot, but Mrs. Eggleston would never have guessed just how unprincipled until that terrible summer. That was all behind them, she thought thankfully. Now Christopher and Nicole were both adult, and perhaps something good and worthy would come out of this odd, yet providential meeting of the three of them so far from England! Her mind relatively satisfied, she dozed happily before the fire, truly at ease for the first time since she had left Beddington's Corner all those years before.

If Mrs. Eggleston was at ease and Nicole resigned, Christopher was neither, for he knew that what lay ahead was not going to be as simple as it appeared to the two women. He was satisfied, though, with the way events were going—except for the situation between him and Nick.

And in the weeks that followed he was to curse again and again his growing preoccupation with Nicole. He was continually thrown into her company. Granted, Mrs. Eggleston was there beaming at them as Christopher would gracefully seat Nicole and then for a few minutes exchange the required polite conversation, only to have to do it again because Mrs. Eggleston felt Nicole had been too stiff, too unbending in her movements.

Smiling, her blue eyes kind, Mrs. Eggleston instructed, "My dear, you must learn to relax when in the company of gentlemen. Do not . . . er . . . poker up that way. Now we'll try it again. You meet in the hall as before and Christopher will then escort you in to be seated."

And so they did it again, and this time Nicole was able to move less stiltedly, yet all the time unbearably conscious of Christopher's presence.

Grimly, Nicole threw all her efforts into eradicating the past five years. She learned to smile with just the right degree of friendliness at Christopher as he pretended to solicit her hand for a dance; she became adept at making polite conversation as the three of them dined together; and under Mrs. Eggleston's guidance she overcame the intricacies of afternoon tea. Her scholastic education was not neglected either, although how much she could be expected to absorb in the time they had was questionable. And as Mrs. Eggleston had commented, young ladies were not particularly scrutinized for their well-educated minds! It was their graceful movements, their polite conversation, their pretty faces, and their delightful manners that counted in polite society.

It quickly became second nature for Nicole to expect the services of Mauer and Galena and the deferences shown by the other servants. And only occasionally did she yearn for the freedom that had been hers such a short time ago. But this way of life, too, had its compensations, and Mrs. Eggleston's company made the situation with Christopher much easier to bear. And as the days passed and she exhibited more and more naturally the manners and conversation that Mrs. Eggleston felt were imperative, their social sphere at Thibodaux House widened.

The easiest, and by far the pleasantest, was the first time Hans and his young wife were invited to tea. With a grace and charm worthy of the role she played, Nicole made them at ease, acting just as if she really were Christopher's ward. Dinner at a nearby neighboring plantation was next, and despite a certain nervousness at first, she passed without conscious effort.

Christopher viewed the emerging Nicole with half-admiring, half-hostile eyes, for while he was satisfied with the way she was quickly becoming a model of the well-born young woman, he detested the apparent ease with which she accomplished it. Watching the way she smiled at him, as if he were nothing more than the guardian they

213

pretended, he was reminded painfully of her mother's deceit. So had Annabelle pretended in front of others, smiling at him so disinterestedly and then sneaking away to let him rain passionate kisses on her willing mouth. They were both alike, he thought contemptuously.

Yet, lying awake night after night, knowing she slept just down the wide hall from him, he wasn't so sure. During the day he could cloak himself in indifference, playing the game for Mrs. Eggleston's benefit, but the nights were long, and he found sleep particularly elusive, especially those evenings Mrs. Eggleston insisted upon Nicole's ballroom graces being perfected. It was both an exquisite pleasure and a painful torment to hold her in his arms as they circled around the small ballroom that Thibodaux House possessed.

For Nicole, too, the intimacy of Christopher's arms about her waist, her hand clasped in his, and their bodies almost touching, was an agony she didn't think she could bear for any great length of time. Fortunately Mrs. Eggleston did not believe in spending many hours on such frivolities.

The day finally came when Christopher, after consulting with Mrs. Eggleston, decided that they were ready for New Orleans. Upon their arrival, Christopher immediately called on Jason Savage. Polite conversation quickly covered, Jason said, "You must have read my mind, for I sent you a message yesterday requesting you to return to New Orleans if Miss Ashford was at all presentable. I take it she is?"

Christopher nodded. "Yes, I believe so. At any rate I felt that whatever deficiencies were still to be eradicated, it could be done here in the city. She needs to be out amongst society and not just going through the motions in front of Mrs. Eggleston and myself."

"Excellent! In your absence I have made several arrangements that I hope, will meet with your approval. I must apologize for one which we did not discuss, and I trust you will not consider that I have been rather high-handed."

A certain amount of wariness flashing across his face, Christopher asked quietly, "What is it?"

The two men were seated in the library at the Savage town house, Jason behind his large desk and Christopher across from him. Jason picked up one of the papers from the desk and handed it to Christopher.

It was a short letter, and it took only a moment for Christopher to scan its contents. Keeping his features carefully bland, he said, "So, I am to go as an unofficial representative of the United States. What, may I ask, did you tell Monroe to get him to agree?"

Smiling, Jason leaned back in his chair. "I explained that I wanted to send my own representative to England, to have someone on the scene as it were, but that such an individual would be much more effective if he had some sanction from the State Department. And as you see, the secretary of state agreed with me."

A wry expression about his mouth, Christopher said thoughtfully, "I can see to a degree that this will serve considerably better than my own plan—except that now I will definitely be branded in the American camp. Before there would have been suspicion of that, but with a letter of introduction from the secretary of state of the United States there will be no doubt on which side I have laid my wager."

"Yes, I realize that. But this does not change our plans in any way, it only strengthens what I felt was a weak spot. You still have to accomplish the same task."

"I agree," Christopher interrupted quietly. "Official sanction will indeed pave my way, and perhaps if the English believe that I am nothing more than an observer, they will not be surprised when I ask certain questions. Hopefully, if I am very clever, they will not look too far beneath the surface. These letters of introduction Monroe writes of will make my task both easier on one hand and more difficult on the other."

Dryly, Jason commented, "I'm sure you will rise to the occasion."

"Naturally. Perhaps it will even impart an added appeal—running a rig before the British is something I have grown very adept at."

"It will certainly give credence to your escorting and guardianship of Nicole Ashford."

"Yes, that too," Christopher said flatly, and Jason wondered at the lack of enthusiasm in his voice and the bleak look that passed swiftly across the dark, mobile face.

With apparent idleness Jason changed the subject, drawling, "As you have just returned to the city, I take it you did not attend the Lafitte brothers' sale at the Temple?"

"No, I did not," Christopher returned lazily, but his eyes suddenly narrowed and shadowed, he inquired, "Why this sudden curiosity about my connection with

215

Lafitte?" His voice hardening slightly, Christopher added, "I am not a tool that will be used against Jean."

A grimace of regret twisting his handsome face, Jason admitted, "You can't blame me for testing you, especially not in view of what happened at this latest sale."

His attention fully on Jason, his features betraying nothing except a certain alertness, Christopher asked, "What did happen? Something beyond the normal, I take it?"

"Oh, yes! Very much beyond the normal," Jason grated. "Lafitte went a little too far this time—a temporary inspector of the revenue, a man by the name of Stout, and a force of twelve men were sent to stop the sale. Unfortunately they were ambushed by Lafitte's cutthroats, and Stout was killed and two others mortally wounded. The remainder are prisoners at Lafitte's stronghold on Grand Terre. And as you can imagine, the governor is beside himself with fury—and I don't blame him. Lafitte's actions are an outrage to New Orleans and Louisiana."

"There are others who would disagree."

Sharply Jason glanced at Christopher. "You?"

With his lips quirking in a smile of self-derision, Christopher murmured, "Oh, no, not I. Jean has become too closely linked with the pirates and, as you say, cutthroats at Grand Terre. He has changed from the days when the smuggling was done on a small scale and with a certain amount of respectability attached to it. I've warned him that his day is over if he will not change, but he turns me a deaf ear."

"That is indeed unfortunate. There are many admirable traits in your Jean Lafitte." Jason hesitated and then he asked, "Would you consider going to Grand Terre and trying to convince Lafitte to release the revenue men he holds . . . those that are still alive?"

"I rather expected that request," Christopher confessed wryly.

"You'll do it?"

Christopher shrugged. "Let's just say that I have business of my own on Grand Terre and it will not inconvenience me to convey your request to Jean. I will not promise more—indeed, I *cannot* promise more."

"Very well. That will have to do," Jason conceded grudgingly.

Christopher, believing the meeting over, started to rise from his chair, but Jason waved him to stay. "There was a reason other than Monroe's letter of introduction that prompted me to send for you," Jason began, "but I'm afraid I let our conversation stray from its main point. I have made arrangements with a Dutch ship for you and the others to sail in about ten days' time. The ship is the *Scheveningen*. I am familiar with both the captain and the ship; you should have as pleasant a journey as possible this time of year."

"You don't leave me much time to see Lafitte do you?"

"No. Your trip to England is more important than seeing him. If it causes too many problems, concentrate on preparing to sail."

A gleam of speculation in his gold eyes, Christopher asked, "I don't suppose that while I am away at Grand Terre, you and your lovely wife would consider taking Nicole and Mrs. Eggleston under your wing? After all, they know no one in the city, and Nicole should be out socially."

Jason flashed him a look of amusement shot with exasperation. Finally he said in a tone of derision, "I'll give you this, you're very quick to take advantage of a situation! Yes, damnit, Catherine and I will see to Nicole's further education."

Openly grinning, Christopher rose to leave. "Nicole won't destroy your credit with New Orleans society." He added roguishly, "Of course, I would not trust her where games of chance are played—she seems to rather like gambling with my valet!"

Jason closed his eyes in anguish, visualizing the consternation if Nicole should invade the gaming rooms set aside for the gentlemen. "You had better bring Nicole and Mrs. Eggleston to dinner tonight. Then I will let you know if I dare give her my patronage."

"Very well," Christopher agreed amiably. "What time shall we arrive?"

"Around seven or so. And I hope I haven't destroyed my standing with my wife by inviting last-minute guests. Good-bye—I *almost* look forward to meeting your ward."

Whistling softly and as close to being satisfied as was possible in his current position, Christopher walked quickly to his own house. Flinging off his caped greatcoat, he joined the ladies in the small salon near the rear of the house.

A fire on the hearth dissipated the slight hint of dampness that managed to invade the houses of New Orleans in the winter. Nicole was standing and staring out a pair of French doors that opened onto the normally inviting bricked courtyard, and Mrs. Eggleston was seated on a low, rose-damask sofa, her hands busy with some needlework. Both women glanced over at him as he entered, and Nicole, watching him as he strode across the room to sit beside Mrs. Eggleston, thought it unfair that the very sight of his tall figure could cause her blood to race so crazily. She despised this weakness of hers where he was concerned and wished desperately that he possessed a squint-eyed and pockmarked visage; then perhaps she would be able to combat the physical attraction that continually gnawed at her. Wistfully she admitted to herself that, since Mrs. Eggleston's arrival, he had been all that was polite, treating her with an indifference and careless arrogance that hurt and yet enraged at the same time. If only she could forget those moments in his arms, forget that his long, hard body had taught hers the exquisite pleasure of being possessed by him. If she were still the untouched virgin Mrs. Eggleston assumed, it would not have been so painful, but now she knew the magic his mouth could arouse, and it was an intolerable form of torture to have him act as if they were almost strangers. But what else could she have expected from him, she wondered sadly.

Christopher slanted her an appraising glance, taking in with appreciation the gown of deep Prussian blue that fitted her tall, slender shape admirably. Her hair was in loose ringlets that brushed her shoulders, and in the diffused light of the room there was no hint of red, just a dusky wealth of curls. Her eyes were veiled by the demurely lowered sable lashes, and he wondered how she was going to take his latest news.

She took the information about dinner this evening and the fact that he would be away for a few days without so much as a flutter of those long lashes, but at the news that they would sail within ten days, her eyes flew to his.

"Ten days," she said in a small voice. "Will we be ready by then?"

"Oh, yes, my love," Mrs. Eggleston broke in encouragingly. "You have nothing to fear that you will give yourself away—and as Mr. Savage and dear Mrs. Savage have offered to take us into society, you shall have a splendid opportunity to perfect your manners." She added with a smile, "*If* they need it!"

There was nothing more for Nicole to say, and with a shrug she said carelessly, "If you say so."

Watching her closely, Christopher couldn't tell exactly how the news affected her; she was becoming extremely practiced in hiding her emotions. For a brief second he longed irrationally for one of "young Nick's" darkling looks to be flung at him. This fashionably attired doll that had taken Nick's place irritated him. He knew he should be overjoyed at the transformation, but instead he was angry at it. And because he knew his thoughts were illogical and ridiculous, he was angry at himself. With relief he viewed the unexpected trip to Grand Terre; perhaps there he could find a solution to the situation in which he found himself. Bleakly he hoped so.

Dinner at the Savage's passed off very well. Catherine, a vision in a pale lavender gown that intensified her deep violet eyes, immediately established a warm rapport with Mrs. Eggleston. Nicole suffered a sudden and appalling attack of acute shyness, but she soon found herself responding to the gentle flow of conversation that Catherine kept running throughout the evening.

Leaving the gentlemen to their after-dinner brandies and tobacco, Catherine ushered the other two women into a spacious sitting room decorated in pleasing shades of gold, her mind very busy with conjecture about the relationship between Nicole and Christopher.

What a beautiful girl! Catherine thought with a slight twinge of envy when she compared Nicole's statuesque body to her own petite one. But then she smiled—small women, like herself, invariably wanted to be tall goddesses, and tall women, like Nicole, probably wished to be something else. She wondered which Christopher Saxon preferred.

When their guests had departed and she was preparing for bed, Catherine commented on Nicole to Jason. Jason, lounging in an emerald robe that matched his eyes, was watching her as she brushed her curling black hair. She made an entrancing sight before her mirror, the heavy swath of hair hanging to the still narrow waist—despite the birth of five children. Glimpsing her curvaceous body through her gossamer night rail, Jason wasn't paying much attention to her words until Catherine said in a troubled tone, "Nicole Ashford is one of the loveliest young women I have ever met. I hope that Christopher Saxon does well by her. I wouldn't want her to get hurt—you men can be such unthinking devils!"

Crossing swiftly to her side, his face suddenly very serious, Jason took her into his arms. "I thought you had long since changed your opinion of me."

"Oh, I *have* darling! I didn't mean as you are now, but I can't help remembering how unhappy and miserable you made me at one time. I wouldn't wish for her to endure such pain."

Jason shrugged his broad shoulders. "They'll have to work out their own differences. All I care about is you." Staring down into her face, he muttered thickly, "I love you, Catherine—so much, so *very* much. And right now all I want is to make love to you." Then he bent his dark head and kissed her urgently, and Catherine promptly forgot about Nicole Ashford and set herself to the far more agreeable task of proving to her husband that she entirely reciprocated his sentiments.

20

Approaching Grand Terre in a pirogue, Christopher sensed the difference in the atmosphere even before he sighted the islands. There was nothing tangible to strengthen his feeling that his approach was being watched by hostile eyes, yet instinctively he knew that behind the scrubby foliage Baratarian lookouts surveyed his passage. As he splashed ashore, the same wave of suspicious belligerence hit him, even though outwardly the island appeared the same.

He had discarded his elegant clothing and was once again dressed as Captain Saber. He had not bothered to shave for two days and his face was shadowed with the beginnings of a beard.

No one stopped him as he walked to Lafitte's mansion, but again there was a disturbing feeling of surveillance that told far better than words that the pirates themselves were uneasy about this latest clash with the governor's men. Gambling and whoring still went on, judging from the squeals and laughter coming from the brothels he passed, and the bay was filled with as many ships as ever, but there was undeniably an atmosphere of waiting—that and hostility.

There were changes at the calaboose; a contingent of armed guards patrolled the area, and Christopher had no doubt that Stout's men were held prisoner there. Armed men, Dominque You among them, also slowed his progress to Lafitte's house, but again no one halted him, many no doubt recognizing him as Captain Saber.

Jean greeted him affably, but there was an unfamiliar air of alert watchfulness. Knowing he would gain little by making polite conversation, Christopher asked wryly, "I suppose you know why I am here?"

Lafitte gave a careless shrug. "But of course, *mon ami.* I can think of only one reason why you have returned at this moment, unless you have come to inquire about the spy from *La Belle Garce?*"

Christopher shook his head.

"Ah, I thought not. You have come to seek the release of the governor's men, have you not?"

Risking a smile, Christopher inquired, "Is there anything you don't know?"

His eyes hard, Lafitte said softly, "There are many things I do not know. What I don't know about you, *mon ami,* is how deeply you sit in Claiborne's pocket."

The smile wiped from his face, Christopher blazed angrily, "Oh, for God's sake, you do not believe that I would change my coat so readily!"

Again Lafitte shrugged. "Who knows? It has happened before."

Christopher eyed him assessingly, for once uncertain in his dealings with the man. Lafitte met his stare, the black eyes revealing little. Finally Christopher said quietly, "If that is your attitude, I have nothing to say." He waited a second, and as Lafitte made no response, he rose and asked, "Am I free to leave?"

Rather pensively, Lafitte regarded him, and then with a half-embarrassed, half-angry expression on his face, he muttered, "Sit down! Do not be in such a hurry, *mon ami.*"

Wary now himself, Christopher sank back down in his chair, but curiosity compelled him to inquire, "Do you really believe Claiborne has bought me?"

A snort greeted his words and Lafitte growled gently, "If I did, *mon ami,* you would not be sitting where you are now—you would not have set foot on Grand Terre."

Knowing it was unwise, but unable to help himself, his gold eyes gleaming with mockery, Christopher taunted, "You think you could stop me?"

Lafitte looked undecided whether to be angry or amused, but amusement won and he let out a bark of harsh laughter. "One thing that I have always admired about you, Saber, is your arrogance. And no, I'm not at all certain I could stop you. Maybe yes, maybe no— who knows? But the question does not arise. You are here and I bear you no animosity."

Relaxing slightly, Christopher ventured, "Will you listen to what I have to say?"

"Bah! I know what you have come here for. You are here to beg the release of the governor's men."

"All right, so what if I am?" Christopher returned levelly. "Someone has to negotiate for their return—why not me?"

"Ah, very well then, we talk, but I tell you, Saber, I

am very, *very* displeased with your so pious and sancti-monious Claiborne."

"Jean, you broke the law—you are still breaking the law—and you cannot blame the governor for trying to put a stop to your activities."

Enraged, his black eyes flashing, Lafitte leaped to his feet. "How can you say so? What law do I break? A law passed by your too-fat American businessmen so that they can monopolize the trade? I give you this for your law!" Lafitte boasted, snapping his fingers in the air. "Me, I sell better and cheaper goods to the citizens of New Orleans, and for that I am outlawed! Tell me why the Americans should be favored and why I should pay an importation tax on my goods?"

Grimly Christopher said, "I'm not here to debate with you—I am here to convince you to release the gover-nor's men to me."

Sulkily, Lafitte muttered, "Why should I? They make good hostages."

"You are a fool if you believe that!" Christopher snapped, his gold eyes blazing with exasperation. "Lis-ten, Jean, this time you have gone too far! You have killed three men in the Revenue Service! Do you think Claiborne is going to sit still for that? He's bound to go to the legislature for troops and money to wipe you out. If you release the men, it will soothe some tempers and appear that you are not just some ordinary pirate—murdering and holding for ransom anyone who crosses you."

Lafitte's eyes were sly as he murmured, "I do not think Claiborne will get far with his requests. Gold, *mon ami,* in the right pockets has a way of making certain men in the legislature deaf to the governor's pleas."

His temper rising, Christopher snarled, "Very well, bribe your way out of it—this time! But I warn you, your day is past, Jean. Law and the enforcement of it is growing and you cannot flout it forever. You are a damned jackass for not realizing that public sentiment is growing against you!"

"Bah! What do you know of public sentiment—still they flock to my sales. This latest at the Temple, despite Stout's stupid move, was a tremendous success. Every other day I still ship out contraband by way of Donald-sonville and still I find eager buyers—buyers who do not want to pay the price of your so honest businessmen!

Let your smug merchants compete openly with me, and we shall see who benefits the buyers best."

His jaw set, Christopher rose to his feet. "We will have to agree to disagree. But for the devil's own sake, Jean, release those men to me!"

Lafitte watched him over his steepled fingers. Christopher could see him weighing the advantages of keeping the hostages over the disadvantages. A long silence drew out and then Lafitte said, "Very well, I shall do it, but only to prove that I am an honest man who was protecting his goods and his men."

Christopher was not going to argue with him. All he wanted now were the prisoners and pirogues to transport them back to New Orleans. Coldly he asked, "We can leave today?"

Lafitte shrugged. "If you wish. I can lend you three small boats. A few prisoners are unharmed except for bruises and such, and they will be able to man the boats. I can also, as a sign of my good intent, give you enough food for the journey. My own men will escort you to within a few miles of the city—you have no objections to this?"

He did but there was nothing he could do about it. He only hoped Lafitte's men wouldn't cut their throats in the swamps. Hiding his reservations, he said indifferently, "None!"

They regarded each other across the few feet that separated them. After so many years of friendship they were on opposite sides for the first time. It was Lafitte who said quietly, "It is a pity, is it not, that we are so far from our rapport of only a few months ago. I trust you, my friend, do not betray me."

Christopher didn't answer him. He knew and Lafitte knew that while they might be on opposing sides in the months to come, the past had forged a bond that would be impossible to break.

"What of Allen Ballard?" Lafitte asked suddenly, breaking their uneasy silence.

Christopher shrugged. "I still want you to hold him prisoner, if you will?"

Lafitte nodded slowly. "Of course, we are still friends enough to grant each other favors, are we not?"

Ignoring that comment, Christopher continued, "You can unchain him, but make certain he does not escape. I am sailing for England within the week, and whether or not I return by September, I would like for you to release him then."

Surprise lifted one black brow and Lafitte repeated, "Release him? A spy?"

His face expressionless, Christopher said, "Yes. I made a promise to do so. We have little to fear from him then. The information he possesses will be several months old and useless."

"You have changed indeed, my friend. There was a day you would have ordered his neck broken without compunction."

"Perhaps. It may only be that it pleases my vanity to be magnanimous and free him."

Lafitte gave an expressive wave of his hands. "Very well, it shall be as you wish."

There was little else to keep Christopher on Grand Terre, so he rose from his chair and said, "I'd like to leave as soon as possible, if you don't mind; let's get on with it."

They exchanged no further conversation, and some two hours later Christopher, the prisoners, and their escorts were on their way back to New Orleans.

It was not a difficult journey, although it was unpleasant. At night he found it impossible to sleep, for he didn't quite trust the crude-mannered men Lafitte had sent to escort them. And the prisoners themselves worried him—three or four were dangerously wounded, the others were weak, and he hoped none would die before they reached the city.

None did and he couldn't help the sigh of relief that escaped him when their unwelcome escort left them a few miles south of the city. The final miles were covered in complete quiet, and in the gloom of the rapidly falling dusk Christopher picked out the small pier and warehouse in the wharf area near Tchoupitoulas Street which he and Jason had chosen for their rendezvous.

Silently the three pirogues glided up to the pilings, and as Christopher gained the pier in one supple leap, he noticed a small group of men that had been standing near the rundown warehouse start forward. He recognized Jason in the lead and with surprise Daniel Patterson, his naval uniform looking out of place in the squalid part of the city. He hadn't been certain how the exchange would take place, and the fact that Jason was here, now, filled him with faint misgivings, and his first thought was of Nick—something had happened! But at his questioning glance Jason shook his head slightly and murmured, "No, she hasn't ruined me; I merely thought it expedient if I were here. Patterson isn't well pleased with the way I took matters into my own hands. And how he found out about our little scheme, I'd give a great deal to know. It would seem that the Navy's spies are not as useless as I thought.

"And I do have news for you—you sail day after tomorrow, on Thursday. But enough of that, I'll explain later, and tell me, how goes it?"

By now Patterson's men were swarming over the three pirogues and helping the ragged prisoners onto the pier. Some were able to do it on their own, but others, unable to walk, were quickly placed on stretchers and carried away.

With his eyes on the scene as the men were swiftly escorted from the area, Christopher answered indifferently, "It went as well as I could expect. Jean returns them as a sign of good faith, protesting that he was only trying, as would any good citizen, to protect his merchandise."

Jason gave an exasperated grunt. "It's not that simple, and Lafitte damn well knows it!"

Christopher merely shrugged, but before he could comment, Patterson, his face set, came marching over to where they stood.

Commodore Daniel T. Patterson was an earnest young man. It was obvious from his stiff greeting that he disapproved not only of Jason's interference, but also of Christopher Saxon.

"I would like to have a few words with you, if I may?"

The request was more like an order, and Christopher was just a little bored by the entire incident. An eyebrow flying up as if in rebuke to the other's surliness, he drawled, "Now?"

"Now!" snapped Patterson.

Christopher, casting a gold, unblinking glance at Jason, wondered exactly what that gentleman had let him in for. But Jason's face was unreadable in the falling darkness, and Christopher was left with the growing conviction that Jason was as eager for the questioning as was Patterson.

His resignation apparent, Christopher sighed, "Very well, let's get it over with. I haven't slept for many hours in the past two days and my temper is not at its best, but if you insist . . ."

They entered the building and a wave of damp and mustiness mingled with the faint odor of long-ago stored spices drifted to Christopher. The wooden building was empty, and the sound of their footsteps echoed hollowly as they crossed the building. Patterson ushered them into what must have been the office when the warehouse had been in use. The room was bleak—the only pieces of furniture two rickety chairs long overdue for the rubbish heap and a scarred, ugly desk of pine. The dim light came from a small lantern on the desk, and Christopher suddenly wondered if he hadn't been the biggest fool in nature. He declined to take one of the chairs offered and leaned instead against the wall, his arms folded with apparent carelessness across his chest, his eyes watchful and narrowed, as Patterson shut the door behind them.

Jason, with a familiarness that bespoke of having been here quite a few times before, gingerly opened one of the drawers of the desk and extracted three grubby glasses and a bottle of cheap whiskey.

A sardonic grin on his face, Jason said, "You'll forgive the quality of the liquor, I hope. Most of the inhabitants of this area responded more readily to this type of rotgut than to a smoother, more refined blend. Drink?"

Patterson gave a negative shake of his head, not liking Jason's attempt to put the affair on a more social footing. But Christopher, discarding the instant speculation that the whiskey could be drugged and more to annoy Patterson than because he wanted it, nodded and watched as Jason poured him a generous shot and then the same for himself.

After having waited until Jason had begun to sip the whiskey before tasting it himself, Christopher eyed the two men in front of him. How much had Patterson found out and how much had Jason told him, he wondered. Enough obviously for the man to feel hostile, for it was painfully clear to see that the commodore considered him just one step away from the notorious Lafitte. The questions, when they came though, were not unanticipated and rather what he had expected. How large a force did the Lafitte brothers have? How much ammunition? What fortifications? What routes did Lafitte use to smuggle his goods into the city? How many ships were moored at Grand Terre?

The questioning went on, seemingly for hours, and to all inquiries Christopher merely looked bland and murmured maddeningly, "I don't know! I didn't count them and I'm really not interested enough to think about it to any great extent. You're wasting my time and yours!"

Jason appeared interested in nothing but the contents of his glass, staring at it as if it held the answers Patterson sought. As the time passed and Christopher proved no more cooperative than he had in the beginning, Patterson's temper exploded. "Damnit! Answer me or I'll have you arrested—then we'll see how not interested you are!"

"I've taken enough of you, Patterson," Christopher snarled softly. "Arrest me if you dare! If you are stupid enough to do so, I can promise you that within forty-eight hours you will be meeting me at twenty paces on the Metairie Road at *Les Trois Capelines!*"

Patterson's face paled. Whether from anger or Christopher's sheer effrontery was debatable, but before Patterson could speak, Jason intervened.

"Daniel," Jason said quietly, "there are no charges to bring against him—and he did negotiate the release of those men."

Stiffly Patterson said, "I haven't forgotten, nor have I forgotten that Mr. Saxon has had intimate dealings with that outlaw! That he could, if he wished, enable us to put an end to the Lafitte brothers' infamous operations!"

Sighing, Jason said, "I agree, but I also warned you that Mr. Saxon is a very stubborn man."

He looked again in Christopher's direction, and Christopher, prompted by some imp of devilry, gave an impudent wink and murmured, "True, unfortunate from your point of view, but you must admit . . . I did warn you."

Jason's mouth tightened a little. "Someday, I suspect you will hang—as much from a lawless streak as an unruly and overready tongue!"

Christopher merely grinned at him, displaying his even white teeth. Pushing away from the wall and placing his empty glass on the desk, he asked carelessly, "May I leave now?"

"No!" Jason said grimly. "Patterson is through with you, but I am not! And I wonder at my own wisdom in using such a tool as yourself!"

Patterson snorted, his opinion of Saxon's usefulness obvious, but he said nothing more and departed abruptly after bidding Jason a curt good evening and rudely ignoring Christopher.

When he was left alone with Jason, the impudence died out of Christopher's eyes, leaving them cold and forbidding. Deliberately he said, "I didn't appreciate that. Neither the questioning, nor Patterson's being brought into it."

228

Obliquely, Jason regarded him. "I have made no secret of my feelings about Jean Lafitte and you cannot hold it against me if I continue to pry as much information out of you as is possible." Wryly he added, "I didn't "Jean and I could have connived together. He could you—except that you are a man of your word."

Belatedly it occurred to Christopher that this entire episode had been a test—Jason testing him to see if he could negotiate the freedom of Stout's ill-fated force and again testing his loyalty. Almost absently he said, "It could all have been a sham, you know."

At Jason's sharp glance, Christopher added dryly, "Jean and I could have connived together. He could have released the men to me merely for the look of it, by all appearances assisting me deeper into your confidence."

Bleakly, Jason stared at him. "Do you think I haven't thought of that? I'll confess I can't quite make up my mind about you. I'll sleep easier once you're on your way to England, for I don't quite trust you, friend Saxon, where Lafitte is concerned."

Levelly, Christopher said, "I'm surprised you trust me to go to England. Do you want to change our plans?"

"Don't be ridiculous! Naturally not! It is only with regard to your connection with Lafitte that I have any doubts," Jason exclaimed exasperatedly. Then, a most charming smile lighting his harsh features, he offered another drink, saying, "Enough of our differences. Let us talk of your mission to England!"

Christopher agreed readily enough, accepting the second glass of liquor, although he wondered cynically how the strong brew was going to sit on his empty stomach. "You mentioned that the sailing date has been moved up?"

"Yes. As I said, day after tomorrow. I meant to tell you at our last meeting, but got sidetracked, that Monroe has accepted England's minister of war, Castlereagh's proposal for direct negotiations."

"Mmm. My only comment is that Monroe should have done that some time ago. Now the British will try all the harder to grasp all they can before the peace is declared."

"I suspect so. Certainly it becomes even more important to have someone in England that is attuned to our side."

"Have we no official representative?" Christopher asked.

"Only a gentleman by the name of Reuben Beasley.

He is our agent for our prisoners of war. I believe Monroe has included a letter of introduction to him for you. And there is also a young secretary of Albert Gallatin's staying now in London. I believe he is there merely to observe and let Gallatin know the temper of London. Like you, he is there unofficially—more so than yourself —and he has no letters of introduction from the secretary of state."

"Do I see him?"

"No. I do not feel he would be of any use to us. But I will give you what information I have on him tomorrow."

Another round of whiskey was poured, and swallowing it slowly, almost enjoying its stinging bite, Christopher decided that he was going to be drunk as a wheelbarrow if he stayed much longer. But Jason appeared to be in no hurry to end the conversation and said with amusement, "I must congratulate you on your ward."

Almost with misgiving and definitely suspicion Christopher repeated, "Congratulate?"

"Yes. You said she wouldn't shame me and she didn't —she did beat me at cards, though, she *is* very good at them! And it's fortunate that you are sailing on Thursday, for the suitors will be clamoring outside your house. Her manners are delightful. We dined at the governor's mansion on Saturday and Claiborne himself was very attracted, but only in an abstract way, you understand, as he is unusually devoted to his wife. And Sunday we took her to the opera. The opera itself was not a great success, but Nicole certainly was! I vow I thought I would have to fight our way clear."

A glitter gleamed in Christopher's eyes that couldn't be defined by Jason, but there was no mistaking the deadly smoothness of his voice as he asked, "And did Nicole find anyone who took her fancy?"

"That, I couldn't tell you. But I'm certain you will discover it for yourself—she is, after all, your ward."

"Perhaps." And abruptly Christopher changed the subject. "If Monroe has accepted Castlereagh's offer, has a place for the actual negotiations been settled upon?"

"No. Remember that Monroe wrote his reply barely a month ago—it hasn't even reached England yet. There has been a new commission appointed for us also—John Adams will be the leader and the others are a Federalist by the name of James Bayard, our speaker of the house, Henry Clay, Jonathan Russell, and Albert Gallatin. Madison finally appointed Campbell to Gallatin's post as secretary of the treasury. It is an imposing group."

"But can they accomplish anything?" Christopher asked sarcastically.

Jason shrugged. "Well, Gallatin and Bayard are at the czar's court in Russia at this very moment supposedly negotiating for peace with England. Who knows what they will accomplish? You, I hope, will certainly have more success than they have had so far."

They stayed talking quietly for several more minutes and decided on two final and vitally important items. The first, and by far the easiest, was a simple code to be used for what news Jason could send to Christopher. Knowing the various improbabilities of the mail during the war, they had acknowledged that the letters might never reach England. But Jason had agreed that he would try to keep Christopher abreast with events in New Orleans.

The second item was more difficult. Leaving England in this time of war with the United States was something they discussed at length. Obviously no British ships were sailing to American ports. If Christopher were successful in obtaining any documents of value, speed would be of utmost importance, and there would be no time in which to take a more circuitous route—to go from one port to another before heading to the United States.

After much thought and argument it was agreed they would make use of several privateers known by Jason to be plying the waters off the coast of England. Christopher jibed Jason about it, finding it vastly amusing that he would make use of them in view of his feelings about Lafitte. But Jason snapped, "These, my young friend, are honest privateers!" Christopher wisely held his tongue.

The most difficult obstacle was the timing. Neither had any idea how long Christopher would be in England. They dared not set just one date for a rendezvous. There would have to be several different times that Christopher could meet with an American ship. Finally it was decided each month, starting April 25, a privateer would be tarrying off the coast of Sussex, near the tiny village of Rottingdean. The ship would remain for several hours of darkness and sail with the midnight tide if Christopher's signal did not appear. The date would change each month, the next month's date being a day later than the previous month's. The captain would know nothing except that he was to pick up one or two passengers and then immediately set sail for New Orleans. A simple lantern signal would be used.

It was perhaps not the best arrangement—it was risky and left much to chance—but it was the best they could do.

The problems solved to their satisfaction, they had another glass of the rotgut whiskey, and it was only when the bottle was finished and they were both as drunk as lords that Christopher and Jason began to stroll in the direction of their respective homes. It had started to rain, and swearing with discomfort, Christopher pulled his thin jacket closer to him. Seeing his actions, Jason laughed, "Wait until England, my friend. Wait until it rains in England."

PART THREE

THE ROGUE AND THE VIXEN

"I hate and I love. Why I do so, perhaps you ask. I do not know, but I feel it and I am in torment."

—Catullus

21

In February, while Christopher and Mrs. Eggleston had been drilling Nicole in deportment, London had been gripped by the longest and hardest frost in centuries. The Thames River between London Bridge and Blackfriars became a road of solid ice, and the populace traveled across its frozen expanse by way of "Freezland Street."

At the ends of local streets signs were mounted announcing that it was safe to cross, and before too long there sprang up a "Frost Fair." It was a marvelous affair to see; crowded side by side were booths for bakers, butchers, barbers, and cooks. There were swings, bookstalls, skittle alleys, toy shops—exactly like a regular fair. But the "Great Frost" ended, only to be followed by a tremendous fall of snow that continued without intermission for six weeks.

The weather was still beastly on one of the last days of March when Christopher and his party disembarked. Cursing the wind and rain, Christopher had promptly and efficiently removed them to Grillions Hotel, a fashionable hotel on Albemarle Street.

All in all the first three months of 1814 had been bitter and icy in England, but beyond that swirling curtain of snow and ice, across the Channel, Napoleon's empire was in ruins. Schwarzenburg led his Austrians, and von Blücher his Prussians, into Paris. Wellington defeated Soult at Toulouse, and on April 6, 1814 Napoleon finally conceded defeat and abdicated. He left Paris at midnight on the following day on his way to exile on the island of Elba, and Louis, the Bourbon, who had become old and fat in exile, was now King of France, Louis XVIII.

By April the cruel winter was over, the long war with Napoleon was over, and in England there was exuberant rejoicing with the white cockades and the flags of the Bourbons everywhere. Despite the festive atmosphere, neither Nicole nor Christopher felt any sense of home-coming. For Christopher it was understandable—he had left unwillingly, under painful and brutal circumstances. England was simply a foreign country to him, one that was at war with his own adopted country. Nicole had no strong feelings for England, having left it so many years before. But she was glad to leave the ship's confinement, for she had been tortured by Christopher's nearness during the long voyage.

Of the three of them only Mrs. Eggleston was truly happy at the return to England. She was home again—and she had Christopher and Nicole with her! During the week following their arrival they had absorbed all the latest news and gossip circulating about the city. With something like dismay Christopher had heard the news of Napoleon's abdication. The end of the war with the French Empire freed British troops for service in America, and bitterly he cursed the necessity to act cautiously. For the moment there was little he could do but smile and act the part of the returned native son.

The first week of April passed swiftly. Christopher was taken up with a variety of mundane but time-consuming affairs—seeing a banker in the city, establishing his credit, the hiring of horses and carriage, the selection of an agent for whatever business he might have, and finding his feet in a strange city.

The ladies had promptly discovered the delights to be found in the shops on Bond Street and proceeded, after a certain amount of reluctance on Mrs. Eggleston's part, to add a number of elegant trifles to their wardrobes. Christopher took out a subscription from Colburn's Lending Library for their amusement and even managed to escort them on a few sightseeing tours: the National Gallery, the London Museum, and the wild beasts at Exeter to name a few.

There were two notable and curious omissions in all Christopher's activities; namely, he did not present any of his letters of introduction nor did he seek out Nicole's guardians. He undertook one personal task his second day in London, paying a quiet visit to Somerset House, that monumental institution where the records of all births, marriages, and deaths were kept and discovered to his relief and satisfaction that Simon Saxon was still the sixth Baron of Saxony. His grandfather lived, and not for the first time, Christopher wondered how the irascible old gentleman was going to take his return.

Yet knowing his grandfather was alive, he kept the knowledge to himself, and beyond discovering that Simon Saxon was presently staying in his London residence, he did nothing to bring about a meeting between them. He was busy adapting to London, discovering the temper of the populace, familiarizing himself with the city itself, and absorbing the currents, rumors, and news that flew like wildfire. After about ten days he knew he could no longer remain in the shadows.

His first official call was to Alexander Baring, head of the great banking firm of Hope and Baring, which served American interests in Europe. Baring was also a member of Parliament and had campaigned vigorously against the war with the United States and for the repeal of those damaging Orders of Council that gave Britain the right to stop American ships and remove at will whomever they desired. He greeted Christopher cordially, and after producing a chair, cigars, and some refreshments, he proceeded to read Monroe's letter of introduction. Glancing up from the letter he remarked, "I do not mean to be discouraging, but there is little I can do for you at present. You are here unofficially and we are still at war with one another. I can introduce you socially, but I'm afraid that will be the extent of my patronage."

Christopher nodded. "Of course. It is no more than I expected and I appreciate your difficulties." He smiled, the gold eyes very bright. "I can only hope you will continue your efforts on our behalf in Parliament."

"You may be assured on that point, but it is a damnable situation that I can do little to change. At least your American commission has been appointed for the peace talks." A grim smile on his mouth, he added, "Now if only we British will do the same and finally settle upon a place for the talks."

Looking startled, Christopher said, "I beg pardon! I thought the site of the talks was to be in Gothenburg, Sweden."

Baring shook his head. "No, not any longer. At first this was true, but now there is a movement, God knows why, to move the talks to Ghent in East Flanders."

"I see," Christopher mused slowly. "And this change of site will no doubt delay the start of the talks a few months, or at least several weeks?"

"I'm afraid so. But bear this in mind—Britain *does* desire peace."

Christopher agreed politely, unwilling to share his

237

very different views with Baring. Baring was, after all, a member of the British Parliament and as such, while perhaps wishing for peace, was naturally watching over his own country's interest. Christopher said little more and took his leave shortly thereafter. He returned to his rooms at Grillions and spent some minutes pacing the floor of his elegant parlor.

Britain might wish for peace, he thought sardonically, but not before she had one more brilliant victory in America. A master stroke that would show those brazen colonials who was the actual power. The fact that the peace talks site was in question pointed to delay. Also, although Monroe and Castlereagh had finally agreed on direction negotiations and the Americans had appointed their delegates, it appeared Britain had done nothing, thereby creating a further delay. A delay that would perhaps enable them to capture New Orleans. Christopher snorted derisively. Though it was up to him to find proof, he cursed the fact that there was little he could do at present except allow himself to be absorbed into English society and hope eventually to stumble upon something or someone that could provide the information he wanted.

He joined the ladies in the drawing room of their suite for tea. It was Mrs. Eggleston who raised the question of his family. "And when do we call upon your family, Christopher? We have been in London over a week now, and I feel it is very rude of us not to have apprised some member of your family of our arrival before now."

Christopher regarded her with something like consternation. He had avoided his family simply because he wasn't certain he was prepared to be plunged into the possible recriminations and ugly repercussions that might result. How was his grandfather going to react to his return? And Robert . . . dear, kind Uncle Robert . . . planning some new underhanded plot? His family was a complication he didn't really need at this time, he thought with frustration.

Unfortunately Mrs. Eggleston was not going to give him much choice! "Well, Christopher?" she asked as he continued to remain silent.

Stifling a curse in his throat about interfering old women and yet knowing she was right, he said reluctantly, "I suppose, I could call at Cavendish Square this evening and at least leave my card if no one is at home."

Mrs. Eggleston gave him a searching look. But before

238

she could pursue the subject, Nicole asked the question that she, too, like Christopher, would have preferred not to have answered. "Do my aunt and uncle know that I am returned? Have you written to them or am I to do it?"

Nicole, too, had been content to drift, but Mrs. Eggleston's very proper question made it impossible for her to avoid her own uncertain situation.

Christopher swore silently to himself at Nicole's unexpected query. His deliberate avoidance of informing the Markhams of their niece's return had its roots in a perplexing problem: he was simply unable to deal with the idea that Nicole would no longer be under his protection! He told himself grimly that this feeling would pass soon enough, that the reason for it was their many years together, the shared adventures on the sea, and because he had seen her grow, helped her grow, he admitted cynically, from an impetuous Nick into the extremely desirable young lady seated across from him.

And like most males confronted by two determined women asking questions he would rather not answer, he was feeling harassed and slightly exasperated. "No, I haven't informed them, damnit! I didn't realize you were so eager to return to their bosom!" It was unfair, and Christopher regretted it the moment the provoking words left his mouth.

Nicole's eyes darkened with sudden anger, and Mrs. Eggleston instantly thrust herself into the role of peacemaker as she murmured soothingly, "I'm certain dear Nicole meant nothing of the kind, and really, Christopher, you should not use such language in front of ladies."

Choking back his unaccountably rising temper with an effort, he said tightly, "I apologize. And since you ladies are dissatisfied with my arrangements, I shall immediately see to your expressed wishes!" He gave them both a stiff bow and departed.

"Well!" Mrs. Eggleston exclaimed, considerably startled at the uncalled-for display of bad temper. "Whatever was wrong with Christopher? I have never known him to behave so."

You don't know the half of it, Nicole thought angrily. She set her teacup down with a clatter, showing her own temper.

But the smile she bestowed upon Mrs. Eggleston a second later was all that could be wished for in a well-bred young lady. With a pretty shrug of her shoulders she said lightly, "Perhaps he is not feeling well, or it could be that his visit to Mr. Baring this morning was not to his liking. There's no telling."

Doubtfully, Mrs. Eggleston concurred. "Yeees, I suppose that could be true. I feel, though, that there is something more behind his unseemly display of temper than a morning gone wrong!"

Of course Mrs. Eggleston was correct. Christopher, to his dismay, was finding himself compelled to do several things he didn't want to do. Leaving the ladies, he cursed his bad luck for ever having set eyes on Nicole Ashford, her mother—that damned and bewitching Annabelle!—his Uncle Robert, and Jason Savage.

In his rooms over the following hours he composed many letters to the Markhams but ended up screwing them into knots and throwing them on the empty hearth. He had no excuses or reasons for not having notified them of Nicole's return before now. And as he was aware, the longer he postponed informing them, the more suspicion would be cast on their tale. He reached once again for a clean sheet of paper and then with a curse crumpled it and tossed it aside.

Grimly, he finally acknowledged to himself that he was not going to write to her relatives—not now, and his reason for not doing so was his own business! And damn anyone who questioned him—Nicole included!

It was impossible, he knew, to keep her in his bachelor household much longer, even with Mrs. Eggleston's chaperonage. Legally and even morally, he should have written the Markhams the instant they arrived in England, and legally, once her guardians knew where Nicole was, he could do nothing to stop them from whisking her away.

Christopher had been playing for time with regard to both his family and Nicole's guardians, but time was obviously running out. Thoughtfully he stared at the gleaming shine of his top boots. Alone he could not hope to do anything for Nicole. But his grandfather was a lord, the Baron, and if all Nicole had told Allen was true, Lord Saxon *could* exert a great deal of influence on her behalf. Influence enough, perhaps, to have the guardianship set aside? Possibly. But the question remained—if the Markhams were to be stripped of their authority over Nicole and her fortune, who would take their place?

Eventually a husband would fall heir to those duties, Christopher mused aimlessly. Realizing suddenly the train of his thoughts, he jerked up as if someone had stabbed him. Husband? To Nicole?

Good God, *no!* It was ridiculous! They disliked each other, except for the strange chemistry that ignited between their bodies and that, Christopher thought with a sneer, *that* would fade. No, he was not going to offer marriage as a way out of her difficulties. He came to no solution as he sat there in his room, but he did come to one decision—he would seek out his grandfather immediately!

Ringing for Higgins, he dressed for the coming interview with especial care. Breeches of light drab, a pristine white single-breasted waistcoat, and a black velvet jacket with flat gilt buttons completed his apparel. The thick dark hair, worn at present longer than was fashionable, was brushed and gleamed like a blackbird's wing in the sun. With his tall, lithe body, his hard, handsome features, and his easy manner, he was a grandson that most men would be proud to acknowledge . . . but would Lord Saxon?

Christopher approached the tall, stately home in Cavendish Square with a variety of emotions. He did not fear either his grandfather or Robert, but he was slightly wary and uneasy. Simon was perfectly capable of having him ejected from the house, and Robert, if he thought he could get away with it, would take delight in identifying him as a deserter from the British Navy.

There was, too, a certain typical, devil-may-care tilt to his head. If Simon didn't want to acknowledge him, well—damn him! Yet underlying all his feelings was a desire to make his peace with his grandfather.

His firm rap upon the heavy oak door was received with polite disdain by a very stiff butler. Without comment the man received Christopher's card. Feigning indifference, Christopher said crisply, "I would like to see Lord Saxon this moment . . . if he is at home. You may say that it is a personal matter."

There was for just a second the faintest flicker of interest in the pale eyes as the butler read Christopher's name. "If you will wait here, sir, I will see if Lord Saxon is available," he said. Then he disappeared down the long white and gold hallway.

Now that the moment was upon him, Christopher felt himself filled with impatience. Restlessly, with short nervous steps, he paced the inlaid tile floor, oblivious to the elegance of his surroundings.

Suddenly he stiffened as a door banged open and a well-remembered voice roared, "Where the blazes is he? You bettle-headed sapscull! Don't leave him waiting like some ragtag Bartholomew baby—he's my own grandson come home!"

A tall, gaunt figure, dressed in evening clothes much like Christopher's, his eyes flashing like burnished gold, the swarthy skin lined and seamed with age, and the thick dark hair at variance with the creases in his face, erupted into the hallway. The similarity between them, Simon and Christopher, was incredible—so Christopher would look in forty years' time; to Simon it was like peering into the past, with his own face. once again smooth and hard, staring back at him.

An abrupt silence fell. They surveyed each other without words. Christopher, his pulse unaccountably jumping, bit back an eager smile, as a feeling of joy replaced his earlier fears.

"Well," the old man said testily, "I see you're back—and high time too!"

This time Christopher's lips did twist in a grin. "So I assumed! You look the same, sir, if I may say so."

His grin fading, his eyes searching the dear familiar features, Christopher said slowly, "I expected from what I had heard to find you greatly changed. I'm happy to see you in health, sir."

Regarding him from under heavy brows, not quite able to hide completely the pleasure he felt, Simon lashed out aggressively, "You young devil, what did you mean disappearing like that? You were very nearly the death of me! And now you have the impertinence to ask after my health! Bah! I've a good mind to send you packing!"

The words had hardly left his mouth when he whirled on the waiting butler and barked, "And you, you chuckle-headed creature, what are you standing there for? See that rooms are prepared for him!" His fiery glance swung to his grandson and he demanded, "Where are your valises and baggage? Don't tell me you travel that lightly!"

Not a bit disturbed by the half-angry, half-conciliatory tone of voice, Christopher replied coolly, "I'm presently staying at Grillions, and before you make further plans I should warn you that I am not alone!"

"Married, hey? Well, that's all to the good m'boy. Provided of course she's a good gel. I'll not have any custom-house goods brought into the house—your wife or not! But come! Come into my study!"

One hand clutched Christopher's arm in a death grip, while the other pounded him heartily on the shoulders as Simon led him into his study. "Damn me, boy, but this is a most welcome surprise," he finally muttered as if the words were torn from deep inside him.

Alone they stared at each other again. Christopher realized with pain that his grandfather had been totally unaware of his fate until this very moment, and he found himself at a curious loss for words. What does one say after almost fifteen years?

Simon, too, was wondering much the same himself, but for the moment he had no need of words. He was content to feast his eyes on those beloved features, which he had feared he would never see again. And he was proud of what he saw. Thank God, the boy was safe, he thought. Safe and come home to me.

Gruffly, concealing his deeper emotions, Simon commanded, "Sit down! Sit down! Don't just stand there towering over me!" He walked to a liquor cabinet in one corner and poured generous portions of fine French brandy into crystal snifters. Handing one to Christopher and seating himself, Simon demanded bluntly, "Well, now, you young jackanapes, tell me why you ran off like that. You must have known I'd get over my anger! Damn me, boy! If you could have waited, I would have explained matters to you."

Startled, Christopher stared blankly at him. "Explained matters?"

"Of course! Damnit, Christopher, what was I to do but go along with Adrian Ashford? There was Annabelle weeping all over us, swearing you had raped her. Adrian was ripe for murder, and I simply had to act as I did." There was a note of entreaty in the older man's voice. "I know I was harsh on you and you didn't deserve it." He paused as he intercepted Christopher's stunned look. "I had to say what I did to you—I couldn't very well tell Adrian that his wife was a liar and a spread-legged little slut, and that it was my son who was her lover, rather than my *grandson!*"

Speechless, Christopher stared. At last he rasped, "You knew?"

"Of course I knew! Oh, not that they planned to use you as a scapegoat. But I had been aware for some time that Robert had an alliance with Annabelle, and I knew

243

that she was playing up to your calf love. I never suspected, though, that they intended to cuckold Adrian into believing that you were the man!" Regretfully, he added, "I certainly never suspected that you were to take the blame. I'll be honest . . . I *was* furious that day, with you for being such a romantic young fool, with Annabelle and Robert for creating the situation, and with myself for not having nipped their little plan in the bud." His eyes fixed with painful intensity on Christopher, he asked softly, "Was it so necessary for you to disappear like that? You must have realized that I would never have condemned you like that without first hearing your side—your side alone and in private. Why did you never in these past fifteen years let me know where you were? Didn't you think that I would care? Could you not know I would be half mad with fear?"

It was the most awkward moment of Christopher's life; he was completely unable to justify himself. It was obvious that Simon had no inkling that Robert had literally almost sold him into slavery. Nor, it appeared, did his grandfather have any knowledge of his own attempt five years ago to reconcile the differences between them. As much as he hated and despised his uncle, he could not betray him to Simon. It simply was not in him to return like this to vilify Simon's only living son. Knowing the truth would nearly destroy the old man before him, Christopher made a grim decision—what was between him and Robert would remain private. Looking steadily into his grandfather's eyes, a rueful smile tugging at the corner of his mouth, he lied, "I'm afraid, sir, that I took you at your word when you said you never wanted to see me again."

Simon's face twisted with pain, and Christopher cursed his clumsy tongue. Earnestly he pleaded, "I beg you, sir, do not be distressed. It was my own folly that caused the entire situation, and I was in the devil's own temper when I left you. No one could have prevented me from doing what I did that day—even if you had called me back an instant later, I would not have heeded you. Don't blame yourself." Seeing some of the anguish fade from the lined face, Christopher continued on a lighter note, "It was for the best, you know. I did as many another young man and offered my services to the Navy. I must say that I have done rather well by my decision too—even if I have lived somewhat precariously at times."

"The Navy, hey?" Simon snapped, as his eyes searched Christopher's face.

Disliking himself intensely, Christopher answered blandly, "Why, yes. After I flung out of the house, I stormed into that little village beyond Beddington's Corner. And I happened to meet with several sailors on leave. Their life sounded so exciting that before I knew it, I had asked to join." Firmly he added, "And I have never regretted it, sir, except for the fact that I departed from you with such bitterness."

Simon waved aside the attempted apology. "Enough! It is behind us and you are home again. A good thing, too," he growled, "You're my heir, don't forget. When I die, the title is yours and all that goes with it."

Once again the thought occurred to Christopher that Robert may have had another more sinister motive in wishing for his disappearance and death. The entailed Saxon fortune was extremely large and not to be dismissed lightly. The title Baron of Saxony was an old and respected one, one that any man would be proud to hold . . . but would Robert kill for it?

Christopher's expression gave no clue to his thoughts. He swiftly said, "I am too soon returned for us to talk of your death. I trust that it will be many years before I become Lord Saxon."

Simon snorted, "Ha! Little you care, I could have died anytime these past years and you would have never known it! At least I can acquit you of being unduly interested in the state of my health!"

Christopher merely grinned, knowing that Simon tended to hide what he really felt behind a crusty, sometimes rude, exterior. Simon would never have let Christopher know the extent of his emotions at the reappearance of his eldest grandchild. The nearest he could come were those half-apologetic statements concerning the events that had led to Christopher's departure and those reproachful questions about Christopher's whereabouts during the past years.

Seeing Christopher's grin, Simon snapped, "If you're going to come back and just sit there grinning like some half-wit at a fair, well, I would just as soon you take yourself off again!"

An uncontrollable crack of laughter greeted his words, and after an affronted second a reluctant smile curved Simon's lips. "Now stop that, you young devil, and tell me all!"

245

Some of Christopher's amusement vanished, and rather hesitantly, taking care to stick to the truth when possible, he regaled his grandfather with his adventures. It was difficult in some places, especially trying to explain why, after eagerly joining the Navy, he had jumped ship and never returned to England.

Simon obviously disapproved of the fact that Christopher had abandoned a naval career so easily. And Christopher, without implicating Robert, was powerless to excuse his actions. So he merely shrugged his broad shoulders and said, "I had served my time and in the process discovered that a British seaman's life was not for me."

"And of course you never thought that I could have seen to it that you became an officer!" Simon retorted bitterly. "Damn it, Christopher! If you had written, just one word, I would have seen that you were properly placed. I tell you, it goes against the grain to think of a grandson of mine, my heir, as a mere seaman, when by now you could be a captain or even higher! A Saxon, the future Baron of Saxony, a lowly sailor! Disgraceful!"

Idly, Christopher wondered how the old man would take the knowledge that not only had he been a lowly sailor, but a pirate as well! In the ensuing hours he cleverly wove a tale of ships and the sea, of winning a fortune in New Orleans, and of his desire to return home. Of his privateering, he passed over lightly, leaving the impression that the bulk of his wealth and land had come on the turn of the card—which in fact, a goodly portion had. And as fortunes passed thus every night in the exclusive gaming clubs to be found in Pall Mall, there was no shame attached to this.

When he finished his story, Simon stared levelly at him for several unnerving seconds, and Christopher wondered how much of his tale his grandfather really believed.

Actually, the only part that Simon felt was positively true was the portion dealing with the fortune won at cards; the rest, while telling himself it could be true, he reserved judgment on, for despite a gap of fifteen years, Simon detected an element of falseness in Christopher's account. But Simon was shrewd and kept his thoughts to himself, merely saying, "At least you've had the sense to come back home where you belong."

It was on the tip of Christopher's tongue to point out that he was here only for a visit and that his home was

246

now the plantation house in Louisiana. But it was unthinkable to say such a thing. He would have to wait, and trust that in time he could bring his grandfather to realize that he could not step back into his old life. Thankfully Simon said no more on that subject but turned to one just as delicate.

"Now," Simon commanded, "I noticed you made no mention of your wife. Why?"

Smiling disarmingly, Christopher murmured, "Because I have no wife, sir. I must explain my circumstances to you more fully."

"Well, get on with it—don't dawdle!"

So Christopher began to speak of the coincidental meeting with Mrs. Eggleston and Nicole Ashford, but he had barely mentioned Mrs. Eggleston's name when he noticed a peculiar expression on Simon's face.

"Letitia Eggleston?" Simon demanded impatiently. "Letty, you know where she is?"

Surprised, Christopher blurted out, "Letty? You mean Mrs. Eggleston?"

"Damnit, of course I do! I never called her anything but Letty in my life! And if she hadn't been such a hot-tempered article that wouldn't listen to reason—" Simon broke off in mid-stride to glare at his mystified grandson. "Don't you be fooled by that butter wouldn't melt in her mouth air she affects! But if she hadn't been the most stubborn woman alive and if I hadn't been such an arrogant, hot-tempered young fool, she would have been your grandmother!"

Staring dazedly at his grandfather, Christopher was thunderstruck at the notion that proper, sweet Mrs. Eggleston could have ever been called hot-tempered and that his fractious grandfather had once contemplated marrying her. He swallowed and asked faintly, "You were engaged to her?"

"Yes. Damnit, haven't I just said so! But we had a god-awful row about something, and like a jingle-brained weanling, I took off in a pelter, vowing I would never see her again. Two weeks later, out of sheer spite, I offered for your grandmother. That, my boy, was the biggest mistake of my life!"

Fascinated by this unknown piece of family history, Christopher prompted, "And?"

Simon moved uncomfortably. "I never loved your grandmother, I'll not deny it, but people of our station seldom marry for love and I was good to her. But Letty was always the only woman for me." Angrily he mut-

247

tered, "I could have throttled her, though, the day she married that court-cad Eggleston!"

Bitterly, Simon stared at the untouched brandy snifter in his hand. "Don't you make the same mistake, boy! I've had to suffer because of my actions and probably caused a few other people to suffer along with me!"

Christopher wisely remained silent. Simon, belatedly aware that he had unburdened himself to an abnormal degree, shot his silent grandson a chilling look, as if daring him to comment, and growled, "I dare say, this is all very boring to you, and truth to tell, it is! Now, tell me how you come to have Letty traveling with you."

Christopher passed on the story that he had concocted to explain just that situation. Simon heard him out in silence; not even Nicole Ashford's presence seemed to disconcert him.

"So, the chit's been with Letty all this time," Simon muttered at the end of Christopher's story. "I wondered about that myself. Knew Letty was fond of the child and knew that aunt and uncle of hers were a pair of Newgate birds, the first and only time I met them! Now what's to do?" He peered at Christopher's deliberately bland face and snorted, "Want me to take 'em in, hey?"

"If you will," Christoher replied promptly and truthfully. "It is not proper for me to continue to withhold Nicole's whereabouts from her guardians. And I know the instant they are notified, they will descend like locusts and no doubt incarcerate her in the country. Certainly they will not allow Mrs. Eggleston to accompany her."

"No doubt. I can tell you this, m'boy—they're going to kick up a devil of a dust! They've been living for years on her fortune, everyone knows it. Even tried to have the gel declared dead last fall. But the courts denied it, said they'd have to wait until what would have been her majority, her twenty-first birthday, before making that decision. The uncle didn't like it, but the young cub, Edward was furious about it!" Simon gave a malicious chuckle. "Like to see *his* face when he finds out the chit's back!"

Somewhat grimly, Christopher smiled. "He'll find that he has me to answer to, if he has any comments to make about it."

Oh, ho, Simon thought with glee, sits the wind in that quarter. His eyes suddenly gleaming, Simon said, "It's too late this evening to bring the ladies, but first thing tomorrow I expect you three to be here."

By God, Simon thought to himself after Christopher departed, but this was going to be most enjoyable. Christopher home, Letty with him, and the battle for the little Ashford gel for some spice. Gleefully he decided that outfoxing the Markhams would provide him with more amusement than he had experienced in years!

22

The removal to Cavendish Square went smoothly. Christopher, despite his ready agreement to Simon's demand, had his own reservations. He did not like the idea of taking advantage of his grandfather, but he consoled himself with the knowledge that Simon would have been grievously wounded had he refused. And there was the irritating knowledge that there was no other path open to him.

When apprised of the plan the next morning at breakfast, Mrs. Eggleston, too, had reservations, but hers were more of a social nature. "But, Christopher," she asked, "is it proper? It is for you, but Nicole and I are no relation at all to Lord Saxon. Might people talk of us living in his house?"

It was a valid question, one Christopher had not considered. Mrs. Eggleston provided more than adequate chaperonage for Nicole while she lived under his care, but who was to provide that same act for Mrs. Eggleston while she lived in Simon's house?

It was an unusual situation, as neither he nor his grandfather was Nicole's legal guardian, and there was going to be enough speculation as it was. They certainly did not need the gossips and scandalmongers wondering about Mrs. Eggleston's role in the affair. Considering the ages of the two involved, it was a ridiculous circumstance, but in view of that long-ago engagement—and there were bound to be people who remembered it!—it was a problem that had to be resolved.

Fortunately Simon was more quick-witted than either Mrs. Eggleston or Christopher, and when Christopher paid him a visit that morning and explained this new complication, Simon snorted, "Just thought of it, hey? Well, m'boy, I thought of it last night!" A delightfully smug expression on his lips, Simon continued, "Made arrangements for m'sister Regina to come for a visit. She's widowed, y'know, lives in a tidy, little home at Chigwell

250

in Essex. I sent a groom to her after you left last night, and not above ten minutes ago he arrived back with her answer. She'll arrive tonight, so everything is right and tight!"

Christopher returned to Grillions and informed Mrs. Eggleston of Simon's actions. Almost lovingly she murmured, "So clever of him, but then he always was." And so the servants began to prepare for the transfer to Cavendish Square.

Nicole had remained pensive throughout the morning. She could not understand why Christopher seemed to have no intention of informing the Markhams of her presence in England. Why? It occurred to her that he might have developed a fondness for her, but she banished that thought. She was not going to be mislead by him again!

Nicole was finding it very easy to drift with the currents created by Mrs. Eggleston and Christopher. She had lost the will to fight. Her life was a pleasant one —Mrs. Eggleston, kind and concerned; Mauer, competent and amusing; Christopher, for the most part considerate, almost avuncular, seeing to all the arrangements. It was nearly impossible to do anything but what was asked of her—all anyone demanded was that she dress beautifully and behave charmingly.

She found it harder and harder to remember the days of *La Belle Garce* and to recall the hoydenish creature she had been. Even the times that Christopher had possessed her had taken on a dreamlike quality. She almost believed she was the demure and quiet young lady she appeared.

Simon greeted them politely and promptly absented himself, as he hated to see the household in an upheaval.

By five o'clock that afternoon the ladies were ensconced in an impressive suite of rooms on the second floor, each with a separate bedroom and dressing room. They shared a handsome sitting room, decorated in soft shades of yellow with a striking deep-toned sapphire-blue rug. Christopher's rooms were down a wide ruby-carpeted hallway on the opposite side of the house and presumably as elegant as Mrs. Eggleston's and Nicole's. The servants had their rooms, as did most of Lord Saxon's staff, on the third floor.

Regina's arrival that evening, nearly three hours after she was expected, created quite a stir, for she traveled with a personal maid, a dresser, and her very own page boy, in additition to her groom and driver.

Lady Darby was a tall, stiff-backed woman whose features would be described as handsome rather than beautiful. She had a long nose, a wide mouth and a chin that brooked no opposition. Like her brother, Simon, she had dark hair, but while she was some fifteen years the younger, her raven locks were liberally dusted with strands of silver. Divested quickly of a fashionable pelisse lined with crushed silk, she was dressed in a gown of deep puce. Her hair, with its silver wings, was brushed back into a severe, but extremely attractive chignon that emphasized the magnificent bones of her face. Regina exuded a sense of majesty and aloofness. But it was all a sham—she was as good-hearted as she was formidable.

Sweeping into the drawing room, she exclaimed, "My dears! I am so dreadfully sorry to be so late, but I simply could not arrive here sooner." Flashing her brother a teasing glance, she scolded, "Really, Simon, you would think at your age you would not be so impetuous!" As he spluttered and glared, Regina wisked across the room to enfold a slightly startled Mrs. Eggleston into a fond embrace. "Dearest Letitia! How absolutely marvelous to see you again! How *could* you have departed as you did? It is *so* good to see you once more, and how wonderful that you are staying with Simon! We will have plenty of time for several comfortable cozes."

Leaving Mrs. Eggleston in a state bordering on bemusement, Regina's eye fell upon Nicole standing politely near a stylishly low sofa of striped satin. "My dear! What a delightful child you have become! The gentlemen will be living on our doorstep! You shall be all the rage in no time at all. Oh, I'm going to enjoy myself, I just know it! I vow that within a fortnight we shan't have an evening free."

Nicole was enchanted. What a darling Lady Regina Darby was! She dropped a graceful curtsy. "Thank you for your gratifying words. It is so kind of you and Lord Saxon to take us in. I do hope I shan't be a disappointment to you."

"Disappointment? My dear, I am never disappointed! No one would *dare* disappoint me!" Regina returned with a twinkle.

As she turned slowly, Regina's inquiring glance took in Christopher, lounging carelessly against the mantel. Dressed in his customary black velvet jacket and light breeches, he was a man to catch any woman's eye. What Regina thought of him, she did not betray, but only re-

252

garded him intently. "Well, Christopher?" she said coolly, "Have you returned to stay? Or do you intend to disappear without warning and nearly destroy your grandfather again?"

"Regina!" thundered Simon.

"Oh, my!" gasped Mrs. Eggleston, dismay creeping into her eyes. Everything had been going so pleasantly, she thought unhappily, only she had forgotten Regina's *very* forthright tongue.

Nicole, standing just a bit away from the others, viewed the unfolding scene with more than a little interest. Captain Saber, as she still occasionally thought of Christopher, had always been an enigma to her, and try as she might, she could not remember ever meeting him at Beddington's Corner, although she knew she must have. She was intensely curious about him, and this was her first chance to learn more of his shrouded past. So it wasn't at all strange that she watched closely as Christopher, apparently not disturbed at all by his great-aunt's barbed words, bowed and, with a mocking smile curving his beautiful mouth, said smoothly, "I've just returned. Do you think it apropos to greet me with concern about my departure?"

"*Touché!* I'll grant you this, young man, you've certainly become a very handsome devil with a glib tongue. But don't try to bamboozle me!" Regina retorted tartly. And as Simon opened his mouth, she turned on him, exclaiming, "Oh, shush, my love! We are all family and families *always* ask embarrassing questions! Come now, in vulgar parlance—feed me! I vow, I am positively starving to death!"

The evening passed swiftly, as Regina regaled them with gossip. She asked few questions about their sudden arrival, and she appeared to take their opportune meeting at face value. But Christopher was very wary of Lady Darby; he sensed that his aunt was the least likely to swallow the tale without reservations. Several times he was aware of a speculative, appraising gleam in her dark eyes when she regarded him.

Christopher found sleep elusive that night; a sense of frustration and doubt churning inside him. I must be the most arrogant fool alive, he thought disgustedly, to have believed I could return to England, divest myself of Nicole and Mrs. Eggleston as if they were a bit of troublesome baggage, deceive my grandfather, ferret out the plans for an attack on New Orleans, and then blithely sail away.

The next morning he and Simon had planned to stroll down to St. James Street; Simon wished to show off his grandson at the various men's clubs to be found there. But when Christopher descended for breakfast, he found a hand-delivered note waiting for him. After scanning it quickly he frowned. Why would Alexander Baring want to see him as soon as possible? Then he shrugged, he'd find out soon enough.

Seeking out Simon, he made his excuses and left for the Baring residence in the city. Arriving at the Baring house some minutes later, he was shown into the library, where Baring was conversing with a middle-aged man. They were seated comfortably in two high-backed chairs of red Moroccan leather, and as Christopher entered Baring rose to his feet.

"So good of you to come this soon. I hoped you would. But come, I have what I believe will be a pleasant surprise for you!" So saying, Baring led Christopher over to the older man who had remained seated.

"Albert, this is the gentleman I was speaking of. Monroe, I might add, writes highly of him. Christopher Saxon, may I present Mr. Albert Gallatin. Albert, you'll be interested to know that Saxon arrived here not above two weeks ago from New Orleans. I'm certain you'll have much to speak of later."

Christopher stared at Gallatin in astonishment, and after they had shaken hands, he exclaimed, "Sir! I never expected to see you in London. The last I heard, you were in St. Petersburg, Russia."

.Gallatin smiled grimly. "So I was—kicking my heels and playing the tourist for months. As I was accomplishing nothing, Bayard and I decided to leave. I was hoping that when I arrived here Alexander would have some good news for me, but it appears that nothing has been done."

Baring looked uncomfortable. "I've explained in my letters, my government absolutely refuses mediation. It is felt that foreign interference in our domestic quarrel is unwarranted. And at least now your Mr. Madison has agreed to Castlereagh's plan of direct negotiations, so one of our stumbling blocks has been removed."

Gallatin grunted. "And the impressment question?" he asked dryly.

Looking even more uncomfortable, Baring said, "We simply cannot accept your demands without losing our Navy. It is useless and unrealistic to discuss it as an abstract question of right when it is one of necessity. Damnit, Albert, we've been fighting for our lives!"

Gallatin did not appear moved by Baring's impassioned comments, but Christopher found them intriguing. The United States had declared war ostensibly because of impressment of American seamen, and it now seemed that though peace talks were in the offering, Britain was refusing even to consider that topic in the negotiations! Coolly Christopher inquired, "You think it right for your warships to stop our ships on the high seas and take off American citizens, forcing them to serve in the British Navy?" It was a question that struck deeply into Christopher's being—hadn't he been impressed himself? If the experience had embittered him, how much more so must it an American?

Baring said nothing to Christopher's question. He did not approve of the practice, but he could do little to stop such activities. And there were British deserters on those American ships who were needed in the war against Napoleon. Few American seamen, he felt positive, were actually being taken and he had his doubts that any had been taken.

It was Gallatin, a patient and temperate man, who banished the slightly hostile air that had entered the room by stating calmly, "I don't think it is a question of right so much as a question of, will it stop?" He gave Baring a searching glance before continuing, "So we are not to discuss the impressment issue, yet our two governments have agreed to direct negotiations. What *are* we to discuss? The weather?"

"I know, I know," commented Baring exasperatedly. "I don't have any certain idea what direction the talks are to take. For the moment I'm content to know that the way is being made for the negotiations to begin." Smiling, he added, "You know how these things are."

Gallatin did indeed know. First there had been the czar's offer of mediation during which the Americans, according to Ramonzov, the Russian chancellor, had shown "rather too much ardor in pursuing peace." Now they had agreed to direct negotiations and appointed a new commission, only to discover that the British faction had not only not appointed their commission, but also wanted the site changed. Sometimes he felt they would never get to the peace table at all. Hence, his and James Bayard's unorthodox visits to England.

They had accomplished nothing in the months in Russia—absolutely nothing. And having grown tired of waiting, he and Bayard had left John Quincy Adams in his role as United States minister to Russia in St. Petersburg. The whole Russian trip, Gallatin admitted to himself, had been a fiasco. He and Bayard had arrived nearly a year ago in St. Petersburg to discover within the hour that the British had refused the czar's offer. Intending to leave immediately for the United States, they found to their dismay that diplomatic form obliged them to stay. As commissioners to the court of St. Petersburg they had to be received by the czar and present their credentials. Thereafter it was for the czar to decide when his efforts at mediation might be considered at an end. And for the past nine months, Gallatin and Bayard had been involuntary tourists. Yes, he did indeed know "how these things are."

Christopher, too, had his own idea how things were. Gallatin might think that the delay was caused by mere circumstance and form, but Christopher had the uncomfortable growing conviction that the British were deliberately stalling, playing for time in which to strike a mortal blow against the United States. Yet, he could hardly make any such statement in front of Alexander Baring. With that thought, before he departed, he managed to make arrangements to meet privately with Gallatin.

Gallatin's and Bayard's arrival in London was something neither he nor Jason had considered. It could do no real harm and in fact could lend more credence to his own professed reason for being in London. He wondered, though, what the two men thought they could accomplish.

Like himself, they were visitors without diplomatic status in a hostile nation. Naturally they would be excluded from all official receptions, and it seemed they would be in a position to do little but exist on the fringes and glean what information they could. For himself he expected as much, but then his purpose was to infiltrate and, by whatever means were necessary, find out exactly what the British plans were for the South, New Orleans in particular.

Gallatin and Bayard were in a different situation entirely. They were appointed peace commissioners, both directly serving the United State government. In his case he was serving private interests, his own and Jason Savage's, despite Monroe's fine letter of introduction.

Impatient for the meeting with Gallatin, he was restless and on edge for the remainder of the morning. And because he wanted no one to interfere with the coming meeting, he avoided Cavendish Square and managed to waste the hours until it was time for the meeting by wandering aimlessly throughout the streets of London.

He presented himself at Gallatin's address some fifteen minutes earlier than he was expected and was gratified when Gallatin had him instantly ushered into his suite.

Christopher eyed him closely, not unnaturally curious about this former secretary of the treasury, whose appointment to the commission had been held up for so long and had caused such a furor in Congress. Albert Gallatin certainly did not appear a man who would normally be found in the middle of a partisan congressional fight. He was a patient, temperate man, a thorough thinker, and one not given to rash action. Christopher hoped that the other appointees were of the same caliber.

Smiling in welcome, Gallatin waited until Christopher had seated himself across from him before asking, "Now, young man, what can I do for you?"

"I'm not so certain you *can* do anything for me. I merely wanted to speak to you in private."

Gallatin looked somewhat surprised. "You have something to say that couldn't be mentioned in front of Baring?"

Feeling at a disadvantage but determined to express his own views, Christopher said, "Yes. Yes, I do. I believe that Mr. Baring is working very sincerely on our behalf, but I also feel quite strongly that this delay is deliberate." And feeling that he might as well be hanged for a sheep as a lamb, he finished defiantly, "I think Castlereagh's government is willfully keeping the peace talks from getting started. I feel very strongly that the British want another outstanding victory in America to bolster their hand at the peace table."

"Oh, I'm quite certain that's exactly what they are planning."

"You are?" Christopher said, his confusion at Gallatin's calm acceptance plain to see on his face.

Gallatin sighed tiredly. "Oh, yes, my young friend, I'm more than a little certain our British companions have territorial conquest in mind. They have a strong hand as it is, with the war with Napoleon at an end, but I'll also agree that they would like to firmly trounce us."

This will teach me, Christopher thought sardonically, to play at intrigue. He had, it appeared, underestimated the quiet Mr. Gallatin.

Gallatin, regarding him closely, guessed at his thoughts and said slowly, "I am getting used to people saying one thing and doing another. I don't believe there is anything that you and I can do about it. I am writing to Monroe of my suspicions and hope he will realize that we will be lucky to hold onto our boundaries as they were before the war. I intend to warn him very strongly that the British will launch a massive offensive sometime this year and that we would be wise to make peace as soon as possible. We may be in grave danger as a nation if we do not. We had best forget any thought of the conquest of Canada, before we find ourselves under British rule again!"

"My idea exactly! I am relieved to know that you will be writing to the secretary of state on this matter. Everywhere I go I see proof of British supremacy," Christopher said earnestly. "And I'll confess I have indeed been troubled over it. Our Congress must be living in a dream world if they think we can gain anything further from this unpractical war."

Gallatin sent Christopher a wry look. "Our Congress *does* live in a dream world." Then as there seemed little more to add, he said, "I appreciate your calling on me and letting me know your opinion—you have had more opportunity to observe the state of things than I have, and I'll admit that it is comforting to know that I am not alone in what I suspect. I only hope I can convince Monroe and Madison."

"I, too, express the same hope." Rising to his feet, Christopher added, "Sir, if I can be of service to you, please do not hesitate to let me know. I would be happy to do anything within my power to serve you." It was a sincere offer, for Christopher instinctively respected and admired Gallatin.

Rising to his feet also, he extended his hand. "I shall certainly call upon you if the need arises. And don't you waste a second in coming to me, if I can be of some help to you. We Americans must stick together, you know."

Christopher smiled. "Especially when we are in a country that is at war with our own!"

With a laugh Gallatin agreed, "Especially, then!"

It was a pleasant ending to the meeting, and Christopher went away feeling more confident and assured that he was not on a foolish quest. There *was* going to be an invasion. But when? And most importantly, where?

Understandably, Simon was somewhat angry at Christopher's desertion on his first day in Cavendish Square, and when Christopher appeared only moments before dinner, Simon barked, "Well, now, it's kind of you to join us this evening. Couldn't think of anything else that you had to do?"

Christopher only grinned at him, which made Simon scowl all the blacker at him. The ladies arrived a moment later, and the other object of Simon's displeasure came under scrutiny. Glaring at his sister, he snapped, "What's this nonsense I hear of a grand ball next month? Damnit, Gina, I warn you, I won't have my house turned topsy-turvy by your machinations! You're here as my guest, don't you forget it!"

"Oh, pooh! This was once my home too! And how," she inquired reasonably, "are we to present Nicole, if not with a grand ball? Anything else would be paltry. Even Letitia agrees with me!"

"Oh, yes, Simon, it is most necessary," Mrs. Eggleston broke in. "You don't really mind do you?" she begged, her blue eyes very big and fixed painfully on Simon's face.

Something that perilously resembled a blush crossed Simon's lean features, and in stupefaction Nicole and Christopher stared, as Simon melted beneath Mrs. Eggleston's appealing look. Drowning in anxious blue pools he muttered, "Ahem . . . ah . . . I don't suppose *one* ball would be too much of an ordeal." Then frowning fiercely, he tore his eyes from Mrs. Eggleston's and growled at Regina, "But remember, I don't want this house draped in pink silk or some other such nonsense!"

Regina merely smiled angelically, pleased with the outcome. But then she had never doubted its conclusion for a moment—Simon had always been a fool where Letitia had been concerned and Regina had quite shamelessly made use of the fact.

Not a little startled at Lord Saxon's abrupt turnabout-face, Nicole glanced at Christopher as if he could solve the mystery, and Christopher, guessing her perplexity, mouthed, "Later."

It wasn't until much later in the week, though, that he had a chance for private conversation with Nicole. This particular evening, his grandfather had dined at his club with several of his cronies, and after dinner in Cavendish Square, Mrs. Eggleston and Lady Darby had closeted themselves in the blue sitting room, busy with plans for the ball.

Nicole, time heavy on her hands, had been listlessly

practicing on the pianoforte in the music room when Christopher, on his way out for the evening, entered, expecting to find all three ladies present.

Seeing Nicole was alone, he hesitated, but as the relationship between them had been almost amicable of late, he judged that there was no cause to leave abruptly. Shutting the door behind him, he walked across the room to where she sat behind the highly polished rosewood instrument.

"Are you planning on a musical career?" he asked, teasingly.

Nicole grimaced. "Hardly! It is just that your great-aunt and Mrs. Eggleston have banished me from their schemes after I asked why it was so important to invite Princess Esterhazy and the Countess Lieven."

"Why is it so important?" Christopher inquired interestedly.

An impish twinkle in the topaz eyes, Nicole said demurely, "Well, you see, they are both patronesses at Almack's, and Lady Darby says I simply *must* be granted vouchers! There is a list made up for the invitations each week and if my name is not on it, if I am denied, I will be ruined socially!"

At Christopher's expression of scornful disbelief, Nicole said earnestly, "It's true! Lady Darby even quoted a little verse about it. Let me see if I can remember it." Frowning a moment, Nicole concentrated, and then her face lightening, she said triumphantly, "I have it!"

"All on that magic list depends;
Fame, fortune, fashion, lovers, friends:
'Tis that which gratifies or vexes,
All ranks, all ages, and both sexes.
If once to Almack's you belong,
Like monarchs, you can do no wrong;
But banished thence on Wednesday night,
By Jove, you can do nothing right!"

Christopher smiled in cynical amusement; Mr. Henry Luttrell's little ditty certainly seemed to have made a lasting impression on Nicole. Dryly he asked, "And your entire success depends totally on that list and those two ladies?"

"Yes, as far as the list is concerned, but there are more patronesses. Lady Darby mentioned a Lady Jersey, who she said is very flighty, and a Lady Cowper. Lady Cowper is supposed to be extremely nice. There are others too, I believe, but those are the only names I can remember right now. Lady Darby says there should be no trouble, but if Princess Esterhazy or Countess Lieven prove awkward, because of my aunt and uncle and this unorthodox situation, then she'll have to approach Lady Jersey." A wry smile curving her lips, Nicole finished, "Apparently, Lady Jersey likes to cause a stir and she might like to patronize me, if for no other reason than to disturb the others. And your great-aunt is very certain that if all else fails, Lady Jersey will do just that."

"Hmm. It appears my great-aunt has events well in reins." An expression of mocking dismay on his face, Christopher mourned, "I sincerely hope she doesn't decide to take me in hand!"

Nicole giggled, feeling completely at ease with him for the first time in years. "I know. She is the most managing woman ever—but so delightful about it that one cannot help but agree with her plans. Even your grandfather, I noticed, does not deny her."

"Now, there you are wrong!" Christopher retorted derisively. "It was Mrs. Eggleston who arranged for him to give his consent for the grand ball, as you well know! You were there!"

Dropping her gaze from the laughing eyes, almost deferentially, she asked, "Was there something between them? I don't mean to pry, but your grandfather so obviously agreed to the ball because of Mrs. Eggleston that I couldn't help but wonder."

Christopher, standing carelessly beside the pianoforte, staring upon Nicole's downbent head, was suddenly aware of the charming, artfully tangled mass of curls and the view of the soft white neck afforded him. He had an almost irresistible impulse to lean over and kiss that appealing little spot where her neck joined the silky shoulders, and with an effort he restrained himself. In this demure, nearly shy mood that had overtaken her, Christopher found himself enchanted. So enchanted he caught himself staring at her as infatuatedly as Simon had stared at Mrs. Eggleston, until Nicole, uncomfortable as the silence continued, glanced up, and he instantly recovered himself. Cursing inwardly at his own stupidity, he said coolly, "Yes, there was something between them. It seems that in their youth they were engaged. Due to some argument or other, it was broken off by Mrs. Eggleston and they each married someone else."

"I see," Nicole said slowly, not really seeing at all. It was rather difficult to imagine Mrs. Eggleston having an argument with anyone, and especially an argument that led to a broken engagement. An engagement was not to be taken lightly, even in this day it was almost as binding as marriage, and almost fifty years ago it would have been more so. But a long-ago engagement couldn't have made Lord Saxon so visibly Mrs. Eggleston's slave, Nicole thought quickly, and in surprise she blurted out, "He's still in love with her, isn't he?"

Christopher's mouth twisted in a satirical smile. "So it would appear. Incredible, don't you think? A Saxon loving anyone and for any length of time?"

"Don't!" Nicole cried, inexplicably angry at his disparaging remarks. "Why do you have to say things like that?" she demanded passionately, her eyes stormy. "I think you enjoy creating disturbances, making cynical statements like that!"

"And you don't?" he shot back tightly, for some reason just as angry. "I should think that you have more disturbances than I ever have!"

"That's unfair! Oh!" Tears unaccountably glittering in her eyes, she spat, "Oh, I hate you Christopher Saxon! *I hate you!*"

With a muscle jumping along his jaw, Christopher stared at her one long moment, and then forgetting all his good resolutions, he dragged her into his arms and muttered thickly, "Well, here's something else to add to your hatred!" His mouth hard and merciless captured hers in an angry kiss that held no passion, no gentleness, but as Nicole struggled violently against him, that searing bittersweet flame of desire that seemed to always leap between their bodies flared into being.

To her shame Nicole felt herself instantly pressing ardently against the muscled length of him, and she took a perverse joy in the pain of his angry embrace. But then, just as his kiss deepened and warmed, Christopher abruptly thrust her ruthlessly from him as if she were something vile and ugly. His eyes blazing with contempt and something like hatred, he spun on his heels and flung out of the room without another word, leaving a stunned Nicole staring after him.

Shaken as much by the kiss as the unexpected ending of it, she sank slowly down on the stool behind the pianoforte. They'd been so easy with one another, she thought numbly, so comfortable for once, without any undertones, any treacherous currents, and then without warning it had all exploded into something dark and violent and unpleasant. Would she ever be able to remain unmoved by his nearness? she wondered bleakly. She caught her breath in anguish, realizing that she hated him almost as much as she loved him. Why, she thought unhappily, does it have to be him? Why do we have to have all those ugly memories to destroy us?

Christopher, striding furiously in the direction of his club, was wishing that things were different. But he believed that no matter what, he would still have distrusted Miss Nicole Ashford on sight, still have wondered how much like her mother she really was beneath the innocent and tantalizing exterior. He knew, he told himself angrily, from his own observation that she resembled a chameleon, changing so rapidly before his eyes from Nick to Nicole Ashford that he marveled at her duplicity.

But tonight, try as he might, he could find no blame in her actions. It had been he who had destroyed the fragile peace between them. There had been no cause to say what he had, and having said it, no reason to goad her further on to fury. If only she weren't so damned desirable, he thought jerkily, and he weren't so bloody eager to have her again. That look of contempt and hatred he had thrown at Nicole had been as much for himself as her—contempt that he could not keep his hands off her, that she could still move him; and hatred that *any* woman could shake him from his icy indifference.

Scowling blackly and in an ugly temper, he joined some new acquaintances at a faro table in one of the gaming rooms at Boodle's. Christopher had not been idle these past few days. Under his grandfather's auspicious recommendations he had been granted membership not only at Boodle's, but at White's and Brook's as well.

Simon had also naturally introduced his grandson to the sons and nephews of his friends, and as a consequence Christopher was now fairly well-known to the members of the *ton*. But intent upon finding the proof of the invasion that he needed, he had quietly gravitated toward the military element. And because he disliked intensely the thought of using Simon's friends, he placed those he met on two distinct levels. There were those gay blades about town, who were concerned with the cut of their coats, horses, and gambling, whom Christopher joined for the sheer enjoyment of their antics. With the military set he fixed his sights on those he suspected would have access to the information he needed and possessed an indiscreet or corrupt nature.

More a man of action than of guile, his present situation left him feeling hamstrung and helpless—a circumstance that tended to keep his temper barely below the simmering stage. But despite everything he was making some progress. He had managed to scrape up a meeting with an Army captain presently stationed with the Horse Guards, and then there was the young lieutenant in the Navy, home on leave, recovering, from a wound received at Orthes.

Captain Buckley, Christopher surmised, was inclined to be indiscreet, and he hoped that Lieutenant Kettlescope would prove to be corruptible.

His mind wandered from the faro table as he thought of the days ahead, of the nights to be spent drinking and gaming, listening for any bit of information, any casual gossip that might turn into solid fact. He groaned inwardly, cursing Jason. Then he grinned, for he knew that once the idea had been presented, nothing could have prevented him from demanding his part in it all.

But underneath all his worries and concerns, ran a deep satisfaction at seeing his grandfather again. Great-aunt Regina he still had reservations about. But the one member of the family whom he had both looked for and yet almost dreaded meeting had not appeared, nor had Simon or Regina mentioned him. Where the *hell* was Robert?

23

As Christopher played at faro, Robert Saxon was driving his team of chestnuts furiously toward London. His handsome features, marred by signs of dissipation, were further distorted by his black expression.

Damn him! he thought viciously. Why didn't he die and Simon too, that old fool!

In Robert's breast beat very little affection for anyone, except himself. He was a cold man who had hungered after only two things in his entire life. One had been denied him, simply because he had been born the second son, and the other because of an unkind trick of fate.

But Robert was not a man to let such minor things as an older brother stand in his way, nor the fact that the woman he wanted had a husband! His brother had been by far the easiest to remove. When Gaylord and his wife had left on a pleasure trip to Cornwall many years ago, Robert had accompanied them—until they reached a particularly treacherous stretch of coast road. At the posting inn where they had stopped for a last change of horses, Robert had suggested he remain behind to wait for several friends who were joining them. Gaylord had been an easygoing handsome man, and he had readily agreed, never thinking that his younger brother might have had an ugly motive for his actions. And so waving carelessly, Gaylord and his wife had driven off, unaware that Robert had partially cut the traces to the coach. Two miles down the road the cut leather had severed, and the coach had plunged into the sea, leaving Gaylord's young son, Christopher, the only obstacle in Robert's path. But Robert was a patient man, and he was confident that he would hit upon a plan that would take care of his nephew.

The accident that had claimed Gaylord's life had worked rather well for Robert, but neither he nor Annabelle had planned on *her* death in the apparent yachting accident that would claim her husband, leaving the beautiful young widow free to remarry. No one would ever know the bleak fury and searing anguish Robert had suffered when the news of Annabelle's death had reached him. That and suspicion—what the hell had really gone wrong that day? Why had the brat, Giles, been with them? Had Adrian discovered their plot too late to save himself and seen to it that Annabelle died with him? Or had Annabelle drowned as she tried to save her son? Those were questions that would never be answered, and like acid, they had for six long years eaten into his soul, corrupting whatever good had existed within him.

With Annabelle gone, he had become a man driven by demons; his only real satisfaction was knowing that at least his remaining desire was within his grasp—*he* would be the next Baron Saxon. But then five years ago Christopher had returned, Christopher whom he had hoped was dead at sea, and he had been forced to try again to rid himself of the one person who thwarted his ambitions. That time he had planned outright murder, but again Christopher escaped.

Robert's eyes narrowed, and with a savage stroke of his whip he lashed the straining horses to greater speed. His mouth twisting in a cruel smile, he promised venomously, *this* time you won't escape, my dear little nephew! This time you *won't*—even if I have to do it with my own hands.

Simon's note telling of Christopher's arrival had reached Robert while he was visiting friends in Kent, late in the afternoon. Making his excuses, he had left as soon after dinner as was decently possible, overriding their very reasonable objections against night travel. Robert had been adamant, though he knew he wouldn't make London tonight. He needed this swift flying ride through the night-darkened countryside to gather his forces for the confrontation with Christopher.

He had no idea of what tale Christopher might have told Simon, and his father's note had been singularly unrevealing, stating only that Christopher was presently staying with him in Cavendish Square. Robert had paled as he had read those unwelcome lines. Christopher returned and alive! And it wasn't hard to read between those noncommital lines to guess that they had been reconciled. Cursing, Robert had thrown the note violently away.

The relationship between Robert and his father was one of guarded indifference. Simon lived in Cavendish

Square for part of the year, enjoyed the season at Brighton, and then when these amusements palled, retreated to the quiet and tranquillity of Surrey. Robert, too, lived in London; he had a very elegant and expensive suite of rooms on Stratton Street. But he and his father seldom encountered one another, usually only when Robert's bills became too pressing or a nasty scandal looked like it might ruin him. Otherwise their only meetings were at certain, notable affairs of the season in London or Brighton.

Robert's wife, always sickly, had died seven years ago giving birth to a stillborn child, and it was her death that had prompted the idea of Adrian's accidental death to Robert as a way of at last freeing Annabelle. Robert had often thought it bitterly ironic that it was his own plan that had caused him to lose the one person who mattered to him.

His surviving children, for there had been two offspring of his marriage, had no more love and affection for him than he had for them. His daughter, Anne, was happily married to a dashing young peer of the realm and was in York awaiting the birth of her third child. His son was still at Eaton, and Robert fully expected Simon to sponsor the boy and see to his allowance when the young man left his school years behind and came to London.

If Christopher had wondered aloud why Robert's name had not been mentioned, Regina would have told him rather tartly it was because his uncle was such a cold, unfeeling beast! Robert, while he possessed to a degree the Saxon charm and could be extremely fascinating to the unwary, had not endeared himself to his family. Simon loved his youngest son, but he was not blind to Robert's excesses and faults—too often he'd had to rescue him from unsavory dealings. But no one knew the true extent of those faults. Even Regina, seeing beyond Simon's father love, never would have suspected her nephew of murder. But Robert did indeed have murder in his heart this night, as his curricle thundered toward London.

Another of Simon's notes had also aroused fury and consternation.

"My God, I don't believe it! Nicole has to be dead! That must be an imposter that Baron Saxon writes of!" Edward Markham had exclaimed angrily when he had been informed by his parents that evening of Simon's disturbing news. "What is she doing in London, if it *is*

Nicole? She would have presented herself here at her home! It must be a sham! I don't believe it!"

Simon's missive to the Markhams had been couched in the politest terms possible, but, like the note to his son, he had written little beyond the barest facts. Miss Nicole Ashford, their niece, was at present visiting at Cavendish Square. She had returned to England a fortnight or so ago from America. Perhaps, if it were convenient, the Markhams would care to call?

"Visiting?" Edward shouted wrathfully. "Visiting is she? Well, she will be leaving Cavendish Square the instant I get my hands on the little slut! Who does Lord Saxon think he is? You are her guardian, not he!"

Edward had grown used to believing that Nicole was dead and it was only a matter of time until all her wealth and lands became his. The entire Markham family had grown quite complacent over the years, certain that Nicole must have been the victim of some foul play.

The entire family was greatly shocked to learn of her whereabouts, shocked, chagrined, and slightly apprehensive. William, her uncle, had over the years funneled a large amount of rents and moneys due to Nicole's estates into his own properties, and he was not looking forward to an accounting of his guardianship. Edward, thinking that everything would be his—his without a bothersome wife tied round his neck—was furious. And Agatha disliked intensely the thought of having to share her role of Mistress of Ashland with Annabelle's detested child. None of them, though, had any doubt that their original plan for Nicole and Edward to marry wouldn't now be carried out. Edward would marry Nicole, and there would never be any awkward questions of how and where moneys had been spent during the time of her minority. And so, much in the manner of a pack dog determined to retrieve a particularly fat and juicy bone, they began to prepare to leave for London at the earliest moment.

Simon had penned both notes with malicious glee and was waiting with lively anticipation for the results of his work. He had toyed with the idea of warning the visitors at Cavendish Square of the probable invasions by Robert and the Markhams but had discarded it, thinking it much more diverting to let everyone be taken by surprise.

Robert arrived in London the following morning and went to his rooms on Stratton Street to snatch a few hours' sleep after driving through the night. Upon waking in the afternoon, he dressed with his usual careless style for the call at his father's home.

At forty-three Robert Saxon was still a fine figure. Despite his air of dissipation, the deep sardonic grooves in his face, he had great appeal to the feminine sex. Standing just over six feet, his body was as muscled and lean as it had been twenty years ago. The black hair was highlighted by two handsome wings of silver at the temples, and like Christopher, his complexion was as swarthy as a gypsy's. His eyes were an odd shade of color—neither green nor gold; his mouth was thin and tight, the very opposite of Christopher's with its sensuous curve, yet Robert was a deeply sensual man.

As Robert dressed for his visit, all of the inhabitants of Cavendish Square were at home for tea. They were gathered in the main salon, a handsome room that featured an Adam fireplace of Italian marble and pale gray silk-hung walls. As hostess, Lady Darby was pouring from a heavy silver tea urn, while Nicole, in a willow-green gown of jaconet, was sitting next to Mrs. Eggleston on a Chippendale double-chair sofa upholstered in rose brocade.

Simon was seated somewhat to Lady Darby's left with Christopher standing beside his chair. The two men were conversing amiably when Robert was announced.

The three ladies looked up, only faintly surprised, although Regina wondered with exasperation what Robert wanted from Simon this time and crossed her fingers that he wasn't going to create an unpleasant scene. She surmised that he might be disappointed at Christopher's presence, after having thought himself Simon's heir for years, but hoped he would behave as a gentleman for once in his life.

Robert had himself well in hand, his first surge of insane rage having passed. He was far too crafty to show his displeasure. But then something happened that drove all thought of Christopher from his mind.

Regina's appearance behind the tea table was not notable, for she often stayed with Simon. But Simon had made no mention in his note to Robert of Mrs. Eggleston's and Nicole's presence, and Robert was totally unprepared for Annabelle's daughter.

He would have known her anywhere. It was true, he thought as his gaze roved hungrily over Nicole sitting so demurely by Mrs. Eggleston, that her hair lacked the fiery red of Annabelle's, but the dark auburn glow of the sable locks was an unmistakable reminder of her mother. The similarity was in the petal texture of the warm apricot skin, the teasing tilt to the slender dark brows, the tantalizing curve of her lips, the straight, almost arrogant nose, and the slim full-bosomed body. In the color of the eyes lay the greatest difference. They were not Annabelle's deep pools of emerald, yet the shape was the same, and Robert suddenly found himself lost in their great topaz depths.

With an effort he tore his gaze away and focused blindly on Mrs. Eggleston. Vaguely he remembered her, and during Regina's introduction he was able to bring himself under control.

A cool smile on his lips, he remarked, "What a pleasant surprise to see you again, Mrs. Eggleston. I hope you will enjoy your stay here in London."

Mrs. Eggleston stammered some reply, for Robert had always tended to fluster her. Having acknowledged Mrs. Eggleston, he was now able once again to feast his eyes on Annabelle's daughter. Unable to help himself and further infuriating Christopher, who was watching them closely, Robert held Nicole's hand longer than was strictly necessary, kissing her slender fingers.

Under Robert's intent stare Nicole couldn't subdue the faint wave of color in her cheeks, but with an uncertain smile she openly met his look. Robert was bewitched, and in that moment the passion he had felt for Annabelle was transferred to Nicole. He forgot everything but the girl before him, and it was only Simon's curt voice that called him to order.

"Stop exercising your undoubted charm on my guests and come say hello to your nephew!" Simon demanded testily.

The purpose for his being in Cavendish Square came flooding back to Robert, but he skillfully disguised his rage, and with a sardonic smile curving his thin lips, he pivoted to face them. Calmly he said, "Forgive me! But it is so seldom you have visitors of such a delightful nature that I forgot myself. Hello, Christopher."

The antagonism between the two men was instant and tangible. Resembling two powerful beasts of prey, their gazes met and clashed like jagged lightning in a black sky, as the air nearly crackled with the force of dark emotions tightly leashed.

Christopher had frozen the moment Twickham announced Robert, but now, his face deliberately shuttered, his eyes bright and challenging, he bowed with studied grace, murmuring dryly, "Uncle. How satisfying to see you again after so many years."

Robert's brow quirked. "Satisfying?"

Smiling mockingly, Christopher replied, "Yes! You

have no idea how ardently I have looked forward to meeting you—again."

His eyes narrowing at the double meaning, Robert shrugged and said with apparent lightness, "How gratifying! I shall see that you are not disappointed!"

"I'm sure you will! I look forward to . . . ah . . . accommodating you!" Christopher promised with polite menace.

Robert tensed, but before he could answer, Simon, feeling this peculiar conversation had gone far enough, interrupted.

"Harrumph! Well, m'boy, you're looking fit. Hadn't expected, though, to see you before next week."

"Now that I rather doubt!" Robert retorted with a grim smile. "You must have known curiosity about Christopher's arrival would bring me posthaste. After all, it isn't often that one risen from the dead, so to say, returns to the ancestral mansion."

Of all the occupants of the room, only Christopher caught the underlying animosity in Robert's words. But Christopher had decided on his course of action, and he let the remark pass. A moment later the conversation was general, and he allowed himself a sigh of relief, almost glad that the first difficult meeting with Robert was behind him. His mouth tightened, though, and he shot Simon a dark look. That old rascal is going to have some explaining to do, he thought.

Later in the evening Christopher sought to have a private word with his grandfather, but Simon, whether by design or accident, quickly disappeared to his club and Christopher was thereby forced to postpone his interrogation.

Lying in his bed that night, he went over and over the conversation with Robert, knowing that Robert still hated him and was infuriated by his return to England. For a long time, he lay there in the darkness, knowing that his presence in Cavendish Square was anathema to Robert. And all the ugliness and hatred he had thought conquered, now engulfed him. Thrashing and tormented, not only by old memories but by the scene of Nicole smiling up at Robert, he twisted in his bed, unable to separate Nicole from Annabelle. Seeing Robert and Nicole together this afternoon had been too reminiscent of those old scenes.

Ah, Jesus Christ! I'm mad, he thought sickly. Mad to let the past destroy me, and mad to entangle myself with such ancient history at a time like this.

Christopher was not the only one tossing that night. Simon had been most disquieted by the confrontation between Robert and Christopher, aware that, for all their polite words, there was something dangerous and ominous between the two men.

Simon had hoped the unexpected meeting with Robert would shake Christopher into some revealing action. But, he reflected glumly, his grandson knew to a nicety how to hide his emotions, and beyond a slight stiffening of his body and the shuttered expression on his face, Christopher had betrayed nothing.

What did you expect? Simon asked himself. What did you want? Christopher to fall on Robert's neck with affection? Bah! Just because you suspect Robert may have had more to do with Christopher's sudden desire for the sea is no excuse to look for proof of what doesn't exist. And what will it gain you, he thought, to have your suspicion confirmed? To know that your son is an even greater blackguard than you already know? Would that make you happy?

Because no father wishes to believe evil of his own offspring, Simon would think no further on the subject. Christopher was returned to him and that was all that mattered.

The next morning immediately after breakfast, Christopher requested a word in private with his grandfather. Expecting such a request after Robert's appearance, Simon readily agreed and led Christopher to his study. Shutting the door behind them, Simon, never precisely his best first thing in the morning, demanded crossly, "What is it? What's biting you so badly I can't even be allowed to eat my breakfast in peace?"

Knowing that Simon had been finished eating a good half hour before he approached him, Christopher ignored the complaint. Waiting until his grandfather was seated behind his desk, Christopher said seriously, "It is nothing of great importance, but I suspect that you will not like what I have to say."

Simon stiffened, fearing that at last he would hear the truth of what he already suspected. And so braced was he for the abhorrent words he was certain must come, that for a second after Christopher ceased speaking he only stared. Then as the simple words sunk in, he repeated slowly, "You wish to move out? To have your own set of rooms?"

That was exactly what Christopher had in mind. In all his twisting and turning last night one decision had come to him. Staying with Simon was out of the question. In the coming weeks, more than likely, he would be doing a few things and seeing some people that he wished no one to know about. If he were to accomplish anything, he needed freedom of movement, freedom to come and go as he pleased at odd hours and times with no one to comment or wonder what he did or why.

Spies, he had decided somberly in the early hours of the morning, worked best in the shadows. But there was another reason he longed for his own lodgings. He had no wish to view again Robert bending solicitously over Nicole's hand. It was too vivid a reminder of Robert and Annabelle. Nicole, herself, haunted his dreams against his will, and her nearness could still bring about an instant physical longing that he despised as weakness. He was not adept at fighting temptation, and he thought it best to remove himself from his own personal temptress. He had done what he had intended in returning her to England. She was no longer his responsibility. Whatever had been between them was finished. *Dead.*

Christopher had expected an argument, but Simon surprised him by saying carelessly, "Do what you wish. You're too old now for me to order about." Eyeing Christopher's slightly startled face from under heavy brows, he inquired dryly, "You will call occasionally, I trust?"

"Of that you can be assured! I take it then you have no objections if I consult my agent about suitable lodgings for myself?" Christopher asked politely, both of them knowing the question was mere form.

"Oh, I've objections aplenty, but I doubt you'd heed them. I'm only thankful you're not determined to wrest young Nicole and Letty from me!" A fond smile on his lips, he confessed, "In the past week I've grown quite attached to that child. Thank God she is nothing like her mother! Nicole is a pleasure just to watch and a sweet, nice young thing to boot." Aware of the suddenly indifferent expression on Christopher's face, he hastily switched the subject. "Of course, Regina will have us all in a fret with this ball of hers, and you're wise to seek the safety of a different residence! Don't blame you a bit! Do it myself, if this wasn't my home!"

Laughing with real enjoyment at the almost regretful tone in his grandfather's voice, he tempted, "Join me?"

But Simon only laughed and said, "No, I'll not run from Regina." Though Christopher smiled, he felt a pang as he regarded Simon. The signs of his past ill health were more obvious than Christopher had first noticed—

he used a cane now and then, and his tall frame was somehow frail. The skin of his face seemed worn and thin, stretched tight across the prominent cheekbones. Suddenly Christopher hated the deception and lies and half-truths he was embroiled in and wished with all his heart the tale he told were true. But there was no going back, so he said lightly, "Well, if it becomes too much for you, you know my door will be open."

Simon only snorted. "Ha! I'll wager fifty pounds you'll take bloody well care that I *don't* move in with you!"

The dancing amber-gold eyes at variance with the mournful expression, Christopher cried reproachfully, "Grandfather! To think me capable of such a thing!"

Staring hard at the handsome face, Simon said abruptly, "I think you're capable of many things. Things I'd rather not know of." And deciding that he might as well be taken for a wolf as a lamb, he added deliberately, "You're like Robert in that manner."

Instantly the laughter fled Christopher's eyes, and in a flat voice he attacked, "You're capable of quite a few things yourself! Didn't you think I would be interested to know that you had written to him?"

Simon had the grace to look embarrassed, but he blustered, "*I* knew I had, and I'm the only one that needed to know, you young jackanapes!"

There was no comment from Christopher, seated on the corner of his grandfather's desk, one long leg swinging negligently as he appeared to be examining the few black hairs that grew on the back of his hand. The moments passed, and still saying nothing, he leisurely straightened the white cuffs of his shirt. Not looking at Simon, he asked carelessly, "Is there anyone else you may have written to that you don't feel it is necessary to tell me about?" And swiftly flicking his gaze to Simon's face, he caught the slightly guilty expression that crossed it.

"The Markhams, perhaps?" he purred in a silky tone.

Defiantly Simon retorted, nettled by the cat-and-mouse game, "As a matter of fact, yes! Yes, I have!"

"And you didn't think I'd be interested? That I wouldn't want to be prepared?" Christopher snapped, his eyes blazing with exasperation.

"*I'm* prepared!" Simon growled. "And I'm the only one who needs to be!" As Christopher continued to regard him without pleasure, Simon said in a more conciliatory tone of voice, "There is no reason to upset the ladies. They'll only fret and worry and will be unable to do anything in the end anyway. When Markham and that cub of his arrives, I'll take care of them. You see if I don't!"

Christopher contemplated the glitter of excitement in Simon's eyes, and enlightenment dawned. "You're enjoying this!" Christopher accused, sudden laughter not far from his voice.

Glowering at his grandson, Simon loftily made no reply, but after a second his lips twitched into a grin. "Perhaps," he admitted grudgingly. Then his face the picture of hypocritical piety, he said somberly, "There are so few pleasures left a man of my age, and you would deny them to me."

Laughter bubbling in his throat, Christopher shook his black head. "Oh, no, grandfather! You have my blessing to amuse yourself however you see fit—especially when it is the discomfiture of the Markhams that pleases you!"

Unaware they would be viewed with amusement, the Markhams were prepared to descend upon Cavendish Square. Astonishingly though, after their arrival in London on Thursday, Edward suddenly reversed himself and declined to accompany his parents to Lord Saxon's. More astute than either William or Agatha, he surmised correctly that Lord Saxon had no intention of tamely releasing Nicole into their hands. He could also picture the confrontation that would result—Lord Saxon arrogantly adamant and his father raging and blustering while his mother proceeded to have hysterics. No, he thought with a shudder, he would *not* accompany them.

He would instead let his parents do all the threatening and abusing, and he, appearing with all cousinly candor, embarrassment at their actions barely hidden, would proceed to woo Nicole on his own. There was, Edward decided with self-satisfaction, no reason to put all of one's eggs in a single basket. If his parents failed to gain custody of Nicole one way, he would do it another. He had no wish to be part of an uncomfortable scene that Nicole would no doubt remember with distaste.

William and Agatha were not unnaturally disturbed by his about-face. It was especially provoking in view of how angry and furious he had been at first. Now he seemed indifferent, and they could think of no reason for it, Edward having declined to tell them of his own personal plans.

Consequently on Friday morning, the morning after Christopher's meeting with Simon, it was only William and Agatha who came to call at the elegant house in

Cavendish Square. They were met by an extremely supercilious Twickham. Simon had instructed him to be as high-stomached as he pleased, so he looked them up and down disparagingly and murmured with disdain. "If you will wait, I shall see if the master is receiving this morning."

He left them standing in the hall and with stately movements disappeared down the hallway. Finding Simon alone in the breakfast room, a conspiratorial gleam in his eyes, Twickham, in a voice hushed with anticipation, said, "They have arrived, sir! I have left them waiting in the hall."

"Ha!" Simon snorted with satisfaction, the light of battle leaping in his eyes. Thoughtfully he regarded Twickham. "Think we should keep them waiting more than thirty minutes?"

Reflecting with pleasure that his master had not been so lively for some time, Twickham allowed his punctilious features to lapse into the semblance of a smile and said calmly, "Yes, sir, I believe around thirty minutes would be sufficient. The gentleman was already somewhat impatient. He should be nicely browned by then!"

Almost rubbing his hands together in glee, Simon remarked, "You know, Twickham, I'm going to enjoy this! Damn, but it's a good thing my grandson has come home! Haven't had as much sport in years!"

24

While the Markhams waited in the hall with growing choler, Simon settled back to savor the coming meeting. Twickham busied himself about the study, thinking with fondness and satisfaction how fortunate it was that the young master had come home.

Upstairs in her dressing room, ignorant of the pending encounter, Regina was thinking much the same. Christopher's return had done a world of good for her brother and for that she was thankful. She was especially thankful that Christopher had so opportunely met with Letitia Eggleston.

Regina preferred the single state herself, but could not bear to lay eyes on an unmarried man without instantly devising schemes to change his way of life. A bachelor was somehow a personal affront to her honor, and she felt it was her duty quickly and efficiently to rectify such a deplorable state.

She had for years nagged Simon to remarry and had gone to great lengths to introduce him to suitable widows and spinsters. To her mortification Simon would have none of them. When Colonel Eggleston had died she had, after a tiny pious thought for his departed soul, been almost indecently overjoyed. She had been sure that, after a proper period of mourning, Letitia would marry Simon as they should have done years before. When she learned of Mrs. Eggleston's abrupt and unexpected departure, she could have bitten off her tongue in vexation. But now all would be well. She would see to it!

Christopher's unmarried state did not interest her at the moment to the same degree that Simon's did. But she did give it a passing scrutiny and decided judiciously that once her brother was safely settled she would see to Christopher's affairs. As she had grown very fond of Nicole, it was only logical to conclude that a match between Christopher and Nicole was something to be greatly desired.

Nicole, sitting in her room, was staring blankly off into space, her spirits unaccountably low. Earlier she had listlessly allowed Mauer to dress her, and when Mrs. Eggleston had popped into her room to inquire if she wished to go to Colburn's Lending Library, she had apathetically declined. Even the news that Christopher would be escorting the two of them, if she cared to come, aroused no response.

A little worriedly, Mrs. Eggleston had acquainted Christopher with Nicole's refusal, but Christopher had only shrugged his shoulders, and a moment later he and Mrs. Eggleston had left the house on their way to the library.

Knowing Mrs. Eggleston and Christopher were gone from the house, Nicole wandered around her room in a sudden fit of restlessness, wishing that she had accompanied them. Anything would have been better than her own company. Unable to bear her own lonely society a second longer, she started down the stairs in search of Regina, not realizing that Regina was still hovering over her morning toilet in her dressing room.

Nicole, concentrating hard on why she was so spiritless and malleable lately, was halfway down the stairs leading to the main entrance hall when she became aware of the man and woman standing there. She stopped in surprise, for it was unlike Twickham to leave someone standing there, and as she looked at the waiting couple with growing curiosity, recognition was instantaneous.

A gasp of surprise and dismay escaped her, and at the sound William and Agatha, who had been busy whispering angrily to one another, glanced up.

If Nicole had recognized her aunt and uncle instantly, it took them a moment or two longer to realize that the tall, lovely young woman in the stylish lavender gown of French cambric was their niece. An intangible air of grace and elegance about her gave them pause, and in those few measuring moments the inconsequential thought crossed Nicole's mind that five years hadn't changed them very much.

Agatha was fatter, her hair a brighter, more improbable shade of gold, her dress still as indecently snug, this morning's choice being an unflattering puce silk. And William, well, William, if possible, was redder in the face, his lank, nondescript hair thinner, and his girth greater.

Staring unblinkingly at the slim young woman on the stairs William felt a swift rush of fury, suddenly aware that it might not be as simple as they had thought to crush this objectionable creature into submission. She was obviously no longer a child to be ordered at will, nor was she totally at their command—she had Lord Saxon's protection. She could no longer be scolded and dismissed lightly, nor would her money spill unquestioned into his hands. The thought of what an inquiry into his guardianship would reveal increased his sense of ill-usage, and his anger, kept barely below the boiling point, burst its bounds as with an oath he vaulted up the stairs.

Grasping a startled Nicole in a painful grip around her wrist, he attempted to drag her down the stairs. Throwing Nicole a malevolent look, he commanded, "You'll come with me, miss! And this instant! How like you to run away and embarrass us so. After all we did for you, you ungrateful little snip. I can promise you, you're going to regret that you ever shamed us so. Come along now, I say!"

Nicole, after her first astonishment, was furious, and twisting her wrist in his hand, she struggled violently to free herself. Promptly forgetting all the precepts drilled into her brain by Mrs. Eggleston, she spat, "Let me go, you slimy eel, or I'll darken both your daylights!"

Flabbergasted at such unladylike language coming from a picture of refinement and elegance, William's grip loosened, and Nicole immediately slapped him across the face and, for good measure, gave him a crippling kick in the shins.

Howling with rage and pain, William seized her arm and shook her brutally. "Why you little slut! I'll—"

Simon had just motioned to Twickham to show them into his study when William's angry howl vibrated in the air.

The sound galvanized Simon into action, and moving with the speed of a man half his age, he thrust the speechless Twickham aside and marched out into the hall. At the sight of Nicole fighting desperately with a man he freely stigmatized as a grubbing maw worm, his temper exploded.

"How dare you! Unhand her this instant, you blackguard!" he roared in a voice that shook with fury. His eyes spat sparks of molten gold as he advanced into the hall. "How *dare* you!" he thundered again, his voice carrying throughout the house, bringing on the run several of the servants and Regina. Regina, stopping at the head of the stairs, took in the situation in a glance, but knowing that her brother abominated interference, she held her tongue.

279

William, queasily aware that he had exceeded himself beyond all limits, ventured a sickly ingratiating smile, while Agatha speedily fell into hysterics. Babbling incoherent excuses and crying in noisy gulps, she stood in the center of the hall completely ignored except for one or two nervous glances sent her way by one of the younger servants.

If William had been content just to focus his apologetic manner on Simon, the scene might have ended differently, but he made the fatal error of trying to redeem himself with Nicole. With the same ingratiating smile in his face, he patted her arm and muttered, "Now, now, this is not what it appears. Little Nicole and I were just having a minor disagreement, weren't we, my dear?"

Nicole, her temper still flaming, and genuinely horrified by what had happened, but wanting the unpleasantness over as soon as possible, probably would have followed his lead and smoothed over the incident if William, his smile fading a trifle and an ugly look in his eyes, hadn't tightened his hand threateningly on her arm and prodded, "Isn't that so, my dear?"

Distastefully she shook off his hand and in a cold voice said clearly, "Please release my arm this instant! No, we were *not* having a minor disagreement! You attacked me and were trying to force me to leave with you."

There was a concerted gasp from those assembled, and Simon, his anger barely under control, approached the stairs with stiff-legged strides. One foot on the bottom step, he stated in a dangerous tone, "Leave my home, immediately, and do not *ever* show your face here again! If you are unwise enough to do so, I shall have you beaten from my door like the cowardly jackal you are!"

Inflamed by Simon's barely concealed contempt, William's face went dark with rage, and spinning on Nicole, he snarled, "This is all your fault, you wicked jade! But I am your guardian and you will come with me!" Flashing Simon a look of dislike, he sneered, "You forget yourself, my lord. Nicole is my niece and I am her legal guardian. You have no right to stop me from removing her from this house!"

And William proceeded to compound his already precarious position by once again laying an ungentle hold on Nicole and ordering loftily, "Come along, now. Your belongings can be sent to our lodgings later."

Knowing that Simon could do nothing to help her unless she made the first move, Nicole thought swiftly. She knew Simon would not allow her to be taken against her will, but he could do nothing if she didn't fight herself. William's overbearing tone and manner had shown her unmistakably that her uncle had certainly not changed in the passing years, and as he gave her a vicious yank down one stair, her decision was made.

Drawing herself up proudly, she said quietly, "I have no intention of going anywhere with you." Then twitching her arm quickly away from his grasp, she whirled and sprinted up two steps, intending to avoid further conflict. But William, cursing and swearing, caught her by the shoulder. Wrenching her around, and oblivious to Regina at the head of the stairs and Simon and the others staring at him, William struck Nicole a savage blow across one cheek and shouted, "We'll just see about that, miss! You'll learn who is your master after I get through with you!"

Any restraint Nicole may have tried to put on her temper vanished, and with the imprint of William's hand burning her face, in a voice full of loathing, she spat, "Why you fat toad!" and returned his violence with a stunning wallop to his left cheek.

William rocked on his heels, and Nicole, deciding she was damned as it was, gave him a punishing right to his protruding stomach.

Everything had occurred so swiftly that those watching were momentarily stunned, but as William stumbled backward, Regina, upon whom Agatha's histrionics were beginning to wear, started determinedly down the stairs. Simon, his cane held like a club, rushed angrily up the stairs and commenced to give the already reeling William several smart blows about his shoulders.

The added attack was enough to overbalance William, and with profanities streaming from his mouth he tumbled ungracefully down the eight or nine steps to land in a crushing heap at Agatha's feet.

"Ha!" Simon grunted satisfactorily, his eyes bright with elation. Nicole glanced at him, and the audacious wink he sent her caused a sudden glint of laughter in her eyes. Looking quickly away to keep from giggling, for Simon was so blatantly satisfied with their combined endeavors, she watched as Regina sailed passed the recumbent William and the sobbing Agatha to snatch up a vase filled with roses and efficiently throw it in Agatha's face.

The shock of the water stilled her noise, and even William was startled enough to cease his string of gutter language. Silence reigned in the hall at Cavendish Square.

Then in her most awesome and grand fashion, Regina

said calmly, "Twickham, see that these callers are removed, at once!" Sending a stern pair of eyes in which an imp of amusement danced to the two culprits still standing on the stairs, she commanded, "Nicole go to your room, we'll discuss this later. Simon, I believe you had better retire also. Remember, the physician has said exertion is bad for your health."

Picking up her cue instantly, Simon muttered, "Yes, yes, you're absolutely right." He and Nicole beat a hasty retreat up the remaining stairs and out of sight.

William, seeing his prey vanishing, staggered to his feet, crying hoarsely, "No! Nicole is to go with us."

Regina fixed an admonitory look on him and said dispassionately, "That, I hardly think so, sir! You have entered, uninvited, my brother's home; harrassed and abused our guest; treated myself to a display of the type of language I hope never to hear again; and your wife has nearly deafened my ears with her ill-bred screechings. With those events fresh in my mind, I can assure you that Nicole Ashford will never be released into your hands. Further, I am thinking seriously of laying charges against you and your wife. You would be wise to leave before I make my decision!"

Speechless for once, William stared open-mouthed at her, and before he even realized it, Twickham, with the help of the under-butler, had skillfully piloted both the Markhams out the massive front door and bolted it behind them.

Bowing with deep respect to Regina, Twickham said solemnly, "If you will permit me to say so, madame, that was *very* well done!"

"Well, yes, I rather thought so too!" Regina agreed with her usual modesty. "Simon, where are you?" Regina called. "I know you're probably hanging over the upper railing like some vulgar housemaid. Come down!"

"Ha!" Simon barked, appearing so promptly that Regina's unkind cut was proved true. In an aggrieved tone he went on, "What else could I do when you ordered me about so? And in my own home too! I tell you, Regina, I won't put up with your overbearing ways!" Unfortunately he ruined this reproachful tirade by a delighted chuckle. "Clever of you to hustle them out that way," he admitted. "Always said you were a great gun for a woman!"

His sister only gave an unladylike snort and asked, "Where is Nicole?"

"Here I am," Nicole called and followed Simon down into the hallway.

Aware of the interested stares of the still-assembled servants, Simon whisked the two ladies into his study. Twickham, he knew, would see to it that nothing of this morning's incident was bruited about among the servants, but he suspected that for the next few days there would be many snickers in the kitchen and stables. While it had afforded him a certain amount of enjoyment, he was uncomfortably aware that it had been a very serious affair.

Nicole, too, was conscious of the gravity of the situation, and feeling she had disgraced herself she was thoroughly ashamed of her own part in the fracas. In a low, mortified tone she said. "I must apologize for my share in that deplorable scene. I should not have lost my temper, and I should never have struck my uncle. If you throw me out into the street, it will be no more than I deserve."

"I quite agree. You acted little better than a fishwife," Regina replied amiably, a twinkle deep in the dark eyes, however, taking the sting out of the words. "But I must own that in this case I can hardly blame you. What a disgusting creature your uncle is! No wonder you have no wish to return to his roof. But," she said with a frown, "what has occurred is a most serious event. What are we to do now, Simon?"

The two ladies were sitting on a red-brocade couch while Simon was seated across from them in a high-back chair of black leather. His face was stern and thoughtful, and Nicole, filled with guilt at her shocking conduct, was certain that despite the conspiratorial wink on the stairs, he was disgusted with her and meant to ban her from his home.

Until this moment she hadn't realized how very fond she had grown of Lord Saxon and his sister, Regina. Being thrust away from them would be anguish, almost like losing her family again. Bitterly she regretted her actions, and once again she attempted to apologize. But Simon held up his hand and did not allow her to speak. He gave her a measured scrutiny, and then when she thought she could bear it no longer, Simon grinned at her.

"Aha!" he snorted with gratification. "What'll we do, hey? Well, we'll fight!" He shot Nicole a piercing glance. "Won't we, gel?"

The cold fear around her heart melting, Nicole smiled tremulously. "If you say so, sir."

"Of course, I say so! Why I wouldn't let that . . . ah

283

. . . fat toad, I believe you called him, have say over one of my dogs!" Thoughtfully he added, "He *does* resemble one, doesn't he?"

Regina gave an exasperated sigh. "Fat toad, or not," she began determinedly, "he *is* Nicole's legal guardian. We had no right to deny him. Legally, he can remove her from this house and order her to do as he pleases." Looking at Nicole, Regina, always forthright, asked, "I don't wish to wound you, my dear, but how is it that you have two such dirty dishes for relatives?"

"They are not really related to me at all," Nicole answered truthfully. "Aunt Agatha is my mother's stepsister, and when my parents died, there was no one else."

"I see," Regina said slowly. "That means that their guardianship of you could be overthrown. Especially if someone like Simon were prepared to push the issue. Are you?" she asked Simon.

"Of course, I am! Didn't I just say so?" he barked testily. "Now that the Markhams have arrived in town, I'll go around and visit my friend Judge White in Russell Square. He'll have the ticket—I have no doubt of that! Very knowing fellow, Judge White. Besides," he added thoughtfully, "the Markhams ain't going to do anything. I've a suspicion that your uncle has been playing ducks and drakes with your fortune, and I'll wager he don't relish an inquiry. We'll just sit tight. It's my guess that for a while at least they'll bide their time and keep mum."

"Hmmm. For once I rather agree with you. Particularly if there is anything illegal in his handling of the estates," Regina remarked reflectively. "Certainly they won't seek a court's ruling. And even if they did—today's contretemps would definitely put them in a bad light. There are several of us who can swear that he struck Nicole in a rage, and I think the fact that he is no relation would weigh against them. Especially if Nicole's fortune is a great deal more than their resources. Is it, my dear?"

"I think so," Nicole replied uncertainly. "I really have no idea."

"It is," Simon said dryly. "William Markham is barely a gentleman farmer. His property would provide his family with a comfortable living, nothing more. Nicole's father was a wealthy man. He could have bought and sold someone like Markham a dozen times over and never even noticed it. As I see it, all we have to do is outwait them. Nicole will reach her majority in less than three

284

years, and if she marries before then, she'll come into her fortune even sooner."

"But I can't live off you for three years," Nicole exclaimed, feeling that Simon had already done a great deal for her.

"Why not?" Simon growled. "I see nothing wrong with it. You and Letitia will be my pensioners and I'll gladly stand the nonsense. You'll not break me, you know."

Biting her lip, Nicole was driven to protest, guiltily aware that she was already in Cavendish Square under false pretenses. "It wouldn't be right. I can't allow you to do such a thing. There must be a simpler way."

"You can't allow me?" Simon burst out irascibly. "Listen here, missy, it's either letting me do so or going to your uncle. Now you can take your choice!"

Two spots of hot color burning in her cheeks, the topaz-brown eyes no longer soft, Nicole's volatile temper flared. Stiffly she said, "You know there is no question of choice! But I must insist that you keep a strict record of your expenditures on my and Mrs. Eggleston's behalf, and when my fortune is my own, I will repay every penny!" Having again forgotten that young ladies of quality hardly spoke and acted as she was doing, she rose angrily to her feet and swept from the room.

Once the door was shut firmly behind her, Regina and Simon silently regarded each other. Finally Simon smiled ruefully. "Got spirit, that little filly! I suppose I shouldn't have been so blunt?"

"Exactly!" Regina answered promptly. "Really, Simon, you do alarm me sometimes. There was no reason to be so tactless."

His moment of compunction disappeared instantly, and Simon scowled at his sister. "Bah! Don't you start now with one of your famous scolds. The morning has been lively enough!"

"I quite agree," she snapped. Rising to her feet, she continued, "When will you see Judge White? I don't feel that you should delay it too long. After all, the Markhams may have an entirely unblotted copybook, and may go directly to a lawyer and start proceedings against *us!*"

Simon grimaced. "This afternoon. I'll send a note over this morning to see if it will be convenient. Does that satisfy you?"

Regina permitted herself to smile. "Yes, my dear, it does. But Simon, remember not to tax yourself too far. I know you don't like anyone to speak of your health, but you *did* nearly die with that last seizure five years ago.

And your physician says you mustn't overtire yourself."
Ignoring the gathering storm on Simon's face, she added,
"Why don't you have Christopher see the judge instead?"

"Damn you, Gina! If you and that mealy-mouthed
sawbones are going to coddle me, I might as well be
dead! Besides," he finished with a very youthful grin,
"I'm enjoying myself!"

Shaking her head and smiling, Regina dropped an affectionate kiss on his dark head. "I know you are, you
old devil! But for my sake, don't overdo it."

"Ha!"

With a laugh at his usual bad-tempered retort, she left
the room. But her smile faded as she walked slowly up
the stairs. The situation was grave. If Nicole were compelled by law to live with the Markhams, there was no
doubt in Regina's mind that her life would be wretched
indeed. Wretched and dangerous, she decided thoughtfully, recalling the ugly look in William's eye and the
savage manner in which he had struck the girl. Like Simon, though, she believed that for the moment the
Markhams would do little except grumble. If they were
wise, she reflected without enjoyment, they would put
forth a smiling face and pretend that Nicole, with their
blessing, was visiting with the Saxons and say no more.
As long as there were no immediate demands for an
accounting of his stewardship and no requests for money,
Mr. Markham would probably not press too hard in
changing the situation. It was unfortunate that there were
three years in which the circumstances would remain
unresolved, because she was certain there would be several more repellent scenes with the Markhams before Nicole's majority was reached—unless Nicole married . . .

Regina stopped in mid-stride, her expression suddenly
very pleased. Yes. The very thing! An objective in sight,
a pleasant one at that, Regina smiled happily to herself
and walked toward her room to finish her interrupted
toilet.

It was nearly an hour later when she descended the
stairs again, feeling she now looked her best, especially
with the silver-streaked hair caught up in a fetching chignon and her dress of Devonshire brown twilled sarcenet
fitting her angular body admirably. She had stopped for
a moment in Nicole's room, but Nicole, she was informed by Mauer, was in the conservatory downstairs.
Staring thoughtfully at the thin-lipped dresser, she had
asked, "How is she?"

Mauer had hesitated then admitted bluntly, "She'll

have a nasty bruise for a few days where that monster struck her. She didn't say much about it."

Frowning, she had left the room. Deciding to leave Nicole to her own devices for the time being, she headed for the morning salon, not certain what she was going to do—a most unusual state of affairs for someone of Regina's temperament. But before she had a chance to think very deeply or become bored with her own company, Christopher and Mrs. Eggleston arrived home.

Mrs. Eggleston was rosy-cheeked and full of enthusiasm for the several books she had selected.

"Oh, Regina, just look here! I was most fortunate to obtain a copy of Lord Byron's *The Corsair*. It has just been published, you know."

"How very nice, my dear. I do not care for that young man's work, but he has been very popular since his *Childe Harold* was published a year or two ago."

"Oh, yes, I was quite excited to find a copy of it just after we arrived. Such an admirable young man!"

"I won't argue with you, but you have been out of the country for some time and know nothing of his carryings on. The way he and Caro Lamb have been behaving is beyond belief. Although," Regina added with satisfaction, "I believe that little affair is now over. I have heard that he means to offer for Annabella Milbanke. You know she turned him down once already?"

Mrs. Eggleston's blue eyes wide with interest, she breathed, "Why, no! However do you hear all these things?"

Christopher, realizing that the two of them were ready to sit down and brew some scandal broth, stifled a grin and remarked, "If you ladies will excuse me? I have an appointment with my agent to view some lodgings, and I don't wish to keep him waiting."

Mrs. Eggleston gave him a dismissing smile and repeated again how very much she had appreciated his company, but Regina, gossip instantly the farthest thing from her mind, said, "I would like a word with you first, Christopher. Letitia, please excuse us for a moment, won't you?"

Bewildered, but correctly divining that Regina wanted a word in private with her grandnephew, Mrs. Eggleston quickly murmured something about seeing to her tea and faded gracefully from the room.

Her departure created a momentary silence, and Christopher, his relaxed, smiling manner gone, a wary expression in his eyes, asked after a second, "Well, Aunt, what is it?"

Regina hesitated, knowing she should probably leave the telling of this morning's events to Simon. But she wanted to see for herself how Christopher took the news of the Markhams' arrival, and more interestingly William Markham's attack on Nicole. So bluntly and succinctly she told him what had transpired. For all the reaction she got from him, she might as well have saved her breath. There was the tiniest flick of muscle in his right cheek and an odd flash that lit his gold eyes for the briefest second to reveal that he felt anything at all. Regina searched his handsome dark features intently, hoping for some further sign that Markham's striking of Nicole had affected him, but there was nothing. And when she had finished speaking, he merely drawled in an indifferent tone, "And where is Nicole now?"

Frustrated by his lack of emotion, Regina almost didn't tell him, but thinking better of it, she snapped, "I'm sure I don't know why you should wish to know, but she is in the conservatory."

Christopher raised one heavy brow at the tone of her voice and only added to her sense of disappointment by saying smoothly, "Well, then, if Nicole was well enough to leave her room, she can't have been too upset by the Markhams' visit." With an infuriatingly mocking smile on his beautiful mouth, he added, "And if I know Nicole, she probably enjoyed herself thoroughly. Now, if you will excuse me?"

Regina glared at him, wishing violently that she could read what went on behind those thickly lashed gold eyes. But she could not and had to console herself with the small knowledge that while he had not given much away, that telltale bunch in his lean cheek and that momentary glitter in his eyes boded ill for someone.

As he left his aunt, his air of disinterest vanished; his face was suddenly hard and ruthless. Taking the stairs two at a time, he quickly reached his rooms. Declining Higgins's help, he swiftly changed into a pair of buckskins and riding boots. It took only a second, and on the point of rushing out the door, he threw over his shoulder in a curt voice, "Find out where the Markhams are staying. As soon as I've seen Nicole, I'll be paying Mr. William Markham a visit!"

The conservatory was at the rear of the house and it was the pride of Lord Saxon's head gardener. The domed roof was all of glass, and a profusion of greenery and blossoms enchanted the eye and titillated the senses. A miniature waterfall and fishpond were cleverly constructed in one corner of the huge room, and there were stone benches scattered throughout the seemingly natural paths that crisscrossed the area. It was like finding a beautifully cared for private park under glass. Unfortunately it was seldom used or displayed, only being in demand when a ball or some important function was in progress. Nicole had quickly discovered it was one place that she could always find privacy, and she often escaped to its quiet and peace.

Christopher found Nicole seated on one of the stone benches near the fishpond. She didn't hear his approach, and for a moment he watched her as she stared, apparently engrossed in the orange and gold fish that swam in the shallow depths. She was still wearing the lavender gown, and her hair, worn loose today, hid part of her face as she bent forward.

He said her name softly, and with a start of surprise she jerked around. Her eyes flew to his and she knew instantly that he had already been told of this morning's affair. What his response had been she couldn't quite determine—his features were carefully controlled. But then Christopher always kept himself in perfect command of any situation, she thought bitterly. Nothing ever perturbed him or set him back—damn it!

She greeted him coolly, her own emotions held firmly in check. All she needed now, she decided tightly, was another scene to send her screaming to Bedlam.

But Christopher seemed to have no intention of creating a scene as his eyes carefully scanned her upturned face. Without comment he noted the pale complexion and taut curve to her usually soft mouth. Then he reached out and slowly tipped up her chin, and stared keenly at the disfiguring bruise that marred one perfect cheek. His hand, incredibly gentle, brushed it lightly, and when she flinched, his lips thinned and an angry glitter entered his eyes. But Nicole, unable to stand the silence or his touch, was too conscious of her emotions to notice his, and she slapped his hand aside, snapping outrageously, "I've already been mauled once this morning, do you intend, now, to gloat over it?"

Christopher's expression didn't change except, perhaps, to grow harder, and Nicole experienced the familiar surge of resentment at his ability to remain aloof and unmoved. Her resentment didn't abate one bit when, his eyes mocking hers, he said coolly, "I don't recall that I have ever gloated over your misfortunes, Nick."

Her eyes sparkling angrily and the faint flush of temper blooming on her cheeks, she taunted, "At least I should be used to being struck—you did it often enough! Do you think William does it as well?"

For just a second Nicole wondered if she had pushed him too far. But he made no move and said instead in a scathing voice, "I may have boxed your ears, which you richly deserved upon occasion, but I'm afraid my memory falls short of remembering ever hitting you so hard that I bruised your face in such a fashion!"

"No!" she retorted sweetly. "Instead you seduced me!"

A muscle knotted in his jaw, and Nicole had the hollow satisfaction of knowing she had gotten under his skin. Her mixed elation was short-lived, however, for Christopher countered levelly, "Yes, I did that. But I think I am more sinned against than sinning. How was I to know that you were no more than some little tart after adventure or that you hadn't been Allen's mistress? I did no more than any other man in my position would have. And," he added cruelly, his own temper slipping its leash, "I seem to recall that you enjoyed it!"

Nicole's face paled, and without thinking, she leaped to her feet and struck Christopher full force with an open palm across the mouth.

His eyes shutting instinctively in protection, he stepped back in surprise—surprise and anger. When he opened his eyes a split second later, anger was very apparent in them.

Rebelliously, Nicole awaited his reaction, hating herself and him for the seemingly effortless way he could arouse her to fury and blind action. What was there about him, she wondered fiercely, that drove her to defy him, to goad him until he reacted as blindly as she did.

For a long minute Christopher surveyed her; his lips twisting into a tight smile, he said at last, "No wonder your uncle struck you! If you behave with him as you do with me, I think I should offer him congratulations instead of a sword point!"

Warily, Nicole eyed him, well enough acquainted with his actions to know that, despite his careless words, he was furious and that her maddened blow would not be allowed to pass so easily. "What do you mean by that?" she asked, frowning at his words.

His expression bland, he answered quietly, "You don't

think William is going to get by with merely a scold from my grandfather, do you?"

Dry mouthed at the implication of what he said, her eyes very big, Nicole whispered, "You're not going to challenge him to a duel?"

Christopher's mouth smiled, but his eyes remained cold and deadly and she read her answer there. Forgetting instantly their own argument, she placed a pleading hand on his arm and said breathlessly, "Oh, Christopher, do not! He is a dangerous man, and he will not meet you without first having taken steps to assure that he will win! He will kill you! It was only a blow—not a mortal insult. Let it be!"

Unemotionally, Christopher removed her hand from his arm. "I rather think it is up to me to decide whether it was a mortal insult or not," he replied dryly.

"Oh, but . . ."

His face darkening with rage held barely in control, Christopher cut off her further protest by grasping her by the shoulders and snarling, "Shut up, Nick! You may be willing to overlook his actions, but I'm afraid I am not! No one strikes you, while you are under my protection. I may do it if you drive me to it, but I will not allow that piece of offal to do so!" Lips curling in a sneer at her look of disbelief, he added, "Oh, yes, even you I will not have mistreated—except perhaps by myself."

In confusion she stared at his angry face, wishing desperately that she understood him, but beyond the cold anger in his eyes, his features revealed nothing. She couldn't help herself from feeling a twinge of fear for him and softly said, "Be careful, Christopher."

His hold on her tightened painfully and his mouth curved in a crooked smile. "Concern for me? Now that I find hard to believe!"

The ready anger came flooding back, and she fought violently against the hands that held her prisoner. "You utter beast!" she panted. "Let me go!"

"Oh, no, my dear, I owe you something for that little display of bad manners a moment ago." A thread of amusement in his voice, he stared down at her furious face.

Nicole froze, but angled her chin at him defiantly. "Go ahead then, strike me! There is obviously little difference between you and my uncle!" she sneered.

"Oh, but there is, my little vixen," he promised softly. "A great deal of difference." And jerking her against him, his hard mouth caught hers in a punishing kiss.

Nicole frantically sought to suppress the wild surge of pleasure that coursed through her veins at the tormenting pressure of his mouth, but even knowing he was kissing her to chastise, to hurt, she melted into the warm strength of his body, her lips parting under the demanding assault of her senses. Christopher's body responded instantly to the soft crush of hers, and with something like triumph, she felt his desire leap and grow as their locked bodies strained closer together. His hand moved tantalizingly down her back, urging her nearer, caressing her hips. The dull ache of passion in her loins became almost unbearable as his tongue explored and probed the sweet wine of her mouth, and she knew if he wanted her, she wouldn't stop him.

He raised his head slowly, and from the desire-blurred look in his eyes Nicole knew he was experiencing much the same wild senseless emotion. Somewhere in the back of Christopher's brain a warning was hammering, a warning that discovery could happen at any moment, but he was beyond the point of being able to draw back, and with a groan he pulled Nicole to him, suddenly not caring if the king himself were to find them. His mouth found hers with a frightening urgency, and lost to coherent thought they slowly sank down beside the quiet fishpond.

In the tight grip of aching desire, Nicole made only a soft murmur of resistance when Christopher lifted her gown and pushed aside the lacy chemise, his hand warm and compelling as he sought the softness between her thighs. Blindly he found the delicate triangle, and at his touch, as he stroked and fondled, probing deep within her, the last remnant of sanity fled them both, leaving only the need to join with the other.

He took her swiftly, the swelling pressure of his manhood as he drove compulsively into her welcoming softness, flooding Nicole with pleasure and filling her urgent desire. Their bodies came together in a sensual tempo, each rushing to meet the thrust and lunge of the other, oblivious to anything but the heedless flame of passion that engulfed them. There were both exquisite pleasure and bitter anguish in this mindless driven desire that burned within them; neither was willing to admit that it had its roots in something deeper, finer, and more lasting than animal lust.

At this moment Christopher was only conscious of the smooth, sinuous, twisting body beneath his, and Nicole of the hard muscled force that was buried within her. The first swirling mists of fulfillment were already dimming Nicole's brain, and as the aching pleasure washed over and flooded her body, her moan of intense ecstasy was muffled by Christopher's hungry mouth. Replete, she lay there, unable to move, feeling with a stab of queer tenderness Christopher's own eruption of desire. For many moments they stayed there locked together, their mouths gently mingling and tasting.

Eventually Christopher moved slightly and lifted his body away from hers, and for a timeless second he stared down into her face. A troubled, uncertain expression coming and going on his features, he said, "Nicole, I . . ." But then as if aware of their situation, he jerked up abruptly. Standing, after quickly rearranging her clothing, he reached down and absently pulled her crushed gown into place. Helping her to her feet, he still said nothing, his face once again a mask.

Passion gone now, Nicole was suddenly ashamed and furious with herself for what had just happened. And in this moment she hated herself and Christopher more than she had at any other time in the past. With a hand that shook with pain and embarrassment she finished straightening her dress, unable even to look at Christopher, fearful his features would be bearing their usual sardonic expression. And when at last she braced herself to glance at him, what she saw filled her with anger and despair.

His face was empty and cold, the gold eyes bleak and remote. Even his voice when he spoke was lifeless, as if he had fought a terrible battle and lost. "I apologize for what happened. You needn't fear it will happen again, I can promise you that it won't."

His words did nothing to soothe the confusion of shame and anger that rioted through Nicole. She wanted something more from him than a mere apology that sounded as if it meant nothing to him, as if it were mere form. Her eyes shimmering with unshed tears, she spat, "I won't accept that! You seem to believe that you can do as you will and then a few words will undo everything! Well, it won't!" Her emotions were so raw she had no thought for his, never realizing that he was as ashamed and angry with himself for what had transpired as she was.

Her words stung him, though, and with a savage gleam in his eyes he snarled, "And what about you, my dear? I didn't notice that you fought so very hard! Goddamnit, Nick, I'm only a man! I'm sorry. I didn't mean for that to happen. And you can rest assured that I regret it more bitterly than you can ever know. I made a vow I wouldn't ever touch you again, and I broke it. How do you think that makes me feel?" Bitterly he added, "You're the *last* woman I want to become entangled with!"

They faced one another angrily, not thinking of what they were saying or even of what they were doing. Hurt and stunned by the knowledge that he hated her so much, Nicole struck him in a sudden painful fury across the cheek.

Christopher made no retaliation, but his jaw tightened and his eyes went icy. "That, I think, will be enough! I'll admit you had provocation, but don't push your luck too far!" he said softly.

Horrified by the ugliness of what she was doing, Nicole spun away from him. Her back held ramrod-straight, staring blindly in another direction, she said tightly, "Leave me, Christopher. We don't seem to be able to act like normal people when we are alone together. We either fight or"—a hysterical little gurgle of laughter escaping—"we do something that resembles making love." She turned back to look at him and said sadly, "But we don't, do we? We make hate."

His face bleak, Christopher made no attempt to deny her words. He merely nodded, whether in agreement or good-bye she couldn't discern. Then he left her, striding with catlike grace from the conservatory.

But what had happened between them, he didn't leave behind. He took it with him, and there was no relief from the grotesque war that raged within his breast. She was like Annabelle. She was. She was *her* daughter. Like mother, like daughter, the thought thundered in his brain. And in the fashion of two powerful serpents, the emotions of love and hate were locked, writhing and twisting together in a battle within him. So entwined were they that Christopher was blind to reality, unable to distinguish one emotion from the other, love from hate, the present from the past.

25

The Cavendish Square house seemed deserted as Christopher walked from the conservatory. Twickham replied to his careless inquiry that his grandfather had left to visit a Judge White in Russell Square and the elder ladies had gone to see Mrs. Bell, Regina's dressmaker. Christopher hesitated a moment and thought of joining his grandfather, but then deciding he would gain more satisfaction and release from his pent-up fury by facing Markham, he nodded curtly to Twickham and sprinted up the stairs.

Higgins was waiting for him. "The Markhams are staying at a hotel in Piccadilly. I have the address here," Higgins said, handing Christopher a scrap of paper.

Christopher barely glanced at it. "Thanks." Then suddenly remembering the appointment with his agent, he groaned, "Higgins, go see this fellow Jenkins. I should have met with him almost an hour ago! Apologize for me. Think of something and look at the lodgings he has to offer. I'll leave it to your judgment. But for God's sake, find me somewhere else to stay before I go mad!"

Startled, Higgins stared at his usually imperturbable master. "That bad, eh?"

Christopher threw him a wry grin. "Worse! I am in danger of losing whatever sense I was born with, and retreat is not only necessary, but desperately desired!" With that he flung from the room, leaving the bewildered Higgins to stare after him.

Christopher found William Markham with no trouble. Nor was William surprised when Christopher was announced. He had been prepared for some additional communication from the Saxons, but he was not prepared for Christopher's intimidating presence, nor had he expected him so soon.

William had figured that it would take the Saxons a day or two to decide on their future action. He had expected their decision to take the form of a written acknowledgment of his rights from Lord Saxon's lawyer. Consequently when Christopher, a dangerous glitter in his eyes, was shown in, William suffered a definite shock and a feeling of unease.

There was something so menacing in the way this tall broad-shouldered young man stalked into his room, that William was assailed by a momentary qualm and found himself wishing apprehensively that Edward had not gone to Long Acre to buy a tilbury this particular afternoon.

Christopher halted just inside the room, making no attempt to hide his contempt for William. In a peremptory tone he inquired, "You paid a call to my grandfather's home this morning?"

"Well, yes," William began defensively. "Yes, I did." His sense of injustice renewed, he said more forcefully, "And I'll tell you this, young man, I was treated most cavalierly! Miss Ashford is my ward, and your grandfather, even if he is a lord, had no right to interfere."

"Even when you strike her?" Christopher asked in a silky voice.

William swallowed somewhat nervously. "She was impudent, and as her guardian," he began to bluster, "as her *legal* guardian, I have every right to reprimand my ward! She was impertinent, sir!"

Almost caressingly, Christopher ran the riding crop he held through his hands, his gaze never leaving William's increasingly red face. "You are mistaken," he stated flatly. "Nicole Ashford is no longer any concern of yours —she hasn't been since she ran away from your tyranny five years ago."

William stiffened with anger, but Christopher ignored him. "I'll give you some free advice, Mr. Markham," Christopher said pleasantly. "If I were you, I'd forget about Nicole Ashford and return to my farm. She'll be well taken care of by my grandfather. And, of course, if you don't follow my advice," he paused, an unpleasant smile curling his lips, "I'm afraid that it will be our unfortunate duty to request an inquiry into the management of her moneys during your guardianship."

William nearly choked on his rage. "How dare you threaten me! I'll have you thrown from this hotel, young man, and when I see my lawyer, you'll discover that it is unwise to spout slander at an innocent man!"

"Innocent?" Christopher mocked. "I hardly think so. And I'm certain we'll be able to prove otherwise."

Knowing full well that he could not withstand any investigation, William protested, "Now, look here! Let us discuss this!"

Christopher murmured dryly, "But I thought we were."

"Yes. Yes." Attempting to save face, William said conciliatorily, "Just sit down and we will see if we can come to an agreement."

"Only one course is acceptable. You and your wife retire to your farm and forget about Nicole Ashford. You will also," Christopher went on in a hard voice, "turn control of her fortune to my grandfather. If you don't," he growled dangerously, "you will, I promise, regret it greatly."

Nearly gagging on the fury that shook him, his face darkening alarmingly, William agreed in a strangled tone. "I understand." It galled him, but he was at a standstill. He could not afford to have his accounts examined. It was far better to lose Nicole and her fortune and keep what he could than to gamble all on winning against the Saxons.

"Fine!" Christopher said with a snap. He pivoted on his heel, then, as if remembering something, swung slowly back to face William. "Ah, yes, one more thing." And deliberately he slashed William deeply on the cheek with the riding crop. His eyes mere slits of gold, he snarled softly, "Don't *ever* lay a hand on Nicole Ashford again. Next time, I'll *kill* you!"

Stunned, William stared speechless as Christopher bowed with exaggerated politeness and departed. Once he was alone in the room, his hands clenching into fists, he nearly howled aloud his chagrin and rage. But he stifled the emotions, suspecting that he was fortunate that young Saxon had not challenged him to a duel. And if he escaped a legal inquiry into his affairs, he was doubly lucky.

The stinging cut on his cheek was throbbing painfully as he barged into Agatha's chamber and ordered her to pack—they were leaving for the country as soon as Edward returned! He offered no explanation, and when Agatha timidly asked what they were to do about Nicole, he roared at her in such temper that she promptly went into a swoon.

Having thoroughly unnerved his wife, he stormed from the room and proceeded to drown his disappointment and humiliation in several glasses of dark, strong ale. And as the hours passed he became more resigned and viewed the future with a more reasonable mind. His rage had not abated, but he was able to see the advantages of leaving town and salvaging what he could from Nicole's fortune.

Edward, though, when informed of the change of plans, merely looked at his father in a bored fashion and said languidly, "Very well. You and mother retire to the country."

The cut on his face now a livid bruise, William growled, "And you?"

Edward smiled sweetly, and flicking a bit of imaginary fluff from his sleeve, he murmured, "Oh, I intend to try my hand at wedding the heiress."

William grunted. "Well, I wish you the joy of her. She's a regular little hellcat! She'll make a hot-tempered shrew of a wife, and I'll warn you, it might not be worth the fortune."

Edward stared blandly at his father and said softly, "That may be, but I doubt that my dear bride will survive her honeymoon!"

Gazing intently into his son's limpid blue eyes, William shivered. There was something about Edward that frightened him occasionally, and hastily he muttered, "You do as you see fit."

"I intend to."

Edward had grown up to be a very eligible and handsome young man. He was almost beautiful, with fair hair of gleaming silver curls and smoky blue eyes framed by silky lashes, an aquiline nose of classic proportions, and a passionate, full-lipped mouth, all complementing his fairness. He was taller than average, and his body was as muscled and sleek as the rest of him. Oh, yes, Edward was an astonishingly beautiful young man and could be most charming and engaging. He was the hope of many a mother with a marriageable daughter and the despair of those very eager young ladies. But Edward's polished surface concealed an evil nature; he was inordinately, poisonously selfish and cared for no one but himself.

William was aware of that unpalatable fact, and rising heavily from his chair a moment later, he repeated, "You do as you see fit. But remember, from now on the Saxons will be controlling her fortune. I dare not fight them on the issue. Your mother and I leave tomorrow for the farm."

His son waved him away with a negligent flick of his hand. "I'll bid you good-bye then."

Alone in his own chambers, Edward debated at length what his next step should be. More permanent lodgings, of course, but a servant could see to that. The most important thing at the moment was Nicole Ashford.

With a serpent's grace he glided through his apartment, torn between the necessity of presenting himself to Nicole's notice at once, and the prudent notion that it would be wise to wait until the unpleasantness of his parents' intrusion had faded.

But necessity won. It was vital that he make Nicole's acquaintance before she was presented—an heiress never wanted for admirers, and Edward was not blind to that fact.

He entirely discounted Christopher as a threat. To Edward's way of thinking, if young Saxon had designs on the heiress he would have compromised her and compelled her to marry him before returning her to England.

The attack on his father disturbed him not at all, nor did it arouse any desire for revenge. He was furious with William's stupid handling of the affair and cursed his parents' fumbling ineptness.

After several hours of careful plotting he decided he would, after all, call at once on his cousin, professing to be newly arrived in town. He would naturally be shocked and horrified when he learned what had happened. Composing his features into an expression of sorrow and horror, he stared into his mirror. Exactly. That looked excellent! It gave his profile that appearance of manly embarrassment so endearing to the ladies.

Intent upon creating a favorable impression on his cousin, Edward prepared himself with extreme care the next morning. He chose a coat of deep blue superfine; pantaloons of buff-colored duck; shining Hessians with long, silky gold tassels; a white cravat starched to perfection; and a tall curly-brimmed beaver hat and malacca walking stick. With pleasure he surveyed himself in the tall mirror in his room and then gracefully sauntered out to bid his parents good-bye.

Edward wafted a careless kiss to his mother's cheek, shook hands perfunctorily with his father, saw them to their coach, and watched dispassionately until it disappeared down the cobbled street; then he turned and stepped languidly into his own waiting vehicle—a tilbury purchased just the prior afternoon. As it was now some minutes after eleven o'clock, he drove directly to Cavendish Square; his confidence was such that it never crossed his mind that he might not be welcome at Lord Saxon's home.

Twickham read the proffered card with something like

amazement, for there was no denying this young Adonis bore little resemblance to the older branch of the family. Fastidiously Twickham showed Edward into a small parlor just off the entrance hall.

Edward nodded pleasantly and spent the intervening moments assessing the worth of the furnishings in the room. He had just decided that Lord Saxon must be very warm in the pocket, judging by the plush carpet and velvet chairs, when Simon entered the room.

"Why do you want to see Miss Ashford?" he barked aggressively.

Edward allowed his features to take on their most winning expression. "Oh, I do beg your pardon, sir, but if it is not too very inconvenient I would like most awfully to see my cousin." Looking slightly embarrassed, he went on, "I must apologize for my parents' actions yesterday morning. I have just arrived in London this morning and regret that I was not here to prevent such an unfortunate scene from occurring. I hope most sincerely that my cousin does not blame me."

Uneasily Simon eyed the young man before him. Twickham had warned him, but mere words could not convey Edward's good looks. Simon, like many of his generation, distrusted such blatant masculine beauty. He would have been more favorably impressed if Edward had some physical flaw to mar the perfection of his features. But Simon was fair-minded and the boy seemed sincere. And he was Nicole's cousin.

"She don't!" Simon finally said, grudgingly answering Edward's question. "But you can't hold her to account if she's not eager to meet you. Your father, I'm sorry to say, cut up mighty rough yesterday. No doubt you've heard what happened."

Exhibiting an ashamed countenance, Edward manfully bit his lip. "Of course. I understand. And you may tell her for me that I have convinced my parents to return to the country. They are, as I am, deeply distressed by what occurred."

"They should be!" Simon snorted. And as Christopher had not yet told anyone what had transpired between himself and William Markham, Simon was inclined to be well disposed toward the young man who had caused the elder Markhams to retreat from the field. He shot Edward another penetrating glance, and then having decided that Nicole might be pleased to meet this charming cousin of hers, he commanded, "Come with me then. Your

300

cousin is in the morning room with Lady Darby, my sister, and Mrs. Eggleston."

When he was ushered into the morning room a moment later, Edward's charm was at its height. With apparent deep respect he bowed to Lady Darby and Mrs. Eggleston and said to the latter, "How fortunate for us that my cousin was in your safekeeping, madame. I can never thank you enough for returning her to England unharmed. I must add, too, that we missed you intolerably once you had left Beddington's Corner."

Mrs. Eggleston, while having a momentary qualm, remembering that he had not always been particularly pleasant to herself or Nicole as a boy, was inclined to be bedazzled, by his perfect manner and seemingly sincere smile. Regina, having nothing to go on but his parents' deplorable actions, was willing to be lulled by his delightful character. Only Nicole regarded him doubtfully, when at last he approached her.

She was standing near an open window that overlooked the town garden, and the bright sun, streaming in on her hair, had blazed a fiery glow in the depths of the dark curls. Wearing a gown of pale yellow muslin that gently clung to her breasts before falling in graceful folds to her feet, she appeared like a young goddess.

Not surprisingly, Edward was taken aback. Not only by the tall slimness, but by the almost haunting beauty of the delicately boned face. "Nicole?" he asked uncertainly.

His astonishment was obvious and Nicole dimpled in enjoyment, her straight white teeth flashing as she smiled. "Yes, cousin, it is I."

Edward, thinking suddenly that marriage with his cousin might not be as unpleasant as it had first appeared, grinned at her with delight. "I simply cannot believe it! It is, I know, ill-mannered of me to mention it, but, cuz, you have changed all out of recognition!" Edward said with an easy laugh.

"An improvement, I trust?"

"Oh, yes!" Edward breathed, for once sincere, though hardly besotted. He would freely admit Nicole was beautiful. He would also admit that many a man would be more than fortunate to wed her, money aside, but all she represented to him was a great deal of wealth. A wife wasn't high on the list of things Edward yearned for—even a beautiful one.

During the following hour he exerted his not inconsiderable charm to ingratiate himself not only with his cousin, but with Lord Saxon and Lady Darby as well. It proved a successful endeavor, and he was flushed with satisfaction when he departed an hour later with one of the gilt-edged invitations to Nicole's coming-out ball tucked in a pocket.

The elder ladies of Cavendish Square were most dismayed by Edward's appearance. "Really!" Regina cried vexedly the moment they were alone. "You would think Simon would have more sense than to bring about a meeting between Nicole and that gorgeous cousin of hers! Sometimes I wonder where his brains are!"

"Oh, dear! He is so very handsome," Mrs. Eggleston agreed sadly. Then brightening, she added, "But Christopher is so much more . . ." She groped hopelessly for a word.

"Virile? Masculine? Forceful? Potent? *Sensual?*" Regina asked dryly.

"All of those!" Mrs. Eggleston said with a blush.

"Well, that's all well and good, but proper young women are not supposed to notice such things!" Regina snapped. "They are supposed to be wooed gently by polite phrases and beautiful manners, not swept off their feet by a man like my grandnephew!"

"I know, I know," Mrs. Eggleston muttered agitatedly. "But sometimes, Gina, I wonder . . ."

Her eyes narrowing, Regina demanded, "You wonder what?"

Flustered, Mrs. Eggleston admitted, "It's just that I can't help but feel that . . ."

"That . . ." Regina prompted impatiently.

"That they have been *intimate!*" Mrs. Eggleston gasped in a rush, feeling like a traitor to Nicole and Christopher. In growing trepidation she waited for Regina to erupt in a deluge of disgust and shocked disapproval.

"Hmmm, you think so?" she asked with interest.

"Yes. Yes, I do," Mrs. Eggleston confessed and in bewilderment watched a pleased smile curve Regina's mouth. Curiously she asked, "Aren't you displeased?"

"Naturally I am. It is very deplorable! But don't you see, you goose! If Nicole and Christopher are already involved, we have nothing to fear from the likes of Edward Markham. If Christopher *has* compromised her, it shouldn't be very difficult to wring an offer from him. It is the gentlemanly thing to do."

"You think so?" came doubtfully from Mrs. Eggleston. "I don't think," she added honestly, "that Christopher could be forced to do anything he didn't want to—gentlemanly or not."

Smiling kindly, Regina patted Mrs. Eggleston's hand. "Don't worry, my dear. Leave it to me. Remember, Christopher has had, as it were, Nicole all to himself. But now if he finds that there are other men interested in her, interested and offering marriage, well," she said confidently, "well, I'm certain he will be more than willing to declare himself. Jealousy," she added wisely, "has prompted more than one proposal. And it is up to us to see that Christopher becomes extremely jealous indeed!"

"Oh, Regina, you are so clever," sighed Mrs. Eggleston admiringly.

"Yes, of course I am, my dear."

The older ladies needn't have worried about Nicole's reaction. Edward was indeed a beautiful young man with winning manners, but Nicole had a very good memory. Without the least strain she could tick off all the mean and spiteful tricks Edward had played on her in their youth. No one changes *that* much, she concluded thoughtfully.

She remembered all too well the bleeding sides of her horse when Edward had finished riding it; the sly jabs and the times he had deliberately created trouble for her with his parents; and most of all, she could recall that sordid little affair with the housemaid in the stables at Ashland. And Nicole was astute enough to realize that it was wiser to let Edward play his little game than to send him roughly about his business.

Impatiently, she dismissed Edward from her thoughts her mind going irresistibly to yesterday's disastrous meeting with Christopher.

What is wrong with you, she thought with despair. The moment he touches you, shows the least concern or kindness, you melt over him like some lovesick fool! She caught her breath in pain, thinking of the wanton way she had given herself to him. That he already thought her little better than a common slut of the streets, she knew, and yesterday by her own actions she had proved him right.

Closing her eyes in sudden anguish, she pleaded vehemently, ah, dear God, let this thing between us be severed. Let me live my life without his shadow always at my back. *Please!*

Blindly running to her bed and hurling herself face down on it, she beat the silken coverlet with impotent fury, swinging from one painful emotion to another. She hated Christopher for what he was doing to her . . . hated the power he seemed to wield over her, she concluded fiercely. Hated him, she thought passionately, for awakening her to the powerful emotion of love and then carelessly throwing it back in her face . . . hated him for arousing the wanton side of her nature, for being able to drive her to reckless and irresponsible depths.

But Nicole was a strong-willed young woman; she was also not one to waste time bemoaning those things that cannot be changed. Sighing, she sat up, her fury gone as quickly as it had come. With an unsteady hand she straightened her tumbled curls, thinking tiredly, I have wasted my last moment on Christopher Saxon. He is not the only one who can be so infuriatingly indifferent. I, too, shall be the same, and one day, one day, she vowed grimly, I will be whole and immune to his spurious charm. *I will!*

The rooms Higgins had examined while Christopher was having his confrontation with William Markham had met first with his approval and then Christopher's. By the time another week had passed, Christopher was no longer living in the Saxon home, and he was particularly pleased that it removed him from Nicole's orbit.

The abandon with which he had reacted to her in the conservatory had rattled Christopher, and he wanted desperately to become indifferent to the inexplicable emotion that raged between them. That desire had partially prompted his original plan to find his own lodgings, and Christopher was determined to place as much distance as possible between himself and Nicole.

He could visit with Simon at one of their clubs or accompany the old gentleman as he attended his various amusements. It required little effort to discover when the ladies were not at home, and he could then call at Cavendish Square with no fear of coming face to face with Nicole. If they met occasionally in passing, he was able to act with equanimity, offering a few words of meaningless conversation before departing.

Regina, unaware of what had happened, as was everyone, was furious with the situation; Christopher was proving as elusive as the will-o'-the-wisp. To add to her feeling of frustration, it seemed that whenever Nicole was absent from the house, at a fitting at the dressmaker's or perhaps riding with either Robert or Edward in attendance in Hyde Park, Christopher would appear and laze away hours with his grandfather or pass the time of day with herself and Mrs. Eggleston, only to disappear minutes before Nicole returned. No matter how often she attempted to throw them together, to halt his departure, to demand his escort, or to discover when next he would call, Christopher always outwitted her, and not unnaturally she was vastly put out with him.

If Christopher guessed that his great-aunt was set upon making a match between himself and Nicole, he gave no sign. Even when Regina, driven against the wall, began to sing Edward Markham's praises, insinuating slyly that Nicole seemed much taken with him, Christopher balked her further by murmuring disinterestedly, "Really?"

Denied satisfaction from one source, she proceeded to dangle Robert, whom she privately detested, as a possible suitor to Nicole's hand, simpering over his charming attributes until she thought she would gag. All to no avail. Christopher remained unmoved, and it appeared he was singularly indifferent to Nicole and her suitors.

In reality Christopher called no more than was strictly necessary at Cavendish Square. Living in a very satisfactory suite of rooms on Ryder Street, with his own widening circle of friends, Christopher lived the life of many a young aristocratic gentleman in town, and visiting with relatives was not a desired pursuit.

And so the weeks and months began to pass, as Nicole took her place in London society, striving desperately to forget Christopher. Christopher spent his days and nights cultivating the military set, listening intently for any scrap of gossip that would give him a direction in which to search for proof of the British plans for the invasion of New Orleans.

In May Nicole's coming-out ball was held, and it was praised as the social event of the year. Even the prince regent attended, his corset creaking alarmingly around his girth as he bent over Nicole's hand. Nicole was her most scintillating; her gown of white satin spangled with threads of gold, pearls gleamed at her throat, her dark-fire hair was dressed high; she became instantly the most admired and wooed young lady to grace a season in years.

Christopher was there, naturally, but he was not part of her court that night, or any other for that matter, and only stood up with her for one dance, a lively country reel, before departing discreetly into the card rooms.

The vouchers for Almack's were obtained without a murmur from Countess Lieven, and Nicole's success was a foregone conclusion.

On the political front, in May Wellington rode into Paris as the British ambassador, and at last Albert Gallatin's official credentials as a member of the peace delegation arrived.

Gallatin and Bayard, sponsored by Alexander Baring, had been well received in private circles and were doing their best to open unofficial channels of communication, hoping to get the peace talks at Ghent started. Finally, after weeks of inactivity, the British appointed their commission—three men of such distressing mediocrity that even Gallatin was dismayed. The British negotiation panel consisted of an obscure lawyer, William Adams; Henry Coulburn, an undistinguished under secretary for war; and Vice Admiral Lord Gambier, the leader of the mission, a competent, if uninspired, sailor. And perhaps most discouraging of all, Anthony St. John Baker, already loathed in Washington, was appointed secretary.

The outlook for the success of the peace talks was not good.

In June along with what seemed half the population of England, Christopher watched grimly at Dover as a procession of rulers, statesmen, and military commanders of the Quadruple Alliance disembarked from the *HMS Impregnable*. The czar of Russia in a form-fitting, bottle-green uniform lavishly laced with gold; the king of Prussia, his white breeches straining across a massive rump; Prince von Metternich, chancellor of the Austrian Empire; Field Marshal von Blücher, chancellor of Prussia—they were all there, moving down the quay that was lined in fine military splendor by the Scots Grey and three great light infantry regiments, the 43rd, 52nd, and 95th, heroes of the victorious British Army. It was a fine sight and the crowds shouted and cheered, but Christopher felt only impatience and a nagging sense of inadequacy.

It was in June, too, that Christopher received the first of the coded letters from Jason Savage, and he opened it with surprise and pleasure. But as he scanned the missive his pleasure turned sour, and with a low curse he read of Pierre Lafitte's arrest in April by a platoon of dragoons. Bail had been denied, the custom officials had seen to that! John Grymes, the district attorney, had created a furor when he resigned and joined Edward Livingston to prepare a defense. Christopher wondered how Jean had reacted to his brother's arrest. But then he shrugged his shoulders—the news was months old and he was an ocean away.

A particularly persistent rumor of twenty-five thousand

British troops sailing for America sent him for one last meeting with Gallatin. The meeting was gloomy, and on the basis of Christopher's information Gallatin wrote to Monroe stating his own personal feelings that these troops would be used to attack Washington, Baltimore, and New York. Gallatin and Christopher decided that it was folly for the Americans to hold out for any extravagant concessions on the part of the British once the peace talks got under way. The British were too strong, and coming victorious out of the long war with Napoleon, they were filled with a feeling of invincibility. Gallatin, finally realizing that there was nothing further he could do in England, on July 6, 1814, joined his fellow American commissioners in Ghent, leaving Christopher to do his best.

Nicole continued to reign as the belle of the season; no fashionable gathering was complete until she arrived. Edward's and Robert's rivalry for the hand of the newest heiress had not gone unnoticed, and in the gentlemen's clubs bets were being laid as to the eventual winner. The advent of the heir to a dukedom in the circle of admirers surrounding Nicole increased the betting to a fevered pitch as the month wore on. Even Christopher, a sardonic slant to his lips, had placed his wager in the betting book at Waiter's—his money on the dukedom.

Weeks passed without Nicole and Christopher meeting, and when they did it was only for a brief moment. Each would nod politely or flash a meaningless smile as they continued to fight their private battles.

At last on August 8, 1814, the peace talks in Ghent began. Christopher felt relieved, but his frustrations were growing with every second. He was more than ever convinced that the British were planning an all-out attack on some major city in America, but he was no longer even certain that New Orleans was the target.

One night when his spirits were at their lowest, one of his deliberately cultivated Army friends, a Captain Buckley, his tongue loosened by brandy, began to needle Christopher about his American ties. Buckley dropped hints of troop shipments and went so far as to imply that a powerful offensive in the Great Lakes region would be only a feint—the true battle was to be fought at New Orleans. Christopher covered his excitement and mingled dismay and grinned carelessly, "What do I care, my friend? I am here in England. Another drink?" But reaching his room shortly thereafter, he sat down and penned the information to Gallatin, hoping it could be of use in the negotiations.

The late nights, drinking bottle after bottle of brandy, the smoke-filled gaming rooms and rakish pursuits were beginning to tell on him. His face was leaner, tighter, his temper shorter and more explosive with each passing day. Rumors, gossip, and idle talk were fine, but he had nothing solid on which to build any proof.

In desperation he had taken to visiting at the War Office and the Horse Guards where he had become a familiar figure, but he hoped not suspiciously so. Idly he would scan the various offices, wondering if what he wanted was behind a particular door. It was frustrating work, and worse, his conscience had a way of stabbing at him unexpectedly.

Though Christopher had managed rather adroitly to keep his several and varied companions on two very distinct levels, now and then they overlapped. It was during those times that he felt the most uncomfortable, for it brought it home that he was in reality a spy, using all of them for his own ends.

But he was able to ignore such prickings with a certain amount of ease by reminding himself how he would feel if New Orleans fell to the British. To a point the attitude of most Englishmen toward the war in America reinforced his own conviction that, for the most part, they couldn't care less what happened on the other side of the ocean. Somewhat to his astonishment he had discovered that the greater part of the populace was indifferent to, even uninformed of, the war in America.

The majority of the British population had been more concerned with and caught up in the terrible war with Napoleon to waste much thought on the trifling affair with those hotheaded Colonials. The knowledge that most everyone viewed the war as merely a domestic scrabble —one that Britain would promptly settle—only added to Christopher's determination to see that precisely the opposite happened.

His grandfather had not helped matters when Christopher, out of perverse curiosity, brought up the subject, and Simon, looking startled, asked, "Are we at war with America?"

Casting his eyes heavenward in exasperation Christopher snapped, "Yes, and have been for two years!"

Simon, uncomfortable, muttered, "Well, I knew something was going on over there," which just about summed up the general attitude of everyone in England.

By the middle of August Christopher was almost ready to concede defeat. He had been in England nearly five months, he had surmises aplenty, rumors by the roomful, and gossip, Jesus Christ, the gossip, he thought angrily. But no goddamn *proof!* That thought reverberated through his brain daily like a cannon, and he knew he was ripe for mischief or murder—which it might be wasn't important, either would relieve his growing sense of futility.

26

Over the months Nicole convinced herself that whatever attraction had once existed between her and Christopher was well and truly dead. She could now meet him socially without any loss of composure, and if her heart still jumped in her breast when their eyes met unexpectedly, she told herself that eventually even that would fade.

To a large degree Robert Saxon was responsible for this apparent change. He was witty and urbane, and enough like Christopher to capture her interest, and he was a welcome departure from her young and ardent suitors. He was tantalizing and aloof, yet managed adroitly to let Nicole know that she was the object of his desire.

Nicole enjoyed Robert's company. He could make her laugh at his outrageous remarks, and yet, by the glitter deep in those sea-green eyes, he made her blood run just a little swifter, and she found herself dreamily wondering what it would be like to have him kiss her.

If she found Robert attractive, she deliberately kept Edward at arm's length. She had no intention of falling for his specious charm, but nor did she wish to enrage him. Too well she remembered his petty revenges from childhood. But Edward seemed impervious to her hints, and without creating an ugly scene, she had to submit to his wooing. She found it a chore, more than once having to bite back an exclamation of disbelief at Edward's blatant flattery. She found him a little too charming, a little too gracious, and too obviously smitten for her to think him sincere. He was also extremely vain and inclined to preen himself unashamedly. He thought himself very dashing and brave, making certain that Nicole learned that his malacca cane was actually a cleverly constructed sword cane, and rather pompously intimating that she had nothing to fear when *he* was in attendance. Nicole was hard pressed not to burst out laughing—did he think

Lord Saxon or Lady Darby would let her go anywhere there was the least chance that she would be in danger? Somehow strolling through Hyde Park with all the members of the *ton* bowing and scraping politely, she thought it seemed a ridiculous place for one to sport a sword cane. But then Edward *was* a trifle ridiculous. After she kept Edward at bay, bored with his posturings and banal conversation, it was no wonder she turned with relief to the mature and exciting courtship of Robert Saxon.

With Robert she was not on her guard, she could be easy with him, and she found herself looking forward to those moments when they could steal away from Regina's watchful eye. There was a promise in his gaze that made Nicole very aware that she was a woman and that Robert Saxon was an extremely attractive and fascinating gentleman.

Fascinating and brazen too, she thought with amusement one night at Vauxhall Gardens, when he very deftly whisked her out from under Mrs. Eggleston's and Lady Darby's presence and down one of the many winding paths that offered privacy and seclusion.

She was looking particularly lovely this evening in a white, gauzy gown, her hair worn in a cloud of soft curls around her smooth, milky shoulders. Her hand rested lightly on Robert's hard-muscled arm, and the topaz eyes were bright with laughter as she said gaily, "You are acting most outrageously! Behaving, I must say, most improperly—you know Lady Darby is going to be furious with us?"

"As long as *you* find no fault with my actions, that is all that matters to me," Robert replied. The moonlight intensified the handsome silver streaks in his dark hair, and dressed this evening in a dark coat with jewel buttons, he was looking most distinguished.

"Oh, I don't mind," Nicole answered truthfully. "Sometimes I feel so hemmed in, I could scream with the silliness of it all. I don't see why we can't even go for a walk without a chaperon! It's perfectly ludicrous!"

Nicole was used to freedom, freedom that would have astonished those who knew her now, and the stiff conventions of England's upper ten thousand frequently made her resentful. She disliked intensely the constant supervision of either Lady Darby, Mrs. Eggleston, or her maid if no one else were available. She could not even walk through Hyde Park by herself or go to the library or to her dressmaker's without some sort of escort, and when she thought of the careless freedom of the days of the

La Belle Garce, her indignation sometimes became almost uncontrollable.

Some of what she was feeling showed in the expressive face, and Robert, his eyes resting on her tempestuous features, felt his heart tighten, and without thinking, he swiftly drew Nicole into his arms. Staring down into her startled face, he said lightly, "Chaperons are definitely needed for young women as beautiful as you are, my dear. And they never let you out of their sight because they fear this will happen." And deliberately he kissed her on the mouth.

It was a questing kiss and did not assault her senses as Christopher's kisses did, but it was very pleasurable after all.

A shy smile on her lips when he released her, she asked demurely, "And what is so terrible about that?"

Robert had thought he could control himself, but the soft yielding sweetness of Nicole's mouth was his undoing, and muttering, "Because it leads to *this!*" he swept her into a passionate embrace, his lips compelling hers to part, allowing him to drink hungrily of the honey within. Nicole returned his embrace unstintingly, her bruised heart healing and reviving under Robert's heady kisses. He kissed her a long time, and at last, his eyes nearly black with passion, a leaping tenderness gleaming in their depths, he released her momentarily. He stared at the lovely young face before him and, his breathing jerky, muttered thickly, "I love you, Nicole! I adore you, my dearest darling!" Sweeping her once more against his tall frame, he covered her face with passionate kisses, finding her mouth at last in a long urgent taking of her lips. It was thus that Regina found them.

First shocked and then furious, she stared unbelievingly at the locked figures a second before bursting out in an angry tone, "Have you gone mad, Robert? What is the meaning of this?"

The two figures parted, admittedly slowly, and Nicole, bemused by the knowledge that someone as handsome and polished as Robert Saxon could love her, looked blankly at Regina, while Robert, a pleased smile on his mouth, started forward and said soothingly, "I know, my dear aunt, that this is extremely unorthodox, but Nicole and I—"

Regina, her face thunderous, snapped, "I'll have a word with you in a minute! Nicole, you return immediately to Lord Saxon and Mrs. Eggleston! You I'll talk to as soon as we reach Cavendish Square. You are a disappointment to me, miss, I can tell you that! Now go!"

Reality came flooding back abruptly, but her chin set mutinously, Nicole was prepared to do battle, until Robert said, "Go, my dear. It is better that Lady Darby and I discuss this between us."

Sending Lady Darby a speaking glance, she complied and disappeared quickly down the path. She was barely lost to sight, when Robert, turning to face his aunt, said coolly, "Was it necessary to speak to my affianced wife in that tone?"

Astonishment threw Regina off stride, and she repeated in a stupified voice, "Your affianced wife?"

"Yes. I have not spoken to my father yet, as I should have, but there can be no possible objection," Robert explained impatiently. "And if you wish, I will wait until after I have spoken to him before formally approaching Nicole, but it seems rather a ridiculous state of affairs. I mean to marry her and I'm fairly confident that she will accept me."

"You are mistaken!" Regina said icily, drawing herself up proudly. "There is a prior understanding between Christopher and Nicole—your father has already given his approval for the match." It was an outright lie, but Regina never let such trifles stand in her way. She had made up her mind that Nicole and Christopher should marry, and nothing would deter her.

Robert's face darkened with chagrin and rage. "I don't believe it!" he burst out furiously. "Why, that young whelp hasn't come near her a half dozen times this entire summer. I have been the one constantly at her side, not he! It is to me that she looks, not him!"

Regina merely looked bored. "My dear nephew, that has nothing to do with it! If you chose to make a cake of yourself over a chit younger than your own daughter, that is your affair, but put Nicole Ashford out of your mind, for she is not for you. She will wed Christopher, you mark my words."

Dislike glittered in his eyes and his mouth thinned in a tight, ugly smile as Robert bowed stiffly, "We will see, my dearest aunt, we will see."

Regina watched him as he strode angrily away. Robert, she could see, was going to be difficult. It was such a pity, she thought unemotionally, that his fancy had to alight on Nicole. But then she shrugged her shoulders dismissingly, a setback would do him a world of good. But if *her* plans were not to suffer a setback, she must tackle

313

Simon immediately. He must be convinced to go along with her mendacious story. She hoped he would not prove *too* awkward.

Simon did not prove awkward at all, although he did give Regina a momentary fright. She was coolly polite to Nicole for the remainder of the evening, and as the constraint between them was obvious and as Robert had left their party so unexpectedly, it was not a difficult matter for Mrs. Eggleston and Lord Saxon to grasp the fact that *something* had occurred.

At Cavendish Square Nicole was sent summarily to her room by Regina, apparently in disgrace, and then as the three older members of the party settled in the blue salon for a few minutes of conversation before retiring, Regina divulged all—including her mendacious story.

There was a gasp of dismay from Mrs. Eggleston at Nicole's wanton behavior, and her mouth a round *O* of surprise, she heard the remainder of Regina's tale. Frowning a little, she inquired timidly, "Have you countenanced the match, Simon?"

"Of course he hasn't!" snapped Regina. "I made that up!"

"Oh!"

After his sister finished speaking Simon said nothing; he merely regarded the amber-hued brandy in his glass for several moments. Finally he lifted his eyes and from under those scowling black brows stared fixedly at her. "Ever stop to think that the chit might prefer Robert to Christopher?" he asked quietly.

Appalled, Regina gaped at him. "*Simon!* You cannot mean you would rather see Nicole married to *Robert!* I don't mean to hurt, and I know he is your son, but you cannot deny he led his first wife a dreadful dance. I often think she died just to escape him!"

Simon nodded. He was under no illusions about his youngest son but felt he had to say some word in his defense. "Robert didn't want to marry that pale-faced little thing, but I insisted upon it. It was," he said with a painful smile, "an excellent match. I forced him into it, thinking I was doing it for the best." His face suddenly sad and haunted, he glanced at Mrs. Eggleston. "You would have thought I'd have learned better, considering I had done the same thing myself."

Mrs. Eggleston smiled mistily at him. "Don't let it distress you, my dear, it *is* in the past."

Regina watched them, torn—retreat and let them work things out or stay and fight for Nicole, even if the little

314

baggage didn't want her to? Fighting won, simply because any fool could see that it was only a matter of time until Letitia and Simon worked out their own future, something, she acknowledged with a faint pang of regret, that they could do without her help, whereas Nicole . . .

"That's all very well and good!" she said briskly. "But it still doesn't make Robert a proper husband for Nicole."

"Hmm, no, it don't. But I'll not have that young filly forced into marriage with my grandson, simply because we three think it a capital idea. If she wants Robert, I won't stand in her way," Simon said heavily.

Regina could have shaken him. Of all times for Simon to turn romantic! People of their station had been marrying without love for centuries, and here he was objecting just as if she were intent upon thrusting the girl into marriage with a man half in the grave and repulsive as a toad, instead of a fine healthy animal like Christopher.

"Very well," she said coldly. "If you are not willing to help, there is nothing I can do." Then her icy front melted instantly, and she wailed, "But, Simon, Nicole doesn't want Robert, she only thinks she does! Even Letty believes that Nicole and Christopher are in love, but too stupid and proud to admit it!"

Simon glanced at Mrs. Eggleston. "That true, Letty?"

Mrs. Eggleston nervously pleated her pale blue satin gown. She wouldn't look at him as she said softly, "I believe so. We were once as they, and let our pride blind us."

Simon paled, for it was the nearest they had ever come to discussing their own abortive love affair. But first things first, he thought determinedly. "I'll compromise. I will not deny, nor confirm to Robert that there is an agreement between Nicole and Christopher, and I will withhold my consent for the time being for a match between Robert and Nicole."

It was the most Regina could hope for and with it she had to be content. At least, she thought comfortingly, Simon would not, for the moment, allow an engagement between Robert and Nicole to take place.

Christopher's day started simply—a morning's fencing at Angelo's. Christopher had spent several hours over the months boxing at Gentleman Jackson's salon at Number 13 Old Bond Street, but while he enjoyed the gloves, his real love was the sword. He was frequently found at Angelo's with a rapier in his strong hand as he worked off some of his pent-up energy.

315

This particular morning he had stopped in with Captain Buckley and Lieutenant Kettlescope for an hour or two with the foils. Perhaps a dozen or so gentlemen were in the studio, several watching the little Frenchman Angelo as he revealed the intricacies of a rather involved parry.

There was an exchange of greetings, and Christopher and Captain Buckley walked to the changing rooms. Lieutenant Kettlescope, a slender young man with sleepy blue eyes, decided suddenly that he really didn't feel like exerting himself after all and ambled to a seat in the box window that overlooked a courtyard.

Captain Buckley cast a merry smile at Christopher. "Anthony, I fear, is truly a lazy fellow. I wonder how he manages to fulfill his duties when on board ship?"

Christopher merely shrugged, not in the mood for idle conversation. He was still struggling with his conscience over using Buckley and Kettlescope for his own ends, and he sometimes found it difficult to respond to their careless, lighthearted conversation. Today was no different, but some of his moroseness vanished when they met in the arena a few minutes later.

Christopher was already a formidable opponent, an accomplished swordsman few would care to meet in a real contest of skill. Captain Buckley, a few years Christopher's senior, was no novice himself, but shorter, just under six feet, and more compactly built; what he lacked in height, he made up for in fury.

They bowed mockingly at each other, then the tips of their buttoned foils kissed briefly, and *"En garde!"* During the next half hour they filled the air with the whistle and clash of expertly handled steel blades.

Captain Buckley, breathing heavily and powerless against Christopher's blade, eventually called a halt. "Damn you, Chris, why don't you ever lower your bloody guard? I thought I had you with that *flanconade,* but you were too fast for me—blast it!"

The two of them were at the moment the only ones using the wooden-floored fencing arena, and they noticed that all the gentlemen, including Angelo and some others, were gathered near the front of the building, laughing and exchanging jests.

Captain Buckley, never one to be behind the times, immediately strode toward the group and demanded good-naturedly, "What is so interesting that you are all clucking like a gaggle of geese over a crust of bread?"

"It is Daventry! He has the drollest story about Brummell and the regent. Come listen!"

Christopher, not overly interested in the latest conflict between Prinny and his greatest of dandies, remained standing where he was. He paid little attention to the story being told; his gaze wandered over the group—and suddenly fell on Robert.

Robert was lounging at the edge of the circle, evidently having accompanied the gossipy Daventry, for Christopher was certain his uncle had not been there earlier. Apparently Robert was also uninterested in the current story, for as their eyes met he sauntered slowly toward Christopher.

It was an accident that Robert was here at Angelo's this morning. Past the age of wild, youthful spirits, he seldom felt the need to exhaust himself in any such activities. But he was an excellent swordsman and had watched intently the last few minutes of Christopher's exchange with Buckley.

Robert's pursuit of Nicole had made him willing to let his feud with Christopher wait for a more opportune moment, but last night's exchange with Regina had pointed out rather painfully to him that Christopher could still thwart his plans. The thought that Nicole was to be Christopher's wife woke all his sleeping rage. Seeing the object of his hatred standing negligently before him, so much nearer Nicole's age than his, so tall and handsome, he experienced a terrible burst of fury. He mastered it, but his eyes were hostile. "You handled that foil rather well . . . for someone so obviously untrained," Robert sneered, his jealousy driving him half mad.

Christopher eyed him coolly. "Now how would you know whether or not I am trained? I thought I did very nicely for myself."

Robert shrugged his shoulders and reached carelessly for one of the many foils that lined the walls of the studio. "Oh, no doubt you've picked up a parlor trick or two," he offered contemptuously, running a limber, deadly rapier through one hand. "But I, my nephew, have killed my man in a duel."

"How?" Christopher inquired derisively. "A thrust in the back?"

"Damn you!" Robert snarled through clenched teeth. And not stopping to consider his actions, he flipped the button from the tip of the foil and then, without even giving the fencer's required warning *"En garde,"* lunged at Christopher with the unsheathed blade.

Like a cat, Christopher leaped away, swiftly parrying

Robert's wild attack. There was a savage flurry of rapid movements, but Christopher recovered quickly.

Concentrating on evading Robert's naked blade, Christopher retreated unhurriedly before several vicious feints, parrying them expertly, almost lazily. After a moment, when it was obvious that Robert meant to continue this uneven fight, Christopher commented in a level tone, "The button is off your foil, or hadn't you noticed?"

Robert smiled. "Really? I'm afraid I don't know what you're talking about." He lunged violently forward on his right foot, launching a flying attack, but Christopher easily deflected the aim of Robert's blade.

Their faces momentarily close, Christopher, his own temper rising dangerously, taunted, "You'll have to do better than that, Uncle. Or is it only with the weak and foolish that you appear to advantage?"

Robert drew in his breath with a hiss of rage and disengaged their blades. "I can promise you, you will regret that statement."

"Oh. Another meeting with a press-gang, or did you have something more . . . ah . . . honorable in mind this time?"

The blades met with a clash, and Robert, his eyes cold and furious began a series of deadly and deliberately false attacks, attempting to lure Christopher into a premature parry.

Coolly, Christopher assessed the situation. It was inconceivable that Robert was so far from reason that he would attempt to kill him in a room full of gentlemen, but something was eating at the other man, making him totally irrational. Christopher spared a lightning glance at the oblivious chatting group at the opposite end of the room, but for the moment no one was paying them any attention. He could call for help, but he dismissed the notion the instant it crossed his mind—his pride would not allow it.

As they fought fiercely, Kettlescope suddenly shouted, "My God! Mr. Saxon, the button is off your foil! 'Ware! 'Ware!"

Kettlescope had been sleepily contemplating a fly on the windowsill when the furious tempo of the exchange between Christopher and Robert caught his attention. It happened occasionally that the buttons did come off foils accidentally, and Kettlescope not unnaturally assumed that this was what had occurred, as did the several other gentlemen who now looked in the combatants' direction.

Thinking that Robert would cease his attack now that

attention had been brought to them, Christopher lowered his guard. Robert, unable to resist the tempting target, allowed himself a spiteful and deliberate lightning thrust; Christopher's quick and instant recovery deflected the aim, but the foible glanced along his arm, leaving a bright, welling red slash.

Kettlescope reached them first, and Buckley was not two steps behind him. The others, now alarmed, were streaming across the wooden floor.

There was, however, no doubt in anyone's mind that it was an accident—a terrible accident that could have happened to anyone. It had looked as if Robert, apparently unaware of his naked blade, had not stopped his last thrust. His sense of self-preservation overpowering the hatred in his heart, Robert was quick to take advantage of the misconception. Throwing his blade aside, a tragic expression on his face, he cried in a loud voice, "Oh, my God! I had no idea! Nephew, are you much hurt?"

It was all Christopher could do not to skewer him as he stood there, but the wound was not as slight as it appeared and he was losing blood at an alarming rate. Kettlescope, efficiently whipping out his large white handkerchief, was binding Christopher's arm, staunching the flow of blood, when Christopher said in a low, taut voice, "I'll live! Unfortunately for you!"

Kettlescope glanced up sharply, but Robert was already walking away and saying in a worried tone, "I must find a physician. Angelo, where is the nearest surgeon? My nephew must be seen to at once!"

Ignoring the adjurations of the group, Christopher grimly proceeded to change into his street wear, only consenting to remain still once the physician arrived.

The physician pursed his lips and looked sour when he examined the long, deep slicing wound in Christopher's muscled arm, but after dressing it with an antiseptic powder and rebinding it in soft bleached muslin, he stated gloomily that there was nothing wrong that a few weeks of rest would not cure. Giving Christopher the further instructions that the dressing should be changed twice daily for a few days and that the arm should be supported in a sling until the cut was healed enough not to break open again, he repacked his leather bag and departed.

Robert had used the intervening time to good avail; his face wore such an expression of avuncular concern that it set Christopher's teeth on edge. No one questioned Robert's apparent worry, and once Christopher, accompanied by his two companions, had departed, the incident was forgotten—after all, it was just an unfortunate accident, wasn't it?

The news of Christopher's wounding reached Cavendish Square before noon, and hearing of it, Nicole felt a queer lurch in her heart. For the briefest second it crossed her mind that she was in some way responsible for what had happened, but then telling herself it had to have been the accident everyone said it was, she was left with only the forlorn knowledge that Christopher still had the power to move her, whether she wanted him to or not.

Lord Saxon wasted little time in going around to Ryder Street to see for himself how his grandson was. Robert, intent upon excusing himself, had brought his father the news, but after a blistering explosion between them no one had any doubt that Lord Saxon blamed his son for the accident.

Christopher was resting fretfully in bed when his grandfather arrived. He was pale from the loss of blood and his eyes looked heavy and feverish, but seeing the concern in his grandfather's face, Christopher roused himself and sent the other man a lazy smile.

"What a silly thing to have happened!" he said with just the right note of ruefulness. "I don't know which of us felt more the fool—Robert for not realizing the button had slipped off his foil or myself for not being more nimble."

The light, careless words calmed the fear in his grandfather's breast as they had been meant to. The last thing Christopher wanted was for Simon to know of Robert's deliberate attack on him. The knowledge would only distress the older man, and so he determinedly set about making certain that Simon did believe it had been a careless accident. Robert he would settle with at a later date.

Regina, while sparing a thought for Christopher's wound, was almost delighted with the situation. With today's contretemps any chance of Robert asking for Nicole's hand was blasted away. Simon would never countenance the suit now! And surely Nicole's tender heart would be wrenched every time she thought of poor Christopher lying on his bed of pain?

But setting her lips in a straight, uncompromising line, she decided thoughtfully that it wasn't enough to hope that Christopher's illness would touch Nicole. She, Regina, must see to it that Robert was no longer allowed to run tamely about, free to court Nicole whenever he pleased.

It wasn't until Thursday morning, two days later, that the fact that she and Robert were to have no future private conversations was brought home rather firmly to Nicole. Robert often took her riding in the park, and at breakfast she said idly, "I'm so glad today is going to be delightful. I shall enjoy riding with Robert in the park today."

But Nicole was somewhat disconcerted when Regina said coolly, "I'm afraid you will not be riding in the park or anywhere else in Robert's company for some time to come."

"I beg your pardon?" Nicole asked blankly. She knew Regina had been displeased with her conduct that night in Vauxhall Gardens, but after receiving a thundering scold and having suffered Regina's strictures on her unladylike principles for the last two days, she had thought the unpleasantness was behind her.

Regina, her eyes snapping impatiently, said bluntly, "You both have shown a deplorable lack of manners, and obviously you are not to be trusted. We have decided it best if you see less of my nephew."

Nicole's eyes narrowed and the soft mouth went hard. "You are forbidding me to see him?" she asked in an ominous tone.

"Oh, no, my dear!" rushed in Mrs. Eggleston gently. "Do not think so! It is just that his pursuit of you is most marked, and we feel you should not let him take up so much of your time. It is not seemly, you know."

Furious, and seething with rebellion and resentment, Nicole finished her meal; the toast tasted like sand and the tea like bilge water. If she had felt restricted before, this morning's conversation had rather forcibly pointed out how very little freedom a young woman of her station was allowed. Her fingers trembled with suppressed temper as she set down her cup with a decided snap. Hiding her anger, she asked woodenly, "Then if I am not to ride in the park, what am I to do?"

Mrs. Eggleston smiled at her kindly. "Come now, my dear, have you forgotten that Lord Lindley mentioned he would come to call this morning?"

Nicole pulled an unladylike face. She had forgotten, and she wasn't so certain that she wanted to encourage Lord Lindley's very definite interest in her. But shortly, when Lord Lindley and an acquaintance were ushered into the morning room, there was no hint of reservation as she greeted the two young men very prettily. Mrs.

321

Eggleston, watching fondly, beamed at her, and Nicole could have stamped her foot with temper.

Usually Lord Lindley was a shy young man, but this morning he was full of enthusiasm, and it was all about the retiring gentlemen who had accompanied him. Fairly burbling, Lord Lindley said, "I do hope you forgive me for bringing Jennings-Smythe with me. But he has just returned from America and I am doing my best to make him feel at home in London. He is by way of being a hero you know." At Nicole's almost-bored look of inquiry, he continued, "It is true! Why just last year, a notorious privateer, a Captain Saber, attacked his ship and captured him. It was only by Jennings-Smythe's ingenuity that he was recently able to escape."

Hiding the trepidation and sheer fear that coursed through her body, Nicole sent the reticent young man at Lord Lindley's side a faint smile. Hoping desperately she had misheard Lord Lindley, she asked stupidly, "Is that true? Did this man capture you?"

Jennings-Smythe smiled eagerly, "Oh, yes, Captain Saber of *La Belle Garce* very nearly sank my ship and we were forced to surrender. I was taken with all the others to some squalid little island where eventually I managed to escape. It wasn't a prison I escaped from, merely some smuggler's den."

"Is that so?" Nicole returned with a blank smile. More frightened than she cared to admit, she asked carelessly, "Did you see him, this Captain Saber?"

Jennings-Smythe frowned, looking somewhat pompous. "Well, only once, but I can assure you I would recognize him again. He is not a man one forgets."

Smiling sickly, Nicole made some comment and was inordinately thankful when Regina and Mrs. Eggleston joined in the conversation, both ladies making much of Jennings-Smythe.

When she could at last escape, Nicole hurried to her rooms—her one thought that she must warn Christopher. Wary of putting too much in writing, she decided it would be best to tell Christopher in person. Consequently the note she bribed Mauer to have delivered to his rooms stated only that she must see him at once!

She had debated over the signature, and fearful that Christopher might not realize the urgency and importance of her summons, she signed it simply Nick, hoping he would understand that her request had something to do with Captain Saber.

It was only then that she realized with a jolt that was

half elation and half fear that if Jennings-Smythe had escaped Grand Terre, Allen might have too! For the first time she felt a wave of guilty contrition—she had been so caught up in Christopher, in London, that she had given Allen little thought. That Allen might be free filled her with joy, that he might be in England was an entirely different matter.

Oh, Allen, forgive me, she thought with anguish, but please, *please* be safe and free somewhere else—anywhere but here in London where you would recognize Christopher!

Nervous and restless, she paced her rooms anxiously waiting for his reply. When it came she was both limp with relief and understandably vexed. Mr. Saxon, she was informed, was with his manservant in Sussex for an indefinite period of time.

27

Christopher's decision to drive to Sussex had not come to him lightly. It was only in London that he had any hope of discovering any useful information, but London was not the best place in which to convalesce.

He had a lively horror of his great-aunt and Mrs. Eggleston descending upon him with possets, as well as having to suffer his concerned grandfather's calls nearly every day. His friends, he thought crossly, were more likely to cause a setback in his recovery than to speed it up. Determined to cheer him, they had crowded into his rooms, drunk his brandy, laughed and talked and finally passed out drunk as owls on his bedroom floor. No, London definitely was not the place for someone who needed several days of quiet and rest.

More importantly he had decided he had been chasing after a will-o'-the-wisp. It had been a half-mad dream of his and Jason's to think he could discover anything of importance. He had known that it was not likely to be successful before he had even consented to the improbable scheme, but he had been hopeful that somehow, someway, with a little luck he might be able to overcome the nearly insurmountable odds. Now even hope was gone, and he had come to the bleak conclusion that he had wasted enough time in England. There were things he could be doing in New Orleans, that would accomplish more than he could in England. It was a bitter decision, but his mind was made up, and if he were to sail back to New Orleans, he would first have to establish a point from which to depart—hence Sussex.

Christopher's wound gave him an excellent excuse to leave the city, and no one would think it strange that he wanted a few days on the coast for peace and quiet. He used the time to good purpose, despite the pain and discomfort of his arm, letting an isolated cottage on the beach.

He decided that once his arm had healed he would try

for one last time to discover the British plans for New Orleans. He leased the cottage until the first of October, as September thirtieth was one of the dates he and Jason had decided upon for a rendezvous with the privateer. If he remained unsuccessful by that date, he would signal the ship and leave empty-handed, except for what rumor and current news he had.

Feeling at last that he was taking charge, he stabled his horses and carriage at the local inn and actually did relax and rest. The time he and Higgins spent at the cottage passed swiftly; Christopher grew stronger with each passing hour. The days were spent idly exploring the coast; he even risked swimming in the cold ocean water, exercising his wounded arm gently; he rested afternoons on the rocky outcroppings near the shingle and evenings slept soundly after a day of fresh, invigorating sea air. The only jarring note came one day when he discovered, a few miles down the coast from his cottage, a handsome residence that he recognized instantly as the house Robert let while he stayed in Brighton.

He had forgotten that fact, and the house brought back memories of his youth, when with his grandfather he had come to Brighton in the late summer and had often visited with Robert's wife and children at that same house. How strange that he had forgotten it. But then he pushed it to the back of his mind, wanting no thought of Robert to disturb the peace he had found.

Christopher had much time for quiet reflection. Lying on the sand, his shoulders propped against the cliffs that faced the sea, the wind ruffling the dark hair, he would watch the ever-changing ocean by the hour, sometimes his thoughts far away, drifting in lazy rhythm like the waves that pounded on the shore. He had no deep regrets for anything he had done so far in his life, he discovered with surprise. Oh, perhaps he wished he hadn't been such a silly young ass over Annabelle or that he had handled Nicole more gently, but even those were no more than merely passing quirks. His dislike of the role he was playing in England he dismissed cynically; if it had been truly distasteful to him, he simply wouldn't have done it, he told himself.

His thoughts did turn briefly to Nicole, but he was, despite everything, a ruthless young man, and he had locked her away in the deepest recesses of his mind. She should be grateful to me, he decided with sardonic amusement; I gave her adventure and excitement enough to last the rest of her life. When she's married to some dull and worthy gentleman, surrounded by a pack of brats, she'll probably remember me with fond nostalgia. Thinking of that, he gave a sudden harsh shout of mirthless laughter, frightening away a curious gull. And what did it matter? In little more than a month he would be sailing for home, and Nicole, well, Nicole would probably be deciding on which of her many suitors to bestow her hand and lissome body.

An unexpected vision of that supple body rose before his eyes, and with sheer fury he felt his body's instant response. Cursing, he leaped to his feet, stripped, and threw himself into the sea. The water was icy and numbing and his wounded arm made vigorous swimming awkward, but grimly he propelled himself through the water until common sense made him swim toward shore. He walked unconcernedly to where he had been lying and flung himself down on a worn blanket. The plunge in the sea had effectively banished Nicole from his thoughts, and now as he sat once more staring out to sea, his mind dwelt on Simon.

Having decided to leave in September, he wondered with real distress how he was going to tell his grandfather. He could not sail out to sea without a word, slinking away like a dog in the night.

He would have liked to banish the idea of the coming departure just as he had his unwelcome thoughts of Nicole, but this was something that had to be faced. Displeased by the trend of his musings, impatiently he threw a pebble into the foaming surf and wished he could dispose of his troubles as easily.

He could not say casually, "I've had a nice visit with you, grandfather, but now I must return to New Orleans." Hardly! No solution presented itself, and after a while, frustrated and growing angry, he gave it up—when the time came he would think of something—he had to!

The long walks along the beach with only the murmuring surf and occasional gull wheeling overhead had been good for him. The sea wind blew out the fumes of too many nights spent drinking in smoke-filled rooms, the hot sun intensified the bronze of his skin, and his eyes lost that world-weary cast that had been evident of late.

One week became two and Christopher found himself curiously loath to return to the noise and crowds of London. He and Higgins had been alone and undisturbed the entire time, except for Higgins's necessary trips to Rottingdean to replenish their food supplies. The tiny cottage had been kept as meticulously as his captain's quarters on *La Belle Garce.*

But at the end of the second week, the wound a thin red line of which he was hardly conscious, Christopher made the decision to return to London. With a definite date now for departure fixed firmly in his mind, he felt a compelling need to make that last attempt to turn his ill-fated mission into a success.

Arriving at his lodgings in London at dusk the next day, Christopher found a pile of notes, cards, and invitations waiting for him. He glanced disinterestedly through a few and then shrugged his shoulders. After dinner he would discover if there was anything that merited his attention. He took a leisurely bath, and then wearing only a brocade dressing robe, he sat down to one of his landlady's excellent meals. A cigar and a glass of brandy polished it off nicely, and it was only then that his attention turned again to the pile of correspondence lying on the corner of a mahogany sideboard. Consequently it wasn't until after ten o'clock that he discovered Nicole's message.

Frowning, he reread it. What the devil did it mean? As he stared at the signature, his frown deepened. He could think of only one reason for her to have signed it "Nick." Whatever she had to see him about must concern Captain Saber. And the damned note was two weeks old!

He tossed aside his half-smoked cigar, and calling impatiently for Higgins, he began to dress hurriedly. In an astonishingly short time he was on his way to Cavendish Square. But to his frustration his quarry was not at home. Miss Ashford, he was informed by Twickham, was attending an assembly at Almack's with Lady Darby and Mrs. Eggleston.

Cursing under his breath, Christopher sped down the steps, glancing at his watch. Not yet eleven; with luck he would make it to King Street before the doors were shut firmly against latecomers. *No one* was admitted after eleven P.M.—not even the great Wellington himself. Fortunately he was wearing knee breeches, for it was an inflexible rule that only knee breeches were acceptable. More than one mortified gentleman in pantaloons had been loftily turned away at the door.

Christopher made it to Almack's by one minute to the hour. Leaving off his hat and gloves, he entered the ballroom an instant later, his gaze searching for Nicole's auburn head. He found her easily enough as she stood near one end of the ballroom surrounded by a bevy of admirers. Her bare shoulders were pale apricot above a gown of dull gold silk with an overdress of spangled gauze. The blazing chandelier overhead brought to life the fiery glimmer of her sable hair.

For a long moment Christopher stared at her across the length of the ballroom, his intent gaze occasionally obscured by the constantly shifting kaleidoscope of women in bright silk and satin gowns and gentlemen with white starched cravats and velvet jackets. With something like shock he realized for the first time that Nicole was more than just a tantalizing wench who had haunted his dreams against his will. And the unpleasant thought occurred to him again, that he had been a fool to put her out of his reach. But then he shrugged—women were women. Yet even as that cynical premise crossed his mind, he noted Robert standing by her side, laughing into Nicole's upturned face, and his eyes narrowed. His nostrils flared like those of a tiger about to defend its territory against an encroaching marauder; a swift and powerful emotion swept through his body. He did not recognize the emotion; he only knew that he wanted his arms around that tempting baggage, and he wanted her away from Robert.

With a long, determined stride he quickly stalked across the ballroom floor and approached Nicole just as Robert was about to lead her onto the floor for a waltz that was beginning. A mocking gleam deep in the gold eyes, Christopher deliberately blocked their way and, after bowing politely, murmured, "My dance, I believe!" And before Robert or Nicole could guess his intentions, he swept Nicole out onto the ballroom floor.

The unexpectedness of his appearance, as well as the feel of that familiar hand around her waist as they danced to the lilting music, made Nicole's heart thud with short, rapid strokes, a fact she was instantly fearful that Christopher would discover. But then meeting the audacious twinkle in the thick-lashed eyes staring into hers, she couldn't control a spurt of genuine laughter. A hint of amusement in her husky voice, she scolded, "Christopher, how could you! Robert will be furious!"

With a smile tugging at the corner of his mouth, Christopher shrugged his shoulders as they whirled down the polished floor. "What do I care, as long as you are not angry. Are you?"

Puzzled, she looked up into the dark, handsome features just above her. There was something about him tonight that was different, something she couldn't put a name to, and as she continued to gaze at him, an odd expression flickered momentarily in his eyes, making her suddenly giddy. "No," she said at last. "No, I'm not." And she smiled up at him so sunnily and naturally that Christopher felt a queer, startling leap in his veins, and he muttered thickly, "When you smile like that at me, it's fortunate we are in the midst of a crowd or I'm afraid I would not be responsible for my actions."

Feeling lighthearted, Nicole sent him a demure glance from under her long, curling lashes. "Oh? Pray what do you mean?" she teased. Her breathlessness increased at the glitter that flared in his eyes, and she looked away in confusion as Christopher's grip tightened momentarily. But then recalling that they were waltzing in the sacred precincts of Almack's, he relaxed and smiled lazily.

"You know very well what I mean, minx! Sharpen your claws on someone else!" he said evenly, although the bright gleam was still in his eyes.

They danced in silence for a moment, Nicole very aware of his body moving in effortless rhythmn with hers. He held her hand lightly in his clasp and his touch was sure and deft at her waist. As they waltzed around the room Nicole was suddenly beset by memories of those hands, hard and caressing, moving over her body, and unconsciously she stiffened. As if reading her thoughts, Christopher said softly, "Relax. I don't intend to pounce upon you." Adding dryly, "You're safe enough, *here!*"

Unable to help it, she shot back tartly, "But not, I fear, in your grandfather's conservatory!"

Christopher's face tightened; his expression was cool and mocking as he answered readily enough, "You always had a quick tongue, Nick. I seem to recall, though," he continued crushingly, "that you didn't exactly repulse me that day."

Nicole swallowed painfully, torn between rage and shame. Not meeting his derisive eyes, she hissed, "Why do you remind me of what we had both best forget?"

"Because," he snarled savagely, "I can't forget it! You're a devil of a temptation," he went on in a hard voice, "to any man, and for all my faults I am very definitely a man!"

Both of them were disconcerted by his vehement words. Christopher looked away, appalled at the admission, and asked abruptly, "Why did you want to see me?"

"Jennings-Smythe from that English packet you took last year is here in London!"

Christopher betrayed no surprise, although his eyebrows drew together in a slight frown, but then aware of the eyes on them as they danced, he appeared unworried. His voice was crisp as he asked, "Are you certain?"

Nicole nodded vigorously, oblivious to those who might be watching. "Oh, yes!" Then suddenly recalled to the danger of the situation, she gripped his hand tightly. "He is here tonight, Christopher. I saw him earlier."

He appeared unmoved by her disclosures, and she could have slapped him for his indifference. For the benefit of any onlookers, she smiled at him and said through clenched teeth, "He may recognize you, as Saber, have you thought of that?"

"No. But you obviously have. Do you think he will denounce me? If he does, you should enjoy it! What a revenge you will have then, watching them drag me away in chains. There is, I think, still a price on my head. Why, you might be able to collect it for yourself!"

"Oh, be quiet!" she snapped, hating and loving him at the same time. Almost pleadingly she raised her eyes to meet his sardonic stare. "Christopher, be careful. Jennings-Smythe is *here* tonight, can't you understand that? And if he were to see you and realize who you are, you *would* be dragged away in chains!"

"And would you care?" he asked gently, his eyes holding hers steadily. All her hard-won composure, her infatuation for Robert crumbled in an instant, as she thought painfully, it would be heaven to admit, yes! Yes! I would die if something happened to you! But caution checked her passion, helped her fight her instincts, as she replied carelessly, "Well, it would be awkward, you know. After all, if you were arrested, someone might wonder at my connection with you."

His face froze, his eyes were suddenly icy.

"Oh, Christopher . . ." she said contritely, hating herself for disrupting their intimacy, wishing she had bitten her tongue before telling such a brazen lie. But the damage was done, and as the waltz ended he promptly returned her to Robert and bowed without a word. As he turned, he looked back at her and said, "Thank you again for telling me of Lieutenant Jennings-Smythe's presence. I must go and make his acquaintance!"

Frightened by Christopher's recklessness, conscious only of danger, she said sharply, "Don't be a fool!"

But Christopher only smiled, not a nice smile, and walked away, leaving Nicole feeling at once furious and scared half silly. The stubborn ox-headed jackass! she thought with a quiver of fury. But her anguished heart screamed silently, "Oh, for God's sake, Christopher, *don't!*"

There was no stopping him, though, and uncaring that Robert was staring at her with open speculation, she watched with dull misery as Christopher sought out an introduction to Jennings-Smythe. Nicole's hands clenched and her body went rigid with anxiety, as she watched a smiling Christopher shake hands with the slightly startled Jennings-Smythe.

Nicole could not hear what was said, but it seemed that her apprehension and terror had been unnecessary. Jennings-Smythe did not recognize the tall, lithe gentleman standing so negligently before him.

Incensed and yet relieved, Nicole looked away at last. Robert Saxon, upon whom nothing had gone unnoticed, remarked carefully, "My nephew appears to have upset you."

She sensed that it was imperative to turn Robert's attention away from what had passed between her and Christopher, but she was too distraught to think of anything to say. But then realizing that as Robert stared, others were doing the same thing, she gathered her twisted emotions together and sent him a blinding smile. "Oh, fudge! I'll admit though, that your nephew is outrageously arrogant. Imagine, whisking me away in that manner, he is so droll!"

Robert subjected her to a probing stare, but Nicole had a tight rein on herself once again and her unconcerned countenance allayed his jealousy. But with the knowledge burning in his brain that Nicole was meant to marry Christopher, it was all he could do not to ask her outright if there was in fact a match between her and Christopher. He knew that a crowded ballroom was hardly the place for that kind of conversation, and he was certain that Regina would be bearing down on them any second, so he lightly changed the subject.

Nicole was almost unbearably thankful when Lady Darby swept up to her a moment later and suggested in a tone that brooked no argument that they leave. Meekly Nicole followed her from the ballroom. At Cavendish Square she declined a proffered cup of chocolate and retreated to the privacy of her room.

If she was distracted and uncommunicative, Mauer thought nothing of it as she helped her undress. Miss probably had a headache and would be her usual spirited self in the morning. Alone, attired in a soft cambric nightdress, Nicole prowled unhappily throughout her

331

rooms; sleep eluded her as her thoughts raced angrily around her brain.

What a damned bloody fool he was to court danger so blatantly, she decided scornfully. And she was a fool to have worried over him. Let him hang! I'll dance under his gibbet with glee, she promised, her eyes bright with temper and unshed tears.

While Nicole fumed in her rooms, Christopher was beating a rapid retreat from Almack's. After his first rush of black, savage anger at Nicole's provoking prattle, he knew that by seeking out Jennings-Smythe he was courting danger. However, approaching Jennings-Smythe at a moment when he was prepared and the other man was not had been the wisest course open to him. But having made his acquaintance and remained unscathed, he intended to avoid that young man in the future.

He was fairly certain that Jennings-Smythe had not recognized him. But given time it was probable that he would connect the privateer Captain Saber with the London Christopher Saxon, and Christopher wanted no part of the denouement that would follow.

The hour was late, but the idea of sleep was not particularly appealing, and searching for a way to pass the time, he sought out Buckley and Kettlescope.

After a fruitless search of several clubs, he found the two of them in Kettlescope's lodgings. There were two members of the Horse Guards with them, and the four were rather the worse for drink.

Kettlescope regarded him with a bleary eye and offered him a glass of wine. Though resigned to joining them, Christopher drank his wine with little enjoyment. But his distaste for the scene vanished and his eyes narrowed in concentration when Buckley muttered, "Been celebrating—Kettlescope's going to sea!"

"Really? Where are you off to?" Christopher asked indifferently.

Kettlescope gave him a sleepy grin. "Thash a secret! But I'm to report for duty and hold m'self in readiness!"

Buckley, holding his liquor excellently, snickered, "A pony to a monkey, you're off for America! Everyone knows we're launching another offensive."

A beefy member of the Horse Guards piped in sagely, "No one knows yet who'll lead the attack, but I've heard that Wellington turned it down and that Pakenham is hoping to escape the American campaign. It's anyone's guess who'll be the commander in chief."

Staring into his wine, Christopher murmured dryly, "I wonder if anyone really knows *anything* about the American attack. I've heard for months that one is planned, but no one seems to know for certain when or where." Smiling disarmingly, he added, "I think my friends, you were just looking for an excuse to get blind drunk!"

"Not so!" Buckley growled disagreeably. "I tell you, I saw the memorandum by accident on Major Black's desk yesterday."

"Oh, yes, another famous memorandum!" Christopher mocked, but his eyes were alert and his thoughts racing. Buckley was just drunk enough to be indiscreet, and the conversation had sprung up so naturally and opportunely that Christopher couldn't tamp down the certainty that tonight he would learn something.

"It's true! It was all there, the troops, the destination, and the date!"

"Really?" Christopher asked, his disbelief plain. "If that is so, which I doubt, my friend, suppose you tell us what it said."

Buckley opened his mouth, then shut it with a snap. "That's secret information," he muttered, recalling himself. "I shouldn't have mentioned it."

"Exactly!" Christopher agreed. Then almost as an afterthought he said, "But if Major Black leaves this memorandum lying about so carelessly, it's surprising that it hasn't been lost."

One of the Horse Guards laughed. "God, Saxon, that's rich! The War Office is always losing their damned precious memorandums. One was lost just a month ago concerning a supply shipment needed in a bloody rush, and it took them almost two weeks to find it! In the meantime one of the ranking officers was screaming it had been stolen. Very embarrassed he was when it turned up in a file on his desk!"

Christopher joined in the ripple of amusement, but inwardly he cursed the interruption. Without being obvious he had to get back to that damned memorandum. It was the first real piece of evidence he'd heard of since he'd been in England, and he sure as hell wasn't going to let it slip by. Laughter crinkled his eyes as he said idly, "Well, let us hope Major Black's memorandum doesn't suffer a similar fate!"

And his luck was riding high as Buckley took the bait. "Ha! Not bloody likely! The major now has it locked up tight as a virgin in a nunnery!"

"Oh?" Christopher queried sardonically. "I seem to

remember that more than one blushing virgin went missing from some of those old stone nunneries."

Buckley smiled patronizingly. "That may be, but in this case our little virgin is locked up tightly in an iron safe in the major's office!"

Apparently losing interest, Christopher shrugged and said, "Perhaps so, my friend. Perhaps so."

He forced himself to remain for another hour, laughing and drinking, but he was already working on a plan. Walking slowly toward his lodgings in the predawn hours he knew he was going to steal that memorandum. Steal it, and soon. But not too soon, he thought with frustration, remembering unpleasantly that September thirtieth would be the date of the next American ship.

With his thoughts in turmoil, he entered his rooms and absently undressed. If he were to steal the memorandum immediately, he would be in the unenviable position of having in his possession a document that could hang him. To hold it for almost thirty days was madness!

But to wait could be disastrous. He knew where the memorandum was at this moment, but would he be able to say the same thing in a week or two?

Lying sleeplessly on his bed, he mulled over the night's revelations and searched for a way to put what he had learned to his advantage. There was no question that he would have to allow a day or two to elapse before wandering casually over to the War Office and casually inspecting Major Black's office and the iron safe. The safe gave him little concern—his agile and sensitive fingers could open any lock.

Stealing the memorandum posed few problems; it was the timing that was his greatest obstacle. With a groan he cursed the fate that dropped this plum in his hand two days *after* the August rendezvous! He dared not wait before stealing the memorandum for obvious reasons, but what in the hell good did it do him if he had to wait nearly thirty days before he could set sail for New Orleans?

28

A sleepless night presented no solution, and the next morning Christopher sat staring blankly at nothing in particular, still seeking a way out of his dilemma. Only one thing was a certainty—the knowledge that before the week ended he was going to have the memorandum in his possession. The only way he would be able to conceal the memorandum's theft was to replace the original memorandum with a fake and hope no one would detect the difference. To effect such a forgery, however, he would have to bring in another person, and this he had no desire to do.

The obvious course was to bring in Higgins. Not only was he absolutely convinced of Higgins's loyalty to the United States, he knew Higgins to be a master forger—indeed it was this talent that had led to his being in the British Navy in the first place, prison having been his other choice.

Though Christopher had not confided in Higgins, he often suspected that the older man had a very good idea why they had actually come to England. But not wishing to involve anyone else in what could be a very dangerous scheme, Christopher had kept his valet and friend deliberately in the dark.

But it did not take Christopher long to realize that he had no choice but to include Higgins; he was the only person who could be trusted.

Once the British found the memorandum gone, or once it was decided that it had been stolen, there was no doubt that their plans would be changed—which would make the memorandum he held useless. So there simply *had* to be a forgery lying in that damned safe.

For a long minute he considered telling Higgins immediately, but hoping another solution would present itself, he put it off. If nothing else came to him by the time he was ready to steal the memorandum, then and only then would he tell Higgins.

Shaking off his abstracted mood, he dressed quickly, exchanging only the most commonplace remarks with Higgins. As usual Higgins read his master's mood. Idly he inquired, "Something in the wind, Guvenor?"

Christopher sent him an affectionately exasperated look. "Nothing that won't wait. I'll talk to you about it later. Right now I'm going to call on my grandfather. He'll know by now that I am back in town, and unless I want a thundering scold, I had better go and set his mind at ease." Shrugging into his jacket, he finished, "Tell the landlady that I'll not want dinner here this evening and do as you wish for the rest of the day. Don't look for me before midnight."

Christopher arrived at Cavendish Square well before the hour that social calls began. Consequently he caught Nicole and Simon still at the breakfast table; Regina and Mrs. Eggleston had not yet descended from their rooms.

Simon was delighted to see him, and much relieved by his vigorous appearance. He started to order another place set for him at the table, but Christopher forestalled him by saying lightly, "Don't bother. I have already eaten this morning. A cup of black coffee would not be amiss, though."

Nicole ignored him, concentrating fiercely on her rasher of bacon and poached egg. The sudden breathlessness that assailed her at the unexpected sight of him infuriated her and made her even more determined to have nothing to do with him.

Last night she had vowed she would dance beneath his gibbet and, by heaven, she would keep that vow, she thought grimly. She was *not* going to continue with this silly infatuation for a man who obviously cared for no one.

Unfortunately she couldn't leap to her feet and sweep regally from the breakfast room, it would be too distressing to Simon. And despite Simon's apparent willingness to condone Regina's attempts to keep her and Robert apart, Nicole was very fond of the old gentleman and had no wish to upset him. Determinedly she kept her eyes studiously averted from the dark-haired devil across from her.

Though he seemed to pay her no attention, Christopher had certainly noticed the uncompromising set to her fine jaw. He had seen Nick assume that expression too often aboard *La Belle Garce* not to recognize it. But if the stubborn expression reminded him of Nick, certainly nothing else about her did.

Almost leisurely, only one ear attuned to his grandfather's comments, Christopher appraised her as she sat there so pointedly pretending he wasn't at the table. Wearing a gown of apricot jaconet with ivory lace ruching down the front, and with the burnished curls framing the stormy features, she looked particularly fetching. And Christopher knew a sudden urge to catch her in his arms and to make her as aware of him as he was of her. As he sat staring at her his gaze was drawn involuntarily to the sultry curve of her lips and his mind strayed from what Simon was saying.

Aware that he no longer had Christopher's attention, Simon hesitated then rambled on, watching the two of them with growing interest. As he continued to talk, just as if his grandson were listening avidly instead of barely conscious that he was in the room, Simon discovered with satisfaction that it was as obvious as the nose on his face that those youngsters were definitely drawn to each other. It was also exceedingly apparent, he decided disgustedly, that they were either too obdurate to admit it or too stupid to realize it. Pigheaded fools, the both of them! I wonder if I . . .

Hastily Simon drew back from that thought. No, he'd be damned if he was going to turn into a meddling old busybody. Let the pair of them work out their own solution, he wasn't about to stick his head in that hornet's nest! But it did relieve him to see that there was a foundation to Regina's contention that Nicole and Christopher were not indifferent to each other. It made it easier for him to continue to nourish the anger he had felt against Robert when he learned of the accident that had led to Christopher's wounding. And as long as he remained angry with Robert, Robert couldn't very well ask him about the truth of the engagement between Nicole and Christopher, he reminded himself. Besides, he admitted ruefully, he wanted Nicole and Christopher to marry! Deep in his heart he acknowledged that he did *not* want Robert to win Nicole's affections under any circumstances.

Christopher, realizing abruptly that he had been only half listening to Simon, jerked his gaze away from Nicole and said, "I beg your pardon? What did you say? I'm afraid I was thinking of something else."

A wicked twinkle in his eye, Simon barked, "Well, pay attention then! I asked if you were going to join us at

Brighton for the remainder of the season. We're leaving on Monday and I don't expect we'll be back in London till the spring." Seeing Christopher's look of surprise, Simon added by way of explanation, "After a few months on the coast at Brighton, I always end up at Beddington's Corner for the winter, swearing I'll not step foot from it again. But come spring, the urge to come to London grows too strong for me, and I find myself once again in Cavendish Square. Then the whole damned cycle starts all over again. You'll probably discover it is the same with you."

Christopher merely smiled noncommittally, thoughtfully absorbing this new information.

Brighton was the favorite sea resort of the prince regent, and since the prince had begun to patronize it several years ago, the small village had become the preferred haunt of the members of the *ton* during the fall months. And Brighton, Christopher remembered with mixed emotions, was not more than a few miles from Rottingdean and his rendezvous with the American privateer. Almost thinking out loud, he said slowly, "I have a cottage near Rottingdean, you know—it's where I have been these past weeks. Rather than join you at Brighton, I think perhaps I will stay there and ride in each day for whatever delights the town has to offer."

"That's ridiculous! Now I understood your desire for privacy in London, but really, Christopher, it is silly for you to ride in each day from some tatty cottage when you can live in comfort and style. I had been looking forward to having you under my roof again at least for a few months."

Christopher was tempted, if only to please his grandfather, but he declined with a great deal of politeness. "I appreciate your offer, Grandfather, but I do already have a residence nearby, and I would prefer to keep my own household as I have done in the past." A mocking glint danced in his eyes as he added, "If you will have me, though, I shall be delighted to stay overnight occasionally. Will that satisfy you?"

It wasn't what Simon had in mind, but he was wise enough to accept it without further argument. Burying his nose in the *London Times,* he was heard to mutter something nasty about hell-born cubs and their lack of duty to their elders. Christopher grinned and murmured, "I have said I will make it a point to stay overnight now and then."

Simon glared at him a moment before snapping, "See that you do!" and then stuck his nose back into the paper.

Nicole, after having forced herself to finish the food on her plate, very carefully laid her napkin on the table and, standing up, said in a quiet voice, "Excuse me, please. I have some things to discuss with Mauer."

Christopher looked directly at her, a curious gleam in the gold eyes, and surprising both of them, he drawled, "Must you leave now? I was hoping to persuade you into coming with me for a ride. It's a lovely morning and I have a new gig that I would like to try out. Come with me?"

Nicole's face betrayed no hint of the riot of emotions his request aroused. An eager yes trembled on her lips, but with a flash of inward violence she ruthlessly squashed the word. No! She was not going to let herself be mesmerized by the coaxing note in his voice, she thought angrily, remembering the anguish she had experienced over fear for his safety and how callously he had flaunted himself before Lieutenant Jennings-Smythe. No! She would not be a fool a second time—if one didn't want to get scorched, one stayed away from the fire. But she was aware that Simon, for all his apparent preoccupation with the newspaper, was keenly interested in their exchange, so she infused a note of regret in her voice as she said prettily, "Oh, I'm so sorry, but this task must be taken care of this morning and I already have plans for this afternoon."

Christopher detected the falseness of her regret and returned sardonically, "Some other time then. Perhaps at Brighton?"

Smiling in his direction and feeling that she had taken the first step away from his dark fascination, she replied vaguely, "Perhaps."

Before he could press her further or think of a suitable retort, Mrs. Eggleston entered the room; she looked especially engaging this morning in a smart French cambric gown in a pleasing shade of blue and a little lace cap on her silver curls. When she saw Christopher there was instantly a warm welcoming smile on her lips, which was reflected in the kindly blue eyes. Christopher was reminded irresistibly of a small good fairy from some child's tale, as, her cheeks pinkening with pleasure, she said in a soft, lilting tone, "How nice to see you, Christopher! It seems that what with all the balls and parties we seldom have the enjoyment of your company. I'm so happy that you called this morning. You must do it more often."

Simon, who had lowered his newspaper at Mrs. Eggleston's entrance, growled, "That's a stupid thing to say, Letty! The boy just got back to town last night as you well

339

know! And he can't come to call on us much longer because you know we are leaving for Brighton on Monday." Throwing his grandson a dark look, he finished sarcastically, "Fortunately he has deigned to visit us there for a night or two."

Not a bit disturbed by Simon's gruffness, Mrs. Eggleston only smiled approvingly at Christopher. "How pleasant! At least there we will see you more than we have here in London."

Nicole, whose retreat had been stalled by Mrs. Eggleston's entrance, now took advantage of the lull and said hurriedly, "If you'll excuse me?" And after sending a blank little smile in the random direction of the other three, she departed from the room. Christopher stared meditatively after her, slightly perplexed at his impulsive invitation and the feeling of dissatisfaction that swept through him at her answer. Impatiently he shook off the old sensation of disappointment and decided that it was just as well she had refused him. After all, she meant nothing to him, didn't she?

Mrs. Eggleston paid no heed to the glance Christopher shot after Nicole, but she asked anxiously after his wound and his stay in Sussex. Then she said, "I was so disappointed when Nicole mentioned that you had been at Almack's and I didn't see you. Were you there long?"

Christopher returned a light answer; he did not particularly want to discuss it. But Mrs. Eggleston seemed determined to talk of nothing else. He ignored her prattle, but she caught his attention when she said, "Of course, Lord Lindley wasn't there last night, but he has been quite obvious in his attentions lately, and I wouldn't be surprised if he makes an offer for our lovely Nicole."

Hiding his inner conflict at this piece of news behind a bland smile, he asked idly, "The son of the Duke of Strathmore?" At Mrs. Eggleston's affirmative nod, he finished lightly, "Well, she should do very nicely for herself. Imagine, Nicole a duchess."

"I'm sure she'll be a lovely one," said Mrs. Eggleston with uncharacteristic tartness.

Christopher smiled, knowing full well why she was so annoyed with him. Rising to his feet, he said teasingly, "But don't set your hopes on it. Who knows, someone else—even myself—might oust the worthy Lord Lindley."

Both Simon and Mrs. Eggleston looked up immediately in response to his remark, and he wished he had simply bitten his tongue. Irritated with himself, he made his excuses to leave very shortly thereafter. A bewildered Mrs.

Eggleston peered anxiously at Simon, unsure of what to think.

If Regina had been there, she'd have known how to interpret it, but at the moment her thoughts were on Simon and Letty. Over the months the situation between Mrs. Eggleston and Lord Saxon had not progressed to any great extent, much to Regina's exasperation. And it provoked poor Regina no end that Simon, having Letty at last under his roof, appeared content to let things remain as they were. If only Letitia would make more of a push to get Simon to declare himself, she reflected vexedly, as she was seated at the breakfast table.

Mrs. Eggleston, however, was neither vain nor ambitious, nor was she given to easy flirtation. It had not occurred to her that she might marry again, nor that Simon might think of marriage to her. When she looked at herself in the mirror each morning, all she saw was a faded little woman, hair silvered with age. She missed the sweet serenity in her blue eyes, and the soft appealing curve of her mouth. Even at almost seventy years her delicate face gave a hint of the charming young woman she had been, and of the genuine warmth and kindness that radiated from her. But Regina's mind was made up—this unsatisfactory state of affairs between Simon and Mrs. Eggleston was not going to drag on any further. *She* would see to it!

Once Regina was seated and her breakfast deftly served by the silent Twickham, Mrs. Eggleston breathed with pleasure, "Oh, my dear, I think Christopher is finally going to make an effort to fix his interest with our darling Nicole. He was just here, and from what he said, I do believe he is seriously considering marriage with Nicole." She added dreamily, "A December wedding would be ideal, don't you agree?"

Simon remained ominously silent behind his newspaper, but Regina looked at Mrs. Eggleston with a calculating gleam in her eyes. Mrs. Eggelston, Regina decided judiciously, looked most delightful this morning; the excited pleasure over Nicole and Christopher added a pink glow to her cheeks and an increased sparkle to the clear blue eyes. She is truly the sweetest person, Regina thought fondly. Her gaze shifted to the end of the table, and there, she fumed waspishly, was Simon hiding behind his wretched *Times* instead of paying court!

A devious and mendacious scheme leaped to her mind, and she said after a moment, "How delightful! And how wonderful for you! I expect you shall be overjoyed to be on your own once more and not have to be at Nicole's beck and call."

Regina knew this was the biggest untruth. Mrs. Eggleston was not at Nicole's beck and call; she was treated just like a beloved member of the family. And Regina, by determinedly whittling away at Mrs. Eggleston's reserve, had gotten some idea of her circumstances.

She knew that parts of Mrs. Eggleston's history were hazy. Why drag a child like Nicole with her, when she had absolutely no money? And she must have been extremely fortunate that her employers allowed the child to stay with her. She was certain Mrs. Eggleston was in dreadfully straitened circumstances, and that if Nicole's and Christopher's patronage were withdrawn, she would be thrown into the world to make her way.

Regina knew there was no danger of this. Neither Nicole nor Christopher would allow it, nor would she herself for that matter, and Simon, well Simon would absolutely move heaven and earth to prevent it . . . if he knew. Regina was also well aware that Mrs. Eggleston would never so much as breathe a hint of her financial state to Simon.

Regina's statement had a startling effect on Simon. "What nonsense is this?" he said, slamming down his paper. "Letty has no need to think of leaving!"

"Oh fiddle!" Regina retorted carelessly. "A newly married couple certainly wouldn't want an old woman around, no matter how much they thought of her. Don't you agree, my dear?" Regina asked, looking directly at Mrs. Eggleston.

Mrs. Eggleston's smile faded as she thought of no longer having her dearest Nicole and Christopher nearby, and the notion of not seeing Simon each day was anguish. Pulling herself together, she said slowly, "Oh, yes, I do!"

What Regina said, she realized sickly, was true. She certainly could not intrude on a honeymoon, nor could she remain here at Cavendish Square alone with Simon. Her sunny future vanished in a moment, leaving her chilled and frightened. What was she to do?

Regina firmly ignored the faintly stricken expression in Mrs. Eggleston's eyes and said bracingly, "You see, Simon? Letty understands. No doubt she has already made plans for such a contingency! Do you think you will travel abroad, my dear, or will you go back to America? I'm certain that after all the interesting places you've seen you won't want to remain in England."

Simon's face grew darker and his eyes hard and stormy,

while Mrs. Eggleston fought bravely to present an unmoved countenance. Inwardly she was shrinking, unable to believe that dear Regina, who knew her circumstances, could be so cruel. She realized with dismay that she had unconsciously depended upon Regina's patronage in those far-off days when Nicole had no further need of her services, such as they were. But those "far-off" days were suddenly and frighteningly in front of her, and it was obvious that Regina intended to play no part in her future. Gathering her failing forces with an effort, Mrs. Eggleston said brightly, "Yes. Yes. I expect that is precisely what I shall do!" Then afraid she might disgrace herself by bursting into agitated tears, she rose hastily from the table, murmured distractedly, "Excuse me, I have some things to do!" and fled, her distress rather obvious.

Pretending that nothing of any importance had just happened, Regina buttered a piece of toast, biting daintily into it with real pleasure as she waited for Simon's wrath to break over her head. She hadn't long to wait.

"Well!" Simon burst out after a moment of menacing silence. "I certainly hope you are satisfied with yourself! I never thought I would see the day that you would treat an old friend so coolly. I am ashamed of you, Regina! Why you might as well have told her to pack her bags and leave at once! How could you?"

"Oh, pooh!" Regina replied irrepressibly. "Letty understands. Besides what else is she to do? Nicole certainly won't need her once she is married!"

"Ha! Just because Christopher makes some careless remark is no reason to assume he and Nicole will marry! And in December at that!"

"Letty was the one who suggested December," Regina said in dulcet tones. Simon was visibly shaken and angry, and surreptitiously Regina crossed her fingers, hoping it was because he now realized that some day, and soon at that, the cozy group at Cavendish Square would be split up.

Damn Gina, Simon thought crossly, why couldn't she mind her own business! Everything had been so dandy and fine and now look at it! Blast all meddling women! Grumpily he snatched up his paper, but Regina was not about to let this promising conversation languish.

Her voice was very reasonable as she said, "Perhaps we are wrong in pinning so much hope on one statement of Christopher's, but Letty should be thinking of what she shall do in the event Nicole marries anytime soon. Anyone can see it is unlikely Nicole will face the New Year, if not married, certainly unbetrothed!"

"Oh, I'll not deny it, but that was no reason to put the idea in Letty's head that she should go galavanting off all over the world!" Simon retorted heatedly.

Opening her eyes very wide, Regina asked with well-feigned astonishment. "Why, what else should she do? There is nothing for her in England! Oh! I expect she will visit me once in a great while and Nicole also. But really, Simon, she is not chained to us!"

Looking at his sister with open dislike, Simon snapped, "I know that! But I don't see why she couldn't find a cozy little house near you in Essex." Warming to his theme and feeling suddenly pleased with himself, he continued, "You know, Gina, I have never cared for your living by yourself, but if Letty were with you, why, it would please me a great deal."

"I'm sure it would," replied his sister dryly. And that was precisely what Regina was bent on avoiding. If Simon could place Letty in her household, it might be months yet before he declared himself, and that was something she was determined would not happen. Mendaciously, she added, "But it would never work, Simon. I enjoy Letty's company but day after day I'm afraid it would drive me to distraction. You know how I prefer my own way, how I gad about all the time. Poor Letitia would be fagged to death keeping up with me. No, it would not do."

Simon glared at her, not liking the implied slur against Letty. Almost aggressively he snapped, "Funny thing, Letty hasn't bored you these past months!"

"That may be true, my dear, but there has been such excitement, what with the season and all, that no one could have bored me!" Regina returned glibly, but once again the conversation appeared on the point of dying as Simon picked up his newspaper, his mouth set in a tight line. Desperately playing her last trump, Regina said in a distressful tone, "Oh, what a goose I am, Simon! It completely slipped my mind. Oh, poor Letitia, what have I done to her! Poor, poor dear!"

"What? Damn you, tell me!" Simon demanded, his interest fixed intently on his sister.

Assuming a diffident expression, Regina murmured, "Poor Letty! She had absolutely no fortune you know. The Colonel died with debts and she has worked for her living these past few years. And like a fool I prattled on about her traveling abroad. What must she think of me?" Regina gave a sigh. "It is a pity it is so, but she will, I suppose, have to start looking for some position to keep her. I must write to several of my friends—one of them is bound to need a governess, or perhaps a companion." Simon opened his mouth, and suspecting what he was going to say, she rushed on, "Unfortunately *I* could never offer her such a position with me, for she would immediately guess that it was charity, and you know how touchy her pride is." Her face thoughtful, Regina said, "Now let me see . . . Oh, I have it, the very thing! Mrs. Baldwin mentioned just last week that she was considering looking for a companion." Rising to her feet she continued, "I shall tell Letty at once! Poor little thing, I know she must be crushed imagining that I would do nothing to help her!"

"Sit down!" The words thundered from Simon, and there was no mistaking the violence underlying his tone of voice. "Mrs. Baldwin?" he said with loathing. "That old harridan is the rudest, most overbearing woman in London and you would put Letty at her mercy!"

"But, Simon, what else is there to be done?" Regina asked reasonably. "Mrs. Baldwin will pay her handsomely, you must admit."

"Yes! And then treat her like a slave! Unthinkable!"

Regina smiled sweetly. "I agree completely. But perhaps some other method will present itself. After all, it is not as if something must be decided today."

"Bah!" snorted Simon, and with surprisingly youthful strides he stalked from the room, slamming the door behind him.

An angelic smile on her lips, Regina contentedly sipped her tea.

Simon did not immediately seek out Letitia. He retreated to his office to think over all that Regina had revealed. The thought of his little Letty working to support herself these past years was abhorrent, and that she might be forced to do so again, why *that* was simply intolerable!

Simon had been a widower for over twenty-five years, and never during that time had he given any thought of marrying again. His marriage had not been *un*happy, but it had not endeared that state to him. And Mrs. Eggleston, the one woman who could have changed that notion, had departed the country before it had really dawned on him that they were now both, in their twilight years, free to marry each other.

All his protective instincts had been at once aroused by Regina's disclosures. And he was afraid that Letitia would depart as clandestinely as she had from Beddington's Corner five years ago. Remembering his pain and disbelief then, he paced the room, a tall, still handsome man not many months from seventy.

Marriage, he knew, was the answer. He had wanted to marry Letitia since he was a dashing seventeen and she a blushing sixteen. But now that the moment was upon him, he was beset by the same fears and uncertainties that plague any man at any age the moments prior to a proposal: Did she love him? Would she accept?

She must marry him, he thought fiercely. He had loved her all his adult life, and he could not bear to think of living out the remainder of his years without Letty at his side.

Determinedly, he sought her out and discovered her after several moments in a small room at the back of the house. Mrs. Eggleston had her back to him, for she was staring blindly out a window that overlooked the small town garden, her thoughts bleak and miserable. There was a dejected slant to her small shoulders, and seeing them so, Simon felt a leap of protective tenderness. But he hesitated, strangely at a loss, all his fears and doubts submerging his usual confidence. And as he dithered, the heartrending sound of a faint sob reached his ears. Instantly all other considerations were thrown to the winds, and he rushed to Mrs. Eggleston's side.

"Letty, Letty, my dear, you must *not* cry!" he pleaded. His harsh, lined features were soft and wretched as he turned her gently to face him, and his big, gnarled hands rested warmly on her frail shoulders.

"Oh, d-d-dear!" Mrs. Eggleston stammered, valiantly attempting to recover her composure. But it was no use, she was feeling so unwanted, so alone and completely deserted that the sight of Simon's dear face, so worried and solicitous, was her undoing. The big blue eyes filled with tears, and the maidenly precepts practiced for all her life vanished as she threw herself into his arms and wailed, "Oh, Simon! I am so dreadfully unhappy! What am I to do?"

Simon's arms closed instinctively and possessively around her small body. "Letty, Letty," he murmured tenderly into the soft white curls that brushed against his chest. Feeling her in his arms at last after all the long, interminable years that had gone before, his confidence returned full-blown, and almost agressively he said, "Why, you will marry me! You should have years ago! And I'll not have you say nay to me now!" On an incredibly

346

tender note, he added, "The years we wasted, my love. Please, don't let us waste those that are left to us."

"Oh, Simon, no! We shall not! I've always loved you and I could not bear it if we had to part again. I think I should die!" Mrs. Eggleston said earnestly, her face pale and upraised to his. Unable to resist Simon bent his head and fervently kissed his Letty for the first time since their youth.

Perhaps the kiss did not have the fire and passion of fifty years ago, and certainly Letitia had lost the smooth, silken curves of a maid of sixteen and Simon the powerful muscles of a youth of seventeen, but it was as sweet and as satisfying as any kiss between lovers can be.

"Oh, Letty, I love you so! We were such fools!" Simon said at last, Mrs. Eggleston still protectively cradled in his arms.

Her small hand reached up to caress tenderly his lined cheek. "Oh, yes, we were, but, Simon, at least we have now," Mrs. Eggleston whispered softly, her face radiant, the blue eyes bright and a becoming flush to her cheeks. But then an unwelcome thought intruded. Her eyes fixed painfully on his and she asked, "Simon, has Regina said anything to you?"

With his face perfectly blank, Simon asked in apparent surprise, "Regina? Why, what does she have to do with us?"

Mrs. Eggleston gave a breathless little laugh, reassured that it was not pity or charity that prompted him. "Oh, nothing, Simon dear. Nothing at all."

She glanced up at him almost shyly, and Simon couldn't help kissing her again. But beneath his happiness ran the fear that Letty would discover that Regina had indeed said something to him, and so when he had seated Letty on a small rose-velvet sofa and had sat down beside her, he said briskly, "We will marry at once. I shall obtain a special license and on Sunday you will wed me!"

"Oh, but, Simon, should we? What will people think?" Mrs. Eggleston protested, genuinely shocked at such indecent haste.

Simon clasped one of her hands in his and implored, "Letty, does it matter? At our age?"

"Oh, Simon, no! No, it does not!" she replied breathlessly, her eyes shining with love.

And what could he do but kiss her again, after such sweet, longed-for capitulation?

29

Nicole had left the breakfast room earlier with no particular destination in mind, seeking only to escape Christopher Saxon's disruptive presence. After wandering aimlessly through her rooms and finding nothing there to banish the picture of Christopher's mocking face, she rang for Mauer and, after slipping on a soft russet cloak of twilled sarcenet, left word that she was going for a walk in Hyde Park. As was the case whenever she stepped out of the house in Cavendish Square, she was accompanied by a servant, a circumstance she considered irksome. But as the servant was usually Galena, she managed to suffer her company without too much resentment. After all, she reminded herself time and time again, it wasn't Galena's fault!

Galena following sedately behind her, Nicole's features were introspective as she walked slowly along one of the pleasant paths in the park, with no eye for the late-blooming cornflowers or the pungent-scented daisies that brightened the ground near her feet. What a terrible coil she had made of things, she thought with a spurt of annoyance.

She had left England to escape from one trap, and she was just discovering that she had fallen into a far worse snare. Now the things that she would otherwise have accepted without question grated and irritated her until sometimes she thought she would go mad. The chaperons, the lack of privacy, having to account for her every minute, her acquaintances first having to be approved by Lord Saxon and Lady Darby, the places she simply could not go because, "My dear, it is not done!" left her feeling as if she were smothering.

Lost in her thoughts, she continued to walk, unaware of the admiring glances sent her way, or the warmth of the sun shining brightly overhead.

She could not, she acknowledged unhappily, continue to live much longer in this rigid unyielding social order that dominated the lives of her peers. She hungered with a growing fierceness for the freedom to be herself, to put aside the facade that was the heiress Nicole Ashford, and to let Nick, Nick of the ready tongue and impudent manner, Nick who dressed as she pleased and pleased only whom she wanted, come bursting out of this prison.

Bleakly, she admitted marriage was her only escape, unless she were willing to be completely shunned by all she knew. Not surprisingly, Nicole did not want to live the life of a recluse or set tongues wagging more than she already had by her unorthodox return. What she wanted was a compromise, and perhaps marriage would give it to her, she mused slowly. Married women had much more freedom, were allowed more license, and if she were to live in the country, where the day-to-day living was more casual, more relaxed, then she might not feel so stifled and trapped.

A wry smile curved her soft bottom lip. Marriage—to whom? There was only one man she could think of, and marriage to Christopher was *un*thinkable! If only she were still living in that fool's dream of infatuation with Robert! But she knew now that what she had felt for Robert had been just that—infatuation. Marriage with a man she did not love was out of the question. Besides, she reminded herself heavily, Robert had been as close to being banished from Cavendish Square as anyone could be. Certainly marriage to Robert would not be acceptable to anyone. And as for the rest of her suitors, well, Edward was not even worth counting, and while she enjoyed Lord Lindley's company, she had no desire to spend the rest of her life with him. There were others too, but none whom she couldn't bear to have go out of her life.

Perhaps at Brighton she would feel differently, she mused. But then she sighed. Whom did she think she was convincing? Christopher would be there, and whenever Christopher was in her vicinity there was no peace for her. Wishing she could either love him completely or detest him totally and not be torn apart by the conflict within her breast, she determinedly shook off her gloomy thoughts. There was Brighton to look forward to, she reminded herself firmly, and she was a little fool to brood over things she couldn't change.

Deciding she had been gone long enough from Cavendish Square, she turned and was about to tell Galena that they would be going home now, when Robert's voice stopped her.

"By all that's holy! Nicole!" There was no mistaking

the pleasure, nor the delight in his tone, and with a smile Nicole looked up at him as he expertly guided his gig to her side.

"Hello, Robert. How are you this morning?" Nicole returned easily, aware that this was the first time they had met without Regina's watchful eye on them since the night he had kissed her.

Robert was very conscious of it too, and without hesitation he said, "Come for a ride with me? You can have your servant meet us at the south gate. And while my aunt may not approve of *my* escort, she can find nothing improper in a ride through Hyde Park."

Nicole agreed readily, a surge of rebellion against Regina and Lord Saxon making her determined to exert her own independence. Seated beside Robert a moment later, she laughed, "You know, we shall both be without honor as far as Lady Darby is concerned."

A warm light was in his strange sea-colored eyes, and Robert retorted, "And what do we care? It is a beautiful day and we are together—that is all that matters."

There was a time such frankness would have pleased Nicole, but not this morning, not knowing she could never return his affections. Suddenly sensible that riding with Robert might not have been the wisest move, especially since she might have to repulse his advances, she wished she had not accepted so eagerly his invitation. A slight note of reserve in her words, she replied, "Yes, it is indeed a lovely day and it was very kind of you to offer me a ride."

Robert caught the note of reticence in her voice and his first flush of exultation vanished. Frowning, he asked bluntly, "Would you rather *not* ride with me?"

Nicole swallowed uncomfortably, very conscious that in the past she had led Robert to believe she did not find his attentions disagreeable. And now she was faced with the unpleasant proposition of trying to make him understand that while she liked him and enjoyed his company, he would never mean any more to her than just a friend.

Robert was quick to sense her constraint, but putting it down to another reason, before she could compose a reply, he asked harshly, "Is it true then? You are to marry Christopher?"

Nicole's complexion went white and her eyes were two huge topaz jewels in her face as she whispered, "Marry Christopher?"

Looking ahead at his horse's ears, he said savagely,

"Oh, yes, haven't they informed you yet? My dear aunt made certain I knew, that night at Vauxhall Gardens!"

For several seconds Nicole was speechless, divided between a wave of blind fury and a surge of exquisite hope. Fury won out, unfortunately, and grasping Robert's arm tightly, her face stormy with temper, she demanded, "What are you talking about? Christopher is the last man I would marry! How dare they say that I will wed him! I know nothing—no one has said a word to me!"

Robert shot her a calculating look, his eyes lingering on the angrily heaving bosom and the wrathful slant to the full mouth. Relaxing slightly, eminently pleased and reassured by her reaction, he drawled, "So it would appear." His gaze sharpening with curiosity, he asked, "You had no inkling? No hint that my aunt and, I must assume, my father had already worked out a marriage agreement with Christopher?"

Her jaw tensing, Nicole snapped, "Absolutely not! Why they must be insane to think that I would . . . And Christopher, why he barely tolerates the sight of me!"

"Oh, I wouldn't say that," Robert muttered dryly. "Last night at Almack's he seemed to do more than tolerate you!"

Nicole dismissed his statement with a vehement shake of her head. "Christopher is capable of pretending whatever emotion he feels is necessary at the moment. Don't *you* be fooled by him!"

"Very well, my dear. But what are you going to do? Regina says the marriage is all arranged."

"We'll just see about that!" Nicole spat furiously. "Take me to Galena. I intend to discover what has been going on behind my back immediately! Your aunt and your father will explain to me precisely what they have planned, and I shall enjoy informing them that they can just *un*plan it!"

Robert shrugged his shoulders and complied without further comment. He didn't envy Regina and Simon the coming interview, and some of the tight ball of rage that had been his companion these past weeks lessened. Nicole had been too angry, too surprised not to be telling the truth. Obviously she had known nothing of what Regina had claimed, and just as obviously, she wanted no part of marriage with his nephew. Feeling more sanguine than he had in weeks, he watched with satisfaction as she and Galena set off in the direction of Cavendish Square.

Nicole literally marched along the street, so angry she paid no attention to Galena's plaintive pleas for her to

351

slow down. Angrier than she could ever recall being in her life, she swept up the stone steps of the house, and after flashing Twickham a fiery glance of sheer fury, she snapped, "Where is Lord Saxon? I wish to see him at once!"

Slightly taken aback by this glittering-eyed young virago, Twickham fumbled for a reply and finally said, "Lord Saxon has taken Mrs. Eggleston to meet with the Bishop." And unable to contain himself, his lofty, haughty exterior melting instantly, he beamed, "Miss, they are to be married—on Sunday!"

For a moment Nicole didn't quite believe him; then some of her anger fading before the rush of delight that spread through her body, she repeated in a stupefied tone, "Lord Saxon is marrying Mrs. Eggleston?"

Nodding vigorously, Twickham fairly burbled, "Oh, yes, miss! It is so romantic! He proposed to her not more than an hour ago and she accepted. I can tell you, that I couldn't be more pleased." Then hastily recalling himself, he said in a more stilted voice, "They have gone to see about a special license and Lady Darby is at the engraver's hoping to find a suitable announcement to send to their many friends." Then forgetting himself again, he said earnestly, "It will be a small wedding, you know. There is absolutely no time to prepare for more than just a few friends and relatives."

Slightly dumbfounded, Nicole nodded in unspoken agreement and like one in a trance slowly walked up the stairs to her rooms. Mrs. Eggleston and Lord Saxon married! It came as no surprise and yet in another way she was almost numb with astonishment. To think of someone of their age falling in love and marrying was somewhat difficult, but the more she considered the idea the more logical it became. What could be more reasonable than Lord Saxon wishing to claim his long-lost love as his bride? What did age have to do with love? At least their future loomed bright and beckoning before them, she thought with a small sigh, and with an angry start she remembered why she had come home in such a furious rush.

Momentarily thwarted from venting her furious objections about marriage to Christopher by their absence, she paced her room. How dare they! And Christopher! Just wait until she saw him! Just wait! Suddenly, her eyes narrowing, she stopped her indignant pacing. Lord Saxon and Lady Darby might be out of her reach at the moment, but by heaven, Christopher wasn't!

Her mind made up in an instant, she rang once again for her cloak, and not stopping to consider the wisdom of her actions, she ignored Twickham's startled protest and flew out the front door.

With her chin set stubbornly, and hot, angry, irrational thoughts clouding her brain, she set out for Christopher's lodgings on Ryder Street with a belligerent stride. The perfidy of which he was capable enraged her beyond belief. To think that while treating her to his sneering comments, and after ignoring her for months and acting as if she were some money-grubbing little tart, he should have agreed to marry her was like tinder to flame, and Nicole was in a rage by the time she reached Ryder Street.

It was a flabbergasted Higgins who opened the door and admitted her into Christopher's rooms.

"Why, Miss Nicole, whatever are you doing here? You should not be here! Especially unescorted—is no one with you? No maid? No servant?"

Nicole threw down her reticule on a large overstuffed leather chair. "I want to see Christopher! And I want to see him now! What I have to say to him is private, and I am sick and tired of being escorted everywhere I go!" Her eyes kindling with further injustice, she continued heatedly, "I am perfectly capable of finding my way about the city, as you well know! Now, where is Christopher?"

Quite truthfully Higgins answered, "I have no idea. He left this morning to call upon his grandfather, and from there he gave no indication where he would be going. He did say not to have dinner prepared for him, so I do not expect him back until late this evening."

Balked, but still furious, she faced Higgins, and in a voice that quivered with outrage she demanded, "What do you know about this absurd notion that Christopher is to marry me?"

Higgins's rather round eyes went even rounder, his face wore an expression of the utmost astonishment, and he gaped at her. "You and Christopher are to marry?" he finally asked, a note of undisguised pleasure in his tone.

Nicole flashed him a look filled with scorn. "Absolutely not! But Robert Saxon told me this morning that a marriage agreement between Christopher and I had already been settled, and I mean to make it clear that under no circumstances would I consent to such a match!"

Dimly, somewhere beyond her flaming temper, Nicole was aware she was guilty of cutting off her nose to spite

353

her face, but at the moment she was in the grip of such scarlet, unthinking rage that it mattered little to her.

"Well? Do you know anything?" she snapped at the staggered Higgins.

Higgins rapidly recovered himself, and at the mention of Robert's name a displeased frown wrinkled his forehead. "Robert Saxon told you this tale?"

And Nicole, forgetting that she was Miss Nicole Ashford, the heiress, and that Higgins was nothing more than a valet, found herself answering automatically, "Yes. I met him this morning by accident in Hyde Park, and he told me that Lady Darby had informed him some time ago that the match was all settled, that Lord Saxon had given his permission."

Higgins cast her a look of mingled disappointment and disgust. "And you believed him?" he inquired caustically.

A flicker of doubt in her eyes, the first hint of uncertainty in her voice, Nicole replied, "Why shouldn't I? Why would he lie about something like that? He is Christopher's uncle you know, not some gossipy scoundrel!"

Higgins eyed her thoughtfully, suddenly very pleased at the way events were turning out. For a moment he had been inclined to believe that Christopher had not confided in him about his marital arrangements, but the instant Robert's name had entered the conversation, he knew otherwise. He decided in that moment that it was time he enlightened Nick about several things. Telling her about her mother was going to be a bit difficult, but it had to be done. After all, he reminded himself silently, Annabelle had been dead now for about seven years, and Nick had only been a child when she had lost her mother, so time should have blunted her emotions somewhat.

Adopting the authoritative manner of the first mate aboard *La Belle Garce*, Higgins ordered Nicole to sit down and to stop prowling about the room like a half-scalded cat. After a silent contest of wills, with something resembling a snort, Nicole sat down, her body rigid against the comfortable padding of the small sofa in Christopher's sitting room. With the light of battle still flaming in the topaz eyes, she said stiffly, "Why should I disbelieve Robert Saxon? He has been all that is kindness to me—something that I can't say about Christopher!"

Higgins sat opposite her, his hands resting lightly on his thighs, the elbows at right angles to his wiry frame. Leaning forward, a stern glint in the usually merry brown eyes, he started almost gently, "Now I'm going to tell you something I don't think you know. You're not going to like it, and I can't say as I'll blame you. It happened a long time ago, and maybe once you know about it you won't be so eager to speak so highly of Robert Saxon. Or, I might add, think so badly of Christopher."

Nicole couldn't help looking skeptical, yet respect for the little man across from her kept her silent. She trusted Higgins. He had never lied to her, had always treated her fairly and justly. And so she waited for what Higgins would tell her, positive he would tell her no lies, and yet when he began, when he first mentioned her mother, her mother and Robert, she recoiled and fought against his unemotional declaration that her mother and the man she herself had considered marrying had been adulterous lovers. It left an ugly burning taste in her mouth, but after a grim painful struggle within herself she accepted Higgins's word.

She had to. It explained the suddenness and single-mindedness of Robert's pursuit, that queer glitter that frequently entered the sea-green eyes, and the intensity of that passionate declaration at Vauxhall Gardens. Feeling slightly sick to know she must have been a substitute for the illicit desire he had held for her mother, she fixed her eyes unhappily on Higgins's sympathetic face. In a tight little voice she said, "Go on. I suppose it gets worse?"

"That it does, Nick, that it does," Higgins answered sadly, and with a curious uncertain gesture he absently rubbed his hand over the thinning patch of graying brown hair, as if at a loss how to continue. Finally apparently steeling himself, he looked directly at Nicole and bluntly told her the remainder of the tale—of Christopher's seduction by her mother, of the way Robert and she had used him as a shield, and ending with Robert's final monstrous act.

There was silence when he finished, and unable to look any longer at Nicole's frozen, stricken features, he got up and nervously busied himself, shuffling a few bills and vouchers that rested on the mahogany sideboard. "You see now why Robert Saxon is not to be trusted. And do you understand now why Christopher often appears to act irrationally where you are concerned?"

There was no censure in his voice, only a sort of sad pity, and lost in her own obscene nightmare, Nicole barely heard him. She tried to speak, but no words came; they were locked at the back of her throat. She swallowed convulsively, attempting to push away the ugly, monstrous things that Higgins had said about her mother and Christopher and the vileness of Robert's actions. But the grotesque thoughts kept crowding back, leaving her no peace, stabbing like little knives, as she sat there, her face white and strained, her eyes begging Higgins to call back those damning words. A shudder of revulsion shook her at the repulsive knowledge that her own mother had lain with Christopher and had known that dark magic of his body moving on hers, had, in fact, *taught* it to him. Her mouth trembling, she tried once again to speak, to denounce what Higgins had told her, but the words would not come. They would never come, she realized sickly, because deep in her heart she knew that Higgins told the truth. It had to be the truth, no lie could be so monstrous and abhorrent. It gave the reasons for so many unexplained things—the barely leashed animosity between Robert and Christopher, the queer times Christopher had looked at her as if he hated her. It revealed the motivation behind those moments of deliberate brutality between them . . . Christopher had been punishing her for her mother's actions.

With an anguished little moan she buried her head in her hands, and Higgins, deeply troubled by her obvious distress, hurriedly poured a small goblet of brandy and with rough fondness forced her to take it.

"Now, Nick, there is no cause for you to take on like this. It happened long ago and you are not to blame," Higgins said gently, regretting now that he had ever decided upon this course.

After forcing herself to take a sip or two of the brandy, she stared into Higgins's kindly face and said dully, "Christopher blames me."

Higgins sighed. "Aye, that I don't doubt," he admitted heavily. "But don't you see, Nick," he began eagerly. "Now that you know the truth, perhaps you won't be quite so inclined to think of Christopher as such a brute. And when you think better of him, you'll act better toward him, and he, well, Nick, you must confess that when you are fair with Christopher, he meets you halfway."

The numbness was receding somewhat from Nicole and wryly she asked, "Higgins, are you by chance trying your hand at matchmaking?"

Higgins had the grace to look guilty. "Well, now, Nick, you can't deny that you and Christopher make a most handsome couple," he said brazenly.

Nicole swallowed the rest of the brandy and, standing up, remarked grimly, "Handsome is as handsome does and even you will admit that what Christopher and I do is not handsome! I think you have been drinking a little too much of Christopher's wine, Higgins."

As he said nothing, she said tiredly, "Never mind, I shouldn't have made such a poor jest. I don't know whether to thank you or curse you. I think for the moment I shall thank you though, because if nothing else, the reasons behind a lot of things are now understandable to me." She stopped speaking, a little frown creasing her forehead. Almost apologetically she muttered, "I can see why Robert's word is suspect, but, Higgins, I believe in this case he was telling me the truth. The truth as he knows it, and I mean to get to the bottom of it. *Someone* must have told him there was to be a marriage." She paused, trying to remember Robert's exact words. "Lady Darby," she said slowly at last.

She and Higgins had been too intent on their own conversation to pay a great deal of attention to what was happening around them, and consequently they were both startled when the door to Christopher's rooms swung open and Christopher himself walked in.

To say which of the three occupants in the room was the most startled would be impossible. Certainly Nicole and Higgins had not expected him, and from the expression on Christopher's face he clearly was astonished to find Nicole in his rooms. It was equally clear that he was extremely displeased with what he found.

"What in hell's name are you doing here?" he demanded forthrightly, casting an inquiring glance around, obviously searching for either Lady Darby or Mrs. Eggleston.

Nicole licked her lips, frantically groping for the right words. Higgins very meanly suddenly thought of something that required his urgent attention, and with a mumbled excuse he bolted out the door. The two faced each other and Christopher demanded again, "Well? Would you kindly explain yourself?"

Wishing she weren't so very conscious of him as a male, a male seduced by her own mother and one who held an almost irresistible appeal for herself, Nicole hesitated, and as those gold eyes regarded her with growing impatience, she blurted out, "I spoke to Robert this morning and he says that it is arranged that you are to marry me."

Thunderstruck, Christopher stared at her, dozens of wild improbabilities racing through his brain. "Don't be ridiculous!" he snapped finally. "Believe me, there is no agreement, at least," he added truthfully, "none that I know of."

Fighting back the knowledge of his past that shrieked like a whirlwind through her mind, she persisted stubbornly, "Robert said Lady Darby told him that it is all arranged. Even your grandfather has given his consent."

His lip curling derisively, Christopher remarked skeptically, "Now that I rather doubt! Simon may be overbearing, he may want his way in everything, but he is not without common sense! And only someone totally without any sense at all would be so foolhardy as to arrange a marriage between *us!*"

Nicole swallowed the hot retort that sprang to her lips and muttered, "That may be, but Robert was quite positive about what Lady Darby had told him."

Resigning himself to the inevitable, Christopher motioned for Nicole to sit down, and after she had done so, he asked levelly, "Suppose you start at the beginning and tell me what you know? When did Regina tell Robert?"

Nicole hesitated, suddenly not wanting to continue this awkward conversation. Her eyes did not meet his as she said jerkily, "A few weeks ago we were at Vauxhall Gardens for the evening. Lady Darby had a few moments alone with Robert and she told him then."

His eyes narrowing, he leaned negligently against the mahogany sideboard, his arms crossed loosely over his chest, and regarded Nicole's averted face intently. "Now why did she do that, do you suppose?" he queried in a dangerously silky tone.

"I have no idea!"

Apparently not satisfied with her answer, Christopher reached over, and his fingers tightening about her chin, he forced her to look at him. "It couldn't be that she had found you two in a compromising position, hmmm? And perhaps wanted to warn Robert off?"

Nicole's flaming cheeks were answer enough, and with something like disgust leaping to his eyes, he released her chin abruptly, as if her skin suddenly burned him. His voice was cold as he said, "Knowing my great-aunt, if she caught you and Robert acting indiscreetly, she would be perfectly capable of lying to suit her own purposes. I have been aware now for several weeks that for some unknown reason she would like to see us married! And I suspect she said the first thing she thought of. Rest assured that at the moment I have no intention of marrying you! So you can put Robert's tale from your petty little mind and in the future pay no attention to gossip!" His eyes hard and mocking, he taunted, "Believe me, if I wanted to marry you, you would know it—I'd make damn sure of that!"

358

The soft mouth thinned and Nicole leaped to her feet. Clutching her reticule so tightly her knuckles showed white, she spat, "Thank you very much! It relieves my mind no end to know that I can face the future knowing I shall not be married to such an utter swine as you!"

Staring at her vivid features, at the topaz eyes flashing sparks of tawny fire, a curious expression flickered across his face, and softly, almost threateningly, he murmured, "I said *at the moment* I had no intention of marrying you!"

Nicole caught her breath in a gasp of pure rage. Forgetting that marriage with Christopher was something she longed for with all her heart, or that only moments before she had been torn apart, agonizing over the great wrong done him by her mother and Robert, she cried furiously, "You beast! Do you honestly think, you have only to change *your* mind! That I won't have something to say about it?"

A lazy smile on his mouth, he levered his body away from the sideboard, and before Nicole had time to guess his intention, she was locked in his arms. With the mocking mouth hovering just inches above hers, he teased, "Oh, I'm certain you'll have a great deal to say about it! But there are ways of dealing with recalcitrant young women who don't know what's best for them."

Nicole jerked as if stung, but Christopher only tightened his hold and deftly caught her mouth with his, his lips hard and warm, almost hurtfully demanding a response from her. His kiss was the familiar half-savage, half-tender assault on her senses, and with a soft moan of part shame, part answering desire, she yielded her lips to him, offering no resistance as his tongue ravaged her mouth. Painfully aware of the solid muscular promise of his body against hers, of the hard thrust of his thighs against her legs and the strength of the arms that bound her so closely to him, Nicole fought against the traitorous urge to return his caress, to allow this urgent, hungry embrace to end as nature demanded it did—to let him sweep her into his arms and carry her through the doorway to the bed she knew lay beyond, and to feel again that exquisite dark enchantment of Christopher's body possessing hers.

But then even as her hands began to caress feverishly the dark head, the insidious memory of what Higgins had told her came slithering back like some venomous reptile from a black cave, and suddenly filled with revulsion,

359

revulsion that her mother had known that same magic, she twisted frantically out of his arms.

Christopher made no attempt to recapture her; instead, his eyes mere slits in the dark face, his chest heaving slightly, he said icily, "If that is how you act with Robert and if that is how Regina caught you, I am not surprised she lied as she did!"

Nicole glared at him. "At least Robert had the decency not to force himself on an unwilling woman!"

"*Un*willing?" Christopher taunted, unable to help himself. "Don't try that line of defense! You were as willing as I!"

"Have done!" Nicole muttered angrily. "I didn't come here to wrangle with you! Believe me, despite what might seem actions to the contrary, I really have no desire to be seduced by you! And if you were any kind of a gentleman you wouldn't put me in such an invidious position."

A rueful smile creased Christopher's lean cheek. "I agree, but we both have already agreed that I am no gentleman and that you, my little firebrand, are certainly no lady! I think we are each equally as guilty as the other for this present confrontation."

The fight suddenly vanished from her body at his disarming manner, and Nicole nodded and in a weary voice said, "At least there is something we *can* agree on! And now I think it best if I leave before we say anything that destroys this momentary accord."

For a seemingly endless minute Christopher stared at her, noticing the hint of strain that clouded the topaz eyes. He was aware of an inexplicable urge to take her into his arms and to demand that she allow him the right to resolve whatever difficulties had caused the air of sadness that clung to her. But then jeering at himself for being a fool and a madman, he shrugged his broad shoulders and said out loud, "I will order a sedan chair for you and escort you back to Cavendish Square; if we are lucky no one will ever guess that you have been here. What did you tell them when you left the house?"

"I didn't say anything, I just left," Nicole answered quietly, undecided if Christopher's help was what she really wanted. She was extremely conscious of the debt she owed him, of the wrong done him by her mother, and for the first time in their relationship she found herself ashamed and contrite for some of the things she had thought about him. Higgins's revelation had given her a different view of Christopher, and she hadn't yet had the time to accept the idea of his being vulnerable, of Christopher Saxon's being capable of being duped, of his having the same failings as any other person. An odd wash of tenderness for him clutched at her heart, and for one wavering humble moment she almost forgot herself and tried to express some of the conflicting emotions that were warring in her breast. But one look at his face and that impulse died. In a queerly docile mood she let him take charge of her and followed his lead.

They were able to return without undue incident to Cavendish Square. Nicole's unusually obedient manner nettled Christopher, and somewhat exasperatedly, the moment they were alone he said, "Will you please let off with these die-away airs! They don't become you, I can tell you that!"

Wrenched abruptly from her unpleasant musings, Nicole sent him a lowering look. "If you don't like it, you can leave!" she shot back.

His mouth tightened angrily, but he said nothing further on the subject; instead he asked, "Where are my grandfather and the ladies?"

And with a shock Nicole remembered the exciting news that Twickham had imparted earlier. Her constraint vanishing, for a moment the topaz eyes suddenly sparkled with mischief and she said almost happily, "Oh, Christopher, I did not tell you! Your grandfather and Mrs. Eggleston are to be married! This Sunday!"

If Nicole had thought to startle him she was disappointed, for he displayed neither astonishment nor surprise. "I wondered when he would get around to it!" Christopher replied lightly.

"You expected it!" Nicole returned almost accusingly.

Smiling sardonically, he merely remarked, "Of course I did—anyone who knew either of them would have been aware it was just a matter of time until Simon proposed. And there was never any doubt that Mrs. Eggleston would accept him. Even *I* could see that!"

Hunching a shoulder in displeasure, Nicole said sulkily, "Well, you don't have to be so conceited about it. *I* am prodigiously pleased with the news, and I won't let your cynicism spoil it for me!"

Dryly, his eyes hard and disbelieving, he retorted, "Could I spoil *anything* for you, Nicole?"

With something like horror she heard herself saying in a tortured tone, "You know you can, Christopher! You've known it all along."

Christopher froze; his eyes were like golden daggers

slashing across Nicole's quickly averted features. The very air in the room seemed to crackle with electrifying suspense as Christopher digested those impetuous words, unwilling to trust what they hinted at. And Nicole, unable to bear the intensity of his narrowed gaze, terrified he would tear out the secret in her heart, muttered distractedly, "I don't like to be always at odds with you— especially since I am living with your grandfather and I owe so much to you. I wish that we could be friends, that we could put aside the past and treat one anther with courtesy and the fondness that one has for those who are dear acquaintances."

"Dear acquaintances!" he snarled. The crazy mad longing to read something vital and revealing in her statement died instantly like a snowflake under the desert sun. Crossing the room with lithe strides, he grasped her arm in a painful grip and with one long-fingered hand turned her face brutally up to his. "Friends!" he spat. "There can never be friendship between us! Forget that you owe me anything, Nick! Remember that, will you, the next time your sordid little conscience pricks you!"

With a contemptuous movement he released her, and walking over to the door, he said in a sarcastic tone of voice, "Now that you have expressed your gratitude and I have calmed your fears of a marriage between us, I think it is time for me to leave. Give my congratulations to the newly engaged pair when they reappear, will you?"

He slammed out of the room, intending to put the length of London between himself and Nicole, only to be brought up short by Regina's entry into the house.

"Oh, Christopher, there you are. Have you heard the news? Isn't it thrilling?" Regina babbled, wondering with one part of her mind why his face wore such a scowling black frown.

Stiffly Christopher replied. "Yes. I have heard. As a matter of fact Nicole just told me."

Ignoring the fact that he obviously had been on the point of leaving, delighted that he had apparently come to call on Nicole, Regina rushed on, "Do stay a bit longer, won't you? I am full of plans for the wedding, and as you are his grandson, I would like to discuss them with you."

Almost rudely Christopher retorted, "I'm quite certain Simon can manage his own wedding, and what he can't, you, my dearest aunt, will be more than capable of handling. If you will excuse me?"

Regarding him with exasperation, Regina snapped,

"Really, you are the most boorish young man of my acquaintance! It is too bad Robert didn't let a little more of your hot, bad-tempered blood!"

Christopher bowed with insulting politeness. "Madame, shall I seek him out and request that he rectify his oversight?"

"Oh, don't be silly! You know I didn't mean what I said," Regina returned peevishly. "Really, Christopher, you are enough to drive a saint to the devil. Tell me, how is your arm?"

"Very well, thank you. It was only a scratch you know." And his gaze suddenly sharpening, his attention caught by something she had said, he added, "Perhaps I shall stay. There is something I would like to ask Nicole."

Very pleased with the change about-face, Regina said graciously, "Well, do rejoin her and I shall be with you both in just a moment. I simply have to rid myself of my cloak and to have a word with the cook about tonight's dinner."

Christopher reentered the blue sitting room so abruptly that Nicole gave a decided start. Still slightly stunned by the unexpectedly ruthless manner in which he had received her frail attempt at mending the past differences between them, she eyed him suspiciously as he shut the door and approached her. And it wasn't so unreasonable of her to put the protection of one of the low damask-covered sofas between herself and Christopher as he walked toward her.

With a derisive smile curling his lips, he murmured, "Don't run away, brat! I want a word with you and we haven't much time." He added enlighteningly, "Regina is home and will be joining us."

Her jaw clenched with anger at his careless tone and the arrogance of his actions, and Nicole replied tightly, "I think you and I have said enough today!"

"Mmmm, that may be, but unless you want an unholy row breaking over your head, you had better listen to me!"

Mistrustfully Nicole asked, "What do you mean by that?"

"Simply this: I think it advisable not to mention what Robert told you." At her expression of doubt he said reasonably, "Regina made that up on the spur of the moment, of that I am certain, and to bring it out in the open will only cause complications I think we can both do without." With disarming candor he admitted, "I don't relish telling her, or my grandfather for that matter, that they are both living a fool's paradise if they think they can arrange a match between us. Especially since it all may be nothing more than a fond wish on Regina's part —one she unfortunately expounded on to Robert. To save all of us an awkward time of it, it is best for the time being to ignore the rumor, because, believe me, that is all it is!"

After a moment's hesitation Nicole nodded her head. "Very well, I shall say nothing," she agreed listlessly, wishing only for the privacy of her room, for the time to refocus her thoughts, to come to terms with all that she had learned this traumatic afternoon. But Christopher now seemed in no hurry to depart, and when she glanced inquiringly at him, he said, "There is one more thing I want to discuss with you. Tell me, precisely which night was it that Robert found out about this supposed engagement between you and me. Can you remember exactly?"

Her forehead wrinkled in a frown of puzzlement, and she queried, "Why do you want to know that?"

"Because," he answered curtly, "I think it will explain something that has been baffling me for the past fortnight or so. Do you recall when it was?"

For a second longer Nicole stared at him, trying to discover why the date was important to him. And then with appalling clarity she connected two apparently unrelated events with one another. Her heart lurched sickeningly in her breast, the topaz eyes widened with ugly realization, and she whispered, "The night before your accident. It was the night before you were wounded."

Christopher smiled grimly. "Thank you, my dear, that explains a great deal."

"Oh, Christopher! He didn't! He wouldn't have done it deliberately, would he?" It was a cry for reassurance, but Nicole, with Robert's earlier base action burning in her brain, didn't really expect Christopher to answer any differently than he did.

The gold eyes cold and impenetrable, he drawled, "Now that remains to be seen, doesn't it?"

30

Having discovered what he wanted, Christopher would have preferred to depart from Cavendish Square immediately. But he had committed himself, and reconciling himself to the inescapable, he gained a queer sense of enjoyment from the afternoon, even going so far as to accept Regina's invitation for dinner that night. It was the least he could do—tonight's dinner would be a celebration, and it would have been churlish to refuse. For a brief while he was able to forget that tempting memorandum that lay just out of his reach.

It had been because of the memorandum that he had returned so unexpectedly to his rooms. Wary of approaching Buckley too soon after last night's indiscreet conversation, he had avoided his usual haunts, but finding no place in which to do some hard thinking, he had returned to Ryder Street, intending to plot a course of action. Nicole's untimely presence had put an end to that, and once he had connected Robert's attack on him with Nicole's news of the alleged marriage arrangement, he knew he couldn't leave Cavendish Square without discovering if his deduction had been correct.

Watching Regina at dinner that night, he wondered wryly if she had any inkling of what her deliberately mendacious remarks to Robert had caused, or that it was her careless inquiry after his wound that had led him to connect the two events. As it was, he hadn't really needed Nicole's confirmation of the date to convince himself of the devils that had driven Robert to attack him. He briefly toyed with the idea of letting Robert know that Regina had lied to warn him off, but then he discarded it; unfortunately he was incorrigible enough to leave Robert with that mistaken information. It gave him wicked amusement to think of the heart burnings Robert must be suffering.

Dinner was a pleasant affair; Christopher and Robert were the only additional guests at Cavendish Square.

Robert took the news of his father's approaching marriage with careless indifference and murmured all the appropriate offers of congratulations in a tone that did little to conceal his disinterest. Christopher, on the other hand, was quite sincere and unstinting in his approval of the match. He was also guiltily aware that Simon's marriage fitted in very nicely with his own plans—with Letitia as his bride Simon wasn't going to miss his departing grandson a great deal, and that thought soothed Christopher's uneasy conscience.

If Robert was disinterested in the news of Simon's second foray into the married state, he certainly displayed no such disinterest in Nicole. Delighted by the invitation to dine at Cavendish Square, Robert spent the entire evening trying to fix his interest with Nicole, but Nicole was singularly elusive and unreceptive. Frowning, he regarded her across the room, as for the second time this evening she had escaped his attempt to have a private word with her. Not unnaturally he wondered if her sudden and obvious distaste for his company had anything to do with this morning's conversation. She had been so positive and vehement in her denial of any agreement between her and Christopher that he was more than a little puzzled by her actions. Did the agreement perhaps exist, and had his aunt and his father brought enough pressure to bear that she had given in to their demands? It was an unsettling thought, but after a moment's reflection he dismissed it. So why did she avoid him? Why did her eyes not meet his? Why was there more than a hint of reserve in her manner with him—almost as if she found his company distasteful?

Glancing suspiciously at Christopher, he caught the gleam of knowing amusement that flickered in the gold eyes and felt a shaft of rage whip through his body. It was obvious that Christopher knew the answer to Nicole's strange behavior, and Robert experienced again that blind rage of hatred against his nephew. Someday, he promised fiercely, someday I will be rid of you, just as I rid myself of your father! And soon, Christopher, it will be soon, have no doubt of that.

Almost as if he could read Robert's mind, Christopher smiled at him grimly and lifted his glass of wine in a mocking toast.

Armed with her new knowledge of Robert, Nicole could barely stand the sight of him. The thought that she had once considered marrying him filled her with revulsion. Watching the two men from under lowered lashes,

366

she wondered how Christopher could act so nonchalantly, how he could smile so coolly into Robert's face without giving way to fury.

That ability came from many years of concealing true emotions, of mastering the wild, dark hatred that ate at his soul like some foul cancer. Christopher had lived with Robert's betrayal a long time, and like a hunting tiger, he could wait. There was no doubt in his mind that in time Robert would be his, and he would have no mercy. And so Christopher smiled at his uncle, and after the last toast to the newly engaged pair had been drunk, he prepared to depart, promising that he would attend the wedding on Sunday.

It was only when Christopher was standing in the hall bidding his grandfather a further good night that the subject of the removal to Brighton came up. Almost as an afterthought Simon remarked, "The plans for going to Brighton still stand, although Letty and I shall not be there until some time toward the end of September." Giving Christopher a half-defiant glance from under his heavy brows, Simon went on, "She and I are going to Beddington's Corner on Monday. Thought it best that we have a few weeks by ourselves before joining Gina and Nicole at the Kings Road house."

Christopher smothered a shout of laughter, and with mocking amusement glinting in his eyes, he murmured dryly, "And you can't wait to show her off!"

"Bah! That has nothing to do with it! Every man is entitled to a honeymoon and I am no different. Besides Letty has expressed a desire to see Beddington's Corner and I see no reason to deny her. She has a lot of friends in the area, you know, friends she hasn't seen in years. Don't forget we grew up there together. Did our first courting there." His eyes were suddenly almost dreamy as he finished softly, "It holds a lot of memories for us."

Christopher made no reply, for none was needed. After a moment Simon seemed to recollect himself and said in his usual testy manner, "Edward Markham and Robert are going to escort Gina and Nicole to Brighton. Are you going to join them?"

At the mention of Robert, any desire to go to Brighton vanished for Christopher. Simon's presence had been his main reason for agreeing to go, and without Simon there the motivation for traveling to the popular sea resort was no longer valid. He had been having second thoughts about the wisdom of leaving London too far in advance of the rendezvous with the American privateer. It was possible he might be able to learn something more of the British plans by remaining precisely where he was, and knowledge that Robert would be in Brighton made up his mind for him. Carelessly he returned to Simon's question, "I don't believe so. I find that I have too many commitments at the moment to tear myself away." Seeing the thunderous lowering of Simon's black brows, he added hastily, "But rest assured that I shall be in Brighton by the time you and Mrs. Eggleston are finished with your honeymoon."

"Too many commitments, hey!" Simon growled. "A little blond opera dancer would be nearer the mark!"

Christopher bit his lip in vexation and wondered how Simon had heard that bit of gossip—he thought he had been most discreet. "That may have been true last week, but Sonia and I have parted—she was, I fear, too greedy by half!"

Simon only grunted and grumbled as Christopher turned toward the door, "Well, I expect I should feel honored that you will even come to Brighton when I am there!"

"So you should!" Christopher shot back, a fond smile curving his lips.

"Bah! Get out of my sight you young rascal—and see that you are here on Sunday!"

Christopher took his leave and as the hour was not unduly late, just past ten, and the night a fine one, he was wide awake and restless by the time his carriage deposited him at his lodgings. To his surprise, upon entering the rooms, he discovered Buckley, pacing the floor like a caged wolf.

"Ah, there you are! I thought you would never return! Your man told me that you were attending a family dinner, but I never expected you to be this late," Buckley growled by way of greeting.

Inexplicably wary, Christopher smiled politely and, as Higgins entered the room, ordered that a bottle of brandy he procured from the landlord's excellent cellar. With his eyes fixed intently on Buckley's florid face, he inquired casually, "Now, what brings you here?"

Buckley looked uncomfortable and somewhat ill at ease and Christopher's watchfulness increased. Now what the devil was biting the captain?

He didn't find out for several more moments during which Buckley, obviously a man with something on his mind, prowled about uneasily, indulging in the most commonplace conversation.

Higgins returned with the brandy, and after pouring the two gentlemen glasses of the amber-colored liquor, he busied himself at the far end of the room, ostensibly paying no attention to the others, though in actuality he had his ears trained on what they were saying. Master Christopher might say that nothing was in the wind, but he knew differently.

Buckley glanced over at Higgins, and for a moment Christopher had the impression he was going to demand that the other man be dismissed. But apparently thinking better of it, he leaned confidentially toward Christopher, now sprawled negligently on the sofa, and said softly, urgently, "About last night, I hope you will forget that conversation we had. We were all pretty well in our cups and I wouldn't like to think anything was said that shouldn't have been."

His face a clever mask of apparent mystification, Christopher regarded him. "My dear Buckley, whatever are you talking about?"

His florid complexion became even redder, and Buckley muttered defensively, "It is that damned memorandum! I never should have mentioned it! And I would like your word as a gentleman that you will say nothing of it."

Assuming his most supercilious expression, Christopher remarked with deliberate stiffness, "I beg your pardon! I am not some gossiping old woman! Why would I mention such a thing? It was a private conversation between us, and I am not in the habit of repeating all the tittle-tattle that comes my way."

Obviously relieved by Christopher's insulted manner, Buckley made soothing noises and stumbled over himself in his haste to unruffle Saxon's very obviously ruffled feathers. Christopher very nicely allowed him to do so, wondering if Buckley had any idea of the foolishness of his actions. Even if he had not been so vitally interested in the memorandum, Buckley's behavior tonight would have increased his absorption in it. And for one very tense moment he considered the possibility that he was being baited—that someone wanted him to take a very definite interest in what went on at Whitehall. No, he decided thoughtfully, Buckley was very honestly trying to cover up an indiscreet slip of the tongue, and if Christopher had been what he appeared to be, that would have been the end of it.

Buckley's whole desire had been to ensure Christopher's silence on the matter, and having been convinced that nothing more would be said about what had transpired the previous evening, he very shortly made ready to take his leave. Escorting him to the door, Christopher asked carelessly, "Shall I see you tomorrow night at Lady Bagely's ball?"

"Oh, no, not I, my friend! As a matter of fact I shall be out of town for the next fortnight."

At Christopher's look of inquiry, he added almost shamefacedly, "My mother has taken to her couch, asserting most vocally that it will be her deathbed. And as my company commander is a good friend of the family, he has ordered me home for a few weeks to help ease her affliction."

"I hope it is nothing serious."

Buckley laughed. "No, that it certainly isn't; she does this at least three times a year, and I think she would be most affronted if she were to be taken grievously ill—she enjoys the attention too much to be sick!"

Christopher saw him out, his smile vanishing the minute Buckley was out of sight. It seemed he had chosen his tools wisely, after all, when he had decided Buckley and Kettlescope were his most likely prospects from whom to learn anything about the possible invasion of New Orleans. He had been right in thinking that Buckley would be the one to be indiscreet, he mused to himself. Thank God *someone* had been possessed of a loose tongue.

Unaware of the speculative gleam in Higgins's eye, he bid his valet a brief good night and took himself off to bed —but not to sleep. Instead he lay there staring at the ceiling and mulling over the best way in which to get his hands on the memorandum.

Obviously he was going to have to steal it, and a lone thief stood a better chance of escaping undetected than did two. Higgins would not be told—it would curtail all arguments and discussions if he merely presented him with a *fait accompli*. There was no shadow of a doubt in Christopher's mind about Higgins, but he wished to avoid the worry and dismay his plan would cause if Higgins knew about it in advance. Once the memorandum was in his hands would be soon enough to solicit Higgins's talents in preparing the forgery. Besides, if he were caught and hanged, he would just as soon hang by himself. Far better that Higgins be kept as much in ignorance as possible.

The following morning before Higgins awoke Christopher slipped from his bed, and neglecting to shave, he dressed hurriedly in a rough set of clothing that dated back to his days as Captain Saber. Quickly he made his way to Newton and Dyott Streets in St. Giles's parish. He had considered going first to the notorious Whitechapel area of London, but further reflection had deemed St. Giles's the place most likely for his purposes. After all, Newton and Dyott streets were the headquarters for most of the pickpockets and thieves about London, and while he didn't need the services of either, he did need the stock in trade of the latter, namely the implements and tools to open the safe in Major Black's office. The inhabitants of St. Giles's would be suspicious of a swell cove, but a shabby unkempt fellow as he was today would escape curiosity. It took him several false starts before he found what he wanted—a set of tools that any locksmith or nimble-fingered thief, for that matter, would be delighted to own. Before returning to Ryder Street with his curious purchase, he also had the forethought to acquire several locks of varying size and complexity.

Shoving the morning's acquisitions hastily in the bottom drawer of the oak bureau in his bedchamber, he swiftly stripped off his worn and coarse clothing. He then rang for Higgins to lay out a fresh change of apparel and to fetch him some hot water so that he might have a shave.

An hour later no one would have connected the tall well-dressed young gentleman who descended to the street and made his way to the stationer's with the rough-looking rogue who had made several purchases in the back streets of St. Giles's parish. He purchased many differently styled pens, and a variety of inks, as well as a wide selection of papers from a number of stationers. Returning to Ryder Street in time to eat luncheon, he concealed his writing supplies in one compartment of the mahogany sideboard before ringing for Higgins to serve him.

Immediately after fortifying himself, he walked into his bedchamber and there rifled through the drawer that held his various pairs of gloves. Finding a pair he did not particularly care for, he stuffed them in the inside pocket of his jacket and, warning Higgins that he would be home to dine this evening, strolled languidly toward Whitehall and the War Office. Once there he inquired casually for the way to Major Black's office and very shortly, after a brief look at Buckley's deserted office, found himself in that gentleman's domain.

Christopher had met the major once or twice when visiting with Buckley. Consequently he knew him by sight, but until now he had never known the whereabouts of his office. Finding it, he knocked for admittance. Summoning all the careless arrogance and cool aplomb of his aristocratic background, he sauntered in. Sending an apparently vague glance around the room, he murmured, "So sorry to interrupt, but I thought Captain Buckley would be here."

The major, a bluff, hearty fellow, exclaimed, "Why no! Buckley has been given leave for the next fortnight. May I help you?"

Christopher, his sharp gaze having noted the heavy iron safe in the corner, assumed an expression of mock vexation. "Oh, that's right. How silly of me to have let it slip my mind! Actually it was nothing very important; it's just that when he called last night, he evidently left this pair of gloves behind, and as I was in the area, I thought I would return them," Christopher replied lightly, laying the pair of gloves on the Major's desk.

"You may leave them with me, if you like," Major Black offered.

"No, that won't be necessary. Chances are that I may very well see him before you do. Thank you anyway."

His mission accomplished, Christopher replaced the gloves inside his jacket and, as the major was rather talkative, wasted a few minutes more desultory conversation. Christopher put the time to good use, and unobtrusively studied the iron safe that was supposed to hold the memorandum. From what he could see, the safe shouldn't prove too difficult to open—especially if he spent the next few days arduously familiarizing himself with the locksmith tools purchased that morning.

Arriving once more back at Ryder Street, he sent Higgins on several errands about town—errands that were destined to keep the gentleman away from their lodgings for a few hours. Once he was alone in his rooms, he broke out the locksmith tools and spent the afternoon recalling and utilizing everything he could remember about locks and the opening thereof. Higgins's return put an end to such activities. Christopher proceeded to express himself well pleased with the new cravats, the particular blend of snuff he had ordered from the apothecary's, and the swatches of cloth he had requested from his tailor. Higgins was not fooled; he knew he had been deliberately sent chasing all over London, but for the moment he held his peace.

The next two days fell into a pattern for Christopher. In the privacy of his bedchamber he spent hour after hour practicing springing the various locks. After dining early and wrapping himself in a dark cloak, he spent the night observing the activities of the guardsmen in the vicinity of the War Office. Long ago he had ascertained through careless conversation the various routines of the changing of the guard, but now it was vital he be certain of their procedures.

Finally the night came when he knew he must strike. Dismissing Higgins somewhat curtly for the evening, he spent the intervening hours until after two A.M. pacing the floor of his rooms, burning with a feverish impatience. As the clock struck the hour, he moved quickly, almost viciously stripping off his elegant garments and clothing himself in rough dark breeches and a close-fitting shirt of coarse black cotton. Some burned cork disguised and distorted his features. In his pocket he had some flint, a candle, and the small expensive set of tools he had purchased at St. Giles's.

As he approached the War Office, Christopher located the window that he would go through. Entering with cat-like stealth, he timed his deed to avoid the night guardsmen. He was certain his entrance had been undetected, and after obliterating all signs of his forced entry, he sped down the quiet corridors and up the two flights of stairs that led to Major Black's office.

The door was locked. But he had expected that and swiftly he knelt by the door. Keeping one eye on the dim narrow hall, he worked quickly until the door clicked open. Placing a wooden chair under the knob—that would give him a moment's warning if nothing else—he crossed the room and glanced down at the gas-lit street three stories below. A nasty jump, he thought tightly. Gently he unlocked the window.

Having cleared his escape path, he knelt before the massive iron safe. Gingerly he lifted out the locksmith's tools and deftly lit a candle. Even after all his hours of practice, Christopher was surprised and gratified at how smoothly the safe opened.

Once the safe was unlocked, he hesitated and then swung wide the heavy door. By the light of his candle he saw that it was filled with dozens of sealed and beribboned documents. He hoped desperately that the one he wanted was not sealed! After months of spurning him, luck was on his side, for the memorandum was the third document that he touched.

It was only a single sheet of paper, but it held the future for Christopher. As he skimmed it his mouth grew grim, and without wasting another second, he slid the document in an inside pocket and, moving with speed and stealth, shut the safe, relocked the window, and removed the chair from the door, placing it exactly where it had been originally. Out in the hall he pulled the door shut behind him and swiftly relocked it. Except for the memorandum burning like a brand against his chest everything was precisely as it had been.

Making no sound, keeping to the shadows in the gloomy building, he made his way unobserved to the ground floor. He left the same way he had entered, merely minutes before, and dropped silently to the cobbled street.

A quick surge of elation swept through him as his feet touched the ground, but savagely he tamped it down; when he handed the memorandum to Jason in New Orleans, *then* he could enjoy his triumph. Even so, a delicious feeling of satisfaction, of success stayed with him as he walked swiftly and determinedly toward Ryder Street.

Once in the safety of his rooms he laid the memorandum on the table and rather absently wet a cloth from the pitcher of water on the marble washstand and began to remove the traces of burned cork from his face. But the memorandum proved irresistible, and with his face still half-blackened, he sat down to reread it.

Major General Sir Edward Pakenham was to lead the expedition, and as he swallowed that, Christopher whistled. So it would be Pakenham, the great Wellington's brother-in-law, after all. Pakenham who hoped that he had "escaped America." He and his staff and additional troops and supplies would sail from Spithead, sometime during the first week of November, ostensibly under secret orders. Their immediate destination would be Jamaica, where at Negril Bay they would meet Admiral Cochrane's fleet and troops that would be assembling under Major General John Lambert. New Orleans and the surrounding territory would be their ultimate objective. Further orders would be awaiting them at Jamaica.

Thoughtfully Christopher set the memo down. If he were favored by whatever gods watched over such scamps as himself, he would reach New Orleans just about the time Pakenham set sail for Jamaica, provided there were no last-minute changes in the present plan. If all went well, New Orleans would have six weeks—and that just might be enough time. Enough time to show the British what Americans could do when pressed.

The slight click of his bedroom door as it swung open told him instantly that he was no longer alone, and Christopher, shielding the memo on the table behind his body, whipped around to confront a startled and astonished Higgins.

"Sir!" Higgins cried, obviously confounded not only by

374

Christopher's attire, but by the black streaks on his face as well.

Now we're for it! Christopher thought irritably. The time had come to bring Higgins in on their reason for being in England, but Christopher was curiously loath to involve the other man. But there was nothing else he could do—he needed Higgins's skills.

For several seconds the two old friends eyed each other, and then Higgins broke the taut silence by saying calmly, "Did you find the memorandum?" Christopher's eyes widened, but he speedily recovered himself. "How long have you known?"

Looking extremely pious, Higgins murmured, "Only since Captain Buckley's visit the other night when I overheard him talking about a certain memorandum." Almost gently Higgins continued, "I know you so very well, Christopher, and I couldn't help but tell that you wanted that memorandum like nothing else on this earth."

Exasperatedly Christopher snapped, "Well I hope to God that no one else can read me as well!"

"Oh, no, sir! You have nothing to fear. It is only that, well"—Higgins shrugged—"we have fought against the British too many times and been together in too many tight quarters for me *not* to know."

A quick affectionate grin flashed across Christopher's dark features. "That we have, my friend, that we have."

The awkward moment passed. Christopher brought Higgins up to date and then broached the matter of Higgins's art in forgery.

When he had finished, Higgins nodded slowly. "I figured that was the lay, but I wasn't quite certain. Did you really think that I would fail you?"

"No! It is just that I dislike drawing you into something that could very well hang us both!"

"Have no fear of that, I'm too old a flash cove to be picked for a Tyburn blossom! We'll come right, you'll see," Higgins said confidently. With a sly twinkle of laughter brimming in the brown eyes he added, "I was one of the cleverest in the business until Bow Street took undue interest in me."

Clapping the other man on one narrow shoulder, Christopher asked, "Well, my friend, do you think you are still the best?"

"Damn right, I am! And I'll prove it to you when I finish with that memorandum. You won't be able to tell one from the other."

Several hours later when Christopher compared the two

pieces of paper, he saw they were identical, even down to the slight stain across the left hand corner. All that remained was for the fake memorandum to be returned to Major Black's office.

The two men had discussed that aspect minutely. It was risky, as risky as stealing the memorandum in the first place, but it would remove the danger of imminent discovery. Together they decided that rather than have Christopher press his luck too far by attempting a repeat of tonight's feat, he would visit Major Black's office tomorrow afternoon, and when the moment presented itself, and surely it would, he would slip the forgery in amongst the paperwork on the major's desk. His reason for calling again on the major gave them some difficulty, but Christopher said he would think of something—even if it were the flimsy excuse of needing Buckley's home address.

He hoped the memorandum wouldn't be discovered or missed for a day or two, and by then Christopher's visit would be, if fate were kind, long since forgotten. No doubt speculation would arise, but as everyone knew how paperwork continually went astray at Whitehall and the War Office, Christopher was laying odds that careless filing would be blamed when the memorandum was found on the major's desk instead of in the safe.

The following day Christopher called on Major Black and inquired after Captain Buckley's address in the country. He wasted as much time as he possibly could without arousing suspicion, but no opportunity for replacing the memorandum presented itself. He had actually said his good-byes and was thinking furiously about another place to leave the memorandum, when he collided with the major's aide-de-camp, who was just entering the room with an armful of files. The files went flying, and in the ensuing apologies and hasty gathering of papers, Christopher was able to slip the memorandum from his pocket in amongst the clutter.

Christopher offered his apologies again, but the aide-de-camp, a very nice young gentleman, demurred. "It was my fault, sir. I was in such a hurry I wasn't watching where I was going. It serves me right too! Now I shall have to spend hours sorting out these reports, for there is no telling what goes where!"

Christopher sympathized profusely, but as he walked away there was a lightness to his step and a jaunty grin that kept tugging at his lips. The memorandum would be found, and no one would be quite certain *where* it had been!

Now all that lay before him was the interminable waiting. He and Higgins would not leave London until the day before the rendezvous. They would travel down to Brighton in the morning, and sometime after their arrival, but before the next evening, he would have to face his grandfather. It was not a prospect he relished, especially since he could offer no explanations, or even excuses for that matter.

What the hell was he to say? For a moment he considered merely writing a letter, but he dismissed it instantly. No, he would not take the coward's way out—somehow he must prepare Simon for his departure and yet avoid any hint that with the information he now had, it was imperative he return to the United States.

He refused to think of Nicole. She could move him unbearably, fill him with wild, improbable yearnings, but he was adamant that he was not going to fall into the silken trap that she spun so artlessly. But the thought of marriage with her would not leave his mind; instead, like a tantalizing promise, it swirled round and round, driving him nearly to lunacy. Appalled at the trend of his unruly thoughts, he convinced himself that they were best apart, that when he sailed for America, the last lingering tie would be severed. He could hardly ask her to wait for him . . . could he? As if stung by a scorpion, Christopher jerked away from what he was thinking. By God, no! It would never do, not in a thousand years!

And losing himself in the charms of yet another dainty blond opera dancer that night, he was positive he had made the right decision. One woman was as good as another, and time would destroy the odd flashes of something like pain that washed over him whenever he viewed a future without a topaz-eyed vixen in his arms.

31

Cℓ& The wedding of Lord Saxon and Mrs. Eggleston was set for one o'clock, and it was necessarily small, as Letitia and Simon had only two dozen guests. In fact, Simon had advocated marrying in Judge White's chambers with Regina and Christopher as the only witnesses, but Regina had quickly put a stop to that nonsense!

Consequently Simon and Letitia recited their vows in the most elegant and handsome parlor in the house at Cavendish Square. The room had been lavishly decorated with great silver tubs of flowers—early chrysanthemums with shaggy white and yellow heads, pink wild bell heather, daisies, late-blooming blue cornflowers, deep red roses, their heavy scent permeating the air, spicy dianthus, and tall stately stalks of gladiolus. The glass doors had been thrown wide open to permit a glimpse of the small formal garden beyond, and the adjacent flagstone terrace was ringed with huge pottery urns simply filled with flowers of every imaginable kind.

The ceremony was brief. Nicole, observing the tender, almost reverent manner in which Simon placed the ring upon Letitia's finger, felt a lump rise in her throat and for one awful moment was afraid she was going to burst into noisy tears just as Lady Darby had done.

However, once the final words were spoken, Lady Darby had promptly recovered and was again her forthright self, beaming and smiling upon the newlyweds.

The bridal banquet that followed was a gay and merry affair; everyone relaxed and drank numerous toasts to the bridal pair as the afternoon slid slowly into evening.

As the hours progressed, though, Nicole would have been extremely happy if three of the male guests had departed. Robert, she avoided for obvious reasons; Christopher's mocking face, his eyes alight with sardonic amusement whenever their gazes met, infuriated her and twisted a knife blade of anguish in her heart. And Edward, Edward with his fawning manner and ridiculous

378

posturing, was fraying her already overstrained temper. Like a hunted vixen with three dangerous hounds on her trail, Nicole drifted from one smiling, jesting little group to another, keeping a wary eye on her three tormentors.

Christopher was the easiest to avoid, for he was making no attempt to solicit her company and treating her to his usual indifference. And yet, it was Christopher, tall and cynically handsome in a slim-fitting black velvet jacket, the starched white cravat intensifying the dark, lean features, who disturbed her most. Try as she might, it seemed her eyes were inexorably drawn in his direction. She was furious with herself for this display of weakness and with Christopher for having the power to disrupt her control so easily.

Robert, increasingly mystified by Nicole's coolness, watched her intently, from under knitted brows wondering at the change in her manner. Well versed in the art of the chase, he made no attempt to force himself on her. Perhaps she was merely being capricious, he thought impatiently, or perhaps his ardor had frightened her. Whatever the reason, Robert was willing to wait, confident that in time Nicole would be his wife.

Edward, too, had noticed the fact that Nicole no longer seemed to find as much pleasure in Robert's company, and he rejoiced in his rival's apparent rejection. Now Nicole would surely fall for his blandishments, Edward crowed to himself, and his growing fear of languishing in debtor's prison faded.

Edward was in desperate straits. Used to the large income from Nicole's estates, scorning any attempt at living within his reduced means, his extravagances were catching up with him.

No longer was he granted credit at his favorite tailor's; his bootmaker had stated rather rudely that if he had not received a substantial payment within thirty days, he would lay charges against him; and his landlord had somewhat pointedly remarked that if Master Markham did not come up with three months' rent past due, very shortly he might find his belongings impounded and himself in the gaol! His creditors' demands were growing louder, and hinting at an engagement to a well-connected heiress was no longer enough to hold them in check. An immediate marriage with Nicole was the only thing that could save him now from ruin.

But Nicole, even after Robert's banishment, showed no inclination to smile with favor upon him, and Edward was torn between fury and the fear of what failure would mean to him. It was true that there were other heiresses in London, but since his reverses in fortune their guardians took care to see that Edward Markham was not allowed to exercise his blatant masculine beauty in the vicinity of their wealthy wards.

Ignoring his languishing glances in her direction, Nicole wished for the tenth time that her cousin had not been included in the festivities. He dogged her footsteps and was acting so well the role of her smitten slave that she longed to box his ears. Gritting her teeth, she promised herself she would do just that if Edward followed one more of her commonplace remarks with, "How clever of you, cousin! To think that such beauty as yours is allied with a nimble brain leaves one breathless."

Desperate to escape his smothering attentions as they stood for a moment alone, her fingers curling into the palm of one hand, she smiled grimly into Edward's smoky blue eyes and said tightly, "Would you mind fetching me a glass of lemonade, Edward?" And as Edward, playing his role, politely did her bidding, she bolted toward the seclusion of the garden.

It was a delightful night, the air warm, but with a hint of fall crispness about it. The gardens had been decorated with gaily colored lanterns, and the bright lights were like a chain of gleaming sapphires, rubies, and emeralds in the darkness, creating a fairyland setting. A few of the younger couples had taken advantage of their elders' preoccupation with the bride and groom and were wandering slowly down the neatly manicured paths.

Finding a secluded stone seat partially screened by a heavily scented climbing rose vine, Nicole sank down gracefully, hoping Edward would not think of the gardens to look for her. Sitting there quietly, her eyes closed, savoring the night, suddenly she yearned for the sea so intensely that for one moment she thought she could feel the gentle rocking of the ship, hear the soft swish of the waves, and smell the tangy ocean air.

But Edward's voice broke the spell, and with a sigh she watched Edward approach her, a tall chilled glass of lemonade in one hand.

Taking it, she said, "Thank you, Edward." She added somewhat bluntly, "I'm surprised everyone has stayed this long. You'd think they'd have left hours ago."

Impervious to Nicole's broad hint, Edward smiled vaguely and sat down beside her, careful not to disturb the skintight fit of his buff breeches. "Oh, no, my dear! Everyone is enjoying themselves much too much to think of leaving! And you can't really blame them—Lord Saxon has provided such an array of delicacies. You must admit too that it is not often there is a wedding like today's," Edward murmured and ended with an affected little titter that grated on Nicole's nerves.

"That may be," Nicole returned tartly, "but it is gone nine o'clock and absolutely no one has even suggested leaving. Don't forget we are all driving to Brighton tomorrow after Lord Saxon and Mrs. . . . er . . . Lady Saxon depart for Beddington's Corner. I still have some packing to do, and I should think that you yourself have certain arrangements to make."

Edward pretended not to understand the trend of Nicole's conversation. "I have made all arrangements with my landlord; my valet has everything packed, and have no fear, I shall be at your doorstep by no later than ten o'clock tomorrow morning."

The removal to Brighton met with Edward's full approval. Not only would he escape the duns that had begun to haunt his doorway, but Nicole would be removed from her more ardent suitors. Edward was determined that before they left Brighton Nicole would be his wife. Seduction was never far from his thoughts, and as he glanced about the nearly deserted gardens, the idea of creating a compromising situation immediately crossed his mind.

Subduing the malicious smile that threatened to crease his cheek, Edward suggested lightly, "Shall we take a walk, cousin? The garden beckons quite delightfully."

It was on the tip of Nicole's tongue to tell Edward to take himself off for a walk, but after a struggle with herself, she throttled the impulse and fell in with his urgings. After all, she reasoned, walking gave her something to do, and it was a lovely night.

They spent the next ten minutes or so wandering with surprising accord throughout the moonlit gardens—the colored lanterns imparted a carnival glow, the soft night air was intoxicating. As they approached the small white pavilion glistening silver in the moonlight, Edward said with oozing enthusiasm, "How clever of Lord Saxon to have a pavilion here in the town gardens! Come, let us step inside it!"

Nicole saw no danger in stepping inside, although she did wonder at Edward's sudden interest in the building. She soon found out that Edward had apparently mistaken her complacent mood, for they had barely entered when he suddenly startled her by snatching her into his arms.

"Are you demented?" she exclaimed, violently pushing against his shoulders.

And Edward, conscious that he had barely moments to perfect his plan, muttered, "Yes! I am mad for you!" And promptly, deliberately he tore at the fragile lace covering her breasts, ripping the gown at the shoulder. Infuriated rather than frightened, Nicole struggled angrily to escape from the clutching hold he had on her arms, but Edward was stronger than his willowy slimness suggested.

The curls that had been so painstakingly arranged some hours before came tumbling down in charming disarray, and the topaz eyes bright with temper, Nicole spat, "Unhand me, you toad! Have you lost what wits you possess?"

Edward, gazing at the creamy shoulders, the soft curve of breast his attack had revealed, was suddenly swept by a very real sensation of passion. No longer pretending, no longer even caring if the footsteps he had heard seconds ago were coming nearer or not, he said thickly, "Yes! You have driven me witless, dear cuz, and I am afraid you shall have to pay the consequences!"

His mouth found hers unerringly, and Nicole was momentarily stunned by the sheer audacity of his actions. Then nearly shaking with revulsion and fury, she fought to break free of the hurting plunder of Edward's lips, his tongue forcing its way into her mouth, raping and pillaging, his hands digging painfully into her arms. Edward gave her no respite; instead, the twisting thrashing motions of her body excited him even further, and with an intentionally brutal movement he shoved her down onto one of the nearby lounges, his body lying heavily on hers.

Her head spinning with disbelief, Nicole fought to clear her thoughts. Edward was too strong for her, and her only choices were to scream, thereby bringing everyone on the run, or to outthink her attacker. She instinctively shrank from screaming, instantly realizing the scandal that would follow. Well, she thought grimly, she had outfoxed Edward before and she could certainly do it again. Forcing her body to go limp, she suffered kisses and let him think she had become resigned to her fate. Feeling the fight leave her body, Edward was elated, certain his masculine charm had won the day. His vicious hold loosened somewhat; his hands greedily fumbled under her skirts; his lips freed her mouth as they sought the tempting softness of her breast. Nicole's skin crawled at his touch, and only by concentrating fiercely on what her next move would be was she able to keep from betraying the utter revulsion that filled her.

In the dim light of the pavilion she spotted a half-empty bottle of champagne and two glasses sitting on a nearby table. No doubt the remains of an amorous couple's rendezvous, she thought sourly. But with her weapon in sight, she slowly brought up one arm, gingerly caressing Edward as she went, not wanting him to guess her intentions. With her arm free, she gently moved one leg, letting Edward believe it was to facilitate his probing hands, and then when she was positioned to her satisfaction, she struck like a fighting tigress. Her teeth sank deeply into Edward's tender ear, and coolly she brought her knee up sharply and painfully between Edward's legs.

Edward let out a shriek of excruciating pain, all thought of seduction fleeing in the face of the exquisite agony burning between his thighs and the numbing pain in his ear. He doubled up, literally tearing his ear from Nicole's teeth, his hands protecting his groin, and Nicole deftly pushed him away from her and leaped to her feet. Snatching up the champagne bottle, she broke it swiftly against the table, and holding the jagged edge toward Edward, she snarled, "Touch me again, *cuz,* and that handsome face of yours will give nightmares to children for the rest of your miserable life!"

Edward was in such a state of shock—shock that any woman could resist him, shock that a young woman of Nicole's station had not fainted away in sheer shame at his attack, and shock at how incomprehensibly the tables had been turned on him—that he could only lie there moaning, his face white, his ear bleeding profusely on the satin cushions. Nicole regarded him contemptuously for a brief second, and then in a tone of loathing she said, "Pull yourself together, fool! Sit up, I haven't killed you, you jackass!"

"You certainly haven't, my dear, but I'm positive your poor cousin probably feels as if you have," remarked Christopher dryly from the doorway, his face inscrutable in the moonlight.

Surprisingly Nicole's feeling was one of relief that it should be Christopher who had found them. Almost wearily she put the bottle down and said, "My cousin was rather overcome by the night and too much wine. I would suggest that you show him to his carriage, while I return to the house and repair the damages to my gown."

Edward, seeing his chances slipping away, struggled to

his feet and cried hoarsely, "No! I shall marry her!" And seeing that Christopher remained curiously unmoved by his words, he stammered, "Y-y-you can't want a scandal! I'll marry her the instant a special license can be obtained and no one need ever know of what happened tonight. Her honor will be secure!"

"And your fortune made!" Nicole exclaimed angrily. "I have no intention of marrying you, Edward."

Christopher stepped farther inside the pavilion, and taking a lightning assessment of Nicole, he asked, "Are you all right, brat?"

Pushing back one of the tumbled curls, Nicole answered truthfully, "Yes. A bit mussed and torn, but unharmed otherwise."

"Then I suggest you slip up to your room and have Galena or Mauer put you to rights and I will take care of Mr. Markham."

Feeling as if she were being sent away like a bothersome child, Nicole bristled and the topaz eyes shimmered angrily. "Don't order me about!" she said between gritted teeth. "If you will remember, *that* is precisely what I suggested a moment ago!"

"So it is. Why don't you do it then? Or is it that I have mistaken the situation? That this is actually a lovers' quarrel?" he purred menacingly, and it dawned on Nicole that despite his careless manner, he was furious. And dangerous. With a shudder of foreboding she saw the look he sent Edward, and she flew across the room to clutch Christopher's arm. Almost dragging him, she forced him to follow her outside. A step away from the pavilion she said in a fierce undertone, "My cousin is annoying, but he did me no harm! I've grown up with him, Christopher, and I can handle him. What you saw in there is typical of how all our arguments ended as children." Then her face pensive, she added honestly, "Although Edward usually found some way to pay me back."

Examining his nails in the silver light, Christopher asked expressionlessly, "Shall I kill him for you?"

Startled, Nicole looked into his face. "Would you?" she asked without thinking, and her mouth growing dry, she read her answer in the gold tiger's eyes. Swallowing with difficulty, she said, "I don't want him hurt, Christopher. He is foolish, I can barely stand him, but don't harm him."

His gaze rested coolly on her face as he said tightly, "You realize that if he persists in his offer to marry you, if he goes to Simon with the tale of tonight, you may very well find yourself shackled to him? My God!" he burst out angrily. "If anyone else had stumbled across that little scene you would be before Simon at this moment, a ruined woman, and there would be no choice but to give you to Edward!"

Shaken by the unexpected possibility, Nicole looked away from the naked anger in his face. "I hadn't thought of that," she mumbled, studying her satin slippers. "But no one else *did* find us," she said at last, looking again at Christopher. Beseechingly, she laid a hand on his arm. "Let me go to the house and tell Simon myself. And if you were to help Edward—"

"Simon may believe you, but how are you going to keep your cousin's mouth shut? How are you going to make certain you are not the conversation in every club along Pall Mall? That you are not shunned and refused to be acknowledged by polite society?" Christopher demanded angrily. Grasping Nicole's shoulders, he shook her. "Don't you realize he can ruin you?"

"What do you care?" she shot back defensively, confused by his concern and giddy with the nearness of his hard, warm body.

Christopher slanted her a derisive glance, and setting her from him, he bit out savagely, "God knows!" Running a hand through the thick black hair, he muttered, "Go to the house, and don't say a word to anyone. Leave Edward to me—and take that look off your face, I'm not going to hurt him. Just scare the sweet hell out of him!"

Nicole wasted no further time in conversation and glided like a wraith into the darkness. His face blank, Christopher watched until she disappeared, and then with a swift movement he turned and stepped back inside the pavilion.

Edward had recovered a certain amount of his composure and was standing warily by one of the tables when Christopher reentered. As soon as Christopher came in, he babbled, "I know it was wrong, but, Saxon, I love her! I mean to marry her! I shall do the honorable thing by her, believe me!"

The gold eyes were mere slits in the dark, dangerous face. Christopher snarled softly, "You will *not*, my friend, not if you want to live! You will leave and you will say absolutely nothing about what transpired here tonight. For some reason your cousin wishes to protect you, but let me tell you this, if it weren't for Nicole, you'd be a dead man! Now get out of my sight and keep your mouth shut! And, Markham, if I hear one whisper, one hint, one word of what went on tonight, I will kill you, make no mistake of that! I may anyway, so stay away from me!"

Bravery not being one of his strong points, Edward wilted and scuttled like a frightened rabbit from the pavilion, overwhelmingly thankful to escape with his life, not caring at the moment if he had lost in his attempt to marry the heiress.

Unfortunately that mood did not stay with him, and by the time he had reached the safety of his rooms and had drunk several glasses of brandy, he had convinced himself that Nicole's interference on his behalf had been because she did, in fact, hide a *tendre* for him, and that Christopher's ugly threats had been just that—threats. Why, he couldn't hurt me, Edward thought scornfully, absently caressing the sword cane that was ordinarily by his side but which he had not worn today because dress had been more formal than usual. Ah, my beauty, he cooed to himself, if you had been with me tonight, Saxon would not have been so arrogant and brave. We would have seen to that! Having convinced himself that Christopher Saxon was an overbearing bully whom he could take care of anytime he choose, and that his suit with Nicole was prospering, Edward planned to go on just as if nothing had happened.

Christopher remained at the pavilion for several minutes after Edward had disappeared, struggling with a primitive urge to follow him and break every bone in his body. How dare he lay a hand on her, he thought furiously. And yet when he remembered how ludicrous Edward had looked bent over double, and how fierce and ready to defend her honor Nicole had been, a quiver of amusement shook him. Vixen! Edward probably would have suffered less at his hands than hers! He would only have killed him, while Nicole would have maimed him for life! Chuckling to himself, Christopher leaned carelessly against the doorjamb of the pavilion and stared down the path that Edward had used to make good his escape.

As fate would have it, Robert and Lord Lindley's friend Lieutenant Jennings-Smythe, having escaped to smoke a cigar, were wandering toward the pavilion by one of the several paths that ended there, and most disastrously Christopher was unaware of their approach. His profile was presented to them; with the lower half of his face in shadows and the moon intensifying the blackness of his hair, highlighting the heavy eyebrows and the flaring nostrils, the resemblance to Captain Saber was unmistakable.

Christopher didn't hear their approach, lost as he was in his own thoughts, and Jennings-Smythe had several seconds of unobstructed viewing of his lean profile. Jennings-Smythe could not believe his eyes and was so startled he blurted, "Captain Saber! Your nephew is a damned American privateer!"

Christopher, hearing voices, but just far enough away not to understand what was being said, looked in their direction and smothered a curse of exasperation. It had been to avoid Jennings-Smythe that he had been in the gardens in the first place, well aware that sooner or later, he might recognize him. So far Christopher had been adept at evading face-to-face confrontations and generally managed to keep a room full of people between them. It appeared, though, that his luck had just run out. Straightening, he lounged away from the pavilion and leisurely strolled up to them as they stood in the center of the path.

"Taking the night air?" he inquired lightly. Suddenly uncertain when he looked at Christopher's aristocratic features, Jennings-Smythe mumbled some trite remark.

And Christopher wasted little time in removing himself. He returned a polite comment and then with deceptive indolence began to walk to the house.

Frowning, he slipped into a small deserted room in the back of the house. He would have to work out an alternative plan just in case Jennings-Smythe did recognize him, he decided thoughtfully. As long as someone, either he or Higgins, was there to meet the ship at the end of September and was able to get that memorandum to Jason in New Orleans, that was the important thing. If he were arrested, Higgins would have to take it to America. And if he, Christopher, weren't clever or adroit enough to convince everyone that Jennings-Smythe was entirely mistaken, well, then he would deserve to hang, he told himself cynically, never doubting his own ability to avert disaster. His thinking was correct as far as it went, but what he hadn't taken into consideration was the fact that Jennings-Smythe had inadvertently betrayed him to Robert.

Robert had watched that scene with undisguised interest, certain at last that he had stumbled across something that would bring about Christopher's ultimate downfall. He remained silent until Christopher had disappeared, and then looking at Jennings-Smythe, he asked idly, "You say my nephew is a privateer? This Captain Saber? Why didn't you say something to him?"

The thought that Captain Saber and Baron Saxon's grandson could possibly be the same man was so preposterous that Jennings-Smythe was feeling extremely silly, and he said apologetically, "I must have been mistaken and I feel a perfect fool. It was just a trick of the light, you know, for now that I've seen him full face, I realize that there is nothing more than a superficial resemblance."

If it had been anyone but Robert Saxon, Jennings-Smythe's explanation would have sufficed, but Robert was hungry for anything that would discredit Christopher, even a lie. In his own rooms that night Robert reviewed what he had learned, and for the first time in months he felt a flash of triumph.

He would have preferred to begin investigating the truth of what Jennings-Smythe had said immediately, but everything was already arranged for the removal to Brighton, and there was not enough time in the morning to pay a visit to the Admiralty Office—not if he wished to escort Nicole and his aunt to Brighton. Certainly he had no intention of allowing Edward to be their sole protector for the journey, not when it was glaringly apparent that Edward had covetous eyes for Nicole!

Robert had waited this long for his revenge, and he was willing to wait just a little longer—primarily because at this particular moment it was more important to Robert to retrieve himself with Nicole—to discover what had gone wrong between them, to have her smile warmly at him once again. *That* was much more imperative than for him to remain in London ferreting out possibly discreditable information about his nephew. There would be time for that! Soon enough it would be worth his while to pay a call at the Admiralty Office and discover what was known about this Captain Saber!

PART FOUR

TRACES OF LOVE

"Le coeur a ses raisons que la raison ne connaît point."
The Heart has it reasons that reason knows nothing of.

—French Proverb

32

Brighton was not a happy place for Nicole. It had been here that her parents and brother had drowned, and when she and Regina had driven past the handsome Ashford manor one day, she couldn't suppress the shudder of pain that shook her as she remembered that day. Regina had suggested she might like to wander through the house to see if the Markhams had done any alterations or damages during their guardianship, but she shook her head violently. She didn't think she could bear to go through that house, especially not to step out onto that balcony where she had sat that terrible day watching wide-eyed with terror as the gleaming white sloop had plunged into the sea.

Time had deadened her pain, but she could not help associating Brighton with unhappiness. She missed the new Lady Saxon dreadfully, although Regina was kindness itself, evidently having forgiven her the lapse with Robert. But Regina was no substitute for Lady Saxon's sweet, understanding manner nor Lord Saxon's sarcastic gruffness, and the house seemed dull and empty without the newlyweds.

There were certain advantages to Brighton, she admitted to herself. For one thing, she could hear the crash of the ocean just beyond the seawall, and with Galena in attendance Nicole found a certain solace in walking along the edge of the ocean, the sea breeze ruffling her hair and kissing her pale cheeks with color. There was a more relaxed air in Brighton, despite all the members of the *ton* from London who crowded into the small city this time of year, and Nicole found herself with somewhat more freedom and with fewer restrictions. Perhaps, she thought wryly, I have at last grown used to this life and now will fade into a vapid existence, no longer straining against the restraints of polite society.

As she sat in her room one mid-September afternoon, her mind wandered to Robert and the rather strange situation that existed between them. She tolerated his company much as she did Edward's but her cool manner seemed in no way to disturb Robert as it did Edward. Edward continued his pursuit of her, but he was more inclined to reveal his true character these days, having finally realized that his ardent display the night of the wedding had done him no good, and that Nicole was not a bit taken in by his loverlike air. Consequently whenever Nicole refused his invitations to dance, or sought the company of others rather than converse with him privately, he tended to pout and show his displeasure, but with Robert it was an entirely different matter.

Robert took all of her snubs with good grace, smiling quizzically at her, his eyes gently asking why she had changed toward him. But she could not tell him that she no longer trusted him, or that she could never forget that he had been her mother's lover and, worse, that he had so brutally betrayed Christopher. Robert never pressed her, but like Edward he never abandoned his more refined and disarming wooing.

On the surface Robert had taken Nicole's withdrawal without any sign of anger, but underneath he was seething with jealousy. He had attempted to lure more information out of Jennings-Smythe about this Captain Saber, but he always turned aside with a laughing comment, mocking himself for his mistake. He learned a little more from casual inquiries, but nothing that would connect Christopher with the American privateer Captain Saber. Robert finally decided that the hiring of an inquiry agent was his only option, and in the middle of the second week of September he did precisely that.

On the twenty-fourth of September Simon and Letitia arrived in Brighton, both looking incredibly happy. With their return the house on Kings Road suddenly seemed to wake and shake off its slumbering air and resounded now with lively laughter and gaiety as various friends and acquaintances came to call, offering their congratulations and welcoming them to Brighton.

The air of passiveness that had overtaken Nicole vanished with their return, and she found she could bear with equanimity Edward's persistent and increasingly annoying suit and that she could even occasionally smile at Robert Saxon. She told herself firmly that this new vigor, this bubble of excitement in her breast was because Lord Saxon and his wife were once again part of the household, but it was only her unruly heart that acknowledged the feeling might have something to do with the fact that in less than a week she would see Christopher again.

Simon and Letitia had both noticed instantly that Robert was no longer greeted with the same degree of warmth and cordiality he had been in the past, and both were more than a little curious as to why Nicole had changed her attitude toward him. Simon, thinking it some work of Regina's, had taken her to task for it the first moment they were alone.

Glaring at his sister, he demanded, "Now, Gina, what is going on here? What have you said to Nicole to make her avoid Robert so? I told you to let the gel be, that if she wanted Robert, I wouldn't throw a rub in her way. And I meant it! I don't want her to marry Robert, but I've learned my lesson and I'll not be a party to forcing them apart."

Regina drew herself up stiffly. "You wrong me, Simon! I do not know what you are talking about! Certainly I have said nothing to Nicole to give her a distaste for Robert. I haven't had to! She had been disenchanted with your son since before the wedding had you cared to notice!"

"Just so you haven't been meddling!" he barked after a moment.

Somewhat huffily Regina replied, "Meddling! Why I would never do such a thing!"

Simon grunted disgustedly. "Now don't give me that! You are an unscrupulous woman, Gina! And you are perfectly capable of telling an outright lie if it suits you!" Seeing his sister was becoming highly incensed, he added somewhat hastily, "Well, that is enough of that! Perhaps Letty can find out why the chit had taken such an obvious aversion to Robert."

Letitia was indeed able to find out what had happened when Nicole unburdened herself. Regina had gone to visit her close friend Lady Unton, and Simon was closeted with his man of business, leaving Letitia and Nicole to their own devices, and they were seated under the spreading leaves of an elm tree at the side of the house, enjoying a glass of lemonade, when Nicole haltingly told Letitia what she had learned from Higgins.

She hadn't meant to tell anyone, but Letitia's gentle probing about Robert loosened her tongue and the story came tumbling out. All of it.

Letitia, the faded blue eyes round with astonishment and dismay, listened in silence, her only comment when Nicole halted, "Oh my! How dreadful!"

"Yes, it is. It's been rather beastly too, knowing that my mother was such a depraved creature." Her face averted, Nicole said in a choked voice, "I've tried to make excuses for her, tried to remember her as I thought she was, but I just can't! All I can think of is that not only was Robert her lover, but Christopher as well!" Her eyes were anguished as she looked into Letitia's compassionate features and cried, "How could she! How could Robert share her with Christopher! Oh, I know it was to distract my father, but you would have thought if Robert were in love with her, he wouldn't have wanted to share her that way."

Letitia looked away and said very carefully, "Perhaps Robert didn't know."

Nicole stared at her. Finally she asked in a dull tone, "You mean, mother also betrayed Robert? That he thought those meetings were innocuous, arranged solely for the look of the thing?"

"Yes, my dear, I'm afraid that is precisely what I mean." Letitia clasped Nicole's hand. "My dear, listen to me! Your mother was like a spoiled child. I knew her from a babe, and she absolutely *had* to have the adoration of any man, young or old, whom she met. I don't believe she ever really loved anyone, but that didn't make her entirely wicked! Oh, dear, what I am trying to say is that she wasn't malicious, she just did these things." Sadly she continued, "Christopher was so obviously suffering from a terrible case of calf love that I think it was beyond her to resist seducing him! She and Robert probably meant to use him as a blind, but her vanity drove her to make the lies she told her husband reality."

"Mrs. Eggleston!" Nicole burst out, so shocked she had neglected her new title. "How can you say that! Are you excusing what they meant to do?"

Flustered, Letitia twisted her hands together, "Oh, no! What I am trying to say, is that your mother was selfish and thoughtless and that she used people, but in the way that a child uses people. She didn't think what she was doing to Christopher. She and Robert needed a scapegoat and he was available. She saw things only as they affected *her!* Can you understand what I mean?"

Frowning, Nicole gazed off into the distance. "I think so. But it doesn't lessen what she did."

"Oh, no, I never meant it did! I was only trying to explain how Annabelle would have looked at things. It probably never even occurred to her that she was being unfair to your father by being unfaithful, or that she was

394

betraying Robert by taking Christopher as her lover. She simply never *thought*."

"And Robert?" Nicole inquired tiredly.

"Oh, my!" Letitia murmured unhappily. "I don't wish to be brutal, my dear, but Robert would never have done for you. He was jealous and spiteful as a child, and I must admit that I never liked him. From what you have told me, I blame him for what happened. It was probably his idea to use Christopher, and certainly it was his doing that sent Christopher from England. And I cannot say in this case that it was something done without a lot of thinking and planning. Robert meant for Christopher to die, and I'm certain he wanted Christopher disgraced more than—" she broke off suddenly, as though she had gone too far.

Nicole smiled sadly. "But we can hardly say this to your husband."

"Oh my, no! Robert has caused Simon enough grief as it is. It is over with and finished; there is nothing any of us can do to change it. All we can do is to forget it and go forward." Her eyes misty with tears, she leaned forward and said earnestly, "My dear, do not let it destroy you! Put it from your mind and forget it."

Nicole gave her that sad smile. "I think I will now that I have talked to you. I feel more at ease about it, less confused and angry. Perhaps in time I shall view it more objectively."

"Yes, that's it, my love! *Do* try!" Lady Saxon urged her affectionately.

Nicole discovered that she had spoken the truth; it was as if the conversation with Lady Saxon had lessened the hurt.

But if Nicole's pain had been lessened by that coversation, Lady Saxon was in agony. The sight of Robert Saxon filled her with wrath, and without even being aware of it, she glowered at him every time he even looked at Nicole. She was tormented by what she learned, and could not bear the thought of the horrors Robert had inflicted on those she loved.

By the night after her conversation with Nicole Lady Saxon's distress was so acute that even sleep would not come to her. It suddenly seemed clear to her that she must do something to confront Robert with her knowledge, but she had no idea what she could do that would not somehow involve Simon.

She shifted miserably in her bed, trying not to disturb her sleeping husband. She almost jumped out of bed when his voice pierced the darkness. "Letty! What is it? You've been fidgeting for hours!"

"It's nothing, Simon. I've had the most dreadful headache all night and cannot sleep. I had hoped I would not disturb you." Her voice quavered slightly.

Simon heard that quaver and reached out to enfold her in his arms. "What is it, my dear, what is distressing you?"

Determined to keep the truth from him, she made some light comment, but Simon would have none of it. With paralyzing intuitiveness, he asked, "Is it Robert? I noticed that you have been somewhat strained in his company since yesterday."

Letitia went rigid, and instantly aware of it, Simon said sharply, "Tell me what he has done! And, Letty, don't fob me off with some feeble excuse about a headache! I know you too well and it is obvious that Robert has done something to upset you. Now tell me what it is and no nonsense."

For a moment Letitia still hesitated, but then Simon kissed her gently on the cheek and said in a pleading tone, "Please, love, tell me."

What could she do except tell him after that?

When she finished Simon said nothing for several seconds, and Letitia's heart ached for him. He set her from him gently with a heavy sigh. "I feared all along that it was something like that," he said in a sad tone. "I suspected it, but I didn't want to believe it. Why? Why, Letty, is Robert this way? I have always tried to treat him fairly, and God knows I have always loved him and protected him. To treat a boy that way! His one nephew! To sell him into certain death!" Agonized, he burst out, "I tell you, Letty, I don't think I can bear the sight of him anymore. This time I cannot forgive him."

"Simon, Simon. Do not distress yourself. Please try to sleep. Remember it happened so long ago."

Absently he rearranged the tangled bed clothes, his movements slow and painful, and Letitia was filled with pity for him. Now it was she who cradled him, her arms enfolding him, her lips pressing tenderly against his temple. "Simon, don't let it eat at you. Robert is what he is and you cannot blame yourself. Know in your heart that you have done the best you could, and put the rest aside. He is a man full grown, and he was a man full grown when he and Annabelle planned their charade and when he sold Christopher to that press-gang. It is not your fault; you taught him what you could, and if he chose not to learn, there is nothing you can do about it. Put it from you," she pleaded.

"I shall try, Letty. I shall try. But I doubt I can be as forgiving as you—or as Christopher appears to be."

Letitia stirred uneasily. "I don't think Christopher has forgiven him, Simon. Sometimes I think he is merely waiting like a tiger does for his prey to make a mistake."

In London, Christopher did resemble a tiger—a caged tiger. Waiting was not easy for him, and the thought that Jennings-Smythe could bring about disaster anytime he cared to open his mouth, did nothing to improve his temper.

Anticipating his departure, Christopher had already let it be known that he was leaving London and traveling to Brighton. He left his plans deliberately vague, alluding carelessly to travels on the continent.

He had paid his debts, informed his landlord of his date of departure, and completed his packing. The memorandum itself was in a thin leather pouch strapped around Christopher's waist. He was ready.

The days of September had lagged. He had still not come to any firm decision concerning what he would tell his grandfather, and it knifed him with increasing and painful frequency. He was not ashamed of what he had done, but would Simon, if he knew, understand? More than ever Christopher was aware of his invidious position, but his worst moment came on the morning of the twenty-eighth of September.

He had risen late, after having spent the previous evening drinking and whoring with Captain Buckley and Lieutenant Kettlescope as a sort of farewell to London. His head was aching, and his mouth tasted like the floor of a stable. He had just finished his fourth cup of very strong coffee when Higgins entered and thrust the *London Times* under his nose. "They've burned Washington!"

With a feeling of incredulity, Christopher read the bold black headlines, WASHINGTON BURNED! His face white, he swiftly devoured the article.

Captain Harry Smith had just returned from America in a phenomenally short amount of time—twenty-one days—and with him came the dispatches reporting the capture and burning of Washington. During the week of August 19, the British had fought back the American lines and driven them from the capital city. British troops had then poured into the city, looting and sacking at will. Major General Robert Ross had personally ordered the destruction of the White House, the Capitol, the Treasury, the War Office, and the National Archives.

With black fury in his heart, Christopher continued to read of the terrible havoc wreaked on the American capital by the invading British troops, and any remorse he might have felt died.

Sick with impotent fury, Christopher slammed the paper on the table, snarling, "By God, they'll regret this infamous act!" With barely leashed violence he promised softly, "Let them come to New Orleans—we'll teach them that no one attacks our capital with impunity!"

Christopher and Higgins left London early the next morning and arrived at Brighton shortly after lunch. Simon was delighted to see his grandson and made no attempt to hide it.

"By heavens, boy, but it is good to see you!" he thundered as Christopher entered the library where Simon had been sitting, idly leafing through the latest racing magazines.

"The same to you, sir! I can see that the married life must be most agreeable. You look like a happy, contented man and Lady Saxon is positively blooming!"

Simon looked inordinately pleased. "She is, isn't she?" he replied with simple pleasure. "We did enjoy ourselves in Beddington's Corner. We've decided to go back there the first of October. Gina can show Nicole the sights here in town if the chit don't want to bury herself in the country this early in the year."

Christopher smiled noncommittally and wondered if he should take advantage of this unexpected private moment to tell his grandfather that tomorrow night he would be leaving. He sought vainly for the words, but they stuck firmly in his throat. He could not, within moments of arriving, spring it on the older man that he was leaving for an indefinite period of time. Deliberately he pushed the distasteful task from him and instead sat back and savored those precious minutes alone with his grandfather.

Simon, too, had been struggling for words—but of a far different nature. He longed to tell Christopher that he knew the full story of what had happened all those years before, but somehow he couldn't quite make himself bring the subject up. Christopher had obviously not wanted him to know, and Simon was quite sure his grandson would not be pleased that the sordid story had come to him through the women of the family. For a second Simon frowned, suddenly realizing how the past could very well be an insurmountable obstacle between Nicole and Christopher, and his heart hardened further against his son. Not only had Robert nearly been the death of Christopher, but it appeared that even now his wickedness could destroy any hope that Christopher and Nicole had of happiness. Ah, damn! Why did it have to be that way, he thought with sad vexation.

"Something wrong, sir?" Christopher asked, his eyes watchful on Simon's face.

"Eh?" Simon grunted, hastily pulling himself together. "No, I was just lost in a daydream." Smiling with apparent sheepishness, he added, "I find myself going off at the oddest times. Must be that my age is catching up with me. Next year, I shall probably be absolutely senile!"

"Hardly!" Christopher snorted, not entirely satisfied with Simon's excuse, but he let it be. If it were something important, he would discover it soon enough.

Nicole hadn't known Christopher had arrived until she joined the guests Regina had invited for tea. Seeing him unexpectedly, she felt her heart lurch, but she forced herself to smile politely when he approached.

"Well, brat," Christopher taunted lightly, his assessing gaze taking in the charming gown she wore and the brilliance of her eyes. "You're looking very beautiful. Brighton must agree with you."

With a dazzling smile she said sweetly, "Brighton? Oh, I put it down to being away from you!"

His eyes darkened and for one wary second she thought he would retaliate. Instead he shrugged his powerful shoulders. "Still the vixen's tongue, Nick," he commented dryly. Without further conversation he sauntered away.

Edward came strolling up just then, and Nicole lost sight of Christopher as she tried politely to ignore her cousin.

Edward Markham was becoming truly desperate, and later pacing his room, he reviewed his staggering debts and again came to the realization that he was totally without financial resources. As he pondered his situation again and again, only one thing became clear—he must marry an heiress. And the one he wished to marry had spurned his suit. "Damn, Nicole," he hissed. He had been so sure before that incident at the pavilion that winning Nicole's hand would be an easy trick, but now it was quite obvious that he had misjudged her.

He cursed Nicole again, but more he cursed the folly that had led him to that ill-fated card game on the previous night. He had been certain that luck was with him at last, and that he would be able to recoup enough money to keep the duns at bay. Instead when he rose from the gaming table in the early hours of the morning he was several thousand pounds in debt.

It was impossible to think of reneging. He would be ruined if he did not pay that debt—within the week.

It had actually occurred to him to murder Nicole, so great was his resentment of her, but as he assessed his situation he realized that it would be easier to marry her —to force her to marry him.

Once his decision was made, he set about perfecting a hasty plan. The hiring of a coach and four would take the last of his ready money, but that he was willing to risk, considering the fortune at stake.

How to get Nicole into the carriage? He could hardly kidnap her off the street in broad daylight! She wouldn't meet him anywhere feasible, but what about meeting someone else? But whom? And why a secret meeting? Desperately he racked his brains, but as the hours passed he came to no solution. Nicole would not meet just anyone, and certainly even fewer people in clandestine circumstances. Yet he had to have her in some private place. He could think of dozens of places that would suit his purposes, but the prickly question remained— how the hell to get Nicole there, and alone.

Eventually he hit upon a rather haphazard scheme. Nicole, he knew, was in the habit of walking every afternoon in the park, usually with one of the maids from Lord Saxon's establishment accompanying her. All he would have to do was meet Nicole as she started home, race up to her with the frantic message that Lord Saxon had suffered a fatal stroke, and then before she had time to think, whisk her around to his waiting coach—without the attendant maid. By the time Nicole questioned his ability to have at his disposal a coach and four and realized that they were not traveling toward Kings Road, it would be too late. He was rather pleased with his final strategy. The only real flaw he could see was the uncertainty of Nicole being alone with the mail. He would have to leave it to chance—that and the unthinkable prospect that for some unknown reason Nicole would not take her usual walk tomorrow afternoon in Brighton Park. But he knew she would. Fate could not continue to be so unkind to him.

33

Christopher faced his last day in England with mingled excitement and dread. Most of all he dreaded having to tell Simon that he was leaving, and the thought of that farewell was unbearable. He had no idea how he would explain that sometime between the hours of dark and midnight he would be sailing back to America.

Already, the older man was expounding on the delightful and merry Christmas they would have this year at Beddington's Corner. He had even made sly hints that perhaps the town house in London could be totally turned over to Christopher since he and Letitia preferred the quiet of Beddington's Corner.

Morosely Christopher wandered about the Brighton house. Once he laughed out loud at himself. To think that he, just like an erring schoolboy, dreaded the coming, and come it must, interview with his grandfather. England, he thought derisively, had certainly changed him. He felt that he was overcivilized—and somehow less of a man. Why else this occasional conscience that pricked him and this dislike of leaving, this actual dismay at telling his grandfather good-bye? As for Nicole . . .

Nicole at the moment was reading in the library, but as was common recently, anytime she was left alone her thoughts were on Christopher. With a sigh she closed her book. What was the use of thinking of him? Of torturing herself over someone she couldn't change?

Suddenly she could not bear to be alone and strode determinedly toward the door. She had almost reached it when the door swung open, just missing her.

"My God, Nicole, you might have given me some warning that you were in here! I could have hurt you badly when I opened the door," Christopher snapped exasperatedly as he halted his progress into the room.

Her ready temper rising, Nicole shot back hotly, "And how was I to know you were about to come barging in like a bull with a wasp in his ear?" she snapped.

Warily they regarded each other. Christopher gave her a crooked grin, and then laughed. "Pax, little vixen! Pull in your sharp teeth."

"You started it!" she retorted defensively, angrily conscious of his masculine presence. His face looked leaner to her, harder, and there was an air about him that she couldn't quite place—an aura of recklessness that caused her to wonder exactly what he was doing in Brighton. She managed to ask calmly, "How long are you to stay with us?"

Christopher hesitated a moment, but then he shrugged and replied easily, "I'm afraid I won't be staying here at all." At her look of surprise he said slowly, "Higgins and I will be staying at my cottage near Rottingdean tonight." Flashing her a careless smile, he finished lightly, "As for tomorrow who knows where we'll be." It was as close as he could come to the truth.

But Nicole knew him too well and a premonition chilled her, and with her eyes fixed intently on his, she asked tightly, "You're leaving aren't you? You're going back to Louisiana."

Christopher drew in his breath as if struck a deadly blow, but his face remained impassive as he replied. "Yes. Yes, we are, Nick." The admission shocked him. He had not meant to tell Nicole at all, and certainly not before he had spoken with his grandfather. Yet, when she had unerringly guessed, he could not lie to her. I wonder if that's an improvement, he thought cynically, being unable to lie is supposed to be a virtue.

Nicole froze as a terrible sense of loss spread throughout her entire body. He was leaving. No more Christopher to taunt her and drive her mad with passion and fury. She should be glad, she told herself staunchly. Pride stiffened her spine, and glibly she retorted, "Well, that's very nice!" The big topaz eyes blank behind black spiky lashes, a set smile on her wide mouth, Nicole continued on a determinedly cheerful note, "You must be delighted to be rid of me at last. I have never thanked you for the many things you have done for me, and I hope now that our ways are finally parting that you will allow me—"

"Shut up, Nick!" Christopher snapped tautly, a muscle jumping in his cheek.

Nicole shook her head and the dark fiery curls danced on her shoulders as stubbornly she went on, "No! You must let me! I must tell you—"

Christopher stopped her in the only way he could; his hands roughly grasped her slender arms, pulled her tightly against him as his mouth captured hers. He kissed her a long time. A long, hungry, urgent assault that left her weak and trembling in his crushing embrace. Then cradling her head against his shoulder, his mouth moved with aching tenderness across the soft curls beneath his chin, and he said thickly, "Don't say another word. Words don't mean much to you and me. We say things we don't mean, and we let our tempers rule us too often. Someday maybe we'll be able to talk like sensible human beings, but God forgive me, for where you are concerned, I am not rational."

Astonished, Nicole jerked her head up to stare up at him. She opened her mouth, but no sound came out, and Christopher driven as much by the knowledge that tomorrow he would be putting an ocean between them as by her yielding body, couldn't control the urgent need to taste her mouth once again. Her lips parted sweetly, and at the unexpected surrender a muffled imprecation broke from him. He gathered her slim form nearer to him; his hands caressed her back and hips, making Nicole forcibly aware that he wanted her. But then Christopher, remembering against his wishes where he was, gently pushed her away and said with a wry smile, "You're more potent than any wine, Nick. You make a man lose his head and do things he regrets."

Nicole, not unnaturally, misinterpreted what he was saying and stiffened, but Christopher gave her no chance to reply; instead he compelled her to sit down. After seating her in the center of an elegant fawn-velvet sofa, he lounged negligently on one of the arms, one long leg swinging restlessly. Shooting Nicole a queer look, a look of brooding regret and yet strong resolution, a look of mockery and arrogance, he began slowly, "I haven't always treated you as I should. I won't apologize for what I have done, though." Eyeing her wickedly, he confessed brazenly, "Heaven help me, given the same set of circumstances, I'd probably do the same thing again! I wanted you then, I want you now, and I'll admit that no woman has ever quite had me so entangled and confused as you have! Believe me, minx, I'll be glad to see the last of you!"

The careless words hit her like a slap in the face. She had always known that he would be happy to see the last of her, but she was stunned by his easy admission. Aimlessly she played with the silk of her gown to hide her trembling hands and kept her face averted from him,

403

fearful she would betray how deeply his indifference hurt her.

Christopher was watching her face intently, the expression in the gold eyes shadowed by the dark lashes. He was painfully aware that he was handling this scene badly, but he was powerless to change it. His usual ready address failed him completely with Nicole. He said the wrong things, did the wrong things, and even when it was the last thing in the world that he wanted, he always seemed to provoke an unholy argument. Trying for the light touch didn't seem to be the answer either, judging from the rigid set of her features.

Nicole, oblivious to Christopher's intent stare, knew she should make some offhand remark, some laughing rejoinder, but the words stuck in her throat. Eventually pride came to her rescue, and with a fixed, bright smile she said, "Well, I suppose confusing you, as you say I have, must be some sort of victory for me!"

"Damnit, Nicole! There is no war between us!" Christopher growled, wanting something more than just a glib statement from her, yet uncertain precisely what it was he sought.

But Nicole, lost in her own bitter battle with her heart, did not hear the odd note of entreaty in Christopher's voice. All she registered was the barely hidden anger on his face. With piercing resignation, she knew why there could never be anything but anger and ugly recriminations between them—because of her mother. Nausea curled in her stomach when she thought of Christopher's brutal betrayal at her mother's hands. Could she blame him for hating her? For hurting her?

Resignedly she said, "Oh, Christopher! Have done with this pretense between us! I know what happened to you all those years ago and I know why you hate me so. You say there is no war between us, but you lie." Some of her spirit came rushing back, and passionately she continued, "There will always be a war between us! My mother saw to that! I could try for a thousand years to make you forget it, I could let you trample me in the dust, but it would never soothe all the hate you've filled yourself with."

Christopher went still, very still; the heavy black brows contracted into a frown above his narrowed eyes. "Exactly what are you talking about?" he asked coldly.

Nicole leaped to her feet; with her fists clenched tightly at her sides, she stated baldly, "Higgins told me about you and my mother! About how Robert and she tricked you and about how he sold you to the press-gang."

Christopher, more icily furious than she had ever seen him, swore long and with astonishing fluency. The gold eyes glittered dangerously, the fine mouth was thin with fury as he snarled, "And is that why you are being so understanding? So willing to have me kiss you? Because that old sad tale has aroused your sympathy? Well, spare me *that!*"

He stood up abruptly, and throwing Nicole a glance of utter dislike, he muttered fiercely, "You forget about what happened in the past! I have! And certainly I don't need Annabelle's daughter mewling over me like I'm some half-drowned kitten!"

"Mewling!" Nicole spat. Any regret, any sorrow for her mother's actions, even her own anguish over his departure vanished as her temper rose. Her face white, the great dark eyes sparkling, she stepped swiftly forward and before Christopher could guess her intent slapped him open-handed across one cheek. "Why you ass-eared whelp!" she cried furiously, tears of anger glittering in her eyes.

Furious himself, Christopher caught her shoulders, holding her prisoner in a deliberately brutal grip as she fought to free herself. "This, I believe," he said tightly, "is where I came in. And since we seem to have said everything that need be, I'll bid you good-bye. If we're lucky, we won't have to see each other before I leave. Rest assured I'll damn well take care to stay out of your way!"

Dimly aware that she was hiding behind her anger, Nicole, her temper now in full blaze, sent Christopher a look of mingled despair and defiance. "You do that!" she choked belligerently. "By God, I'll bless the day you sail away. It can't be too soon to suit me!"

With a queer flicker in his eyes he studied her stormy features for a moment, almost, she thought oddly, as if memorizing them; then his lips twisted into a mocking grin, and he said coolly, "Now that's the Nick I remember. And here's something else for you to remember me by!"

Jerking her into his arms and catching her half-opened lips possessively, his tongue ravening her mouth, he pinioned her body against his. His lips seemed to sear hers like a flame, commanding, demanding that she respond to this deliberate cold-blooded arousal. Blindly, Nicole fought desperately against the insidious languor, the blaze of urgent desire that spread through her body. His mouth allowed no escape; his lips compelled her to yield, to give in to the physical craving that washed through her veins. Unconsciously she molded herself closer to him. Damn him! she thought furiously with one part of her mind. Damn him, for making me want him. *Damn him!*

Christopher was fighting his own battle; rigid with barely leashed desire, he wanted Nicole unbearably for one last time—just once more to lose himself in that flesh, to feel her shudder beneath him, to have the taste of that silken skin in his mouth, that perfume peculiarly hers in his nostrils. Ah, Jesus, he wondered with dull rage, why her of all women? Hadn't he learned once that an Ashford woman was a beautiful witch of uncanny power, a creature of lust and lies, of passion and betrayal? Frantic himself now to break the tenuous silken web around him, Christopher tore his mouth from Nicole's and with a jerky movement set her away from him. He was breathing heavily, his eyes still blurred with desire, but his voice was detached as he said, "I think we'll each have something to remember of the other, Nick—whether we want to or not!" He spun on his heel but then, as if recalling something, stopped and glanced over his shoulder. "I haven't as yet made definite plans for leaving and I haven't said anything to my grandfather. I would appreciate it if you would say nothing to anyone, until I have told him myself."

Nicole couldn't bear to look at him, afraid of her own emotions. She nodded dumbly, concentrating on fighting back the foolish tears that shimmered in her eyes.

Unable to help himself, Christopher gave her one long last look, sealing the achingly beautiful picture she made away in some buried part of his heart. Almost hungrily he stared at her, taking in the flawless features, the mass of dark flaming curls, the wide-spaced topaz eyes, the willful, passionately full mouth, and that tall, slender body that fitted his so exquisitely. Oh, God, he thought with a tearing pain in his gut, why does it have to end like this? He took one more look, and without another word he stalked to the door and left the room.

With the sound of the slammed door ringing in her ears, Nicole sank down slowly on the sofa. He's gone, she thought dully. No, that's not true, she argued feverishly, it'll be a few days yet. A few days in which I'll have to act normal, smile and laugh and pretend that I'm not dying inside. She closed her eyes tightly in anguish, thinking of the bitter facade to come. I'll do it. I can! And someday I'll forget him. I will! I have to.

Driven by different emotions than those that beset Nicole, Robert Saxon had been making inquiries all over London in search of the elusive Captain Saber. He had learned that indeed there was a Captain Saber, and yes, he was an American privateer, and yes, there was a price on his head. But beyond Jennings-Smythe's startled remark, Robert had nothing to go on. He had no doubt that Christopher was Captain Saber, and he longed to throw that information in Simon's face. He would see that everyone did know the truth, see that all of them learned what a scoundrel Christopher really was!

Robert called in the afternoon to speak to Nicole, hoping he could coax her into taking a short ride in the country. That it was nearing five o'clock when he arrived at the house on Kings Road, bothered Robert not at all. Darkness did not fall until almost seven and he would have Nicole home long before that.

But he was disappointed. Nicole, he was informed, had gone walking in the park and wouldn't return home for a half hour. Undeterred, Robert was on the point of leaving to seek out Nicole as she took her walk, determined to convince her to accompany him, when Simon spoke to him.

"Robert, I'd like a word with you if you don't mind!" Simon demanded.

Annoyed, Robert glanced at him. "Does it have to be this very moment? I was just leaving to find Nicole."

"She can wait," Simon retorted testily. "I have something to say to you, and I want to say it now!"

Robert shrugged and followed his father into the study. The small study was a pleasant room, paneled in oak. A Boulle cabinet in ebony inlaid with a tortoise-shell pattern gave an Oriental effect to the room, but the curled maple desk that Simon seated himself behind was definitely English in design. Robert, clearly impatient to be off, stood aggressively in the center of the room, his York tan gloves and small chimney-pot hat held carelessly in one hand.

"Well," he interrogated irritably, "what is it? I haven't much time."

"Sit down," Simon said quietly, his eyes cool and contemptuous as he pointed to a nearby chair. Somewhat reluctantly Robert did so, alerted by his father's odd manner that all was not well.

Simon had spent the two days since Letitia had told him what had passed between his son and grandson in great mental agony. He had loved his black-sheep son, despite many disappointments throughout the years, but the infamous act against Christopher he could not forgive. When the first horror and repugnance had died away, he had thought he could bury it—that while his affection for Robert would never be the same, he could, in a fashion, continue to view him with some fondness. But after two sleepless nights, tortured by what his own flesh and blood had done, he knew it was not true. Whatever love he had borne his son had died, and he felt it only fair and right to tell Robert precisely why he would no longer be welcome in his home. It was the hardest decision of his life. But he had finally in his heart acknowledged that Robert was a bad one, rotten throughout, and that he could never change that. Nor could he ignore it and thereby condone his son's despicable actions. It had been a bitter, painful admission and now that the moment was upon him, he found he was curiously unmoved by it. He had dreaded this time, had feared he would not be able to do it. But it was not so.

His face was cold and stony as he said unemotionally, "This will be the last time I shall have you in my home —any of my homes. I have put up with a great deal from you throughout the years—I have suffered scandal after scandal with you: I have paid off debts, intervened for you on countless occasions. But that is finished. You went too far, Robert, with what you did to Christopher. I cannot, may the Lord God forgive me, pardon you for it. It was bad enough that you and Annabelle Ashford used him to hide your adulterous liaison, but to sell him! To sell him into what was almost certain death! *That* I cannot tolerate!" Simon's formidable control broke, and almost pleadingly, he asked, "Why, Robert? Why in God's name? He was so fine a youth, such a joy to me. He did you no harm. I tell you, I will never understand how you could have done it." Simon paused, his face suddenly heavily lined and very sad. "You could have been the cause of his death. Doesn't that engender some feeling of remorse?"

Robert had blanched at his father's first words, his worst fears at last realized. Christopher had turned his own father against him! An intense surge of bitterness swept through him, and sullenly he retorted, "It didn't hurt him. You can see for yourself that he profited by what happened."

Disbelievingly Simon stared at him. With a shudder of revulsion, he realized that Robert saw no wrong in what he had done. A sense of futility crept along his veins, and tiredly he admitted, "Yes, it appears he did profit by it. But that wasn't what you had in mind, was it?" Knowing the answer, weary of the scene, Simon said harshly, "Good-bye, Robert. Thank God that despite what he has been through, Christopher has grown into such a fine young man. At least I have a grandson I can be proud of, if not a son."

His sense of ill-usage breaking its frail bonds, Robert leaped to his feet. With a wild look in his eyes, he shouted, "You're wrong! You think he is so wonderful. Ha! He is nothing but a common pirate. A sea rogue wanted by the Admiralty for his crimes against our own ships. Ask your precious Christopher about Captain Saber! Ask him! You'll see. You'll see that he is not the godlike being you think. He's a bloody pirate!"

"Silence!" Simon thundered, his face dark with rage. "You're lying, casting aspersions on him, to exonerate yourself. I will not have it! Leave my house this instant! This instant, I say, or I shall wrench your lying tongue from your throat!"

Beyond rational action, Robert placed both hands on the desk and, thrusting his face near Simon's, ranted, "It's not fair! He is the one you should treat so. He is a pirate! Lieutenant Jennings-Smythe recognized him." Frantically fabricating his story as he went on, Robert continued passionately, "It's true! He told me! If you don't believe it, ask him! You'll see!"

For a long minute Simon stared at him. Robert was so earnest that it gave him pause. With startling insight he acknowledged that Robert's accusations didn't really disturb him. Christopher could very well be a pirate—it made little difference to Simon. Hadn't Sir Francis Drake been labeled such? Yet he felt as one last concession to his son, he should face Christopher. Quietly he said, "Very well, I will. But whether he is or not, does not change the situation between us. Once I have spoken to him, you will leave this house and spare me the distasteful pleasure of ever seeing you again." Rising from his seat, Simon strode swiftly from the study, intent upon finishing this painful affair as soon as possible.

Spitefully elated, a satisfied smile curving his thin lips, Robert sank back into the chair. Now let Christopher wiggle out of this one, he thought malevolently. I may be shunned and banned, but Christopher will also share the same fate!

Simon, refusing to have one of the servants find Christopher for him, shortly ran him down in his room. When Simon burst into his room Christopher was comfortably perched on the corner of a mahogany table, watching Higgins put a shine on a pair of Hessians.

At Simon's forceful entry Christopher straightened instantly, a wary look crossing his face.

Simon glared at Higgins and said with his usual sharpness, "You leave! I want a word with my grandson."

Higgins glanced at Christopher and at Christopher's slight nod bowed and left the room.

Idly, Christopher asked, "Was it necessary to speak so rudely to him? I value Higgins rather highly, you know."

"Bah! Don't fob me off with such trivial conversation. What I have to say is extremely private and personal, and I don't want anyone else to overhear us. If you wish, I'll apologize to him later."

An eyebrow cocked sardonically, Christopher echoed, "Apologize to him? Now that I must see! You have never apologized to anyone."

"Damnit, quit trying to turn me away! Robert is down below in the study, and he had made a most damaging statement against you." Eyeing Christopher from beneath scowling heavy brows, Simon said bluntly, "He says you are a pirate! A Captain Saber and that there is a price on your head. Is it true?"

Their eyes met, gold clashing against gold. "Well, are you really this—this Captain Saber?"

His gaze never wavered as Christopher nodded curtly, "Yes, I am." He stated the words flatly, offering no explanations, no excuses. What was he to do? Express hypocritical regret? Cry out it was not his fault, but circumstances? Not bloody likely, he thought fiercely.

The admission, despite his earlier emotion of indifference, was a shattering blow to Simon. He hadn't really believed it—hadn't wanted to believe it. The gold eyes dimmed just a little, and slowly, like a worn-out old man, he sank down into a nearby chair. Heavily he said, "I feared it was so."

Knowing that some explanation would have to be offered, if not the entire turth, Christopher had dreaded this moment. He had hoped he could leave England without Simon's ever learning of Captain Saber. Certainly he had never meant to tell him, had hoped with savage intensity that he would never be hurt by this knowledge. No matter how many times he had rehearsed this scene in his mind, the reality of Simon's weary, almost broken manner was far worse than anything he could have imagined. His teeth clenched, a muscle jerked in the taut jaw; he stared at his grandfather, groping for words that would lessen the blow.

Unable to bear the sight of him so apparently devastated, without the usual thunder and fire spilling from him, Christopher muttered thickly, "Grandfather, I would have spared you this, if I could have. I cannot change what I am or what I have been." Dropping to one knee, his strong brown hand tenderly covering the blue-veined one that still clutched the ever-present ebony cane, Christopher said harshly, "I cannot even ask forgiveness for what I have done. But I did not do it to hurt you or to bring shame on you." With a note of pleading in the deep voice, he went on, "Each of us must live as he sees fit. I do not expect you to approve of what I have done, but for God's sake don't condemn me for being myself, for being what I am—a privateer, an American first by circumstance and then by choice."

Simon's head snapped up at the words, the faded gold eyes boring into the deeper, brighter golden ones fixed so earnestly and purposefully on his.

"An American?" he barked testily.

Christopher nodded tersely. Steadily, his gaze unwaveringly on Simon's face, he declared vehemently, "New Orleans is my home now! My land, my fortune, my future all lie in the United States. And yes, I have been a privateer, the Captain Saber that Robert claims. Yes, I have attacked British ships, I have even," he added deliberately, "sunk them. But whatever I have done, I did not do it to cause you pain or distress." Bleakly he finished, "There was a time I never thought to see you again, when I hated anything, everything British. I've lived my life by my own rules, and I can't claim that I'm sorry for it."

"Admirable," Simon remarked dryly.

Christopher stiffened and stood up. Curtly he said, "I did not mean to bore you."

"Ha! Never said I was bored, did I?" Simon snapped irascibly. "Now you listen to me, coxcomb! American you may be, privateer you may have been, but you're my grandson before all else and my heir, too, for that matter!"

Assessingly, Christopher eyed him, partially encouraged by the irate note in his voice, but still uncertain as to how deeply the confession had cut into him. Simon

411

appeared to be recovering somewhat, even though what he had just learned must have been a terrible wound. Simon did not, however, give him the chance to say more. Sitting bolt upright on the chair, his cane held firmly in one hand, he scowled ferociously at his watchful grandson. "Now then," Simon began aggressively, "I have a few things to say to you sapscull! First, you're my grandson and don't you ever forget it! Second, I don't give a damn what you've done—" He stopped abruptly, remembering Robert and what he had said to him. Pursing his lips in concentration, he said slowly, "Provided you've not deliberately harmed innocent people—and I don't mean those that might have come to grief in the course of your privateering. That is war and that I understand. Unless you have fought unfairly or been cowardly in your attacks." He hesitated, shooting Christopher a gloomy glance. "I am not saying I wouldn't rather you were not this Captain Saber or I don't wish that your first loyalty lay with England. But since it don't I am not one to repine over what I can't change. Point is, you are, as you said, what you are, and I'd be all kinds of a silly fool if I denied you because we disagree politically."

Christopher grinned at him ruefully. "Do you think Robert is going to take that enlightened view?"

Simon snorted. "You leave him to me. That Canterbury tale of his is going no further. I'll see to that!"

"I don't think it will be that easy, sir. There is," he paused, then said carefully, "a certain enmity between us, and I don't believe he will simply shut up because you order him to." Christopher hesitated, uncertain of his next move. He had not planned his denouement, but with the thought of time slipping by and the knowledge that in a matter of hours he would be meeting the American privateer, it seemed his only opportunity to tell Simon of his impending departure. But he could not baldly divulge his plans—Simon would guess instantly that this trip to England had been more than just a personal visit, and it would cause him even more pain. Captain Saber he might be able to forgive, but a spy? Christopher thought not. Inspiration saved Christopher as he realized he could use Robert as his excuse for departure.

"I think," he said slowly, "it would be best if I left for America. Tonight. Before Robert has any chance to cause trouble. Once this war is over"—he threw Simon a mocking smile—"this war you pay little heed to, my privateering activities will cease to be a danger. Then I

412

can return. Until then, I'm afraid, sir, I can't risk staying."

At Simon's balky look, Christopher said candidly, "Jennings-Smythe knows who I am. He recognized me and can point me out as Captain Saber."

His jaw thrust out stubbornly, not quite convinced, Simon asked, "How will you leave? There are no ships sailing for America."

"I can leave tonight for France. From there I can catch a ship sailing for the West Indies. Or Cuba. Whatever it doesn't matter; eventually I'll manage to reach an American privateer sailing in those waters or a ship that is going to run the blockade of the Gulf. Don't worry, I'll get back to New Orleans. It'll just take time." Coolly and deliberately he stifled any remorse at these lies— better his grandfather believed this than know of that American privateer.

Simon didn't like it, but he saw the danger clearly. Still, not wanting to see him go, he argued, "Why must it be tonight? Why not tomorrow or the next day?" He knew the answers as soon as he spoke the words. Any delay, now that Robert was speaking openly of Captain Saber, could be fatal. An icy fear clutched his heart at the thought of Christopher in chains and on the gallows, and Simon said almost inaudibly, "You're right. You must go tonight."

The soft words tore at Christopher, knowing as he did how much the older man must be dreading this parting —didn't he dread it as much?

"Grandfather," he coaxed persuasively, "it will not be like the last time. This time you know where I am headed and you know that I will be back. Soon. I promise."

Without haste Simon stood up. He could not say the words of farewell, not yet. They would have another moment alone before this evening ended and Christopher left. Then perhaps he could bid the boy adieu without this silly moisture in his eyes.

Without meeting Christopher's eyes, he muttered gruffly, "After dinner tonight, I'll want another word with you in my study. After that you may slip away. In the meantime I'll talk to Robert. Tell him I couldn't find you and that his story is a Covent Garden farce. Tell him he'll have to say it to your face in front of me before I'll believe it's not just a spiteful tale. That should keep him quiet until tomorrow sometime. By that time you

413

should have reached Dover. I warn you, though, to waste no time. I will try to keep Robert at bay as long as I can, but the very most I can fob him off will be a day or two."

Christopher nodded. "And the ladies? What will you tell them?"

Simon let out his breath in a rush. "Simply that you have been called away to France on urgent business and they are not to talk of it. Anyone else that asks after you will get the same answer. Sooner or later they'll stop asking." Then regarding his boots, he muttered fiercely, "You just get yourself back here safe as soon as you can."

Christopher stared at his grandfather, not bothering to hide what he felt. With that charming warm smile so few people ever saw on his lips and the usually hard gold eyes soft with unhidden love, he said haltingly, "I'm sorry it has to be like this. And I'm sorry you'll have to make excuses for me. Next time, I promise you, there will be no need for such a hasty departure."

"By God, there had better not be!" Simon barked irascibly. His eyes bright with suppressed emotion, he stumped from the room growling, "I don't know why I waste my time with you! Here's Robert waiting in my study for me, and now thanks to you I have to go turn him up sweet to keep his mouth shut. And just when I was warming up to a grand disinheritance scene too!"

For a long time, a very long time, Christopher regarded the doorway through which Simon had disappeared. There was a sadness within him, a dull ache in his heart. Roughly he pulled himself back to the task at hand and rang impatiently for Higgins to rejoin him. Jesus, he decided derisively, he was getting like a maudlin milkmaid, and deliberately he switched his thoughts, wondering idly how Robert was taking Simon's orders.

Unfortunately when Simon reached his study, it was empty. A sharp inquiry of Twickham elicited the puzzling information that Master Robert had departed with Nicole's maid Galena.

"With one of the maids?" Simon repeated. "What is he doing with one of the maids?"

"I really couldn't say, sir," Twickham replied politely. Catching the fire in Simon's eye, he added quickly, "I did hear Miss Nicole's name mentioned though, and Edward Markham's. It was something to do with Brighton Park. Perhaps Miss Nicole sent Galena with a message for one of the coachmen to fetch her and Mister

Markham from the park and Master Robert decided to go instead."

"Perhaps," Simon agreed noncommittally. It seemed unlikely, yet Robert *had* spoken of seeing Nicole. Perhaps they had gone for a ride. At this hour? With Edward Markham? Now that sounded odd. Very odd.

34

It *was* odd. Edward Markham was with Nicole, but not at her invitation, or even pleasure. He had indeed put into effect his plan to abduct her—and luck seemed to be on his side.

The hiring of the carriage had been done with a minimum of effort. Even the weather smiled on him, the afternoon being a lovely fall symphony of crisp biting air and gold and scarlet leaves. Nicole did come to the park escorted only by Galena and exultantly Edward had watched them disappear down one of the many pleasant walks in the park. From his vantage point just outside the park he waited impatiently for Nicole to complete her walk, refusing to think of the dismal possibility that she might join friends in the park.

Nicole took a longer stroll than usual, her thoughts on Christopher and the scene in the library. The brisk walk cleared her head somewhat and released a portion of her pent-up frustration and unhappiness.

She was glad, she told herself fiercely, that Christopher was leaving. It was best. With him gone, with no possibility of seeing him, knowing he was on the other side of the world, and more than likely with a number of new female conquests, she would at last be free of this silly, lingering emotion she had for him.

It was Galena who finally curtailed the walk. Galena did not like walking and thought her mistress mad to walk when she could ride, and after suffering in silence for quite some time, she finally said to Nicole, "Miss Nicole, don't you think we should start home now? It's almost five o'clock and you did not make arrangements for anyone to meet us with a carriage."

"I suppose you're right, Galena. Very well, home we will go."

Shortly thereafter they reached the main gate to Brighton Park and started the long walk to the house on Kings Road. They had not walked but a few steps when

Nicole was genuinely thrown off balance by Edward's distracted and distressed air as he almost literally ran up to her.

"My dear!" he cried affectingly. "I have such dreadful news! I do not know how to tell you! But they felt it best if you heard it from one of your own family."

Nicole blanched, her first thought being of Christopher. The topaz eyes nearly black with apprehension, she clutched Edward's arm in a painful grip. "What is it? Tell me, damn you! What is it?"

"Lord Saxon!" Edward said dramatically. "He is dead! Not but a short while ago he suffered a fatal stroke. Come, they need you! Hurry!"

In something like shock Nicole numbly let Edward hustle her across the busy street into the waiting coach. Such was her very real sorrow and anguish that she paid no heed to the fact that Galena had been left standing dazedly in front of the park, nor spared a thought as to why the inhabitants at Kings Road had thought him the best person to break the news to her.

Nearly paralyzed by the staggering news, Nicole, as Edward had counted on, paid very little attention as to where they were going. Blindly she stared out the coach window; at first she did not realize that they were traveling swiftly in the wrong direction.

Edward watched her covertly from his seat on the other side of the carriage. Now, dear cuz, you won't fob me off! he thought maliciously. In two days' time or less we will be married—sooner than that you will no longer be the innocent virgin you are now. I'll see to that! He smiled a very nasty smile as he contemplated the pleasures that would soon be his. Time enough to break her to his will, he thought with satisfaction, and a spiteful expression crossed his face.

Nicole saw that expression and it woke her instantly to several things—Galena was not with her; they should have reached Kings Road some minutes ago; and finally sitting up and taking a quick reconnaissance of the passing scenery, she realized in a flash that they were not even traveling in the right direction. They were heading north!

Slowly she sank back against the seat, her face smooth and bland; stemming the furious flood of anger that was boiling in her veins, her brain was functioning at an almost-frenzied pace. Edward had obviously duped her and bitterly she cursed her own stupidity. She should have suspected him to try such a trick sooner or later—

it was so like him, she thought contemptuously. He must plan on a Gretna Green marriage . . . unless he had murder on his mind. She could not totally discount that possibility, and Nicole regarded him with consideration. No, she decided finally, not murder—he was too cowardly for that! But even cowards will murder if driven too far, she reminded herself uncomfortably, and Edward must be desperate indeed to have undertaken such a rash scheme.

Suddenly she frowned. Not so rash if Lord Saxon had truly suffered a fatal stroke. It would be hours before anyone would even have a moment to spare for her, to wonder at her continued absence. Had Edward cleverly seized upon a tragic event to serve his own needs? It was a frightful thought, and all the fear and sorrow she had felt when he had first given her the news of Lord Saxon's death came rushing back.

"Edward," she said at last, "I know we are not going to Lord Saxon's. I gather we are eloping to Gretna Green. But tell me the truth, is Lord Saxon truly dead or did you merely say that to get me into this coach?"

Edward had expected all sorts of recriminations from his cousin. He certainly hadn't planned on her calm demeanor, nor on any real concern about Lord Saxon. And because it caught him unprepared, he told the truth. "To my knowledge Lord Saxon enjoys his usual robust health."

At Nicole's look of scorn he added defensively, "Well, I had to tell you something that would shake you, throw you off stride. What else was I to do?"

"You spineless jellyfish!" she spat contemptuously. "What else could you do? I'll tell you what else you could do—you could order this carriage stopped immediately, and I will pretend this distasteful episode never transpired. You may have me in your power at the moment, but I'll tell you this, cuz," she drawled the word cuttingly, "nothing will make me marry you! You are going to look rather silly when I refuse to repeat the wedding vows."

With an ugly expression in the blue eyes Edward snarled, "I wouldn't talk quite so bravely if I were you! By the time we reach Gretna Green, you will be more than happy to marry me . . . especially since by that that time you may well be carrying my child! Certainly I shall have done my part to insure that it is so. I am taking no chances, cuz, of being thwarted, so don't look for help from the Saxons! Unless they overtake us within the next few hours, which isn't likely, they will be of no use to you. Not even Lord Saxon would stand behind you once he realized that you were a maid no longer and that there was the possibility of a child."

Bitterly Nicole choked down the furious words that clogged her throat, not wishing to infuriate him into action—not yet. Edward was a fool if he thought he could get away with this madness. She would never marry him! Never! And he would not find raping her easy. But even if he succeeded, even if she were to become pregnant, she would never marry him. She would face the scandal, the gossip, the disgrace, and somehow she would rid herself of the unborn child.

"Nothing to say, my dear?" Edward jeered, his words breaking into her thoughts.

Nicole shrugged, not willing to open hostilities until she had decided precisely what she meant to do. Almost indifferently she said, "What is there to say? You have obviously thought of everything."

"So I have," Edward agreed complacently. "So I have. And you are very wise to see the folly in being obstructive. The whole affair will be much less of an ordeal to you if you cooperate." With an egotistical smirk on his lips he added boastingly, "I am said to be quite, quite competent in the art of lovemaking, and I am sure you will more greatly appreciate my skill if you do not fight me. There are, you know, several women who would gladly trade places with you."

"Oh, really?" Nicole returned noncommittally, and surreptitiously she glanced around the carriage, searching for some object that could be used as a weapon. By pitting her own strength against Edward's, she might gain some minutes' respite, and there was the outside chance that she could prove the victor in a test of wills between them, but she wouldn't disdain something that would put the odds more in her favor.

At first there appeared to be nothing she could use. The carriage was empty except for them; whatever baggage Edward had packed was strapped outside to the roof. Her reticule lay on the seat beside her, but she quickly discounted it—there was nothing in it that could help her. Biting her lips, she took one last desperate glance around the carriage and then she saw it! Edward's malacca cane! The sword cane! Hungrily her eyes caressed the slim deadly object lying so innocently on the seat beside him.

Nicole had never felt so alone and helpless in her entire life, and as the miles passed and the fading late afternoon sunlight gave way to the silvery glow of the moon, she grew more frustrated and angry. She was not frightened, nor did she fear Edward, but with every passing hour she realized that time was running out for her—that soon her cousin would make good his threat and force his unwanted attentions upon her. She shuddered as she imagined the feel of his hands roaming freely over her body and his mouth ravishing hers.

As if guessing her thoughts, Edward smiled at her in the dim gloom of the carriage. "Nervous, my dear?" he asked blandly. "Don't worry, you have a few more minutes before my baser instincts take over."

Her mouth dry, Nicole inquired levelly, "What are you waiting for? More moonlight in which to view your performance?"

"Now that is a possibility! But no, you are wrong. There is a particularly narrow and curving stretch of road coming up, and I would not like to be swung about this way and that at a most crucial moment. You'll appreciate my consideration when you see what I mean."

Weary of hiding her contempt and anger, of pretending a resignation she didn't feel, Nicole snorted derisively, "I doubt you have ever considered anyone in your entire selfish life!" Almost conversationally she went on, "You know, Edward, you are endangering that life by what you are doing. Do you think that a marriage will stop one of the Saxons from calling you out?" She gave a gay little laugh at Edward's sudden look of uncertainty. It was obviously a point he had not considered. There was a mocking cat-yellow gleam in her topaz eyes as she continued slowly, savoringly, "Let's see. First there is Lord Saxon himself—still quite handy with a pistol from all accounts. And then there is Robert. Robert should be quite good with the swords, don't you think? And as for Christopher, well, I have heard it said that he is very good with both!" Her voice unexpectedly harsh with loathing, she spat, "Do you really think they will let you get away with it? Especially if they overtake us?"

Edward laughed nervously. "Oh, don't be ridiculous! None of them are foolish enough or care enough about you to challenge me to a duel. And no one is going to overtake us!"

At that moment, as if to disprove his words, the coach gave a sudden vicious sway, hurtling Edward against the door and sending Nicole clutching for one of the leather handholds. They had no chance to recover before there was another sharp lurch that sent Edward cursing and sliding across the floor of the coach, while Nicole, clinging tightly to the handhold, was barely able to keep from tumbling into the aisle. Seeing that her cousin was taken up with regaining his balance, she wasted not a moment, but swiftly bent down and snatched up the cane that had bounced onto the floor near her feet. In a trice it was concealed in the folds of her pelisse.

The coach, after an ominous grinding of the wheels and one bone-shaking bump, came to an abrupt halt at an uneasy awkward angle. Outside Nicole could hear the coachman shouting to the postilion in an agitated voice, and Edward, finally righting himself, flung open the door. The coach was at an odd slant, forcing him to climb up to climb out. Safe at last on the ground outside, he demanded in a furious tone, "What the hell is going on!"

There was an exchange of voices, all of which Nicole listened intently. Apparently there had been an unexpectedly deep rut in the road, and swerving to miss it, the coach had inadvertently swung off into the roadside ditch. One of the back wheels was off the road, firmly embedded in the loose dirt.

Nicole smiled to herself in the empty coach. She had no idea if any of the Saxons were even in pursuit, but any delay was to her advantage. She rather thought that help would be on the way though, for Galena was bound to return to Kings Road, expecting her to be there with Edward—and Lord Saxon dead! When it was discovered that Lord Saxon was still very much alive, the alarm would be sounded and someone—her heart leaped crazily in her breast, when she thought of Christopher's dark, angry face—someone was certain to realize what had happened. They were on the main road heading north, the most direct route to Scotland, and it was the first avenue any rescue would take.

As the minutes passed and the men worked to free the trapped coach, her spirits rose. Edward, from the sounds of it, was not endearing himself to the coachmen as he shouted and cursed their unsuccessful attempts to get the coach back onto the road. Glancing about the moonlit countryside, she wished fervently her door were not jammed. Perhaps, she thought, hopeful, they would have to remain here all night. Now wouldn't that be a fitting outcome to Edward's dastardly plot! But her hopes were dashed, for the next moment the coach lurched violently; the wheel spun madly for a second, then sprang free of the dirt. Rocking wildly, the heavy vehicle reeled triumphantly onto the road.

Nicole's heart sank as the coach righted itself, but comfortingly she fingered the concealed sword cane. Edward, she decided, with a tight little smile curving the generous mouth, was in for a nasty surprise.

The object of her thoughts clambered aboard the coach a moment later and said in a disagreeable tone of voice, "Those incompetent fools! You would think for the money I'm paying them, they'd know how to drive."

Nicole made no comment; her heart beat rapidly in her breast. She would act now, now while he was still slightly agitated by the unexpected accident and before they traveled a great deal farther. Her eyes bright with determination, she waited only until Edward had seated himself. Before he had time to realize what had happened, she struck swiftly, the sword held unerringly in her hand, and he found himself staring down two feet of naked blade. Instinctively he shrank back against the seat, and Nicole commanded with deceptive softness, "Stay, Edward. Do not startle me or I may accidentally skewer you."

Edward froze, his eyes riveted on the blade barely inches from his face. Nicole had wisely chosen his face as her target, knowing Edward would do just about anything to protect his beautiful features from being mutilated.

Scornfully Nicole regarded him as he vainly attempted to melt into the cushions of the leather seat, thinking unaccountably of Christopher's insolent actions when she had held a pistol to his head in Allen's cell that night on Grand Terre.

Not bothering to hide the contempt she felt, Nicole ordered, "Call your coachman and have him turn the carriage around. We are going back to Brighton."

Seeing all his hopes for a rosy future disappearing, Edward was so moved he forgot about his face, and furiously he jerked up, only to be halted instantly when the blade nicked him very delicately on the cheekbone. "Damn you, Nicole!" he swore viciously, frantically dabbing at the minor scratch with a fine white linen handkerchief. "Damn you if you have scarred me!"

Her eyes narrowed, the lips were a grim line, and she replied evenly, "And damn you, my dear cuz, for what you tried to do to me! Now order this coach turned around or next time I shall mark you permanently. Do it! *Now!*"

Reluctantly Edward complied, pounding against the wall for the coachman to stop. The coach halted, and a moment later, Edward's eyes burning with hate, he angrily spat out the command to return to Brighton.

The driver and postilion exchanged resigned glances —gentry! Mad as hatters and never knew what they wanted. But as the coachmen had already been paid for the long journey to Gretna Green, gold that would *not* be returned, they were willing without further argument to drive the much shorter distance back to Brighton.

The coach was wheeled about, and Nicole permitted herself a brief sigh of relief as the horses picked up speed heading toward Brighton—and home. She did not allow her guard to drop, realizing Edward was more dangerous now than at any other time. If he were somehow to gain the upper hand—God help her! Instinctively her grip on the sword cane tightened. She would kill him before she would let herself fall into his power again.

They rode in silence—Edward sullen against the seat, and Nicole's eyes unwavering on him—the sword a deadly barrier between them.

She had no idea of the time, nor how long or how far they had traveled; but it was long after dark, the silver moon was high in the black sky. Help, she felt certain, must be on the way. Galena would have returned long ago and the alarm sounded. Even now Christopher or Robert would be in pursuit of them. At least she prayed it was so. Edward was intimidated for the moment, but Nicole knew her cousin well. While she was confident of her own abilities, especially with the added force of the sword cane, she would be relieved to have the protection of the Saxons once more. How dependent upon them I have grown, she thought with a wry smile.

As the miles passed, the rocking motion of the coach had a soothing effect upon her, and Nicole relaxed slightly, only to stiffen and to watch Edward narrowly as he moved restlessly across from her, the sword following every movement.

Irritably he said, "Oh, put that damn thing down! I'm not about to try anything as long as you hold a sword. I'm not a fool, you know!"

Nicole smiled without amusement. "Oh, but you are! No one but a fool would have attempted such a stupid way out of his difficulties. Did you truly think me so much of a ninnyhammer that I would go along with you? I could see you trying this trick on some young foolish maid already half in love with you. But me, Edward, of all people! How could you be so ridiculous?"

Edward shot her a look of pure hatred. "Because," he said furiously, "you cheated me out of a fortune! It was *mine*, all mine, and then you had to come back. I needed it—you didn't! Why you could marry any number of rich men, men richer than you are, and you would have no use for it."

Her voice was hard as Nicole replied, "I think it is up to me to decide whether I need my fortune or not. Certainly not you! Your family has grown rich enough off of me during the past years, and I think you are more than just a little greedy to want it all. Remember, except by marriage, we are in no way even related. I may call you cousin, but it is a courtesy title only, and to want the entire fortune that my family has amassed over many years is, I fear, the height of avarice. I did not 'cheat' you out of a fortune, I merely returned to claim what was rightfully mine . . . and you would do well to remember it!"

There was nothing that Edward could say to her cutting words, and resentfully he gazed out the window of the coach, damning the unkind fate that had so misled him. It wasn't fair that he should come this far and then be thwarted by a mere female, he thought indignantly. If only he could snatch that damned weapon from her —then everything would be right again. Only this time he wouldn't wait to defile her, nor would he treat her with politeness. This time she'd learn that it wasn't wise to interfere with his plans.

Some of his confidence returned, and Edward shook off his earlier cowardice and covertly assessed Nicole. She was only a woman.

Nicole, ever wary, like a hunted vixen, knew the moment Edward's attitude changed. She sensed it in the air the way an animal does, and her body tensed. Unafraid, she faced him, her beautiful features betraying no sign that she suspected him of action, and as Edward shifted position, she said levelly, "Edward, I wouldn't try anything if I were you. I am not some missish female who faints at the sight of blood—I have seen blood before and seen men die before. I can and will kill you if I am compelled to . . . the choice is yours. But know that you are not dealing with some hysterical female—force me and I will skewer you without regard."

Edward swallowed painfully, slightly taken aback at

the determined tone of her voice. It gave him pause, but his situation was too desperate now to heed her warnings. If Nicole escaped him, not only would he still be in debt, a debt he could not pay, but the scandal this abortive escapade would create would completely and utterly ruin him—he might even face criminal charges if the Saxons wished to face the furor such an action would engender. This was no prank that could be explained away, nor could he buy his way free—once in Brighton he would have to face the consequences of his actions, something he had never done in his entire selfish life . . . something he had no intention of doing now. He would teach this stupid bitch a lesson—*his* moment would come before they reached Brighton. And he'd be ready for it, she would see. Just wait, dear cuz, he thought malevolently, just wait, you'll not outtrick me!

Edward's moment came not five minutes later, although it wasn't what he expected. The wheel that had skidded off the road earlier had been damaged in the mishap. The momentum of the carriage and a particularly sharp curve were its undoing, as the damaged wheel's hub could not bear the combined onslaught and with a grinding shudder simply disintegrated, the spokes snapping like brittle straws. Without the spokes for support the rim of the wheel crumpled like old parchment; the now unbraced rear axle tore up a deep furrow before the cursing driver brought the horses to a stop.

Outside there was chaos—the horses plunging and fighting against the reins, the front pair of animals entangled in their traces, and the coach, tilted at a drunken angle, right in the center of the narrow road. Inside Nicole and Edward were locked in a deadly battle for the sword cane; neither knew what had been the cause of the sudden unexpected violent lurch and the final tremendous jolt that shook the carriage when the axle hit the ground. At the first rattling jar Edward had gathered his courage and leaped for Nicole, and Nicole, literally hurled from side to side of the carriage by the accident, fought like a vixen at bay, the topaz eyes nearly yellow with fierce concentration. The erratic motion of the coach gave Edward a slight edge, and he took instant advantage of it and launched himself bodily at her, deftly avoiding the blade as Nicole struggled to regain her balance. It was an ugly battle; Edward cursed as Nicole twisted in his murderous grip, his body heavy on hers, pinning her against the seat, his face thrust next to hers. With a shudder of distaste she felt his hot breath on her cheek and struggled even more violently to free herself. Edward had both her hands captured in his and exerted all his pressure on the wrist of the arm that held the sword, but Nicole, breathing rapidly and painfully, ignored the shaft of burning agony that ran up her arm, and thrashing like a wild creature, she managed to bring a knee up between their straining bodies. Viciously she kicked Edward in the groin area, smiling grimly at his howl of pain. His aching hold on her wrist slackened slightly, and Nicole, giving him no chance at all, with the swiftness of a striking snake quickly drove the sword deep into Edward's shoulder.

A shriek of agony broke from him and he fell back, one hand clutching his groin the other his shoulder. With disbelief he stared across at the disheveled young woman as she held the sword ready to strike again. At the sight of the few smears of blood on her pelisse, Edward closed his eyes and moaned, "I am dying! I know it. You have killed me, cousin!"

"Hardly," Nicole returned dryly. "You are *wounded,* cousin, and not fatally, I can assure you. I did warn you, so you have no one to blame but yourself. Feel thankful I didn't kill you . . . because the thought had crossed my mind."

The sudden sound of an approaching vehicle distracted her attention, and ignoring Edward, she leaned forward, listening intently. It took her only a second to recognize Robert's irritated voice in the darkness, and with one last contemptuous look at Edward, she threw the sword cane at him, opened the door, and sprang gracefully from the carriage.

"Robert! Stay! It is Nicole!" she cried almost elatedly, thankful for rescue so soon. She had not relished remaining there in a disabled coach with a wounded and petulant Edward throughout the night while the postilion went for help, and while she would rather have had just about anyone other than Robert Saxon be her rescuer, she wasn't in a mood to quibble.

Through the silver light of the moon Robert peered at her and exclaimed, "My dear, is it really you? I had not thought to overtake you for at least another hour or more."

Nicole gave a shaky laugh. "We have had a series of accidents; the latest you can see for yourself." Then with a throb of relief, she added, "Oh, Robert, I am so glad to see you! Please take me home! Are they very much worried at Kings Road?"

426

Robert started to reply, but Galena, seated at Robert's side, could contain herself no longer, and tumbling from Robert's gig, she ran up to her mistress. "Miss Nicole, I have been so frightened! I hurried home the instant you disappeared with Master Edward. I met Master Robert in the hall and learned that Lord Saxon was alive!" Throwing Robert a troubled look, she went on, "When I told him what had happened, he guessed instantly that Master Edward was planning a runaway marriage, and we came after you. No one even knows where we are. Master Robert felt not a moment was to be lost, and he said that when we overtook your coach that you should have me with you for appearances' sake."

Nicole smiled reassuringly down at her worried face. "You've done the right thing, Galena. Let us leave this place and go home. I am so tired and it seems all I have done is live on the ends of my nerves for the past hours."

Robert took the cue from her words, and stepping down, he helped Nicole up into the gig. She took one glance at the broken-down vehicle and shuddered. Thank God she was out of Edward's clutches!

After having seen the women seated, Robert, a grim cast to his features, started purposefully toward the other vehicle, but Nicole called him back, "Robert! No! Let him be!"

At Robert's stunned look of disbelief she said persuasively, "He can do nothing further tonight. I have wounded him with his own sword and tomorrow will be time enough for us to take action. Please, for my sake, let us be off?"

"My dear, I would do anything for you, but I cannot stand the thought of that fellow escaping with nothing more than a wound given to him by a woman! He needs to face a man!"

"He will, Robert, he will. But tomorrow, please? The hour grows late, and as no one else knows where I am, they all must be frantic with worry, so please, please take me home?"

Robert's face was turned away from her, and so she didn't notice the peculiar expression that flitted across it. Apparently taking one last look at Edward's disabled coach, he said, "Very well, my dear, if that is what you want. I shall have my satisfaction of him later. That you cannot deny me!"

"Nor would I want to, Robert. Nor would I want to."

Without further ado Robert climbed swiftly back into the gig, turned his horses, and once again, Nicole was on the way back to Brighton, this time in much, much more convivial company, and actually enjoying it, despite the cramped seating and the bite of the cool night air. She spared no thought for Edward, only thankful that she had escaped with so little injury.

Nicole erred in her judgment of Edward's state. She should have realized that Edward was an extremely desperate young man. Edward had recognized Robert Saxon's voice, and clutching the sword cane, he had slipped out the other side of the disabled coach and hid behind it. Facing an angry and furious Saxon was more than he could bear at the moment. He needed time to gather his flagging courage once more about him. Oh, he would fight to keep Nicole, but not here, here on a main road, with four witnesses.

From his place of concealment he watched narrowly as Robert swung his gig about and started on the journey back. Feeling safe from retribution, he stepped out boldly from behind the carriage, and ignoring the twinge of pain in his shoulder and the bloodstains that marred his beautifully cut pale blue jacket—he demanded that one of the horses be cut loose—he would go for help! He definitely wasn't sitting the night out in a cold uncomfortable carriage waiting for them to do something.

There was a brief acrimonious argument, but eventually Edward got his way. A few moments later, precariously astride a strapping barebacked coach horse, he set off down the road, presumably on his way for help.

Edward had no intention of going after help. Marriage to Nicole was now out of the question—but murder wasn't. With the sword cane strapped firmly to his waist by a strip of leather from the harness of the coach team, he set off in pursuit.

It would be a tragedy, he thought proudly, a mysterious tragedy. Lord Saxon's son and Miss Nicole Ashford and her maid murdered on the Brighton Road by an unknown assailant! Brilliant! The answer to all his problems. And no witnesses. Precisely how he was going to get the three of them calmly to let him stab them to death was a point Edward had not yet decided upon. At the worst, his identity hidden behind the handkerchief that would be tied across his face, he would just make a wild thrust for Nicole and escape.

Unaware of the desperate stalker a short distance behind them, Robert and his passengers made their way toward Brighton. Except Robert, like Edward, had very different plans from the ones stated.

Robert had not started out on this journey with any real plan other than to rescue Nicole from Edward's dastardly plot. It wasn't until he had Nicole safe that his decision not to return her to Kings Road was made. Instead he would take her to the small house of his near Rottingdean. There he would convince her of his love and make her realize that she must marry him!

Nicole had no idea of what Robert was planning, but she had been uneasy from the moment she had learned that no one else knew what had happened. Her liking and admiration for Robert had long since died and she was wary and suspicious of him. But he had rescued her from a very dangerous situation and for that she was grateful. Resolutely she quelled the disobliging wish that her rescuer had been someone other than Robert Saxon. And as they traveled down the moonlit road, Robert made polite, relaxing conversation, deftly turning her thoughts away from the trauma of the night. She felt a prick of remorse—he was being so kind.

Her feeling of remorse lasted for all of thirty-five minutes. Then as Robert casually guided his horses off the main road onto a side road leading to the left, she asked sharply, "Where are we going? Brighton is ahead of us, not this way!"

"I know, my dear, but I thought we should stop by my house. It is much closer. You are chilled to the bone, and my housekeeper will prepare a hot mulled wine that will drive the cold from your body," he replied smoothly, his eyes on his horses. "There will be a fire on the hearth to warm you, and I shall immediately send one of my servants with news of your whereabouts. As you said, they all must be worried beyond belief about you. When my message reaches my father, I'm positive it will not be many minutes before they all arrive at the house. Then instead of a cold and drafty gig to take you home, you will travel there in comfort, surrounded by my relieved family."

It was an enticing picture, but Nicole mistrusted it. And unless Robert's house came into view very shortly, she would mistrust his words even more.

Edward, cold and decidedly uncomfortable, but still following doggedly behind them, had whistled silently in surprise when Robert turned the gig off the main road. What was Saxon up to? A sneer curved his mouth, and he laughed to himself. A little seduction, perhaps? It would serve Nicole right, he thought viciously. Whatever reasons Saxon had for following this particular road, they suited Edward admirably. A deserted country lane this time of night was far more appropriate for cold-blooded purposes than the main road to Brighton.

Fondling the sword cane, he kicked his horse viciously on the sides, intending to overtake the gig and have the business done. But his mount, trained as part of a team of coach horses, proved recalcitrant. Not only did the animal not respond to Edward's urgings, but it began to wheedle and cavort, fighting against the reins. Fearful of falling off, for Edward was no expert rider, he instantly desisted and with growing fury had to allow the horse to proceed at his own pace, an unwavering, steady plod. Sometimes Edward feared he would lose sight of his quarry altogether. But while the gig would occasionally disappear around a curve or down a dip in the road, somehow Edward always managed to get just enough speed from his horse not to lose track of his prey.

As the miles went by them it was obvious, at least to Nicole, that in one respect Robert had lied outright. By now if he had stayed on the main road, they would have been home, and her uneasiness grew. Galena must have sensed her uneasiness, for like a child she had slipped her small hand into Nicole's.

Robert was driving to the southeast toward the sea, and Nicole could smell the scent of the salt-laden air. Turning her head to look at him, she asked quietly, "Exactly where is your house?"

Robert smiled charmingly down at her. "Not more than a mile from here. It is on the sea; I often lie awake at night listening to the pounding of the surf." Lowering his voice, he said softly, "Your mother claimed it was one of the most delightful houses she had ever visited."

Nicole felt her stomach lurch at the implication, but not wishing to bring up the whole ugly story at the moment, she forced herself to give a careless shrug. Fortunately Robert's house came into view approximately a mile down the road.

35

Robert's house was not large, but it was extremely cozy and comfortable. The entrance hall was tiny, but the drawing room where Nicole was ushered by one of Robert's servants was handsomely appointed. A fire leaped merrily on the stone hearth, and Robert's housekeeper instantly served her a steaming cup of hot spiced wine.

Her stained pelisse was thrown carelessly on a nearby chair, and standing in front of the fire, Nicole warmed herself and sipped the hot liquid. Eyeing Robert over the rim of her cup, she asked steadily, "When are you going to write to your father? Shouldn't you be doing it before the hour grows much later?"

"Ah, yes, my dear, I shall do it, this very moment," Robert agreed swiftly and, sitting down at a rosewood-inlaid desk, proceeded to do so. Sending her a smiling look, and taking the folded note with him, he walked to the door and stepped out into the hall. Suspicious of him, Nicole flew across the room, carefully slipped the door open a slight crack, and watched him intently.

Robert was alone in the hallway, standing with his back to Nicole. She watched as he methodically ripped the note into shreds and dropped the scraps in a large copper urn. He turned so quickly, coming back toward the drawing room, that Nicole had no time to shut the door and had barely enough time to race across the room to her earlier position before the fire.

It was with a decided effort that she met his guileless smile when he reentered the room. Inwardly she was seething, damning herself for being goose enough not to realize that under no circumstances was Robert to be trusted. Lowering her lashes to hide the furious expression in her eyes, she surveyed the room. There appeared little that would be of use to her. It was simply a masculine room, with a comfortable yet elegant air— the furniture covered in dark shades of leather and dam-

431

ask, the rugs muted pools of gold and brown, with heavy drapes of russet velvet pulled across the windows to keep out the fall chill. With consideration Nicole examined a set of glass doors that apparently led to the outside. A gathered drape of some diaphanous material screened them. For just a moment she had the uneasy feeling that someone was watching her, but dismissed it as a silly fancy.

If the doors were not locked, it would be a simple matter to pluck up her pelisse and run out into the night. This stretch of coast, she recalled vaguely, was rocky and pitted, offering her several places to hide until morning. She began to edge toward her pelisse, but Robert unknowingly blocked that move by walking between her and her objective. Grasping her hand, he brought it to his lips and said, "My dear, you don't know how often I have dreamed of you here with me. Dreamed of you as you are now, your hair in the firelight, shining like flame itself, and your skin bathed in gold."

Nicole swallowed, uncertain whether to laugh or to slap his face. Hastily she looked away, afraid her eyes would betray her, and determinedly she removed her hand from his, stepping back as she did so. Not looking at him, she murmured, "I do hope that Lord Saxon will come immediately! I am so exhausted and I fear that I have a sick headache coming on. You must forgive me, sir, if I do not seem appreciative of your compliments, but I am so distressed by this evening's events that I cannot think clearly." It was a blatant lie, and if Robert had not been so besotted, he would have recognized it as such. Christopher would have snorted with disbelief and told her roundly to drop her missish airs! But Robert was blind where Nicole was concerned; so tenderly he said, "If you would like to lie down, I can have my housekeeper Mrs. Simpkins show you to one of the bedrooms."

That wasn't precisely what Nicole had planned on— a bedroom was the last place she wanted to be with Robert Saxon in the vicinity! Despairingly she glanced around the room, her gaze momentarily riveted by a pair of dueling swords hanging crossed above the mantel. But even Nicole's mind boggled at the thought of stabbing a second man this incredible evening. Besides, she argued realistically, it wasn't likely she would be able to wrest one of the swords down from the wall before Robert stopped her.

The bedroom it would be—but with Galena in attendance. Putting a hand on her head, she cried in fainting accents, "Oh, how my head aches! Yes, I believe I will lie down. But please, please, send my maid to me. She knows how to cope with these attacks."

Her request was accomplished with an ease that startled her. In a matter of seconds she was whisked up the stairs by Robert's housekeeper, an extremely worried Galena in close attendance. Acting like a spoiled beauty, Nicole muttered pettishly, "Oh, please, Mrs. Simpkins, do leave us! My maid knows exactly how to cope with these terrible headaches."

Galena's mouth nearly fell open at such an outright lie, Miss Nicole never having been sick a day since she had known her. She was a clever girl, though, and said nothing, only nodding her head as if agreeing with every word Nicole said.

Mrs. Simpkins, suspecting she was waiting on her employer's intended wife, did exactly as told. No use upsetting the new mistress—this was a good placement and she wouldn't want to lose it. And so she went back down the stairs to her kitchen.

Nicole barely waited until the door closed and Mrs. Simpkins's steps had died away before she sat up impatiently and somewhat disgustedly threw away the lavender-soaked cloth that had been so gently placed on her brow a moment before.

Nervously Galena regarded her as she ran to one of the windows and stared down at the ground below. Then with an exclamation of triumph she raced back to the bed and began ruthlessly tearing down the silken bed-curtains. Unable to help herself, Galena burst out, "Miss Nicole, what are you doing? What is happening?"

Nicole sent her an almost gay look. "We," she said lightly, "are escaping. Come now, help me! Tie these strips to the leg of that heavy armoire. This material should be strong enough to hold our weight."

At Galena's expression of incomprehension, Nicole said hurriedly, "Robert Saxon is not to be trusted! I'm afraid that he means to compromise me, just as Edward did. So we must free ourselves."

Silently Galena helped her, obviously not totally convinced. When she took a look at the three-story drop below, she balked. "Miss Nicole, I can't do it! I'll fall, I know I will. It's too far!"

Grimly Nicole stared at her. She could browbeat the girl, but it would gain her nothing. If Galena felt she would fall, fall she would, probably wailing in a loud, carrying voice as she did so.

"Very well," Nicole said resignedly. "I will do it alone. Give me a few minutes once I've reached the ground, and then go back down to the kitchen just as if nothing were wrong. Tell the housekeeper I have fallen asleep and must on no occasion be awakened. That should gain me an hour or so. By that time I should have been able to find someone to carry a message to Lord Saxon."

"Miss Nicole, you wouldn't go off and leave me!"

"Galena, I have no choice!" Nicole retorted exasperatedly. "Now do as I tell you. You'll be safe. Just remember to act as if you know nothing, and when my disappearance is discovered be as surprised as everyone else. Understand?"

Her eyes the size of saucers, Galena nodded her head slowly. "But, Miss Nicole," she cried protestingly, "you have no pelisse, no cloak. You are sure to catch an inflammation of the lung."

Throwing her a fierce glare, Nicole said harshy, "If I thought walking naked down the middle of Brighton on Christmas Day would save me from Robert Saxon, I would do it! Now stop this nonsense and help me!"

The window opened easily, and without hesitation Nicole slid across the sill, her hands tightly grasping the swath of material. She hung there a moment, and then she swiftly lowered her body to the ground. It took her but a few minutes. The countless times she had climbed like a cat in the shrouds of *La Belle Garce* came to her aid now. Her heart was thumping thunderously, partly from exertion and partly from elation, as she stood on the ground beneath the window. Galena's face appeared, and after giving her a cheerful wave, Nicole lifted her skirts in her hands and sprinted down toward the sea, planning to work her way back up to the road farther down the beach. Rottingdean, she knew, lay not more than three miles to the east of Robert's house, and within the hour she should reach it. There she would find someone to take a message to Lord Saxon.

Traveling down the beach, she idly stared at the ocean and watched without too much interest the tall masted ship anchored some distance out to sea. She smiled to herself again. Oh, for the carefree days of *La Belle Garce!* Those early days before she had become so aware of Christopher as a man, before she and Allen had thought of their mad plans. And with a guilty start she realized that she hadn't thought of Allen in weeks, months. Christopher had said he would be freed. Perhaps at this very moment, Allen might be free, Nicole mused, wanting desperately to believe it.

She felt curiously carefree as she walked on the moon-lit sand, the breeze tangling the sable-fire hair. But reality pressed on her, and she turned her back on the pounding surf and began to climb up the rocky sloping cliffs that led up to the road.

Increasingly aware of the chill bite of the air, and trying to ignore it, she focused her thoughts on the warm fire that would be waiting for her when she at last returned home to Kings Road. How glad she would be to be there once again! The explanations, though, she decided gloomily, would be dreadful, for how was she to tell Lord Saxon that his own son had played a part in tonight's ugly and dishonorable occurrence.

It wasn't a pleasant prospect, nor was the prospect of meeting Christopher's contemptuous, derisive eyes. He would think the worst, she thought half angrily, and half miserably.

At first neither Simon or Christopher had thought a great deal about Twickham's assessment of the situation. It seemed reasonable enough, although a bit erratic, on Robert's part to leave Kings Road under the circumstances simply because he wished to give Nicole and Edward Markham a ride home in his gig. And the more he thought about it, the more it bothered Christopher. Four in Robert's gig? Or after taking Galena back with him, did Robert assume Nicole would order the girl to walk all the way home again from the park? It seemed unlikely.

By seven o'clock that evening both he and Simon were more than just a little worried. They had said nothing to the ladies, not wishing to alarm them, and when Regina had asked after Nicole, Simon had muttered somewhat hastily, "Ah, forgot to tell you—I gave my permission for her to dine at Unton's place tonight. You know how smitten Unton's heir is with her and I saw no harm in it. After all, you were just there last night yourself, so you can't say you disapprove."

"Well, no, I don't disapprove, it's just that it's unlike Nicole to go off like that. Did she say how late she would be?"

Simon hesitated and Christopher broke in smoothly, "Rather late, I suspect. There was some talk of a midnight charade, because of the full moon. I wouldn't worry about her; Unton and his son will see to her."

Simon shot him a thankful look and the subject was dropped—dropped but not forgotten by either of the gentlemen as they sat alone in Simon's study a few minutes later. Dinner was to be served at eight, and Christopher, after a quick glance at his pocket watch, said, "I'm going to take a ride by the park and then go to Markham's lodgings. Perhaps he is there and can tell us something." He stood up, started toward the door, and then stopped. Revolving slowly to face his grandfather, he added determinedly, "I am also going to find out if Robert is at home—so don't expect me back for dinner."

"Christopher! Do you think that it is wise—considering how he feels about you?"

The gold eyes were hard, the firm mouth taut as Christopher retorted exasperatedly, "I am not afraid of Robert! He obviously is the one who knows precisely what Galena said, and probably the only one who can tell us what happened and where Nicole is. It's not more than an hour's ride out to his place, so I should be back before ten o'clock. Don't worry—I have been taking care of myself for a long time."

Higgins, when informed of the plan, disliked it even more. "I'm telling you you're mad! Nick can take care of herself. I'm not saying that if we didn't have that ship to catch I wouldn't be in favor of trying to find out what happened too. But damnit, man, we have to sail on the midnight tide! You shouldn't be galavanting over the countryside searching for a tough little varmit like her! She is probably perfectly safe."

His face shuttered, Christopher replied levelly, "Shut up, Higgins, and do as you're told! Do you have everything packed?"

Knowing there was no swaying him when he was in one of these damn-all moods, the older man answered sourly, "Yes. There wasn't all that much, after all."

"Very well then. You will come with me. Robert's place is not but a mile or so from the rendezvous point. I'll go ahead and take you . . . and the memorandum there."

Staring fixedly at the dark features, Higgins asked slowly, "Are you telling me that you're not leaving? That you're staying and I am to return alone?"

"No!" Christopher bit out angrily. "I will be there, but I may have to cut it fine and if—" he stopped, then continued harshly, "if for some reason I am delayed, you and the memorandum will still reach New Orleans safely."

There was no moving him, though Higgins tried his best during the time it took them to survey the closed and deserted park, Edward's darkened and empty lodgings, and especially during the long ride out to Robert's house. The impassioned exhortations, the curses and insults that Higgins hurled at him left Higgins exhausted and Christopher completely unmoved.

At Robert's house Christopher discovered from the servant who answered the door that Master Robert was not at home at present, but was expected for a late dinner. Christopher left no message and merely tossed off some remark to the effect that he had called for no important reason and would see Robert tomorrow. Casually he added that there was no need to tell Robert that he had called. The servant bowed politely, and a moment later Christopher and Higgins were on their way to the little cottage they had stayed in while Christopher had recovered from his wound.

The parting between the two men was brief. After depositing Higgins at the cottage, Christopher merely said, "I will be back by midnight. If I am not—do not wait for me. See that the memorandum is delivered to Jason Savage the instant you reach New Orleans." At Higgins's gloomy, unhappy expression he said lightly, "Higgins, I'll make it, but if I don't—I'll do as I've already told my grandfather and head for France. I'll be there in time for the battle—that I promise you."

He made the ride back to Kings Road in good time, his thoughts unwillingly on Nicole. She was probably sitting at home warm by the fire, he decided angrily, as he reached the outskirts of Brighton. And if she is, she had better have a damn good reason for disappearing like this, he thought furiously.

Simon pounced on him the instant he entered the house, dispelling any notion that Nicole had returned in his absence. "Well, what did you find out?"

Stripping off his driving gloves and warming his hands before the fire in the study, Christopher admitted, "Nothing. The park was deserted, Markham not at home, but Robert is expected home for a late dinner."

Taking a deep breath, his jaw tight, Christopher looked over at his grandfather. "I still have to leave tonight, you know. Nicole's disappearance doesn't change anything." Then turning his back away, he snarled, "I could damn well strangle her for this! If I didn't know better I'd swear the little devil had done it on purpose." A harsh laugh broke from him. "What am I saying? Hell, I don't know better!"

Simon regarded him sharply. "It seems," he said calmly, "that you are taking this much too personally. I see no reason to change your plans—Nicole will be found and there is probably a logical explanation for her absence. Whether you are here or not makes little difference."

Christopher let out his breath in a rush. "You're right, and if I am to depart, I shall have to do it before the hour grows much later. Are the ladies still up? If they are I had better bid them good evening—it's the least I can do, considering they don't know it is really goodbye."

Simon nodded and sat alone in his study while Christopher walked to the blue drawing room and said his good nights to his new stepgrandmother and his great-aunt. Neither lady suspected he was bidding them good-bye, although Regina did wonder at the way he gave Letitia a quick hard embrace before leaving the room. But then she dismissed it—Christopher was given to strange fits and flights; any young man, she thought resentfully, who would turn his back on the chance to marry such a charming heiress as Nicole must be a little strange.

Christopher entered the study slowly, his face serious and a little drawn, knowing that the time for the final good-bye had come at last. Simon, seated behind his desk, also knew that the moment of farewell was upon them, and with an aching, sorrowful heart he watched as his tall grandson crossed the room to stop before the desk.

Idly Christopher's long fingers skimmed the polished surface, and his face bleak he stared down into the worn features so like his own. "Grandfather," he began haltingly, "I do not like to leave under these circumstances, but I must, and within a very few minutes. Higgins is already waiting for me at Rottingdean and from there we will travel to Dover and then to France." Inwardly Christopher cursed himself for being such a ready liar and wished that at least for this moment he could put the lies and half-truths aside. But it was imperative that Simon believe he was heading for France, and so ruthlessly he quelled his conscience. The lie behind him, he was able to say more easily, "I shall miss you," adding with a quick, endearing grin, "and my new grandmother too!" More seriously he continued, "I feel certain that a peace between England and the United States will be negotiated in Ghent before many months have passed. I may be back by next summer, and so while I am saying goodbye now, remember it may only be for a few months."

Simon, his emotions temporarily well in hand, snapped, "Bah! Don't molly coddle me! I expect Letty and I shall do very well without you." Not looking at Christopher, but staring ferociously at the top of his desk, he said casually, "I've been thinking about it and this is really best. Letty and I are just married, and it's not good for a man to start marriage cluttered up with a lot of relatives and such. When you return next summer, Letty and I will be well settled, and *then* we'll have the time to appreciate your company! You'll not understand what I mean, never having been married before, but I doubt Letty and I will miss you too much during the next several months."

Christopher could hardly choke back the gust of laughter that shook him at Simon's outrageous words. With barely disguised amusement in his voice, he replied, "Ah, yes. That point of view had not occurred to me. Perhaps it is even fortunate that things have fallen as they have."

Simon glared at him. "Yes. Yes, it is! And now if you're going—get!"

Hearing the raw pain in Simon's tone, Christopher's amusement fled, and reaching over the desk, he extended his hand, and as Simon grasped it tightly, he said simply, "Good-bye, grandfather. Look for me come summer."

"I will—and you had damn well better be here!"

Neither man spoke of the dangers involved in the long sea journey, nor did Christopher allow himself to think of Simon's age. Christopher said softly, "I will be. Depend upon it!" The clasped hands tightened a moment longer and then Christopher was gone.

The night was growing colder, Christopher thought to himself, when at last he urged his horse in the direction of Rottingdean. If everything went as planned, in less than two hours he and Higgins would be on their way back to New Orleans.

Nicole's whereabouts vexed him not a little, and even though there was probably a reasonable explanation for her continued absence, he would have liked to know precisely what had happened to keep her from returning home. There were dozens of reasons that occurred to him, but none of them found any favor with him. He was beset with a nagging premonition that Nicole was in some kind of danger, and no matter how often he told himself that she had gone for a ride with Robert and that they had probably lost a wheel or stayed overlong visiting with friends, he was never quite satisfied. And because he was worried, a fact he would not admit to himself, he was also blazingly angry with Nicole for acting in such a reprehensible manner. Baggage! he thought cynically, running about the countryside with two men, just like a common little trollop! He'd not waste another moment on her. Let Edward Markham and Robert fight over her—he was getting the hell out.

Having followed Robert's gig to the house, Edward had hovered about outside for several minutes, unable to decide precisely what his next move should be. He had not yet discarded murder, and he was searching for an entrance into the house, when he saw Nicole and Robert through the glass doors of the drawing room. Outside in the darkness he had watched intently the scene being acted—Robert's writing of the note, Nicole's dash across the room, and eventually her departure. A wolfish smile on his lips, he undid the sword cane. Such a little actress his cousin, he was going to enjoy her performance when he at last drove this blade through her black heart. But first there was Robert. Gently testing the glass doors, he discovered to his delight that they were unlocked. Silently he opened them and slipped into the room while Robert was momentarily gone.

Hearing approaching footsteps, Edward quickly hid behind a pair of russet drapes and watched with satisfaction as Robert returned and seated himself before the fire. His back was to Edward, and taking instant advantage of that fact, Edward crept across the room, until with the blade pointed at Robert's neck, he said softly, "Don't move! If you do, I'll kill you!"

Robert stiffened, but remained perfectly still. "Is that you, Markham?" he asked at last, having recognized the voice.

Edward chuckled with malicious satisfaction. "Is that you, Markham?" he mimicked. Keeping the blade on Robert, he walked around in front of him. "Of course it is! Who else did you think it was? Did you really believe that I would let Nicole escape me so easily?" Drunk with success, the blue eyes almost feverish, he taunted, "Not so eager to meet me now, are you? I heard what you said to Nicole out there on the Brighton Road—said I needed to meet a man. Well, I've met a man and what does he do, but sit there!"

Coolly Robert eyed him, taking in the bloodstained

coat and the occasional slight sway that told of a loss of blood. Almost politely he asked, "May I stand? If we are going to talk for any great length I would prefer to be nearer the fire."

Suspiciously Edward stared at him. Deciding it seemed a harmless request and feeling magnanimous in his power, he graciously assented, watching with an owllike gaze as Robert, a glass of wine in one hand, stood up and walked to the fireplace.

Civilly Robert asked, "Now tell me, Markham, precisely what it is that you want?"

Edward giggled, the blood he had lost making him light-headed. "I'll tell you what I want," he said thickly, waving the sword cane about erratically. "I want Nicole. You send for her!"

Unhurriedly Robert took a sip from his wineglass and then, when Edward took a menacing step forward, flung the glass and its contents into his face. As Edward bawled with fury and surprise. Robert leaped for one of the swords crossed above the mantel, quickly wrenching it free. Then Robert stalked Edward around the room, the sea-colored eyes queerly bright.

The situation had reversed itself so swiftly that Edward was still reeling with shock as he stumbled away from Robert's steady advance. Haphazardly he parried Robert's murderous attack; his short sword cane was useless against the long, deadly blade the other man wielded so effortlessly. It was like killing a rabbit in a trap, and Robert smiled to himself as he drove the sword into Edward's unprotected throat.

There was an odd little gurgle from Edward, and then he slid to the floor. Absently, Robert wiped his sword clean and looked broodingly down at the corpse. Now what the devil was he to do with a body? The sound of the sea caught his attention and he smiled again. Of course, the sea.

But as he reached down and began to pull Edward's body toward the open glass doors, he heard the sound of an approaching horse. Tensely he waited for the animal to pass, but it did not.

Christopher had not meant to stop at Robert's house again that evening, but he could not put aside the thought of Nicole. Where in God's name had she gone, and why? Simon was right, though, he reminded himself grimly— where Nicole was at the moment made little difference to his plans—she would return home eventually whether he was there or not. That thought should have dispelled her from his mind, but it didn't, and so when his horse approached Robert's house, Christopher couldn't withstand the impulse to satisfy his curiosity.

Dismounting and tying his horse to the post, he glanced over at the large coach horse standing near the corner of the house and wondered idly what the animal was doing here. The front of a gentleman's residence was certainly an odd place for it to be.

Everything was odd, he thought impatiently—Nicole's going off like that, Robert's walking out in the middle of an important discussion with Simon, and now a horse with no saddle, parts of its harness still strapped to the body, was calmly cropping the sparse grass that grew near the house. His interest aroused, he walked over to the animal and ran his hands knowledgeably over the broad back, feeling the slight lingering dampness. Been ridden quite a distance, he concluded. He gave the animal one last pat and started to walk up to the front door, when he noticed the glow of light spilling out from the side of the house.

It was obvious from the intensity and amount of light being shed that a door was open, and after a brief hesitation Christopher went down the same path Edward had followed, and halted just outside the pool of light, staring into the drawing room.

Strangely enough, when Christopher looked into the room, the first thing he saw was neither Robert, nor Edward's sprawled body, but Nicole's pelisse, still lying carelessly on one of the chairs near the doors. He recognized it instantly, having selected it and paid for it in New Orleans. Little bitch, he thought savagely, little goddamn bitch! He took an angry step forward and then in that second realized that the room was not empty.

Robert was there and Edward Markham too. A very dead Edward Markham, he discovered without surprise, as Robert bent down once again and began to drag the body toward the open doors.

For a moment Christopher almost turned his back on the entire scene, revolted by the ugly conclusion that flamed across his brain. Nicole was obviously with her lover, and it appeared her lover had killed the rival for her affections. It was so tawdry and sordid it sickened him, and was just the sort of thing that Nicole's mother, Annabelle, would have reveled in. Nicole, it seemed, was not much better. He took a step away but, remembering Simon's worried, apprehensive face, decided to intervene not for Nicole's sake, but for his grandfather's—or so he told himself. What Robert did with Markham's body he didn't care to waste much thought on, but the apparent relationship between Nicole and Robert ate at him like acid, and fondly he imagined Nicole's slender throat in his hands.

Christopher must have made some sound, or Robert, his nerves already agitated by the cold-blooded killing of Edward, sensed him standing there just outside the drawing room and glanced up. For a long timeless moment their eyes met and held. Then with a half-pleased, half-mad smile on his face, Robert dropped Edward's arm and stood up.

"So," he said, "it appears we will meet at last."

There was no need for explanations between them; each was aware that this night would see the final deadly battle between them. All the old wrongs, the ugly hatred between them would be settled . . . in blood.

Christopher nodded at Robert's words and with a long, easy stride walked into the room. He didn't look at Robert as he shrugged out of his greatcoat; instead, his assessing gaze traveled almost idly around the room. Rolling up the sleeves of his white linen shirt, he asked briefly, "What will it be, swords or pistols? Here or on the beach?"

Equally businesslike, Robert replied, "Swords. Yours is there above the mantel. I already have mine. As you may not have noticed, it has served me well once already this evening."

Christopher's lips moved in something that might have been called a smile. "I had noticed. But where do we finish this farce? Here?"

"Why not? The furniture can be pushed aside."

Both men set to work with deadly amiability, shoving the heavy furniture against the walls of the room until a large empty space was cleared. Still without speaking, both men sat down and removed their boots and stockings, each wishing for the extra balance and mobility afforded by bare feet.

His boots off, Christopher strode over to the mantel and plucked down the remaining sword, running it lightly through his hand, checking the perfection of the blade, the weight in his hand. Turning to Robert, now also with a sword in his hand, he said in a level tone, "Your choice in weapons is to be applauded. This is an uncommonly fine blade."

Robert bowed mockingly and answered with a sneer,

"Did you ever know me when I did not have the finest? Be it swords or women?"

A cold light entered Christopher's gold eyes, making them glitter in the firelight. Deliberately he murmured, "But do you have her, Uncle? Or rather I should say . . . can you *keep* her?"

It was a studied insult, and Robert's hand tightened around his sword, his mouth thinning with fury. "By God, you'll pay for that!" he spat. *"En garde!"*

Christopher met Robert's attack eagerly, their blades singing in the air. Instantly disengaging his sword and leaping nimbly away from Robert's maddened thrust, Christopher taunted, "Come now, Uncle, you'll have to do better than that! After all, this time we are evenly matched. Or is it that you only show to advantage when your opponent is relatively unarmed?"

Robert's teeth ground together in rage, but he held onto his temper, guessing that Christopher was consciously infuriating him. Smiling grotesquely Robert hissed, "Brave words for a man who runs before my sword. Come closer, Nephew, and we shall see the truth of your taunts."

Christopher made no reply; his expression was deceptively lazy as almost contemptuously he parried Robert's furious lunge and danced easily away from the older man.

"Damn you! Come to me and fight!" Robert snapped, breathing heavily.

"I will, Uncle, I will, have no fear of that," Christopher replied coldly, and then suddenly reversing his defensive actions, he charged Robert, his blade flashing in lightning strokes, driving the other man before him.

They fought grimly and silently, except for the soft thud of their bare feet on the carpet and the occasional clash of their swords, the firelight gleaming on the flashing blades. There was a deadly atmosphere in the room that increased by the second, as time after time, Robert was just able to turn aside the swift and wicked thrust of Christopher's blade. But Robert was tiring and he knew it—knew too that there was no escape from this attack, that this was no fencing master's display, no polite duel with its punctilious niceties.

For each of them nothing existed except the other, and the hatred they shared; nothing was real except the other man's sword, always feinting, thrusting, and parrying, each always avoiding the one little lessening of the guard that would allow this inevitable meeting to end. They were two tall men, two handsome men, evenly matched in many ways, and the rage both had contained for too long was now in full blaze, racing uncontrollably through their veins.

Their breathing was quick and hard as the fight continued. Robert barely parried a lunging thrust aimed at his heart. He moved too slowly, and Christopher's blade clashed against his, before sliding over his guard and slashing along his arm, leaving a long, welling, bloody slit.

With a tigerish smile on his lips, Christopher muttered softly, "I owed you that, Uncle!"

And because this was no simple duel to be decided by a single hit, to be ended by first blood, neither checked, but each relentlessly wielded his sword against the other. Hard pressed, Robert feinted in high carte and thrust in low tierce, but his blade met only the opposition of Christopher's.

Breathlessly, but very clearly, Christopher asked, "Where is she?"

It was Robert's turn to smile. "Upstairs in my bed . . . where else?"

He regretted the words instantly, for Christopher's blade easily and deliberately stung him on the cheek. "And how does she arrive there? What was Edward doing here?"

Robert had no strength remaining to waste on attack; he could only parry the increasingly dangerous thrusts of Christopher's sword, his arm aching from shoulder to wrist, the sweat rolling off his face.

"Answer me! How does Nicole find herself here and with Markham?"

In a gulping, panting gasp, Robert spat, "Markham abducted her and I got the story from her maid. I overtook them and brought Nicole here."

Christopher could figure out most of the gaps in Robert's story, but not all. And his eyes narrowed in grim concentration; his point flashed under Robert's guard, checked, and withdrew. "And your bed?"

Tauntingly Robert panted, "Have you ever known me . . . to boast . . . of my . . . conquests?"

It was the last thing Robert Saxon ever said. He had no breath left with which to speak; all his energies were concentrated on avoiding that final deadly thrust he knew would finish this struggle.

A moment later Robert saw it coming—a straight lunge aimed for his heart; he made a desperate attempt to parry it, but was too late to deflect the fatal thrust. Unerringly, Christopher's point sunk deep and deadly into Robert's heart, ending forever the duel between them.

Unemotionally Christopher viewed Robert's body, surprised to discover that he felt nothing. Robert had been someone he had hated and despised for almost his entire life; to win against him should have given a sense of victory, but he was empty, numb, indifferent to the body lying there on the floor.

He must have stood there for several moments, and what it was that eventually roused him from his queer blankness he never quite knew. Perhaps it was the crack of a burning log on the hearth or the crash of a breaker on the beach. At any rate he gave himself a mental shake, realizing at last that the monstrous hatred between him and Robert was finally over—but at a horrible and bitter price.

The chiming of the clock on the mantel roused him still further, made him more aware of the passing time, of the ship that was waiting for him beyond those same breakers pounding on the sand just below Robert's house. Grimly he surveyed the scene, Robert dead at his feet, and Edward's body stretched out on the floor not four feet away. It was the proximity of the bodies that first gave him the idea—that and a deep-rooted desire to save his grandfather more grief. Robert's death would be a blow enough without the added knowledge that his grandson had killed his son. His mind made up in a lightning flash, he walked over to Edward's body and deftly substituted his own sword for the sword cane, unconsciously thrusting the sword cane into his waistband.

It took him but a moment longer to unroll his sleeves, put on his boots, and slip into his greatcoat. He glanced once more around the room, increasingly conscious that he must leave—the tide was on the turn and time was passing swiftly. But the thought of Nicole sleeping soundly in Robert's bed upstairs would not leave him, and he knew before he could depart, he had to see her, to see for himself that she was indeed the lying jade he had damned her for being.

A timid knock interrupted his thoughts, and swiftly he crossed the room to press himself flat against the wall near the door. The knock came again and after a brief hesitation the door opened slowly.

Somewhat cautiously Galena entered the room, her soft brown eyes wide with apprehension and worry. What she was doing was unheard of, but nearly sick with worry about her rash young mistress, she had whipped up her

446

courage and was now intending to confess to Master Robert what Miss Nicole had done. She had wrestled unhappily with her conscience, but her concern for her mistress had won. Perhaps, she told herself staunchly, Miss Nicole had misunderstood the situation. Surely Master Robert was not in the same mold as that wicked Mister Markham. And besides, she excused herself, if she didn't do something, Miss Nicole was likely to freeze out there on the beach with no cloak, no pelisse.

Galena had taken not more than two steps into the room, when Christopher, moving with that pantherlike grace of his, shut the door with his shoulder and swiftly clamped a hand over her mouth.

"Hush!" he ordered softly in her ear. Shooting a sharp glance over to where the bodies lay, he noted with satisfaction that from this angle, they were hidden by one of the couches. Quickly he hustled a petrified Galena over to Robert's desk and, still holding a hand against her mouth, spun her to face him.

Her eyes opened even wider if possible, and silently her lips formed his name.

Placing a finger to his lips in a gesture of silence, he slowly removed his hand.

"Master Christopher!" she breathed with a sigh of relief. "I knew you would come!" Then recalling instantly her reason for being there, she cried, "Oh, Master Christopher, you must save her! She has run away down the beach. You must find her and bring her back!" She added irrelevantly, "She has no cloak to keep her warm."

Christopher thought quickly, mistakenly assuming that Nicole had somehow learned of his presence and was even now racing away to escape the retribution he would undoubtedly deliver. Spying a piece of paper and a pen on Robert's desk, he quickly scrawled a note to his grandfather.

> Grandfather,
> I write to you in haste—leaving for France immediately as planned. I have Nicole safe—but at a terrible price!
>
> Christopher

Snatching up Nicole's pelisse, he dragged Galena from the room, deliberately making certain she had no view of the bodies, and hurried her along the path he had followed such a short time ago. Reaching his horse, he literally pushed Galena into Nicole's pelisse, pressed the note into her hand, and tossed her up onto his mount.

"I sure as hell hope you can ride, Galena," he said with a grin. "You're going to go to Lord Saxon's and give him this note. Don't worry about your mistress—I'll take care of her." He hesitated, then he said slowly, "Galena, I would appreciate it if you didn't tell anyone but my grandfather that you saw me here tonight. If anyone asks, you slipped away all by yourself. Understand?"

Like one in a trance Galena nodded; then Christopher slapped the flank of the horse, and she clutched the reins as the animal sprang forward. Christopher watched until she was well on her way and then turned and leaped down toward the beach, his one thought to find Nicole and when he did . . .

Miss Nicole Ashford was at the moment in a very unhappy predicament. She had grown careless in her confidence and had to her disgust managed to stumble over a half-buried rock in the sand and twist her ankle badly. The pain was excruciating, but that was nothing to the burning humiliation she felt at being stopped by such a silly and feminine accident. Fuming, she sat in the sand, having nearly given up her futile attempts to climb to the small cottage just a short way above her. Her ankle would not hold her weight, and beyond crawling on her belly, there was little she could do except smolder at such an unkind fate. She was determined to continue and had seriously considered traveling on her hands and knees when she noticed a flash of blue coming from the ship she had seen earlier. Mystified, she glanced back up at the cliff, and in the moonlight she could make out the shape of a man.

For one wild second she thought she recognized the shape but dismissed it as fancy. Higgins wouldn't be out here at this time of night exchanging signals with a strange ship. Or would he?

Suddenly she jerked upright, remembering Christopher's mention of a cottage near the sea—that and the fact that he was leaving. Intently, she stared out to sea, not at all surprised when a few minutes later a small boat was lowered into the water and the men aboard her began to row toward the beach.

Higgins's appearance coming down from the cliff top not a second later she viewed almost with amusement. Tonight was certainly her night for stumbling into one scrape after another. Christopher would kill her if he found her here, she thought with a half-hysterical giggle

448

—but she would rather Christopher throttle her, than live as Robert's wife.

Higgins was just even with her, when she called to him, "Higgins! I know this is an awkward time for me to call, but would you please tell Christopher that I am here."

Higgins not unnaturally nearly jumped out of his skin. "Miss Nicole!" he said in an agitated tone, when he squinted in the moonlight and recognized her. "Whatever are you doing here? Christopher is out looking for you—in fact, he is going to miss the ship, because he is looking for you!"

With something like horror, Nicole regarded Higgins's extremely apprehensive face. "Oh, Lord!" she muttered softly, realizing precisely what must have occurred. The thought of Christopher murdering her was no longer very funny, especially since there appeared a very definite possibility that he would do exactly that when he caught up with her.

Biting her lip, she watched as the small boat drew nearer. "What are you going to do?" she asked at last. "Tell them you aren't going?"

Higgins shot her an uncertain glance. "No. I am returning with them. This ships sails for America, for New Orleans, and Christopher has given me orders to make it without fail."

"I see," she answered slowly, seeing a great many things she would rather not. This rendezvous must have been planned even before he had left New Orleans, and the thought that she was the cause of his failing to keep it filled her with dismay. But damnit, she thought rebelliously, it isn't my fault! I didn't ask him to go haring off all over the countryside looking for me!

"Look!" Higgins cried excitedly, interrupting her thoughts, and with a sinking heart Nicole recognized instantly the long-legged figure striding so furiously down the beach. It took him only a moment to reach them, and there was a curious expression on his face when he looked at Nicole, still seated on the sand.

"Well, well," he drawled sarcastically, "what have we here? A maiden in distress? Or my uncle's runaway mistress?" Giving her no time to answer, he swooped down and pulled her to her feet.

Warily, she eyed him, ignoring the stabbing pain of her ankle. Almost meekly she said, "I hurt my ankle, or I wouldn't be here. And Christopher," she went on with quiet desperation, "I didn't mean for this to happen."

Christopher stared at her silently, a victim of so many

449

conflicting emotions that he wasn't certain what he felt. He had thought the only emotion she could arouse was disgust and lust, thought he had said his final good-bye to her in the library. But he discovered that some other indefinable feeling for her was tearing him apart.

There was a stiff breeze blowing now, lifting the sable-fire curls and tumbling them wildly about her shoulders, molding the thin material of her dress against the slim body, making Christopher remember things he wanted to forget. He didn't want her, he told himself savagely. She was trouble—had been trouble since he had first discovered her in that cove in Bermuda—and now she had nearly been the undoing of months of planning. As the moments passed and still Christopher said nothing, Higgins, with a discretion that further endeared him to Nicole, left them and walked down to the surf to wait for the nearing boat to make it through the breakers.

Nicole swallowed, slightly unnerved by the hard, unrelenting features above her. For once her temper had fled before the tightly leashed fury that emanated from Christopher, and falteringly she said, "I . . . I . . ,"

"You what?" Christopher snapped explosively. "You're sorry? Isn't it a little late for that? Two men are dead because of you! Jesus Christ, Nicole, I leave you alone for less than a month and what do I find? Chaos and mayhem. And now what am I to do with you?"

Her eyes a stormy topaz in the moonlight, she flared back, "You aren't going to do anything with me! I've managed to get this far by myself, and I sure as hell don't need any help from the likes of you! Meet your damn ship!"

She spun away momentarily, having forgotten the injury to her ankle. But a shaft of tearing agony reminded her forcibly of it, and smothering the gasp of pain that rose in her throat, she took another stumbling step before Christopher's hard hands closed around her shoulders.

A shout from Higgins jerked Christopher's head around before he could continue further, and with a low, vicious curse he swung a kicking, fighting Nicole up in his arms and carried her down near the surf. Standing her none too gently on the damp sand, he snarled, "Now you stay here and you listen to me! Robert and Edward are both dead! And if you didn't do the actual deed yourself, you are directly responsible for their deaths." He finished bitterly, "You are so like your mother!"

Nicole's face went white, her eyes huge enormous pools of darkness. The news of the deaths was a staggering shock to her, but what stunned her most was that Christopher was blaming *her!* She had known he would take the worst possible view, but this? It was so damned like him, she thought with a burst of blazing fury, to couple her with her mother, to think that they were alike! "If I were a man, you'd not say that! And if I were a man, you'd meet me on the field of honor before the sun rises. How dare you! How dare you condemn me! Condemn me without a hearing, without even knowing what happened. You arrogant beast—I hope your bloody ship sinks!" It was a childish taunt, and Nicole bit her lip in frustrated fury, wishing she could command a blistering attack that would leave him speechless.

There was just enough justice in her words to give Christopher pause, but there was no time—no time for further conversation, no time to settle the disagreements between them. Harassed, torn apart by emotions he could not name, or would not name, he was for the first time in his life swayed by indecision. And this one woman was the cause of it all. There was no denying that he still wanted her; even now, knowing Robert had lain with her, had tasted that sweet mouth, he still wanted to feel her slender body naked against his, to feel that exciting quiver her body gave when he entered her. And unbidden the thought leaped in his mind—why leave her behind?

It was madness even to think it, but once the idea was born he could not shake it, and considering he gauged the nearness of the boat. It had reached the breakers, and now within seconds he would have to make a move. Higgins was already beginning to wade out into the foaming surf to meet it and he must join him any moment. He turned back to stare down into Nicole's tempestuous features, his eyes lingering on the ripe fullness of her mouth. And in that second Christopher Saxon vanished, leaving only Captain Saber.

Christopher Saxon had planned to leave her safe with his grandfather. Knowing she was secure with Simon, Christopher could have sailed off to America and tried to forget her. But Saber never denied himself anything he wanted, and he wanted this slim woman desperately.

The wind whipping his blue-black hair about his head, the gold eyes glittering with emotions and instincts that had been tamped down and denied during the long months in England, Christopher's gaze swept down the slender length of her body. He made his decision and swooped down on Nicole before she even guessed his intention. He gave her a long, hard kiss on her half-opened lips, and then effortlessly he tossed her over his broad shoulder.

Ignoring her scream of pure outrage, oblivious to the fists pounding fiercely on his back and the thrashing legs, he plunged into the surf and strode eagerly forward to meet the incoming boat. He met it in thigh-deep water and almost cheerfully pitched Nicole onto the wooden planks. A second later, with an enthusiastic hand from Higgins, he levered himself aboard. He took one last look at the deserted, moon-washed beach, aware that now he could truly leave England without regret. Turning to one of the crew, he said lightly, "We're all aboard. Now let's get the hell out of here before a British warship finds us!"

There was a brief hesitation from the men, and then with a resigned shrug they began rowing toward the ship. One of them couldn't help muttering, "No one said anything about a female. Captain Baker ain't going to be best pleased when he catches sight of her!"

Christopher glanced down into Nicole's furious features, and carelessly stroking her curls, he replied evenly, "Sorry for the extra passenger, but the lady and I have some very important unfinished business to discuss—and New Orleans is just the place to do it."

36

The long sea journey back to New Orleans was a nightmare. Twice they were menaced by British warships, once fired upon, and only a drifting fog bank saved them, enabling Captain Baker to slip away unseen. The weather was foul; gales and storms seemed to follow the ship every mile of the way, making short tempers even shorter.

Understandably the captain was provoked by the unexpected and unwelcome addition of a woman to his ship, and Nicole spent the entire journey isolated in a tiny cramped cupboard of a room. There was no privacy, absolutely no comfort, and as she had left England rather precipitously, she grew to hate the bronze silk gown with the ecru lace that she was wearing. She and Christopher exchanged the minimum of words, each aware that now was not the time to begin another of their acrimonious arguments. Higgins provided a much-needed buffer zone between them, quickly and efficiently changing the conversation when it threatened to flare into a full-fledged battle.

Day after day Nicole stalked the confines of her small prison, her temper smoldering. She was caught like an animal in a trap, a trap that she at once wanted furiously to escape and yet . . .

Christopher fared not much better, although he did have the freedom of the ship, and as he had known he was leaving, he at least had a change of clothing. The lengthy journey seemed endless to him; the miles and miles of churning sea stretched out interminably before him.

The only satisfaction he gained was the knowledge that the longshot he and Jason had counted on had paid off, and he had been able to bring back proof of the British plans to invade New Orleans. But then he smiled wryly to himself—the past weeks the newspapers had been full of that sort of thing.

He could do nothing about Nicole but curse the crazy

impulse that had driven him to such reckless lengths. What in sweet hell am I going to do with her? he thought angrily as the ship plowed its way through the stormy seas. What was he going to write to his grandfather? That particular unpleasant aspect had not occurred to him before, and broodingly he stared out at the tossing, surging waves.

Simon must guess that Nicole was with him. His note to his grandfather had obliquely implied it—and he had told Galena he would see to her mistress. For a brief second the incredible thought occurred to him that even then he had been subconsciously planning to take Nicole with him—if he found her. Even more preposterous and displeasing was the feeling that he would not have left England *without* finding her.

Christopher was in the most tormented quandary of his entire life—he despised the whim that had overtaken him, damned Nicole for being such an overpowering temptation, but he could not deny that he still wanted her, wanted her so badly that he could not envision life without her. And *that* was what really ate at his gut, infuriating and torturing him until he could barely look at her without the urge to close his hands around her slender neck and break once and for all this web of unwilling desire and unnamed emotions that bound him to her.

The long weeks at sea did nothing to resolve his difficulties. The promixity of Nicole and his inability to feed the physical hunger that gnawed at his vitals drove him to pace the deck night after night, his thoughts irretrievably on Nicole, snug in her little cabin.

Oh, he could have forced his way in and taken her, could have ordered Higgins from the room anytime during the day that he wanted, and satisfied his hunger, but he had reached the distasteful point where he craved something more than a swift physical release from the passion that welled inside him. Violently, like a man unexpectedly grasping a white-hot poker, he recoiled from the absurd notion that what he wanted from her was love. The whole idea was ridiculous, and with frustrated loathing he thrust the problem behind him, unwilling to face what was in his heart, what had been in his heart since the night of the thunderstorm at Thibodaux House all those months before.

Their arrival at New Orleans in the second week of November was greeted with relief by everyone. The weather in New Orleans, though, was no more appealing than it had been at sea. A particularly cold, driving rain was blowing in from the coast and whipping across the area, making it an extremely inclement day. The roads were quagmires of mud.

At Christopher's elegant mansion in the Vieux Carré an especially warm and welcoming fire danced on the hearth in the main salon when he and his two companions arrived a short while after docking at the port. A hastily written note carried by one of the many dockside loiterers to the house in the Vieux Carré had prepared Sanderson for their arrival, and in a matter of seconds Nicole found herself efficiently escorted away to the room she had stayed in before they had left for England, while Christopher was instantly served a steaming mug of warm rum punch as he stood by the fire.

Wasting little time, Christopher finished his punch while exchanging the latest news with Sanderson. Almost immediately he departed for the Savage household. He had debated the wisdom of sending a servant around to inquire if the Savages were in residence, but restless and impatient, he had decided not to waste the time. Instead he fought his way through the blowing rain the few blocks to the Savage town house.

Fortunately Jason was at home, somewhat unenthusiastically scanning some business papers, when Christopher was shown into the library. An eager and welcoming smile flitted across Jason's harsh features as he stood up and energetically extended his hand. "By God," he said with half mockery, half seriousness, "it is about time you returned! I had begun to wonder if perhaps my instincts had betrayed me."

Christopher merely grinned as they shook hands and said lightly, "Believe me, there were times I wondered if we were not *both* mad to have considered such a scheme!" Then unable to help himself he announced elatedly, "It worked, Jason! I was at my wit's end, nearly certain I had failed, when events worked out splendidly. Read it for yourself." Handing the memorandum to Jason, he sat down casually on the corner of the desk and added, "It isn't much—but it *is* proof of an invasion and it does give us some desperately needed information."

"Hmm, yes, yes, I see what you mean," Jason commented as he quickly skimmed the brief facts of the memorandum. "But this is exactly what I was hoping for! I must get this to Claiborne immediately—he has been nearly frantic these past months. And the newspapers have not helped matters. It seems every day I read of the imminent invasion of New Orleans, and yet nothing appears to be done about it. The city is still woefully under-manned and the few defenses that exist are totally inadequate."

"Nothing seems to have changed then in the months I have been away," Christopher observed disgustedly.

"Oh, I wouldn't say that!" Jason replied with a slight smile. "Certain things have happened, you know. John Armstrong resigned as Secretary of War and Monroe took over his office. Despite the burning of Washington, we haven't done too badly these past months. The news may not have reached London before you departed, but Sir George Prevost's campaign to invade the United States by way of Lake Champlain and the Hudson Valley came to nothing. One of our young Lieutenants was responsible for that little victory. With only a makeshift flotilla of four ships and ten gunboats, he destroyed the British naval support near Plattsburgh, and Prevost was forced to abandon his plan and return to Canada. And while this news is even older, August, I believe it was, General Andrew Jackson *very* efficiently put an end to the Creek War—so that is one less problem. On the other hand, you have heard no doubt that the country is in deep financial trouble—the Treasury is bankrupt, and it is becoming increasingly harder to find the money to pay for this fiasco. But, all in all, we are managing to hold things together, and given time and a little luck we should come about somewhat tattered but whole."

Christopher only grunted, his lips twisting derisively. "If we can't defend New Orleans against Pakenham's forces, we definitely will not be whole! The British would like nothing better than to take over the entire State of Lousiana and control the Mississippi River. Unless we get some troops here, and soon, they stand a very good chance of doing so. Admiral Cochrane's fleet in the Gulf will provide naval support to Pakenham, and combined with the Army, the British will be damn near capable of running over us like a pack of wolves over penned sheep!"

"Not quite," Jason said slowly. "There is one more piece of news I neglected to pass on—General Ross is dead. He was killed in September during the assault on Baltimore, which failed, I might add. You see, we have been showing a few teeth of our own."

Christopher sighed. "Perhaps you are right—but the outlook is not particularly encouraging. Don't forget that the peace talks in Ghent are traveling at a cripple's pace, and as far as Ghent is concerned, I would not look there for any speedy remedy."

"I agree. But come now, with this memorandum we are certain to convince Andrew Jackson that New Orleans is indeed in peril. And once convinced of that he and his army will be here. Jackson is not about to allow the British to take Louisiana."

Christopher looked skeptical. "I trust you are right. In the meantime what do you advise?"

Jason leaned back in his chair. "I want you to come with me when I give this memorandum to the governor," he said after a moment's deliberation. "Since you were instrumental in obtaining the information, I feel it is only fair to give credit where credit is due. And more importantly, the governor needs every able man on his side." With a bitter smile Jason added, "Our Creole population is, as usual, ignoring the situation, and except for a few Americans most people in the city are pretending that there is no danger. And that is part of what Claiborne is fighting against—apathy and ignorance."

Christopher pulled a face. "I certainly hope you know what you are doing—knowingly sponsoring a ragtag privateer like myself to the governor! Aren't you afraid if he finds out my connection with Lafitte it will ruin your standing with him?"

A peculiar expression crossed Jason's face, but then he seemed to recover himself, for, the green eyes bright with mockery, he drawled, "My dear fellow, it would take more than a scamp like yourself to ruin me! And you must remember that part of my usefulness to the governor is the very fact that I know so many ragtag privateers!"

An answering gleam of mockery danced in Christopher's eyes. "In that case I am at your service, sir!"

The meeting with the governor was arranged immediately, and watching Claiborne as he read the memorandum, Christopher was never quite certain whether the news contained therein pleased him or alarmed him further. Claiborne's face was totally expressionless as he finished reading the memorandum and laid it carefully on the highly polished surface of his desk. Calmly he folded his hands before him and with bright eyes regarded the two men seated in front of him.

"Well," he said slowly, "if this doesn't rouse Jackson, nothing will! I only hope he will realize that the British objective *is* New Orleans and not Mobile. He and Monroe both believe that the British will try to attack through Mobile, and consequently they are concentrating their efforts in that area." Claiborne's soft Virginia accent, even after eleven years in New Orleans, was still evident as he continued, "I myself am of the opinion the attack will be from the coast. But then I am only a mere civilian," he finished glumly.

There was little either Christopher or Jason could add to what he already knew and after several minutes of polite conversation, during which, much to Christopher's discomfort, the governor praised his accomplishments, the two men departed from Claiborne's house on Toulouse Street.

The rain had stopped, but after glancing at the leaden skies above, Christopher remarked, "If we hurry we might make it to our respective homes before another downpour overtakes us. I suggest that unless you have something further to discuss, we do precisely that."

Casting a wary eye at the gathering rain clouds, Jason agreed. "From the looks of the sky, we may end up swimming, *mon ami!* And for the moment I think we have done all that we can. Claiborne will do what he has to, and as soon as I learn anything, I will send you word." Jason hesitated, a curious expression flitting over his face. Almost diffidently he asked, "Would you care to dine with Catherine and me on Thursday? There have been certain events that have taken place in the New Orleans area that I would like to talk over with you. Now is not the time and I am not free until that evening."

Ignoring the few splatters of rain that were beginning to fall, Christopher regarded Jason consideringly. "Is it important? Something I should take action on?"

Again there was that odd hesitation about the other man, and Christopher had the impression that Jason was holding something back. But before Christopher could demand bluntly what Jason was hiding, Jason said, "You may consider it important and you may feel compelled to do something." And as Christopher frowned, Jason added, "I do not mean to be mysterious, but quite frankly I haven't the time at the moment to go into a great deal of detail. You may hear it before I tell you, and I ask that you keep an open mind and do not fly off in a rage. Remember the Creoles love gossip, and rumors are not always the truth of the matter."

Christopher's jaw took on a stubborn slant and the gold eyes narrowed as he snapped, "You may not be trying to be mysterious, but from where I stand you're doing a bloody damn good job of it!"

A brief smile tugged at Jason's full mouth. "I know, my friend, I know, but bear with me. It is definite then? You will come to dine on Thursday?"

"You know damn certain I'll be there!"

Jason strode off and Christopher began to walk slowly toward home, his thoughts on Nicole.

Hot-tempered to a fault, a bewitching little slut, as beautiful as she was mercurial, and probably hating the very sight of him, he wanted no other woman—at least not for the moment, he thought hastily, unwilling to look beyond the next few weeks . . . perhaps months?

He absolutely refused to think too far into the future, obstinately determined to take each day one at a time and not bother himself with what eventually happened between them. He never had with any other woman, so why with Nicole?

Predictably, Nicole was not in any frame of mind to follow a course of "wait and see." She was understandably furious at Christopher's actions—furious, and yet on the other hand deplorably aware that with him was where she most longed to be. But not like this, she thought angrily, not thrown over his shoulder like some piece of booty and carried off to shame and disgrace.

If the choice had been hers, if she had deliberately chosen to sail with him, if he had said, "Come," and she had made the decision herself to follow him, then she would not have resented so bitterly the position in which she found herself. Shame and disgrace were something she could have faced, faced gladly if Christopher had given her the choice. But he had not! He had callously ignored her wishes, her emotions and literally torn her from England. It was, she decided heatedly, another example of his arrogant, high-handed actions.

Not adept at hiding her feelings, her face grew stormy, and it was only when she noticed the apprehensive expression on the face of the young black girl hurriedly pressed into service as a lady's maid that she forced herself to think of something else. Throwing the girl a charming smile, she said, "Please, don't be frightened of me! I occasionally scowl rather blackly, and I have a terrible temper, but I seldom vent it on my servants. Now, tell me, what is your name?"

Shyly the girl murmured, "Naomi, ma'am. Mister Sanderson says I am to be your maid until he can hire someone else."

Watching as Naomi deftly arranged for a bath to be drawn and reverently laid out one of several gowns left behind for various reasons when she had sailed for England, Nicole decided privately that the services of this girl were all that she would need. There was no reason to hire another Mauer—this time she was not going to be entering polite society. A mistress—and she was guessing that was the role Christopher had picked for her—was a very different position from that of a ward! A tiny tight smile curved her mouth, and she thought grimly that Christopher would find her a damned uncomfortable lady-bird! She'd make certain of *that!*

Naomi's announcement that the bath was ready for her broke into Nicole's thoughts, and pushing aside the problem of her future battle with Christopher, she let herself be undressed and helped into the large brass tub.

The bath was sheer heaven. After the many weeks at sea, of making do with hurried saltwater sponge-downs, the hot fresh water was like paradise. Luxuriously Nicole submerged her slender body, delighting in the caress of the delicately scented water. Sighing with pleasure, she leaned back and, resting her head on the rim of the tub, decided it was almost worth going without a bath for weeks to have one feel this good. Eventually, though, the water began to cool, and after scrubbing herself from head to toe, she had Naomi help wash her hair.

Feeling cleaner and more relaxed than she had in weeks, Nicole sat wrapped in a large fluffy towel before the fire in her room, as Naomi patiently brushed and combed the long strands dry. The soothing constant motion of the brush nearly put her to sleep, and once the waving hair was dried to Naomi's satisfaction, Nicole decided to lay down for a while.

It was late afternoon by now. The dark sky promised more rain before the day ended, and the thought of stretching out on a *real* bed was more than Nicole could resist. She slept soundly, waking to a darkened and silent room some hours later. The thick feather mattress was like a cloud, and with a low purr of enjoyment Nicole snuggled back down into its welcoming softness, unwilling to leave the warmth and comfort. But Naomi's entrance just then, a lit candle in her hand, put all thought of sleep from Nicole's mind.

"Yes? What is it?" she asked.

"Oh, ma'am, I didn't mean to wake you! Master Christopher just wanted me to see if you were still asleep."

"You didn't wake me. I was just on the point of ringing for you," Nicole replied untruthfully.

Reassured that she had given no offense and deciding that waiting on Miss Nicole was going to be pleasant work indeed, Naomi lit the lamps and proceeded with ready skill to help her new mistress dress.

The gown laid out earlier was of soft worked muslin, in a particularly pleasing shade of pale green. It was a beautiful gown, but Nicole, thankful to be out of the hated bronze silk she had worn for the past several weeks, would have adored it if it had been made of cotton sacks.

The one item of clothing not left behind had been shoes, and staring at her bare feet peeping out from under the flounces of her skirt, she was reminded painfully and poignantly of that evening in Bermuda. *How different my future might have been if I had followed Allen's advice*, she thought regretfully. And again she wondered about Allen's fate. Christopher had promised he would be freed, and in this instance she wanted desperately to believe he had kept his word. There were bitterness and recriminations enough between them without having the added burden of Allen's death dividing them. Allen *must* be free—free and with the British. Deliberately Nicole closed her mind to any other explanation, unable to think of Christopher intentionally lying to her and coolly turning Allen over to the Americans to be hanged as a spy. There was a great deal she would believe of Christopher Saxon, but not that!

The problem of the lack of shoes was solved simply by wearing the slightly disreputable bronze silk slippers she had brought with her. A spangled shawl draped carelessly around her shoulders completed her attire, and after a brief glance at herself in the mirror, noting with satisfaction the clean shine to the gently waving locks, Nicole slowly descended the stairs to the main salon.

Christopher was there before her as she expected, but what she hadn't expected was the shaft of half pleasure, half pain that shot through her when she saw him standing casually before the fire, one arm resting on the creamy marble mantel.

Glancing up from his contemplation of the leaping flames, Christopher inquired politely, "Did you sleep well?"

"Yes. A genuine bed was something of a novelty after the accommodations provided by Captain Baker," Nicole replied evenly, not certain of herself or his mood.

He appeared very much at ease; his dark features were unreadable as she stared at him. Dressed in a pair of slim-fitting yellow pantaloons and an exquisitely cut coat of bottle green, he was enough to make any young woman's heart pound in her breast, and unfortunately Nicole was very much aware of his tall, hard body as he strode across the room and courteously offered her a chair

461

by the fire. She hesitated, then deciding that she, too, could act as if there was nothing between them, graciously consented to be seated.

They were both stilted in their movements and conversation, both acting much in the manner of two strangers meeting for the first time. Civilly Christopher asked, "Would you care for a glass of sherry? I believe we have plenty of time until dinner is served."

Feeling like a stuffed doll, a painted inane smile on her lips, Nicole murmured quietly, "Yes. Sherry will be fine."

Christopher walked to the other end of the room, to where a tray with several crystal decanters was placed, and in silence poured out a small glass of the pale amber liquid. Still in silence he came to her side and handed the sherry to her, their fingers touching as the glass was placed in her outstretched hand. Both reacted as if stung; Christopher's hand abruptly fell away and Nicole's fingers nearly jerked the glass from his grasp.

The silence between them was uncomfortable; both were almost unbearably aware of the other, each waiting for the other to make the first move, to say the first word. Neither did.

The silence was like a third presence in the elegant room; the crack and pop of the fire burning brightly on the hearth echoed in the uncomfortable quietness, intensifying the silence. As the moments passed, Nicole shifted uneasily on her chair and, for something to do, cautiously sipped the sherry, not really wanting it.

Christopher had returned to his position by the fire; his profile was presented to her as, apparently ignoring her, he once again seemed fascinated by the leaping yellow and orange flame. A half-finished snifter of brandy stood on the mantel. As Nicole watched him, noting idly the way his blue-black hair seemed to curl more crisply in damp weather, he reached for the snifter and in one motion tossed the contents down. Straightening, he turned to look directly at her.

With a quizzical smile tugging at the corner of his mouth, he asked mockingly, "Well? Don't you have anything to say? I've been waiting these past moments for that scathing tongue of yours to annihilate me. Don't tell me you have lost the power of speech. Come now, expectorate your spleen, as I'm certain you have been longing to do for weeks!"

Nicole stiffened, her topaz eyes beginning to flash with ready temper. With difficulty she controlled the strongest urge to do exactly as he said, but instead she said levelly,

"Railing against you will gain me nothing. I have, I hope, outgrown some of my foolishness, and losing my temper is one thing I have no intention of doing, despite the provocation."

One thick black eyebrow flew up derisively. "For the moment I'll take your word for it," Christopher replied dryly. "But I'm sure you *do* have something to say. Some condemnation of my conduct?"

Nicole stood up and very deliberately placed her unfinished glass on a nearby table. "Yes, I have something to say, but more to the point I have a question to ask. May I?" she inquired sarcastically. At Christopher's curt nod, she requested bluntly, "What do you plan to do with me?"

From the bronze slippers on her feet to the top of her head Christopher's eyes traveled over her, almost caressingly, halting for a brief second on the high bosom, the fiery gleam of the dark hair, before finally coming back and stopping on her full mouth. "Oh, I can think of several plans for you, my dear," he murmured, "but I doubt you would agree with them." His eyes still on her mouth, he walked over to her, standing so close that there were barely inches between their bodies. "I want you, Nicole," he muttered honestly. "I want you as I have never wanted any woman I have ever known." The gold eyes were bright with sudden desire as he said quickly, "You were willing to be Robert's mistress, so why not mine?"

As Nicole stood frozen with icy anger before him, he continued rashly, "I gave you your chance to lead a respectable life. I saw you safely launched into society, but no, that wasn't what you wanted. Oh, no! You were willing to throw it all away just to become Robert's plaything. Well, my dear, you'll be much better off as my plaything than Robert's. Believe me, I shall be extremely generous with you—your own house on the ramparts, your own carriage, servants, anything you like. Just name your price."

The topaz eyes, like two great golden-brown jewels in her pale face, shimmered with anger, as she spat, "You overestimate your charm! If I were dying and you had the gift of life, my answer would still be the same—absolutely not! Be your mistress? Ha! I would rather whore along Tchoupitoulas Street, submitting to any man who wanted me, than to suffer *your* embrace!"

Christopher's jaw went taut, his lips thinned as angrily he reached for her. "So you say, madame!" he snarled against her mouth. "So you say, but your body tells me something different!"

Brutally his mouth closed over hers, forcing her lips apart. His arms tightened unyieldingly around her, instantly awakening memories of other times in his arms, of other moments shared between them. If he had continued to kiss her in such a cruel manner she might have been able to resist him, but as if sensing that sheer force would avail him nothing, Christopher's mouth slackened its painful assault and began to move gently across hers, urging and yet demanding an answer to his rising passion.

Feeling the familiar curl of desire swirling in her stomach, Nicole fought desperately against it, for once determined not to allow him to sweep her into his dark power. But Christopher was too much for her; his hands tightened around her waist, drawing her nearer to the warmth of his body, making her physically aware even through the restraint of their clothing of how much he did indeed want her. His hands left her waist, gently exploring her hips, traveling up her slender spine in one long exquisitely tantalizing caress; his lips, warm and desire-drugging, were still locked on hers, and Nicole felt what control she had slipping.

Christopher, blind to anything but the desire scorching his veins, oblivious to the battle raging within the woman in his arms, drew her gently and inexorably down on the sofa near the fire, his hands instinctively finding the silken flesh beneath the muslin gown. At the touch of his hand on her thigh Nicole gave an anguished moan, wanting him to take her with every fiber of her being, yet knowing if she did, she was lost. Fighting against herself as much as Christopher, frantically Nicole twisted beneath him, seeking vainly to escape the well of desire into which she was falling. The movements of her body only heightened Christopher's compelling urge to know once again the ecstasy of joining his body with hers, making him kiss her with deepening urgency.

Christopher stiffened at a sudden knock on the door. With a muffled curse he sat up and demanded, "Yes, who is it?"

"Sanderson," was the calm reply. "Dinner is served, sir."

Standing up and straightening his clothes, Christopher snapped, "Very well. We shall be right there." Turning to Nicole, he muttered half teasingly, half angrily, "It appears that this interesting conversation, too, will have to wait until later! Are you ready?"

Not looking at him, with a hand that trembled she re-arranged her skirts and said in a voice that only shook slightly, "For dinner, yes!"

Christopher grinned at her. "But, my dear, what else?"

Resisting the urge to slap his face, Nicole walked stiffly to the carved doors that led to the main hall, allowing Christopher to open the doors for her, her hand resting correctly on his arm.

She and Christopher conversed with ridiculous polite-ness during dinner—partly because of Sanderson's hov-ering presence and partly because neither could think of anything to say . . . except something totally outrageous and provoking. Both, though, had their minds on the eve-ning ahead, and perhaps that explained why the cook was slightly disappointed at the amount of food returned to the kitchen.

After dinner, feeling replete, yet tingling with wariness, Nicole demurely allowed herself to be led back to the salon they had occupied before dinner. Seated on the sofa that had nearly been her undoing, she accepted with pleasure the demitasse cup of sweet black coffee that Sanderson offered from an ornate silver tray. Not so Christopher; with a careless hand he waved the butler away, preferring instead a snifter of brandy.

Dinner had been a time of truce, an uneasy truce, but a truce nonetheless. And Christopher made that perfectly clear the second the door closed behind Sanderson. "Well?" he asked peremptorily. "My proposition still stands. And now that you have had a few moments in which to consider it, don't try to fob me off with the usual feminine prattle that you need time to think!"

It was an unfair attack—both knew that Nicole had never even consented to think over his offer. Her eyes gleaming with resentment, the soft mouth hardening with resolution, she snapped, "There was never any question of my considering your less-than-respectable proposal! I told you then and I'll tell you now—I will *not* become your mistress!"

Her bosom heaving with agitation, she stood up abruptly, and her voice was shaking with suppressed emo-tion as she continued hotly, "I am surprised you even want such a depraved creature as myself near you! After all, I am so without gratitude that I would turn my back on the very agreeable life you had arranged for me, insult the hospitality of your grandfather, align myself with a man unworthy of the name, a man who was my own mother's lover!" The topaz eyes shimmering with unshed tears, the full red mouth trembling with the effort to hold back those same tears, she cried in anguish and anger, "Oh, yes! Let us not forget that I am my mother's daughter! And we both know what she was like—a liar, a betrayer, and an adulteress! And, Christopher, I promise you —if you force me to let go I shall show you exactly how like my mother I can be! For God's sake let me go! Give me the passage back to England! Send me away from you so that we both can find peace."

Christopher whitened at her words. Bitterly he snarled, "I cannot. I have thought of all that you say—it has torn me apart day after day, night after night! But let you go, I cannot!" It was an admission he had not wanted to make, an admission he had tried to hide from himself. And furious that he had given her, as he thought, another weapon over him, with a jerky movement he swallowed the brandy in one long gulp. Slamming the empty snifter down on the mantel so hard that it splintered, without another word he stalked swiftly across the room to the door, his anger and rage apparent in every step he took. Standing with his hand on the door, he glanced back at Nicole standing frozen by the sofa; then there was just the banging of the door as he departed. That look he sent her the last moment before hurling out the door was one of such loathing and fury that she recoiled from it, and yet, and yet, for just a moment there had been a flicker deep in that golden gaze of something, something like . . . like . . .

Tossing on her bed that night, again and again Nicole relived those tense, revealing moments, unable to believe that he had said what he had. To know that Christopher, too, felt that invisible bond between them was encouraging, but that he also hated and resented it bitterly was very obvious. What am I to do, she thought unhappily. Stay? Hope that in time he will come to love me, if he is even capable of love? Or continue to fight against him, try to make him understand that we are better off apart? But would you be? her mind whispered insidiously.

Her dilemma was unanswerable. Prudence, common sense, past experience, and a lively sense of self-preservation clearly dictated that she flee. But her heart, never a very reliable organ, twisted from the idea of deliberately cutting him away from her.

Restless, heartsick, undecided, and bedeviled, she gave up the pretense of sleep and left her bed. Barefooted, wearing only a thin, nearly transparent nightdress of cream-colored cambric, she prowled around her room. The fire had nearly died, and for something to do she added a few small logs from the tidy pile laid to one side of the hearth, stirring and blowing on the glowing embers until the fire caught and began to flicker and leap with a life of its own. The room was in darkness except for the shimmering of the flames as they danced and painted shadows on the walls. A faint gleam of moonlight crept through the shuttered windows, and as she pulled the wooden shutters aside she discovered a full silvery moon high overhead. The rain had stopped once again, but the dampness and wet lingered, tickling Nicole's nose as she took a deep breath.

Sighing, she turned back to her bed, knowing that sleep would not visit her this night. Sitting on the bed, her knees drawn up under her chin, her hands clasped lightly around her ankles, she stared blankly at the fire. What was she to do? She had no money of her own. She had no place to go. England was far away, too far to offer an immediate solution to her problem. Dismally she acknowledged that as long as she loved Christopher Saxon there never was going to be a solution to her dilemma.

She had never stopped loving him, she admitted sadly. Yes, she had tried to convince herself otherwise, but there was no denying that she had fooled only herself, herself and her foolish heart. Whatever he was—brutal, arrogant, one minute tender, the next savage—she unfortunately loved him. What was she going to do about it?

Surprisingly, considering the state of her heart, she longed most desperately to leave. There was nothing that she could see to be gained by staying except more heartache, more disillusionment. Christopher would never love her. He wanted her, that she would not deny, but wanting had little to do with love, and love was what she wanted most.

She bit back a half-hysterical giggle when she thought of the expression on his face if she were to say, "Love me! Want me not only with your body, but with your heart as well. Love me, damn you!"

But what was the use? She wasn't even certain in her own heart that she could forgive everything that had passed between them—especially his latest high-handed actions. Then she smiled cynically; there she went again, fooling herself. As much as she wished to pretend otherwise, if Christopher lifted one finger, gave her one indication that he wanted more than just a warm body in his bed, she would fling aside all the doubts, the bitterness, the past, everything and leap willy-nilly into his arms. She *loved* him, goddamnit!

Lost in her own unpleasant thoughts, the abrupt opening of her door caught her by surprise, and she couldn't quite control the small gasp that escaped her at the sound. Her startled gaze fell on Christopher as he stood reeling slightly in the doorway.

It was obvious that he was half drunk—his hair, rakishly disheveled, spilled onto his forehead; the pristine white cravat was no longer so neatly arranged; the bottle-green jacket was swung carelessly over one shoulder; the tail of his shirt was freed from the yellow pantaloons. With a decidedly wicked leer he slammed the door shut, causing Nicole to flinch and to eye him warily as he stood there. Only by the greatest control was she able to remain precisely where she was, stoutly refusing to be intimidated by his looming presence. Every instinct called out to scramble away as he approached, but caution counseled she do nothing to enrage or antagonize him, and so outwardly serene, she looked up at him. Coolly she asked, "What do you want, Christopher?"

A crooked grin curved his mouth. "Ah, now that is a very good question, my dear," he replied levelly, the words perfectly clear. Casually, as if he did it frequently, he sat down on the corner of her bed, throwing the jacket on the floor, and beginning absently to take off his cravat. He said slowly, "I've thought about that a lot this evening. What exactly *do* I want?" Not looking at Nicole, he finished with the cravat, wrenched off his boots, and began to undo the shirt.

Her mouth dry, she watched as a rabbit watches a rattlesnake, fearful of moving, knowing a swift retreat is the only safety, yet frozen to the spot by the other's mesmerizing quality. When the shirt joined the other clothing on the floor, he stood up, and as he commenced to unfasten the yellow pantaloons, some of her rigid control broke and she croaked indignantly, "What do you think you are doing?"

Not stopping or hesitating in the least with what he was doing, he glanced over at her. "Well, now," he murmured, "that question has a direct bearing on what I want. I *want* you, my dear. And I *think* I am going to have you!"

"You're drunk!" Nicole accused, unconsciously beginning to edge away from him.

"No. You're wrong there," he answered quite without heat. "I have been drinking, drinking a great deal, but

I am not drunk. Besotted, mad perhaps, and filled with longing for a bewitching creature who gives me no peace" —his voice lost some of its detachment and hardened— "now *that* I am!"

Sliding inch by inch away from him, Nicole swallowed nervously; she had never seen him like this before. Maybe he wasn't drunk, as he said, but he was certainly behaving queerly. He bent over, pulling off the pantaloons, and surreptitiously Nicole angled one foot toward the floor. But quick as a striking snake Christopher's hand struck, capturing her wrist. "No," he said quietly. "You are not going anywhere—at least not until I have finished with you."

Her cheeks rosy with temper and apprehension, she fought against the hard iron grip. "Damn you, let me go! And get out of my bedroom." Her eyes met his, and what she read in the gold depths increased her now-desperate struggle to escape him.

Unmoved by either her words or her actions, Christopher only said softly, "No," and quite, quite deliberately with his other hand ripped the cambric gown from her body.

There was never any question of her escaping him, though she fought as fiercely and furiously as she was capable. Ignoring the blows she rained about his head, oblivious to the vicious movement of her knee, he simply pulled her into his arms, the thrashing of her naked body against his only adding to his heightened awareness. Effortlessly he found her mouth, feeding on the soft lips like a man with a long hunger to assuage, his tongue exploring and tasting the sweet wine within.

Despising herself, Nicole could feel her body beginning to awaken to the sensual magic of his as he continued to kiss her. His hands, when not holding her prisoner, lightly caressed her. His mouth left her lips, traveling with a trail of fire down her neck to her breast, and breathlessly Nicole whispered, "Don't, please, Christopher, don't do this to me."

He stopped and stared up at her, beguiled and enchanted by the beautiful features so near him. "Stop?" he muttered thickly. "I cannot. You say you do not want me. But you lie, Nicole, you have always lied. If you did not want me, *this* would not happen." And gently his hand caressed her breasts; the nipples, betraying her, hardened instantly into tiny mounds of desire. "Nor this!" he added softly, his hand insidiously sliding between her legs, touching tenderly the yielding softness he found.

With a low, ashamed moan of pleasure, Nicole melted, unable and unwilling to deny that she, too, wanted the physical meeting of their bodies.

It was like the night of the thunderstorm—both of them submerging all their doubts and questions, reality being only the touch and caress of the other. Nothing else existed except this world of warmth and softness, tenderness and savagery—love and hate.

Nicole did not deny him; her body responded as always to his lightest touch—nor did she remain passive and merely let him have his way. She, too, wanted him, wanted that glorious release that only Christopher could give her. Once she had lost the battle against him, her hands eagerly explored the hard, muscled body sprawled next to her.

Like a wondering child discovering some wondrous enchanted land, her fingers traveled over the curiously soft hair on his chest, down across the flat, taut stomach, delighting in the way his body shivered at her touch.

"Ah, Jesus, Nicole," he groaned softly, when at last she found the rigid, pulsating hardness of him. "You're a witch, my love. A witch with a terrible power over me."

Hungrily he drew her next to him, his body straining against hers, his hands ferverishly moving along the slender spine, gently fondling the gentle swell of her hips, until not content with that, he shifted their bodies so that he half lay across her, his mouth able now to taste and excite the tempting honey of her body.

He was like a starving man at a feast, Nicole's long-limbed, slim shape his only sustenance as hungrily his mouth burned a trail of desire down her body. Kissing the madly beating pulse at the base of her throat, his lips slid down her chest to her breast; his teeth gently nibbled on the hardened upthrust nipples. One hand tangled in the burnished fire of her hair, the other lightly caressed and kneaded her flat stomach, tantalizing her, teasing her, by deliberately not reaching where she was throbbing and most hungry for his probing touch.

She was aflame with desire, too long denied his possession and driven by an emotion as old as the world; without volition her body betrayed her longing by the sensual motions she made, her back arching to meet Christopher's hand, her hips twisting helplessly in erotic rhythms.

Slowly Christopher slid his body over hers, slipping easily between her thighs, his knees holding her legs outstretched. But he did not take her, nor did his mouth reach for hers again; instead his lips traveled lingeringly down her smooth skin, past her stomach, filling her with a giddy anticipation as the warm mouth slipped lower and lower until . . .

Nicole's entire body leaped with half-shocked, half-stunned pleasure when his lips found the delicate silken flesh between her thighs, his hands lifting her to meet his searching mouth. Instinctively she recoiled from this new and intoxicating havoc Christopher was lavishing on her, but he would not let her escape; his hands tightened on her hips, holding her to him, as softly his tongue caressed and explored her. The touch of his mouth, there where she never dreamed of it, was exquisite agony. Nearly maddened by the unfamiliar, and yet so well remembered, sensations engulfing her, Nicole was an abandoned creature, aware only of Christopher and what he was doing to her, her head twisting frantically from side to side, her body arching and rushing up to greet eagerly the darting of his tongue. Sobbing aloud her intense pleasure, trembling with the near ecstasy that was beginning to shake her body, blindly she reached out for him, wanting violently to touch him, to taste him, to feel him, to communicate somehow to him this wild, fierce enchantment. Her groping fingers encountered the crisp darkness of his head enfolded between her thighs, and with a low animallike purr of satisfaction, she clutched the black hair, reveling in the very texture of it. Unconsciously she urged him on, unaware that her soft cries of pleasure were as potent as any caress, driving Christopher to increase the tempo, until Nicole felt wave after wave of the most powerful and acute surge of ecstasy break over her, leaving her gasping and shuddering, her body floating in some blissful newly discovered world of physical enjoyment.

Limp and satiated, too replete to move, she was only dimly aware of Christopher's body covering hers, his mouth finding her lips unerringly as quickly and gently he penetrated her. She could taste herself on his lips, smell the faint muskiness of herself as he kissed her deeply and hungrily, his body moving slowly on hers. With a jolt she felt desire begin anew to flood her; the earlier lethargy vanished abruptly, leaving her eagerly thrusting up to meet the plunge of Christopher's hard body, her lips moving sweetly against his, her tongue a small brand of fire as she returned his searching caress.

With the taste of her still on his tongue, Christopher was oblivious to anything but the slender body beneath his, the searing caress of her hands as they roamed at will

471

across his scarred back down to his driving hips. And in that instant every other woman he had ever known faded forever from his mind and there was only Nicole, Nicole with her welcoming softness, her proud young bosom crushed under his chest, and her hands driving him nearly wild, until he could bear it no longer, and with a deep, husky growl in his throat he spilled himself into her.

Nicole felt the eruption of Christopher's held-back passion, and the jump and convulsion of his long body against hers was bittersweet. Her own body uncontrollably throbbed and shook with the force of another piercingly sensual gust of fulfillment, proving once again how effortlessly he could lift her to the heights of passion, how powerless she was in his arms.

37

The cold gray light of winter dawn was filtering into the room when Christopher awoke. For several seconds he lay there, not quite certain where he was. Then as Nicole moved lightly in her sleep, her slender body pressing closer to his, awareness and the memory of last night came hurtling back.

Gently, so as not to disturb her, he shifted his big body away from her and, propping himself up on one elbow, stared intently down into her sleeping face, wondering bleakly why she of all women should be the one he wanted most in the world. And want her he did. Just watching her as she lay sleeping was enough to make his pulse stir, his breath come faster, his body harden with desire, and not even conscious that he did it, he slowly slid the blankets from her body, his eyes caressing her. Ah, Jesus, he thought dully, she was fashioned by the devil to make men mad, and I have no defense against her. What in hell's creation am I going to do? I cannot tear her from me, she has sunk her fangs in too deeply, has twisted herself around me, until all I know is that I want her . . . that she is mine.

For a long, long time he stared down into Nicole's face, noting, with a derisive smile at his own enchantment, the way the long curly lashes lay like great dark shadows upon the pale cheeks. Her lips were bruised ruby, the soft fullness inviting, but with a great effort Christopher stilled the sudden impulse to lean over and kiss her awake.

Chilled by the cold air on her naked body, Nicole stirred uneasily in her sleep, and not wishing to awaken her, Christopher gently replaced the blankets and determinedly left her bed. If she woke, he would make love to her again, and while his body was eager for her, his mind wanted time—time in which to think, to puzzle out this dilemma in which he found himself.

Slipping quickly into his scattered clothes, he departed silently from her room and walked quietly down the long

473

carpeted hall and crossed quickly into his own room. He tossed his jacket and crumpled cravat on a chair and dropped his boots near the door. With deft, unhurried movements he stripped off the remainder of his clothing and crawled beneath the blankets of his own bed.

Sleep was the farthest thought from his mind as he lay there, his hands behind his dark head, his eyes fixed blankly on the heavy damask canopy of the bed. Last night he had hoped to resolve something, and instead he was more deeply entangled in his own emotions.

When he had said he was not drunk last night, he had told the truth. He had gone out to a waterfront dive to put Nicole from his mind, but he discovered to his horror, and not a little anger, that she was still there, tempting and tantalizingly out of reach. The later the hour grew, the more he convinced himself that he had only to take her one more time, to feel once again that exquisite shudder she gave when, despite herself, she was swept along with his lovemaking, and then he would be free. Then he could set her aside and live as he had done in the past.

And so with that determination firmly and stubbornly fixed in his brain, he had proceeded to do exactly that. Unfortunately his actions had not given him the answer he sought. His mouth curved with displeasure as he sourly acknowledged he still wanted Nicole, wanted her as badly as he had last night.

And the new and startling knowledge grew that not only did he want her body—he wanted her! All of her, her thoughts, her laughter, yes, even her stormy fits of temper. For just a moment he tried to envision a life in which there was no furious, topaz-eyed vixen to hurl herself angrily at him. It was not possible. Whatever Nicole was, he wanted her. And despised himself for doing so.

You *are* mad, he decided without rancor. Like Nicole, he found no solution to his dilemma, only more confusion and uncertainty.

He was still lying there, his mind exhausted and weary from the seemingly unresolvable problem, when Higgins entered.

Glancing at the bed and seeing that Christopher was awake, he said cheerfully, "Well, good morning to you, sir! Would like some coffee brought to you or would you prefer to wait until you have dressed?"

Christopher merely grunted, and taking the sound to mean no, Higgins began to pick up the clothing strewn about the room. Having put the room to rights, the little man crossed to the shuttered windows and briskly opened them to let what daylight there was come filtering into the room. Looking outside at the sky, Higgins observed, "Hmmm, I think we'll have another day of rain, by the size of those black clouds crowding the horizon. If you have any plans for going out, I'd suggest that you cancel them."

Knowing further concentration was useless, Christopher threw back the blankets and walked over to a marble-topped washstand. Throwing some cold water onto his face, he said disagreeably, "Since when has the weather ever deterred me? And now since you're so goddamn eager to get the day started, make yourself useful and lay out some clothes for me."

An hour later a freshly shaved and bathed Christopher Saxon slowly sipped a cup of strong black coffee and watched dispassionately as Higgins laid out his apparel for the day. It was very fashionable town wear—a vest of flowered silk, skintight pantaloons in pale gold broadcloth, and a long coat of dark forest green.

He left the house about nine o'clock and sauntered to Maspero's Exchange. At this time of the morning it was not very crowded, and with ease Christopher found a table in one corner of the long wooden building and ordered *café au lait*.

Christopher did not remain seated by himself for long; his coffee had barely arrived when Eustace Croix sauntered over to the table and joined him.

"Ah, so you are back," Eustace began by way of greeting, a wide smile revealing two rows of startling white teeth. "You know, *mon ami,* you have a disconcerting way of disappearing and then as calmly reappearing. I have remarked on it often during the years, but you always brush me aside. This time I will have an answer! Where in the devil's name have you been for the past six months or so? Exciting things have been happening in our city, I can tell you that!" Eustace finished with a wink. His black eyes were bold in an olive complexion.

A heavy dark eyebrow was cocked at him. "Oh?" Christopher inquired dryly. "What? A new cock that is the strongest and fiercest around? A horse that can run like wind? Or, yes, it must be! You have a new quadroon mistress!" Christopher ended with a grin, his gold eyes dancing with mockery.

"*Mon ami,* you wound me!" Eustace cried dramatically, his own gaze bright with laughter. Sobering suddenly he said, "Have you heard of Lafitte? Of what has befallen him?"

Christopher stiffened, going very still. "No," he said casually. "What has our friend Jean been doing lately."

"Hiding," came the blunt reply. "The so proper and patriotic Commodore Patterson and Colonel Ross of the Army have destroyed Barataria. In September they attacked the stronghold and overran the place." With a satisfied expression on his face he added, "But the victory was not as complete as if should have been—neither Jean nor Pierre was there."

"Pierre?" Christopher queried sharply. "The last I heard he was in the calaboose."

Eustace grinned. "Ah, yes, for a while perhaps, but have you ever known the Lafittes not to manage to free themselves? Pierre along with three negroes escaped not many days before the attack on Barataria, much to the consternation of the military. According to the rumors I have heard, though, Pierre is quite ill. And Jean is in hiding—Dominique You and scores of the others are currently cooling their heels in the calaboose, and Barataria is in the hands of the military."

Christopher's face was grim and hard as he asked, "And Claiborne? I suppose he is extremely pleased with himself?"

"Now there you have me, *mon ami.* I must tell you that there is some mystery about the entire affair." Leaning forward confidentially, Eustace said, "I have heard that Lafitte actually wrote to the governor prior to the attack. Certainly it is known the governor called a meeting of his advisors to discuss something very important to do with Lafitte, that I know. Gossip has it that Lafitte offered to help defend our fair city, in the event that the British actually attempted to descend upon us." Carelessly Eustace revealed the Creole contempt for such an idea, "Me, I do not think such a thing is possible. Claiborne is a nervous old woman, seeing wicked things where there are none."

Controlling his temper with difficulty, Christopher remained silent, furious with both Eustace's attitude and with the knowledge that Savage had deliberately not informed him of Lafitte's fate. Savage must have known, must have even sat in on this meeting that Eustace spoke of. And probably, he thought viciously, decided along with the others to authorize the attack on Barataria! Goddamn him!

He had known that he and Jason were on opposite sides when it came to Lafitte and his activities, but he had not thought that the Barataria situation presented such a problem that it required the efforts of the United

States Army to solve it! He supposed he was not thinking very clearly, but the news had been an unexpected and unpleasant shock, and he had a certain amount of loyalty to Lafitte. He was regretfully angry and bitterly resentful to think that while he had been in England, ostensibly with the same goal in mind as Jason and the governor, they had been plotting to destroy a man known to be his friend.

It cost an effort, but after a moment Christopher said indifferently to Eustace, "So Lafitte is no longer at Barataria and his men are in the calaboose. Very interesting, my friend. And as you remarked earlier, things have been happening while I have been gone."

"Yes. And that brings me back to my original question. *Mon ami,* where have you been these past months?"

Christopher returned a light answer, adroitly turning the conversation to less personal matters, and after a bit Eustace was busy passing on bits of tittle-tattle that Christopher barely heard, his mind still on the news of Lafitte's destruction. He finished his coffee, and in no mood to be entertained by Eustace's lightly malicious chatter, he excused himself, claiming a prior appointment.

Jason's peculiar manner yesterday came back to him, and with a mirthless smile he recalled the advice not to jump to conclusions. Well, he wouldn't, but Jason had better damn well have a good explanation, and he sure as hell wasn't waiting until Thursday to talk with him! Savage would see him today, or else . . .

Jason was in the midst of a meeting in his home when Christopher's card was presented to him a few minutes later. Irritably he glanced at it, having a very good idea of why Saxon was here. Wisely he realized there was nothing for it but to see him immediately. He didn't relish the thought of what Christopher was capable of doing if he pushed him too far. Murmuring an apology, Jason left the room and walked impatiently to the small salon where Christopher waited.

One look at Christopher's tight-lipped features was enough to tell Jason that his hunch had been right. Resignedly he asked, "You've heard about Lafitte, I take it."

"You're damn right about that!" Christopher spat, his eyes gleaming gold between the dark lashes. "Why in the hell didn't you tell me yesterday? Why did you have to be so goddamn mysterious about it?"

"Because, *mon ami,* I simply did not have time to soothe your indignant feathers. I do not have the time now, but you have forced this meeting on me. Take that

477

scowl off your face while I explain a few things to you."

Feeling slightly chastened and not liking it at all, Christopher sat down stiffly on a couch of red Moroccan leather. Common sense reasserted itself, and he said calmly, if coldly, "I apologize for inflicting myself upon you like this. And I am sorry if it is inconvenient. If you would like, I can call at a more suitable time, but I intend to see you today. I want to know exactly what happened and I am"—a wry smile crossed his face—"willing to listen to reason."

Relaxing at Christopher's less aggressive tone of voice, Jason replied easily, "I, too, owe you an apology. I should have told you immediately about Lafitte and not have let you find it out, along with all the half-truths, from someone else."

Taking a small gold watch from his vest pocket, Jason glanced at it, saying, "I shall be in this meeting until luncheon. Will you come back at, say, two o'clock? I really am afraid I cannot see you before that time." He added grimly, "Claiborne is in such fidgets over that damned memorandum that my life is no longer my own."

Christopher inclined his head in agreement. Together the two men walked out into the hall, and after shaking hands, Jason strolled back to his meeting and Christopher departed.

He had no inclination to return to Maspero's, nor did he wish to seek out Dauphine Street and the unresolved situation that awaited him there. Instead he walked aimlessly along the muddied wooden sidewalks, letting his feet take him where they would, his mind on Lafitte.

That first surge of irrational anger had faded, and Christopher was able to view the event more sensibly. Lafitte was, despite his standing in the city, a smuggler, and he did break the law every day. And there was no denying that in his crew there were men who could only be labeled outright pirates. I warned him, Christopher thought savagely as he continued to walk. By God, but I warned him.

Unfortunately that knowledge gave him little comfort, and without surprise he found he had wandered to the ramparts. Lafitte had a small cottage nearby, and a moment later Christopher found himself standing in front of it.

The wooden building appeared deserted, but as he remained there, the conviction grew that someone was watching him. A faint movement, barely discernible through the barred and shuttered windows, convinced him of it, and with a determined stride he walked boldly up to the door.

At first there was no answer to his sharp rap on the door, but when he repeated it a second time, very slowly the door opened. Stepping inside, without any astonishment at all he stared at Lafitte, as he stood negligently by the door. Lafitte was the first to speak.

"Well, *mon ami,* we meet again." With an irrepressible twinkle in the black eyes, he murmured, "But in vastly different circumstances, hey?"

"Very," Christopher replied dryly, watching as Lafitte shut the door and walked over to a simple scrubbed oak table.

Waving him to one of the sturdy wooden chairs placed near the table, Lafitte said, "Sit down, *mon ami!* Sit down and tell me why you have come to call. I do not think that I am in a very good odor with most people in the city these days, and I am amazed you even bothered to seek me out."

With brutal honesty Christopher replied, "I did not know that you were here—I just had a hunch that you might be. And I couldn't imagine you running away with your tail between your legs."

"Ha! After Patterson and Ross were finished with Barataria, I almost didn't have a tail to put between my legs!"

"I know. And I'm sorry, Jean," Christopher said quietly, adding slowly, "I don't want to insult you by offering you money, but if you need it, you know that I will supply you with it—that and anything else you may need."

A rueful smile curved Lafitte's mouth. "I have not reached the point yet where I must exist on charity. But I thank you for your offer, and it pleases me that despite your yearning for respectability, you are not willing to desert me."

Christopher grimaced and said carelessly, "You helped me when I needed it—I am only returning the favor."

Lafitte nodded. "Yes, that is so. But come let us talk of other things. I presume you would like to know what happened to the good Allen Ballard, would you not?"

With a derisive gleam in the gold eyes, Christopher admitted coolly, "Actually I had not given Mr. Ballard another thought. Did you release him as planned?"

Lafitte looked almost smug as he said with grandeur, "I did better than merely release him, *mon ami!* I will not go into details, but the opportunity presented itself to me to politely place him in the hands of a few of his fellow British officers, and not one to overlook opportunity, I quickly seized upon it. I would guess that he is now somewhere on his way back to England . . . or more likely safely ensconced with the British fleet currently harrying us on the Gulf." Sending Christopher a laughingly reproachful glance, Lafitte murmured, "The shifts I am put to by my friends!"

There were a dozen questions Christopher would have liked to ask about Allen's return to the British, the first being the circumstances of Lafitte's meeting with British officers. But Lafitte had already stated he would give no details, and from past experience Christopher knew he would gain nothing by persisting. Lafitte had told him all he intended to . . . for the moment. Yet he could not let it rest entirely—there was definitely something there that he did not like, something he could not put his finger on. The question of Allen's fate aside, Lafitte's entire attitude troubled him. Jean was simply too carelessly indifferent, too cheerful. A man who had lost everything did not act as Lafitte did—not when he was reduced to hiding in a small cottage near the ramparts. Frowning, Christopher demanded bluntly, "Jean, what are you going to do now? Let the Americans hound you from New Orleans? And what about Dominique You and the others?"

Lafitte's face instantly went smooth, a calculating gleam in the black eyes. "Do you ask that for yourself or for your friend Jason Savage? Savage who whispers into the governor's ear?"

His own face suddenly hard and angry, Christopher said levelly, "I think you know the answer to that question. I have told you before how I stand."

"So you have, *mon ami*, but considering the circumstances, you will forgive me if I am suspicious. After all, I have no reason to love the governor, and word has already circulated that you and Monsieur Savage called upon him yesterday. I wonder if you will tell me of that meeting?"

Caught off guard, having forgotten that Lafitte's spies were some of the most adept, Christopher stared at him, suddenly wishing to hell he had never started this conversation. Telling Lafitte of that meeting was out of the question, and yet if he did not, Lafitte would never trust him again. And for some unknown reason Christopher instinctively felt that it was vitally important that Lafitte continue to look upon him as a friend. Trapped in an unpleasant situation, Christopher took the only way out that someone of his nature could; with his jaw set stubbornly, he said bluntly, "I cannot."

Surprisingly his answer seemed to please Lafitte. "I know that, *mon ami*. If you had told me what you know, I would never have trusted you again. A man who will betray one secret will betray many."

"You are turning into quite a philosopher," Christopher drawled wryly.

"Ah, yes, it happens occasionally," Jean agreed lightly. Studying his hands clasped together on the table before him, Lafitte said slowly, "You ask what I am to do and I tell you I do not know. Barataria is in ruins; my warehouse, my ships are burned and in the hands of the Americans; many of my men are in cells in the calaboose. But I am not beaten. The Americans know nothing of the men that escaped and that are waiting my command at the Isles Dernieres, nor do they even guess that there is another, a secret warehouse of flints and ammunition, easily accessible to me." Bitterly, the black eyes bleak and hard, he finished, "They will regret it, *mon ami*, that they turned down my offer of help."

Alert and slightly puzzled at Lafitte's words, Christopher asked sharply, "Your offer of help?"

Lafitte sent him a mirthless smile. "You have not heard? The British approached me, with the intention of having myself and my men join their ranks, and as you will instantly guess, it was then I gave them Ballard. I did not give those same officers an immediate answer; instead, like a fool, I notified Claiborne that I was willing to repulse the British proposal and fight on the side of New Orleans if he would allow me to do so." His voice thickening with injustice, Lafitte spat, "You see the result of my offer!"

Watching Lafitte's ruthless face, Christopher thought exasperatedly, By heaven, Savage, I hope you and Claiborne know what you have done!

He said as much to Savage when he met with him later. The instant the two men were alone in Jason's library, Christopher snapped, "I've seen Lafitte. Would you mind telling my why the governor refused his help? We need any help we can get, and you know damn well that Lafitte's men are already war-hardened. My God, Jason, from what we know we will be outnumbered almost three to one, and you and Claiborne turn down a force of nearly a thousand men!"

Jason sighed heavily. "I know. And all I can say is that I did not vote with the others for the attack on Barataria. I believed those letters Lafitte sent were genuine. But Patterson and Ross had been preparing for the assault on Barataria for weeks and they overruled everyone else."

The hard, handsome features were hostile and slightly disbelieving; Christopher requested sourly, "Suppose you tell me exactly what did happen? From the beginning, if you please."

Settling back in his chair, Jason did precisely that. "The first I heard about it," he began slowly, "was when I received a note to come immediately to the governor's house on the fourth or fifth of September. When I arrived there, I found that several others also had been sent a similar message. Major General Jacques Villere, Patterson, and Ross were present acting as Claiborne's naval and military advisors; Collector Dubourg, in charge of the customs for the government in New Orleans, was naturally there, as well as myself and one or two others. John Blanque was there too—his presence, I assume, comes as no surprise to you."

It did not. John Blanque, a lawyer-banker and a member of the legislature, was known to be extremely sympathetic toward the Lafitte brothers. There were even well-founded rumors that he had financed several of the vessels owned by the brothers, and there was no denying that he was very definitely their friend.

At Christopher's curt nod of agreement, Jason continued, "Lafitte had sent certain letters to Blanque of a purported British bid for his services, along with a letter to the governor expressing his desire 'to return to the sheepfold.' And he wrote, I remember exactly, 'that the only reward I ask is that a stop be put to the proscription against me and my adherents.' We all found it a little hard to believe," Jason commented dryly. "But before the meeting ended, I for one was convinced that letters of the British offer for his services were genuine. I did still have some doubts as to his sincerity, but, as you said, a thousand armed men, even of dubious loyalty, fighting for the city was better than none at all! I was willing to consider the matter, as were one or two of the other men. Unfortunately Claiborne relied entirely on his military advisors, asking them only two questions: Did they think the letters genuine? And was it proper for the governor to enter into any correspondence with Lafitte or his associates?" Jason paused, his face somber as he looked across at Christopher. Then in a weary voice he said, "Villere voted vehemently yes, while Patterson and Ross voted no. And that ended it, *mon ami*. The governor decided that Lafitte's expulsion from Barataria was more urgent than to give any credence to what might only be a trick on Lafitte's part."

"You didn't think that."

"No. I did not," Jason agreed. "But I am not the governor. He did as he saw fit. And you really cannot blame the man for falling in with his military advisors. After all, that is why he has them! Patterson and Ross did not believe the letters genuine, and I cannot say that I hold it against them. Now, though, with what you have brought back from England, I am even more certain that the British *did* attempt to bribe Lafitte and that those letters were, in fact, precisely what Lafitte said they were. Unfortunately Lafitte is now our enemy, and we may come to regret bitterly that we acted as we did," Jason finished dispiritedly.

Christopher's tone was thoughtful as he murmured, "Lafitte is certainly not overjoyed at what has happened, but he may still be brought over to our side. And God knows we need him! He has men and more importantly a warehouse of flints and ammunition."

Christopher had debated telling Jason that, but feeling he would betray nothing that could be used against Jean, he felt relatively safe in mentioning the men and arms. It might even help, if Savage was willing to listen to the plan beginning to take shape in his head.

Tentatively he inquired, "Could you find out if the governor is still unwilling to negotiate with Lafitte? It's possible we may yet be able to turn this to our advantage."

The emerald eyes alert, Jason regarded Christopher. "You have something in mind?"

"I do. But it depends on the governor." Then Christopher frowned. "Or," he said slowly, "Jackson."

Jason shook his head decisively. "Nothing there. Jackson already knows everything about the entire business, and he had dismissed Lafitte and his men as 'hellish banditti.' He thinks they should have been run out of the Gulf long ago and applauds what Patterson and Ross have accomplished. You'll not find him inclined to deal with Lafitte, I can tell you that! At least," Jason tacked on reflectively, "not at the moment. Perhaps when he sees how poorly equipped we are to beat back a concerted British attack, he will feel differently. That memorandum of yours will certainly help convince him of how strong the effort to capture New Orleans will be. By the way, Claiborne sent it to him by special messenger immediately after we left yesterday. So now all we can do is wait and see what the general decides to do."

Christopher pulled a face. "That seems to be what I have been doing for months," he said disgustedly. "First in England and now it appears that is what I shall be doing here in New Orleans—wait and see. It should be my middle name."

Jason laughed. "I know exactly how you feel. It has been a trying time for us all. We know the British assault is coming; we know there is great activity by the British fleet in the Gulf; but when or even precisely where they may strike has everyone glancing nervously over their shoulders."

"At least now I hope everyone knows in *which* direction to look over their shoulders," Christopher commented tartly. Straightening from his relaxed position, he said, "Well, I won't keep you, and I apologize for acting so angry earlier. Since we won't have to discuss the Lafitte situation now, do you still desire my company at dinner Thursday?"

"Why not? I did not invite you only to discuss Lafitte, you know." A smile crinkled the corners of his eyes, and Jason added, "I am most anxious to hear of Nicole's conquest of England. Do tell me, did you leave her well established, with every eligible male in London at her feet?"

Christopher's easy manner vanished in a second; a certain wariness entered his bearing. Oh, Jesus, he thought angrily, why didn't I think of the all awkward questions that would be asked? There was no use lying about the situation—he had made no attempt to hide Nicole's presence in his house, and Jason was bound to find out about it, sooner or later.

His voice was void of any expression at all as he said slowly, "As a matter of fact, I didn't leave her behind. She is with me at Dauphine Street."

Jason astutely regarded the hard, closed face, wishing fervently that he had minded his own business. Christopher had made no mention of marriage, no mention of a wife, and his demeanor certainly indicated otherwise; so evidently Nicole had returned as his mistress. And that, Jason decided regretfully, was going to be a problem. He had liked the girl, so had Catherine for that matter, and she had been introduced to some of the finest and proudest families in New Orleans, but now . . . What a cursed affair! It didn't bother Jason a tinker's damn that Nicole had become Christopher's mistress, but one could not in all politeness offend other acquaintances not quite so broad-minded. There was a rigid social line between an eligible young woman and a mistress, and there were going to be quite a number of ruffled feathers when it dawned on certain people that the young woman they had met and admired as Christopher Saxon's ward had returned as his kept woman.

The pause that had greeted Christopher's words became very noticeable, and almost haughtily Christopher demanded, "Well, haven't you anything to say? No further questions?"

"What do you want me to say?" Jason hedged, remembering suddenly and unaccountably how he had felt in those early days with Catherine, when he had been torn between the desire to put his hands around her throat and put an end to the torment she provoked, and the equal desire to possess her. Intuitively he sensed that Christopher found himself in much the same position, and he sympathized more than a little. It was an exquisite torture that he would not wish on even his worst enemy.

Aware that Christopher was like a banked fire ready to burst into flame, and uncertain of his own ground, Jason asked, "Do you want to talk about it?"

"God, no!" Christopher exploded, leaping to his feet and taking several short, agitated steps about the room. Bitterly he said, "Talking will do no good." Then as if contradicting himself, Christopher threw Jason an arrogant look, one daring him to offer pity, and muttered, "I find myself in the most damnable coil, and no matter which way I turn I see no escape."

No doubt you do, my young friend, no doubt you do, Jason thought understandingly, recalling vividly his own frustration and anguish. And I suspect you would rather have died than to admit it to me.

It was a ticklish predicament that Jason found himself in. He could not be positive, but he suspected strongly that Christopher and Nicole had fallen into much the same trap that he and Catherine had all those years before. But without knowing for certain, he could hardly say, "Look here, Saxon, the same thing happened to me and this is what I did." If he were wrong, he would be revealing more about himself than he cared to, and for no reason. Of course, on the other hand, if he read the signs correctly and did say his mind, he might very well present Christopher with a way out of his painful dilemma.

He watched the other man consideringly as Christopher stared outside, his back to the room, the broad shoulders squared as if for battle. You bullheaded young animal, Jason thought with sudden surprising affection, you are so like me in so many ways that I know precisely what is eating at your gut. We are such blind fools where our women are concerned. And for you, my young friend, I will offer one piece of advice. I wonder if you will be wise enough to take it?

Before Jason could say anything, though, Christopher spun on his heel and, like an edgy golden-eyed panther, stalked over to the desk. Furious with himself for having burst out as he had, he wanted only to escape, to deny once again that Nicole presented any difficulty. Certainly he did not want to discuss the situation with anyone—especially not Jason Savage, in spite of the odd air of sympathetic understanding that seemed to flow between them. Right now Christopher felt naked and exposed, too proud and arrogant to say, "By God, yes, let's talk about it. I need someone with a clearer head than mine!" Instead, as always when he was confronted by adversity, he withdrew into himself.

Outwardly indifferent, he stood in front of Jason and, deliberately ignoring the present subject, said coolly. "I shall see you on Thursday as planned, unless I hear differently from you. Now if you will forgive me, I am afraid I must be about my business. If you hear news that you think would be of interest to me, please do not hesitate to send a messenger to Dauphine Street. And if I can be of further service to yourself or the governor, you know that I will be more than willing."

Almost amused by Christopher's stubborn refusal to face what was bedeviling him, Jason merely nodded and replied lightly, "Fine. Catherine and I look forward to seeing you. And rest assured, should I have need of you, I will demand your presence immediately."

Christopher bowed politely and had walked as far as the door when Jason's soft drawl stopped him abruptly. "You are a rather obdurate young man, you know," Jason said reflectively and without heat. With a hint of laughter lurking in his voice, he added, "I'm going to break one of my cardinal rules and give you a little unasked-for advice, my mule-headed friend. I once found myself in a dilemma much like, I suspect, the one you are in now. And I solved the matter," Jason finished almost complacently, "simply by marrying it!"

Throwing Jason an exasperated look of half vexation

and half-mocking amusement, Christopher stalked from the room, unwilling to speak further on the subject. Damn him, he thought with annoyance, as he walked in the falling rain, was there *nothing* that escaped the man?

Unwilling to consider seriously Jason's suggestion, he deliberately dismissed it and instead turned his mind on the problem of Lafitte—Lafitte and New Orleans and the coming battle with the British.

Finding one of the smaller, quieter coffee houses, he settled in a dark corner and, his eyes on the rain splashing and hissing against the windows, reflected on what he had learned today.

On the face of it none of it looked good. Claiborne had alienated Lafitte by ignoring his offer of help. Lafitte, understandably incensed, had the weapons and men that could turn the tide against a concerted effort by the British. How in the devil was he to reconcile them? Jason, he knew, would be doing his best with the governor, but he rather suspected that the answer would lie more with Lafitte—would he be willing to forgive the governor and fight with the Americans?

The problem appeared unresolvable. But what about Jackson? As a military man and one who had not been involved in the feud between Claiborne and Lafitte, perhaps he could provide the answer. Provided he was willing to put aside his feeling about "hellish banditti"! Christopher smiled grimly to himself. When Jackson saw the defenses of New Orleans, he was more than likely to open his arms to the devil himself than to worry over the less-desirable traits of some of Lafitte's men. The flints alone should make him willing to turn a blind eye to past lawless activities. Yes, Jackson was the answer. Somehow, he must arrange a meeting between Lafitte and Jackson . . . with Lafitte in the right frame of mind of course! Jackson would need no priming from anyone—New Orleans's lack of strength and armaments would be argument enough.

On Lafitte's news concerning Allen Ballard he wasted little time in speculation. His only thought was Nicole would be pleased Ballard was with the British.

That brought him face to face with what he had been avoiding all day—Nicole. He swore under his breath as her image rose before his eyes, blasting every thought from his mind. And Jason's words came back to burn across his brain—marry her!

Coolly he forced himself to think about it, reminding himself that this time last year he had been in Bermuda on the verge of offering for Louise Huntleigh. And Louise never moved him, infuriated or delighted him as did Nicole. So why not marry her? It would please his grandfather. And if arranged instantly and with secrecy, it would silence the social flutter that Nicole's unmarried state would arouse. The Savages would not betray the fact that he had married Nicole *after* they had arrived in New Orleans. If he moved quickly, by tomorrow night Nicole would be his wife. Thursday's dinner would be the first social appearance of his bride.

The same reasons that had prompted him to consider marrying Louise still existed, he thought unemotionally, and Nicole was far more well connected and possessed a fortune that dwarfed the Huntleigh estate. Why not marry her?

She was beautiful, tantalizing, and everything he wanted in this world. Whether or not she had given herself to Robert no longer mattered. That she was Annabelle's daughter he dismissed impatiently; he even began to his horror to make excuses for Annabelle's despicable behavior. Ah, Jesus, he thought angrily, you really are a besotted fool. Marry her, you jackass, but for God's sake never let her know how easily she could wrap you around her little finger. Never, *never* allow her to discover that you have committed the unspeakable folly of falling in love. He was, he acknowledged miserably, passionately, irrevocably in love with Nicole Ashford.

There! he had admitted it, but it brought him no pleasure, no joy, no relief, just the bitter taste of defeat. How she would laugh if she knew. Laugh and taunt him and make his life a living hell. But marry her he would. And even try perhaps to make her love him? That he even considered such a possibility showed how deeply his heart was committed.

All the wild, and yet gentle, emotions he had scorned were now pounding in his breast for one woman, and that one woman wanted nothing of him—except her freedom! What an ironic jest on himself! He who had laughed and jeered at unrequited love, sneered at love, denied such an emotion existed, was now himself a victim of it.

There would be compensations, he reminded himself bleakly. Nicole would be his, and someday there would be the child that he wanted. Oh, yes, there would be compensations, he decided, as the picture of a topaz-eyed daughter rose in his mind. A daughter on whom he could lavish all the love and tenderness he dared not reveal to her mother for fear of having it thrown back in his face.

His decision made, he rose from his chair, tossed a few coins on the table, and headed for Dauphine Street. If they were to marry he had better damn well set about arranging it. He deliberately refused to think of Nicole's reactions.

He proposed with arrogant tactlessness. He did not ask Nicole if she would marry him; he told her. To make matters worse, he gave no hint that the marriage was anything more than a matter of convenience. It would please his grandfather, he said. It would save her embarrassment, he said. It was time he married and had a heir, he said.

Ignoring the blazing light in Nicole's fine topaz eyes, he continued blindly to dig a pit beneath his feet, as impassively he trotted out practical reason after reason why Nicole should fall gratefully into his arms.

Christopher had not been the only one to make some decisions that day. Nicole, waking long after he had left her bed, had come to some bitter conclusions on her own. She loved Christopher Saxon, and she wanted him on any terms, at least she did when she could think about it coolly. This morning she had decided with a calmness that was shocking that if he wanted her as his mistress, well, he would have her. It was useless to rail against him, to shout she hated him when all he had to do was touch her and she melted like snow in the sun. She could not forget those odd moments that occurred occasionally, when she glimpsed something flickering in the gold eyes that left her breathless. It was possible all he wanted was her body, but now and then the queer thought crossed her mind that Christopher might be motivated by an emotion other than lust. It was a comforting idea to cling to, and that thought more than any other helped make her decision. Someday he might grow to love her, and she was willing to risk her entire future on that frail hope.

Throughout the long day she had paced the confines of the house, waiting for his return, determined to burn all her boats, determined to tell him of her decision before she lost her courage and bolted like a wild thing for whatever safety she could find. She had been understandably nervous when, shortly after dark, Christopher had at last returned to Dauphine Street, and when he had requested that she join him in the library, her mouth had gone suddenly very dry. Then her chin held proudly, and squaring her shoulders, she had walked with an outwardly brave step to the library.

Christopher had been standing, staring down into the

fire when she entered, and after sending her an appraising glance that took in the soft hair piled elegantly on top of her head and the deceptively demure gown of emerald wild silk, he had brusquely ordered her to sit down. There had been an awkward silence for a moment, and Nicole had the curious conviction that Christopher was uneasy, even nervous.

When he had informed her that they would be married, her heart leaped within her breast; shock mingled with hope and relief. If Christopher had then swept her into his arms, she would have blurted out the shameful fact that she loved him. But Christopher had proceeded to undermine his own cause by coldly explaining the businesslike reasons for their union.

Trembling with disappointment as much as icy rage, forgetting her earlier resolution, Nicole sprang to her feet before the last word had left his lips. With her hands clenched at her side, the topaz eyes glittering with unshed tears and fury, she spat, "Are you mad? Marry *you?* I would rather die!" The genuine anger in her voice almost robbed the words of their triteness, and Christopher, his own temper smoldering into a blazing flame, shouted, "Goddamnit, woman, what in hell's name do you want of me? I've offered you marriage, what more can I do?" The odd note of half rage, half bewilderment in Christopher's voice totally escaped Nicole.

And because she was so angry, she spoke without thinking. "What about love, Christopher?" she cried, her face pale and the soft mouth set in a hard line. "Doesn't love have anything to do with marriage? Must everything be calculated and done for the advantage one gains?"

Christopher froze, staring very hard at her stormy face. Like a man in a trance, he slowly reached out to touch Nicole's cheek. "Love," he whispered, "what do you know of love?"

Suddenly appalled at how close she had come to betraying herself, Nicole's eyes fell from his, and she missed the flicker of naked emotion that had sprung to life in the golden gaze. Not looking at him, yet unbearably aware of the warm caress on her cheek, she jerked away and muttered, "Oh, never mind! I don't want to talk about it."

"Ah, but I do," Christopher retorted ruefully and drew her stiff body back against his. His arms about her, he cradled her next to him and, bending his head, murmured into her ear, "Could it be that you are already in love? That there is someone who has captured that wild, stubborn heart of yours?" Deliberately he said slowly, "Succeeded where I failed?"

Nicole's whole body went very still, and nervously she toyed with the material of her dress, wanting desperately to confess to that coaxing voice, wanting with all her heart to believe in the note of tenderness in Christopher's tone. They had fought too often and too bitterly for her to trust him, and yet she was powerless to tear herself away from him, to destroy this suddenly fragile mood. Even when the silence spun out and Christopher sat down on a couch before the fire, gently drawing her onto his lap, she did not resist. She was frightened, frightened and filled with an exquisite anticipation, a tantalizing feeling of expectancy, that if she wanted, if she were clever and for once did not fly out in a rage, she would discover something incredibly important.

Quizzically Christopher prodded, "Aren't you going to answer me? Or don't you know the answer?"

Nicole swallowed, keeping her eyes on the leaping flames of the fire, giddily conscious of his hard arms holding her next to him, of the muscled thighs beneath her and the warm breath gently stirring the hair at her temple. One of Christopher's hands began slowly to explore her arm, and she mumbled, "Does it matter? I mean is it important whether I am in love with someone or not?"

"It might be," Christopher returned equably. "It depends on who it is?"

Cautiously Nicole replied, "Well, suppose I am in love with someone?"

"Hmmm, well if it isn't me, then I suppose I would have to let you go," Christopher said, adding dryly, "Let you go and somehow help you be reunited with your loved one."

Astonishment swiveled Nicole around to look into the dark face. "You would do that? If I said I were madly in love with . . . with . . ." she groped helplessly for a name and when none came finished lamely, "well, with someone, you'd let me go?"

Christopher regarded her steadily for several moments and then, holding her gaze with his own, said softly, "I'd have to, wouldn't I? You see when I marry, I want no ghosts in my marriage bed. I want the woman that bears my name and eventually my children to want only me, when she sleeps to dream only of me." He was gambling, gambling everything on the mad chance that he had not misread the cause of Nicole's sudden fury and the reason behind her angry outburst.

Warily they stared at each other, Christopher committed as far as he could go without further encouragement from Nicole, and Nicole uncertain of how to reply. With all her eager young body she yearned to fling herself into his arms and beg that he let her be that woman, but the past had taught her caution, and carefully she asked, "When you told me that we were to marry, just now, did you think of me that way?"

His eyes narrowed, and with a thread of amusement barely discernible in his voice, he returned, "What do you think?"

Her face was troubled as she looked searchingly into the mocking features. "I don't know what you thought," she admitted honestly. "I've never known how you felt about me." As Christopher opened his mouth to reply, she broke in, "Oh, I know you wanted me, you've always made that very clear. But I've never known *why* you wanted me. Except to use me as you would a bought whore, and that's not a very good reason for marriage, is it?" There was a note of sadness in her words that stung Christopher, and harshly he said, "If I had wanted a whore, I would have bought one! Oh, Jesus, Nicole, don't tell me you can't guess? Must I say it out in words of one syllable?"

"Yes. Yes, in this case, I think you do," she replied steadily, and with sudden confidence leaned into him; her full mouth barely inches from his, she demanded, "Tell me, Christopher! Tell me!"

The soft, warm body was too much for him, driving out the last remnants of stubborn pride, and thickly he said, "Witch! May God help me, but I love you. *Now* will you marry me?"

His answer was in the ardent mouth that met his, in the fervent melting of the slim young body against his. For a long time there was silence in the library except for the crackle of the fire and the muttered endearments that lovers exchange. Explanations could come later, explanations and understanding, and with those forgiveness, but right now there was just each other—no tomorrow, no yesterday, just the present.

38

They were married the next day, a Wednesday, in a small town some twenty miles above New Orleans, by a justice of the peace, with Higgins, grinning broadly, as one of the witnesses. The justice's wife had been hastily summoned as the other witness, and as she later told her husband, she had never seen such a handsome couple or two people so obviously in love with each other.

Christopher quite frankly could not keep his gaze off Nicole, almost as if he expected her to vanish, and Nicole made no effort to hide the love shining out of the topaz eyes. She could have wished that Lord and Lady Saxon had been there, but all that really mattered to her was that Christopher loved her, loved her enough to marry her, even if it was a hurried, secret, simple ceremony.

They rode back to New Orleans in silence, the persistent rain making it a damp, uncomfortable journey despite the warmed bricks to keep the feet warm and the tight construction of Christopher's elegant carriage. Higgins, displaying his usual tact, had elected to brave the weather; blandly ignoring Christopher's and Nicole's protestations, he sat with the coachman during the four-hour journey back to New Orleans. Ordinarily it would not have taken so long, but the rain had turned the roads into quagmires of mud and silt, and the carriage could gain no speed.

Inside the coach the silence was companionable, both occupants for the first time in their relationship almost at peace with each other. There were difficulties still ahead of them, but with patience, understanding, and love they would overcome them, provided, as Christopher had said with a laugh last night, "We can keep from flying at each other's throat the first second one of us says something the other takes violent exception to!"

They arrived just before dusk at Dauphine Street, and Christopher wasted little time in assembling his staff and presenting Nicole as his wife, and their new mistress. La-

493

ter he made it extremely clear to Sanderson that he would appreciate it if the actual marriage was said to have taken place in England, today's ceremony merely a re-affirmation of their vows.

His features crinkling into a wide, white-toothed grin, Sanderson had replied, "I understand perfectly, sir. There will be no gossip. I will see to it!"

Christopher had grinned, dismissing him with a care-less flick of the hand. Nicole's position was now secure as his wife, and Sanderson would see to it that no one dared raise any awkward questions, either in his own home or in the homes of others.

Before he could put the present aside and concentrate on the far more agreeable subject of his *very* new bride, he sat down and wrote two short messages. One was sent round to Jason Savage's with the less-than-cryptic mes-sage that he and his wife, Nicole, would be delighted to dine with them tomorrow evening.

The second letter took a little longer to write and would take weeks, even months, to reach its destination in En-gland. It was to Lord Saxon; he wrote simply that he was once again in New Orleans and that Nicole was with him —this time no longer his ward, but his wife. After a fond inquiry as to the state of his grandfather's health and that of Lady Saxon, Christopher closed the brief note with the promise that come summer, he and his bride would return once again to England. Tomorrow he would find out from Jason if there were any ships due to run the blockade of the Gulf that might take the letter to his grandfather.

His most pressing tasks seen to, he was able to sit back in the quietness of his library and with a bemused expres-sion recall that he was now a married man.

A tender, half-amused smile on his mouth, with an eager step he left the library, intent on finding that tempt-ing creature, who was now his wife. He found her sitting prosaically in the main salon, idly studying some dress pattern plates.

At his entrance she glanced up, and sending him an almost-shy smile, she put down the plate in her hand and asked, "Did you finish your business?"

"Yes, I did. The Savages have been informed, and I'm certain they will do their part to stifle any awkwardness that might arise. I don't foresee any—after all, we have been back in New Orleans barely three days and you have made no social appearances. I seriously doubt that any-one outside of the members of my household and the

Savages even knows you are here. I've spoken to Sanderson to make certain none of our servants prattle. Few people are even aware that I am back in the city, so I think we can safely put aside the worry of gossip."

Slightly surprised at what had constituted the important business he had stated that he must see to immediately, she questioned gravely, "Why are you so concerned about gossip now? You never have been."

Christopher gave her a twisted smile. "I've never had a wife to worry over, either, and I will not have you the object of every scandalmonger in the city. Especially since the fault of your predicament was largely due to me."

A warm little glow of gratification spread through Nicole's body when she heard those words. More than she would have cared to admit she had dreaded the furor their unorthodox marriage would have caused. Not so strangely too, it gave her the unusual feeling of being protected to know that Christopher, abandoning his usual indifference to what people thought, had immediately taken steps to insure that no one could create a disagreeable situation for her. And with a smile hovering about her lips she remembered the old adage that reformed rakes make the best husbands. She fervently hoped it was true.

Seeing her smile, Christopher drawled quietly, "That amuses you? The fact that I want no one to besmirch your name?"

"Not that! I was just thinking of that saying about reformed rakes, and wondering if you were going to run true to form."

Christopher seated himself beside her on the sofa, and lifting one of her hands, he pressed the palm to his lips. "I intend to try, m'dear. I intend to try."

Breathless, Nicole could find no words to say, and after a second Christopher asked quizzically, "Aren't you going to say the same? That you're going to try too to make our marriage work?"

"Oh, I will!" she promised instantly, leaning against him, her mouth unconsciously beckoning. And unable to help himself, Christopher caught her close in a fierce embrace, his lips searching hers, demanding a response. Nicole gave it unstintingly; the fiery tip of her tongue slipped into his mouth, and with a smothered groan Christopher was the one who ended the kiss. "Witch!" he said in a husky tone. "This is not the time to start that kind of thing! Later this evening will be soon enough. I can tell

495

you I do not intend to sleep alone in my bed as I did last night!"

A teasing light in the topaz eyes, Nicole murmured, "Why did you? You've never let the lack of a wedding band stop you before."

A frown wrinkled Christopher's forehead as he said slowly, "I admit being guilty of that! But knowing we were to be married today, somehow I didn't want the memory of the night *before* the wedding to interfere with *the* wedding night." Almost ashamedly he added, "A most odd sentiment coming from me, my love, but there you have it."

The most incredible suspicion that underneath the habitual cold exterior the world saw of Christopher Saxon, lay a romantic heart was taking hold of Nicole, and a delightful gurgle of laughter broke from her. "Christopher!" she spluttered. "Next you shall be telling me that you are sorry you treated me so cavalierly in the beginning."

Slanting her a mocking look, he retorted bluntly, "No, I am not sorry about anything I have done to you in the past. My only regret is that the moment I saw you I did not recognize my fate and haul you before the nearest minister and marry you instantly! I would have saved myself a great deal of heartburning and uncertainty."

Unable to help herself, softly Nicole taunted, "And did you suffer great heartburning?"

Christopher pushed her gently down on the sofa, and leaning over her, his mouth barely touching hers, he muttered, "And what do you think? First there was Allen to keep me tossing and turning in my bed, wondering if the two of you were together somewhere lying in each other's arms!" The half-tender, half-teasing note vanished as he said in an entirely different tone of voice, "Then there was England. Harshly, he snarled, "Yes, by God, I suffered heartburnings—heartburnings, jealousy, rage, hatred. I suffered the lot, you little devil!"

His face had that shut-in expression she had seen so often in the past; his eyes were suddenly cold and inimical as he stared down at her. She met that gaze this time without flinching, and very gently her fingers traced the chiseled outline of his lips. "You didn't have to, you could have given me some sign of what you were feeling." He started to twist away, but Nicole held him to her by the simple act of twining her arms about his neck. "Listen to me, you fool!" she whispered against his ear. "There was never anyone for me, except you! But how could I let you know? The one time I tried, you threw it back in my face. I was certain you felt nothing for me." Her mouth curving wryly, she added, "Except for a certain amount of animal passion."

It was Christopher's turn to look wry. "I felt a *great* deal of animal passion for you, my dear! I don't deny it. But at the same time, I had never wanted a woman to belong to just me. I had never felt compelled to protect one or see that her future was secure—even if it meant denying myself. And I had never experienced such a destroying emotion as jealousy before. I could have killed Robert and all the others just for looking at you." His face hardened again, the gold eyes were suddenly bleak, and he finished, "And I could have killed you when I discovered you were with him that last night in England."

Searchingly Nicole's gaze traveled over his features. In a very careful tone of voice she said, "Robert was nothing to me, but a good friend, Christopher. Later when I learned his part in what had happened to you, I loathed him."

Christopher's face did not change, nor did he give any sign he believed what she had said, and Nicole's heart tightened painfully. There was so much that had to be said between them, but Christopher was not about to discuss the past. As if in confirmation of her thoughts, he sat up and said lightly, "Enough of this. Sanderson will no doubt be informing us that dinner is ready in no time. Would you like a glass of sherry or shall I pour you something stronger?"

Reluctantly following his lead, she smiled with false brightness and indicated that a sherry would be fine. Consideringly she studied the tall, lean body, as with his back to her, he decanted some brandy for himself and a light golden sherry for herself. He was so dear and handsome, and yet she knew they could not simply pretend that the past did not exist. Christopher might have confessed that he loved her, and she believed that he did—but she also knew he hadn't wanted to love her and that he still harbored certain suspicions and doubts about her. Doubts and suspicions that could destroy the fragile beginning they had at the moment. She wasn't even positive that he believed her avowal of love. Last night there had been a faint gleam of cynicism in his eyes when she had blurted out what was in her heart. And today, despite the fact of their marriage and the way he looked at her, there was a hint of wariness in his manner, and she wondered with a shiver of sadness if he was already regretting not only what he had admitted to last night, but their marriage as well.

That thought was uppermost in her mind all through the delicious dinner that Ruth-Marie had prepared for them, and this time, thinking hard, Nicole did grim justice to the delectable array of dishes placed before her. Swallowing the last bite of a melting almond macaroon soufflé, she made a fierce vow to herself that Christopher was going to have to face not only the truth about her mother, but about Robert as well. Because until he did they could never share the kind of love and marriage that she wanted—that she was determined to have. He had said he wanted no ghosts in his marriage bed, well neither did she!

With a determined sparkle in the topaz eyes, she entered the main salon, expecting Christopher to follow her shortly. When an hour later he had still not made an appearance, she summoned a servant to discover his whereabouts and was slightly nonplussed when the terse message was relayed to her that the master had gone out! Torn between the desire to laugh and a strong urge to throw a tantrum, Nicole spent the remainder of the evening by herself, not unnaturally speculating on where her exceptionally new husband had gone.

By ten o'clock and still no sign of Christopher, with a heavy step she ascended to her bedroom, wondering dismally if that now she was his wife, he no longer wanted her, that she was doomed to endless evenings spent by herself. Common sense told her she was being silly, but their relationship was so delicate, as yet so unexplored and untried, that it took very little to shake her confidence.

Her room had been changed during the day; what clothing and personal effects she had at the moment had been moved into a large elegant suite of rooms that adjoined Christopher's. Ordinarily she might have taken pleasure in the spacious elegant appointments, the thick ruby carpet, the soft gleaming yellow walls, and the rich velvet drapes of sapphire blue, but tonight none of them held her attention. Not even the warmth of fire leaping on a hearth of polished olive slate could melt the iciness that was running through her veins.

Dismissing Naomi almost immediately and ignoring the flimsy negligee of lush amber silk lying enticingly on the coverlet of sapphire velvet, she stared bitterly at the double louvered doors of natural oak that separated her suite from Christopher's. How dare he do this to me, she questioned with increasing anguish. And slyly the thought slid into her mind—you believe he loves you, is this how you prove it? By doubting him? So soon?

Instantly angry with herself for being so quick to judge, so quick to look for slights and injustices, she turned away and with a determined stride walked to the bed. There was a very good reason why Christopher had gone out tonight. And he would tell her what it was when he returned.

Holding firmly onto that thought, she deliberately made herself prepare for bed, just as if she knew that Christopher would be coming to her in a short while. She was not going to greet him in fury and with recriminations —at least not until she had given him a chance to soothe away her doubts and fears. If he didn't . . .

Almost lightheartedly she stripped off her gown and, having bathed that evening before meeting Christopher in the salon, slipped into the amber silk negligee, enjoying the luxurious feeling of the material. From a fat crystal flacon she liberally splashed herself with a heady scent that reminded her of spices and carnations. A tortoiseshell hairbrush in her hand, she seated herself on the rug before the fire and slowly, caressingly began to brush the heavy sable hair, the flames on the hearth bringing to life the fiery glow in the wavy mass.

That was how Christopher found her when, a few minutes later, he quietly opened the louvered doors that separated their rooms. She was bathed in gold, the fire flickering over her body and hair, turning her skin to molten gold, the amber silk negligee to the gold of a morning sunrise, and her hair to dark flame. He caught his breath sharply at the unconsciously sensual picture she made—the negligee in the firelight revealing as much of the slender body as it hid, the steady stroke of the brush in the long silken hair spinning the flame-struck strands about her shoulders.

He made some sound, never afterward certain what it was, her whispered name or the click of the doors as he shut them behind him, and Nicole turned slowly to look at him. The blinding smile she sent him then left him feeling curiously lightheaded.

He crossed the room to her side in an instant and, kneeling down on one knee, reached out to touch the sable-fire hair, and with an odd catch in his voice, he muttered, "Ah, God, you are so beautiful! You remind me just now of some pagan goddess who has wrapped a golden chain around my heart, and no matter how I try, I cannot break it! You're an enchantress!"

The warmth and unconcealed tenderness in Christopher's eyes swept away all her earlier doubts. And because he was near her once again, his hand gently caressing her hair, his mouth just a heartbeat away, she was able to tease impishly, "Is *that* why you went off and left me alone all evening? Because I am such an enchantress?"

Amusement crept into the gold eyes. "Witch!" he mocked. "You have a wicked tongue too." Seating himself on a chair near the fire, he extracted a narrow oblong box from under his jacket. With a diffident quality to his voice, he said as he handed the box to her, "I had not gotten you a bridegroom's gift. Every bride, even one as hastily married as you, deserves something from the man she marries to mark the occasion. And because, I must confess, unfortunately I did not think of it until after dinner tonight, I had the devil's own time rousing a jeweler." To cover his deeper emotions, he drawled lightly, "You have no idea of the trouble you have put me to finding this bauble. I hope it meets with your approval."

It did. Opening the box with a trembling hand, Nicole sat staring misty-eyed at the magnificent necklace and earrings. Suspended on a finely wrought chain of precious gold was a pear-shaped topaz surrounded by glittering yellow diamonds; the matching earrings of smaller stones had a loop of the yellow diamonds that would dangle and dance against her cheek when she wore them. "Christopher!" she breathed at last. "It's positively the most lovely thing I've ever seen."

"Mmmm. I wanted a rare stone for you, but when I saw these, I was reminded so vividly of your eyes gleaming with the same color that I knew I had to have them for you." The words were said softly, almost as if to himself, but Nicole heard him and, setting the box away from her, threw her arms about his neck.

"I love you," she said fiercely. "I think I have always loved you, even when I was a child and you were so brutal to me on *La Belle Garce*. And I will love you until I die."

Christopher's arms tightened around her, his mouth instinctively seeking hers. She was warm and yielding in his arms as never before. It went to his head like a most potent wine, and with a low groan, he gently moved to lay her down before the fire, his own hard body lying next to hers. And like a man savoring the taste of heaven, his mouth slid gently over hers, his tongue questing and probing between her lips, before moving on to explore and touch, to incite and arouse.

500

With feverish hands Nicole pulled his jacket off; the cravat followed a second later, and brazenly she undid his shirt. Her fingers were like tongues of flame caressing the hard chest, the broad back. The pantaloons gave her trouble, her fingers fumbling for the fastenings, until with a smothered laugh, Christopher rolled away, and standing up, he removed the remainder of his clothing himself. Dropping naked beside her, he teased, "I can see that you haven't undressed many men, my love."

The words were said lightly, but they struck a chill in Nicole, and sitting up and pushing her tumbled hair from her eyes, she said steadily, "I've never undressed *any* man."

The teasing gleam in the gold eyes vanished, and as if driven, he demanded harshly, "Not even Robert?"

Taking a deep breath, Nicole replied evenly, "Not even Robert." But he didn't quite believe her, she could see that from the way his jaw tightened and the faint gleam of skepticism that flickered deep in his eyes for just a moment. Exasperated, her voice sharpened, and grasping his shoulders, she shook him impatiently. "Christopher, listen to me! Why do you condemn me without even hearing what happened that night? We've never spoken of it; never once have you told me how you came to find out that Robert and Edward were both dead, nor did you ask me how I came to be there at Robert's house." Her eyes blazing with growing anger and pain, she said bitterly, "How can you possibly say you love me, when you don't trust me? Believe in me?"

Christopher's face was expressionless, and in a frighteningly deliberate manner he took her hands from his shoulders and said, "Very well, tell me what happened."

"Damn you!" Nicole cried passionately. "No! Not when you're prepared to doubt my every word! And you are! I know that look on your face too well. You've already made up your mind that I'm lying." Twisting the knife in her own heart, she finished softly, "That I am my mother's daughter."

That seemed to evoke some response from Christopher; a spasm of what could have been pain crossed his face, and with a nervous gesture he raked his hand through the black hair. "I don't know what to believe anymore," he admitted dully. "I love you. I want you. But I cannot help but remember that your mother nearly destroyed me once—that she held me in her arms and whispered that she, too, loved me." Throwing her a glance of dislike, he said brutally, "She taught me how to make

501

love, how to arouse a woman, how to make her beg for a man, and all the while crying out that she loved me! That I was the only one who had ever made her feel that way." He laughed harshly. "And after I had left her, she met Robert, telling him the same lies, kissing him with the same passion and fire that she had me, giving herself to him with the same abandon. And you're her daughter." Coldly he demanded, "Tell me, Nicole, wouldn't you be just a little suspicious?"

She couldn't bear to look at him, to see the suspicion, the hate and bitterness that she knew was in his face. He loved her, but until she was able to exorcise the past for him, to burn clean the ugly memories, there would be no peace for either of them. Broodingly she stared at the fire, groping for the right words with which to answer him. There was no use in further protestations of her innocence, that she sensed. She could cry until the last trumpet that Robert had meant nothing to her and Christopher wouldn't believe her—because he compared her to Annabelle. And so she had to convince him somehow that she and Annabelle were two very different women, that she was Nicole. Nicole with her mercurial and volatile temper, Nicole who eagerly gave herself to him, not Annabelle, who lied and cheated and betrayed. It seemed a hopeless task, and yet as she sat there staring at the leaping flames, conscious of Christopher's big body behind hers, dimly an idea came to her. Taking a deep breath, she said cautiously, "You keep reminding me of my mother and what she did. And you say that I am her daughter. I agree—Annabelle with all her vanities and vices was my mother. I cannot help that, but because she was my mother is it necessarily true that I must be exactly like her? Have I ever given you proof that I am not to be trusted?"

Christopher stirred restlessly behind her. "Yes," he said flatly. "The code books. Have you forgotten them?"

Her fingers biting into the tender flesh of her palms, she admitted, "Yes. I had forgotten them." Flashing him an angry glance, she said hotly, "All right, I tried to take them, but I didn't betray *you!* Stealing those books was not harming you. They didn't even properly belong to you; you had stolen them in the first place." Honesty made her add, "Feeling the way I did then, knowing what I did then, and given the same circumstances, I would probably do the same thing again. You had no right to them. Allen and I were merely returning them to their rightful owners. Besides," she added childishly, "I wanted to get back at you. To thwart the omnipotent Captain Saber."

With a thread of sudden amusement in his voice, Christopher said softly, "Well, you did that, you little devil! You've done nothing *but* thwart me since Bermuda."

Her eyes shimmering with angry tears, she rounded on him. "Don't you dare laugh! I've admitted why I tried to take the books, and I'll even go so far as to say maybe I was wrong, but that doesn't mean I'm like my mother!" And desperately she played her last card. "Because she was my mother you say I have to be like her, but tell me, was Robert like your grandfather? The same adage should hold true—like mother, like daughter, like father, like son. Was Robert *exactly* like Lord Saxon?"

"Of course not! Absolutely not!" Christopher burst out furiously. "You cannot even begin to compare them! Robert was vile and selfish, while my grandfather is—" Christopher stopped abruptly, an arrested expression in the gold eyes. For a tense moment he stared at Nicole, his jaw taut, the heavy eyebrows meeting in a scowl. "I see your point," he said at last.

Nicole smiled bleakly. "You see it, but you don't agree?"

With a gentle hand Christopher reached out and cupped her face. "I don't know what to believe any longer. I've nursed this feeling against you for so many months that I can't seem to let it go. Give me time, my love. Time to come to understanding within myself. Will you grant me that?"

It was a humble request, and while he still might have to battle within himself, there was no hiding the love she saw on his face. Mutely she nodded, knowing that time was on her side. Time and love. And it gave her a queer feeling of tenderness to know that despite thinking she could be as wanton and wicked as Annabelle, he loved her anyway—loved her and had married her. Perhaps, she mused pensively, that was a greater sign of love than believing in her explicitly.

Gently Christopher drew her next to him and asked simply, "Tell me about that last night in England." And hesitatingly at first, her voice growing stronger as she continued, she told the tale of kidnapping and trickery. When she finished speaking, there was a long silence; both of them stared at the flames on the hearth, as if the answer they sought was there in the leaping tongues of fire. His arms tightening around her, Christopher murmured into

503

her hair, "I believe you, wildcat. That was too wild and improbable a tale for it not to be true. I just wish I had known and had been the one to rescue you—not Robert."

Twisting in his arms to face him, she said gently, "Well, you did in the end, you know. If you hadn't come along the beach just then I would have been in sorry straits. Higgins certainly wasn't going to do anything with me. He was too intent upon catching that ship. So you see, you really did save me from a fate worse than death." Her voice husky with emotion, she said against his lips, "Living without you would have been like dying."

With a groan Christopher pulled her even closer to him. "Keep loving me, Nicole. I'm a brute, a jealous madman where you are concerned, but I love you so much." His voice breaking just a little, he muttered, "I've loved you it seems like forever—you were always in my thoughts. First as an impudent cabin boy I couldn't help teasing and then as a wanton creature that haunted my every moment. Waking or sleeping, you were always there, a torment and an odd sort of joy." Pushing her away slightly, he stared intently into her face. "I can't put the past from me totally, but give me time. Teach me to love without looking for motives, without questioning, without doubting what I see before my very eyes. Teach me to trust you. And oh, Jesus," he growled thickly, "love me and go on loving me."

His mouth descended on hers hungrily, urgently, and Nicole met the hard caress of his lips eagerly, her body suddenly aflame to know again that sweet-savage possession of his. There was no holding back with either of them, no hiding their emotions, just the sweet enchantment of the other.

Slowly, as if he were discovering her body for the first time, Christopher's hands slid over her, marveling at the silken texture of her skin. Lazily his mouth left hers, and with a frankly sensual expression in the gold eyes, his gaze swept the slender body; the flickering firelight caressed the gentle upthrust of her breasts, shadowing the taut stomach and turning to gold the long, slim legs. Entranced, he glanced at her face, the sable hair splayed out like a flame-shot banner of silk on the ruby carpet. Her eyes were half closed, the high cheekbones highlighted by the fire, the full mouth generous and waiting for his kiss. With a muffled groan of desire, he sought her lips again, his hands touching and caressing the proud high bosom, delighting when he felt her nipples harden with hunger as consuming as his own.

Nicole, the blood roaring in her ears, reached for him, wanting more intensely this time for him to take her . . . this time, for the first time in love, not lust. She needed no arousing; her body already trembled with the demanding hunger he evoked so simply and fiercely, her body arched up against his hands, telling him without words that she was on fire for him. Instantly he covered her, filling her, her body expanding eagerly to take all of him.

It was like every time they had made love before combined into one urgent joining—their bodies meeting eagerly and hungrily the thrust of the other, their hands seeking to pleasure the other, their mouths mingling and tasting the other. And this time, this time when that exquisite, shattering explosion of the senses was fading, when they became aware of the world again, there was just each other—Christopher to cradle her body next to his, whispering soft words of love in her ear, and Nicole to press herself to him, her lips gently and tenderly slipping across his face.

It was a beginning between them. The beginning of something so fragile that the merest breath could destroy it, and only the coming months, and perhaps even years, would tell if what was between them now could grow and gain strength, flourish and take root, until not even death itself could destroy it.

39

There was little doubt in anyone's mind that the British were determined to take New Orleans, seize control of the lower Mississippi, and open the subcontinent nearby to the British crown. Even the peace talks in Ghent added to the British desire to take the city from the Americans; Lord Liverpool had remarked to the Duke of Wellington that "it is very desirable that the American war should terminate with a brilliant success."

Fortunately Andrew Jackson was now very much aware of the British intentions with regard to New Orleans, and he had written to Colonel Butler that "there will be bloody noses" before he would allow the conquest of New Orleans to happen. But Jackson made the dangerous assumption that when the attack came it would not be from the coast. He believed that the attack would be mounted from Mobile, and based on that surmise, he ordered mobilization of militia in Mississippi, Tennessee, and Kentucky.

Jackson was on the move from that point on. He ordered fresh supplies, men, and guns to a strategic fort on a long east-west spit that all but closed the mouth of Mobile Bay, reinforced Mobile itself, and sent more troops to Baton Rouge. On November seventh he marched into Spanish Florida and with some four thousand men stormed Pensacola, capturing Forts St. Rose and St. Michael; the English garrison withdrew to ships offshore after blowing up Fort Barrancas. That victory, while having diplomatic repercussions, gave the Americans their first view in months of the British in retreat. Feeling he had done his best to enmesh the British, Jackson departed for New Orleans to prepare the city for any eventuality.

Christopher was seated in Jason's library on the day the news came that the general was on his way to New Orleans. Straightening from his relaxed position, he remarked, "Well that's something! Maybe now our citizens will shake off their terrible apathy."

Smiling almost ruefully, Jason commented, "Do you think so? I tell you, *mon ami*, I have my doubts. The legislators are bickering amongst themselves, the committee of public safety is competing with the committee of defense, and although Claiborne has mobilized the militia, that order has been ignored by anyone who does not wish to serve! We are in a sorry state, and I wonder if even such a magnificent general as Jackson can do anything to change matters."

There was too much truth in what Jason said to dismiss it lightly, and Christopher was still mulling it over in his mind when they joined the ladies about half an hour later. Nicole, quick to sense his mood, sent him an inquiring glance, and while Christopher smiled at her reassuringly, she was not fooled.

The Saxons' visit to the Savages' was a combination of pleasure and business. Christopher and Jason had disappeared into the library to discuss the latest military developments, while Nicole and Catherine enjoyed each other's company. The friendship between the two women had grown rapidly, because they were English, and because they were married to extremely provocative and dynamic men. At first Nicole had been shy with the older woman, but as the days passed, she had discovered that behind Catherine's ladylike air, were a lively sense of humor and some shockingly unorthodox ideas. They had not reached the point where they laid bare all the secrets of their pasts, but Catherine made Nicole feel relaxed and often made her giggle at the tactics she used so blatantly to circumvent her autocratic husband. That Jason Savage was like clay in his wife's small hands and that she adored him grew more apparent each time she saw them, and wistfully she wondered if someday she and Christopher would be as close and so obviously in love as the Savages.

After their call on the Savages Nicole and Christopher sat before the fire in one of the smaller, cozier rooms of the Dauphine Street residence. Nicole was still concerned about Christopher's preoccupation after his conversation with Jason, and she asked abruptly "What did Jason tell you that was so worrisome?"

Christopher glanced up in surprise from some business papers he had been quietly reading. "Nothing very important, sweet," he said carelessly. "Merely some political news, and nothing for you to bother your beautiful head over."

Exasperated, Nicole glared at him and snapped, "I am not an idiot! Why do you treat me like one? And if you don't want to tell me what was said, why don't you just come out and say it?"

Christopher sighed, staring at the charming portrait she made sitting across from him on a couch of rose damask. Her hair was demurely pulled back into a chignon of curls at the nape of her neck, revealing the fine delicate bones of her face, and a discarded embroidery frame lying near her gave the deceptive impression of domesticity. What was he going to tell her?

He hadn't meant to treat her like an idiot, and he didn't really blame her for being somewhat angry at his non-committal answer to her reasonable question. But by the same token, he had no intention of discussing the current situation with Nicole, for two reasons. First, he didn't quite trust her; he was not sure precisely where her loyalties lay. He knew it was highly unlikely that she would find a way to pass any information to the British, but he was taking no chances. His second reason was simply that he did not want her to worry; in fact, he would have preferred to install her safely at Thibodaux House until all danger was past, but he knew Nicole would want to be right in the middle of whatever overtook the city. Hiding in the background was not her way, and he would not have had her any other way.

Seeing his smile, Nicole's temper rose, and she demanded, "Well? Aren't you even going to answer me?"

With a laugh Christopher said, "Calm down, spitfire! You have the hottest temper I have ever known! Yes, I'll answer your question." Rising leisurely from behind the desk, he walked over to where she sat and joined her on the couch. With one arm along the back of the couch, he drawled, "I'm sorry you think that I treated you like an idiot, but I can't see why you are interested in what Jason and I discussed."

A little ashamed at how quickly she had grown angry, Nicole muttered, "I do not mean to be a prying wife and I don't really care what you two discussed. What I cared about was that you were obviously perturbed about the conversation. Is it so wrong of me to want to know what was disturbing you? If our positions were reversed wouldn't you feel the same way?"

She had him there. Reminding himself that what he had learned today would be common knowledge within a matter of hours, he said lightly, "General Jackson is finally on his way to New Orleans. If all goes well he should be in the city in about a week."

"Is *that* what was bothering you?" she retorted disgustedly. "Don't you want him here?"

"Oh, yes, I want him and the troops he brings here. What worries me is the apathy and fear that is in the city. Even the best general cannot fight the combined forces of an enemy within as well as without." It was more than he had meant to tell her, but it seemed he could keep nothing from her—not when she was determined to force it from him.

Resting her head on his shoulder and absently playing with the gilt buttons on his bottle-green jacket, she asked in a small voice, "Is the city really going to be attacked? I know the newspapers have said so, and that the governor has called up the militia—you can see the troops drilling everyday in the Place d'Armes. But there aren't very many of them, are there?"

"Which question shall I answer first?" Christopher teased, suddenly more interested in the soft strands of hair under his chin. Nicole pinched him, and he said hastily, "All right! Yes, I do believe the city will be attacked. I think Jackson is wrong in his belief that the British will start their campaign at Mobile, but he is a general and I am a civilian. And yes, there aren't many troops. But Jackson will be bringing more troops with him, so I wouldn't let it worry you. Satisfied now?"

She shook her head slightly. In a voice barely above a whisper she asked the question that had been at the back of her mind for days. "Will you be in the fighting?"

Christopher sighed and gently smoothed the fire-dark head. "Yes, I'm afraid so," he said honestly. "You wouldn't expect me not to be, would you?"

Her throat tight, she looked up at him. "You'll be careful?"

Christopher sighed and gently smoothed the fire-dark caressing her cheek, he murmured, "When I have such a delightful bride waiting for me, you think I'm going to be taking any chances?" And then his mouth captured hers in a gentle kiss. At least it began gently, but her soft body so close to him was more than he could resist. His lips hardened with desire, and impatiently his hands sought out the fastenings of the gown.

Nicole responded as always to his lovemaking, yet conscious of where they were, she asked against his mouth, "Sanderson?"

The glitter of passion in his eyes, he promised thickly, "Anyone opens that door and I'll break his neck!"

A soft gurgle of laughter shook her, and without another thought she gave herself up to Christopher's demanding body.

It was only later, much later that night, that she recalled the conversation and a little chill crept around her heart. Lying in her bed, Christopher's sleeping form curved protectively next to hers, she touched him, as if reassuring herself he was still there, that the battle everyone knew was coming had not yet taken him from her.

This wouldn't be the first time they had been under fire, but this time it was different; this time he would be out there amongst the cannons and muskets, and she would remain behind. For just a minute she considered disguising herself as a boy to follow him, but knew it was a wistful, impractical idea. Besides, if a British bullet didn't kill her and Christopher found out, *he* would kill her!

Her loyalties about the coming battle were unclear even to herself. She knew that she wanted Christopher unharmed, but whether New Orleans was in the hands of the British or Americans made little difference to her. She had been just a little surprised and shocked to discover how deep Christopher's feelings were about America, and Louisiana particularly. Feeling slightly guilty that she could not summon up the same fierce loyalty that burned in Christopher, she sighed unhappily. She hated this war; it was as though brothers were warring against each other. It depressed her unbearably to know that perhaps some of the young officers she had met and liked while in England were going to be locked in mortal combat with her husband and her neighbors and friends.

Not surprisingly she thought of Allen. He was in her mind frequently these days, not only because Christopher had admitted carelessly one night last week that Lafitte had turned him over to some British officers, but she would have liked him to know that she and Christopher were married, that her seeming sacrifice hadn't been such a sacrifice after all. Her mention of Allen had pointed out how far they were from erasing the past. Christopher hadn't liked it when she had questioned him further about it—his eyes had narrowed, and suspicion and jealousy gleamed in the golden depths.

She stirred uncomfortably under the quilts, thinking that while she and Christopher were closer than they ever had been, there were still a great many pitfalls in their path. Time after time she had seen how a thought-less word could shatter the peace between them.

Despite Christopher's avowal of belief in her story of that last night in England, she sometimes wondered if he had really accepted it. An innocent mention of Robert's name was enough for that shuttered expression to cross his face, and whether he still believed she was like her mother she didn't know. And while they had loved glo-riously these past weeks, they had also fought and argued hotly, both proud, both still a little wary of this ac-knowledged emotion between them.

Christopher was the worst, she decided almost angrily. He shut her out whenever something he didn't want to face was mentioned, and infuriatingly she was confronted once again by the cold and sardonic Captain Saber. But then she smiled. At least it was Christopher who made love to her, ending most arguments in the age-old masculine manner by making violent love to her until she no longer cared what the argument had been about or who had been right. It was only later, like now, that all the doubts came back.

Sleepless and bedeviled, she twitched restlessly in the bed until she accidentally woke Christopher. Irritably he demanded, "What in the hell is wrong with you? I feel like a wiggling puppy has invaded my bed!"

He propped himself up on one elbow, and when Nicole saw his tousled hair tumbling across his forehead, his muscled naked chest, she felt a wave of love sweep over her. Christopher caught the look and his irritation van-ished, and with a smothered laugh he reached for her under the quilts. "If you wanted me to make love to you, why didn't you say so?" he teased and proceeded to do just that.

On December second General Jackson arrived in New Orleans and the inhabitants took heart. Some of the apathy disappeared, although the Creoles still couldn't seem to comprehend that they were going to have to de-fend themselves. Besides, they argued, New Orleans had seen so many flags flying overhead in the past, what did one more mean?

On December third General Jackson reviewed the gor-geously beplumed battalion of New Orleans volunteers in the Place d'Armes. Tall, gaunt, his iron-gray hair worn long and drawn back from his sallow hawklike face, he watched expressionlessly the pitiful number of men that marched before him.

511

Christopher, too, stared at those same pitiful troops and decided to tackle Lafitte once more. First, though, he would have to see if Jason could put the general in a receptive mood.

At first Jason was skeptical. "Look, I know we need those men, but Jackson sided with Claiborne earlier. What makes you think he'll have changed his mind?"

"Because," Christopher retorted levelly, if a little heatedly, "he doesn't want New Orleans to fall to the British and without those men, it surely will!"

Jason regarded him sourly. "Very well. I shall talk to the general."

"Today?"

"No," Jason replied decisively. "The general must first see for himself that using Lafitte's men is the only way to save the city. *Then* I will approach him about Lafitte."

Christopher didn't like it, but Jason was unmoved. He merely smiled and said mildly, "Why don't you go prime Lafitte? That should satisfy your urge for action."

Unable to decide whether to laugh or smash his fist into Jason's sardonic features, Christopher stormed out of the room and headed for Lafitte's cottage on the ramparts.

"Come in, *mon ami,*" Lafitte cried happily. "I was wondering when you would come back to see me."

His lips twisting disagreeably, Christopher lounged down in one of the wooden chairs and snapped, "I suppose you know why I have come?"

Looking seraphic, Lafitte murmured, "Let us say I hope I know why you come? The Americans need me rather badly, don't they?"

"Goddamnit, yes!" And forgetting all his careful arguments for convincing Lafitte to throw his forces in with theirs, he demanded, "Are you going to join us?"

His eyebrows rising in mock surprise, Lafitte admitted, "But of course! Did you doubt it?"

Narrowly Christopher regarded him. "What is your price? Surely it is not sheer nobility of purpose that motivates you?"

"Ah, well, there is that, but you are right, *mon ami*— I do have my price." Suddenly very serious, Lafitte said, "I want my men freed, I want my goods returned, and I want no more interference by Claiborne."

"I cannot guarantee you anything," Christopher admitted candidly. "What I can do, I hope, is arrange a meeting between you and General Jackson—between you, you will have to work out your differences."

Lafitte nodded. "That is fair enough. Jackson, I have heard, is not an unreasonable man . . . nor is he in much of a position to be particularly high-stomached about where his ammunition and added men come from."

Christopher could agree with that, and after confirming Lafitte's willingness to meet with the general as soon as it could be arranged, he departed, feeling as useless as he had to begin with.

From that point on the New Orleans area was a hive of activity. One of the general's first orders was for brigades of axmen to block the swamp-hemmed watercourses that surrounded the city with fallen trees. Because Christopher was spoiling for action and knew those areas well, due to his time with Lafitte, on Claiborne's recommendation to Jackson he was appointed as one of the men in charge of the hurriedly assembled army of axmen. Though the work was hard, Christopher was pleased that at last there was a concerted effort being made to protect the city.

On Lake Borgne Commodore Patterson was posted with five gunboats to act as the general's "eyes" for the defense of the eastern routes into the city. Having decided not to attempt any defense of the river below Fort St. Philip, Jackson inspected the fort, and on his orders the inflammable wooden barracks were demolished and the existing cannon were augmented by the addition of a thirty-two-pounder. Two new batteries were erected, one across the river at the derelict old Spanish Fort Bourbon and the second a half mile upstream.

At English Turn, below the city on the Mississippi River, he ordered the immediate construction of batteries protected by earthworks and another battery to be mounted at a point covering part of Bayou Terre aux Boeufs.

Jackson was out of the city for six days during his inspections, but there was a constant stream of orders relayed back to his engineers in New Orleans, and demands to the governor and requisitions for troops and stores. On his order the slaves of riverside plantations were called in to throw up earthworks and erect batteries. With gladness he accepted Pierre Jugeat's offer to raise a battalion of friendly Choctaw Indians and approved the request of Jean Baptiste Savary to form a battalion of free men of color from the refugees from Santo Domingo.

In the city Nicole watched the activity with growing unease and dismay. She longed desperately for Christopher and worried constantly. She cursed herself a dozen times a day for her silliness, knowing in her heart that Christopher was enjoying himself immensely in the swamps, and that he would have detested being a mere spectator. She supposed it was her own restlessness that made her so inclined to worry about him, and ruefully she admitted she envied him.

Jackson returned to the city on the tenth, but set out again two days later to inspect the routes from the head of Lake Borgne. And as a result of his inspection a battery was mounted on Chef Menteur Road, and Fort St. John was strengthened and reinforced. He had done what he could and with what he had to work with; now there was little he could do but wait.

Jackson had barely returned to the city again, when on December 13, the news reached him that British ships were dropping anchor off Cat and Ship islands at the mouth of Lake Borgne. Unwisely he wrote to Major General John Coffee at Baton Rouge, "I expect this is a feint to draw my attention to that point when they mean to strike at another," never realizing that the British did intend to attack through the lake. So Jackson settled down to wait, confident the lake was too shallow for big ships to anchor within sixty miles of New Orleans.

Christopher himself was back in the city by the second week in December, tired and irritable. His moroseness disappeared when Jason informed him that the general was agreeable to a meeting with Lafitte.

In a private meeting between the two principals in Maspero's Coffee House they agreed that Lafitte would fight for the Americans. Upon hearing the news, Christopher felt a wave of hope sweep through him. With only five thousand men to face an enemy of twice that number, it was definitely encouraging to know that there would now be ample ammunition and that some of the best-trained fighting men in the world were on their side.

And now there really was nothing else to do but wait —wait and wonder where the British would begin their assault.

Christopher, at Claiborne's recommendation, was appointed to the general's staff as the liaison between him and Lafitte and his men. It both gratified and pleased him, for now there was something he could definitely get his teeth into.

Nicole found the waiting excruciating and wished she possessed some of her husband's enjoyment of the preparations. Like the other ladies, she had been busy making bandages, but for the women there was little to do except wait and tend to the absentminded, distracted men who were their husbands, brothers, and lovers.

Then the stunning news reached New Orleans that the British did indeed mean to attack by way of Lake Borgne, having captured Patterson's five gunboats. Jackson was enraged. Not only had he lost his "eyes" and valuable men, but now the British had the use of his shallow-drafted vessels to transport their troops. From his Royal Street headquarters he wrote frantically to Major General Coffee: "You must not sleep until you reach me."

The citizenry was panic-stricken at the news of the British attack on the lake. On December 16, Jackson declared martial law.

Major General Coffee and his men arrived on the twentieth, and on Wednesday of the same week Jackson called a briefing session at his headquarters. Christopher was in attendance, and as Nicole had a fitting at Madame Colette's just down the street, they had decided that Christopher would meet her there after the meeting.

The briefing lasted longer than either of them had expected, and Nicole, growing weary of waiting, told Madame Colette to explain to her husband when he arrived that she had gone home. Her cloak fastened securely around her, Naomi in attendance, she walked out and accidentally bumped into a neatly dressed young man.

Laughing, she stepped back and exclaimed, "Excuse me! I'm awfully sorry, but I didn't see you, if you can believe that!" And the next instant the color drained from her face as she found herself looking into Allen's features.

For a frozen moment neither of them said a word, Allen Ballard's face as white as Nicole's. Unaware that she did it, Nicole reached out to rest her hand on his chest, as if to reassure herself that it was not an apparition. "Allen," she said at last in the merest whisper. And Allen, after throwing a sharp glance around, grasped her hand and said urgently, "I have to talk to you. Is there someplace we can be private?"

Still stunned by the unexpected meeting, still not quite assimilating what his presence in New Orleans on the eve of the British attack might indicate, she shook her head slowly. Then looking at Madame Colette's, she murmured reluctantly, "I suppose Madame would let us use one of the fitting rooms."

It wasn't what Allen wanted, but it would have to do. Thrown as completely off guard as Nicole, he was still fighting with the shock that she was here in New Orleans and not in England as he had been led to believe. She

515

had to be silenced—at least long enough for him to escape the city and report to his commanding officer on the city's woefully inadequate defenses.

Allen hadn't wanted to be sent to spy out the city, but he was the only one who was totally familiar with the area, and reluctantly he had agreed. He had been aware that he might be recognized, but was relying on the frail hope that not everyone had known he was a British spy during his imprisonment on Grand Terre. Besides, dressed as he was as a young man of the city in a tight-fitting coat of Spanish blue, buff pantaloons, and highly polished boots, the brown hair cut short and wearing a cocked hat, he had thought it unlikely that anyone would connect him with the Allen Ballard who had sailed on *La Belle Garce*. But then he hadn't counted on Nicole Ashford to be tripping merrily down the banquettes of New Orleans either. It was the devil's own luck, he thought exasperatedly; another half hour and he would have been safe.

At that very second Christopher was strolling in the direction of Madame's when he was brought up short by the unpleasant sight of his wife making overtures to a strange young man. Then as the two of them turned and walked back into Madame's, his eyes narrowed in disbelief. Allen Ballard! What in God's name was he doing in New Orleans? It took Christopher less than a second to realize the reason, and his mouth went grim as he approached the dressmaker's.

His wife consorting with a damned spy! By God, for all he knew this wasn't the first time they had met. Perhaps that betraying little bitch had been supplying Ballard with information all along. In the grip of raging anger Christopher was blind to anything but the fact that Nicole was with Allen and acting in a furtive manner.

For just a moment he considered reporting that a pair of British spies were meeting at Madame Colette's. Let Nicole pay the price for her duplicity! But in his heart he knew that he could not. Whatever she was, she was his. That knowledge twisted like a knife in his gut, destroying the peace and contentment he had felt these last weeks, making him bitterly aware of how easily he would have succumbed to her spell. He had begun to believe her protestations of love, to believe that she was as different from Annabelle as Robert had been from Simon, and now *this!*

He hesitated only a moment outside Madame Colette's, his mind coldly made up. Nicole must be protected from her own deceit and guile. She was still his wife, and he would not have her dragged into the gutter by the likes of Allen Ballard. Ballard would have to die before he could implicate Nicole.

Almost nonchalantly Christopher entered Madame Colette's just a second later, having decided to act as naturally as possible until he could get his hands around Ballard's neck. But his plans suffered a check the instant he entered the premises, for Madame Colette, her finger to her lips, had hurriedly led him to the back of her shop.

Madame had been profoundly shocked and disillusioned when Madame Saxon had returned with a young gentleman in tow. She was even more disapproving when Madame Saxon had dismissed her maid and requested the use of one of the dressing rooms for a few minutes of private conversation. And while her dressing rooms had often been used as rendezvous places by many married ladies with their lovers, she had not suspected Madame Saxon of being that sort. The wad of notes Allen had quickly put in her hand would have kept her quiet about the meeting if Monsieur Saxon had not suddenly appeared.

Now Monsieur Saxon had been a valuable client in the past. It was likely he would be a valuable client in the future—far more valuable than Madame Saxon—and she had promptly decided on whose side she would align herself.

Bluntly and to the point, she informed Monsieur that his wife, she was sorry to say, was meeting a strange young man in the front dressing room.

In that dressing room Nicole's mind was working furiously. Once her first shock had fled, it hadn't taken her but a second to realize why Allen was in the city. She could not allow Allen to leave, not when she guessed that he had information that might mean the death of her husband. Nor could she turn him over to the authorities, knowing that the gallows would be his fate. Too vividly did she remember the upward spiral of that shark, and she knew she could not live in peace with herself if she were the cause of Allen's death. She must render him incapable of leaving the city until after the battle.

With an elated gleam her eye fell upon the warming brick that sat so innocently in the far corner. If she could grasp that and strike Allen unconscious, she could then, with Madame's help, tie Allen and hide him somewhere in the city until his knowledge was no longer of any value. *Then* she could set him free.

Allen was thinking much the same thing, except he had

decided to overpower Nicole, gag and tie her, and then beat a hasty retreat from New Orleans. By the time Nicole was discovered he would be safe.

Christopher was making his own plan. He had to get Madame out of the shop while he silenced Allen, and the only way he could do that was to send her after the military. But then, he surmised, that would work very well, although instead of a live spy they would find a very dead one—one who could tell no tales. Christopher explained to Madame that when he stormed into the dressing room, she was to race immediately to the authorities.

It did not go as anyone planned. By dropping her reticule, Nicole had managed to get her hands on the warming brick and hide it in the folds of her cloak. Allen was on the point of forcing himself to deliver a powerful blow to Nicole's delightful chin, one which he hoped would knock her out, when Christopher, murder on his mind, burst through the thin door, and Madame, faithfully following his instructions, darted from the shop, speeding after the authorities.

At the sound of the shattering wood Allen jerked in that direction, and Nicole, taking advantage of his distraction, coolly brought the brick up and aimed it at his head. Unfortunately her aim was rather bad, and instead of connecting with Allen's head, it landed very painfully right in the middle of her husband's chest, knocking the wind from him and causing him to stagger back into the other room.

Allen, now intent only on escape, leaped from the fitting room, while Nicole wasted a precious second staring in horrified disbelief at her husband as he reeled from the room. But then realizing that Christopher would be absolutely no help for a moment or two, she shot after Allen.

Allen was almost to the door, and the only way she could reach him was a headlong tackle. She made it despite her long skirts, and wrapping her arms in a stranglehold about his knees, she bought Allen cursing and tumbling to the floor.

To Christopher, his breath coming in painful little gasps, it looked as if the two of them had been trying to escape, only Nicole had tripped and fallen, dragging Allen down with her. Wasting little time on speculation, he heaved himself away from the wall, and as Allen struggled to his feet, seeking to escape from Nicole's embrace, Christopher landed him a mighty punch on his chin. Allen crumpled, and Nicole, with a satisfied sigh, loosened her grip.

Christopher dropped to his knees, his fingers itching to close around Allen's throat and still forever his tongue, but Madame had been more than fortunate in meeting one of the patrols that Jackson had ordered to enforce the martial law, and just as Christopher was about to reach his goal, Madame and a patrol came rushing into the shop.

With resignation, and knowing he had lost his chance, Christopher rose painfully to his feet and said in a dull voice, "This man is a British spy . . . I recognized him. Take him away and inform the general that I will report to him later this evening."

Nicole, her heart heavy in her breast, watched with shadowed eyes as they complied with Christopher's orders. But the real anguish of what had happened didn't occur to her then. It was only when Christopher's steely fingers closed cruelly around her arm and she glanced up at his face in surprise that she saw his disillusionment, contempt, and anger.

"But I . . ." she began helplessly.

Christopher's lips thinned and he snapped, "Shut up! Don't say another word until we are at home."

There was nothing she could do, and confused and slightly resentful, she allowed Christopher to hustle her away. She tried once more to explain, but Christopher's cold, "I said later and I meant later!" froze the words on her lips.

By the time they reached Dauphine Street Nicole was in a fine simmering temper. Christopher couldn't believe that she had purposely met Allen at Madame's! How vexingly stupid and absolutely ridiculous! If that was all the faith he had in her, well she just wasn't going to put up with it!

Standing in the center of her bedroom a short while later, she faced him and demanded, "What is the matter with you? Don't you want to know what happened?"

Taking a deep draught of the brandy in his hand, Christopher replied bleakly, "No. I already know what happened and I don't need your lies to distort the truth!"

Drawing her breath in with a sharp gasp, Nicole cried, "Then suppose you tell it to me! Obviously there is something I don't know about or don't understand."

"In that case, madame, I'll tell you," Christopher began in a cold voice. "This afternoon I was walking to meet my dearly beloved wife"—he grated out the words—

"when it was my unpleasant chance to see her openly caressing a strange man on the street. And then if that wasn't enough, the two of them slunk away, like two alley cats, into a snug little rendezvous. What's more, the man my wife was so eager to meet and touch was none other than an English spy. Tell me," he asked sneeringly, "have you been supplying him with information? Is that why you have been so interested in what I have been doing? You were gathering it for your confederate?"

Nicole blanched at the venom not only in his tone, but in the hard gold eyes that bored into hers. That he believed her capable of such perfidy left her feeling sick and drained of every vestige of fight. Wearily she said, "Very well, if that is what you believe, I'll not try to change your mind. Tell me, do you intend to turn me over to the authorities also? I would like to know so that I may pack a few things to take with me."

Her calm acceptance of his accusations left Christopher staring at her in angry dismay. No, he wasn't going to turn her over to the authorities, he almost shouted, she was his wife! But what was he going to do? And did he honestly believe those terrible things he'd thrown at her? As some semblance of coherency trickled back into his thoughts, he realized that there were certain things about what had happened this afternoon that were decidedly odd. For instance, the lunacy of meeting at Madame's when he was expected at any moment. And that warming brick that had been hurled at him. There had been no warning that he was about to burst in on them, so what was she doing with it? The ugly surmise crossed his mind that Allen had been making a nuisance of himself and that Nicole had been protecting her honor. And if that were so . . .

Christopher swallowed painfully, as it occurred to him that this time he had well and truly leaped to very wrong conclusions. Hesitatingly he said, "Nicole, I . . ."

But it was too late. Heartsick, wounded more than she could have thought possible, Nicole regarded him hostilely. "What?" she spat. "Have you thought of further crimes to add to my list?"

"No. I . . ." he fumbled, his ready address failing him in the face of the enormity of his accusations.

Her eyes were scornful as Nicole regarded him. "Oh, have you had second thoughts?" she asked sweetly. At Christopher's curt nod, her face blazed with fury, and crossing to stand in front of him, she gritted, "Well, it's just too damn late! I'll never convince you that I am not

520

my mother's daughter, will I? You have to cling to that idea, don't you? I hope it gives you pleasure, and don't worry that I'll try to change your mind—I would sooner try to roll back the tide than to waste my time with the likes of you!" Her voice breaking just a little, the topaz eyes bright with tears, she said in a small voice, "Get out of my room and stay out of it. Right now I don't think I ever want to see you again."

Christopher made a move to touch her, but furiously shrugging off his hand, she whirled away and, running to the bed, flung herself face down on it, the tears uncontrollably slipping down her face. In a muffled sob she said, "Get out! Leave me alone and let me be."

Still he hesitated, but knowing she was too hurt, too angry to listen to him now, Christopher did as she requested, shutting the door quietly behind him.

His own anguish was almost unbearable; he was aware that with one jealous, thoughtless action he had shattered the fragile bond between them. But I'll make it up to her, he thought unhappily. Somehow I'll make her understand, and maybe if I'm lucky she'll forgive me.

But if the passing days were anything to go by, Nicole wasn't going to forgive him, he decided wretchedly. She treated him as if he were a leper, and he, so very conscious of that wrong he had done, was helpless to bridge the widening chasm between them. Was this to be the end of their frail beginning?

Avoiding his own home, Christopher spent more and more hours at Jackson's Royal Street headquarters, and because of that he was there on December 23 when Major Gabrielle Villere, Colonel de la Ronde, and Dussan La Croix burst into the general's headquarters with the appalling news that the British were encamped on the Villere plantation just nine miles from New Orleans.

Jackson, his body wasted by disease, his face thin and yellowed by jaundice, swayed for a moment at the news but then straightened proudly. To Christopher watching intently from the doorway, it was as if he suddenly took strength; the lines of pain smoothing from his face, vitality springing from some unknown inner source, he was like a different man—a fighting man with fire in his eyes and bravery in his heart. Taking a sip of brandy, he calmly ordered the assembly of his secretaries, aides, and other members of his staff. And standing before them, he said, "Gentlemen, the British are below. We must fight them tonight."

EPILOGUE

40

What happened in the following days on the plains of Chalmette below the city of New Orleans is history: Andrew Jackson won a most decisive victory over the British. There is no denying that the outcome might have been vastly different had it not been for Jean Lafitte, his men, and his ammunition and flints.

The Battle of New Orleans was actually two battles with scattered fighting in between, the main and final battle taking place on January 8, 1815, in the cane fields of the Macarty plantation. The loss of life was terrible; the British lost over two thousand men in only two hours in a vain attempt to breach the earthen barriers that Jackson had strewn before them. American losses were a mere seventy men, although those seventy men were as important to the Americans as the two thousand had been to the British.

The British also lost two of their most able leaders, Major General Samuel Gibbs and Major General Sir Edward Pakenham. Casualties among the more junior officers and sergeants were crippling—one regiment alone lost twenty-four officers, including its colonel and twelve sergeants.

Indecisiveness and lack of communication between commanders cost the British the Battle of New Orleans. They should have won it: they outnumbered the Americans almost three to one; they had a powerful fleet to supply them and protect their rear flank; and they were fighting against a polyglot army of untried men. Creoles and English-speaking citizens of New Orleans; lean Kentuckians carrying their rifles in the crooks of their arms; bronzed Acadians from the prairies and bayous; small companies of mulattoes and Negroes—"free men of color"; Mississippi dragoons and Tennesseans in homespun coats; Lafitte's Baratarians and a small band of Choctaw Indians, indeed a polyglot army—but an army that brought the British lion to her knees.

Ironically the Battle of New Orleans was fought after the Treaty of Ghent was signed by the British and United States negotiators on December 24, 1814. Word of the treaty agreement did not reach the United States until February, and by then the Battle of New Orleans was an accomplished fact.

The United States ratified the treaty on February 16, 1815, and it is ironic that there is no mention of British impressment of American seamen in the treaty—and that was presumably one of the overriding reasons for the War of 1812.

Christopher and Jason exchanged wry glances when at last a copy of the treaty reached New Orleans. But neither saw any reason to comment on that curious, and yet not so curious, oversight. America was at peace again and for the moment that was all that mattered.

Walking slowly toward Dauphine Street a short while later, Christopher ruefully admitted that all he wanted now was peace within his own household—peace between him and that stubborn little spitfire he had married and loved.

For almost three months now, they had lived in a state of armed hostility—Nicole, unbending, met his attempts at reconciliation with icy contempt. And Christopher, uncertain how to proceed, withdrew behind a mask of indifference.

He was very conscious that he had misjudged her, very aware that the wrong had been his, and because he feared as he had feared nothing in his life to alienate her further, his behavior was exactly the opposite of what it should have been.

They appeared to live separate lives—Christopher busy with his affairs and Nicole drawn into the lively social circle of New Orleans. They attended functions together, but only for the look of it, riding to and from the various affairs in deathly silence, and at their destination promptly finding their own groups of friends, most times never meeting until it was time to depart.

At home they avoided each other. Christopher was up and gone many mornings before Nicole arose, and most evenings he dined out with other acquaintances, leaving Nicole to find her own amusements.

In the beginning Christopher had tried to break through her wall of silence and disillusionment, but because he had proceeded gently and delicately, instead of with his usual arrogance and ruthlessness, Nicole had viewed his attempts as only halfhearted.

He had done one thing, though, that warmed her heart slightly and made her wonder if perhaps all was not lost. Shortly after the final bloody battle with the British, he had arranged for her to meet with Allen. It had been a short visit, and staring unhappily at Allen through the bars of his cell, conscious of the guard a few yards down the hall, Nicole had been vividly reminded of the similar circumstance on Grand Terre.

For several moments the two could think of nothing to say, but then Allen, with a crooked grin, had murmured, "Either I am a singularly inept spy, or your husband is my nemesis."

Nicole swallowed, thinking uncomfortably that this time it was more her fault than Christopher's that Allen was behind bars. Awkwardly she said, "Allen, I'm sorry I didn't let you escape when you had the chance." Her eyes were huge and beseeching on his blue ones as she said huskily, "But I couldn't let you go—not knowing you might be the cause of Christopher's death! Please understand!"

Allen smiled almost gently. "I do, little one. I do. Although I don't really relish the thought of hanging, I can't blame you for what you did." His eyes filling with mockery, he added, "I could wish that you were not quite so agile and hadn't such grim determination to stop me, though. What a little bulldog you were."

"Don't tease!" Nicole cried. Her hand curling around one of his as it rested on the bars, she muttered, "I'll try to help you. Maybe they won't hang you."

"Maybe they won't. But they sure as hell aren't going to exchange me with the other prisoners either! Spying is a little different than fighting on the honorable field of battle." There was a certain bitterness in his tone that he couldn't conceal. But shaking off the bleakness that crept through his bones, he said lightly, "Mayhap you can get that husband of yours to do something to lessen my punishment. From what I hear, he is very close to Claiborne and Jackson both, and a loving wife has swayed more than one man."

Nicole gave him a watery smile. Allen had enough to contend with without knowing that he was the direct cause of the present terrible estrangement between her and her husband. There had been little more to say, and with a quick, bone-crushing clasp of hands they had said good-bye.

They had not met again, and Nicole dared not ask Christopher what Allen's eventual fate would be. She had

not been blind to the fact that behind his fury and accusations that last night had laid jealousy, and she dared not awaken it by questions about Allen. And because she knew him to be jealous of Allen, his actions in arranging the meeting between them had been all the more puzzling. What had he hoped for—that they would somehow give him the proof he wanted? Yet astonishingly she had thought for a second there had been an almost kind expression in his eyes when he had informed her that she was to see Allen. Christopher *kind*? Ridiculous! Quelling the promptings of her heart, she cloaked herself in righteous anger, telling herself that Christopher was unworthy of her love and not to be trusted.

But in so doing, Nicole had backed herself into a corner, and now to her horror discovered there was no way out of her predicament. She was ensconced in her castle of icy disdain and Christopher showed every sign of letting her stay there!

During the weeks that followed the Battle of New Orleans, with the cessation of fear of attack, Nicole had had time for cooler reflections. Without the worry of assault on her mind, there had been room for more introspective thought—and it was not pleasant.

Did she really want to live out the rest of their days in this state of armed indifference? Did she never want to feel Christopher's body take hers again? The doors between their rooms had remained securely shut, Christopher denying himself even the rights of a husband. Was all her pious fury worth never again having the laughter and love that had been hers for those few short weeks? That glimpse of paradise that had beckoned to both of them? The answer was a resounding and heartfelt *no!*

And brutally honest with herself, she admitted that if she had come across Christopher and any other woman in the same sort of situation that Christopher had found her and Allen in, she would have leaped to precisely the same conclusion. And if she would have thought that, could she really blame him for believing as he had? Again the answer was an unpleasant no. Seated in her elegant room, staring out glumly at the budding leaves on a huge pecan tree, Nicole found herself in an appalling situation.

She had repulsed Christopher's attempts to explain or mend the breach between them with such icy scorn that he no longer tried. She had been so proud and fiery in her disdain that Christopher had gradually withdrawn into himself, ignoring her, treating her with cool politeness.

How was she to climb down from this seemingly impenetrable tower in which she had locked herself?

One sunny March day a note was delivered to Christopher from his overseer, Bartel. As he read it, an idea began to take shape. The note was brief, mentioning only that the spring planting had begun, but that there were several things he wanted to discuss. Usually Bartel would come into the city, but Christopher, his mind instantly made up, decided he would remove his household to Thibodaux House. Perhaps there, faced only with each other's company, and without the distractions of the city, he and Nicole could find their way back to each other. His decision made, he wasted little time in informing the staff and, more importantly, his wife.

There was an air of purpose about him, a new and dangerous vitality that Nicole was instantly aware of when he entered her room, a few minutes later. Gone was the polite man who had been her husband these past months, and in his place was the arrogant, infuriatingly attractive man she had first married.

His gold eyes enigmatic, Christopher stared at her as she sat in a small chair by a window that overlooked the courtyard below, a shaft of sunlight flaming the sable curls and intensifying the topaz gleam of her eyes between the black curling lashes. Appreciatively his gaze roamed over her, making no attempt to hide the appraisal in his eyes.

The russet gown she was wearing today was rather lower cut than usual and displayed an enticing amount of smooth, milky flesh, and Christopher felt a tremor of desire sweep through him. Damn the little vixen, he had only to look at her and his body was instantly aflame, he thought with a small spurt of anger. And he had denied himself too long, he decided sourly. It was time Madame learned that this was certainly not how *he* had envisioned their marriage.

Made uneasy by the prolonged stare of the gold eyes, Nicole rose to her feet, and still unable to drop completely her haughty air, she asked coolly, "Yes? What is it?"

Christopher grinned, leaning negligently against one of the posts of her bed. "What?" he mocked. "No welcoming embrace? No sweet greeting from my bride?"

Nicole's head went up angrily, forgetting immediately her resolve to end the estrangement between them. "If you have come merely to taunt me, then I wish you

529

would leave!" she replied heatedly, a becoming flush staining her cheeks.

It was tempting to continue baiting her, but Christopher stifled the desire and remarked idly, "I thought you would like to know that the war with Britain is officially over. I've just come from Jason's and we've seen a copy of the treaty." Unable to help himself, he added sneeringly, "Rest easy that your beloved Allen will not hang now."

Nicole couldn't quite hide the relief that swept through her, and seeing it, all the jealousy he had tamped came surging to the fore, until he could taste it, like burning gall at the base of his throat. It had not been easy for him to allow Nicole to see Allen, but he had been trying to show her that he loved her and that he trusted her, that he could, and had, overcome his raging jealousy. But it hadn't mattered; all the pain he had suffered in winning the terrible battle within himself had been for naught—Nicole had gone gladly to see Allen, but she had not softened, nor made any indication that she realized the reasons, or even the effort it had cost him to allow that meeting. And now he could no longer control the bitter rage and jealousy that had eaten him for months. He had tried being compassionate, being understanding, tried to explain himself, had ignored his baser instincts and treated her gently, hoping in time she would see his outburst for what it had been. But it had availed him nothing and he was through being the polite, courtly gentleman!

Staring at her almost with dislike, he said cruelly, "I wouldn't look quite so happy if I were you—he'll still stand trial and more than likely will spend several years in prison. Hanging might have been preferable."

Her face draining of all color, Nicole grasped the back of a chair for support. Not looking at Christopher, she asked in a low voice, "Can you do nothing to help him?"

"Why should I?" Christopher jeered. "I can't say that he has ever done anything to endear himself to me! Now, perhaps in your case it's different."

Looking squarely at her husband's dark face, Nicole said slowly, "He saved my life, once. We were swimming in one of those lagoons in Bermuda, and a shark . . ." She stopped as the horror of those moments washed over her. Forcing herself to continue, she said, "Allen didn't have to dive in to save me. He was safe. But he risked his life for mine, and if he had not been there or if he had hesitated a second, I would not be here this moment

—I would be just poor Nick who had got eaten by a shark off Bermuda. Now do you see why I will do just about anything for him? It's not love, you fool," she cried hotly. "It's *gratitude!* And you're too pigheaded to realize it!"

The shaft struck home and Christopher stiffened, seeing again where his own blindness had led him. Instead of burning with jealousy over the undeniable affection between Nicole and Allen, he should be thanking God that Allen had been with her that day. It was ironic, he thought bitterly, that the one man he had viewed as his most dangerous rival had, in fact, given Nicole to him.

Nicole could tell nothing from his face. Christopher pushed away from the post and said, in a voice that was carefully bland, "Well, then, it seems I must do something for Mr. Ballard, mustn't I? After all, without him you wouldn't be here now."

Warily she watched him, unable to take any comfort from his words. Cautiously she asked, "What do you intend to do?"

Christopher's shoulders squared but his voice was weary. "Oh, I'll have a word with Jason, and perhaps through him we can see that something is worked out. I'll see to it this afternoon." He started to leave the room, but then he turned and looked back at her. "What I really came up to see you about, though, was to tell you," he said slowly, "that we will be going to Thibodaux House at the end of this week. Please have your maids start packing whatever you think you will need."

Nicole nodded mutely, uncertain whether the news was pleasant or unpleasant. In a way it would be a relief to leave New Orleans, but to return to Thibodaux House with the future unsettled between them was daunting.

Christopher had not been making idle conversation when he had said he would speak to Jason about Allen. But he had known there was really very little he could do. Allen had been caught as a spy, and even the cessation of the war between Britain and America did not lessen that fact. And Jason told Christopher as much, when he brought the subject up that afternoon.

"Hmm. I don't really see that we can do anything, *mon ami,*" Jason had said. "In this case, I am afraid that justice must run its course. Monsieur Ballard is not just another prisoner of war, you understand. I will see what I can do, but I doubt my intervention will accomplish a great deal."

And that seemed to be it. But not one to give up eas-

ily, Christopher paid a call at the calaboose. He did not visit Allen at first; instead, he spent an inordinate amount of time viewing the outer walls of the calaboose itself, and then appeared to be having a serious and important conversation with one of the guards. An observant man might have noticed the wad of notes that were quietly passed between them, but no one paid any attention.

The interview between Allen and Christopher was brief and, to a certain degree, strained. The two had very little to discuss, and Allen had the curious conviction that Christopher was more interested in the construction of his cell than in talking to him. And Christopher's parting words left Allen staring after him with bewilderment. What in the hell had he meant by, "I certainly hope you are as quick-witted as I think you are"?

That night, Madame and Monsieur Saxon dined at home together for the first time in weeks. Their conversation was stilted and wary, but it was a conversation, something they had not had in months. Nothing was resolved between them; Christopher disappeared immediately after dinner, presumably to one of the coffee houses or gambling rooms.

Sitting alone in her bedroom, Nicole regarded herself angrily in the mirror as ruthlessly she brushed the curling sable-fire hair. What in hell's name was she to do? She had to break down the walls between them someway, and glancing at the tall, slender body reflected in her mirror, she smiled a secretive catlike smile. It was brazen and without scruple, but somehow she was going to get Christopher into her bed, and then she would show him without words how silly was this continued estrangement.

Making the decision to deliberately seduce her husband was easier than actually doing it. She would have preferred to do it gradually, to let him see in little ways that she was now ready to accept his advances, except she knew in her heart that they had gone beyond that point. No, she was going to have to take very blunt and forthright action; Christopher wasn't about to let her take the easy way out. She quailed at the thought of rejection, of the cool contempt she might find in his eyes, and so for the next few days she did nothing.

The night before they were to leave for Thibodaux House she steeled her spine and prepared for battle. She scented her bath with a musky odor of forests and spices, brushed her hair till it crackled, and carefully dressed in a flimsy gown of emerald silk.

She waited impatiently and with growing apprehension

in her veins for Christopher to return home that evening, and when at last she heard his movements in the next room, her heart leaped into her throat. Rising from her bed, she took one last look in the mirror, suddenly shocked at the gown's transparency. Her skin gleamed like ivory through the folds, the faint rose of her nipples was obvious, the darkened shadow between her legs was hazy and mysterious. She swallowed, then straightened her shoulders. She wanted to enflame him, didn't she?

There was no hesitation in her walk as she approached the doors that separated their rooms, and with a steady hand she reached for the knob only to have the doors suddenly swing wide.

Christopher, in a robe of dull gold, stood there, apparently as surprised as she, but then as enlightenment dawned on both faces, he grinned and murmured, "Your bed or mine, madame?"

Nicole caught back the splutter of laughter in her throat; a fierce gladness rushed through her veins that all unknowing they had met halfway. Melting easily into his arms, she whispered, "Yours, I think. Mine has memories enough, while yours has none . . . yet."

His eyes suddenly blazing with the love that had been hidden these past months, Christopher swept her up into his hard arms. Against her mouth he promised softly, "Oh, we'll make memories tonight, love. We'll make memories to last a lifetime."

He kept his promise, his body taking hers with such gentle fierceness she would remember it through all the years of their lives. Years that would be spent together in love and tenderness, for there was no longer doubting that—it was there in every movement of his body, in every kiss, in every caress.

Sometimes, Nicole thought sleepily, when at last they were both satiated with the other, sometimes it's easier to say things without words, to say them with actions, with your body and your eyes, with . . .

How long she slept she didn't know, she only knew that dawn was still only a promise when Christopher rudely prodded her awake. Groggy, she stared at him uncomprehendingly, noting vaguely that he was already dressed in breeches and top boots.

His teeth very white in the darkness of his face, he teased, "Get up, lazy bones! We have one last task to do before we leave the city today."

"What are you talking about?" she complained, at-

tempting to roll back over and bury her head beneath the pillows.

But Christopher would have none of that, and callously he ripped away the covers and grasped her shoulders. "Wake up! Wake up or I'll leave you behind and you'll never know what happened to Allen."

Wide awake in an instant, Nicole stared at him. His eyes were filled with lazy amusement, his mouth tilted in a reckless smile.

Pointing to the pitcher of water on the washstand, he murmured, "If you hurry, you won't miss it."

Without a word she leaped from the bed splashed water over her body, and scrambled into the pair of breeches and shirt Christopher handed her. Puzzled, she looked at him. "Breeches?"

"Breeches, my love. I don't want anyone to guess at those very feminine curves."

"But why?"

"You'll see," was his infuriating answer.

They left the house within seconds and slipped across the deserted courtyard to the stables. There were three horses saddled, and with something like bemusement, Nicole was thrown carelessly onto one of them.

They rode in silence through the empty, spongy streets. Christopher led the third animal, the horses' hoofbeats muffled by the still-damp ground. It was only as the calaboose came into view that a suspicion of Christopher's intentions crossed her mind, and the full import of the third horse and the stout rope across his saddle burst across her brain like a rocket.

"You're mad!" she hissed.

"Mmm, I agree, mad about you," he replied softly, his eyes caressing her features.

She reached for him urgently, her fingers tightening around his arm. "Listen," she said earnestly, "Allen is important to me, but not at the risk of your life. I love you, Christopher—you don't have to do this. You could be shot, or just as bad, we could both end up in the calaboose with him."

Christopher grinned, his eyes bright and glittering with excitement, and the thought occurred to her that he was enjoying himself. But his voice was serious as he said, "It's possible, but the sergeant in charge has been paid very handsomely to ignore what is happening in a certain cell. Until, of course, Allen is free; then he is to fire a few warning shots in the air for the look of it."

"Christopher, you don't have to, you know," she repeated fiercely.

A curious expression flitted across his face. "Ah, but I do, my dear. Now let's get the good Allen out of there, mmmm?"

Nicole waited near the huge old cypress where Christopher had left her, holding the reins of the extra horse. Helplessly she watched as he swiftly tied the heavy rope around the bars of one of the cells, and with her heart in her mouth, she unconsciously strained with his horse, as with a slow, steady pressure the bars one by one were pulled out.

Allen's head appeared and then his shoulders, and following Christopher's instructions, Nicole urged her animal forward at a quick pace, dragging the unmounted horse behind her. Out of the corner of her eye she saw a soldier coming around the corner of the building and threw the reins to Allen with a frantic, "Hurry, the alarm has been sounded."

Allen wasted not a moment and vaulted easily onto the horse's back, and then wheeling about, the three of them galloped down the deserted dawn streets just as the first shots rang out. With something like horror Nicole felt her horse scream with pain, stumble, and go down. Luckily she was thrown clear, and before she had time to do more than to stagger to her feet, Christopher's arm, like a band of steel, was around her waist and she was thrown effortlessly across the saddle in front of him.

They rode like the wind, leaving New Orleans miles behind. At last Christopher motioned Allen to follow him and turned the horses from the road into the apparent maze of cypress swamps. They rode in silence for several moments, following a barely defined trail that ran along a dark, sluggish bayou.

Nicole wiggled uncomfortably, and Christopher reached down and shifted her weight until she sat in front of him, her back resting comfortably against the steady beat of his heart. Eventually Christopher halted his horse and dismounted. He turned to Allen, his expression unreadable. He said curtly, "You'll find a change of clothing in that pack strapped to your saddle. I suggest you get into them!"

Allen's nod was equally as expressionless as Christopher's, and disappearing with the bundle, he reappeared a few minutes later in a pair of breeches and a reasonably well-cut jacket.

Warily the two men faced each other, and it was Nicole who broke the silence. Slipping from the horse, she walked to Christopher and, putting her hand in his, asked softly, "What do we do now?"

Christopher's hand tightened on her, and he smiled down at her. The tenderness she saw there made her heart beat like thunder.

Christopher glanced over at Allen before saying, "We go our separate ways now. We're going to Thibodaux House and the good Allen will find his way to England." Speaking directly to Allen, he said coolly, "You'll find money in the right saddlebag, food and a weapon in the left. I trust I can leave the remainder of your escape to you?"

Deliberately ignoring the other man's provoking manner, Allen smiled wryly. "I think so. Since the war is officially ended, I shouldn't have too much trouble finding a ship for England and rejoining what is left of my regiment."

Christopher said brusquely, "Fine. You'll excuse us, please? We have a long journey ahead of us and I still have to find another horse for my wife."

Christopher turned on his heel, yanking Nicole with him, but Nicole, casting him a pleading look, released herself and ran to Allen. Throwing her arms about his neck, she gave him an impetuous hug and said softly, "Go with God, my friend. Perhaps someday we'll meet again."

A gentle hand on the burnished head, Allen agreed, "Perhaps someday. Be happy, Nicole."

She gave him a blinding smile and then spun quickly on her heel and rejoined her husband, who despite his best intentions was scowling blackly. Nicole touched his cheek lightly and a rueful grin twisted his mouth. Christopher mounted and reached down to pull Nicole up behind him. Allen quickly mounted his horse and asked, "Which is the best way for me to go from here to escape the patrol?"

Christopher nodded toward the east. "Follow this path about two more miles in that direction and you'll find it lets out on a main road. From there follow it northerly and eventually you'll find yourself in Baton Rouge."

They parted without any further conversation, Christopher and Nicole riding slowly and aimlessly away, Allen setting out with a brisk pace toward the east. It was several moments later that Christopher stopped their horse

again and, dismounting, pulled Nicole down to sit on a fallen tree trunk.

Holding her hand in his, the gold eyes warm and caressing on her face, he asked simply, "Questions?"

"One," she said with a smile, the love in her gaze almost tangible. "Why?"

He hesitated and then, his features intent and troubled, he admitted, "I don't really know exactly myself. But I think it's because I wanted to give him back his life, because he saved yours, and to try to show you how much I love you . . . to prove that I didn't really believe all those things I had accused you of. And most of all to say I'm sorry, I'm sorry for being the pigheaded ass you've rightly called me so often."

Demurely Nicole murmured, "And you'll never be so again?"

Christopher shot her a considering glance. "Now that I can't answer; I can only say I'll *try* not to leap to conclusions, I'll *try* to listen first to what you have to say, but I can't promise that I'll not be arrogant, upon occasion, and that I won't ride roughshod over your demands. What I can promise," he said huskily, one hand gently caressing her cheek, "is that I will love you until the day I die. You're in my blood, Nicole, like a sweet wild magic that I don't ever want to lose."

Her eyes locked on his; her own love shining and filling him with delight, she asked curiously, "And the past? My mother?"

His face tightened. "The past is behind us. And I was wrong there too—you are not like Annabelle in any way." The gold eyes were almost bleak as he said slowly, "I can't say that the future will be all kisses and wine; I'm not an easy man to live with—I've shut people out too often and for too long to let you think I'll change overnight into a perfect husband. I doubt I'll ever be a perfect husband. But, Nicole, let my try." Suddenly he pulled her to him, his mouth compulsively seeking hers. "Oh, Jesus," he said softly a moment later, "I do love you . . . and that's all I can offer you for a certainty."

But it was enough. In time, the past would be completely eradicated, and while the days ahead would be stormy, turbulent, filled with passion and fire, Nicole wouldn't have traded one for a lifetime of tranquility.

In silence they remounted, Nicole seated behind him, her arms wrapped tightly around the broad chest. For just a second it came back to her that this was how their

journey had begun all those years before in Beddington's Corner. And her arms tightened more fiercely; then it had been to face a dangerous and frightfully uncertain future, but now, now there was Christopher and their love and a whole new beginning. A beginning and the glorious future they would find together.